Toy Store Boy

Allan Blackthorn

Table of Contents

Prologue: Virginity

I opened the bedroom door. It wasn't my bedroom it was the room that we all were sharing this week. All other thoughts of people and where we were just disappeared out of my mind as the door opened and I saw her standing there. I didn't know she was in the room when I had left the pool, but there she was none the less. I was downstairs swimming in the pool when that dumb ass song came on, that stupid dumb ass song. I could feel myself getting hard as that washed up pop star sang, so I slipped away as fast as possible.

I was pissed that at age 19 that Dumb ass song was still affecting me like I was 12 years old. I had planned to just go jack off really quickly and then head off to lunch, but there was Katie standing in the room. Opening the door to see her standing there wearing only a pair of pink swim suit bottoms with a daisy on the front, she looked at me as if I had walked in on her intentionally, she was leaning over to pick up a shirt off the bed her breasts hanging down looking soft and supple.

We stood there for what seemed like an eternity, I couldn't take my eyes off her nearly naked body, it had been so long since I had seen her this way and my need was more than evident. The obsession I had felt for her all those years caused me to jump into an erection so hard that it hurt, yet I still couldn't say anything to her or shift my gaze. She was so beautiful, still wet from the pool her body glistening, her full breasts, nipples tightening hard and pointing from the cold air in the room.

I had dreamed of seeing her naked again and now she was standing there topless and there was no way for me to hide that my erection was trying to burst through my loose swim shorts. Even after all the times we had fooled around in the past I still had only seen her as naked as she was now, I longed to see what lay under those panties. I so desired to feel what lay in that hidden paradise.

I wanted to move but was still rendered paralyzed. She too seemed to be in some kind of shock because she was saying nothing or moving herself. I wished I could know what thoughts were running through her head as we stood there staring. I was so worked up that I thought I was going to die of embarrassment until I realized that she wasn't looking at me in the eyes but she was looking at my shorts.

She had a look on her face that I couldn't place it slightly resembled the look the day she was 14 in the back of the toy store. In the 6 years I had really gotten to know her since then, I thought I understood her, but she was looking at my erection and all I could tell was that it wasn't a look of embarrassment.

I don't know what took me over in that moment but I grew suddenly bold, I pulled my pants down letting them just drop to the floor, but not stepping out of them. I stood there nude and the first real look of embarrassment burned in her cheeks but she didn't look away. I was surprised that she was embarrassed because it wasn't as if she hadn't seen my dick hard for her before, that's how we met for crying out loud, but somehow this was different. We were older now and things had been indifferent between us since that night when I was 16.

Then I grew bolder I worked up all my courage and moved across the room to her. Without a word I leaned in and kissed her neck, it was a slow and gave gentle kiss. I could taste the sweat on her

neck and I licked it as I kissed her again. My body was pressing against hers as my kissing grew stronger, she didn't push me away as I feared.

I had expected her to push me away, I expected her to tell me we'd moved past this, years ago, and I expected her to say it was never going to happen again. I was about to pull away when I felt her shudder slightly then she moved my face from her neck and kissed me on the mouth.

Her lips were soft and very warm as we kissed lightly to start. I slowly, nervously, and with great need began to explore the inside of her beautiful sweet mouth, it wasn't long before she did the same back to me and our tongues danced together in a ballet of repressed love we felt for each other. It was the most passionate kiss we'd had since the first night at the barn, back before everything had gone to hell. In this kiss we put aside all the things that had kept us apart for the last 3 years and fell into each other now.

I couldn't believe that I was kissing her I'd wanted this for so long but on so many levels it was so wrong. The problem was I didn't care about right or wrong in that second I was finally getting to kiss Katie again. I was grinding my erection against her thigh now and had worked my erection to point down against her leg; it hurt and felt so good to touch her at the same time.

All I could think about was I could lose my virginity to her right here and now and it was all due to that dumb ass song, that god damn song that always seemed to play at the worst times ever. I had issues with the song before I met Katie but now the song always made me twice as hard because it reminded me of the first time I met her. That dumb ass song was the catalysts to our whole relationship years ago, and would be the cause of so much more problems in the future.

We were still standing and kissing deeply when my excitement became too much and I came on her. It happened without much warning, she was leaning against me still pressing my erection down against her thigh, when all of a sudden I let loose and I shot cum down her leg. I was embarrassed, and I pulled away from her turning my head in shame.

"It's ok, it wouldn't be us without you going off early," she whispered in my ear pulling my face back to hers, "I can't deny how wrong this is but, your my toy store boy and you've always been so........" she spoke softly right before leaning over and kissing me on my neck right under my ear.

"I love you," I told her. I hadn't meant to say it but I just kind of blurted it out. I loved her very much but I was *in love* with someone else. I felt a touch of guilt and knew I needed to stop this. But my need overcame my will power as Katie took my hands and pulled me to her.

"Don't make this worse than it is," she said lightly, kissing me again. She pulled me with her as she lied down on the bed.

"I don't know how much time we have," she whispered in my ear as I lied on top of her.

Despite my early release I was still really hard. There was no way I was going soft at this moment with my oldest dream coming true. She reached down and slid her swim suit off. I moved between her legs looking intently at her beautifully shaved pussy. It was more beautiful than I had ever imagined. I couldn't believe I was finally seeing it.

As I kissed my way up her body she reached down and took my dick in hand bringing me to her love spot. I thrust forward not really knowing what I was doing. She moaned sharply and I came again

after only a few moments of feeling her soft wet folds taking me in. She was tight but and warm it felt like I was thrusting into wet silk, she smiled as I came inside her and ran a hand along my cheek. I didn't, I couldn't stop thrusting inside her and I was on fire.

I'm not sure how long we were together before it was over, but it probably wasn't as long as it felt. I know it was way too short to cover for the 6 years of yearning behind it. I was lost in a world of my own creating. I'd never felt so good or emotional, I couldn't believe I had done this as guilt touched me again. As guilty as I felt right at that moment I still couldn't get enough of her; I began to kiss her neck again when she told me we needed to stop.

"This felt so wonderful, but we should get back outside before someone notices were both missing," she said softly. I could tell there was something else in her mind that she wasn't telling me. Then it hit me, was she dating someone in college she hadn't told anyone about? We really needed to talk.

I rolled off of her putting my arms around her, pulling her close, putting my head on her breasts. I could hardly breathe from exhaustion and both orgasms. She was soft and I felt like I could fall asleep laying there with her. But this would be bad if Ash came back to the room and saw us like this. The three of us were sharing a room this week and it was just pure luck that Ash hadn't come up and caught us already.

"No one will suspect that we were up here doing this. We can hang out here for a few more minutes. We need to talk about this, we've needed to talk since you left for college but we both keep avoiding it."

"I know, your right but we've been up here for a while and I don't want to be found out. It would be bad if.......... we were overheard," She paused and started stroking my hair.

She got up off the bed and her hair fell over her face. I didn't move, she looked at me in a sideway glance her hair covering half her face I couldn't see her expression. It was all starting to hit me what just happened. As my breathing and thoughts returning to normal I started get scared. What were we going to do now? What if someone found out? Oh god I had cum inside her! She could get pregnant. A mixture of emotions started swirling in my head. Love, fear, happiness, and more guilt, I had really made a mess of things today.

"Katie..... I.....?" I started, I was ready to talk to her but I couldn't find the right words. She looked over at me while she got dressed. She was so hot as she was putting on her shorts; they made her legs look incredible. I had always had a thing for the way girls legs looked in shorts; maybe it was because I had a thing for legs in general.

"Don't.......... We should talk about this tonight." She said picking up her shirt off the other bed she put it on without a bra and said, "We have some serious issues to talk about and we don't need Ash walking in asking questions. I'll see you down stairs."

"Ok." I kind of croaked as she walked to the door. She smiled at me weakly as she left the room and I wondered if she regretted what had just happened. I hopped she wasn't ashamed of doing it with me.

I got off the bed and pulled on my jeans and lied back down reliving it in my head. It wasn't so much the fact that I got laid for the first time but the realization that I finally slept with Katie. My oldest fantasy had come true but now I had to live with it. I laid there and drifted off to sleep.

Chapter One: That Dumb Ass Song

I want to start off by saying that this story is true, it's written as it was lived. I changed the names, dates and familial relationships to protect the secrets of the people I've written about here. I wanted the story to start with the losing of my virginity because that is the biggest day of most boys' lives. I wanted to tell that part of the story without judgment as when we get there later it will have a whole different meaning. What's to come may change your perception of the prologue, I hope it doesn't because Katie is on every level my first real love and so important to the rest of my life. This story is about my love for and relationship to Katie and how it impacted the rest of my life and my marriage.

The beginning of this story starts at puberty. I start this story in the most embarrassing time of my life for two reasons. One: That when it comes down to it both sexes really don't understand what the others go through during puberty. I attribute this to the fact that there are so many questions are hard to ask someone and even harder to answer honestly. I mean who really wants to talk about the most embarrassing moments of childhood?

Two: Most of the problems I had during that time can all be traced back to constant masturbation. Without anyone to talk to I had to take this journey on my own, hiding and ashamed thinking there was something wrong with me. I have to start this story at puberty because without going through what I did in that time period I would never have met Katie. I can't speak for all guys out there but for me it all started with that dumb ass song.

I was 12 years old when that song started playing on the radio. Now keep in mind that when I was 12 it was the 1980s and we didn't have the internet yet. Meaning we didn't have very easy access to the amount of pornography that is abundant today. In my time we had to get by on what we could find and what our imagination could fill in to get ourselves off.

On that note when I was 12 they started playing the song on the radio. It was a slow song sang by the queen of pop, in which she sings about justifying sex. I don't want to say any titles for fear of lawsuit but hopefully you can get which one I'm talking about from that clue. Anyway I was smack dab in the middle of that lovely time period for boys when you start getting spontaneous erections and you don't yet know how to control them.

For some unknown reason that dumb ass song would get my motor running I don't know what it was about it for sure, just that it would cause me to BOING as it were. It wasn't like that was the only time I would get unwanted erections as it would happen in class or when watching TV at home, or when it was generally most inconvenient as possible. The only time I could predict when they would come was when that dumb ass song was playing. That didn't make any sense to me either; I didn't find that pop whore attractive at all. The boys at school had shown me a picture of her topless once and as excited as I was to see real boobs, I didn't really find her attractive.

At that point in my life I had a huge crush on me step mom's cousin's daughter. Her name was Beth and she was 11 years old. I wasn't into older women at all so I was just fine with girls my own age like Beth. So yet again I don't know why that song had such power over me. Beth was the only girl I had ever really had a crush on at that time. I liked girls but I didn't find many I really wanted to try to be with.

I was too shy anyway I didn't think I had the nerve to ask one out if I wanted to. I think that's why I hung on to the idea of liking Beth I would never be allowed to date her because we were considered family.

In the early days I would pop up and I didn't know what to do. I would sit where ever and hope no one would notice me crossing my legs and trying to think of something else. These were some of the worst times of my life. If you only got erections when sitting alone in the dark then it would be too easy but life has to kick you when it's most inconvenient.

I'd be sitting in class and a girl next to me would be wearing a skirt and that's all it would take for lift off. But everyone has heard that story before of the poor boy called to the black board while trying to suppress himself. But it's worst then that. It would happen while watching TV with your grandparents. It would happen in church. It would happen at the super market. It would happen at the park or at the movies. It would happen to some boys in the locker room. Luckily that wasn't me. What the other boys did to that kid was bad.

That's another thing, the other boys would prank you if you popped up in the locker room but they would also harass you mercilessly for being too small. Again I'm glad I wasn't that boy either. What they did to him was almost as bad.

With things popping up all the time it was almost like living in fear I was on guard all the time and I didn't want anyone to know it was happening. My parents didn't really talk to me about sex, so at first I didn't really know why it was happening. All I really knew about sex was that the guy puts his into hers; from there it was all a big mystery. My step mom was catholic and sex was not a topic of conversation when anything was ever spoken in our house it was talked about from her as if it was an evil act and you were a bad person for doing it.

When it first started happening I was trying to figure out what was wrong with me and what was causing it I thought if I could figure out what I was doing wrong that it would stop happening. Of course that didn't work.

One day after school I was watching videos on the local music channel and the video for that dumb ass song came on and I went into full lift off in a way that I hadn't before. I sat there unable to change the channel and staring at the screen the whole time wishing it would go away. It wouldn't and I was upset as that slut pop star was half naked in this video singing that dumb ass song. As much as I didn't like her the video was sexy and we didn't have porn access then and you had to take what you could get.

After 20 minutes my erection was still strong as ever and I knew my family would be home soon, there was no way I could get caught with this going on. My step mom would want to know what I had been watching and doing, she would assume that I had been being bad and I would be in trouble.

Getting desperate I unzipped my pants and tried to push on it. Ok I understand how ridiculous that sounds but I really did at the time think that pushing on it would do something.

I had grown up thinking it wasn't ok to touch yourself at all, I should say with only two exceptions if I was peeing or cleaning it with in the bath. I literally thought I would get in trouble if someone found out that I touched it so it's not an exaggeration that I literally never touched myself at all. It sounds so laughable now but I thought that even pushing on it that day would get me in trouble.

However I didn't know what I was doing and I started pushing it down hoping it would go away. I didn't want anyone to come home while I was tenting my pants. As I was pushing on it I realized that I was bigger than I had ever seen myself. That was weird, looking at it in that state really for the first time. It felt weird looking at it and I started having a weird felling as I was pushing on it, not knowing why I began to rub it a little. It felt really good so I was sitting there rubbing it and feeling really ashamed at the same time. I really felt in my head that I was doing something wrong that I was such a bad person for touching it, but I couldn't stop. After a couple minutes I tried putting my hand around it. This felt better but there was something still not quite right.

I was sitting there stroking it for the first time letting the pleasure wash over me yet inside I was upset. I felt guilty for liking the feeling, I mean I really felt guilty and started getting jumpy. I froze every time I heard a noise. I knew about ejaculate only in the sense that's what made babies so I wasn't ready for it the first time. It exploded out all over my hand and it was over I sat there for less than a minute before the guilt overtook me. "OH MY GOD what did I just do?" I thought trying not to get my own stuff on me I zipped up one handed and ran to the kitchen; I was still washing my hands when my step mom came home.

I was so guilty that I couldn't look at her all night. I felt like if I looked at her she would know I'd been touching it. I would be belt whipped and grounded not to mention the embarrassment of her knowing if she knew she would look down on me forever. I was so ashamed about what I had done that over the next couple weeks I would get erections and I went back to crossing my legs and preying they went away.

It was a few weeks after the first time I had stoked myself that the parents had gone away for the weekend; I got left at a friend's house because they felt I was too young to be left home for 48 hours alone. I was awake in the middle of the night when I turned on the TV keeping the volume as low as possible. The family had cable with a cable box; this was something cool to me because we didn't get all the extra channels. I know some of you already know where this is going but what I didn't know then was that some pay channels show soft core porn movies in the middle of the night.

On this particular night they were showing a skin flick, the movie was some poorly written peace of crap that had a number of girls running around half naked. I hadn't seen anything like this before. I was hard in an instant, drooling on myself. I was embarrassed because I was at someone else's house and I didn't want them to walk in. I started caressing myself without thinking; I reached into my pants and started stroking it. Looking at real boobs it only took a minute, I was feeling guilty and ashamed more than ever but a light bulb went off in my head as I began to soften.

I realized two things at that moment, first, it felt good and no one needed to know as long as I could hide it. Second, that jerking it made it go away right away. I hadn't realized that the first time because I had already been erect for 20 minutes before I started stroking the first time, and I had felt so ashamed when it was over that it hadn't clued in.

These revelations were both a blessing and a curse. The blessing came in the form of sexual relief; the curse was the fact that now I wasn't just getting spontaneous erections all the time, I was now masturbating all the time. My guilt and shame were so strong that I felt like I was going to get found out any minute and in my mind that would be the end of the world, but I still couldn't stop now.

When I say I was doing it all the time, I mean ALL the time. This was a really big summer for that dumb ass song, and considering that the song was tied into my first time with myself, it really set off my

erections. When I say all the time I'm not exaggerating. It started out every day after school from the time I got home until my family got home from work. Then I moved on to after school and in bed at night. That was taking a big risk, doing it with other people in the house could get me caught, I would be quiet in my room and freak out if I heard someone start walking around. By the end of the summer it became whenever I was alone in a room and thought I could get away with it, I had some really close calls. One afternoon my step mom just walked into my room a few seconds after I had just tucked myself back into my shorts. I literally still had cum on my hand as the door opened. I slid my hand under my pillow and wiped it off as she began yapping at me about whatever she was pissy about that day.

From there I started taking more risks. For some reason, the feeling of ejaculating started becoming more important than getting caught. Don't get me wrong I was still mortified by the idea that someone would find out, I still felt guilty and ashamed about it but I still couldn't stop taking bigger risks. I really don't know how I didn't get caught, just dumb luck and loose shorts.

The risks started out small like I would be in our fenced back yard listening to the radio and that song would come on, I would sit in the lawn chair and do it out in the open. That became a regular thing when the parents weren't home; I mean I could have been caught by anyone looking through a knot hole in the wood. Eventually I would do this even if the parents were home. I could hear them walking and thought could pull my shorts leg down really fast if they came outside.

From there I moved on to jerking it in public as it was the next natural step in some ways. It started once when I was waiting in the car at the super market and the song came on the radio, I got hard really fast so I looked around the car really quickly to make sure no one was standing right outside then unzipped my pants, pulled myself completely out and started jerking it right there. I was so scared and thrilled at the same time I was doing it in public and it felt so good. It only took a couple minutes because of the fear of getting caught I finished and looked up to see my parents walking out of the store at that moment, which was to close.

I was a 12 year old monster, out of control and insane. My risks were large and my shame was huge but I couldn't stop, I hated myself for this, I really thought I had some kind of sick problem because I couldn't stop.

This is the point of why I'm writing this part of the story, I didn't have anyone I felt I could talk to, I couldn't tell anyone I was doing this. How do you talk to someone about something like that? Who would understand? I mean this is something forbidden and taboo, I could never admit to another single person that I did this. I really thought at the time nobody else did it themselves, At least not good normal people.

With no understanding things just progressed worse and I had to live with myself as bad as I was, if I was out in public shopping I often would slip away from my step mom and pretend that I was trying on clothes so I could go into a changing room and jerk myself right there in the store. It was thrilling on some level to hear the people in the store talking and they had no idea what I was doing in the booth.

As I became 13 things didn't slow down I had learned to live with it and I no longer felt guilty or ashamed by it anymore, yet getting caught was still my biggest secret and fear. I had just come to the realization that I wasn't going to stop; I just rolled with it and continued taking bigger risks. Things like doing it while sitting alone at a bench at the park or at the movies.

I was sitting by myself at the park watching a girl about my age in the distance, she was pretty but it was the fact that she was wearing shorts and had tan legs that had my attention. I was in the party pavilion which was a covered area with benches, four short walls with open corners and about four or five barbeques. I was behind a short wall watching her through the gap and I was hard looking at her.

This wasn't the first time just looking at a girl made me hard but this time being all alone I just pulled back my shorts leg and started stroking. When I was done I splashed my juices across the bench seat and still sat there, I looked at her a while longer but I left before anyone could walk up and find me there sitting next to my spent cum.

I would like to say that the worst risk I ever took was the day at the moves, I was at a PG13 movie one afternoon the theater was almost empty and I was sitting not in the back row but behind everyone else there. During the film a naked girl walks out of the water, as always was wearing my shorts. I looked around and everyone was watching the screen, I pulled my shorts leg back and did it right there during the movie with people in the room. But it was dark and the movie was loud, when I came I let it hit the floor and I moved up one row and over a few seats so no one would connect the cum on the floor to me.

I was unstoppable on my way to getting caught; the biggest risk of them all came when I was still 13. It started while I was walking through a toy store. I had gone out with my step mom to look for a birthday present for some little kid. I slipped away from her to look around the place on my own when that dumb ass song came on. I thought to myself, really? Their playing that in a toy store? I was getting worked up so I began walking to the back of the store to knock it out in a restroom when I saw the girl from the park weeks earlier.

I recognized her right off she was just as beautiful as when I had seen her the first time. She was wearing shorts and a tank top, her breasts were just beginning to come in and the cold air made her nipples hard and I could see them through her shirt. Up close I could see that she had the smoothest legs of any girl I had ever met.

From both the song and the fact that I was looking at the only girl I had directly ever jerked it to, I didn't mean to but I went from getting worked up to completely popping up right there. I looked down at myself for just a second thinking, oh not now. I saw her look down too and I was so embarrassed I slowly started walking away I really needed to find the restroom now. I went to the back corner of the store only to find no rest room there I turned around and looked up to see she was standing a couple of feet in front of me. I was petrified at first, I was sticking up in my shorts and she had followed me to the back corner.

She looked at me, her face red from understanding and embarrassment, I certainty was too. I don't know what possessed me to do it but I pulled up the leg of my shorts and exposed myself to her for only a moment. She turned completely red but didn't look away instead she pulled her tank top down so I could see her small breast and hard nipple for just a second, this just made my erection visibly thicken. I reached down pulling my shorts leg up again but not just showing her this time I started to stroke myself for her, she turned a shade even redder. I wasn't even looking around to see if an adult was in view I was just looking at her and doing the one thing I kept most private in the world.

"You can touch it," I squeaked out somehow. She tentatively came to me and touched it lightly. Being that it was the first time I was ever touched by a girl even just the light caress of her fingertips caused me to cum all over her tank top.

"EWWWWW" she said whipping her shirt and running away. I ran off as fast as I could before she could bring back and adult.

For the first time in a long while the guilt and shame came back to me full force as I realized just how out of control I had gotten. The whole thing could have gone so much worse, I was lucky I didn't get caught. I was lucky I wasn't arrested; all my fears of this being wrong came back to me and I was ashamed of myself and the fact that I really was some kind of pervert deviant.

I didn't do it again at all for at least a week I wanted to stop it all together and be a good person again. One who didn't touch himself? One who didn't take all these risks to get caught but as things go I couldn't hold out forever and I started again. Only this time I stopped taking such big risks I only did it now at home by myself living with the shame and guilt quietly. Still having no one to talk to it affected my whole life thinking that there was something wrong with me.

It wasn't long after that I turned 14 that was the year of creativity; I call it that because as I said I had stopped taking risks but I moved into another phase. That time period was the object phase, I searched my house for anything round and about the right size that I could stick it in and still feel good. I don't exaggerate when I say I tried everything round, this is the time period when some boys will go so far as to use the vacuum cleaner. I heard tails of that when I got older I was just never that guy. Not that the thought had never hit me but for one the hose was too small and I was actually afraid of the suction.

But flashlights, tubes, piggy banks, toys, holes in the couch, bottles and generally anything I could stick my dick into were all violated. It started at my house but progressed on to other's houses too. My grandmother had a guest bed that was decoratively carved that had holes carved though the foot board. I found out that one of the holes worked perfect. I'm guessing it was the object phase my cousin was in when he was caught naked in his room with the dog. Yet again I'm glad I wasn't that guy, I'm very happy I never went down that road.

I've lost track of all the things I tried that year, because it was a lot of stuff. And talk about fear of getting caught, every time I stuck it in that bed frame I was so worried about someone finding me there with my dick in the foot board. I guess it's not as bad as getting caught with a dog but still I would've lost it if someone walked in on me humping away on a bed frame.

The problem was most round objects were either too small or too big. I could never find anything the right size that felt completely good except the holes in that damn bed frame. The down side to that is that was I had to hang out at my grandmothers to get it. I wanted so bad to find that one object that was perfect and it never happened.

That was the same year my father broke up with my step mom. She had cheated on him with his best friend and we moved across town and he started a new job. After all her talk about the evils of sex she banged his best friend, now that's what I call irony. I was fine with it as I hated her and I never understood what they saw in each other in the first place.

My father had been a player until my mother died when I was 4. I had never met him and when she died he had showed up and taken custody. As far as we knew then I was an only child so finding out he had a child had changed his life. He had married my step mom when I was 6. From day one they were opposites. She dragged us off to church and ran the house with an iron fist.

After breaking up with my step mom we stopped going to church and I hardly saw him anymore. He went back into full time dating. I was home alone so much that I had to learn to cook just so there was something to eat. I would come home often to find cash and a note saying he would be back later. At first I would use the money to go get fast food but after a couple months I started using it for groceries and doing the shopping myself.

It gave me plenty of time to experiment during the year of creativity. That's also why I spent so much time at my grandmother's house. With him gone for whole weekends I would get dumped there. I would act like I was mad that I was stuck there on the weekend again, playing the annoyed kid routine. Then every night it was the same thing I would listen for her to go to bed. When I could hear the snoring through the door, I would go around to the foot board and spend half the night with that rounded wood hole.

When I was 15 I had slowly began to take risks again. After spending the last year humping everything in sight I was frustrated with not being successful with finding a portable object so I went back to using my old friend, my hand. I would only take risks in public where ever I thought it was safe. Places like the woods or public bathrooms or changing rooms. It would be years again before I would do it at a park, parking lot or movie theaters.

The girl in the toy store that day was the one and only focus of my mental fantasizes. I had progressed to at least once in the morning shower, once after school and once right before bed. That was if my dad was home. It was more if he wasn't. It would be some days as often as once an hour when I could. At this point in my life just doing it didn't work alone anymore, so I would have to close my eyes and think about a scenario to get off. It was always her in my head, the one girl who had ever seen it or touched it. The only real live boob I had ever seen, even though she didn't have much more than a nipple then. Those two things combined had got me off some times up to 12 a day over two years.

It was months after my parents broke up that to my dismay I went with my father to a wedding, I was so disgusted with him at that point in my life I really didn't want to spend any time around him. I was at the reception and I was bored out of my mind because I didn't know anybody and I just wanted to go home. The wedding was for some coworker of my Dad's named John who was getting married at his parent's farm house; I really didn't give a damn about this guy and figured this damn thing was a waste of time.

The farm itself was laid out on a huge piece of land, it consisting of a main house and a few of different sized barns, and a number of small sheds spread out in different areas of the property. The wedding was centralized on one section of the property; a gigantic tent was put up to hold the wedding and reception. This was done mainly to keep people out of the small house as the party mainly hung out in the tent or around it. I was wandering around outside the party tent just wishing that the whole day would end already when disaster struck and that dumb ass song came on. I cursed out loud as I could feel my dick beginning to harden.

"Oh, come on," I said aloud. I couldn't believe this was still happening!

I looked around and made the decision to walk to the far side of the farm where no one was at and go behind one of the barns. I figured with everyone at the tent I might have a couple minutes of privacy to take care of business really quickly. I practically ran as my need was tenting my dress pants. I rounded the corner so fast that I almost skidded to a stop when I saw her; she was standing there, the girl from the toy store. I was so shocked I actually lost my erection.

She was smoking a cigarette, dressed in a beautiful red dress with her hair done up so a few strands fell across her face. Her breasts had grown quite a bit and her legs had more tone then before but it was definitely her, there was no mistaking her. I was stunned I almost hoped she didn't recognize me as this could end badly if she did.

"It's you, the toy store boy." she said slyly.

"Yeah, I'm......" was as far as I got when she stopped me, she held up her hand and moved the short distance between us. I was nervous as hell when she leaned in and kissed me.

"I don't need to know your name," she said, "I've never forgotten you. You were the first boy that ever got hard for me." I hadn't been going to tell her my name I had been going to apologize to her for the first time we met but she kissed me again and I went with it.

"Look what happened that day.......... I didn't mean to.........." I said pulling away all embarrassed.

"Don't try to explain. It would ruin it. I'm old enough to get it. You thought I was hot and you got hard. You're not the last boy to do that."

"But most probably don't just whip it out and cum on you, right away," I said blushing.

"No they don't," She laughed, "They want to I'm sure, but they don't." She smiled at me and I started to lose my embarrassment. There was an awkward silence and looking at her I began to get hard again in my rented suit. She smiled as she noticed my arousal.

"You still haven't been with a girl have you?" she asked quietly.

"No," I whispered embarrassed, "Have you ever been with a ......" I couldn't finish croaking out the last word.

"Shhhh." she whispered. Her mouth next to my ear, "I've never......... you know, gone all the way. But I have done this," She said kissing me softly. She reached down slowly unzipped my pants and pulling me out. I was so hard and bigger then I had ever been before. I couldn't believe this was real and I was so worked up I could feel my balls tightening already. I willed myself not to cum yet and tried to calm down.

"You've grown virgin boy," she whispered. The whispering in my ear was making me hotter.

"Warn me this time." she said and my sex addled mind had no idea what she meant until she dropped to her knees and took the head of my dick into her mouth.

As close as I was to letting loose just from her touching me, her tongue running across the head of my cock in her mouth didn't help me last very long. It felt like she had just started when I found myself starting to say I was going to cum, but it happened before I could speak it.

"Uuck, I hate that part. I told you to warn me." She wasn't really angry as she turned and spit out all my cum just a little grossed out. She stood up again and lit another cigarette. I reached down and somewhat sad that it was over, zipped myself up again. I was in shock I tried to get some words out but I couldn't seem to find any to speak.

"I'm sorry I tried to......... I didn't mean to......... that fast," I finally managed.

"It's ok. It's always that way with virgin boys. I just love that look on your face."

"Why did you.......... not that I'm complaining but........... Why?"

She smiled at me and told me that the time in the toy store was the first time she had seen a boy get hard and it had done something to her. It made her curious, it made her want to try to make other boys hard and it made her want to do more than lightly touch a boy.

She said that not long after the toy store she had started dating this guy a couple years older than her who ended up forcing her to go down on him. She actually liked sucking his cock but didn't like the guy for making her do it before she was ready. She said if he would have waited until she was ready she would have had no problem with doing it for him all the time but he was a jerk. What made things worse with him was after she had blown him he tried to force her to have sex so she felt like she had no choice but to dump him.

Since then she had played around with just virgin boys because she kind of liked giving head and because they were always so grateful never trying to force her to do more. But she said she would only do it once or twice with each of them before moving on, she explained that after a couple times they would push for more and she wasn't ready for that yet so she always moved on.

The way that she had taken care of me had felt really good. I felt it would be disrespectful to ask how many of these encounters she had, had. But I was curious.

"You're not kidding." I told her. "That was fucking awesome."

"That's not the only reason I did that for you," she said looking down almost ashamed, "I've thought about you and that day in the store so many times. I mean I should have been disgusted that day. I should have told some one. But for some reason I was flattered, and I was just as curious as you were bold at that moment. I should have been mad but it ....turned me on." She said the last words quietly.

"I never meant to be bold I just saw you and I don't know what came over me," I told her talking about this was getting me aroused again.

"I don't know what it was in that moment but I felt it to. I wanted to touch it the moment I noticed your shorts lifting up; I think that's why I followed you in the store. I don't know how but I knew something was going to happen. Then you did what you did, I was in shock. When I touched you I was so hot, in my mind I was actually curious to know what it would feel like inside me too. Then you came on my shirt and I freaked out and ran away."

"I ran away too," I said blushing hard.

"Tonight when I saw you it was like you walked out of my head and I got hot and I didn't want to miss out this time," she stopped to finish her cigarette.

"Thank you," I said to her, unzipping my pants again and pulling myself out, "Can I have another chance?"

"Sure," she whispered in my ear as she grabbed me with her hand first, "I love it when you're bold." I loved her whispering in my ear, it fueled my erection to new thickness.

She smiled up at me for a moment before taking me into her warm, wonderful mouth and sucking me again. This time as I hoped it lasted a little longer, we're not talking hours longer but it was at least a good few minute longer this time.

"UKKK, Warning is a good thing," she said spitting and standing up again when I was done. All I could manage was a miserable "Sorry" again.

"Just keep that in mind when you're with a girl, it's nice to give her some warning," she scolded as she lit a 3rd cigarette.

We talked about basically nothing for another 2 hours and she had a couple more cigarettes in that time. She said that she usually didn't smoke that much but she wasn't having the best day. I didn't really hear most of what she was talking about, I was so lost in talking with her that it didn't really matter what we talked about. I had never had such a long open conversation with a girl before. I felt like we had a connection and I never wanted to lose her from my world again.

She explained that her mom was the bride's sister and she hated her new uncle. She claimed that John had hit on her repeatedly since she was 15. Being which I was only now 15 it made me wonder just how much older them me she was. She had been really glad I came along, seeing me again and being able to fulfill one of her longest fantasies had made her day. I was glad because it had made mine too.

Finally she said that we should rejoin the party, I knew she was right but I was sad to see our time together come to a close. I didn't know if I would ever see her again. She pulled out another cigarette saying she was going to have one more before returning to the party. I leaned in and kissed her before she could light it and it fell to the ground. It had been a couple hours now since she gave me head and I wanted at least one last kiss before leaving. She kissed me back hard and heavy and as our passion deepened I pulled down the top of her dress exposing her breasts.

I pulled away long enough to look at her body and commit the image into my memory before kissing her more deeply and rubbing her breasts with my hands. I pushed her up against the barn wall and lifted up the bottom of her dress. This was hot and passionate and I was losing my mind. I slipped my hand inside her panties and my finger inside her; she was warm and wet as I slid my finger back and forth in her tight slit. I had no idea what I was doing as this was the first time I had ever done this but she moaned and grabbed my hand guiding it to touch the right spots.

I couldn't believe this was real, I couldn't believe it was really her. We were kissing and I had one hand on her boob and one finger in her pussy after getting head! I was waiting to wake up; I just hopped that it wouldn't happen before we could finish this dream. I was burning I took my hand off of her breast and unzipped my pants. I moved forward lifted her up against the wall higher and got as far as my penis touching her through her panties. I was doing my best not to cum before I could get myself inside her, I was about to pull her panties aside when she stopped me.

"See," she said panting, "Never fails you blow a guy twice and he wants more."

"I'm....... I was just going with ...." I said embarrassed, I had screwed up again.

17

"I was fucking with you," She said smiling, "I want it too....... I like you....... you're my toy store boy........ That was the most passionate moment I've ever ....I'm just not ready."

"Oh....... I....." I started looking down at myself.

"And yes before you ask I will help you out one more time." She smiled and winked at me before she spun me around so my back was to the wall this time. She got down on her knees and began to lick the head of my cock. She took it slow this time, grabbing me at the base of my cock and licking me all over. I had never felt waves of pleasure like this before and I was so worked up that it didn't take long this time but I did manage to warn her. I had barely just got the words out as I shot my hot load across her face. She pulled a handkerchief out of her purse and wiped her face then picked up her dropped cigarette and lit it.

We stood there in silence until she had finished her smoke and then she said we really needed to get back. I reluctantly agreed and kissed her one last time before leaving. As we walked back to the reception, I was actually light headed from the whole experience and my mind was whirling around, this had been the best night of my life so far. The walk across the farm took a few minutes as it was a big place, once we had reached the outside window to the kitchen someone called to her.

"I got to go," she said winking at me. I had missed the name they had called and it was then that it hit me, I had almost had sex with her and I still didn't even know her name.

I hung around the outside of the tent for a while before going back in. I was wondering around the buffet table looking for some desert and soda when my father rushed over to me.

"Where have you been I've been looking for you for an hour?" He asked. He was really excited about something and I already didn't care.

"Walking around, what's the big deal?"

"I have someone I want you to meet," he told me. We walked over to his coworker John and standing with him was his new wife Linda and another very pretty woman.

"Joey this is Lilly, as it turns out John here married the sister of one of my ex-girlfriends."

"Wow dad, that's cool," I said really flatly not really thinking about what he just said. At this point I really didn't give a damn about some ex-girlfriend, there were lots of ex-girlfriends I didn't see what made this one any different.

"I don't expect you to get excited about that part," He said equally flat, "But I guess when we last saw each other she didn't know she was pregnant. I have a daughter and you have a sister, isn't that cool?"

I knew the rest of it before he said anything. Knowing my dad as I did I know that he would have fucked her a few times then disappeared when another piece of ass came along. I'd seen him do it repetitively over the last six months. He never stayed with one for long. I wouldn't be surprised at all if I had 10 more sisters out there. What I didn't learn for another few years was just how different Lilly had

been as far as ex-girlfriends go, if I had known the significance of their relationship I might have cared more about what was going on that night.

It was then what he had said a minute ago came screaming into my head. Didn't the girl say that her mom was the sister if the bride? But what are the odds? This didn't mean she was my sister she could be the daughter of another sister of the bride right? Unfortunately that is what this story is all about. My toy store girl walked up to us a few minutes later, she smiled at me and winked as she approached. It was all I could do not to lose it, but I told myself not to jump to conclusions yet.

"Oh God Please don't let her be my sister," I mumbled to myself as she gave Lilly a hug. It was then she was introduced to my father and me as Lilly's daughter Katie.

We looked at each other horrified for a minute and it was all I could do to maintain my composure. I tried to play it off like I was just in shock of having a sister but I wasn't sure that it came across that way, this whole situation was wrong, so wrong. I found out Katie was 16 making her one year older than me yet all I could think about was oh my god! I just got head from my sister, three times and almost fucked her!

As soon as we could get away we walked outside together to talk, we both were horrified by the realization that we were related. It was a while before we really spoke and when we did it was real talking. The kind of adult conversation I don't think I had ever had with another person in my life to that point. She said the thought of us almost having sex made her a little sick, I didn't make her sick just the situation.

"I just thank god I stopped you when I did," She said trying to smile.

"Yeah..........." I said quietly.

"You'll always be my toy boy," she said lifting my chin and kissing my cheek trying to cheer me up, "But now things are different."

"Well ....," I started. I was so confused that I really didn't know how to respond, "It's not like we live together....... but I understand your point...... I just don't know if I can think of you as a sister......."

"Look, I can't do it with my brother. I just can't. Everything is weird now. My god I fingered myself to the thought of you, for two years!" She said her face turning red, "And tonight.........."

"I........," I couldn't talk; the shame I hadn't felt for a long time started to come back, because it didn't matter to me that she was my half-sister, I still really wanted her. But I was too scared to tell her how I felt about her.

"Look," she said again, "Let's just put this in the past and try whole brother sister thing, I've always wanted a brother, really."

"Ok," I said thinking that having her in my life some way was better than no way.

We talked more; she figured that since we had only ever run into each other a couple times that we could move past everything and it wouldn't be too weird given time. We talked until it was time for us to leave, we talked about our likes and dislikes and movies and books. We found we had a lot of common

interest and we enjoyed discussing books. We intentionally avoided the monkey in the room as it were and started our relationship as siblings.

It was late when my dad came to find me, I hadn't paid any attention to where he had been all night and when he found us talking he thought it was great that we were getting along already. He said it was time to leave and Katie gave me a quick and innocent hug good bye and said she had my number and would keep in touch.

I rode home in silence that night; I really hated life right now. I had finally found my toy store girl again only to have all my fantasies ruined. How could I ever think of her as my sister? There was just no way after tonight was there? I loved her, not as a sister, as a woman and I knew I was going to have her someday.

Chapter Two: Brother and Sister? Really?

It took about a month before I could get up the courage to call Katie. I was thinking of her still every time I masturbated, I couldn't help it, I knew she was my sister but she was also the only girl I had ever been with. I was conflicted I had thought of her all the time since that day in the park and when you fixate on someone for as long as I had thought of her it was hard just to stop. But worse than that when I closed my eyes I saw her naked body, felt her lips on me and I saw her sparkling eyes looking up at me when she had sucked my dick. I tried as hard as I could but I couldn't get these images out of my mind.

The worst part of it was the wedding had put me into hyper drive, every spare moment I had I was stroking it to the memory of us. She had told me that she thought of me while she fingered herself! How hot was that? This was almost too much for me to handle at 15. She infested my brain every waking minute now, but I couldn't talk to her about it. To make things worse I felt more guilt now than when I started masturbating. Talk about mixed up sex questions, if I had no one to talk to about the jerking off issue then who the hell could I tell about this?

I finally called Katie and asked her if she wanted to hang out, go to the movies or something, she said yes and that she had been waiting for me to call. She told me that she kind of felt weird about things and didn't know how I felt so she had been waiting for my call first.

This was the beginning of us being inseparable, for the next four months we went everywhere together. We didn't even so much as hold hands but we had a blast with one another, she was the most wonderful girl I had ever known. She told me I was the greatest brother she could ever imagine.

Things were utterly perfect in my life for once except for the fact that I still wanted to be with her sexually, take that part out and life was all aces. We went to the movies, book signings, hung out at the library, school functions at both of our schools and even met all of each other's friends. I was so happy having a best friend and just being around her I managed not to think of the sex, except when I was all alone.

What made things even better is when we finally mixed all our friends everyone got along so well it was as if we all had been friends for years. We had a couple of raging parties together and that's how I ended up meeting her best friend Abby.

Abby was a really pretty girl but she simply wasn't Katie. We went to a party thrown by a friend of Katie's by the name of Ted, it was a really big bash and we all had too much to drink. I hadn't gone to the party to hook up as I was still in the middle of my Katie dilemma but one thing led to another. I ended up on the couch making out with Abby, she was a good kisser but I couldn't get into it the same way I did with Katie. It felt weird being with someone else after finally having got the girl of my dreams. I was just trying to respect what Katie wanted and move on.

Katie on the other hand took a liking to my friend Rob, at the same party I made out with Abby I saw them walk into a bedroom and close the door. I asked her later what had happened and she told me they had just talked, but she liked him. I was hurt but I guess this is what it meant to be really trying to do the brother, sister thing.

As far as things went I had completely stopped taking all risks after I turned 16. I had other things going on and almost always had people with me. I wasn't going to whip it out and do it around my friends. I couldn't even admit to them I did it. Even when I was old enough and mature enough to understand everyone does it, I still couldn't tell anyone. I had sat in the room while other guys talked about where they did it and didn't get caught I still lied and said I never did it.

I don't even now understand why I couldn't admit to it with in a group of friends who talked about it like it was no big deal and would have still accepted me. I mean I knew it wasn't a big deal but I still was holding a lot of guilt from my childhood. At the time my guilt over jerking it rolled over into my guilt for wanting to bang my sister. Now with this nearly perfect life I had going on things were bound to hit a bump in the road, when my life hit that bump everything crashed hard.

The first thing that went wrong was Katie ended up dating Rob, I was crushed. Our night together had been almost six months earlier and she had settled down into this whole sibling thing so from her point of view dating my friend was no big deal. I mean I had made out with her friend in front of her so why would she think it was a big deal? I really believe she thought I was in the same place as her and she had no idea that I was so hurt. I just thought to myself at least we don't live together and I don't have to see them dating.

Funny thing about wayward thoughts like that are sometimes they happen. I had so much on my mind the night of the wedding I hadn't given any attention to what my dad was doing, I should have paid attention. I also should have really paid attention to what he was doing after the wedding as well, as again I was stuck in my own world oblivious to his dating at that time.

Apparently seeing each other at the wedding had re-kindled the spark with my father and Lilly and they started secretly dating. Six months after the wedding they sat Katie and I down, they started talking about how happy they were that we got along so well because we were all going to be moving in together. They weren't talking marriage yet but they wanted to see where it went. My jaw hit the floor as I had no idea that they were dating, I had a number of questions on that subject.

Ok this just took things to a whole new level of weird as now Katie was going to be living in my house while dating my best friend. I couldn't think of how this could be any worse, but it did. The girls and my dad and I lived in two bedroom apartments and our parents told us that we were all going to move into a three bedroom apartment.

The new problem came in the form of the girls gave up there apartment and we were all supposed to move on the same weekend, then due to some mix up the new apartment wasn't ready. The girls had to put their things into storage and we managed to keep our apartment for a little while longer. This meant for 3 weeks not only would Katie be living in the house we would have to share a room.

Damn you cruel fate! Now the girl of my dreams was going to be sharing a room with me and I couldn't do anything with her. Not thinking anything of it our parents asked if we would be ok with sharing my full size bed or if we would have to buy a cot or something for one of us. Katie said we could share no big deal she said she thought we were comfortable with each other enough now to handle it.

This proved to only be true for the first week; with them in the small apartment I couldn't find time or space to get myself off. To make things worse Katie only slept in a sport bra and shorts, I was awake and hard for her half the night just looking at her body. I would have jerked off in the shower but we found that the hot water wasn't great for four people in the same morning.

On the 9th day I couldn't take it anymore, it was a warm evening and she had kicked the blanket off herself. I was lying there looking at her trying to fight myself from attacking my hard on, but it had been nine days! She moaned in her sleep and I couldn't stand it one second longer. I pulled my sweats down and couldn't stop myself, I was going at it full force, and considering how long it had been I was lasting a long time.

I closed my eyes for a minute and when I opened them again she was looking at me.

"What are you doing?" She asked quietly.

"I..... I couldn't sleep."

"Oh. I do that when I can't sleep too," she said biting her lip, "I just thought........"

"I ... can stop."

"No. If you need to do that so you can fall asleep," she said looking at my hand, "I understand and I think I'll do it to, to go back to sleep." ARE YOU FUCKING KIDDING ME, I thought to myself as she slid her hand inside her shorts.

She moaned, her eyes closed and her back arched as her hand moved under her shorts. This is so unfair, I thought, I want her so bad and we were here masturbating together when I could just roll over and fuck her yet I couldn't. She slid her hand up under her sport bra and started rubbing her left breast. She was getting so into it she pulled her bra up exposing herself, I couldn't take it anymore, our bodies were so close together that when I came I went off like a gun shot, causing it to shoot out and land onto her stomach.

"Again really?" she moaned referring to the day we met. I was really worked up and started again and she wasn't actually angry that I came on her. I grew bold again and took a chance reaching over and beginning to gently stroke her breast.

"No," she moaned but didn't stop me when I slipped my hand down into her shorts and moved her hand out of the way. She said "No" again but let me continue to finger her, so I moved in and began to suck her nipple. She moaned "No, really no" but didn't stop me instead she grabbed my dick and started stroking.

"What if someone .... comes in....." she moaned between breaths. With my free hand I pulled the blanket over us.

"Ooooh yes!" she moaned softly into the blanket. I pulled her shorts off her and took my sweats completely off, then I climbed up on her and between her legs. She still had her hand on my dick and the head was resting on her pussy! I started to move her hand and she gripped harder.

"No," she moaned, "No........." she rolled me over on my back. She reached under the blanket and pulled her shorts back on. I laid there feeling stupid as she moved her bra back into place; I started to say something when she slid down the bed. I was completely shocked a moment later when she began to lick the head of my dick all over. I closed my eyes and moaned as her lips engulfed the tip and her mouth began to slowly slide down my cock. Her mouth was so warm and she felt so awesome as her tongue caressed the point where my head connected to my shaft. Unfortunately the night had me so worked up I didn't take long for my second orgasm, I burst the last remaining fluid I had in me down her throat as she sucked me in deeper then she had ever taken me before. She scooted back up the bed and coughed slightly swallowing down my seed. She lay down again and I tried to kiss her but she turned her head away.

"I thought you really were just trying to sleep," she said quietly, "I thought we were past these months ago."

"We are," I lied, "I just got caught up in the moment."

"Oh," she said so quietly that I barely heard her; "This shouldn't have happened. I'm your sister and I'm dating your best friend."

"Yeah, I know I just hadn't............. jacked off," I said the last two words quiet and awkwardly, "Since you guys have been here, I thought you were asleep and I was just trying to relive tension."

"Oh," she said quietly again, "It wasn't about me?"

"No." I lied.

"Oh," she said, "I was just caught up too. I've never done that in front of anyone before."

"I have, just once, that day......"

"Oh, yeah, that day..... Tonight I just thought it would be exciting to have someone watch. When I woke up and saw you I was turned on a little too."

"Yeah," I said softly, "I saw you and got more turned on. I never saw a girl do that. I've never seen a live girl's ....pussy, just pictures. With the blanket in the way I still really couldn't see it"

"Oh," she said embarrassed, "I forget you've never had sex." I was taken aback by the way she said it. It was like she had, had sex, but when was that? She never told me she had gone all the way and I know she hadn't when we met at the wedding. Who had she slept with in the last six months? I thought we told each other everything, it had to be Rob. I could feel my cheeks burning with envy.

"Yeah," I said trying to hide my thoughts, "I've come close twice."

"Yeah, I didn't think I should screw my brother. Everything else is bad enough, but we've been there before."

"Well, yeah."

"Maybe we should just go to sleep," She said rolling over

We had an awkward morning after that as she seemed really out of sorts. I felt like a total jerk because I had taken her down a road she didn't want to go. Going to bed that night was really weird, we laid there in silence until I heard her sleeping softy and I rolled over and fell asleep. The next two nights were the same thing we didn't talk and we laid there in silence.

I woke up on the fourth night after to find Katie masturbating next to me. I woke up and she was already into it enough she had her bra pulled up and hand in her pants. Her eyes were closed and she had her back arched. At first I just sat there watching I didn't want to move, I didn't want her to know I was awake and stop.

"What are you waiting for......"she moaned softly. How did she know I was awake? She moaned again as I slid my hand into her shorts and she pulled the blanket up over us. I started sucking her breasts and she kissed the top of my head, she slid her hand in my sweats grasping me hard and started stroking me. I slid her shorts off her again under the blanket; I wanted to see her pussy this time. I really wanted to see a real pussy for the first time.

I started moving lower kissing my way down her stomach. Despite my eagerness I moved slowly trying to make sure not only to give her as much pleasure as I could but to savor every moment of this. I had just made it down to her waist when she pulled my head up to her face. She kissed me on the cheek and pulled my sweats off. OH MY GOD THIS IS REALLY HAPPENING! I thought to myself. I rolled over on top of her and made it as far as my dick was in the hair above her pussy when my excitement got the best of me and I came on her again.

"Really?" she said and pushed me over onto my back.

"I'm sorry."

"I should have expected it." she joked and smiled at me.

"I'm confused........ I thought you were upset. We haven't even talked since the other day?"

"It wasn't you," she said turning her head away, "I broke up with Rob the day after you almost ......"

"He didn't say anything." I wasn't sure where she was going with this.

"The other day just happened. Tonight I've just been upset and I was horny. I knew you were watching me and I know it doesn't take much to get you going. I figured why not."

"So this was just another in the moment thing?"

"Yeah, but when you came on me, again, I realized we were taking it too far."

"Oh."

"You're still up huh?" she said looking down and giving me a playful squeeze, "I'll help you fall asleep." She slid down and took me into her mouth. She sucked me slow and hard until I fell back to sleep.

The next day we talked again, she said that it was getting really weird between us. I lied and told her not to think too much about it, it was all just in the moment fooling around and after we moved it would be ok because we would have our own rooms. She said I was right but we really shouldn't have any more in the moment incidents. She was really upset that she had almost let me have sex with her and if I had cum inside her she could've got pregnant and how would we explain that.

I don't know why but I asked her who she had, had sex with, she admitted that she had slept with Rob the night of the party. They had too much to drink and her boundaries came down, I was so angry inside. I wanted to kill him for getting where I wanted to be but I couldn't be too mad at her because after they had sex he stopped being as nice to her. That was one of the reasons she had broken up with him, she realized that all he wanted from her was sex. I really didn't hear most of what she was saying; I was so upset she had sex with someone else.

Over the next 6 days things were really good with us; it was like things were before we lived together. We went to the movies, hung out at the library and drank coffee at the book stores. We went roller blading through town, and just talked like we hadn't in weeks. Things were so good that I thought maybe I was finally ready to give up and just be her brother. At night we were just sleeping and nothing else, I did wake up and watch her while I masturbated on the third night but she didn't wake up. I wanted to respect her decision to stop all sexual incidents between us but couldn't give up cold turkey.

It was on the last night we before we moved into our new apartment and Rob through a big party, Katie went despite the fact she didn't want to see him. I drank a little too much that night and ended up on the couch with Abby again. We were kissing really playfully, I had her shirt unbuttoned right there on the couch with everyone watching us making out. She was a wild girl and didn't mind as I slid my hand in her open shirt and played with her breasts. Katie came to me at about 10:00 and said that we were already supposed to be home and we needed to go, I somewhat reluctantly pulled away from Abby and left with Katie.

We didn't really talk on the way home, she drove and I tried to sober up as much as possible before walking in the door. The last thing I needed was for my dad to catch me half drunk. To my surprise the parents weren't waiting for us when we got back, we slipped in quietly and went to bed. I had drunk so much and as much as I really wanted to make the best of my last night lying in bed with Katie, I passed out rather quickly.

I woke up to Katie kissing my neck and she was completely topless already, I kissed her mouth going into full gear. Without a word she slid off my shorts and I felt her hand wrap around my cock, I still continued to kiss her enjoying the fact she was lying on me this time. I liked the feeling her breasts on my chest, she began to dry hump me though her shorts. The feeling of her body was so incredible that I got overly excited a little too quickly. I loved the feel of her taking control like that so much so that it didn't take long for me to let loose all over her stomach.

"Is it sad that I was expecting that?" she joked giggling. She slid down the bed and gripped my shaft hard. Slowly she began to lick me, starting at the base of my cock and moving up to the head. She licked the pre-cum off me before she sucked the head into her mouth. I actually lasted about fifteen minutes until I felt the tightening in my balls, I warned Katie and she pulled back and slowly stroked me until I came.

She slid back up my body pulling the blanket over us then she began to kiss my lips again as she wiggled out of her shorts. I could feel her bare wetness on my thigh, she wasn't wearing panties.

"I wanted to get you off a couple of times before I took of my shorts," she whispered in my ear, "The emptier your balls are the less chance for accidents."

She moved over until her pussy was touching my cock and she began to rub herself up against me. I could feel myself wedged between her wet lips and it was all I could do not to grab her hips and push myself inside her. It felt awesome as I kissed her. Slowly I kissed and licked my way lower until I found and began sucking her breasts.   She rubbed her hot wet love lips on me for at least an hour before sliding down my body and again taking me within her mouth. It felt so good and I was so happy but the alcohol from earlier caught up with me again and as she licked my cock I passed out.

When I woke up, not long after, she was lying there with her hand in her panties trying to make herself cum.

"You want me to help you?" I asked kissing her stomach and moving lower. She lifted my head and kissed me.

"With your hand," she moaned moving my hand to her, "If I take anything else off I'll want to do more then let you lick me. I ...." My fingers found her clit and I began to rub her gently and slowly at first. It didn't take long as she had been pretty worked up from our earlier fun. Katie grabbed the pillow from behind me and pulled it over her face as her orgasm hit her. She cried out into the pillow trying to cover her intense release.

"Wow," she said panting as I kissed her neck, "Tonight is our last night in here together."

"Oh, I thought this meant you changed your mind........" I started.

"No," she said softly turning her face away from mine, "I was feeling horny after the party. I just thought since we both were here.............." she stopped as if she didn't know how to finish the sentence.

"Then this was another in the moment thing?" I asked as she pulled her shorts back on.

"You're my brother, where did you think this was going? I told you no sex." she said pulling her bra back on.

"I didn't......." I stammered, "Just the last couple weeks........ They've been the best of my life......... I........"

"Come here," she said pulling me into a hug, "I liked you the moment we met. We both know things aren't meant to be. I've had fun with you but it needs to stop."

"I know....... I know."

"It needs to stop because I want to have sex with you."

"I know......," My heart was breaking.

"We need to find a way to live together in the same house and not do this; I really mean it after tonight it's over."

"I know........ I'm not thinking about a relationship, we just keep doing this because were in the same bed is all." I knew it was the wrong thing to say only because it wasn't what was in my heart, I loved her. I could never tell her that, she would never understand. I didn't know if she could see strait through my lies, if she would have looked me in the eyes she would have known it was all a lie.

"That's all? Just because were in bed together?" she asked quietly.

"Yes. You're a great girl but your right, it's wrong to be like this with your sister," I told her fighting back tears, "But I'm a guy and I just can't hold back when I have a sexy girl in my bed."

"Ok," she almost cried, "As long as it's not..... Anything else."

I laid there for about a half an hour with her face turned away before I kissed neck, she didn't stop me. She turned her head and kissed me on the mouth. We kissed passionately the whole rest of the night finally passing out only about an hour before we had to be up to start moving. We didn't say another word to each other all night.

Chapter Three: Becoming Siblings

The next day we moved into a very nice three bedroom apartment in town, she had her own room and I had mine and our relationship was never the same again. The rooms were on opposite sides of the hall with our doors facing each other, with our parent's room at the end of the hall.

It was only a few weeks later when school started again. Abby's family had moved into a bigger house and she would now be attending school with Katie and me. Both girls were excited to have each other as they were both starting this year at a new school. This excitement was short lived however as Katie started taking the running start classes at the community college meaning she wouldn't be around school much with us. It kind of worked out for Abby and I as we began to hang out all the time.

Within a few weeks of taking classes at the college Katie had started dating a boy there. Before long she found out that when she graduated that she would have scholarships and she would be moving out of state for full time college at the end of the year. I was heartbroken at the news that she was going to be going away next year. I still held out the hope deep in my soul that we would find a way to be together but if she moved it would never happen.

Katie didn't talk to me much about her sex life for obvious reasons but from what I picked up she was hot and heavy with this new guy. I would see them sitting in his car at night when I was coming home from friend's houses and our nights together seemed a million miles away, like a long ago dream that never happened. We didn't have much time to hang out or talk and on the rare moments we were alone all I heard about was college. I felt like I had lost her completely, I realized in her mind I had become just her dorky little brother.

Me on the other hand, I had the women just lining up at the door, ok if you paid attention to the prologue you know that's a crock of shit. I said it there that I had still never been laid and that was when I was 19 at this point in the story I was still only 16. Puberty was over yet I still was masturbating as much as possible, I did it in public again, generally it's a freaking miracle I never got caught.

In an act of need and desperation I kind of started dating Abby. We never went all the way but she was into making out in public and loved the thrill in the idea that we might get us caught together. She got off on the thrill of it as much as I did. We fooled around so many times at her house with her door open and her parents' home, I'm lucky I'm not dead. If her dad would have walked in 90 percent of the time we were in her room he would have thrown me out her window. The funny thing is that he thought if we were in the room with the door open then we wouldn't be doing anything wrong, boy was he mistaken.

As much as I was really beginning to like Abby I never felt for her what I felt for Katie, she was more like a nicotine patch smokers use to give up cigarettes. I know that's a harsh way to put it but I knew then I didn't love her, I liked her a lot but I didn't love her. But what else was I supposed to do? Sit in my room all the time and jerk off to the hope my sister would someday love me. No I decided that I had to make the best of my situation and Abby was a very pretty and sweet girl, I couldn't imagine moving on with anyone else.

Abby liked watching and talking about her favorite movies but I could never get her to talk about or read books. I always felt like something was missing with her, I think when it came down to it I was into her much more because of my own sense of public risk taking. That part of our relationship was really awesome as we took so many chances and played around everywhere we went.

By the next January Katie and I were living together but I saw her less than before we all had moved in, with her trying so hard to get her scholarships she was always at school or with her boyfriend. It had gotten to the point where she often didn't come home for days; our parents were so into each other and their whole romance they didn't even notice.

With everyone so involved with around the house I felt more lonely than ever, so I decided by then to just try harder to make the relationship with Abby work. She was always telling people around school I was her boyfriend, I had just thought we were dating but we had never talked about being officially boyfriend and girlfriend. I just gave in and decided I guess I had my first girlfriend.

We had made out pretty heavy lots of times but she was still a virgin and as much as she liked fooling around in front of a crowd she didn't want to go to fast. One day as the weather began to warm up again we skated quite a ways on the trail and pulled off to a secluded spot to make out, we kissed and I sucked her breasts. I was really starting to like having a steady girlfriend.

I loved playing with her boobs, and the fact that she let me play with them pretty much anywhere anytime. Since we had a little bit of privacy off the trail this time Abby did something really unexpected, as we kissed she began to unzip my shorts. It felt so good when she reached in and began to softly rub me, I begged for more and she pulled me out through my zipper hole and stroked me until I came on my skates. This was the first time she had ever stroked me to completion and it felt so awesome. With the public risks we had taken in the past she would usually just give me a few minutes of rubbing before stuffing me back into my pants.

This new level lead into the next phase of our public playing as from then on she would often pull me out of my pants and stroke me anyplace anytime she thought she could get away with it. I was allowed to play with her any were too as long as I didn't remove her panties, she began to wear skirts most of the time to give me access to her legs and pussy so long as I only rubbed her outside her panties. I had thought we had, had some close calls in the beginning but now that she was pulling me out everywhere we really had an added level of danger now. It was so exciting and I left so much cum on public benches and other places.

The worst of our close call came at the movies, we were in the back row and we got so into it there that I had her tank top and bra pulled down and I was sucking her breasts. She unzipped my pants pulled me out and began to stroke me; I slid my hand up her skirt and fingered her. She shuddered as her orgasm hit her barely able to contain her moaning. She gave me a sexy wink as she pulled my hand away from her soaked panties and slid down her seat and kneeling in front of me, not even fixing her bra, breasts still exposed. She licked my dick tentatively as this was the first blow job she had ever given; she licked me for what felt to me a god awful amount of time before she began to suck my dick.

I almost came as soon as I felt her tongue on the underside of my cock head, the risk we were taking with people only a couple rows ahead of us was almost too much to take. Abby's mouth felt so good as she did her best to please me, it felt so different from what I had felt before. I blasted cum down her throat with rope after rope of bursting in only a matter of minutes. She waited until I stopped letting me fall out of her mouth then she spit it all out into the isle. She sat back up in her seat and ate a mouth full

of popcorn as I sucked her breast again and put my fingers back inside her pussy. When she had cum the second time she fixed her bra back into place and I finally put myself back into my pants. Only moments later a girl usher came in walked up and down the rows doing a regular theater check, we had come so close to getting caught and I was hard again over that.

We were both excited and scared by coming that close to getting caught she said that if her dad would have found out we wouldn't ever be allowed to see each other again. So that was the first and last time we went that far in a movie theater, I really wanted to do it again but I thought it wasn't the wisest of choices.

A few weeks later I finally finished drivers ED and got my license, this opened up new doors for Abby and I. We could make out in my car anywhere we wanted from that point on. We didn't need to sneak around her house or the movies anymore, for her public exposure in a car was her new turn on. For as much fun as we were having Abby felt it was best to still wait to go all the way. She was happy to give me head as much as I wanted but she still held on to that one last thing she thought was most important.

Over the rest of that school year my relationship to Abby progressed to the point where we were fooling around every minute we were alone. We had fun doing things in plain sight at the park on the beaches. We spent so much time making out in my car that we joked that we should have a mini fridge installed in the back seat so we could have something to drink once in a while.

During this time even with all the fun I was having with my girlfriend, I missed my sister very much we lived in the same house but we couldn't have lived farther apart. Things to me couldn't have been worse than my 17th birthday.

It was June and Katie was to graduate, the little comfort I took from the whole situation was that soon she would be leaving for college at the end of August and maybe then I could finally get over her. She came home from school a week prior to my birthday red faced and crying. She said she had broken it off with her boyfriend but wouldn't give any details, I tried to put my arm around her and talk to her but she said no and walked away.

Katie walked into my room not long after I woke up on my birthday; I had just slid my hand inside my boxers for some early morning birthday play when my door opened. It was a Saturday morning and my parents had left early that day to get my grandmother. She lived 4 hours away and was coming to stay with us for a couple of weeks for my birthday and Katie's graduation. We had a big party planned for that night to combine both events.

Katie walked in and stood over me biting her lower lip.

"Hey sis, what's up?" I said kind of jokingly trying to gage what her intentions were.

"I wanted to talk to you......." She had a tear in her eye, "I'm leaving for college soon and........ you haven't really talked to me since before we move in."

"I........" was all I could get out. I was confused and slightly angry. It was her not me that had stopped being close to me!

"I........... Thought you wanted space," was all I could manage.

"No," she said coldly, tears rolling down her face, "What I wanted............ what I've been waiting for.......... Since that night before we moved in here.......... what I've needed to hear............."

"What?" I asked her.

"God you're so.................UUUUHHHH," she cried, "You still can't say the words." I finally understood.

The nights we spent together, sharing a bed. I ran through the conversations in my head as best I could remember them. I realized they had a double meaning. She was saying to me what she thought I had wanted to hear, but I now realized that underneath she was asking me to commit to my real feelings.

It had been almost a year and only now did I understand that she had been asking me to tell her I loved her, I realized that now that nothing on those three nights had been about the sex, it was love. I felt horrible for not realizing sooner I felt so stupid I had hurt her, but how could she be talking about this now? She was leaving and we couldn't have more than the summer to be together and what about Abby? I realized in that moment that I really loved Katie but I didn't want to give up or hurt Abby.

Then my eyes grow big from shock as I realized that she had broken up with HER boyfriend FOR ME, the day after everything had happened with us that first night in my bed. Not only had I never realized that was the true reason for the break up with Rob, I made things worse by hooking up with her friend Abby not long after. I was quiet for so long that Katie turned to leave and I grabbed her arm.

"What now you have something to say?" She was furious.

"Katie...... I ...." I started but couldn't get it out. I was so scared, what would it mean for me to tell her the truth now? I was having conflicting emotions. I loved her, dreamed of her yet I had spent so much time trying to forget all that, focusing on my girlfriend now.

"Katie I've wanted ...." I never got to finish my comment as there was a knock at the front door, "I'll get the door. Go wash your face and I'll talk to you in a couple minutes." I got up and through on a pair of jeans and left my room.

I went to the door and to find Abby there, she jumped at me and wrapped her arms around me. I kissed her and tickled her side and she giggled.

"I missed you so much," she said, "I wanted to come here early so I could give you your special birthday present before your parents get home." She winked at me.

Before I could say a word she grabbed my hand and led me to my room. We lay down on the bed and started kissing. I momentarily forgot about Katie as we sank into our kissing. I didn't mean to forget her but when my girlfriend had winked at me I realized that she was finally ready to have sex. From there my mind just side tracked and I stopped thinking. I was finally going to get sex, I had wanted my first time to be Katie but my mind wasn't functioning right at the moment.

We sank deep into our kissing. She began running her hands over my chest since I didn't have on a shirt. The feeling of her hands was turning me on so much. I moved my hands to the buttons of her shirt. One by one they fell open. I moved my lips lower to her neck as I continued kissing. I ran my hand across her breast over her bra slowly caressing her nipples. I realized without looking she was wearing a

sports bra. After a couple minutes of teasing her nipple I slipped my hand under the fabric rubbing her slowly. Her nipples were hardening as I started rubbing faster.

My free hand found the waistband of her panties under the hem of her jeans. I teased her there with my fingers just inside the elastic for a minute. She started humming softly in anticipation and I moved my hand lower and stopped teasing. I slid my fingers inside her and she moaned loud.

At the same time I felt her hands at my zipper. I groaned in anticipation myself and slid lower to her chest kissing her shoulders. Pulling me out though my now open zipper she began to slowly and softly tease my cock with her fingertips. It was my turn to moan. I lifted her sport bra up and began to suck her nipples as I drove in as deep as I could with my fingers.

Minutes later she rolled me on my back never letting go of my dick. Lying down she unbuttoned my jeans and pulled them off. We kissed deeply and passionately as her hand gripped me and she began to stroke. Moving slowly and deliberately she began to kiss her way down to my pelvis, stopping there kissing just above my shaft, teasing me and driving me wild with anticipation. It was so erotic the way she was taking her time with me, she had never moved this slowly with me in the past and it was the most erotic moment we had ever shared up until that point.

I had on more than one occasion received oral sex from her in the past but she had never done it like this. This time was slow and with so much more love then she had ever given the act. I felt myself getting close, "I'm gonna cum," I told her. I erupted harder than I ever had with her looking right into her eyes as I did so. She smiled at me as she swallowed. I was shocked because she had never done that before.

"That was part one of your gift," she told me pulling away wiping the corner of her mouth. It was so hot I didn't lose any of my excitement after I came; I somehow managed to stay as hard as steel. She noticed as she held me.

"Someone liked that," she grinned, "Now for the second part." She slipped out of her clothes and lay down on her back. She pulled me close to her kissing me deeply.

"I love you," she said to me breaking our kiss. I didn't respond with words, I kissed her deeply again. I couldn't get into that right now; I didn't want to tell her I wasn't there. I was so focused on finally getting laid I wasn't thinking, if we would have stopped to talk of love it wouldn't have happened.

Kissing her I moved from her lips to her neck, I paused for a moment. She was doing this because she loved me. Could I really take her virginity knowing I loved Katie? Could I really take an act of love from her and be that selfish as to sleep with her now?

She grabbed my dick and moved me to her, with one thrust I would lose my virginity. Almost predicatively I was too overly stimulated and I came again on her thigh, she still held me in her hand even after two orgasms I was still hard. This close to getting laid the first time there was no way I would go soft now.

I found out years ago with my self exploration that when motivated I could cum multiple times without losing my erections. Granted each time I came I produced less and less fluid to the point that sometimes it was like a dry heave as it were. My body would send chills through me like an orgasm but I wouldn't have any fluid left.

"I'm sorry........" I started but she cut me off.

"SSShhhhhh, it's ok, I know you're nervous," she said running her hand across my face, "I love you and it looks like you're still ready."

"I......"

"I told you shush," she said softly, "I'm ready. I want this." I was still having my moral debate and it didn't help she kept telling me that she loved me. She moved me into position again, I was about to push in when the door opened. In one motion I rolled off Abby as she gasped and pulled the blanked over us.

"I've been waiting for almost an hour. Who was at the door, Joey?" she asked quietly walking in looking down. Before I could say a word she looked up at us.

More tears came to her eyes and she turned and ran from the room. I felt horrible. I had let my hormones get the best of me and forgotten all about her.

"What was that all about?" Abby asked confused. I was so hurt seeing Katie in tears that I almost didn't hear Abby. I sat there for a moment and finally said,
"She came in here just before you got here and wanted to talk about what had happened when she broke up with her boyfriend a couple weeks ago."

"Oh, poor girl."

"Yeah, I forgot when you got here that I had promised to talk to her about it." I explained.

"You didn't," She said harshly, "No wonder she's upset. She needed someone to talk to and you left her alone." Abby lightly smacked me on the shoulder. I didn't say anything as she started pulling her clothes back on. I just sat there looking at her. I didn't know what else to explain without giving too much away.

"I'm heading home," she said smiling at me, "Go be a good brother, and we will pick up where we left off later." She kissed me on the cheek and left my room. I heard the front door close a minute later. I lay in bed for some time before getting dressed.

Chapter Four: Unexpected Twists

I had just put on my jeans when I sat back down on my bed again. I leaned my head into my hands more confused than I could ever remember. Was it possible to be in love with two women? I really was too young still to have this much emotion running through me and still there was no one to talk to about it.

What had Katie wanted from me this morning? We'd had all year to talk about our feelings for each other. Now that she's leaving she wanted me to admit my love for her? She knew I had a girlfriend, I loved Katie more than anything, and at that moment I really didn't want to choose between them. Katie had said herself we couldn't have a real relationship together, we would have to move far away, and lie to everyone that we weren't siblings. I would do it for her if that's what would make her happiest but I knew how much she loved her mother and she couldn't lie to her for the rest of her life either.

However, Abby had taken our relationship to a new level today and there was an unspoken undertone that she expected me to take the same step with her. She had told me she loved me and I had narrowly avoided the problem, I felt like an ass but I didn't want to lie to her. I knew that the only reason she had been here this morning willing to give herself to me was out of a love she thought we shared, I didn't want to be that guy who used that to hurt her. But I couldn't tell her the truth, I could never tell anyone.

I walked down the hall and knocked on Katie's door.

"Go away."

"Katie, Abby's gone. Can I come in?"

"NO!" she shouted, "I can't even look at you right now." I heard the door lock click as I reached for the door knob, she had never locked me out when I wanted to talk.

"Katie, please I'm not moving until you open your door." I stood there for 10 minutes before I finally sat down; I had meant it when I said I wasn't moving. I thought about what I would say to her anyway, I truly didn't know what to do. I mean I was just a confused teenage boy, even if I told Katie how I felt and she felt the same way, she was still leaving soon. There was no way I was going to get in the way of her college. What kind of relationship would we have when she was cross country anyway?

Abby would be here with me this year and she was already my girlfriend, she was in love with me and she wasn't my sister. Did it matter I didn't love her the way I loved Katie? At least I would be able to have a real relationship with Abby without having to move away and hide who we were. I was starting to realize that Katie had been right a year ago, we couldn't date, even in secret. This whole mental debate was pointless as I clearly had only one course of action.

Abby really was a great girl, nobody would ever compare in my mind to Katie, but anybody would be lucky to be with Abby. No matter how I looked at it, I would someday have to settle down with

someone else I didn't love as much. At that moment it never occurred to me that I would ever meet anyone I could love as much or more then my sister, I thought life was as hard as it could get. I didn't know as soon as that night I would add in a third love of my life.

I snapped out of my thoughts only after I heard the front door open and my grandmother talking. I jumped up and ran into my room grabbing the first shirt I could find; I pulled it on and headed to the door to greet everyone.

"Joey," called dad from outside, "Come out to the car and get your grandmothers bags." I smiled at everyone and headed to the car. My grandmother wished me a happy birthday and gave me a hug. I brought the luggage in and took it down to my parent's room. It had been decided days ago that she would stay in the parent's room and my parents would use the hide a bed couch in the living room.

"Where's your sister," Lilly asked me when I returned to the living room.

"In her room, I think she's upset about her break up." I said as a cover story. It had worked with Abby so I just went with it again, "I'll go let her know you guys are home."

I walked down the hall again and knocked on Katie's door.

"I told you to leave me alone."

"Katie, Mom and Dad are home." I heard a shuffle and the door unlock. I slipped into the room to find her on her bed again sobbing into her pillow.

"Katie?"

"Don't bother nothing you say will change anything," she told me looking up at me, her face was red and puffy, "I can't go out there. How can I explain how I look? I can't tell them I caught you in bed with Abby."

"I already told them you were in here crying over your ex-boyfriend," I told her.

"You covered for me?"

"Well yeah, what was I going to do tell them you caught me and Abby and it upset you?"

"Thanks."

"We really should talk."

"Now really isn't the time," she said wiping the tears out of her eyes, "Come on lets go get your birthday started." She got up without another word and walked to the living room. Grandma took one look at her and pulled her into a hug, asking what was wrong. This led to her making up a whole sob story about how her boyfriend had hurt her. But then again she had never told me why she broke up with him so her story could have been true.

I didn't want to do anything more with Abby until I could talk to Katie, but she was supposed to be coming over tonight. I tried the rest of the day to get one moment alone with Katie that didn't happen. It seemed like she was intentionally trying to avoid the conversation we needed to have.

Before long friends and guests started coming over for the big party, I gave up trying to talk to her. I decided to leave everything alone for now and talk to her about it before she left. I mean we did have all summer and I could hold off with Abby for a little while yet.

We ended up with a packed apartment that night for the party. Everyone gave best wishes to both of us for our futures. Katie did a great job of keeping a smile on her face while often glancing my way; I didn't care about the whole party. I pretended to smile while waiting for Abby come back over.

Lilly's Sister Linda showed up rather late by herself that evening. I was really happy she hadn't brought her husband; I hadn't liked him the night of the wedding because of what Katie had told me about him. There was something more than creepy about a guy who hit on his girlfriend's niece all the time.

As I found out later that night Linda's husband had cheated on her with some young girl who worked at a fast food place. This left the two now separated heading into what looked to be a messy divorce. I felt bad that her life was falling apart but I really wasn't surprised to hear about the young girl.

We had lots of family and friends come and go all night long. Not long after Linda showed up, Lilly's parents arrived. They wished me happy birthday and congratulated Katie on both the graduation and the scholarships. I hadn't met them before but they seemed like really nice people.

There were a number of little kids running around I didn't know, one in particular stood out. She was a little girl about 10 to 12 years old, she had really pretty blue eyes and I remember thinking that she was going to be a really beautiful girl someday.

As the night progressed every time I turned around the little girl seemed to be standing right behind me just gazing at me. I wasn't sure if I should be flattered or creeped out by her. I would've said something to her but every time I looked at her she had the most captivating smile. How could I be annoyed by that adorable face?

"Who is that little girl there?" I asked Lilly after escaping from the child for a minute.

"I knew it wouldn't take you long to spot her," Lilly said flashing me a crooked smile, "That's Ashley." Soon as Lilly told me her name I knew who she was instantly. I just hadn't met her before.

"It's hard not to spot someone who follows you around all night."

"That's cute," Lilly said patting me on the shoulder and walking away. It wasn't more than a couple minutes and Ashley was right behind me again. It annoyed me less knowing who she was, but I still didn't need a little shadow, I just hoped she stopped following me around before Abby got here. I really need a moment alone to talk with her too.

While I spent the night trying to avoid my shadow and waiting for Abby little did I know that my grandmother had invited Katie to drive her home and stay with her over the summer. Grandma had told Katie that she shouldn't let a guy get her so down so she suggested that Katie should just get out of town,

spend the summer with her cousins and have fun before school started. Katie thought it was a really great idea.

I heard the news the next day. That gave us only a week to have our talk. I spent the whole next week trying for one moment to talk to her, it never happened. Every single time I thought that moment had come she found a way to be busy and it didn't happen, again I thought she was avoiding me on purpose.

"You can't leave," I cried out walking into her room a week later. I had, had enough trying to find the right moment. She was packing her bags, "How can you? I............. it was hard enough knowing it would be August, but I'm not ready for you to leave yet."

"Its ok little brother," she said sweetly. She had never called me little brother before, "It's better this way."

"But I think I............. I think I love........" I started and she cut me off. I knew I loved her I just couldn't say it that way.

"Don't make this worse than it already is." She walked over and kissed me on the cheek, tears in her eyes.

"We weren't meant to be," she whispered into my ear.

"We don't know that," I wasn't willing to give up.

She looked at me and nodded and I turned and left her room. As I walked through the door I turned to look at her. She jumped on her bed buried her face in her pillow and began to sob.

Katie left the next morning before I got up. I looked at my watch to find that it was already 11:00. I don't know if I could have held it together to say goodbye anyway. I would have given it all away in front of our parents. I didn't want Lilly to know especially, I couldn't imagine her response if she found out I had almost slept with her daughter. It could break up her and my dad's relationship.

I woke to find a note next to me. I opened it to read;

> Joey,
>
> I know how confusing I've been lately. I'm confused myself. Don't get the wrong idea, I do love you little brother. But there was no reason to make things harder on ourselves then necessary. I need time. We were kids when all this started, I need time to grow up. I'll see you next summer. We'll talk then. If our feelings haven't changed by then maybe we can work on this problem together.
>
> In the mean time I want you to keep seeing Abby. She is my best friend and a great girl. You guys are really good for each other. As much as I hurt inside seeing you together, you've both really grown up this year. Be as good a boyfriend to her as you've been a brother to me. I know what a warm gentle man you're growing into. If you can be all the things I love about you, for her, I will be happy.
>
> Love you always
> Katie

I was upset that I didn't at least get to hug her goodbye when she had snuck in and left the note. But she was right, only one of my relationships had an actual future; I just had to get over myself to realize it. I made the decision to move on at that moment I could always have Katie in my mind and heart, just not in body. That was when she became the girl of my obsessions, not of my reality.

I hadn't talked to Abby all week, and it was about time I did. I had never given her or our relationship the full attention that she deserved. I hadn't even called to find out why she never came back the day of my birthday, I was a horrible boyfriend she deserved better. I decided that from then on I would be better.

I called Abby right away; she actually apologized to me for not calling. She said that there had been some tension going on at home this week and we needed to talk. I was worried when she said "talk" I knew what that usually meant. Was she mad I hadn't returned her confession of love?

I had gotten to know her family quite well over the last year and I knew that her family was all extremely religious. Her father was a reverend at the local church, and her mom played the role of the reverend wife to its breaking point but her parents hadn't gotten in the way of our relationship in the past. Abby played the part of the innocent daughter when she was home but she didn't find herself overly religious, I always figured the exhibitionism a part of her rebelling against her family rule. But as I said they had never interfered with our relationship so when she told me on the phone that morning her mother had told her she wasn't allowed to date anyone now until she was 18 I was more than a little surprised.

I convinced her to have her mom drop her off at the library and I would meet her there so we could talk. She said that a good idea and agreed to meet. I got dressed as fast as I could and stopped at the local burger stand to eat before going to meet Abby at the library, I had a really bad feeling that things were about to get worse for me somehow.

Abby was waiting for me on the steps out front when I got there. I grabbed her hand leading her upstairs to one of the reference study rooms. Closing the door behind us I moved in and kissed her, I couldn't stop myself. The blinds to the room were open and the door had no lock but I couldn't stop kissing her.

Abby responded, she swung me against the back of the door and kissed me passionately. I put all my love, sadness, and sense of loss for Katie into my kissing Abby. I longed to be distracted from my hurt feelings right now. She didn't know any different she took my passion as if it were for her and matched it. Our tongues danced together like never before. We kissed for at least ten minutes before she pulled away to catch her breath.

"God baby," she breathed in my ear, "I should stay a way for a week more often." I didn't respond I attacked her neck. Kissing and licking furiously. She moaned loudly but I didn't care about how loud we were at that moment. I started unbuttoning her shirt with one hand while running my other hand up her leg inside her skirt, I figured if we were going to get caught we might as well get caught for really going for it.

"Yes, baby," she moaned in my ear. I slipped my hand in the side of her panties and began to finger her lips, "Oh god yes." I had her shirt half unbuttoned not wanting to take it all the way off, I

decided that if we were caught at least we could run away fast if we weren't actually missing any clothing. I slid my hand under her bra and found her nipple causing her to grind against my fingers.

Without warning I pulled away from her, she groaned in response. I glanced out the window, seeing no one I slid down the door reaching up grabbing her hips and drawing her to me. As I explained before, Abby had wanted to wait for sex, she could pull me out of my pants I could finger her though her panties but I was never allowed to pull her panties off. She believed also if I were to ever lick her pussy she would lose control and we would end up having sex. I really wanted to eat her out but I had never broken her trust trying to push her too far.

My birthday was the very first time she had ever taken her panties off around me, but she had removed her own panties then. I didn't count it as a break of the rules if she did it herself. I slid down the door grabbing Abby's hips drawing her to me. I moved my head under her skirt and pulled her panties to the side. I couldn't hold out any longer I wanted to taste her, I needed to taste her. To my absolute surprise she didn't complain, I mean it's not like public risk was new to us but just letting me go this far here and now was driving me crazy. Instead pushing me away she opened her stance wider to give me a better angle, and then she braced her hands palm flat on the door behind me for balance.

I ran my tongue across her tasting her wetness, her moaning was getting louder and I knew we would be caught, but I didn't care now, this was so worth it. I was lost in the moment sliding my tongue inside her, thrusting as deeply as I could. I really hadn't done this before and had no real idea of what I was doing, but she tasted so incredible I just dug in with my tongue and hoped she loved it as much as I did. After a few minutes her body tightened up and her thighs squeezed the sides of my head as her peak began to wash over her, she drew her arm over her mouth and screamed into it, as her orgasm fully hit her.

"That was AMAZING baby," she said when she began to calm down. Her breathing was heavy and labored as she pulled me up to her mouth and kissed me hard. She reached down and fixed her panties never breaking our kiss. Her shirt still unbuttoned I slid my hand under her bra again as we kissed. I had leaned forward and Abby pushed me up against the door again. She slid herself down in front of me looking up into my eyes the whole time. She slowly unzipped my pants and reached inside.

She began stroking me as best she could on the outside of my boxers before she finally pulled me out. I looked back at the windows again still seeing no one. I watched as Abby's lips enveloped my cock deep into her mouth. There was no slow teasing and licking this time, it felt like she was trying to swallow me whole as she worked my shaft with her lips and tongue. It felt incredible and I closed my eyes leaning my head back as far as I could, try to enjoy every moment. Considering where we were and how she was working me as fast and deep as possible I shot a huge load of cum down her throat within only a couple minutes. I loved the danger of this kind of fun but it always caused me to go off even faster.

"That's so damn sexy," I gasped out as she swallowed it all down, wiping her face to make sure she didn't miss any juices.

"Don't get used to it," she said pulling me out of her mouth, "I still find it gross. But considering where we are I didn't think it right to spit it somewhere." She rose back up as I stuffed myself back into my pants. We kissed for a couple minutes before she took my hand and led me to the table. We sat down in chairs facing each other still holding hands.

I looked at her for several minutes before she said anything.

"I'm sorry I didn't make it back to your birthday," she started, "I really wanted to but my mom wouldn't let me out of the house."

"So what happened?"

"Well you know Sara, "She started referring to her 14 year old younger sister. Sara was one of 3 younger sisters. He others were Shawna who was 12 and Michelle who was 9.

She explained after she left my house on that Saturday she arrived home to find her little sister crying in their room. It had taken Abby about an hour to find out what Sara was crying about. When the younger girl finally opened up to her she admitted she was pregnant. Sara had gone to her boyfriend that day to tell him the news; he called her a whore and said it wasn't his.

I wasn't surprised. I had seen older guys do the same thing. I didn't think it was right but I had seen it many times. Sara had pleaded with her boyfriend that it was his and in return he broke up with her. I knew I would never do that to someone, I couldn't understand how someone couldn't want their own child. I felt bad for little Sara, I had always felt she was such a sweet adorable little girl.

Abby went on to explain that when she finally got the story out of Sara she told her that she needed to go to their mom. Sara was scared because she knew her mom would over react. Abby agreed but she couldn't think of anything else to do, so she convinced Sara it was the right choice. Abby said that now she wished there had been another option because this was when things went wrong.

Abby walked Sara out to the back yard art studio where their mom had been working all day. Their mom's hobby was to paint portraits of Christian imagery, many of her works hung in the church Abby's dad preached at. The girls walked into the studio and explained to their mother what had happened, to find her painting a last supper rendering.

Abby told me that she had known that her mom would be angry but she hadn't expected the full extent of that reaction. Her mother didn't just go into hysterics she went into a fit of over dramatics, she gathered up all her daughters, making them hold hands and kneel down with her and pray to the lord for forgiveness.

When they were done praying she sat all the girls down at the kitchen table to have a talk about premarital sex. When she had finished condemning Sara she turned her anger on Abby. Their mother told Abby she was just lucky that she hadn't ended up with child herself. Abby tried to explain to her that she was still a virgin, but her mother didn't believe her. She said that being older and with a full time boyfriend she didn't believe at all she hadn't had sex.

Abby tried to argue with her Mom and finally in a fit of anger their mother took the 3 older girls to the doctor. She claimed that Sara needed looked at for her pregnancy to make sure she was safe and healthy. Her mother felt that Abby and Shawna needed to be checked to see if their hymens were still intact. The only reason Abby had agreed to it because she wanted to throw it in her mom's face that she wasn't lying about being a virgin. She was just lucky she hadn't accidentally broken it playing sports like some of her girlfriends.

Abby said that night was one of the worst of her life, it was bad enough that her sister was in trouble but her mom had basically called her a lire, I pointed out that had we had sex that morning her

mother would've been right. Abby flashed me a look as if to say, that's not the point, and I didn't say anything else so she could continue her story.

She told me that they had a church friend who had his own medical practice, her mother called him and he agreed to meet them at his office that night. He agreed to check out Sara for health reasons but he explained to Abby's mom that checking to see if the girls still had their hymens was a very personal thing and sometimes girls broke them accidently. Her mother didn't care, she told the doctor it was her daughters and she wanted the exam done. In the end he agreed to do it.

Abby explained that she had assumed that her mother would let up after she proved to her she was still a virgin. She said of course her mom never needed to know what else she had done, but she could now act like she was innocent. Abby said she was really happy that Katie had walked in on us when she did; I agreed that it was probably the best piece of luck that ever happened to her.

Abby said that after the examinations her mom only minimally calmed down, it was at that point her mother told the girls they were no longer allowed to date until they were 18. Her mother had been happy to find Abby and Shawna were intact but she would be now having her checked every month. Abby knew it was only a threat but she got the point, she couldn't risk having sex until she was 18. Her mom claimed that the family couldn't afford to be raising more babies. I told Abby I could understand her mom's point.

Not long after explaining the whole situation she looked at her watch and said her mom would be coming back to get her soon so she should head back to the front stairs. She re-buttoned her shirt and I leaned in and kissed her, it was just a simple goodbye kiss. Unfortunately it was that moment the door burst open.

"I knew it!" Abby's mom screamed, "I thought it was strange that you'd want to hang out at the library. You don't read!"

"Mom nothing happened!" she yelled back, "I was just telling him about not being able to date anymore."

"That's why I find you kissing and this room smells like you've been having sex?"

"Mom!" Abby exclaimed shocked, "I would never do that in public!" She put on a really good show of being offended by the statement, "And do I have to prove it again already!" Abby made her face look angry and her mom backed down.

"But I still caught you kissing."

"Yeah, He was giving me a break up kiss that's all." I was hoping I was doing a good enough job hiding my embarrassment. If her mom would have really looked at me, my face would have given everything away. I knew that if I was going to keep doing things like this I had to develop a better poker face as it were.

"Ok," she mumbled, "I'll wait outside, with the door open, and you can say goodbye."

"I know you're a good boy, Joey," her mom told me, "But your still a boy. If she told you what's going on, you'll understand why I don't want you seeing her anymore."

"I guess," was all I could say. She left the room and I turned to Abby. I was hurt beyond measure I was losing both the girls I cared about in the same day. I kissed Abby deeply for a few minutes, until she pulled away slightly resting her forehead on mine.

We looked into each other's eyes and in that second after everything that had happened before it; I fell for her in that sweet moment between us. Don't get me wrong I still loved Katie most of all, but I fell for my girlfriend in that moment. She had gone through a deeply personal exam to protect our relationship. I didn't know what I could do that would be that loving back for her, but from now on I would try.

"Don't worry it's not forever." With that said she turned and left. She was right we would have school again this next year to see each other but it wasn't the same.

"Bye Abby," I called after her as she walked out. I closed the door and sat down at the table again literally beginning to cry.

With Katie gone from the house and Abby not allowed out of her mother's sight the summer was the slowest I had ever had. I ran around town trying to find things to do to keep my mind off girls but nothing worked. I found myself falling back into the same routines I had before Abby was around to help me with my needs.

I found at 17 my urge to stroke myself was just as bad as it had been at 15 without a girlfriend to help with that outlet. Doing it myself got the job done but it wasn't anywhere near as satisfying as when I was with Katie or Abby. I was in a strong depression and couldn't hold back. I was spending all my time in my room, meaning all my time was spent trying to stroke myself out of depression.

Most parents would probably have noticed when their kids pulled into themselves and never come out of their room, not my parents. They both worked and Lilly got herself involved in the community center after work 3 nights a week. It was like they almost forgot I was there.

In mid-July just weeks after Katie left to grandma's house, something happened that changed our family forever. Lilly's parents had gone on vacation, a romantic weekend alone kind of thing. They were taking one of those tours by air plane when something had gone wrong and the plane crashed, Lilly's parents had died in the crash.

Lilly left that night to go to Linda's house first then the girls drove to their parent's house. They were gone for about 3 weeks out of state. She called dad every night but I didn't really pay much attention to what was going on. I felt bad for her because I knew what it was like to lose a parent. Granted in my case I really couldn't remember way back before my mother had died but I somehow remembered how it felt. When Lilly came home she had her Ashley with her. I guess I should explain why Ashley was with her, because I never explained who she was earlier.

Lilly's mom died during Linda's birth, the pregnancy had taken so much out of her she didn't make it. Lilly being 6 years older than Linda helped her father raise her sister. When their dad was about 45 years old he met a younger woman in her mid-30s who had one child herself. They dated for about a year before getting married.

They decided that they needed to have one child of their own, a year later Ashley was born. This is one of those things that always piss me off, they already had 3 kids but felt they needed one of their own. I hate it when I see couples get together that have a bunch of kids between them and they need one of their own. With the world as it is I don't see the point.

Anyway so Lilly brings home her step-sister Ashley (who went by Ash), with the reasoning that Linda wasn't in a good position to take care of Ash and neither was Ash's step-brother Kevin, the child of her mother before the marriage.

Linda and John were still going through a messy divorce at the time. He claimed she was just trying to take all his money and was denying the fact that he had cheated on her and the divorce dragged on. Linda was broke and about to move out of state to live with a girl-friend of hers. So they decided that now wasn't the best time for her to try to take on a child so she couldn't take Ash.

Apparently Kevin was in college now and in no way capable of taking care of a child. For some reason, Lilly explained to me, Kevin didn't want any more to do with Ashley. He had moved back to his birth fathers house, he said as far as he was concerned Ash never really was his real sister because they had different fathers. Lilly of course didn't tell her that, Ash was aware there wasn't a lot of love between them but didn't know her brother actually resented her.

Lilly didn't have a problem at all taking in her little step-sister; she really loved Ash and looked at it as an honor. I was less happy about it; I really didn't want a bratty 12 year old following me around all the time from now on. I didn't get a vote, Lilly had called dad and talked it over with him, dad didn't have a problem with it either; it was decided before I even knew it was happening.

They called Katie and told her about the situation and asked if she minded letting Ash share her room. Katie was happy to let her aunt move into her room. With that decided Ashley was here to stay filling the place in the house that should've been filled with the girl I loved.

What made things worse, with Ash going through that boy crazy faze right now so I never got a moments peace. Starting the very first day she started making kissy faces and winking, sometimes she would jump onto my lap as I was watching TV and give me little kisses on the cheek like I was her boyfriend. She was also having a hard time dealing with her parent's death and the transition to our home. One minute she would be flirting with me and the next you might find her in her room sobbing into her pillow.

I did my best to comfort her when I found her crying, but I didn't know how to handle the kissy faces and flirting. She was a little girl and sometimes it made me feel uncomfortable, I didn't want Lilly to see it and think I was doing something inappropriate. After a couple of weeks I actually talked to Lilly about it.

I only brought it up to Lilly because I would never do anything with a 12 year old girl and I didn't want her to think something was going on behind her back. With the way Ash acted toward me at times things could really be misinterpreted. Lilly was kind of touched by my shyness about the subject. I think it just traced back to my upbringing from my over bearing step-mom a couple years ago.

I told Lilly about the little comments, winks, flirting, the sitting on my lap and kisses. Lilly told me to sit down. So we sat on the couch. Lilly took my hand in both of hers and told me that I was such a sweet guy and that was why Ash was flirting with me. She explained that Ash was at a critical point right

now. She was at an age were girls are discovering their sexuality and wanting to feel attractive but at the same time she was having a hard time dealing with the death of her parents. She explained that the flirting wasn't really serious it was a coping mechanism for her grief. She wanted to feel sexy and was seeking approval from me as a way of feeling better about herself.

I asked what I should do in return. Lilly said that it would do the girl a world of good for her self-esteem if I just simply played along. She said to smile back and act like I thought she was cute, she told me there was no harm in me flirting back. She thought it was lucky Ash had turned her attention to me instead of some random guy who would abuse her innocence. She knew I wouldn't cross the line with her, so it kept things safe and harmless. She said as long as I could do that for Ash then maybe it would be enough to keep her from seeking male attention elsewhere.

It kind of made sense to me, I thought about what had happened to Sara, she wasn't much older than Ash only a year and a half. Had Sara simply been seeking validation of her own sexuality when she had sex with her boyfriend? I didn't want to see that happen to Ash. I was still a little uncomfortable with the flirting but I would do my part.

It wasn't long before summer was over and Ash turned 13. Her birthday was 4 days before the start of the new school year. We had a big party for her, inviting all the neighborhood kids, since she hadn't had much time to make friends yet. Linda actually made the drive to be there for her little sister. Ash thought that was one of the best gifts all day, to have both her sisters there with her meant a lot.

I called Abby's mom telling her what was going on and I convinced her to let the girls come to the party. She agreed because she thought it was nice that I cared about Ash's big day and there would be plenty of parental supervision.

We went all out for little Ash's birthday party. We rented the cabana at our apartment complex for more space for guests, that gave us the cabana the apartment and the outside courtyard off the cabana for the party. It was the first big day that had come along since the death of her parents and we really tried to make it a day to remember. Aside from Abby who was 17 like me, most of the kids from the neighborhood were about 10 to 12 years old.

I didn't take more than a couple hours for me to have enough of giggling children. I tried to get Abby alone for a minute but Lilly had promised her mom she wouldn't let us be alone together. I begged for just 5 minutes as Lilly smiled.

"Well I'm going to use the bathroom for about 10 minutes," she smiled at us, "As long as Abby is right here when I get back, I don't know anything." I hugged her and she walked away. I looked at my dad he nodded, "I don't know anything." We ran to my room.

"God I've missed you." I told her kissing her hard.

"I know...... it's been all summer..........." she said thought kisses.

We didn't have much time so all we did was kiss but I was burning inside so badly that I would've made love to her in front of the entire party if she would have let me. After about 5 minutes or so she pulled away.

"I have to go. We made a deal."

"I know…………" I pulled away. She slipped out of the room and I lay down on the bed. I pulled a pillow over my head to block out the noise and the light. I was so hard just from kissing her. I was so tempted to pull out my dick and work it off right there, but with a house full of children I was still afraid of getting caught. Just because I had escaped my step-mother didn't mean I still didn't have the same old fears and guilt surrounding masturbation.

I was lying on my bed trying to resist the urge to stroke myself stupid over the few minutes of kissing, the urge was killing me. I finally just drifted off to sleep when I felt a hand run up my leg. I hadn't even heard the door open or close but I could feel a hand rubbing me through my jeans.

"Found a way to sneak back in huh?" I asked.

"Shhhhhh," I heard the quiet sound then a low whisper, "Just relax." Her hand moved mine away from the pillow when I tried to move it off my face. The next thing I knew hands were sliding up my head covering my eyes with one of my shirts.

"Keep it there like a blind fold," said the low whisper again. Then the hands tied my shirt to my head so it couldn't slip away. Wow Abby was getting fun.

"What happened to the promise to your mom, baby?" I asked her. I was enjoying this game we were playing but I did have a touch of guilt about being lying to her mom and Lilly. We were betraying their trust in us, but at that moment I didn't care.

"Shhhhh," she whispered again. I felt my hands being lifted first one then the other was tied to my bed frame. Wow Abby was getting REALLY fun. I felt my pants unzip slowly. I was so hard and going crazy when I felt a small hand slip into my pants and pull my dick out. I started to worry then; it didn't feel like Abby's hand. Moments later I felt lips on my cock. It really didn't feel like Abby's lips, however whoever it was could really suck cock. She was somewhat inexperienced but there was something in that innocence that made it an amazing blow job. I knew it wasn't Abby because the feel of it was all wrong, but if it wasn't my girlfriend then who was it? OH GOD was it Ash? I was freaking out, it couldn't be little Ash doing this to me but then who?

It was starting to feel really good now so I didn't bother struggling. I hadn't had anything since the library, considering how long it had been and how intense the feeling of a mystery woman felt I was surprised I hadn't gone off yet. Then I heard another zipper and heard rustling of clothes. Seconds later I felt bare skin against my cock. I could feel her pussy rubbing up against my dick. I had, had this done to me only once before.

The last night Katie and I were together she had rubbed me with her pussy without putting it in, just like this. I panicked. I didn't know who this was but it wasn't Katie. As she rubbed me I wondered about her intentions, was she going to put it inside her or just rub her pussy against me. I was conflicted I really wanted to feel what sex felt like, but I didn't want to lose my virginity to mystery girl here and now.

"Bet you liked that," Came the whisper again moving up my body her thigh touching my dick. In response I came on her thigh, "Guess I was right." She giggled quietly.

"My turn," she whispered. I felt her move upside down and take me back into her mouth. She wiggled up on me until her pussy was in my mouth. I attacked it like nothing before. Even after having

one orgasm I was more worked up than ever. I drove my tongue in her so deep I couldn't breathe. I licked her as hard as I could without being able to move my arms. I wanted to grab her ass and pull it to me. I didn't care who it was anymore she had the sweetest tasting pussy ever.

Her breathing went crazy and she tensed up on me as her orgasm broke, causing me to go off again in her mouth.

"That was just what I needed," I said to her. I thought now she would let me see her.

"Me too," came the whisper. I heard cloths rustling and she stuffed me back inside my pants.

"Thank you," she whispered, "You can have me again anytime you want if you figure out who I am." With that she untied one of my arms and ran out of my room. I quickly pulled off the shirt tied to my eyes as the door was closing I had missed who was there.

I untied my other arm and left the room. I scanned around the apartment, all I knew for sure was it wasn't Abby, besides she was still standing with my parents outside. I looked around to see Ash and Shawna were standing outside under a tree talking about something and giggling. I couldn't spot Linda anywhere outside and I hadn't seen her in the apartment when I was exiting. Would she have done that to me? I didn't think so, besides I was pretty sure from the weight of the girl she was young. I also couldn't see Sara or Michelle anywhere, but that seemed almost crazy that I would be one of them. Sara was pregnant and had never showed even the slightest sign she liked me. Michelle was 9 and as far as I knew she still thought boys were icky. That about covered all of the girls I really knew at his party. I shuddered to think about which of the other underage girls it could've been. I wondered would this have happened at all if I wouldn't have happened to have been in there dozing off. How does this just happen at random? Had someone been watching me waiting? That made me think of Ash again, she was always following me around but this girl definitely had more experience then I hoped Ash did yet.

I stood outside, juices still drying on my face thinking I really wanted to know who the girl was. That had been the kinkiest moment of my entire life. My body was aching again already for more. But at the same time I wanted to tell this girl I had a girlfriend and fun as it was, what we had done was wrong. I felt bad that I had been with someone else.

Abby came up behind me and put her arms around me.

"Hey baby," she smiled, "I escaped your parents for a minute. Do you want to hide behind the building and make out for a minute?"

"Yes." I said without thinking. We walked around to crack between the cabana and the apartment building. I started kissing her and she tensed up, the harder I kissed the more she seemed to pull away.

"What's wrong?"

"You've been with someone, don't deny it……. I can taste her on you."

"Abby it's not what you think," I started.

"Who was she Joey?" Her face was red and tears were forming.

"I don't know."

"Don't give me that shit!" She screamed, "Who was the whore you slept with at Ash's 13th birthday party."

"I really didn't sleep with anyone," I wasn't technically lying, "I'm still a virgin like you."

"I can taste her on you! It wasn't there an hour ago when we kissed."

"I really don't know," I told her. I sat down with my head in my hands, "I really didn't cheat on you, I wouldn't, I'm not that kind of guy."

"Go fuck yourself!" Abby screamed. She kicked me in the side as she left. I sat there hiding in the crack between buildings not moving for at least an hour. We hadn't been allowed to spend any time together that summer but at least I had still technically had a girlfriend. I couldn't say that anymore. Thanks a lot mystery girl. I hadn't meant to cheat. At first I didn't even know it wasn't my girlfriend. I watched as Abby gathered up her sisters and walked them away from the party.

It was Ash who finally found me. I don't know how she found me sitting there but I wasn't surprised. She usually didn't let me out of her sight for long. I looked up to see her looking down at me.

"Are you ok Joey?"

"No. Go have fun at your party."

"It's not very fun since Sara left," she said with a slight pout, "Why did Abby make them leave so soon?"

"I can't tell you."

"Really? What did you do Joe?"

"I can't tell you. You're not old enough."

"OOOhh really? Come on don't treat me like a little kid. I am kind of your aunt after all."

"It's not the kind of story I should be telling someone your age."

"Joey, please don't treat me like everyone else," I could hear the need for approval in her voice. I thought back to what Lilly had told me and I don't know why but I started talking to her about how I felt about Abby and what had happened today.

To my surprise Ashley didn't cringe or go "EEWWW" once. I explained what happened and she really seemed to be grown up about it. She asked a few questions and really seemed to want to help.

"You do have to admit that it does sound unbelievable."

"I agree, but I can prove it," I took her hand and led her into my room. When we got there I showed her the pieces of clothing where I had left them after unfastening myself. She looked at everything closely. The only one that still had the knot in it was the shirt blind fold I had pulled strait off my head.

"It's not much proof."

"I know." I lay down on my bed staring at the ceiling. Ashley sat down next to me taking my hand.

"I believe you."

"Really?"

"Yeah," she said softly, "You're the sweetest guy I know. I don't think you would ever intentionally hurt someone." She leaned over and kissed me. I was so shocked I didn't react. The kiss lasted about 30 seconds before she pulled back.

"Was it............ was... it... you?" I asked still in shock. She lies down next to me and put her head on my shoulder, "No, it wasn't me. I don't know if I'm ready to go that far yet."

"Good," I told her. I could see a change in her face. She seemed somewhat sad so I added, "Not that I wouldn't be honored when you are ready." her face lit up again.

"Really?" she giggled.

"Really." She hugged me and left my room.

Chapter Five: Inseparable

My senior year started on a low note. The first time I saw Abby I tried to explain things to her. She wouldn't listen to me at all. She said that no matter what excuse I used I had betrayed her trust. There was no way around that fact and sadly I couldn't disagree.

After her birthday Ash and Sara had become best friends, they hung out after school and Ash would often spend evenings and weekends at Sara's house. Ash tried to have Sara talk to Abby for me, but it only seemed to piss Abby off more. Abby told me I needed to stop trying to turn her sister against her and fight my own battles.

By October she finally let me tell my side of the story. She thought it was bullshit and told me I had, had enough time to come up with something better than that. She said again it didn't matter, what she couldn't handle was the fact that I had my cock in another girl's mouth. She said there was no circumstances were that was acceptable.

I had told her the real truth, well mostly the whole truth. I left out two parts, first the part where I knew it was someone else and just let it happen. The second part I left out was where I had attacked the girl's pussy. I told Abby she had simply rubbed it against my face.

I told her my version of the story then explained that I didn't know it wasn't her until she accused me of cheating, I told her that I had thought it was her being kinky. She said that she wouldn't have done that at a kid's party when she had already promised to not be alone with me. That was the last time she talked to me until we were standing in a hospital on Christmas break.

Things having totally fallen apart with Abby, Ash and Sara had become my best friends. Sara, who had just started her freshman year at my high school, rode shotgun with me every day after school. We went to the junior high and picked up Ash and Shawna. Then we would drive to Abby's and drop off Sara and Shawna, Abby would often hide in the house when my car pulled up.

Ash and I had the house to ourselves for about two hours every night after school. I would help her with her homework and we sometimes cooked dinner together for our family. It was a fun innocent time, despite the flirting Ash still had held back from me in some ways. But after her birthday I started talking to her like a grown up not a little kid, this made all the difference because she really opened up to me now. I found that she was really smart, but it was like she didn't want anyone to know, so she hid her intelligence under a layer of fake innocence. I wondered just how fake her innocence went, I again wondered if she had been my mystery girl.

Without a girlfriend to help me out anymore I had developed a routine where we would come home after school and I would help get Ash started on her homework and I would retire to my room for a while. I would spend about twenty minutes to a half an hour taking care of myself then come back to check on her. Once she had her homework done we would go sit in the living room and find something on to watch until my Lilly got home.

By November Ashley's affections had moved on to her sitting on my lap all the time with her head on my shoulder. I was really glad that I had that talk with Lilly because this could have looked bad under different intentions. If not for that talk I just simply would've been uncomfortable with this in general but knowing it was no big deal I found I enjoyed the closeness of the bond we were building.

Instead of finding her bratty like I thought she would be when they brought her home, she was really fun to hang around with. She really helped me fill the void that Katie had left in me. She was easy to talk to and I really enjoyed her company. I really didn't mind her flirting anymore either. I found it fun to actually be adored by someone. I missed having a girlfriend. For the first time ever felt like a real brother to someone.

We started going everywhere together as I would often take Ash and Sara to the mall or the movies. I got both girls into reading books for fun and not just for school which led to us three spending time at book stores and library's. Sara had told Ash she believed me about Abby and that's why she didn't mind spending time around me; she said I was the nicest boy she had ever met. I was touched a little by that sentiment. It was a fun time for the three of us.

I asked Sara one day why her mom let her hang around us so much without supervision? As rumor had it she was still clamping down on letting Abby out of the house. Sara actually laughed a little; she said her mom didn't mind her hanging around me as long as Ash was with us. Plus her mom wasn't really worried about her sneaking off to meet boys right now because she was already pregnant. I laughed at that, I guess it made sense I just felt bad that Sara's pregnancy was affecting Abby's life.

By Christmas vacation I as ready for a break from school. Word had gone around that I had cheated on my girlfriend right behind her back to the point I stopped even trying to deny it anymore; it was pointless when no one believed me anyway. The fact of the matter was that I had eaten out another girl. I couldn't rationalize that to myself anymore, yes I was tied up but I had attacked that pussy when she put it in my face.

My reputation was destroyed so no girl wanted to go out with me, not that I had one in mind. I still loved Katie in my heart of hearts but I also still had strong feelings for Abby. I still had that moment in the library locked into my mind, the moment when we laid our foreheads together and looked each other in the eyes; some moments are there for life.

Since I was a social leper I had tried unsuccessfully to find a date for Homecoming and ended up not going. I had some girl-friends but they were mostly the girlfriends of by buddies. I was disappointed it was my senior year and I was missing out because of a fucked up situation. Instead of going to Homecoming I ended up taking Ash and Sara to the movies that night just to get out of the house. Ash surprised me by holding my hand all through the movie. I thought it was cute that she trusted me enough to be that comfortable with me. I honestly at the time never really gave it any thought that it might mean more than two friends being close.

The week after Thanksgiving dad and Lilly pulled us into the kitchen for a family meeting. I was fearful, I had no idea what we had one wrong as we never had family meetings. I sat down at the table trying to think of excuses to things I might be in trouble for.

We found out that my parents were going trust us to stay home by ourselves for a few days the first week of Christmas vacation. My Dad had an interview for promotion within the company. To get the promotion he had to go out of state to a corporate function for assessment training. He was taking Lilly

with him and they were going to trust us alone in the house from Monday to Friday. I thought it would be awesome and I was looking forward to it. I just wished I had a girlfriend to make use of no parents.

My main focus however was trying to find a date to the winter formal; I didn't want to miss this dance as I had Homecoming. My friends were all going but they all had dates and as much as I wanted to go I also didn't want to show up without a date. I wasn't looking for a girlfriend or someone to fall in love with, all I needed was a nice girl willing to accompany me and dance for one night. Was that really too much to ask for?

We were sitting around the dinner table a few days prior to the dance when Ash quietly stated that if I wanted she could be my date for the winter formal. I was trying to find the right words to tell her no, without hurting her feelings. It would be more embarrassing to show up with a 13 year old, then no date. As I began to speak up Lilly jumped in.

"That would be so cute Ash!" she cried, "We could go get you a pretty dress and fix up your hair, it would be so cute." The look on both Lilly's and Ash's faces was so priceless that I couldn't say no.

"What do you say Joey?" asked Dad, "It's your dance, it's your choice."

"I don't know," I said really slowly. I could see the sparkle start to leave Ash's eye, that broke me, "Yes you can be my date to the dance aunty Ashley." Lilly smiled and actually clapped her hands in excitement for Ash. Ashley squealed and ran to me hugging me tight, "Thank you, thank you, thank you," Ash repeated to me.

"Alright, get off me," I said jokingly. Ash kissed me on the cheek and sat back down at the table, she had the biggest smile on her face I had ever seen from her.

That night I went to bed feeling like I was the good big brother again. I lay there not really thinking of anything when I suddenly got a major erection. It had been a while since I had sprung up spontaneously like this. I figured since it was saying hello I would just go with it. I reached down and started stroking myself as someone knocked at my door. I felt 12 years old again as I pulled my hand back and said come in. I sat up as the door opened, hoping that the blanket over me would cover it. It was Lilly who came in, I couldn't remember the last time she had come to see me at night.

"What's up Lilly?"

"Nothing," she said looking down at me with a knowing look, "I just wanted to make sure before I bought her the dress that it's really ok. You weren't just being nice out of pressure at the time?"

"No, it's really ok," I smiled at her, "I won't take that away from her now."

"I think you're the sweetest boy in the world. You made her whole month, you know that?" She looked almost smitten.

"Well she is a sweet kid."

"Yeah, but I know some kids will make fun of you. But what you're doing is really good for her. Since our parents died you've been really good with her."

"I'm just doing what you asked me to."

"What?"

"You told me to be nice to her. I found it's not that hard."

"I almost forgot about that talk." She kissed me on the forehead and started out of the room. When she kissed me I had gotten even harder, I found that odd, Lilly was attractive in the same way Katie was but I had never thought about her like that before. Maybe it was the fact that I was hard when she walked in my room.

The next day Lilly took Ash out to find a dress for the winter formal. They spent 3 hours at the mall looking for just the perfect dress. When they came home that night they giggled with each other and I was told I wasn't allowed to see her dress until the dance.

Lilly told me that this dance was a really big deal to Ash; she had never gone to a school dance before or been on a date. I told Lilly this wasn't a real date, she agreed but said to Ash it still felt the same and I was to treat her the same as any other girl I took out to a high school dance. I agreed thinking except the parts were we rent a motel room and lose our virginity's like some of my friends were planning.

At school the day of the formal I told my friends about who I was bringing. The guys laughed and made a couple jokes; they really didn't mean any harm it was all in fun. A couple of girls thought it was the sweetest thing; they said they couldn't wait to see Ash all dolled up in her dress.

By dinner that night I was dreading my decision, I was really starting to want to skip the whole thing but it was too late to back out. I kept having images of people pointing and laughing. I was more worried if people laughed and made jokes, Ash would take them wrong and end up in tears.

The other thing making me dread this event was I realized that Abby might be there with someone else. I hadn't heard any rumors of her dating anyone but I didn't want to find out. I didn't know how I would react to seeing her with another man.

When it was time I put on my suit I got ready and waited in the living room for Ash. I hadn't seen her dress yet, so when she stepped into the room with her hair done up, wearing the most gorgeous dress I was blown away. She looked five years older.

Lilly seemed almost as excited as Ash she made us stand in the living room so she could take a dozen photos. Ash blushed posing with me for the pictures when I put my arms around her. I just kept thinking these were going to be blackmail photos someday.

I drove us to the dance my heart racing in nervousness. As soon as we arrived I took her hand in mine and walked into the auditorium. To my relief no one gave us much of a look that made my fears melt away almost completely.

As it turned out Abby was there but she had brought her sister. Sara ran up to Ash and I explaining Abby had come with her because Abby had turned down all the guys that asked her. Sara said that Abby had told her that the reason she turned them all down was so she wouldn't have to pick one. Sara felt that the real reason was because she wasn't over me yet, I really didn't know how to feel about that.

Sara hung out with us for a while but ended up having to sit down. She was now almost six months along and her energy was warring down. I said I was surprised their mom let them out after what was going on. Sara said that she had dropped them off and with her as Abby's date it was fine. But her mom was going to pick them up as soon as the dance was over.

I took Ash out onto the dance floor and tried to give her the night of her life like I had promised Lilly. We danced every time Sara had to sit down. Ash wanted to be with her friend when she was up and walking. They danced together a few times too; I went to Ash a few times and told her she needed to let Sara rest. I could see something was wrong with her. Sara claimed she was fine but I was beginning to worry. I walked toward Abby to say something about it, yet before I could get to her she turned and walked away from me. Abby spent the bulk of her time leaning against the wall glaring at us. I think that she was a little mad about the fact Sara was spending all her time with us, as it turned out I wish she would've let me talk to her.

We were having such a good time that it never occurred to me that the whole thing could turn in an instant. When we first got there that night and the slow dances came on Ash was a little shy and would dance with me with a gap between us. By the end of the evening we were dancing like a couple. She had her arms around my neck and I had pulled her close with my arms around her back.

It was really nice dancing with her, it felt comfortable, and I liked the feel of her cheek on mine and the smell of her hair. I fell in love with her in that moment, she may have been 13 but she was one of the most wonderful girls I had ever known. This too was a different kind of love then I had felt before. My heart always belonged to Katie, but now it shared space with Ashley.

It was in that wonderful moment, slow dancing with Ash that things went south. I heard the DJ announce that there were only 4 songs left before the end of the night, he said grab that someone special and make the last songs count. I was already holding Ash tight as that dumb ass song started to play. I instantly went hard throbbing against her stomach; I saw her eyes grow wide when she realized what it was. She had no idea it was the song and not her that had done it to me. She had a large smile on her face and I realized that this was probably the first time she thought she had made a guy go hard for her. I remembered how big of a deal that had been for Katie. I had done the wrong thing on that day and I still didn't know how to handle this today. She snuggled her head against my shoulder and I panicked.

I broke our hold and walked quickly toward the back door. I went outside, it was warm for December, or I was warm. I walked to the far side of campus to be alone for a minute. I sat down on the stairs leading to the arts building and tried to wish myself down. I hadn't wished myself down like this in a long time, but I wasn't going to whip it out and stroke it away on the stairs that night. A couple minutes later I felt a hand on my shoulder, I turned and it was Ash, she sat down by me and snuggled her head up to my chest.

"Why did you run away from me, Joe?" She asked softly facing down.

"I.......... it's hard to explain..........." I started.

"Is it because you got a boner?"

"A little bit."

"It's ok. I………. felt special," she said the last two words so quietly that I almost didn't hear them.

"I don't know what to say Ash. I shouldn't be getting hard for you." I didn't want to tell her it was the song, she felt special and beautiful I couldn't take that from her. I knew with the death of her parents and her budding sexuality she was very fragile emotionally. What I did now made all the difference. I know Lilly had told me to go along with things that made her feel nice and beautiful, but I knew she hadn't meant I should go with it when we're talking about my cock being hard.

I was thinking on things when Ash tilted her head up and kissed me on the cheek. This broke me out of my chain of thought, without thinking I turned my head to look at her. The second kiss wasn't as innocent as the first, as she kissed my lips she slightly opened her mouth. It had been months since I had kissed someone and sitting there with a major erection I wasn't thinking straight. I opened my mouth and trust my tongue forward. She squealed in both surprise and delight and thrust hers into my mouth.

She wrapped her arms around my neck and pulled me tighter into her. I couldn't stop. Her lips were so soft. I couldn't stop. I had never kissed a girl that young. We sunk into our kissing and the world around us melted away. I really couldn't stop. I was so into her kiss I hadn't felt her hand move to my zipper. We kissed for what had to be an entire lifetime before we broke apart.

When she pulled away from me I tilted my head back and breathed in the night air. I was coming back to my senses and I realized only then Ash had pulled me out of my pants and was stroking me.

"What are you doing?" I asked trying to snap back to reality but the feel of Ash's hand was sending through waves of pleasure I hadn't felt for so long.

"I'm sorry. I've never seen one for real. I just wanted to………." she said tentatively while kissing my neck and never let go of my cock. As she stroked me I knew it hadn't been Ash, who had been my mystery girl. I could tell by the feel of her hand, Ash felt so very good but inexperienced. She had a soft touch with a slight hesitance of innocent in her motions.

I was losing my train of thought as Ash worked me over. It was Katie all over again, I should have told her to stop but at that moment I couldn't get any more words out. Her hand felt so good, I tilted my head back again getting into the feeling. Ash took this as a hint that I approved and she started stroking harder. I moaned and she leaned in and kissed me again deeply on the lips.

"I'm so………. So close………." I managed. Being outside and the wrongness of the situation had pushed me to a fast resolve. Ash pulled away from our kiss and I felt her mouth on my cock. I really should've to tell her no but I couldn't stop. I needed her to finish then I would tell her how wrong this was. I came in her mouth the moment her tongue touched the tip of my dick. She took it all in until I was done then she pulled off me turned then spit it all down the stairs. I was spent more emotionally exhausted then physically, this was a true moral dilemma I had stepped into, but how to get out without breaking this little girls spirit?

"Thank you," I said panting. I kissed her again showing her as much love as I could ever put into a kiss. I opened my eyes and pulled back leaning my forehead against hers like I had with Abby months ago. I looked into her eyes and I could see the deep blue sparkle shining brighter than I had ever seen it before. I wasn't just lost in her eyes; I swam in a sea of blue, there was no past only future with her and it started in her eyes.

"That was amazing," I said to her.

"I did good?" she asked shyly.

"You did very good." I kissed her lightly.

"I can't believe I made you that excited." I could see the need for reinforcement in her expression.

"In that dress with your hair up like that, you were truly the prettiest girl here." She smiled so bright she was glowing in the dark.

"I love you, Joe." My heart sank. I loved her very much but I knew my love for her wasn't like her love for me. I knew she meant she loved me like I love Katie. I didn't say anything for a long time.

"Ash....... I love you.........very much......." I stuttered slowly.

"But you're in love with someone else." She finished for me looking down.

"I'm sorry baby girl." I put my arm around her.

"It's ok, I already knew that. I know you still love Abby." Well that was partly true. I did have feelings for Abby too.

"Don't be sad." I kissed her again.

"I'm not sad," she smiled at me and the glow was back in her again, "This has been the most amazing night of my life. Thank you for being honest with me. Some boys wouldn't have been, right?"

"No they wouldn't. They would lie and say they were in love with you, to get what they wanted."

"Thank you," she smiled bigger.

"I do love you Ash. You're so very special. I can't imagine living ever again without you." The words came out without me thinking. I didn't know where that statement had come from but I knew I meant every word.

"Thank you," she said quietly tears in her eyes, smile never leaving her lips.

We drove home that night without another word. She held my free hand to her chest with both of hers, the whole ride home. I walked her up to the door and stopped her before we went inside. I leaned in and gave her one deep kiss. She looked up at me, blue eyes shining. She was glowing so strong in my eyes she lit up the whole street.

The next day started Christmas vacation. Lilly asked all kinds of questions about our night and Ash couldn't keep the smile off her face. Lilly pulled me aside and thanked me for giving her the biggest smile she had seen on Ash in months. I just shrugged; I knew Lilly would adamantly disapprove of how I had given her that smile.

Monday afternoon I drove the parents to the airport. At the airport dad made sure to double check with me that I had all the phone numbers and info in case of an emergency. He told me he was putting a lot of trust in me and I better not let him down. I told him things would be fine and wished them fun on their trip.

Ash held my hand the whole ride home; we never spoke of what had happened a few nights before, to me in that moment it seemed like a far off dream. It had happened and brought us closer but we didn't need to discuss it.

I made a light dinner for us that night. Ash was unusually quiet that night and I didn't pry as to what was wrong. Instead I tried to make it a fun evening. We played card games and watched a movie. I let her stay up late and eat junk food like any good big brother would.

I went to bed that night thinking about the end of the formal. Remembering the end of the night had me stroking myself with a fury, the thought of Ash's lips on my dick made me cum with a vengeance. I cleaned myself up with an old shirt I kept next to the bed for such times. I was exhausted this orgasm had taken most of my energy out of me. It was after midnight when I heard a soft knock on the door. Only wearing my boxers I pulled the blanked up to my waist.

"What's up baby girl?" I called to her.

Ashley came into my room; she was wearing only a t-shirt and panties. She looked so good and I instantly got hard looking at those young legs. I was happy I had pulled the blanket up.

"I'm scared being alone in my room." She said more timidly then I had ever heard her talk before.

"Why are you scared tonight? You sleep alone every night."

"Yeah, but my sister and your dad are always home," she said quietly. I understood what was in her tone, the last time she was in a situation where the parents left for a few days they never came back.

"Come here sweetheart," I said to her and lifted up the covers. She looked at me and her eyes went big.

"Sorry," I told her, brining my knees up to hide my erection between them.

"No it's ok," she giggled as she climbed in bed with me. She laid down with her back to me and pushed herself up as tight as she could. I put my arm around her, wishing dick would go soft.

"That's poking me in the back," she said and began giggling uncontrollably.

"I can't help it, unless I roll over."

"NO! Please keep your arm around me."

"Ok then you'll just have to live with me poking you." She reached behind her grabbed me and shifted me into another position.

"There, that's better."

"For you maybe but now it will never go down." I said it without thinking, I really didn't mean it. She reached back and slipped her hand inside my boxers and began to stroke me.

"Does this help?" she asked still giggling I simply moaned in response. I should have told her to stop, but her little hand felt so good and it wasn't like we hadn't done this before so what was the big deal? I was justifying it to myself but I really wanted this. Yet at the same time what we were doing seemed so naughty that I didn't last long.

"I'm gonna................. cum............" I called out after a couple minutes. She spun around and pulled the waistband to my boxers down and took me deep into her mouth just as I started to cum. She let it fill her mouth before she spun her head around looking almost panicky.

"Trash can............" I managed and pointed by the bed. She moved in a flash and spit two or three times into the trash.

"I didn't want a mess."

"It's fine. I love it when you do that."

"Really?" she smiled.

"Yes now come here." I kissed her deeply and laid her down next to me again. She rolled over with her back to me again. I put my arm around her holding her tight.

"That's better, I can sleep now." she giggled hysterically at this.

"You think you're cute?" I asked.

"I know you think I'm cute."

"I think your, a brat," I said with a smile. She rolled over and started kissing me again, and before long things began to get heavy. As deep as we were kissing when she pulled me closer to her body I could feel her heart beating against mine. It was as if the rhythm of our hearts were thumping as one.

She pulled away from me and grabbed the bottom of her shirt. She pulled it off now only wearing a sport bra and panties. I wanted so badly to see her naked but I stopped her as she pulled on her bra.

"Why....."She asked shakily thinking I was rejecting her. It took all of my will power to put things to a stop. I wanted so badly to take her virginity in that moment; I would give her mine and take hers. Two things stopped me. First I still held on to the hope that I would make love the first time to Katie. I loved Ash very much but I knew I wasn't in love with her. It was more like a cross between a big brother and a star crossed lover.

The second reason I stopped is the reason I gave her. I told her we had taken things too far already. I said that I should have stopped her the other night when she began stroking me. She was like my little sister and I loved her too much to hurt her.

"How would you hurt me?" she asked softly.

"I truly believe that the first time you make love it should be with someone who is in love with you. Not just someone who loves you like a brother."

"Playing around won't hurt Me." she said almost like it was a question.

"I'm not rejecting you Ash, I'm telling you, I find you so adorable and so wonderful, if we do more than what we have, I won't be able to control myself."

"I understand," she didn't put her shirt back on but she laid down with her back to me again. This time I somehow managed not to be overly excited as I put my arm around her almost naked body and held her to me. I could feel her skin on my bare chest and feel her breathing. It didn't take long before I drifted off to sleep.

Tuesday happened without incident. Ash and I got up and took our showers, meeting in the kitchen for breakfast. She wanted to cook something special for me. I told her not to make a big deal but he wouldn't listen. She cooked eggs, pancakes and sausage. Breakfast was fun as we ate and joked.

We spent the better part of the day sitting on the couch watching movies. I let her pick the movies which made her happy. She put the first one in and snuggled up next to me. After the first movie we went to the kitchen and made sandwiches. Ash put in a second movie and we ate our sandwiches in the living room. After she ate she leaned against me and snuggled some more.

I woke up sometime later having fallen asleep during the chick flick Ash was watching. She lay with my head on my shoulder; she had slipped her hand up my shirt and was rubbing my chest in her sleep.

I let her sleep and turned off the VCR. I flipped channels for a while but couldn't find something to watch. Ash finally woke from her nap around dinner time. We ate light, just having salads. After dinner she put in another movie and curled up with me.

After two movies we decided it was time for bed. We went to our separate rooms; I stripped down to my boxers and climbed into bed. I was thinking about Ash again. She was such a little angel and I felt really bad that I had screwed around with her. As guilty as I felt the thought of it still made me horny. I reached down and started stroking myself thinking of her. When I felt my balls begin to tighten I grabbed the old shirt off the floor and shot a major blast into it. I was just dropping the shirt back to the floor when Ash knocked on my door.

"Come in, sweetie." Ash walked in only wearing a sport bra and a small pair of panties. My breath caught in my throat. I often question how god can make girls so young look so desirable.

"Can I........." she started and I lifted the covers up so she could climb into my bed.

"Thank you!" she squealed and jumped in bed. I managed to maintain myself as she wiggled right up to me as she had the night before, I'm sure the only reason I had any control was because I had only just finished myself. I put my arm around her and we fell to sleep.

Wednesday was the day that things changed, so much so that it would affect us for the rest of our lives. I realize now that it was only a matter of time before things would've happened, as it was as inevitable as gravity but I'm getting ahead of the story.

We got up Wednesday, showered and met for breakfast in the kitchen again. We only had cereal and sat down in the living room for another day of movies and cuddling. We had just settled into another chick flick when the phone rang, it was so unexpected that we both jumped at the sound.

"I'll get it," Ash said getting up and running to the phone. I couldn't hear her conversation but a couple minutes later I could hear her crying, I walked up behind her and put my hand on her shoulder.

"Ash?" I questioned. She turned her head and gave me a questionable look, tears rolling down her cheeks.

"Ok, I'll talk to Joey. I'm sure we'll be there." She hung up the phone and sat down on the floor.

"Ash, what?" She couldn't stop crying. It took her ten minutes to finally say a few words.

"It's Sara............" She said that it was Abby on the phone and she explained that Sara was in the hospital. That was all she managed to say but it was enough I grabbed my keys and shoes. Ash met me at the door with our jackets and we ran to the car.

We got there and I put my arm around Abby, I was really surprised that she let me do it. I asked her what happened; she took my hand and led me down the hall. The trouble had all started the night of the winter formal, she explained.

"Sara disappeared for a while so I went to look for her. When I found her she was on the ground near the arts building." I swallowed hard. If Sara had been out at the arts building, that meant she could've seen Ash and I.

"When I found her she was holding her stomach and crying," Abby continued, "She wouldn't tell me what had happened to make her start crying. All she would say is that she saw something. She said she had been running away when she had fallen over." I felt really bad now, Sara had seen us and I felt like it was my fault she had fallen. I didn't understand however why she would be so upset by us being together, I felt like there was a big piece of this I was missing.

"Sara had landed on her stomach and skinned her knee. When I picked her up she said that she hurt really badly where she had landed on her stomach." Abby's tears came heavier.

"I figured it was from the fall and she would be ok the next day so I took her home and put her to bed. The next morning I went to check on her but she wouldn't wake up, I went to get mom and dad they couldn't get her up either." Abby was fully sobbing now. I didn't know what to do, I felt numb so I simply leaned in and hugged her.

"Don't!" she said pulling away from me, "We came here Saturday afternoon and we haven't gone home."

"How come you didn't call sooner? You know the girls are best friends."

"We thought we wouldn't call until things got better. But this morning they told us that there was nothing left for them to do...... She not........ Going to make it."

"What did they say happened?" I asked tearing up now too. Sara was a cool kid I didn't want to lose her, it felt wrong to see her taken away so young.

"I don't have all the technical details, the doctors talked to mom and dad. All they really told us was it was some kind of complication with the pregnancy. They did some kind of emergency surgery on Saturday but I guess it she didn't pull through like they hoped. All that matters is that my little sister is going to...... to........."

"You don't have to say the word," I grabbed her and held her to me. I wouldn't let her push me away again, luckily she didn't try. We held each other and she cried into my shoulder. Ash came out of the room and I put my arm around her too. Ash cried on my other shoulder. I found out later as Abby was telling me what had happened Sara's mom had sat Ash down and explained things to her.

We stayed at the hospital all day Wednesday through early Thursday morning. I tried to get Ash to leave for just a little while to get some air and eat something. She wouldn't budge; she said that no matter what she was going to be there for her best friend until the end. I admired her loyalty and heart. If I hadn't already loved her I would have fallen then, it only made me love her more to see her care for her friend.

I left the room after midnight going outside, I needed air myself and I thought I would give the family a little space. There were a number of family members there in the room and it was getting crowded. Abby walked outside an hour later and spotted me. It looked like she was trying to decide what to do before she finally walked over to me. She pulled my arm around her and laid her head on my shoulder.

"This doesn't mean anything's changed," She told me, "I just really need to be held."

"It's fine. I don't want to talk about us anymore," I told her honestly, "I just want to be here for you and Sara right now."

"Thank you," she said quietly as if it almost bothered her to say those two words to me, "As much as I hate you, Sara really adored you. As much as I don't want to admit it, you were always good to her."

"Can we have a truce on the anger?" I asked, "I told you I'm done with the "Us" stuff. Can we try to just be nice to each other?"

"Your right, It's been long enough," She started crying, "Sara loved you the least I can do is be nice to you for her." We didn't speak anymore we just sat on the bench holding each other.

Sara never woke up; Ash sat holding her hand until the end and I was completely lost in guilt. I was too young at the time to understand all the medical reasons for what happened, but it was explained that this would have happened whether she fell or not. I remember thinking something was wrong with her at the dance. I had tried to tell Abby about it.

I hated that her last moments had been seeing Ash and me together. I didn't know if Sara liked me or Ash for that matter in a way that would upset her but I still felt like it was all my fault.

Sara passed away Thursday morning. Abby had just returned to the room and I sat on a bench outside the door. The girls held each other and cried. I left them there and walked down stairs to the hospital church. I'm not at all what you would call religious but I walked into the church that morning and had a long talk with god. I asked him how he could do this to such a little angel. I didn't get an answer.

I took Ash out to breakfast before going home Thursday. We sat quietly eating pancakes. She cried the whole time, tears running down her angelic face. It broke my heart there was nothing I could do to make the pain stop for her. Ash fell asleep on the ride home. I picked her up like a small child and carried her into the house laying her down on her bed. I kissed her forehead and closed her door then I went and lay down on the couch drifting off to sleep myself.

I awoke in the evening; Ash was lying on top of me, at some point she had joined me on the couch pulling a blanket over us. I was just happy to look at her sweet face without tears filling her eyes. I gazed at her for a while until her eye opened; she looked at me and gave me a half smile. I leaned over and kissed her gently to show her things were going to be ok.

When we finally got up and I started to make dinner, it wasn't much I just warmed a bunch of left over's that needed to be eaten before they went bad. We ate without saying anything; I didn't know how to feel right now. I felt bad for Ash, losing someone else she really cared about. I felt guilty for what we did to Sara; I never told Ash that Sara had seen us that night I didn't want her to have the same guilt over it that I did. I felt bad for everything that had gone on this year for Ash it seemed like one tragedy after another. After dinner we went back to the living room and cuddled on the couch watching TV.

We decided to go to bed early that night, neither one of us in the mood to stay up and cuddle on the couch. I stripped down to my boxers as I did every day and flopped down on my bed. I was tired more emotionally then physically, net I didn't fall asleep I lay there waiting for the knock on the door that finally came an hour later.

"Come in." I called to her. I held up the covers before she even entered the room. She walked in wearing only an old t-shirt and panties again, despite everything I couldn't take my eyes off her as she slipped in my bed wiggling up to me as I slipped my arm around her. Tears welled up in her eyes again.

"Please don't cry," I whispered to her.

"I can't stop. She was barley older than me." I pulled her tighter.

"I keep thinking if it were me, there are so many things I would never have done yet. Things I would be missing out on."

"Like what?" I asked.

"Love, and making love," She rolled over facing me, "I don't want to die without ever making love." She kissed me.

I pulled out of this kiss then I pressed my forehead against hers and looked into her eyes. I knew this moment was really big for her and how I handled it could hurt her. I knew enough about girls to know when they got curious about sex; they could potentially do something that could get them physically

hurt as emotionally. Just like Sara had. Here Ash was in my bed asking me to make love to her, as I said earlier I should have seen this coming long before now. I made the decision right there looking into those eyes, I knew I couldn't say no to her but I had to.

"Ash I love you. Very, very much," I kissed her softly, "I'm still technically a virgin too."

"Really?" she asked genuinely surprised, "You never told me that in all the times we talked about sex stuff. I thought you and Abby.......I thought that's why she got so mad when she thought you cheated on her."

"No. That's not why she was so mad. To prove to her mom that we weren't having sex, she let the doctor examine her in an extremely personal way. She only did it to because she loved me and didn't want her mom to stop us from seeing each other. She put a lot of trust in me; to her I betrayed that trust."

"I get it," she blushed, "I accidentally broke mine already. But I don't want to talk about it."

"It's ok," I told her. I knew that happened with a lot of girls.

"I was just thinking that if were both virgins.............we......... could...........help........each other.......... not be........." She said pausing between words.

"Ash, I can't." I could see the tears form in her eyes. She rolled around not facing me anymore

"I'm sorry I just thought you............ would for me. Because you love me and ......" Her tears were rolling down her cheeks again, "I know you're not in love with me but I don't think I will ever meet someone who treats me with as much love as you give me.......... and I love you so much." My heart was aching as she cried. This poor girl had been through so much this year, her parents, her old life, and her new best friend all gone.

"Ash, I don't feel right about taking your virginity. I will promise you two things right now." She turned her head and looked at me.

"I want you to wait until you're a little older. If you still feel for me like you do right now in 3 years, I'll show you how much I love you."

"Three years!" She exclaimed, "That's so long to wait."

"Let me finish," I told her, "On your 16th birthday if you still feel like you do now I will make love to you. I want you to really make sure this is what you want. This has been a hard year for both of us. I've gone through a number of things I haven't told you about as well as everything else."

"Ok, I guess I can wait for you. You'll see my love won't change. It's just that right now I'm so........ I don't know. I just need to be loved."

"That brings me to my second promise, I made a decision tonight," I paused taking a breath, here it was, "I can't resist you for 3 years. I love you so deeply like a brother, but I'm also wildly attracted to you."

"So I'm confused," she said quietly, "Are we going to.........?"

"I've decided that I'm willing to let you have me in every other way except intercourse if that's what you want."

"I want. If we can be with each other that way I can wait 3 years." She turned to me again smiling.

I couldn't hold back anymore so I kissed her hard, she pushed her tongue in my mouth and I returned mine to hers. It was like we were two burning flames joining into each other I pulled her so tight to me I thought I would crack her in half. This just fueled her passion. I pulled away from her face biting her lower lip and pulling it with me, she moaned. I moved to her neck, kissing and licking passionately. She moaned and squealed with pleasure. I gently moved her to a sitting position lowering my hands to the bottom of her shirt.

I moved off her neck only long enough to slide her shirt up her body and off her. I began running my hands over her breasts, she moaned as she wrapped her arms around my neck. I leaned back and gazed just for a moment at her naked breasts. She had a full b-cup already.

I could feel her heart beating rapidly under my lips as I kissed her chest and shoulders. She needed to feel not just loved, but alive tonight. I had always thought making love on the day a loved one died wasn't a sign of disrespect. It was a way of two loved ones to celebrate life. I actually pulled that thought out of a book I read once, but I thought it was really true.

As I kissed Ash I was trying to show her that love she so desperately needed today. I took my time kissing her so she could feel every bit of it, her heart beat, breathing, and physical pleasure.

I had never once felt like this with Abby. I loved her in a way but as I've said before it wasn't like I loved Katie. Tonight I realized I never truly loved Abby. I had never before felt the feelings of love I felt for the beautiful goddess under me now. I felt sadden by that realization so much so that it was only at that moment I finally gave her up, Abby was a great and wonderful girl but she wasn't Katie or Ashley.

I finally gave Ash what she was looking for as I moved lower and kissed her breasts. I was holding the right one gently squeezing her nipple when I brought my lips to her left nipple. Under me her body seized up and she arched her back. She cried out as her body shook.

"Thank you," She moaned, "I thought I'd had an orgasm before, but that was my first real one." She took both of her hands and placed them on the sides of my head pulling me up to her face. I kissed her again.

"That was the best moment of my life," she breathed out the words though kisses.

"Were not done," I told her and moved back down her body.

"I don't know if I can take more tonight, that was intense."

"Sssshhh." I said returning to kiss her right breast this time. I hadn't had enough of her yet. I couldn't get enough tonight. I just prayed that I had the will power to stop myself from taking her virginity when the time came.

I opened my mouth and took her nipple inside; I sucked on it using my teeth very slightly to clamp down on it. She cried out again. While sucking her breasts I slid my hand up her leg and began rubbing her pussy through her panties.

"Oh god, oh, oh, oh god, oh god," she cried out. I gently ran my hands across the sides of her hips slowly removing her panties. Once pulled down her legs to her knees I slid two fingers inside her. Her body began to buck slightly.

"Jesus fucking god," she cried out. I paused for a moment, I had never heard her utter a single swear before. I drove my fingers deeper, driving her into a thrusting frenzy.

I started moving down the bed kissing her sexy flat stomach. This was driving her wild with anticipation. She was thrusting so hard against my fingers I didn't need to move them myself I just let her work her own pleasure. I slowed my kissing of her body just past her belly button. I moved really slow kissing this area for a long time.

I had never gone this slowly with any girl before. I had of course done this, but never this gently and passionately. With Katie it was always hurried because we both knew we couldn't be together. I also didn't have this level of self-control a year and a half ago with her. I would have come at least twice by now back then.

With Abby things had always been more animalistic. I could have slowed down like this and savored every inch of her but she wouldn't have wanted it that way. She always wanted things raw, fast and hard. Not to mention in public as much as possible.

I finally moved lower removing my fingers and letting my tongue taste the first sweet juices flowing out of her. I once wrote that he mystery girls pussy had been the sweetest pussy ever. It didn't compare to Ash, hers was the most delicious thing I had ever tasted.

The moment I placed my tongue on her clit she tensed up again, arching her back higher this time. Her orgasm was so strong she squirted slightly right on my face. For and instant I thought I finally knew how Katie had felt all the times I had cum on her.

"JESUS GOD FUUUUUUUUUUUKING LORD!" She yelled out. Her juices were running down my face. She tasted so wonderful I thrust my tongue deep inside her, drilling in as far as it would go. She hadn't come down from her orgasm yet and I was digging inside her seeking more and more of that sweet taste.

"OOOOOOOOHHHHH GOD!" She screamed this time as her 3rd orgasm took her over. Her hips were bucking on my face, her hands reached down grabbing the back of my head as she squirted more on my face.

"Ok," She panted, "Enough. I can't take anymore." I slid up to her face and kissed her. I thought for a minute she would be grossed out kissing me with her juices on my face, but she kissed me hard digging her tongue into my mouth.

"Did I do good?" I asked with a smile, thinking back the winter formal.

"You did soooooo good," she grinned ear to ear, "I think I'm a puddle of goo now." I kissed her again melting into her lips.

We kissed for a few minutes when I felt a hand slide into my boxers.

"You don't have to do that," I told her, "Tonight was about you."

"Shhhh," she grinned, "Were not done yet." I lay on my back and closed my eyes. She moved down on the bed and removed my boxers. I was expecting a hand job with her sucking out my juices like she had done the past two times, instead as soon as my boxers were off I felt warm and wet across my cock. I looked down to see her sweet angelic face sucking me. It felt indescribable, I had no idea how she could possibly be this good on her first blow job but I didn't question it.

I closed my eyes again and drifted off in the feeling of ecstasy. This was the best blow job of my life, As much as I hated to admit it. But when Katie had done it I was younger and less experienced so it had never lasted that long. With Abby she didn't put in the loving care that Ash was doing. I had sudden jolts of pleasure shooting up from my pelvis and into my stomach area, causing my whole body to twitch when it would happen.

"Ash, get ready baby," I told her. She lifted her eyes to meet my gaze and returned to her ministrations. The eye contact pushed me over. I began to cum what felt like a gallon of seed down her sweet throat, she took all of it looking me in the eyes as she swallowed. I was surprised she hadn't done that in the past, as always I thought it was the most sext thing in the world, and I felt her love for me in that act.

"Wow that was incredible!" I cried out.

"You're still up," she said holding my cock.

"It's such a turn on when a beautiful girl swallows," I told her. To me that was a true statement, for some reason I registered the swallowing as a true act of love and hence was a turn on for me.

"But neither one of us can sleep if your still hard," she giggle and put her mouth back down on me.

"Oh god," I moaned out, "You don't have to"

"You gave me 3," she said smiling going back to work.

I was done after two that night. After all the effort we had both put into giving each other pleasure we both were completely exhausted. When I was done the second time she scooted herself up the bed into my arms. I held her there as we lay naked. I kissed the back of her neck as we drifted off to sleep.

Chapter Six: Secrets

My dad and Lilly returned home that Friday. Ash and I drove to the airport to get them; I really hoped Ashley wouldn't give us away. But I guess she had been affectionate and flirty before so it wouldn't be that obvious.

As soon as the parents got home we told them of what had happened with Sara. Lilly cried, which set Ash crying again, Lil had really liked Sara and hadn't held it against her that she had gotten pregnant. Some people wouldn't like their own 13 year old kid hanging around with at pregnant teen but Lilly had never limited Ash's time with Sara.

Because of the news with Sara and Christmas being only two days away my parents hadn't told us the news they brought back with them. A couple days after Christmas my parents sat Ash and I down to let us know my dad had gotten the promotion and we were going to be moving to another state. I was indifferent about this news. I liked where we lived but I was a social outcast now so a new start might be nice.

According to my dad part of the trip had been to scout out houses. With my dad going to work for the corporate division it meant a considerable pay raise. With the pay raise meant living in a house no more apartments, which suited me fine. We would have a real home with a yard and 4 bedrooms so Katie and Ashley wouldn't have to share when Katie came home this summer. Ashley was excited because the things from her old room were in storage and she had been using Katie's furniture. Now she could have her own room with her own things.

Dad had to fly back right away leaving Lilly to handle the move here. Ash and I told her that we would help as much as possible. We would only be about 3 weeks behind dad. Five days after they returned we drove my dad back to the airport.

Sara's funeral was a week after Christmas. Lilly went with Ash and I. It was really hard to stand there and not break down crying. I wasn't trying to be a tough guy I was simply trying to be strong for the girls so they could come cry on me.

Ash held on to me the whole time crying into my shoulder, I really wished I could take all the hurt away from her. I couldn't stand seeing more tears I wanted to kiss them off of her. I wanted to take her in my arms and kiss her so she would know how much I cared in that moment. Show her the world doesn't always hurt.

I couldn't do that with everyone standing there instead I put my arm around her and held her tight. Lilly came up behind me and whispered, "Thank you." in my ear tilting her head towards Ashley.

When the service was over we were all invited back to Abby's house for memorial pot luck. When we got there Lilly went into the kitchen to talk with Abby's mom and Ash went upstairs with Sara's younger sisters. I was sitting in the living room feeling really out of place, I felt like an intruder standing in their house.

"Joey," Abby called softly.

"What's up?" I thought she was going to be mad I was there. Instead she grabbed my hand and led me up the stairs. We walked into Abby and Sara's room and sat down on the bed.

"I wanted to talk to you," She looked away from me, "I wanted to say I'm sorry." I just stared at her.

"I should've believed you when you told me you didn't cheat on me," She still couldn't look at me, "I should've trusted you loved me."

She turned back to me and I looked away from her. I had been holding back tears all day from everything going on but when she spoke of love I finally lost it. Tears started rolling down my cheeks.

"What?" She said moving my face to look at her, "You don't love me do you?" She started to cry.

"No," I said softly, "I really though I did love you before But never the way you loved me."

"I thought since you brought Ash to the dance you hadn't moved on yet."

"Before we have this conversation, I want to know why you suddenly believe me now after months of me trying to explain."

She got off the bed and walked to her dresser. She pulled out the drawer and removed a book hidden underneath.

"I found this, I shouldn't have read it but I couldn't help it." She handed me a diary, "Sara wrote that she fell for you by watching how you treated me. She decided to find a nice guy like you. She thought she had found that guy but when he got her pregnant, you know the rest." I felt bad. This was the exact mistake I was thinking about when I thought about Ash running out and doing something hurtful.

At that moment I fully thought maybe I had made the right decision to help guide Ash though this time of her life. If only I had known about Sara then. I might have talked to Abby about helping her sister along somehow. Now it was too late.

"Sara was so hurt when her boyfriend dumped her she completely fixated on you. She wrote pages and pages about how much she loved you. She said that spending all her time with you and Ash the last months, she was the happiest she had ever been in her life."

"Then near the end of the diary she goes into detail about Ash's birthday party." I was stunned, I instantly understood. I just had no idea Sara had even liked me. I had always thought she was hanging around us more for Ash then me.

"She wrote that she found you sleeping and tied you up. She said that you thought it was me until the very end when she told you she wasn't."

Abby and I talked after that. I told her that I was sorry I let it happen. She told me she should've believed me. We talked about love. I told her that I really had tried to love her the way she deserved but I found in the end it just hadn't been there. I told her that in my heart I had always loved someone else.

Abby started crying. She said she had loved me enough that she had been willing to give me her virginity. I told her I was sorry but at the time I was still sorting my feelings. I told her we were moving and she cried more. I left her room quietly thinking I would never see her again. It would be a couple years and a couple states away before I saw her again.

It was late the night of the funeral and I had barley dropped the old shirt to the floor when my door opened. I had been thinking about Abby tonight and I came harder then I usually did thinking of her. I was just laying down again when Ashley slipped in. She had been crying again and I lifted the covers for her to join me. I sad up and she sat next to me I put my arms around her and rubbed her back.

"It's going to be alright," I whispered to her. I kept my voice down. I didn't want Lilly to hear us and walk in.

"Can I tell you a secret?" She whispered.

"Yes, if it helps you feel better."

"Will you promise to love me no matter what it is?" She had a pleading look in her eyes. I just told her the truth.

"There's nothing you could tell me to make me love you less." She bit her lip and looked down. I continued to rub her back.

"You're not a man are you," I asked and she actually giggled for a second before returning to tears, "Tell me you're secret."

"I ..... I..... Really liked Sara......" She said softly.

"That's no secret, I liked her too."

"No, I mean I really liked Sara," she said again. Her gaze pleaded with me to not make her say it.

"Oh," I exclaimed understanding, "You liked her like you like me?"

"No. I've never liked anyone like I love you," That statement brought the smile back to her face.

"But you two........ Were you........?" I didn't quite know how to put it without offending her.

"Remember I said that I accidentally broke my cherry?" I nodded.

"I started out telling her one night how much I loved you and she said she had a crush on you too." I didn't tell Ash that I had already found that out.

"She told me she was your mystery girl. She told me about what she had done to you." Her face turned beat red but she continued telling me the story. Ash seemed to really need to explain.

69

They had been talking about sex and talking about what it was like and Sara told her that she could show her. One thing led to another and they had fooled around. Ash said it had felt ok but she felt weird the whole time and she hadn't even gotten off.

When it was over Sara had sworn her to secrecy about their incident and about the one with me and her. Ash hadn't liked lying to me but she had promised. That was why she had tried so hard to get Sara to talk to Abby. She had wanted her to own up to it. The only thing Ash had learned over the whole thing was that she didn't like being with girls. She had just been curious.

I told Ash lots of girls experiment and I wouldn't tell anyone. I told her I didn't love her any less. I told her I understood why she had taken Sara's death so hard. They shared a special secret bond with each other.

"I love you." She said kissing me. We held each other and kissed for a long time before she snuck back to her room.

With us moving in a couple weeks, Lilly didn't make us go back to school. That allowed us to help her get things ready for the move. I was upset inside that I had hurt Abby; she had been my first real girlfriend. I was grateful for the time we had spent together. She had taught me a lot about girls, being a boyfriend, loyalty, stamina and being a lover. I would forever be grateful to her for it all.

Now having sorted out my feelings for Abby that only left me two girls who I really loved, I loved both of the girls equally but in different ways. I needed to have that talk with Katie that we never got in June.

It was after midnight and the movers were coming in the morning, we had a long drive tomorrow and I needed to sleep. It would take us a couple days of driving to get to our new home. I thought it would've been easier to leave the cars here, fly there and buy new cars.

I lay there thinking about the visit Lilly had with me a couple hours ago. She had walked into my room as I went to bed.

"I wanted to talk to you about Ash." I remained stone faced I didn't want to give anything away.

"What about her."

"I wanted to thank you for always being there for her. I can tell she really looks up to you."

"It's no big deal." I shrugged.

"You don't fool me. I can tell you care," Lilly smiled, "How did you get her through everything when Sara died?" I didn't know how to answer. I couldn't tell her I had practically had sex with Ash.

"She was upset. She came in here asking to talk. She was crying. I had her lay down with me and she fell asleep while talking to me."

"See, that's what I mean. You're so sweet to her. I can tell you really love her."

"Maybe a little," I said with my cheeks burning slightly.

"I just wanted to say I appreciate you protecting her. Her own brother doesn't give a damn. It's great she can confide in you." She kissed me on the forehead and left the room.

I lay there now after midnight wondering how much Lilly knew or suspected. Would she have been so nice to me knowing I was treating Ash like a girlfriend? These thoughts were still buzzing in my brain when my door opened quietly.

"Ash what are you doing?" I whispered quietly. She was taking a big risk of us getting caught, sneaking into my room again.

"I couldn't sleep and I wanted to see you." She slipped under the covers with me and wiggled up into me. I couldn't hide my excitement. She reached behind herself and slid her hand inside my shorts. She giggled as she gave me a quick squeeze.

"Ash," I said questionably and she removed her hand. She wiggled her butt closer pressing hard against me.

I asked her if Lilly had talked to her about us, or about the night Sara died. She said that Lilly had asked her some questions and all Ash had told her was that I had been very supportive and helped her through it. I told her what I told Lilly in case she asked. We agreed not to say more to her.

With our cover story settled I asked, "So why did you really come in here."

"I just wanted to feel loved tonight. Everything changes again tomorrow. You told me any time I needed to feel loved."

"Yes it did." I pulled her closer. She wiggled her butt a little and rolled over in my arms.

We kissed passionately I had missed this. We hadn't had a really good moment for a while. It was well after 2 a.m. before she slipped out of my room. We had kissed and rubbed each other without taking any clothes off. I watched her leave and I could still feel her against my lips.

The moving people showed up at 8 a.m. Lilly set them to work. Lilly told me to go ahead and get going. With the long drive ahead Lilly decided that all three of us didn't need to stay and watch over the movers. Ashley asked if she could go ahead and ride with me. Lilly paused for a minute then agreed. It would mean she had to drive out by herself but that was fine.

With Ash with me, Lilly checked twice that I had the maps for the rout and the address for where we were going. She made me promise to call as soon as we stopped for the night at a hotel and let her know where we were. When we were ready Lilly told Ash to go wait in the car she wanted to talk to me.

"I know she was in your room last night." I was shocked, and I remained quiet, "I'm going to ask this only one time. Are you having sex with her?" She looked me dead in the eye when she asked me.

"No. Of course not Lilly, I wouldn't do that to you or her," I told her. It wasn't completely a lie, "She came to me last night because she was scared about moving again. She's been through a lot in the last year and for some reason she trusts me to talk about it." I was hoping I wasn't completely transparent. I could see Lilly visibly relax.

"I woke up and heard you guys talking through the wall last night. I couldn't hear what you were saying but I knew she was there. Then I couldn't hear you guys, but I didn't hear the door."

"She fell asleep while talking to me. I let her lay there I didn't want to wake her and make her move if she was comfortable. I went to sleep and she was gone when I woke up."

"I'm sorry," she replied, "You're a good friend to her I should have known better. I just worry for her." I felt really guilty; I was really betraying her trust. I was just really happy she hadn't decided to check on us.

"It's ok, I understand. She's a pretty, sweet and wonderful little girl." I used the words little girl for a reason as I was trying to point out that I thought of her as a child.

She patted me on the shoulder and told me to go ahead and go. I got to the car and told Ash how close we had come to getting caught. We drove away talking about how we would have to be more careful in the future.

It was a long drive and we talked about all kinds of things. I bought a book on tape to listen to in the car. The book helped our conversation flow as the day passed. We tried to guess what would happen next as the story unfolded. It was a fun way to pass a car trip.

When night came we found a motel to stay in for the night. I tried to call Lilly at the house but didn't get an answer. I hoped that meant she was done and on her way too. I called dad and let him know where we were and he told me that Lilly had called him from a motel in town. She had taken longer to get things done and thought it was smarter to start her drive in the morning. I told him we would be on our way again first thing in the morning too.

I couldn't believe our luck. Lilly had been delayed long enough to give Ash and I the whole night alone. I hung up the phone turned and kissed her.

"We have all night," I told her. She squealed and jumped up on me wrapping her legs around my waist and her arms around my neck. I led her to the bed and kissing her until she dropped down off me. She bounced on the bed. She was wasting no time as she grabbed my belt buckle. She opened my pants and dropped them to the floor. Without a single word she pulled down my boxers and took me into her mouth.

She sucked me harder than she had in the past. I was so hot for her and after almost getting caught last night I shot down her throat in only minutes. She grinned up at me as she swallowed. I was a little disappointed in myself for going off so quick but I figured we had all night to do it again. I took off my shirt and stepped out of my pants. I pushed Ash to the bed and pulled off her jeans and panties I then slid my hands up her shirt and removed it.

I climbed on top of her and started kissing her lips as I removed her bra. I began kissing her neck and moving down her body. I made it to her shoulder when she stopped me.

"I love you so much right now," she said to me pulling my head back up to her lips, "I want to do something else tonight."

"I love you so much right now too," I pressed my forehead to hers, "What I can do to make you happy tonight."

"I want to lie together. I want you to hold me all night. I want to feel more loved then pleasured tonight, if that's ok?"

"Why wouldn't it be ok?" I kissed her again as she rolled her back into my chest. She wiggles her butt up into my erection.

"Because you're still ready," she giggled. She wiggled her butt harder against me. I wrapped my arms around her and kissed her neck.

"Don't worry about that. I love the thought of holding you all night."

"I love you." She kept squirming and wiggling. She was driving me crazy with the bare shin of her ass. I shifted and slid my erection between her upper thighs.

"Ooohhh I love the way that feels," she sighed. She started slowly sifting her thighs in causing a stroking motion on my cock. It was an incredible feeling.

"I'm going to cum again if you keep that up," I told her.

"Good," she whispered. It actually took me about 20 minutes to cum that way, but I came the second time all over her inner thighs. I calmed down after that. Pulling her naked body closer to me I held her as tight as I could. We drifted off into sleep.

I woke her the next morning very early. She was lying against me; I moved ever so gently rolling her body onto her back. I slid down the bed and shifted her legs open. I brought my face up to her pussy lashing out with my tongue. Even asleep her body reacted. I could taste her sweet nectar start to build. I started liking her deeper and deeper as her body lubricated itself to my touch.

I had woke up with a physical need to devour her little body this morning. I was like an addict for her juices. I hadn't been able to get my fix for a month.

"Oh, Oh MY GOOOOOOD," She cried as her hips began to thrash. She grabbed my head with both hands and pressed me tight to her. I dug in as hard as I could my tongue scrapping my teeth trying to go deeper. Her body tensed and her pussy clamped on my tongue squeezing it.

"OH FUCK YESSSSSSSSSS," She screamed. Her whole body arched as she squirted her juices on my face. She fell back to the bed let go of my head and her arms fell to her sides.

"I didn't know it could be that intense." She spoke softly, out of breath, "I would say wake me up that way every morning, but Lilly would catch us, there's no way I could be quiet with that."

I pulled myself up on the bed and looked into her eyes. I didn't say anything to her, I just kissed her.

"Thank you for another wonderful night and morning," She whispered in my ear. I just continued to look into her eyes. Every day I was falling more in love with this beautiful girl. If this continued I would be in danger of losing my love for Katie. That was a scary thought; I was so confused right now.

We finally got out of bed and took a shower together. We had fun cleaning each other. I was just trying to make the most of our night together. With Lilly suspicious I didn't know when we would have another chance to be with one another. I didn't want to let Ash go but I was facing the fact that for the next few years I might have to.

We made the rest of the trip by the end of the night the second day. Our new house was huge, and had a big yard. You walked in to a big open area on the left was a library alcove with shelves and a window box seat. Inside on the right was a large den/office area. Walking in further just past the library on the left was a grand kitchen area, dining room and sunken living room. Further in on the right just past the office was a staircase with stairs leading up and down. Upstairs were 4 bedrooms and a bathroom. The upstairs actually had two bathrooms as the master had its own. The stairs down led to a large rec-room and behind that an exercise room. Next to the exercise room was a small bathroom with a stand up shower instead of a tub.

This house was beyond expectations. I wondered how this was really happening. It seemed too good to be true. As we set up the new house it was decided that the living room was to be set up as a formal living room with no TV and a couple couches for entertaining guests. The rec-room however we set up with all the fun stuff. It was quite large so we put the big TV and the computers in there. The den remained for my dad to do business. I liked having a library in my own house now. I talked dad into putting a couch and a desk in there for kicking back and reading or studying.

We settled into the new house and Ash and I went back to school. We both made new friends in no time. We had to put our relationship on hold for a while. We had, had that close call from Lilly before the move so we couldn't do anything with them home. Lilly hadn't gone back to work since the move and we didn't even have the time after school alone anymore. Life just settled on as the school year came to a close.

As the school year ended I started applying to colleges. I kept getting rejection letters. I finally went in and talked to the school guidance counselor for help. He made some phone calls on my behalf and helped me work out a plan. I signed up for some community college courses for the fall. We figured if I took some strategic classes locally I could reapply in a year.

Linda and my Grandmother both flew out for my high school graduation and 18th birthday. It was a bigger party then we had, had for Katie the year before. It wasn't anything personal we just had the bigger house and more money this year.

I slipped out early from my graduation party hoping nobody would notice. I took off with my new school friends and we went to a high school party on the beach. I hadn't drunk since that last night with Katie a couple years ago so I found that I held my liqueur better then I would've guessed. But that only works for so many drinks. By 1 a.m. I was shirtless and had no shoes and socks. I was running around the beach in just my jeans which were wet from the knees down. I was having the time of my life until I passed out in the sand.

I woke up in my boxers. My jeans wet and sandy hung over a chair behind a desk on the other side of the room. I was confused and my head hurt. I was laying on the edge of a mattress facing away

from the wall. I was in a room I didn't recognize, everything decorated in white. I felt movement behind me and heard a slight breath. I rolled over to see a topless girl lying beside me. She had tan skin and was dressed only in white cotton panties.

I searched my brain, for the life of me I couldn't remember ever meeting this girl before.

"Hi there," She said to me her eyes closed.

"Hi......" I replied.

"Don't worry I don't bite," She said grinning.

"I'm just a little confused," I started.

"Of course you are. You woke up in the bed of a girl you don't know." Now I was more confused, but relived at the same time. At least I wouldn't have to offend her by asking her name.

"How did you know I didn't remember?"

"Side effect of the drug they gave you." She started giggling and I was really more confused.

She finally told me that one of the guys on the beach had slipped a drug into a drink intended for a girl and I had rushed in and drank it while I was running around the beach all drunk. She told me her name was Brooke she was in college and we had met the night before and had been having a good time until I got slipped the drug.

My head hurt this still didn't explain why I was in bed with her half naked. I asked her. She had brought me back to her apartment because she felt it had been her fault as she had dared me to go steal that guys drink. The whole drug thing had backfired on the guy and when everyone else had heard what he had done they kicked the crap out of him. I didn't disagree with that. I didn't like those drugging asshole's who used that to get laid.

Brooke said that after I passed out some friends helped her get me back to her apartment and she had taken my pants off to not get sand in her bed. It made sense to me. Other than that she just went to bed next to me to make sure I didn't get sick from the drug.

I took a chance and leaned in and kissed Brooke. She kissed me back. It wasn't deep and didn't have the love or passion behind it that I was used to, but it was nice. We kissed for a while and I put my hand on her already naked breast. I figured if she was comfortable to sleep topless around me then she probably wouldn't object. As we kissed I was getting really hard, it didn't go unnoticed. She slid her hand inside my boxers and rubbed the palm of her had around the head of my dick. It was a move I hadn't felt before. She wasn't stroking just rubbing but it had been months since the motel room with Ash so predictably I came all over the palm of her hand.

"Wow, you must be young?" She questioned with a little hint of fear in her voice.

"Don't worry I'm 18."

"Wow. I haven't been with an 18 year old since I was 15," she stated, "Even so that was fast for 18." I turned bright red; I could feel my face burning. She licked my sticky cum off her palm and smiled wiping the last bet of wetness off on her leg.

"Sorry," She said quickly looking at me, "Have you never?"

"I've done stuff," I said not wanting to admit to being a virgin, "It's just been a while."

"Oh," She smiled and kissed my neck, "Since you're done, do mind getting me?" She slipped out of her panties and moved my head to her crotch. I was happy to play along. I buried my face in her beautiful tan pussy lapping up all the juices as fast as they flowed out of her. I thought I had understood squirters from Ash but Brooke didn't just squirt she flooded as I ate her.

"OOOOOOK now I believe you've …………done this before," she moaned. Juices kept flowing now much faster than I could lap them up. It took about twenty minutes or so but she arched her back and pushed my head out from her legs and squeezed her thighs together as a huge flood of juices flowed out of her. My face and the bed were soaked.

"Good god damn," She panted, "I haven't cum like that in weeks." I laid on my back my boxer tenting again, and it wasn't unnoticed.

"Just so you know you're not getting laid today," she told me. I hadn't actually been thinking about it. I had been side tracked watching her flood the bed. I had never seen anything like that before.

"I…….. Ok." Was all I could say in a somewhat disappointed tone.

"Just so you know, it's nothing personal," She smiled at me, "I have no problem fooling around on a first date, obviously, but if you want me, you have to really earn it. That's my rule."

"I can live with that," I replied.

"Though after what you just did for me I might have to break that this time." She winked at me. I kissed her again.

"Tell you what, I'm not breaking my rule but I will give you something to make sure you call me again." She leaned over and pulled me though my boxers, "I don't want you to think this is a line, but I really don't usually go this far with someone I just met."

"Ok," I replied simply.

"No really," she looked dejected, "I'm not a slut, and I've only ever been with a handful of guys. I just really thought you were special, so far I don't think I was wrong."

"It's ok," I said to her, "I never had a bad thought. I kind of like you too." She took the complement to heart because with in a second she began running her tongue over my dick slowly and meticulously.

She slid my boxers off and continued her tongue play. I had, had blowjobs before but what she was doing was way beyond that. I had never had a girl take time like this and really tease me in this manor without actually sucking me. She gripped me firmly and lowered her tongue to my balls.

"OOOOOHHHHH MY GOD," I cried as she began to suck my balls. This was something I had never had done before. I liked playing with college girls! I was glad I had already cum because there was no way I could've held back otherwise at this point.

This kind of teasing went on for a twenty to thirty minutes. I would continually get close and will myself to calm down. I didn't want her to stop. Finally at long last she took me into her beautiful mouth. It took maybe three strokes by that point.

"I'm........." Was as much as I managed before exploding in her mouth so hard I was really surprised the back of her head hadn't blown off.

"Wow," she managed swallowing it all down, "That was a lot."

"Thank you," I moaned out. She smiled at me and rolled off the bed, walked to her bathroom and turned on the shower.

"Are you coming," she called and I couldn't run fast enough to join her.

After we showered I put my jeans back on and Brooke drove me home. She offered me a bath robe to cover up a little more, but I told her either way walking into the house I was going to get it anyway.

We talked in the car; she told me she could tell I was a virgin. I turned red again. She said she thought it was a good thing that I had made it to 18 without actually having sex. I told her I wasn't a saint I had come very close many times. She giggled she said close don't count. She said she liked me and if I wanted a chance to earn my way to her body I could call her if not she was great full for the fun morning. She did tell me if I was still a virgin at the end of my first year of college she would fix that for me. She said she believed nobody should leave their first year without getting laid once. I laughed and said I might take her up on that. She giggled and told me I was cute.

To change the subject I asked her how old she was. I explained that she knew how to do things I had never knew possible. But what it really was is that I liked this girl. Not just the fooling around, she was genuinely sweet and just plain fun to be around. I wanted to get to know her better. She grinned and said she had just turned 22. I thought that was cool, I hooked up with an older woman! As she dropped me off at home I told her I would definitely call her again.

It was already after twelve in the afternoon when I walked through the door. My dad was angry at my disappearance last night and how I returned home. Lilly sent him to his office to cool down. I walked up to my room with Lilly following me. When I go to my room I walked in and kicked off my jeans. Lilly was standing in the doorway, she cleared her throat. I didn't really care that much that I was almost naked in front of her. I was losing some of my shyness and after the morning I'd had I was feeling invincible.

Lilly wasn't as mad as dad was but she asked me what had happened. I put on a clean pair of jeans and pulled on a clean shirt. I lay down on my bed and looked at her. I thought about being sarcastic but Lilly had never been anything but nice to me in the past.

I made up a cover story as I went. I told her that some of my friends had stopped by the party last night and convinced me to come pay my respects to another friend at his grad party for just a few minutes. I told her not wanting to be rude I left with them only meaning to be a few minutes. As it turned out they drove me to a beach party. I objected but had no ride back home.

"I'll tell you the truth, Lilly," I said to her, "I met a college girl at the party and I really didn't want to come back home. I'm sorry that I chose a girl over the family but she seemed really cool and I didn't want to miss the chance to get to know her."

"Ok," She replied, "I know you haven't dated since you an Abby broke up, I get it, you're a guy. But that doesn't explain why you're getting home in the afternoon without most of your clothes." This one was a little harder to explain so I went with the truth, well sort of.

"Well....... I had broken down and had a couple drinks since it was my graduation night," I started and she just shook her head at me but didn't say anything, "Somehow I was given the wrong drink and the guy who fixed it got beat up for trying to drug a girl. Then the college girl took me home not knowing where I live."

"Well," she said smiling ear to ear, "Did you at least get laid for all your well-meaning trouble?" I couldn't believe she had just asked me that. I turned red for the third time that day. She giggled at me and said, "Good for you." With that she left my room.

I don't know what Lilly had told dad but he didn't seem to hold the whole incident against me. I was done with school and I now had the whole summer. I wasn't really sure what I would be doing but I was happy to have some time off before classes started again in the fall.

Katie came to the new house a home a week later. Dad and Lilly were out having dinner when she arrived. She looked like a completely different person then the one who had left last year. She was thinner and more tan then I had ever seen her. College life seemed to agree with her. Ash and I were standing in the library talking about the new stories we were reading when the door opened. Katie walked in the door and all my feelings flooded home. She walked in the door bags in hand, I took one look at her turned and walked away.

Katie hadn't even been home for a full minute when I went to my room and closed the door. I heard Ash start talking to her as I was walking away. A few minutes later I heard Ash talking in the hallway, she was showing Katie her new room.

I hadn't turned on the light when I walked into my room, I laid on my bed in the dark thinking how would I make it a whole summer with her if I couldn't look at her for a full minute. I heard a gentle knock on the door a few minutes later.

"Not now Ash," I called to her. She came in anyway. Ash walked over to the bed and lay down next to me. She wrapped her arms around me.

"I saw the look on your face."

"It was nothing," I lied, "I'm just not feeling well."

"Don't lie to me," she said sternly, "I can't handle you lying to me. Not after all we've been through.'

"I can't talk about it."

"You were honest with me our first time. You told me you were in love with someone else. It wasn't Abby was it?"

"I don't want you to think bad of me Ash," I started, "I really liked Abby, for a while I thought I loved her. I wanted to be in love with her. I didn't use her."

"But you weren't in love with her."

"No," I admitted, Ashley was right, she'd never been anything but wonderful to me, she deserved nothing but the truth, "I've been in love with the same girl since I was 13."

"Katie?"

"Yes."

"I thought you told me you didn't find out about each other until Linda's wedding?"

"I met her years earlier."

"Really?" I told her the story of Katie and me. I had never told anyone this story. I didn't go into the details but I told her that some of what is in the story above. I left out the part about the song being a trigger with me. I didn't want her to remember the winter formal and realize that the song not she had turned me on. I didn't want to ruin the memory of our first night together. It did feel good to talk to someone about the bottled up feelings I had been holding for the last 5 years.

"Wow," She said when I was done, "Where do you go from here?"

"That's the problem," I told her, "Unlike you she is my real sister. That makes what we did back then wrong."

"I'm glad we're not wrong," She said kissing me. We kissed or a while until we heard the car pulling up outside.

"Dad and Lilly are back."

"Yeah, I should go." Ash left my room and I went to sleep, not wanting to see any of them the rest of the night. Ash had really helped me come to a real decision. I felt it was time to give up my fantasy and find a real girlfriend. Problem was I really loved Ash. How would she take it if I started dating another girl? Would she be mad if she knew I fooled around with Brooke? I decided for now it was best not to tell her.

Giving up on my fantasy proved to be somewhat liberating that summer. What helped me move past my feelings for Katie were that for starters she had been seeing someone. She called him every night

before she went to bed. At first I would over hear her end of the conversation and I would be so jealous I would want to scream and punch something but after a couple weeks of this I started to mellow out.

The simple sight of her sometimes still set my motor running. She would be running around in shorts and a tank top, or she would come to breakfast some mornings only wearing her sport bra and shorts she wore to bed. I would often have to finish whatever I was doing and sneak off to my room and take care of myself.

For the amount of effort I was putting in to making this work the main part of my resolve was Ash. She was my rock when I grew weak. Because she was the only one who really knew what was going on with me she would see me sneak away and she would often follow behind. We would talk things out and I would calm down. Sometimes if we had a minute alone she would reach into my pants and take care of me to help me calm down when we talked.

I was grateful to Ash in so many ways, and I felt guilty. She was so in love with me and I was so focused on being in love with Katie. I wished I could love Ash the same way she loved me. She deserved that. Mid-summer I talked honestly to her about it. She simply told me she wasn't worried that she knew someday I would feel for her the same as she did for me. She knew in her heart it would happen. She was so much younger than me but in some ways so much stronger and smarter.

By mid-way through the summer I felt like some of the tension that I had with Katie before was slowly slipping away. I could finally spend whole days around her without freaking out, or having to sneak away.

Now that we had all this space the family went together one afternoon and bought a dog. I got out voted and we got a Jack Russell. They named it Jessy for some reason. With the dog in tow we spent whole days in parks playing with Jessy. The three of us kids started spending all our time together and I realized how much of the summer I had wasted brooding in my room over Katie. I decided that some time with her was better than none. She would be leaving again in a short time. I made the best of it.

When we weren't playing with that stupid dog we were at the movies or the mall, drinking coffee at the book store, or rollerblading across town. It truly became one of the best summers of my whole life. I spent it with the two girls I loved more than life itself.

As the summer drew to a close Katie and I had decided to do something really special for Ashley's 14th birthday. She would be starting high school right after her birthday so we wanted to make it fun. We talked to dad and he said because the family hadn't done anything in the way of a family vacation since we all had come together we would do something special.

Dad surprised Ashley a week before her birthday and announced he was taking everyone to Disneyland. It was a great birthday for Ash and a really fun way to say goodbye to Katie as she went back to college. We had a fun filled week full of rides and junk food and laughing. The three of us kids got one hotel room while the parents had one of their own. We stayed up all night and snuck down to the hot tub in the middle of the night. We had more fun than we had ever had together.

The summer ended and Katie left again for college. She was leaving on a Friday morning; we all had school starting the next Monday. I was up early the day she left; I was feeling indifferent over everything. I walked into the kitchen to look for something to eat, when Katie walked in. She was looking for a snack to take on the road with her.

Katie had been trying to sneak out quietly and avoid the whole goodbye thing. We talked while we ate some cereal. I told her that I still had feelings for her but I had fallen for someone. She was happy for me, she said that she actually felt a little jealous but she was truly happy I had met someone. She asked me her name. I told her that I wasn't ready to discuss the details yet. She smiled and said she understood.

She said that she had a secret too. She said she was a little nervous about what the family would think so she hadn't said anything all summer. I told her she didn't have to say anything she didn't feel comfortable with. She came out and admitted that she didn't have a boyfriend. I asked her who she had called every day. She said that she had fallen in love with another woman.

I laughed out load. I didn't mean too and she looked hurt. I told her I wasn't laughing at her, it just reminded of a conversation I had, had with someone before. I let her know I was happy she had fallen in love with somebody. As long as she was happy that's all I cared about.

I told her that she didn't need to hide that from the family. She said she wasn't sure how her parents would react. I told her that dad would probably find it cool. He was very liberal. However I did agree that Lilly might have the harder time with it. Lilly was really big on the whole traditional family thing. But it didn't mean she wouldn't accept her daughter.

Katie asked me to keep her secret for the time being. I told her I wouldn't tell her secret. We hugged before we grabbed her bags and headed to the car. As much as I had put my feelings aside for a fun summer, my heart broke again watching her leave. I'd had her in some form all summer I didn't like giving her up again. After she was gone I went up to my room and sat in the dark.

Dad and Lilly went out that night. After having gone on vacation with us kids they decided that they wanted a night to themselves. They were going out to dinner then off to a fancy hotel with a hot tub. They said they would be back in the morning.

I took this opportunity to have the talk with Ash I had been putting off all summer. She came running into my room and jumped onto my bed. We still hadn't had a real moment alone since the motel room at the beginning of the year.

"Their gone," she said taking off her shirt, "I've missed being with you so much!"

"Ash wait," I told her. She sat there in her bra and little skirt. I was getting hard looking at her. I needed to get this out before I gave in to her.

I told her that with things the way they were in the house I wasn't sure if we should continue. I told her that I loved her so very much but if we were caught it was a real possibility that we would never be allowed to see each other again.

"I'm not sure about Lilly's reaction," I explained, "I get the feeling sometimes she would be really happy to see us get together someday. But I know she would be pissed if she thought we were fooling around now."

"Yeah, Lil thinks you're a really good boy. But I think your right it's only because she thinks you're being a good big brother."

"It's dad I'm worried about. If we got caught he wouldn't understand that we love each other. He would assume I took advantage of you, he'd probably make me move out."

"No! He can't." She pouted with that comment.

"I know, so here's the deal, Angel, after tonight were going to put things on hold."

"On hold? You mean no more anything?" She asked with a look of disappointment.

"If were alone like we are now, we can kiss and hold each other but until your 16 I think that should be it."

"Because it will be legal for you to date me at 16 in this state?"

"Yes. At 16 dad can't do anything about it? I'm willing to wait if you are. I love my sweet little angel and believe me it will be hard but I will wait."

"I love you so much," she sprung on me and through her arms around my neck.

"Ok then we won't talk about it until then," I told her, "If your feelings haven't changed by then, on your 16th birthday I will scream to the world how much I love you."

"Ok," She said, "But I will tell you now my feelings won't change because there will never be someone else. I only have two birthdays to go until you have to keep that promise." She was grinning ear to ear.

I kissed her leaning her back on the bed. I didn't waste time tonight I slipped my hand in her bra and began kissing her neck. She moaned as I played with her nipple. I loved how sensitive her whole body was I knew if I kept this up she would have an orgasm before her clothes were off.

I unhooked her bra still massaging her same nipple. I lowered my lips to her other one but I didn't suck it yet. I applied the same technique I had learned from Brooke on her nipple. I ran the tip of my tongue across her breast without putting any part of it in my mouth. She was moaning loudly in anticipation. That meant this was having the same effect on her as it had on me. I circled the tip of her nipple with the tip of my tongue flicking it lightly every so often. She was squirming under me like she had never done before. I decided to reward her, I took my hand off her other breast and ran it up her skirt. I grabbed her panties and yanked them down her legs she helped squirm out of them.

I slid two fingers inside her dripping pussy, I didn't have to move my hand she began grinding against my fingers herself. I continued my excessive teasing of her nipples, and she thrashed against my hand. She finally couldn't take the teasing any more, she grabbed my head with both hands and looked me in the eyes, "FUCK ME WITH YOUR TONGUE OR FUCK ME WITH YOUR COCK!" he screamed at me. I had only a couple of times heard her use curse words but never like this. I had her motor running good that night.

I slid down and trust my tongue inside her realizing then how much I had missed her taste. Brooke had been good but it wasn't Ashley. I buried my face in her pussy literally biting down on her clit

gently as I came back up from deep tongue penetration. It only took only a couple nibbles to her clit to cause her body to go into a seizure.

"MY FUUUUUUUUUKING GOD!" She screamed as the orgasm took her over. I didn't stop or slow down I continued attacking her pussy as she sprayed my face with her cum. I let it run down my face as I thrust as deeply as I could. I knew the bottom of my tongue would have a sore spot from scrapping my lower teeth tomorrow but now I didn't care. I wanted to be as deep within her as I could. Her body never stopped shaking as I dove deep within her sweet wet wonderland.

The second orgasm came moments later; she screamed so loud and intangibly that I was glad we lived in a house now. Neighbors would have called the cops on that one. I got another quick blast of fluid on my face. I pulled back my tongue and started biting her clit again before she could recover from the second orgasm. I wanted to see how many I could give her.

I ran my fingers inside her again as I nibbled her nub. She still hadn't come down from the first two orgasms yet. Her body was still shaking and she was crying out word fragments. It only took seconds for the third orgasm; she let out a scream that lasted at least twenty seconds. I got the biggest blast of fluid from her yet. I thought about the amount of juice Brooke had produced, with a little time Ash could be like her. I was grateful she only squirted when she came not all consistently like Brooke. We didn't need a full puddle here.

The fourth orgasm came by the time she had stopped screaming from the 3rd. She didn't scream out this time she simply collapsed. She dropped to the bed and stopped moving so suddenly that I had to stop and make sure she was ok.

"Ash?" I called up to her from between her legs. She didn't respond. I slid up her body I could see her breathing, that was good. I got to her face and shook her shoulders slightly. She made a sound and I realized she had passed out the instant the fourth orgasm hit her. It had been so intense for her little body that it had knocked her out.

I lay down next to her my heart was racing and I was almost as exhausted. The front of my shirt was drenched as was the bottom of her skirt underneath her and my bed. The smell of sex was large in my room. I got off the bed and opened my window. It was still the end of August and still warm enough outside. The fresh air felt good, making the wet stain on the front of my shirt feel cold. I took my shirt off and flung it on the floor. I would have to throw all this stuff in the washer before Lilly came back home. I didn't want her to find it. There was no mistaking the smell on my shirt.

Ash woke about an hour later. She smiled at me and kissed me.

"Where did you learn to do that?" She asked softly.

"Improvising."

"Wow, I can't wait to see what you come up with next." She looked over at me and grinned.

"Your turn," she said, I think I'll do some improvising too."

Chapter Seven: Brooke's Promise

My first week of college was already proving to be busy. I had taken a lot of classes on the hope of getting into a real college next year. Katie and I had talked about me coming to the same school as her. After the summer we had together she felt we could finally be together without fear of taking things too far.

I really liked the idea of just being close to her. I was going to have to put in a lot of effort to make that happen. But I still had this thought in the back of my mind that if we went to college together away from our family and people who knew us, maybe just maybe there was a chance for us to have a secret relationship.

I felt in my heart she really did love me, and I had to at least give that one try before giving up completely. However I felt a stab of pain about Ash. I'd told her I would wait for her. But she was 14 and I felt that any day now she was going to come home from school and tell me all about some boy she fell for. That's what 14 year old girls did.

I dreaded that day because it would hurt me terribly when it happened, but I knew that's how girls were at that age. The idea that she would still feel the same way from age 12 when we had met to age 16 seemed unrealistic.

I started spending most of my time at the college. When I wasn't in class I was in the library. I was there some days from open in the morning to close at night. When I wasn't in the school library I was studying in our library at home. Our library had now been set up as my own at home office of sorts. This didn't leave me much time for a social life. Ashley would come by and ask me questions about what I was studying. I didn't mind her interruptions, as it turned out it would help me learn the subject matter if I had stopped to explain it to her. By teaching it to her it stuck better in my brain.

Most nights she would come see me right before bed. She would slip into the library and sneak kisses quickly then say goodnight. I loved those moments. That was my favorite time of day. She made me feel cared about in a way no one else in my life ever had.

If constant studying wasn't bad enough I got an after school job working at the high school 3 days a week doing grounds clean up, landscaping and janitorial. I wanted some extra money so I could go out with my friends a couple times a month. With all the school, work, studying and putting my relationship on hold with Ash, I was feeling kind of lonely. I really needed a night out with a girl.

It was November when I had the thought to call Brooke. I called her up and she was really surprised to hear from me. She said that she had given up the thought I would call her back. I told her that I had kind of been seeing someone in the meantime. But I told her I really would like to take her out. She thought a night out sounded nice.

That as it turned out I wasn't able to take her out until the next week Friday. I picked her up at her apartment and we went out to dinner. It was a nice seafood restaurant, I'm not big on seafood but I had let her pick. Dinner was nice and somewhat romantic. I realized I hadn't really ever been on a really

romantic date of this type before, except for the winter formal. When I was dating Abby we mostly ate fast food and looked for places to fool around.

I found it extremely easy to talk to Brooke. Maybe the fact that we had already been with each other took the edge off the whole first date thing. I liked being around her, she had an air about her that made me feel really comfortable.

After dinner we went for a drive out to the beach where we had met. It was empty tonight, which was fine with me. We walked in the moonlight finally settling down on the bank under some trees. We talked about nothing really for over an hour.

"Are you ever going to kiss me?" she asked finally.

"Oh......... yeah," I had been having such a nice night with her I hadn't really been thinking about that. I really did like talking with her. I kissed her lightly and she attacked my mouth. Her tongue trust forward dancing and teasing, I was surprised as I had barely made contact with her lips when she did this. I gave her my tongue a moment later. We both kept our eyes open the whole time we kissed. We gazed into each other as I ran my hand up her leg and her hand flew down to mine and stopped me.

"No, that's now a good idea," she said pulling away, "Considering what you did to me last time I don't think it's a good idea to get going too far out here. I wouldn't be able to ride home from being too soaked." She giggled with that, and I laughed a little too.

We went back to just kissing laying down in the sand melting into each other. I ran my finger though her hair and slid my other hand up her shirt. She moaned as I caressed her nipple, trying to tease her the same way she had done to me the last time we were together.

"Ok killer," she smiled at me, "It's time to go." I pulled away from her grinning. I liked the fact that I could affect an older woman so much.

I drove her home and she told me that I had earned some really good credit in her book tonight. I just kept grinning. She said if I kept it up she might actually give in one of these nights.

I really liked the thought of losing my virginity to Brooke. She was such a sweet and incredible lover. I still really wanted it to be Katie or Ash, but I wasn't going to turn her down if she ever offered.

Brooke gave me a long good night kiss and paused before getting out of the car. She bit her bottom lip as if trying to decide something; finally she said good night and got out of my car.

As the school year progressed I still had very little time most nights. I came home to late to eat dinner with the family. Most nights I came home made a sandwich and ate it in the library trying to get my homework done. I only saw Ash most days just long enough for her to give me hug and a quick kiss good night. I felt like her and I were growing apart. It looked to me like the thing I had been afraid of was starting to happen as she slowly gave me less kisses before bed and she didn't come in to learn about what I was learning anymore. By Christmas break she would only give me a quick hug before going to bed. Even though I had expected this I was still saddened by it.

I didn't get a chance to ask Brooke out until Christmas break. I called her up and asked her for a date, but she said she couldn't go. She told me that she really liked me but she had started seeing

someone. She said she couldn't just sit around the house waiting for me to call. I explained about my school and job. She said it was no hard feelings, she hadn't taken it personally.

Christmas was on a Monday this year. The Saturday before Christmas I slept almost all day. It was the first full day off I had, had with no school, work or studying needing done. When I woke up I just laid in bed the rest of the day. Lilly finally knocked on my door in the late afternoon. She had been concerned because I hadn't shown my face around the house yet. I told her I was just happy to have a day off. She understood and told me to come down for dinner her and my dad had something to talk to us about.

It was another hour before I got dressed and walked down stairs. Dinner was just getting started as I passed the kitchen heading for the rec-room. It was quite literally the first time I had been in the rec-room since school started.

I dropped down on the couch next to Ash. She was watching a movie. I didn't really care what the movie was I was just happy to have a free moment to sit with her. Despite her pulling away from me lately she moved across the couch and snuggled her head against my shoulder as soon as I sat down. We didn't say a word; we just sat like that until we were called for dinner. We sat down to meat loaf and potatoes and green beans. The meal looked really good.

"Well now that were actually having a family dinner with everyone here," dad said turning to me, "We have an announcement." He nodded to Lilly who was smiling like crazy.

"Were getting married," She said barley able to hold back her excitement. Ash got up running to her and hugging Lilly. The girls were both crying. I walked over to dad and shook his hand and told him it was about time. He laughed at that and said yeah, he really should have asked her long ago. That to me was an understatement I mean they had been living together for 2 years.

The big day was planned for this summer. Dad had already planned the whole thing. I guess he had been putting money aside since he had been promoted last year. He had a reservation booked for to rent this small lodge for a whole week. It was a half a day's drive to get there but the place had lots of rooms, an outdoor pool and spa, and a forest surrounding the whole place. Dad showed us the brochures and it looked awesome.

I thought it sounded like a really fun place to go for the summer. Lilly called Katie after dinner to let her know the news. They would've liked to have told us all together but Katie wasn't coming home for Christmas. Katie was happy for her mother telling her that she couldn't wait until the big event. I realized only then that it was probably an even bigger deal for Katie as it was to me; they were after all both her real parents.

Around late December Ash got asked to the Christmas Eve dance that the school was having. A boy at school had asked her to go and she told him she would let him know. I wasn't home at the time but I heard that Lilly talked her into going and having a good time with her friends. I felt a small twinge of jealousy when I heard about the story. I didn't find out about any of it until the day after the wedding announcement.

It was Sunday and the dance was that night, Ash got dressed up again in the same dress from the winter formal. Lilly had offered to get her a new one but she said no one at this school had seen it and she liked it so much she wanted to wear it again. Ash went with the boy and her friends at about 7:30

Christmas Eve. She was so cute I almost couldn't stand it. She returned just after midnight she was smiling saying she had a good time. I was happy that she had fun, but it only re-enforced the suspicion I had that she was slowly moving on from me.

Christmas break was slow the first week. I had been so used to being busy I didn't know what to do with all the free time I had right now. It seemed unreal. Ash had made quite a few new friends and spent most of her Christmas break away from the house.

My Dad and Lilly had a renewed sense of excitement with each other that week. They were extra flirty and I actually saw them pinching grabbing at each other. I was glad they really loved each other and had found one another again. It would've been a shame for them to not have reconnected. They told us that they were going out on New Year's Eve and wouldn't be home until late in the next day. They asked me if I could stay home and watch Ash. I shrugged and said sure.

New Year's Eve came and I didn't go out I had kind of lost touch with my friends with my schedule this year anyway. I also didn't really want to party this time. The last party I had gone to had been both bad and wonderful in the end, but I wasn't up for any of that. Ash stayed home with me, even though she had been invited to a friend's house. We lay on the couch snuggling until midnight. At midnight I gave her a sweet new year's kiss and I walked to my room to go to bed.

Almost predicatively she came into my room a short time later. She was only wearing her bra and panties. I was in only my boxers. I sprung up at the sight of her. We hadn't been together since the end of summer. Her body had done some more developing in that time. Her breasts I once wrote were b-cups were now at least c-cup now. Her stomach now had more definition as did her sexy little legs.

She climbed into bed without a word. She wiggled herself back into me like she used to do, but didn't acknowledge my hard on.

"I know you said we need to stop everything................. But I really miss your love. I love you still so much," she whispered without looking at me, "I just need you to hold me tonight, please don't send me away." Tears were rolling down her face.

"Ash, I love you so much," I told her, "You can sleep with me tonight. I would never send you away." I kissed the back of her head.

"You still love me?" she asked so quietly. I was surprised by the question. She had been the one pulling away from me.

"I'll always love you, why would you think I didn't?"

"I know you took out that other girl," She almost choked on her words.

"Ash, we talked about waiting to be together."

"That part wouldn't have upset me except around the same time you stopped telling me you loved me." She was sobbing now. Had I really forgotten to say the words to her?

"I'm sorry, angel."

"I would come to give you kisses and you only said good night to me." Her pretty little face was read and puffy. I kissed away the tears falling down her face.

"I thought since you were dating and you weren't saying much to me you had forgotten me." She was crying so hard her chest was heaving as she took in breaths. I hated that I had hurt her. She may have been smart for her age but sometimes I forgot that she was still just a fourteen year old girl.

"I love you so damn much it hurts," I told her, "I'd die without you. I was hurting inside because I thought you were giving me up."

"Really?"

"Yes."

Her whole disposition changed in an instant. She stopped crying and started to smile slyly. She switched gears so quickly I was taken by surprise. She rolled over and kissed me deeply.

"Prove it to me," She whispered. I wondered for a brief moment if what had just happened was real or if she was manipulating me. I was smart enough not to ask that question. If it had been real she would be devastated by me asking, if she had faked the crying she did it to break me of my vow to wait. But if it had all been an elaborate act to make me break our deal to wait until she was 16 it had worked.

She had just asked me to prove my love to her, and she was looking into my eyes. I slid down the bed bypassing her breasts. I pulled her panties off and trust my face into her pussy. She was so wet already that I felt almost as if I was drowning in her. I loved every second of it. It had been so long for her since we had been together that one nibble of her clit was all it took for her to orgasm. Screaming she sprayed my face as I slid my fingers inside her.

Her breathing was rapid as I had done in the past I didn't give her a break. I kept my assault on her going in full force. I didn't lick inside her this time I continued to finger her and nibble her clit. She was trashing now as her second one hit.

"FUCKING.......OOOOOOOOOOOOOOOOOH." She screamed. More juices flowed and I loved her taste I had missed her so much these past few months. I didn't know how I would be able to hold out for two more years. I wanted so bad to make love to her now.

I moved my lips up her body as she trusted against my fingers. I pushed off her bra and took her nipple in my mouth nibbling on it as I had her clit. Her scream shook the room as her third orgasm fired. I knew she was ready still sucking her nipple I pulled my fingers out of her and slid off my boxers. I moved between her legs. I was so hard and excited I came on her thigh as I was moving into place. She shuddered when I came on her.

"YES!" She screamed, "THANK GOD YES." I positioned myself between her and placed my cock to her pussy. I rubbed my cock all over her outer lips. She reached down to grab me and I stopped her by taking my hands in hers, I shook my head. I knew from experience how good and erotic this could feel. I had to be careful; she was so wet that it would only take one slight movement for me to slide into her. I had never done this to a girl before. I had, had it done to me but I used every bit of will power I had to not accidentally slip up.

Her fourth orgasm hit and her hands gripped mine hard before she went limp. If I hadn't seen this before I would have been worried. I rolled over next to her. She was dozing softly almost purring. I thought it was the most beautiful thing watching her chest rise and fall. I loved how she passed out from pleasure spikes. I had never heard of that happening to girls. It was one of the wonderful things that made her Ashley.

I couldn't take my eyes off her. I really and truly was in love with her. Little by little this amazing girl had crept into my sole. I was going to spend my life with her. I really was going to do everything it took to be with her. I couldn't envision myself with anyone else anymore, not even Katie. I wanted more than anything to lose my virginity with her. But I was determined to hold firm on this point I would not do it until she was legal.

The legal thing wasn't so much about the law as it was about giving her time to change her mind. I mean look at me right now in this moment. Up until right this second I had spent from 13 to now dreaming at least in a small way about Katie.

I realized, as I was being honest with myself, Abby had only been a replacement A place to push my love for Katie. Ash and I had started out with a different kind of love for each other, but now it had grown into real love for us both. But if I could outgrow my feelings for Katie that I'd had for so long, then so could Ash. It was only fair I gave her that time.

She awoke around 4:00 a.m. I was still awake looking at her. She smiled big.

"I love it when you prove your love to me," she whispered. I kissed her forehead.

"I love you Ashley."

"I love you Joe." We kissed as we laid there staring into each other's eyes.

The next morning we still lay in bed holding each other. I told her about my feelings from the night before. I told her I was sorry I had gone out with Brooke and I hurt her feelings. I told her I was going to wait for her. If I was going to ask her to wait until she was 16 then I would wait too.

"No." I was shocked that she had said no.

"What?"

"I don't want you to wait for me. I want you to do what your heart truly wants."

"What my heart truly wants is to be here in your arms forever."

"What about Katie?" She asked me firmly.

"I love you Ash. Katie was a dream in a long ago world."

"I don't believe you." She rolled over facing away from me.

"Ash," I whispered stroking her cheek.

"Don't miss understand me," tears formed in her eyes, "I want to be honest with you."

"What is it?" I didn't understand why she was crying again.

"I tricked you last night," she stated, "I wanted us to break the waiting, I wanted to trick you into making love to me. Yet you still held back."

"It doesn't mean......." I began.

"I know you love me. You've proven it to me both physically and emotionally. But after the intensity of what we did together the last couple of times, you still couldn't actually do it last night. Why Joe? Why couldn't you actually give yourself to our love like I've been begging you too? And don't you dare tell me it was my age." She had me dead to rights. It had taken every ounce of me not to penetrate her.

"I don't know."

"Don't lie to ME, Joe," She started crying harder, "Not to me, tell me why? If you love me soooo much, why can't you make love to me? Why?"

"I don't know why I held back with you last night. Your right it was the most intense moment of my life."

"Katie. It was Katie," She rolled over to look at me, "I'm not asking you to choose between us, Joe, but you need to choose yourself. That's why you held back." I kissed her forehead. When had this little girl gotten so much smarter than me? She understood things better than I did myself.

"Your right, about all of it."

"I know." She kissed my cheek and climbed out of bed. She picked up her bra and panties and left my room.

We didn't talk about our relationship again as we spent the rest of the vacation together. We didn't do any more proving of our love, we just sat together and cuddled. Lilly told me one night that she thought it was so cute that we still did that. I made sure to tell Ash every night I loved and cared for her.

For as slow as I had thought the first week of vacation had gone the second week flew by. Before I blinked it seemed I was already back to school. I was taking a few less classes this semester which meant I could spend a little more time at home.

The talk around the house was all about the wedding. There were napkins to pick and seating charts. It seemed dad was giving Lilly the dream wedding he felt she deserved. Every seemingly tiny detail that could conceivably be discussed was planned. I was really happy to be busy at that time; I really didn't want to get involved.

With all the planning going on Lilly didn't want Katie to feel like she was left out. Lilly would call her every night and describe how different things looked to get her opinion on everything. As I write this today I think, Wow the things we used to have to do before we all had phones with cameras. But I digress. Back then thing took 3 times longer to explain without pictures.

One night I heard part of Lilly's conversation with Katie an it sounded bad. I asked her later and she told me that Katie had broken up with another boyfriend. Of course I was the only one in the house that knew Katie had really been dating a girl. Lilly was mad for her daughter. She asked me if there was some broken part of us that made men cheat? I told her I wouldn't know. She smiled and said of course not, she patted me on the shoulder and walked away.

I wondered what Lilly's comment would have been had she known that it was a woman who had cheated on Katie. It made me realize that men and women were just as bad as the other sometimes. I felt bad for Katie, I wished there was something I could do to help her through her latest break up.

I wish I could tell you that point in my life was an exciting time, but it really wasn't. I went to school, I went to work, and I hung around the house. The one fun development was that this semester I ended up having a bunch of classes with Brooke. Because we had that same homework we would often work on it together in the school library. I found I really liked spending time with her. If I wasn't so in love with Ash, I would've liked to take Brooke out again.

I reapplied to all the colleges I had wanted to go to. With my college scores and activities I as actually accepted into a couple. One of which was Katie's. I actually got so excited about that I burnt the acceptance letters to the other colleges and told everyone I had only gotten in to Katie's.

My family thought it was great that I had gotten it at her school. Dad thought now that two of his kids going to school there he would rent us an apartment off campus so Katie didn't have to live in the dorm anymore and I could look after her in town. I didn't disagree.

I was going out of my mind about sharing an apartment that was just me and Katie. What was wrong with me? I loved Ash now didn't I? But I was doing all this stuff to be left alone with Katie. I was just as confused now as I had ever been. I was torn between the girl of my childhood dreams and the girl I loved in the here and now.

The school year came to a close with only one note of excitement. It was the last night before my final exams, I was in the campus library it was really late and I knew it was getting close to time for me to leave before they kicked me out.

Brooke was passing the research room I was sitting in and she knocked on the door. The research rooms were small rooms with a single window in the front and a table under the window. The room had no blinds to hide from passersby's but you could lock the door so you wouldn't be disturbed while working.

I got up and opened the door. Brooke walked in wearing a t-shirt a jean skirt and fur boots. Keep in mind this was years before that style was popular. I loved that look on her tan legs.

We talked for a while she was a little depressed from having broken up with her boyfriend recently. I told her I was in a complicated relationship between two girls. She laughed and told me she didn't think I was the type of guy to date two girls at once. I said that technically I wasn't actually dating either one of them. She said if I wasn't dating them then technically I was single.

She asked me if I was still a virgin. I turned red instantly. She giggled. I asked her why, was she going to keep her promise? She asked what promise. I reminded her of the joke she had made on the morning we had met each other, about not letting me finish my freshman year still a virgin.

"Maybe," she replied grinning, "You've been nothing but sweet to me, the kindest boy I know. I think you may have earned enough points for me to give in to you now." She leaned in and kissed me before I could answer. I let my hormones take over in that first contact between us. I remembered the morning we had first fooled around; she had told me I would have to earn my way into sleeping with her. I actually felt lucky right then for the chance.

As we kissed I thought of Ash. I don't know why I had such a hard time with the thought of having sex with Ash when I had no such problem letting it happen between myself and Brooke. In fact I knew in just a minute I would give in to her when she offered it to me. I was kissing her already thinking about a few minutes from now when I would be sliding it into her as she lay on the table. Then I realized why. This really meant nothing to me. Sure Brooke was a gorgeous and sweetheart of a girl but this was just sex. Like Abby when we had first hooked up at that party.

I started moving her backwards as we kissed. I was about to lean her back on the table when she stopped me.

"Do you have any condoms?" she asked me. I shook my head. I never thought to carry them. I mean really how often did this really happen to me?

"It's ok. Here's what we're going to do," she pushed me down into the chair; "I'm going to get you off first. Then I'll let you fuck my brains out when you're empty." She kneeled underneath the table and reached for my zipper.

"Oh my god………." I moaned as her hand pulled me out of my jeans. She didn't tease me this time she just went straight to work sucking and playing with the tip of my cock with her tongue in her mouth. She was so good at this I couldn't believe I was holding out like I was. Between her tongue and the sense of danger involved here I was holding my own really good.

She sucked me so hard I thought she was going to pull the skin off my cock when she moved up every stroke. It was getting really intense as she opened her stance kneeling on the floor and slid her hand inside her panties. She had juices running down her legs forming a puddle underneath her. She leaked more fluid then any girl I had ever seen, I remembered the last time we had flooded her bed.

I looked up all of a sudden out the window. The lights were going out. The only lights left on were the ones they left on all night. I knew from past nights that meant someone would be around to check for people any minute. Knowing our time was up I came in her mouth strong without warning. She spit it out on the floor in the puddle of juices she had left there. She looked up at me smiling and shrugged.

"We have to go now," I told her shoving my books into my backpack. I didn't want to get caught in the room with our fluids on the floor. We slipped out of the room and ran down the stairs and out the front door without being seen. I then walked her the block to her car. She looked down at her legs they were wet and glistening in the low light. We both broke out laughing.

Now that the mood was over she said she wasn't so horny anymore as much as she wanted a shower and to head to bed. I hugged her and gave her one more kiss. I was sure as we parted ways that night I would never see Brooke again.

The next day I was officially done with my year at community college. I had spent the whole year preparing for the next year. I hadn't participated in any of the usual college things because I really wanted my real college experience to be when I left home next year. Now all my work and sacrifice was about to pay off.

Chapter Eight: Virginity lost

Katie came home for the summer that year and it was the last summer all over again. She looked even more beautiful than I had remembered her. We were having a small welcome home Katie/Belated 19th birthday Joey party that night. That meant some friends were coming over in just about an hour.

Katie walked in and everyone ran to hug her, everyone except me. I was so turned on by the sight of her; I waved at her and went to my room.

I lay on my bed willing myself down. I wasn't angry or love sick for her like I had been last year when she came home, she had just really turned me on today. I reached over and flipped on my radio and tried to focus on the music and calm down.

It was working until that dumb ass song came on. I instantly got hard again. I cursed inwardly this was pissing me off; every time something's going on that dumb ass song plays. I wondered what would happen next. Would someone burst through my door now and fuck me? I mean for crying out loud if it wouldn't have been for that cursed song I never would've met Katie the day at the toy store. I never would've run into her at the barn and I wouldn't had got and erection the night of the dance. That song had started both of the relationships I had with the girl of my childhood dreams and the girl I really loved.

I laid there fighting myself back because I could hear guests arriving already. I decided to just not fuck around anymore I reached over and grabbed my old shirt from by the bed and I unzipped my pants and attacked myself. I was mid stroke when predicatively the door opened. I hated the fact Lilly had removed all the locks from the bedroom doors. I looked up in horror all the old guilt on my face, my fears rising up in me. It only lasted for an instant as it was Ash who entered. She gave me a crooked smile.

"Was it Katie?" she asked knowingly as I grabbed my old shirt and came hard. I dropped the shirt back to the floor and zipped myself up before I answered her.

"Only partly." I said truthfully.

"So if it wasn't just Katie what was it?"

"It was that dumb ass song." Before she could ask I started to explain the last bits I hadn't told her last year. I told her about the song and how it had affected my life. I was honest with her to a point. I still left out the part where the song had been playing at the dance. I wasn't ever going to tell her. If she remembered she could put two and two together herself. She probably hadn't been paying attention to what song was playing when I was poking her in the stomach.

When I was done talking she had a crooked smile on her face. She didn't say a word but simply took my hand and led me out of the room. The party was starting and we needed to make an appearance.

With Katie home now it seemed like Lilly had gone into hyper drive. They had 2 weeks until we went to the lodge and the wedding. With Lilly running her around everywhere I really didn't have much

of a chance to even see Katie. I realized as soon as she had set foot though the door, Ash had been right. The only reason I couldn't commit to Ash was because in the back of my heart I still had a fantasy about being with Katie. I loved Ashley so much I couldn't make love to her without her being the only girl in my heart. But wait did that mean I could make love to Katie with Ashley taking up so much more room in my heart? What any of this all mean? I really did love Ash more now. I spent the next 2 weeks in just this same confused frenzy. I needed to work this out and make a decision.

One week until the wedding Linda came to the house to help and stay with us at the lodge. Lilly was running around like crazy taking Linda, Ash and Katie with her most of the time. The four girls had wedding fever. With them gone all the time I somehow got the responsibility of taking care of the stupid dog. At first I was not happy to be left with the dog, but as time moved on I grew to like walking him or going to the park as an excuse to just get out of the house for a while.

It had seemed like the summer had just started and already it was July. It was finally time for the wedding I found myself in part of a caravan heading to the lodge. Ash had wanted to ride with me, I said yes. She talked the whole way about her wedding day and what she would want. She held my hand the whole ride.

Dad had booked the whole place for the week. We had a number of close friends and family coming to stay during that time. This ended up causing some changes in the sleeping arrangements. There ended up being some last minute scheduling changes and we had more people coming then we had beds.

Ash suggested that since we all live together anyway that the three of us take the upstairs corner room. It had a full size bed and a twin stuffed into a small room. Ash stated that she and Katie could share the full size bed and I could have the twin.

Everybody thought this was a good idea. Katie and I glanced at each other questionably. What was Ash up too? She knew about the tension between us but everyone thought it was a great solution. So here we are again. I'm sharing a room with the girl of my teen fantasies. I hoped this wouldn't back fire.

The wedding was on our second day at the lodge. Lilly looked beautiful, she wore a blue dress, not white. Dad was in a full tux. It was the most dressed up I had ever seen him. The ceremony took place on the side yard of the lodge amongst the trees. It was probably the most romantic looking wedding I had ever seen. I liked it so much in fact that I re-created it when I got married a few years later. This week here at the lodge, because of this wedding changed my life forever so when I had my wedding here it was to honor that. But I'm getting way ahead of myself. My wedding comes way later.

The reception seemed to go on forever. It seemed everyone we ever knew showed up to congratulate my parents. I was happy for dad and I loved Lilly so much I envied Katie that she was her real mother, I wished she was mine.

We finally broke the reception after dark that night. I retired to the room, I was tired and I wanted out of my suit. I got to the room to find it empty. I changed from my suit to a pair of shorts and a t-shirt. I did acknowledge that both girls I was sharing a room with had not only seen me naked but had given me head. But due to the circumstances I chose to put on clothes to sleep in.

I lied down on the bed and fell asleep. I was awaked by Ash some time later. I looked at my watch; it was only 10:20. Ash was shaking me slightly.

"What?" I asked groggy.

"I just really need to be loved right now." I was shocked, we couldn't do anything now.

"Now might not be the best time......."

"Katie is downstairs with my sister. I locked the door. We have a few minutes." She lay down with me and put her arms around me.

"Thank you, Joe," she whispered as I slid my arms around her too, "I just needed you to hold me."

"I love you, Angel."

"I love you too. But we don't have time for this," she giggled squeezing my cock that had grown, poking her leg now, "Just think we only have one year and one month until your promise." I kissed her and she slid her hand inside my shorts and started stroking me.

Now she was appealing to my sense of danger. Anyone could've come up here at any time. Our kissing was growing passionate as she stroked me faster. I was getting so close as we heard the door knob turn. The door was locked so it didn't open. There came a small knock.

At the same time we heard the knob Ash rolled off the bed lightly as to not make a sound. By the time the knock came she leaned over and whispered in my ear, "Pretend to be asleep."

I pulled the blanket over me and rolled on my side away from the door so as not to give away my raging erection. Ash opened to door as I was rolling into place as to not have much delay from the knock to her opening the door. Before Katie even walked in Ash held her finger to her face and ssssshed Katie.

"Joey's asleep," she told Katie quietly.

"Why was the door locked?" Katie asked suspiciously.

"I was going to change and I didn't want anyone to walk in on me."

"You were going to change right in front of Joey?"

"He's asleep," Ash said confidently, "Besides he has his back to us. "

"Good point. We'll see him if he tries to roll over." Katie said as if it were a warning if I were awake. I heard two different zipper sounds and I realized that they were helping each other out of their dresses. I cursed myself for rolling away from the wall I really wanted to peak at them. It had been 3 years since I had seen Katie. I was drooling on my pillow at the thought that for an instant behind me she was naked. I was so hot at the thought of both girls naked together I actually came without touching myself. I felt twelve years old again as wet cum filled my boxers.

I woke the next morning to Ash shaking me. She said Katie had just left and she leaned in to kiss me. I was on my back and standing up in front of her. She giggled and slid her hand in my shorts.

"Kind of sticky in here," she giggled, "Too bad you didn't roll the other way last night. You'd have ripped through your shorts." I had no doubt she was right. She started stroking me with the mental image from last night and the danger of getting caught I didn't last long.

"Angel I'm ...." I said very softly. She pulled up the leg of my shorts and boxers lowered her head on the head of my cock as I came in her mouth. She swallowed it down quickly and removed her hand. She got off the bed and started changing into her swim suit.

"Were all heading to the pool. It's already hot outside." She pulled on her bathing suit a came back to the bed. I put my arms around her.

"Thank you for the wake up."

"We didn't get to finish last night," she whispered in my ear. She knew the whispering was a turn on for me and it was working.

"Ok you have to go before I rip that bathing suit off you."

"Ok but don't take too long .... I'll say changing, up here." she said looking down at the fact I was already up again.

She left the room and I took care of my second orgasm. I put on my swim trunks and headed to the pool. Katie and a number of other girls were already down there. There was more half naked flesh then my teenage brain could handle. It was a good thing I was drained already. Had Ash thought about that for me earlier? I would have to thank her none the less.

Things were going great we had music blasting, everyone was playing and dunking and frolicking like little kids. The water felt amazing to me on this hot morning. It was afternoon before I knew it. Some of the people had gotten out some were tired of swimming some just went to get some lunch. As people were getting out I looked around but had lost track of both Ash and Katie.

It was then disaster struck. If you're smart you probably already realized this is where our story began. I'm running through it again because now that you know who we are, I will imagine this seen takes on a whole different meaning. When I wrote the opening I was trying to hide certain dentals, I now return to where this story began as I tell the extended cut as it were.

I was debating getting out of the pool and getting some lunch myself, when that dumb ass song came on. I could feel myself getting hard so I slipped away as fast as possible. I was pissed this was still happening to me. The last time in my room was bad enough, but now in a pool full of relatives and friends was more than annoying.

That song always put thoughts of Katie in my head and I began getting really worked up as I ran up the stairs. I would just jack myself really fast and head down for lunch. That was the plan until I found Katie standing in the room. I opened the door to see her standing there wearing only a pair of pink swim suit bottoms with a daisy on the front. I didn't mean for it to happen but in that moment there was only me and Katie. I forgot about the party downstairs our parents, our friends, and Ash. All I could see was my sister. Six years of burning lust exploded in me and nothing else existed.

She looked at me as if I had walked in on her intentionally while she was changing. When I opened the door she was leaning over to pick up a shirt off the bed. Her breasts were amazing. Her skin was tan and her hair still damp and clinging to her.

We stood there for what seemed like an eternity, I couldn't take my eyes off her nearly naked body. I jumped into an erection so hard that it hurt, yet I still couldn't say anything to her or take my eyes off her. She was so beautiful, her still wet body from the pool glistening, her full breasts, nipples constricting turning hard from the cold air in the room. There was no way for me to hide the erection trying to burst through my loose swim shorts. She was looking at my erection.

I don't know what took me over in that moment but I pulled my shorts down letting them just hit the floor, but not stepping out of them. I stood there nude and the first real look of embarrassment came across her face, I could see it spread though her cheeks, but she didn't look away.

I grew bolder. I worked up all my courage and moved across the room to her. Without a word I leaned in and kissed her neck. My body was pressing against hers and I felt her shudder. At first she was non responsive I was about to pull away when she moved my face from her neck and kissed me on the mouth. We kissed lightly at first then moving into heavier kisses. I opened her mouth with my tongue and both of ours danced together. It was the most passionate kiss we'd had since the night at the barn.

I reached up with one hand and ran my fingers though her hair, the other I slid behind her back pulling her close to me. I couldn't believe she was letting me hold her. It had been so long, I had so much need for this I didn't care that it was wrong. I didn't care about right or wrong in that second I was finally holding her again.

All I could think about was I could lose my virginity to her right here and now and it was all due to that dumb ass song, that god damn song. We were still standing and kissing hard when my excitement became too much and I came on her. It happened without much warning, she was leaning against me pressing it down against her thigh, when all of a sudden I let loose and I shot myself down her leg. I was embarrassed, and I turned my head away.

"It's ok, it wouldn't be us without you going off early," she whispered in my ear pulling my face back to hers, "I can't deny how wrong this is but, your my toy store boy and you've always been such a good brother," she spoke softly right before kissing me again.

"I think I love you," I told her. The reason I had said, think, in that statement was because at that moment I wasn't sure how to feel. I deeply loved Ash but I couldn't deny that I still had some feelings for my sister.

"Don't make this worse than it is," she said lightly, kissing me again. She pulled away and lied down on the bed. She took my hand and pulled me to her.

"I don't know how much time we have," she whispered in my ear as I lied on top of her. Despite my early release I was still really hard. There was no way I was going soft at this moment with my dreams coming true.

She reached down and slid her swim suit off. I moved between her legs looking intently at her beautifully shaved pussy. It was more beautiful than I had ever imagined. She took me in hand and

brought me to her. I thrust forward not really knowing what I was doing. She moaned and I came again almost right away. She smiled as I came and ran her hand along my cheek. I didn't stop thrusting.

I was inside her and I was on fire. I'm not sure how long we were together before it was over, but it probably wasn't as long as it felt. I know it was way too short to cover for the 6 years of yearning behind it. I was lost in a world of my own creating. I couldn't get enough of her; I began to kiss her neck again when she told me we needed to stop.

"This is so wonderful, but we should get back to the party before someone notices were both missing," she said softly. I rolled off of her putting my arms around her, pulling her close, putting my head on her breasts. I could hardly breathe from exhaustion and both orgasms.

"No one will suspect that we were up here doing this."

"No. But we've been up here for a while and I don't want to be found out. It would be.......bad" She paused and started stroking my hair.

She got up off the bed and her hair fell over her face. I didn't move, she looked at me in a sideway glance her hair covering half her face. I couldn't see the expression on her face. It was all starting to hit me what just happened.

My breathing and thoughts returning to normal, it was then that I started go get scared. What were we going to do now? What if someone found out? Oh god I had cum inside her! She could get pregnant. A mixture of emotions started swirling in my head. Love, fear, happiness, and disappointment our moment was over.

It was then with my rational mind returning I thought of Ash. How could I have done this to her? Granted we had decided to wait to be in an official relationship, but this was Katie, what would this mean between me and Ash if she knew I had finally made a decision and given my virginity to Katie and not her?

"Katie..... I.....?" I didn't know what to say. She was putting her shorts on.

"Don't......... We can talk about this tonight." She said picking up her shirt off the other bed, "I'm just worried that someone will come up here and over hear, I'll see you down stairs."

"Ok." I kind of croaked. I wanted to hold her and she was leaving. I hopped she wasn't ashamed of doing it with her brother. I knew that had been her fear for a long time, a fear that we would end up having sex. I got off the bed and pulled on my jeans and lied back down on the bed it still had her sent on it. I laid there and drifted off to sleep.

It was Ash who woke me. She was kissing my neck and my pants were open she had me in her hand stroking me slowly.

"How do you feel?" She asked.

"Right now both good and scared." I looked at my watch it was 7:00 already. I had slept all afternoon; it had been lunch time when I came up here.

99

"You should stop, we could get caught."

"No, everyone else is way out in the woods doing the bon fire and barbecue thing, besides they think you're sick."

"Why do they think I'm sick?"

"Your dad was looking for you earlier and Katie told him you were up in the room feeling sick. I volunteered to come up here and look after you." I thought it was clever how she had somehow manipulated this situation resulting in us being alone right now, but if it gave us time I was ok with it.

"So how do you feel?" she asked again.

"I'm not actually sick. But if you keep up that slow motion you're doing I'll feel fine in just a couple minutes." She looked at me with her crooked smile.

"No, how are you feeling now that you've finally made love to Katie."

"She told you?" I was shocked. As far as I knew Katie didn't know Ash knew about us and vice versa.

"She didn't tell me, you just did." Tears filled her eyes and she ran to the other bed and curled into a ball rocking herself slowly. I couldn't believe she just played me like that. I zipped myself up and followed her to the other bed. I put my arms around her and pulled her to me.

"Oh Angel, I'm so sorry," I whispered to her, "Something happened and I lost control today." The moment I heard the song I had been thinking about Katie and opening the door to see her naked I lost all control of my senses and my lust took over. In that moment I had not only forgotten about Ash, it was like she didn't even exist right then. Seeing the tears in her eyes that I had caused her I would never forgive myself.

"I'm so, so sorry." I began to cry, "I love you more than the world."

"But you slept with Katie." I couldn't argue that.

"I know baby girl," I hadn't called her that since we got together, "I'll never forgive myself for hurting your."

"Then make it up to me." She rolled onto her back causing me to have to sift my position. She kissed me, I knew what she wanted. I still didn't know if I could give it to her. I lay on top of her kissing her with all my love and passion for her. I had my knees between her knees, palms resting flat on the bed on either side of her breasts. She pulled up her skirt between us pulling her knees together and pulled down her panties. My heart was beating in my rib cage so hard I thought I might die. I knew what she wanted. I wanted what she wanted. But I still hadn't sorted out Katie yet. I couldn't take Ash's virginity without being whole heartedly in love with her. For an angel like her she deserved better. I loved her so much my heart was trying to explode from anticipation. Could I really do this? What was my real fear?

She unbuttoned my jeans. My breathing was heavy, it was like I was the virgin here not her. She unzipped my jeans. My heart beat was hard and I felt like I might pass out. She slid down my jeans to my

100

knees. I almost couldn't breathe. She grabbed my cock and I came on her stomach yet I grew harder as she stroked. I started shaking. I hadn't been this nervous with Katie.

"Calm down," she said running her other hand over my cheek, "I want this more than I've ever wanted anything. I've wanted this since I was twelve." My shaking had turned to a shudder. I knew this was the moment. It was now, today I had never been this scared over anything before. I closed my eyes as I lowered my hips and slid down a little. I kicked my jeans off my lower legs.

"It's okay," she whispered in my ear, "You're not going to hurt me." How did she become the older one in our relationship? I had already made up my mind when she positioned me to her. I had been here before. With other girls, this is usually the time when the lights went out in the library like when I was with Brooke or Katie had walked in the door when I was with Abby.

That was then and she was now. I listened for the sign. Something to tell me if I doing the right thing. No lights went out, no footsteps in the hall. There were no sudden thunder claps or loud thuds I listened for anything but it didn't come. The only sound in that moment was an angelic voice whispering in my ear, "I love you so damn much."

I slid into her delicate pink love petals and she cried out loud. She was so tight I felt like I had entered steel vice lined in silk. She was so warm inside, so very warm she almost burned. She was so warm and so tight, I couldn't believe how so right this all felt. The world felt right, she felt right. My fears melted away with one stroke within her. How could I have waited for this? Ash should have been my first without any hesitation so long ago. I had tried to the right thing for her; this right now felt more right than any moment in my life.

I brought my mouth down on hers after she cried out the first time. Kissing her heavily I backed out slowly and I trust forward again. She cried out into my mouth again. She was so tight and insanely hot inside I thought she would friction burn the skin off my cock if I thrust anymore. But I did, I couldn't stop. I again slowly began to pull back a little and thrust forward.

I was all the way inside my angel and I knew I was the devil. I couldn't believe I was here with her now in this moment. We began to move together. She wasn't thrashing or shaking like usually did when I ate her out. She had what I would call an unusual calm about her as I trust into her. She began to lift her hips up to meet my every movement. My body had caught up with my mind and finally shopped shaking; all there was in the world was Ashley, my love, my angel, and my baby girl. I was going to burn in hell for this but I didn't care anymore. She didn't just moan, but screamed with pleasure with every push forward.

Without warning her body tensed up so tight I couldn't move. It was my turn to cry out into her mouth. I could feel her squirt on my cock, her juices running down us where we connected. Her warm fluid almost had a cooling effect on me where I was exposed from the flame that was her love flower.

I didn't slow down when she came; I sped up the speed and depth of my strokes. I wasn't far after her first orgasm. I shot my seed deep within her. Her body clamped down on my cock again as I flowed into her. I still didn't stop. Somehow I only kept getting harder every time I came. I ran my tongue across hers as I continued my hard thrusting. She was still crying out with each thrust. Her whole body convulsed as her third orgasm hit her. I would've been thrown off her had her pussy not clamped down like a steal press not letting me pull free. More juices flooding the bedspread now. I slowed down again as I regained control and her body stopped shaking. I went back to slow even trusts. She was shaking

unaccountably now. Despite the shaking I couldn't stop. Now that I was inside her I never wanted to stop. I came again inside her and I still couldn't stop; I was never pulling myself from her. Our kissing never stopped as she screamed her shaking got worse and she arched her back experiencing her fourth orgasm.

This is where she had passed out in our past sessions. Her body fell limp but she still had her eyes open. I looked down into those eyes. I still couldn't stop. She was beautiful I kept going slow and lovingly. I couldn't stop.

"I love you so damn much," she said to me. Her voice soft, quiet and full of love, I somehow came inside her a third time. Granted the second and third times for me where far smaller than the last but I had shuddered another small orgasm. I fell off of her onto the bed. My dick was raw, it was sore to the touch as if I had run sandpaper over it. I would feel that tomorrow.

"I love you Ashley."

I was exhausted physically and emotionally. She got up and went to the window and opened it the rush of air felt so good. I pulled my jeans back on just in case someone decided to come back. She wiggled out of her skirt and used it to wipe herself off. She put on fresh panties and a pair of jeans.

After we had put our clothes back on I pulled the blanket off the bed, the upper floor had a laundry shoot and I stuffed the blanket down the shoot and went back to the room to replace the blanket with one from the hall linen closet. With the new blanket in place and the evidence gone Ash climbed back on the bed with me. I pulled her to me kissing her neck.

"That was the greatest moment of my life," I told her.

"Mine too. I'm so happy, even if I'm going to be really sore tomorrow."

"You're so tight I'm going to be sore too."

"So was I good?" she asked giggling.

"So good."

I laid there and thought about the day. Ash hadn't given me much time to reflect before she had been up here to have her first time too. I had slept with both my childhood dream girl and my hearts true love. It had been exciting in an unbelievable way with Katie. But with Ashley it had been so much more. I liked both but I liked it more when real love was behind it.

I looked up and Ash had tears in her eyes.

"I'm sorry baby angel, that I broke my promise to you. This is why I thought we should wait." I felt guilty. I knew she said she really wanted it but she had tears running down her cheeks falling off her chin. I held her rubbing her back. I didn't know what to say to make this moment ok. It had been so great and now the fear and regret were setting in.

"It's ok. I love you so much," I reassured her.

"Because of....... tonight?" she asked and I was surprised by that question.

"No, because of every day." She cried more.

"I wanted today to happen so badly," she cried, "I just never know it would hurt so much."

"I didn't want to hurt you. That's why I wanted to wait," I tried to calm her down but she burst into more tears.

"I didn't know it would hurt me so much to share you."

"Oh," I exclaimed, "I'm so sorry Ash. That should never have happened."

"It's ok, you had to know........ You had to finish what you started with her to ever get past it."

"I didn't need to sleep with her to know I loved you."

"I always thought that was what was holding you back with me. I knew one day you would make love to her. I accepted that. I just didn't know it would hurt me so much to share you."

"Katie wasn't what was holding me back, Angel," I said to her more out of reassurance, but I didn't know if I actually believed that, "I was just waiting until the perfect moment with you, one moment in time where the world was all about us so I could show you what you mean to me. Just like what happened tonight."

She looked me in the eye and pressed her forehead to mine. We sat looking into each other's eyes. Her tears started to subside a little.

"Really, you thought it was perfect?" She asked timidly.

"I will tell you something truthfully," I started, "I had sex with Katie today, but I made love for the first time to you. I know the difference because of you. I could spend a thousand years trying to describe how you felt and never be able to get it out right."

"Thank you," she said quietly her demeanor changing again. She smiled and kissed me. We lay down on the bed together. I figured we could lie together until I heard someone coming back upstairs, then I would send her to the other bed so we wouldn't get caught. We fell asleep not long later.

I woke up early the next morning; Ashley was lying on top of me. I was panicked for a minute until I looked over and saw that Katie wasn't in the room. I slipped out from under her and walked out of the room. I was exhausted and hungry. I hadn't eaten anything all day yesterday and I had worn myself out really good. I noticed the cleaning girl was working on the hall as I past her.

I walked downstairs on my way to the kitchen. I knew the kitchen staff started with breakfast early. I hoped they had something ready. I had made it as far as the lobby when I found Katie. She was curled up in a ball on the lobby couch; she looked like she was freezing. I leaned over and pushed on her shoulder.

"Katie," I called quietly, "Katie, go up to the room." Her eyes flew open when I spoke to her. She glanced around the room seeing we were alone; she slapped me across the face. It caught me so off guard I lost balance and landed on my butt.

"What?"

"How could you, I thought you were better than that!" She growled at me.

"What are you........?"

"You're going to sit there and tell me you didn't use me? Or her?" Now my panic button hit when she said *her*. Did she know about Ash?

"What are you talking about?" I tried not to give up something she might not actually know.

"You told me you loved me yesterday," she started tears forming in her eyes. Jesus Christ, I thought, all I do is make girls cry anymore.

"I do love you."

"Don't say that. How can that be true? How can you love me and take advantage of Ash like you did?"

"I think it's time we finally had that talk we've been putting off for the last couple years."

"I don't want to hear it. I've heard this speech from guys and girls for that matter." I got up from the floor and took her hand.

"Come with me, just for a little while," I asked, "Let's talk, if you're still mad at me when we talk this out, I promise I will never talk to you again if that's your wish."

"Ok," she said tentatively. I led her outside and we went for a walk in the woods. I wanted to find a place where no one would be ease dropping.

I confessed everything to her. I told her about that dumb ass song. I told her about how much I had loved her for all those years. I reminded her of the conversation we had, had a year ago when she admitted to having a girlfriend. I had told her that I had a secret love then, I admitted to being in love with Ashley. I told her the whole story that is basically everything that is this story I'm writing now.

When I was done she was quiet. We lay on the grass together looking at the clouds pass by. I couldn't tell if minutes or hours had passed as I had confessed to her, everything I had done.

"How did you know I was with Ash?" it finally dawned on me to ask.

"I came back to the room to talk to you last night. I walked in and you guys were asleep together, she had her arm around you. Even with the window open I could smell a musty smell in the room and I knew you guys had done it. It was strong enough I knew it couldn't have been from us earlier."

"Oh, did you tell anyone?"

"No, I wanted to talk to Ash first. I thought if you slept with us both then you were just a selfish asshole pig and I wanted her to go with me to mom and dad."

"I didn't mean for any of this to happen yesterday."

"I know. If I would've stopped to think about it," She started, looking down almost ashamed, "I would've realized you always act from your heart, not you dick, like most men."

We sat in silence for another few minutes. Katie moved over closer to me and grabbed my hand. She explained that the reason she had been so upset to find me and Ash was that she thought I had taken advantage of her. Katie said she had, had her share of bad experiences and the thought of me ruining Ash's innocence had set her into a rage. There was no way she was going to live with me if I was a pig asshole who uses the innocence of little girls. She was really happy it was out of love, she could understand me falling for Ash.

I told Katie I loved her. There was no getting around that fact. Every time I tried to put it out of my mind, it flared up worse every time she was around. But as much as I loved her, I was in love with Ash. I told her I could never again be with anyone else.

She teared up a little at the sentiment, but said she understood. She loved her aunt very much. She was happy that we were in love. She was happy about how much I loved Ash. She had thought I was some kind of monster for sleeping with her. But after I had told her the whole story she actually gave us her blessing.

She told me that things had worked out really good for us. She admitted that she had been scared about what I thought this had meant for us. She told me that she hadn't meant to sleep with me. She said she had just lost control in the moment.

She didn't regret having sex with me, she loved me but for the sake of Ash and her girlfriend we shouldn't have done it. I told her I thought she had broken up with her girlfriend. She told me she had. She said she was dating another girl now. She felt bad for having cheated. I understood.

I asked her about her girlfriend, would she break up with Katie for this? I felt bad that I might have cost her another relationship. Katie told me she was in love, real love with her girlfriend and thought she could work it out. I hoped so. I asked her what her new girl was like? Katie smiled and said I would meet her soon enough. That was true it would be hard not to meet someone she was dating if we were living together.

We walked to the lodge still holding hands, we were now for the first time simply brother and sister just a brother and sister that shared a secret bond. When we returned we went to the dining hall and got some lunch. Food sounded so good as I had now missed another meal. Ash found us as I was eating a sandwich about ten minutes after we got back. She had a suspicious look on her face but knew better than to say anything in front of the family.

Ash and I decided to go hiking up the mountain trail that afternoon. We asked everybody if they wanted to hike with us, only Linda had said yes. We were getting ready to go when Lilly talked Linda into going to the hot tub with her. She liked that idea better and decided to stay.

That was fine with us, I told Ash we needed to talk. She said she had expected a talk from me today, more so after seeing me with Katie that morning. I told her what was said between Katie and me. Then I told her that since we had gone ahead and crossed the line already I didn't see the point in waiting anymore to do it again. She hugged me, and said she had been expecting me to tell her we couldn't do it again.

While we hiked found a secluded grassy area and decided to take a break. As we sat I told her I had something else I wanted to talk about with her.

"The real reason I wanted to talk to you alone, Ash, is I have a question for you that I've never asked a girl before," I said to her shyly. I didn't know why I was so nervous I knew the answer yet I almost couldn't ask the question, "Ashley my angle love, would you be my girlfriend officially?"

"YES!" she screamed and kissed me.

"Ok," I said with my heart thumping in my chest, "Wow, you're my girlfriend." I said not for her but for me. I was so overwhelmed with happiness just to have a title on our relationship.

We lay down in the grass and began making out. It didn't take long and I had a need to have her again. I couldn't control myself I lifted her skirt and pulled down my shorts. We started to make love again but both decided we were to sore from the night before to actually do it yet. We kissed some more and continued the trail.

"Joe, can I ask you a question." We had only gone about 70 feet up the trail when she asked.

"What's that my girlfriend?" I asked and she smiled shyly and looked down her feet. I couldn't get enough of calling her my girlfriend.

"You said you never asked a girl before...... to be your girlfriend. But you dated Abby."

"I never actually asked her. We were running around all the time, fooling around. One day she just started referring to me as her boyfriend. I just went with it. I never actually asked her."

"Oh, Ok, I wasn't sure."

We spent the remainder of the week at the pool, hot tub and game room. We played air hokey and shot pool. It was really fun. Little by little our family and friends started leaving for home, giving us more time and places to be alone. On the last full day at the loge we hiked back up the mountain trail to our grassy spot again and made love again. It was just as special the second time as the first. I couldn't get enough of my little lover.

Ashley rode home with me after the wedding. She held my hand the whole time. But unlike the ride up she didn't talk much. Instead she mainly looked out the window. She looked like she had something on her mind. I decided not to pry, she would tell me what was one her mind when she was ready. I drove us home spending half my time looking at the road and half my time admiring my girlfriend.

Chapter Nine: Confessions

The rest of that summer after the lodge was the best of my life to that point. My parents went on a weeklong honeymoon after the lodge. They said after all that family bonding they needed some time just for them. I told them I completely understood. They left the 3 of us at home for the week.

Linda had come back with us from the lodge. She stayed only until Dad and Lilly left for their honeymoon. She had, enjoyed herself so much all of us and didn't really want to leave. Linda told Ash she really missed her and was sad she really hadn't had much time to spend with her over the last couple years. Lilly and Linda decided that Ash would fly to Linda's next summer and stay there until school started again.

Ash and I looked at each other for a minute. Ash agreed saying it sounded like fun. When we talked about it later Ash told me that she really didn't want to go. She had only said yes because she didn't want to hurt her sister's feelings. We both were sad because this meant depending on our schedules next summer we might not get to really see each other. But she pointed out that she would be 16 at the end of the next summer and then we wouldn't have to hide anymore.

Katie had started going out every day to give Ash and I time alone at home while our parents were gone. Katie and I were getting along now better than we ever had. Maybe Ash had been right, she was pretty damn smart, maybe Katie and I had just needed to finish what we started to get it out of our system and move on.

With our parents gone from the house, I made love to my girlfriend every time Katie was gone. I couldn't get enough of Ash. We tried, but she couldn't do it as much as I wanted to. When she couldn't do it she made sure I was well taken care of. We would be naked together all day hiding in my room, making love, holding each other, talking, making love again, tickling, kissing, making love, and sleeping.

I was sad when our week was over. It felt like we were on a honeymoon of our own. When my parents returned home she was actually in my room that morning we had just gotten done making love and were laying there. When I heard the car pull up I told her to grab her clothes and go take a shower. I was glad my window had been open all night.

I grabbed my jeans and a t-shirt and walked down stairs to greet my parents. I asked them how their trip had been and we talked about that until Ash came downstairs from her shower. Her hair was wet and she had such an incriminating grin on her face.

Katie decided to head back for college early. She said she wanted to get all the business about renting and setting up a new apartment done before I came out too. She left the day after Dad and Lilly came home.

Dad said he understood but was sad to see her go. She left mid-day on a Saturday this time. Lilly held her in a hug for at least ten minutes crying, telling Katie she really missed her when she went away and it got harder to let her go each year. Ash hugged her and cried too, Katie shared our secret and that was really important to Ash.

With Katie gone Ash and I made love every time Lilly went to the store, mall, or any place where she would be gone for more than 20 minute. We never risked it with them home. Ash had calmed down a lot since we started doing things all the time, but she was still loud.

We found excuses to leave the house and be alone. We knew our time was coming to a close soon and I would be leaving for college too. We tried to find a way to make love at least once a day on the last week I was home.

Things broke open on Ash's 15th birthday. It had been a month and a half since we had first made love and I was leaving the next morning. I was sad to leave her but I didn't have a choice things were in motion now that I couldn't explain if I didn't follow through with them. I only had about 5 days until classes started.

It was Ash's birthday and this year with the wedding and everything else going on it was decided that we wouldn't do a big party this time; we would just have a nice dinner around the house.

Ash pulled me aside and said we needed to talk. There was something in her tone that worried me. I went to Lilly and told her that I was going to take Ash to the mall and let her pick out a birthday present from me. Lilly said I was too sweet a brother to her. I almost cringed at the word brother when she said it.

I had been planning this for a while anyway. I had already made up that excuse for Lilly to get Ash out for the day. So when Ash told me we needed to talk I already had a place for us to be alone.

I drove us past the mall to the town next door. I had saved some money and rented us a hotel room for the afternoon so we could have one last time making love before I left. We pulled up and I got the key and we made our way up to our room. Ash had looked troubled on the way over, by the time I closed the door to the room she was crying.

"Please don't cry, Angel." I reached into my pocket and gave her a box. I had searched for the perfect gift that said I cared but didn't look like something you would give a girlfriend. She opened it, fell to her knees putting her face on the bed and sobbed into the blanket. Inside the box had been a very pretty necklace she had commented on one time at the mall a couple years earlier. She clutched the necklace as she sobbed.

"Angel, what's wrong?" I asked confused.

"It's all my fault."

"What are you talking about? What's your fault?"

"Do you love me?"

"Yes."

"No matter what I've done?" I knew this had to be bad if she needed reassurance.

"Just tell me." I don't know why but shuddered.

"How do you know you love me?"

"Because I know, that's all I need," I told her. I picked her up and held her to me.

"I think I'm pregnant." I froze, not just my body, my breathing my brain and my hold on her. She fell on the bed as my arms fell to my sides. How could I have been so stupid? We never used condoms, but she had told me once years ago that she had been put on the pill to regulate her cycle. This should have covered us. I finally collapsed landing on the bed next to her. I reached out with my right hand and placed it on her cheek. I wiped the tears away from her eye.

"Then I'll stay here with you this year and we will face the consequences from my parents and we'll have our baby if that's what you want."

"That's really how you feel?"

"Yes. You're my girlfriend, were in this together. I can't leave you behind to face all this yourself." I kissed her forehead and she started crying again. She got off the bed, walked over to the other side of the room and sat in a chair. Her chest was heaving now from crying and as she tried to speak again she stuttered and slurred her wards. I got up to comfort her.

"No, please stay there." I stopped and sat on the bed, "Just listen and please don't hate me."

She was crying so hard that I had a hard time understanding her sometimes. But she began to explain why she was upset. She said that everything we had gone through had been a lie. I asked what she was talking about. She said that she had always loved me from first sight when she was 12. She said she had lied, and tricked and done everything she could think of to get me to love her back since then.

She explained that she loved me instantly but she had really fallen in love with me the night of the winter formal. She said getting dressed up made her feel like a real woman, and the dancing and closeness of the evening had pushed her over the line and she had become full blown in love with me. It told her that was the moment I had fell in love with her too.

She said that she had made up being scared the first night my parents went away that Christmas break so she could sleep in my bed. She was hoping to seduce me then. She told me that every time we had been alone together she had used her tricks on me to try to seduce me. I remembered her tricking me into breaking my vow to hold off until she was 16. I had almost slept with her that night.

She said she was going crazy for me and she planned her worst trick at the wedding, it had worked but now she thought she was pregnant and was having a hard time living with herself. She didn't want to have a baby with a guy who she'd tricked into loving her. She didn't want to end up like Sara.

I asked what her trick had been. She said she had set up the situation for me to sleep with Katie. I asked how that was possible. She said that she was so in love with me and she was so jealous that I looked at Katie the way I did. She knew I would never get over it until I did something about it.

Ash decided the best way for me to get over Katie was for me to be with her so I didn't have the whole fantasy anymore. She thought that once I finally had lost my virginity to Katie maybe I wouldn't be so distracted and I could finally take that last step with Ash and be true lovers.

I hated to admit that she had been right. Everything Ash thought would happen did. She went on to explain that's why she suggested we all share a room at the lodge. That got me thinking about Katie all the time, the next stage in her plan had been to keep me aroused the whole time. That had been why she worked me up when she knew Katie was on her way up to the room that night. She had been expecting Katie to knock on the door that night when she had locked it. Then the next morning she had started my day by getting me off to make sure I was already in that mood. I was in shock at the extent she had gone to trying to make it happen. But I hadn't heard the worse part yet.

Ash said she had been watching Katie at the pool and she knew when she was heading back to the room to change. Ash herself her switched the music and played that dumb ass song. I reacted just like I had told her I had in the past. She figured that once in the bedroom with a major hard on, catching Katie changing I would lose control.

I was mad. I understood why she asked me if I would always love her no matter what. But now I didn't know what was real anymore. Did I really love her or had I been manipulated? If that was the case how far did this manipulation go? Either way my heart was breaking. I was upset because she took something as beautiful as our first time together and ruined it for me. She had tricked me and used my guilt against me to sleep with her that night.

I told her to stay in the room and I would be back. I had said before that she was really smart playing innocent. I had no idea how true that was until right now. She had completely used me. I didn't know what I could trust from her anymore. Did she really love me or was it and act too? Was this love or had she just wanted sex?

I went to the store and picked up 3 different brands of pregnancy tests. I brought them back to the room; Ash was still in the same place sobbing. I asked her why she thought she was pregnant. She said that she should've had her period about a week or so after the lodge. She hadn't had one yet. This made her a month late, and she was never late.

I handed her the bag with the pregnancy tests and told her to use all of them. She went into the bathroom and came out a couple minutes later. It was the longest 15 minutes of my life but when the time was up all three said negative. I actually breathed out hard.

I told her to get back in the car and try to calm down before we got home. She tripped on the way to the car, landing on her knee hard enough to rip her jeans and bloody her knee. I almost wondered if she had done it on purpose, I just didn't know what was real with her now.

When we returned home Lilly took one look at Ashley and asked her what had happened. Ash showed Lilly her bloody knee and they went into the bathroom to look at it. I looked over as they entered the bathroom; Ash had her right hand clenched in a fist. I could just barely make out part of the chain of the necklace hanging from her hand.

Ash was a good little actress and she calmed down enough by dinner. We both sat there with my parents trying to pretend that nothing was wrong. When dinner was over I made an excuse that I needed to finish some packing and loading my car. I left the table and sat in my room one last night. I had everything I was taking in the car already. Since Lilly didn't believe in locks I pushed my bed against the door so it couldn't be opened and I went to sleep. I woke after midnight to hear the knob turning. I knew

it was Ash trying to sneak in and talk to me. I didn't know it then but it would be three years before I would speak to Ash again.

I got up really early the next morning. I decided to put on a pair of loose shorts and a t-shirt so I would be comfortable on the drive. I sat for a few minutes trying to decide if I should wake Ash, I had made a decision last night. One that broke my heart and I knew would break hers. It was very early in the morning and I decided not to wake her up so I wrote her a note:

> Ash,
>
> Nothing will ever change the fact that I love you. It's just right now I don't know how to feel about what we talked about. This is why I had said we should have waited for a few years to see how we really felt. Last week I would've died for you. Today I don't know if we were in love or if it was nothing more than a kid's game.
> I'm sorry if this hurts you. I'm just being honest with my feelings. That's one thing I will never do, I will never lie to you about how I feel. I never wanted to hurt you. I can't stand the thought of more tears running down your beautiful face.
> With me going to college today what we need is time. Time to sort out who we are and what were really feeling. What I'm saying, what I'm feeling, what I want to be clear about, we need to break up. When I come back next summer we'll talk. We can see what we feel after spending a year apart.
> I'm so sorry, angel, but I think this is all for the best. Don't think this means I don't love you. I love you more than life, you were my first *real* love and I will never forget that, ever.
>
> Love you, Baby Girl,
>> Joe.

I moved my bed back into place and opened my door. Ash was asleep in the hallway lying on the floor in an awkward position. Her right hand still clutching the necklace I gave her. I picked her up and carried her to her room, laying her down in her bed. I pulled the covers over her and placed the note in her left hand curling her fingers around it. I hoped it would still be there when she woke up. I didn't know it would be three years when I walked out her door that morning but I wouldn't see her again until I was standing at the wedding under a canopy of trees, holding hands with Abby.

I got into my car and drove about 3 blocks before I had to pull over and cry. I didn't know what to think or feel anymore. I gave up Katie for a love that I thought had been the most real thing in my life. Now I found out it was just a mind game. She only told me the truth because she thought she might be pregnant. That would have been taking things way to far if I didn't really love her like I thought I did. I cried because I had no idea what had been love and what had been nothing but a lie.

When I finally had my composure back I put the car in gear and drove to my new college, to my new life, and down the road that eventually led me to my future wife. I was so depressed on drive for the first hour I didn't turn on my CD player. I was so lost in thought I could hardly drive. I kept missing my turns and had to circle back, or I would almost dive into another lane.

Out of both boredom and hoping to distract my mind to help focus on my driving I turned on the radio. This was at least somewhat of a distraction for the next couple of hours. That helped but I still found my mind wondering as I drove, unable to focus.

Then that dumb ass song came on. I was pissed again here I was on the interstate with my cock poking out the leg of my shorts. I was so depressed that day I didn't care; I pulled my short leg back and stroked myself while driving. It worked for a few minutes as I started to feel a little better. It worked until I shot cum onto the car radio. I thought after all these years of that song pissing me off it was irony that I hit the radio the last bit hitting my leg on my knee and thigh. I didn't care right then I stuffed myself back in my shorts and continued to drive. I had really needed that more than I had realized. It's like fate had known I needed that. I calmed down a lot after I came and was for the first time that day I was really able to focus on my driving.

That was the first time I had ever considered that there was a method to the timing of the song. Could all these random incidents actually have been a design of Fate? I didn't really didn't believe that, yet let's look at the results. If not for that dumb ass song I wouldn't have met Katie when I did. I mean really I loved her but without that song we would never have had a prior sexual relationship when we met at the wedding. I didn't know if I counted that as a win or a loss. Things sure as hell would be easier if I wasn't sexually attracted to her.

Then there was Ash. The reason we crossed the line the first time had been a result of that song affecting me at the dance. The next two years had been awesome due to us crossing the line. Then she used that song against me. I decided to call this a win/lose as well. But at least today it had helped me focus. I didn't know if it was an act of fate or random coincidence but I guess it didn't matter. What was done was done.

I drove until I couldn't keep my eyes open. I pulled over and slept in my car for about 4 hours. I was tired when I woke up, my thoughts returning to Ash. How could she have played me? After everything she played me.

My thoughts stayed on her all day as I finally made my way to my new home. I was happy to get into the city. I was looking forward to seeing Katie. We had our own history but at least we hadn't lied and played each other.

I found my new apartment relatively easy considering I didn't know the area. I had the key Katie had mailed to me; I walked to the door with just a duffle bag of clothes. I decided after the drive I had I would unload my car tomorrow. There was a light on in the window, I smiled inwardly; I was looking forward to talking to my sister. She would know how to help me through all of this. I opened the door to not find my sister but Abby.

I was stunned. She was almost two years older, tanned and had filled out a little more. She was wearing a low cut button up shirt and a cute pleated skirt. Her legs looked so hot; I started getting aroused just looking at her. I was so horny yet exhausted after the drive. I was so surprised at her appearance in the apartment that I dropped my duffle bag.

"Hey sweetie did you get everything you needed?" She asked without looking up. I didn't answer her I just cleared my throat.

"OH MY GOD, JOEY!" She screamed looking up, "You're finally here!" She jumped off the couch and ran at me hugging me tight; I realized in that hug how much I had really missed her. Despite what had happened between us, I still had feelings, whatever they were, for her.

I was holding her in that hug, when she kissed me. It wasn't just a friendly kiss; she reached around my neck and pulled me as hard as she could into her face. I gave in to her with all of my hurt, sadness, displaced love, and need for someone to love me that night.

Abby seemed pleased that I kissed her back. It had been almost exactly two years since the last time we kissed. She pulled me in from the doorway and pushed me onto the couch. She climbed on me sitting face forward her ass sitting on my knees. She wrapped her arms around my neck and pulled us together. We were kissing and I could feel her breasts mashing into my chest.

"Abby, what if Katie comes back?" I managed through kisses.

"Shut up. This should've happened years ago." She said it sweet, yet with firmness to her words. I shut up.

Abby's tongue was dancing in my mouth and I stared to lose control. The way Abby was sitting on me her skirt covered my lap but I could feel the head of my dick coming out my short leg touching the bare skin of her inner thigh. There was no way she didn't feel it. She was kissing my neck now and I willed myself not to cum yet. I didn't want her to stop. I really needed this right now, desperately.

I was lost in the moment as I reached for her shirt and ripped it open, buttons tearing off. I through her shirt at the floor and started rubbing her breast though her bra. This just fueled her harder. She began sucking my neck now. I ripped her bra off and trough it on the floor too.

"Hey," she complained, "That one was expensive." She said giggling then went back to my neck. I took both breasts in my hands and started playing with her nipples. She squealed with excitement. She started grinding her thigh against my cock slowly at first then harder. I reached down and pulled the leg of my shorts back so I was completely free.

Abby was so excited with the feel of me she began lightly biting my neck as she kissed me. She reached between us and moved her panties to the side. My heart was beating hard as she shifted slightly until we were rubbing against each other. It felt so good I didn't want to stop. I pulled her face from my neck and kissing her lips again.

I leaned her back and began to suck on her nipples. After I had given them both a good turn she leaned forward and went back to gently kissing my neck. I tilted my head back as she did so. She felt so good I couldn't hold back and I came on her lower lips as she rubbed them against me.

Abby let out a sexy growl taking my face and kissing me again. She reached between us again and I felt myself slide into her. I could tell she was no longer a virgin. I wondered when she had finally lost it and to who? Was I actually jealous?

"Oh yeah, baby," She moaned, "I've wanted that for so long." She slid up and down my shaft slowly, rhythmically continuing to growl as she did so.

"Abby," I moaned, "Oh baby. You're so tight." She grinned at me. She felt so good; this is what I really needed after the last few days. At the same time I felt a ton of guilt. I had this gorgeous girl riding me and my thoughts were of Ash. I hadn't had a chance to talk to her since I left her the break up note and I was already having sex with someone else. It was only a couple days ago I had rented a hotel room for one girl and now I'm banging another.

As fast as the thought hit me it escaped again as Abby sped up her intensity. This was incredible from a physical stand point but I found it lacked the emotional heart I was used to with the act. I focused instead on the physical stimulation and sunk into the feeling. I began to trust up to meet her. Abby tensed up and I knew she had hit her orgasm. She clamped down on me hard as she arched backwards so hard I had to hold her from falling off the couch.

"That was the best fuck I've ever had," She whispered, "Or it was because it was you and I missed you so much."

"I......" I was breathing so hard I couldn't say anything. This whole thing had caught me off guard.

"Thank you so much," she whispered. She curled up into me burying her head into my shoulder. I was still hard inside her. I gave her a minute and began to thrust upward again. She moaned her approval and started to meet my thrusts in return.

She kept her head on my shoulder moaning as I thrust up into her. It wasn't long before she tensed up again. When her pussy contracted this time I shot into her the hardest blast I'd had in weeks. We came together, both not moving anymore. We stayed in that position with me still inside her. I had gone soft but I still didn't pull all the way out.

We dozed off in each other's arms. As I drifted to sleep I wondered what this would mean later. I always had feelings for Abby but I had never been fully in love with her. I wished I had it in me to fall in love with her. Anyone would be lucky to have a relationship with her. She deserved someone who would treat her like a goddess and love her like one too. I could only give her one of the two.

As much as I hated to admit that I was still in the same place as two years ago, it was true. There were three women in my life that had ever meant something to me, two I loved and one I tried to love. I was looking for words to explain this to her when we had the talk I was sure was coming.

I sat there thinking, about to fall asleep still inside her when the door opened.

"What the hell are you doing with my Girlfriend?" Spoke a loud voice almost in a roar. I snapped out of my thoughts, I would have shot up had Abby not been sitting on my lap. I looked over to see who was standing in the doorway.

"Katie?" I said confused my senses hadn't returned to me yet. Katie looked just as hot as I had ever seen her. She was wearing a pink tank top and a skirt much like Abby's.

"I said what are you doing with my girlfriend?" She asked again but this time much softer.

"Stop screwing with him," Abby said not moving her head off my chest, "His hearts beating so hard he's going to break, you sufficiently freaked him out."

"Ok," Katie giggled, "I see you at least made it to the couch before she raped you." Katie and Abby both laughed. I was more confused, was this planned?

"No, I got him in the doorway and moved him," Abby told her and both girls laughed.

"I'm still not quite sure what's going on here."

"We made a decision on your behalf." Katie said taking off her shirt. I got hard again instantly still inside Abby.

Abby opened her eyes long enough to see Katie topless, "That brought him back to life," She grinned. Abby got off me only long enough to yank my shorts off and pull down her panties. She climbed back on me and slid me back inside her. She didn't move, only sat there both of us enjoying the feeling of being merged together. By this time Katie had taken off her bra and now stood topless. Her body was the ideal of goddessness as she stood before me.

Abby put her head back against my chest as Katie sat down on her knees next to me on the couch facing me. Katie leaned in and kissed me. I was lost in the moment, I had to be dreaming. I was inside Abby kissing Katie. This was more emotional and physical then I could handle.

By the time Katie thrust her tongue in my mouth I already felt like I might cum again. After a few minutes Katie pulled away from my kiss and kissed Abby. They kissed deep and passionately for a few minutes. The sight of them kissing pushed me over the edge; it was so hot watching them it made me cum again. Abby continued grinding against me keeping me hard. I was exhausted with this being the third orgasm in an hour. My body fell limp against the couch but I stayed hard.

"He really liked that one," Abby said grinning.

"I thought he might." Katie returned to kissing me. I kissed her with as much energy as I had in me. Abby stopped grinding and began riding me up and down again. I was completely empty but I had two beautiful girls on me right now. There was no way I was going soft but I didn't have the energy to thrust up into her anymore. I barley had the energy to kiss Katie. Abby tensed up again and fell off me onto the couch next to me. Katie continued to kiss me as I somehow went soft.

"I need a minute," I said fighting for breath. Katie pulled away from me and sat down on the couch on my other side, "I hadn't even made it in the door yet and Abby started trying to kill me." I winked at her and she giggled.

I was confused as to what was going on. I could understand Abby attacking me, she hadn't known about Ash so she probably thought I was single. But Katie knew about Ash and I hadn't had a chance to tell her we broke up. I couldn't understand why she would go behind Ash's back. Then there was the kiss between them and the girlfriend comment?

I woke up not realizing I had passed out. I was lying down in a room I didn't recognize. It was empty except for a bed, dresser and a desk. My duffle bag was on the floor next to the bed. I needed a shower I hadn't had one since before the trip. I literally reeked of sweat and sex. I set my duffle on the bed and opened it up, removing some fresh clothes. I walked out of the bedroom and looked around. I

115

was in a hallway. In front of me was a bathroom to my right at the end was a door to another bedroom. To the left was the living room I recognized from last night.

I hopped into the shower, the water felt good running down my body. I felt like it was recharging me. I thought if those crazy girls were still home I might need as much energy as I could replenish.

After the shower I found the stackable washer and dryer hidden in the bath closet and I threw my clothes from yesterday in the wash. I walked outside to unload my car before it got to warm in the day. I had just brought in the last of my things when I saw Abby in the kitchen. She had on only a bra and a pair of panties. I got hard as I was carrying my last box to my room.

"Well good morning to you too," She exclaimed noticing my shorts, "I made coffee if you want some."

"Good morning, that would be awesome." I walked the box into my room and headed back to the kitchen.

I slid my arms around her from behind and kissed her neck. I still couldn't believe I had fucked her last night. It had felt so good to just be with her again. I might not have the same love for her as the others but I realize this morning I still felt something damn strong for her too. Just what that was I didn't know. I mean I was still picking myself up from being mind fucked by Ash so did I really even have a clue how I felt about anything? All I knew at that moment is she had felt so good last night and touching her this morning was making me happy. She turned her head and I leaned into her, kissing her. She thrust her tongue in my mouth and I returned mine to hers.

"I'm I to expect that every time I walk into a room I'm going to find some part of your anatomy in my girlfriend?" Katie asked playfully. Katie was dressed just like Abby in only her bra and panties.

"Yes," Abby answered and returned to our kiss. Katie giggled and poured herself a cup of coffee.

"That is unless you want some part of my anatomy inside you?" I joked.

"Ok," Katie said taking my hand pulling me away from Abby.

"Hey!" Abby called as Katie pulled me down the hall to her room.

"You had your turn last night," Katie scolded her, "We'll share him later, I want to spend some time with my brother." She pulled me into her room and closed the door. In her room was a queen size bed, two dressers and a desk. I also noticed she had her own bathroom. She had taken the master bedroom for herself. She lay down on the bed and pulled me to her.

"I've missed you," She said kissing me.

"Wait, Kat," I pulled away from her, "I'm still not sure what's going on?"

"I'm trying to get laid, how are you unclear here?" She joked.

"No I mean with you and Abby, I mean for one, how is she here? For two, what's with the girlfriend thing? Three, Abby knows about us and she's ok with the whole incest thing? Four, what's the

decision you made on my behalf? Five, sharing? And lastly why would you hit on me knowing I've been seeing Ash?"

"You are too much. Most boys would just shut up and go with it," she laughed at me, "I promise I will explain it all to you, but I want my turn first........ If you still want me?" She bit her bottom lip in anticipation.

"Hell yes I still want you," I cried out, "You were the girl of my childhood idolatry."

I moved against her putting one arm around her back and one hand behind her head, running my fingers through her hair. I had so many years ago wanted this moment. There were no parents in the next room or downstairs, no one to judge us for being brother and sister.

This was the first time we had ever truly been able to express our friendship, lust and love. I had a knot well up in my chest when that thought hit me. I was in love with Ash. I couldn't lie to myself it would always be her I deeply loved. But I couldn't deny I still loved Katie too. I had admitted it to her just a couple of months ago when we had, had sex the first time. The next day when we had talked I told her I would always love her in some small way but I had chosen Ash over her.

Now a mere month and a half later I broke up with Ash and chose Katie. I gave into her completely at that moment. If I was going to choose this path then I needed to commit to it. I lost any hesitation I might have had then. I washed away my thoughts that I was betraying anyone and kissed Katie with a passion I never had for her before.

I had a new calm wash over me. This was the first time I had ever been with Katie when I hadn't started out as a virgin. I'd had many more experiences now. I was no longer the timid boy I once was, she had set me down that path. I moved my kissing to her cheek slowly moving to her earlobe. I lightly bit and sucked her lobe. She twitched every time I sucked hard. She moaned and I moved lower.

I let the tip of my tongue trail down as I moved to her neck. She shuddered slightly as I began to suck her neck. I grazed her slightly with my teeth, causing her to shudder again.

"You've been practicing," She moaned.

"I......... had a college girl teach me a thing or two about teasing," I said while kissing and sucking her neck.

"I want her phone number," She giggle, "I want to thank her." As I continued to tease her neck I brought my hand back from her head and began running my fingertips lightly over her stomach.

"Mmmmmmmmmmm," She purred, "Really, I need to thank that girl, Abby never likes to go slow like this."

"I know," I replied as I kissed my way back to the other side of her neck. I moved up to the ear lobe I hadn't attacked yet and sucked it hard.

"Oooooohhhh," she moaned, "I didn't even know I liked that before." I grinned at her. I didn't tell her I had never tried it before.

I moved my finger tips from her stomach to her thighs now. She jumped as the light touch tickled her a little. I returned to kissing her mouth, at the same time taking my hands and sliding her bra up off her breasts. She moved to remove her bra completely. I returned to kissing her neck and my teasing. I ran my fingertips along her nipples in slow circles. She moaned and I lightly squeezed her left nipple.

She pulled my face back to hers kissing me hard but I broke her kiss as I slid back down the bed and replaced my teasing fingers with the tip of my tongue.

"OH GOD," she moaned out, "Ash is so lucky she had you as her first." I froze at her name. I knew Katie had said it without really thinking, but hearing her say Ash's name caused me to pause.

"Joey?" She was breathing heavy and I'm not sure she even registered what she had said, "Please don't stop. I'm so wet, I need you so bad." She had a pleading in her voice.

I changed gears, all of a sudden I couldn't hold out anymore. I took her nipple in my mouth and sucked. She cried out as I did. I pulled her panties off her and continued kissing lower. I was finally going to do something I had been waiting for, for six years.

I took my fingers and opened her pussy and trust my face into her pink lips. My tongue trust forward tasting her wetness. I lapped again and again enjoying her sweet taste. Katie's back arched as she trust her hips up and down on my face helping me dig my tongue deeper inside her. I felt her tense up and she fell to the bed

"WOW, little brother," She sighed, "That was awesome."

"Were not done yet," I whispered to her moving up to kiss her again.

"Thank god," she whispered back, "I need more." I didn't wait as soon as I was in position I slowly slid into her. We both moaned out as I entered her. We had done this before, yet this was different. It was like we weren't the same two people we had been just a couple months ago. I came almost right after entering her. She smiled when I filled her pussy full of cum, running her fingers though my hair.

"There's the toy store boy that I remember," She lovingly.

"I love you," It slipped out I hadn't meant to say it, but when she had called me her toy store boy all my old feelings flooded me as I was still flooding her. When I had finish draining myself into her she held me. I was still hard and still inside her. I began to thrust again.

"Thank god you're not done," She whispered in my ear turning me on more. As I've said before sometimes the whispering thing is a major turn on.

I took things slow and rhythmically. Sucking her neck as I trust into her. She was shaking every few strokes now. I brought my hand up and began to tease her nipples causing her to have her second orgasm. Her pussy clamped down on me as her whole body convulsed. I kept thrusting through her orgasm, almost having a second one of my own.

"I've never had a seizure like that before," Said through deep breaths, "I can't take another like that right now." She rolled me off of her, we lay sideways holding each other. That had been how I had

always dreamed my first time with her would be. Our first time had been different because we had been set up. I felt cheated right now that this wasn't our first time. Then I let that thought go. My first time should have been with Ash, it should've been the night Sara had died.

"That was everything I hoped it would be," she said snuggling up to my chest. I thought about the two girls I'd had sex with in the last 24 hours. They were so very different. Abby was like she had been years ago, wild, raw, fast, and hard. Katie was the complete opposite, calm, slow, loving, and soft. Both were passionate in their love making but very different in the execution.

We held each other for a while I looked into Katie's eyes and I discovered something I had never found before. As beautiful as her eyes were, they were just eyes. I stared into them looking for something that I didn't find. I was looking for the ocean of blue to melt into, but I didn't see it there. That ocean only lived in one place. I pulled her to me cheek to cheek to stop looking in her eyes. I tried to stop myself but I started crying.

"What's wrong, Joey?" Katie asked me feeling my tears on her cheek. I didn't know how to start. I'd had all this sex before I had even had time to fully process my break up and move into my new life.

"I broke up with Ash," I said quietly turning away from her.

"I know."

"You knew?"

"Yeah, Well you had a list of questions, I guess we can start with this one," she wiped the tear from my eye, "I love my aunt, do you think I really would've done anything with you behind her back?"

"I guess not."

"Do you think if I didn't know I wouldn't have killed you for fucking Abby last night behind her back?"

"No. You would've ripped my nuts off."

"Damn right. I'd never let you hurt that little girl."

"But how did you know. It only happened two days ago?"

"Who else do you think she talked to about it? Who else knows about you guys, which she can talk to? God, you're really thick some days little brother."

"Yeah, I guess you're right."

"She called me a week ago. She said she thought she might be pregnant. I told her to talk to you about it."

"She did, she wasn't pregnant, we checked."

"I know. She called me in the morning two days ago. She said she woke up to find a note next to her. She read me the note. Surprisingly it sounded strangely familiar." She grinned a little at that. I couldn't help but grin slightly at the parallel situation.

"I couldn't look at her after what she had done."

"That's the one thing she didn't explain, she said that the day before you guys had got into a fight about something. She didn't say what. She just said you left without a goodbye and a note that said you were breaking up with her."

I explained the whole story to her. I hadn't been going to, but since it involved Katie herself, I thought I would just come out and say how we had been manipulated.

"That little Brat!" She exclaimed.

"I know, huh."

"I'm so sorry, Joey, I could see the love in your eyes when you talked about her in July. I know you didn't just love her; you were in love with her in your soul. I could see that then. That's why I didn't rat you out to mom. I saw something real there."

"Yeah," Is all I could get out. More tears welled in my eyes.

"I wish I could say I ever loved someone like that. I've only ever really loved you and Abby."

"Yeah........" More tears came I couldn't stop them. Katie pulled me to her again and rolled me on my back. She took my cock in her hand I got hard for her but still couldn't stop the tears. She got on top of me, slowly sliding me into her. She leaned forward pressing her breasts to my chest, leaning forward to kiss the tears out of my eyes. She was forming tears for me now too.

She began rocking her hips while still lying on top of me. She kissed me gently on my cheek as she grinded herself on my cock. I was so emotionally hurt, and she had found a way to make me feel loved and feel pleasure at the same time. I couldn't contain myself long in the emotional state I was in. I came in her again holding her to me like I thought I would never see her again if I let go.

By the time I had cum she had made my tears stop. I loved my sister so much at that moment. It was in that moment I fell in love with her again, I fell in love with her completely. I fell in love with her as my sister, my warm, loving and caring sister, willing to do anything for the brother she loved just as much.

"I love you; you're the greatest sister anyone could hope for."

"So I'm just you sister now? After all this?"

"You'll never be just my sister," I told her kissing her again, "Thank you for loving me so much."

"I love my brother," she grinned at me, "And I'm willing to prove that every day."

I could hear foot steps behind the bedroom door. I moved up the bed and she slipped off of me. We both sat up against the headboard. There came a knock on the door, and Abby came in.

"It's about lunch time now. Is it my turn yet?" she asked with a fake pout about her. She looked at my face and her pout went away.

"What's wrong sweetie? Did everything cum up ok?" Abby joked, Katie just waved at her and she turned around, "I'll go make us some lunch and we can have it in here." She left the room again.

"What's with her?" I asked, "She's even more a sex maniac then when we dated."

"Once she had sex the first time she became a sex addict. She had some crazy times. Now she's just horny because you're the first guy she's been with since we got together."

"Yeah, about that how did that happen?" I asked. Katie gave an indeterminate laugh.

"It's funny how things work out. You know I've had a few boyfriends in my time."

"Yeah, that's kind of how we hooked up at Linda's wedding. I think you were in a curiosity faze then."

"To say the least, I never told you the half of it," she laughed again.

"Well when I met Teagan she changed my life. I had never even thought about women before that. We became best friends and one night she kissed me. By then I was so close to her as a friend it felt comfortable and I let it happen."

"Wow, that's all it took was one kiss?"

"Well that kiss ended up going all night as it were," she laughed again.

"I get it. So how does Abby just show up then?"

"Well I had always kept in touch with Abby. When I left my first year of college I still called her all the time. She was my best friend, before you guys started dating, if you remember."

"I didn't know you still talked after you left. She never told me."

"Well with her thinking you cheated I'm sure there wasn't a lot of talking going on."

"Yeah, it took me over a month for her to even let me tell my side of the story."

"You're welcome."

"For what?"

"Who do you think talked her into talking to you? I told her you wouldn't ever cheat on anyone. I told her to talk to you. I just forgot that when she's pissed off theirs no changing her mind."

"Tell me about it," I laughed.

"Tell you about what?" Abby asked coming in with a tray of cheese sandwiches.

"Nothing," Katie said quietly. Abby handed the tray to Katie and hopped up on the bed on my other side.

"Hell with this," she said whipping her bra off, "If everyone else is going to be naked in my bed then so am I." We all laughed. I couldn't believe I was sitting naked in bed with two of the hottest girls ever. I wondered for a minute if maybe I had crashed the car while jerking off and died, because right now I was in heaven, sexy heaven.

"So I don't see any more tears," Abby said sweetly, "What happened to make you so sad when you're in here fucking my sexy girlfriend?"

"We were talking about him breaking up with his girlfriend."

"Katie!" I exclaimed, I didn't want the whole world knowing about the fact I had, had sex with an underage girl.

"Don't worry," Abby said taking a bite of sandwich, "I know all about all that."

"What? Really?"

"Don't worry, I didn't betray you. Ash and I talked at the lodge. After I found out about you guys I wanted to hear it from her, that you guys were in love," Katie paused to hand me a sandwich before picking one up herself, "Ash talked to me about everything so I thought it was only fair I tell her about Abby. She said she trusted Abby and I could tell her what was going on."

"So you don't think I'm trust worthy, huh," Abby asked grabbing my balls and squeezing.

"NO! It's fine!" I cried out. Katie laughed.

"That's what I thought," she exclaimed letting go and grinning.

"Anyway," Katie continued, "I was upset when I broke up with Teagan, and I needed someone to confide in. I called Abby."

"Oh I like this story!" She said excitedly, "Can I tell the next part?"

"Ok. I haven't told him about you yet anyway. He doesn't know about what happened to you after he moved."

"Oh yeah that," Abby's face darkened, "I was hurt after you left. I realized I had just lost the nicest guy ever."

Abby went into her story. After I had left she got sick of her mom's rules. She realized that none of what had happened with us would have gone down if her mom hadn't interfered. She said that realistically Sara wouldn't have had the chance to sneak in on me had Abby been allowed to be around me that day. Then we wouldn't have had to waist months not talking before I left.

She started to disobey her mom after I moved, she started dating this guy who had bought her flowers, wrote her poetry, and was always too shy to even hold her hand. Their first kiss she had to make the move on him because he was shaking so much. She said that they had been dating for two months in secret in school and whenever she could sneak out to see him.

That was when he asked her to prom. She was excited to go. She begged and begged her mom to let her out for one night. She was to be 18 in just a week. Her mom relented because it was her senior year and her last prom. She went out and got a fiery red dress and had her hair done up and all that. She loved the dance, and when it was over he asked if she wanted to go to a hotel party with him. She agreed to go thinking it would be fun.

At the hotel someone put something in her drink. I saw where this was going. I had kind of been through this only I knew her story didn't have the happy ending mine did.

Abby went on to tell about how she had gone into a room with her sweet boy. The night had been so perfect, and her need for love so strong she had a physical need to have sex. She said other than kiss she hadn't done anything with anyone since the day in the library. That had been almost a year earlier.

When in the room she started to feel some to the effects of the drug. She started kissing her boyfriend, next thing she knew he pulled her dress off, not to kindly, and had sex with her. She said there was no sweet loving like when she had fooled around with me. He simply pulled her dress off her, ripping it in places, unzipped his pants and took her cherry. She said the physical pleasure of the act had felt nice but, she just didn't like how impersonal he had made her feel for her first time.

Abby teared up a little as she told the next part. It got worse. When he was done he came on her stomach and she realized by then she couldn't move. It was then she realized that they had given her something. She was fully awake but completely immobilized. Then one by one his friends came in and took turns with her. Some were more gentle than others. No one hit her or physically abused her, her assault was all sexual. Just like that they came in had a turn, came on her and left.

When her boyfriend realized she was still awake he told her that the drug was supposed to have knocked her out as well as cause temporary muscle seizure. He looked at her and said, "Sorry babe." Then he simply shrugged at her.

By the time she was able to move again she had lost track of how many she had taken. Some had gone two or three times. She knew it was at least 15. They had all pulled out and came on her in different places. Her boyfriend told her that if she tried to say anything they would all back each other up and say she had been drunk and didn't know what really happened. Abby realized it was pointless to argue she just wanted to go home. Her perfect boyfriend then called her a whore and left her there in the hotel. She locked herself in the bathroom shaking and crying until morning.

Abby had tears now. I felt horrible this had happened to her. I wiped the tear away and kissed her. I pressed my forehead to hers. She smiled.

"I really missed you," she said and kissed me again.

Abby went on with her story. She said that she finally worked up the nerve to take a shower and wash all the boys off her body. She put her ripped dress back on and walked home. Her mom had been worried sick for her. She wouldn't tell her mom what had happened and for once her mom didn't ask.

Her mom saw how Abby looked when she came home and simply hugged her daughter for a long time. Abby went inside and changed her clothes and her mom held her the rest of the day.

The worst part of the incident came next; Abby's mom took her to the doctor the next day to make sure she was ok. After tests had been done it was determined that due to what happened to her in the hotel that night, Abby would never be able to have children.

This was a turning point in Abby's life. She graduated, barley, her grades had slipped the last month so far she was almost held back. She started smoking and skipping classes. She had been labeled a whore around the school. She said she knew how I had felt when everyone had turned on me.

After graduation she had given up her search for a nice guy and had gone through a bad boy faze. She said she wasn't proud of it now but she had partied all the time and slept with a lot of men. She was in a really bad place.

"That's when I called," Katie chimed in, "When I finally got a hold of her she was working at a strip club, living behind the club in an RV."

"Like I said I was in a bad place."

"Well to understand what happened next, we have to back up a little," Katie explained, "What Dad didn't know is I had already left the dorm and moved in here with Teagan. That's why I told him I would take care of finding the apartment a couple months ago. I just signed a new lease under his name."

"This was you and you girlfriend's apartment?"

"Yeah, we lived together for about 4 months. When we broke up she moved back to the dorms and I managed to keep the apartment. I thought I might give it up and go back to the dorms too, when Dad suggested we share a place off campus."

"Lucky I ended up going here," I grinned.

"Why do I think luck had nothing to do with it?" Abby asked. I simply shrugged smiling.

"Anyway, Katie calls me to talk about her break up and I tell her what's going on with me. Katie being the great girl she is tells me she has an extra room and if I want to I can come up, find a job and be her roommate."

The girls tell me about how the first time they see each other after so long they tear up right away and can't stop hugging. Then Abby tells me a familiar story. She said it was her first time moving from home and she got lonely and home sick. She asks Katie if she can stay in her bed with her for one night.

At this point both girls blame the other for who made the first move in bed that night. I laugh at that. But in the end what they agree on is that night they realized they were more than just best friends.

"That was the first time I had ever been with a woman," Abby says and I actually see a blush cross her cheek. I was surprised because nothing ever embarrassed her, "I never did sleep in the spare bed. Katie asked me to be her girlfriend the next morning."

"That's the real reason I came back early a few weeks ago. I felt I had been away from Abby long enough."

"That's so cute," I told them, "You really missed her."

"Yeah, but I was having a hard time with the guilt over what had happened between us at the lodge. I technically cheated on her. I thought she might break up with me. I came home to confess."

"I won't ever break up with her," Abby said leaning over and grabbing her hand, she lifted it up and kissed it.

"I was scared though. I didn't know how or what to tell her. It meant telling her all about us."

"So how did you work it out?"

"We came to an agreement on your behalf. Abby can I tell him the truth?"

"He's not a complete moron, he probably already knows."

"What?" I asked.

"Abby and I are in love. But you still are and always will be her first love." I turned to Abby pulling her into a hug.

"I don't know how to feel about that," I replied, "Don't get me wrong. I wanted so much to be in love with you but when we were dating I was hiding a burning love for Katie. I'm so sorry I tried so hard to love you back." Abby smiled and kissed me more gently then she ever had before.

"It's ok. I know you love me more then you want to admit. If you're not *In Love* with me it's ok. I'm in love with Katie."

"So your agreement?" I asked.

"When I finally got Katie to spit out what her problem was, we talked. She told me everything. I wasn't actually surprised. I saw how you were with each other and I often wondered if I was imagining things. I guess I wasn't."

"I told Abby, I was so sorry I had slept with you. But I had lost control. I had wanted you for so long I broke down and gave in when you started kissing my neck. It's like you knew my weak spot." Katie winked at Abby.

"I loved Katie so much and I totally understood losing control. I told her no matter how much we love each other sometimes you just need a good dick to fuck. I said I would only ever be hurt if she slept with anyone else, except you." Abby winked back at her.

"This brings us to the only question you asked I haven't answered yet." Katie paused and bit her lip.

"When Ash called and said that you guys broke up Abby and I talked and we figured with 3 horny college students in the house, sooner or later one of us was going to break and sleep with you."

"Yeah, since I've wanted to fuck your brains out for years, even more so since Katie came home and told me what happened this summer. It made me so hot, and jealous."

"Anyway, so Abby and I decided that if you wanted, we would all be a couple."

"Really?" I asked, "How is that going to work?"

"Well officially as far as people outside the house are concerned, Abby is your girlfriend, and you and I are just brother and sister. Abby and love each other but were not quite ready to come out to the world yet," Katie explained.

"But at home anyone is allowed to do anything they want with anyone they want." Abby explained excitedly.

I didn't answer. I looked at both beautiful girls; I knew I died in a car crash now. I get to sleep with Katie and Abby anytime I want? How could this be real? I'd be a fucking idiot to turn this down. Yet I still stepped back for a minute.

Sure sex would be awesome, but I didn't love Abby, and my feelings for Katie had matured. But then again my feelings for Ash had changed too. I broke up with Ash. I was allowed to be with these girls. What was holding me back?

"Look he actually has to think about it," Abby said after a couple minutes. She had a joking tone to her.

"He wouldn't be him if he didn't. That's why I love him so much. He's rationalizing it to himself so he doesn't feel like a pig," Katie replied.

"If he has to rationalize it then we didn't fuck him hard enough," Abby joked.

I ignored them; I ate my sandwich while thinking. What I was rationalizing wasn't being involved with two girls. I was asking myself could I really be involved with them so close to leaving my time with Ashley. I was still so hurt. Granted they had done nothing but make me feel better since I had been here, but I was still so very emotionally unstable right now.

Abby finally broke me out of my trance by stroking my dick. After lunch and all that talking I was ready to go again. I slid down to lay on my back. Abby took the hint and climbed up on me. She slid down my cock and started grinding.

"God damn girl, you really know what you're doing." She didn't answer in words she slowly began to lift up and come down grinding on the downward motion. I was losing my mind five strokes in. I reached up with my left arm and grabbed Katie's neck pulling her into me with a kiss. I grabbed her breasts and played with her nipples while we kissed.

After a few minutes of nipple play Katie moved in front of Abby and began kissing her. Their kissing grew heavy as Abby rode me harder and harder as Katie kissed her. Katie swung her leg over me

126

and wiggled her pussy to my lips. I thrust my tongue in her so hard eagerly licking her juices. With the double stimulation of two pussies I my whole body shuddered and seized up. I came harder than I had ever done before. I fell back to the bed.

"Oh no," came two voices, "Were not done yet."

Chapter Ten: Drunken Hook Ups

College life on campus was actually a lot easier than what I had gone through the year before. I was taking optometry as a major and writing as a minor. I had decided that eye doctor was a worthy occupation and dad really liked that idea for me.

I was taking the writing classes for me. I had gotten it in my head lately to become a writer. The writing classes I was taking were more about learning how to tell a story, in the way of characterization, dialogue and plot development. Not so much about the sentence structure and spelling.

Katie was still in school on scholarships and taking a number of classes. I would see her at the school library quite often. Sometimes we would sit and do our homework together. I enjoyed that time with my sister as much as our at home time. She worked a couple nights a week in a law firm doing filing. This gave her enough money for school supplies and groceries.

Abby had gotten a full time job as a waitress when she had come to live with Katie and spent her days at the restaurant. This helped out with the grocery money along with the fact that she often brought home dinner from work. That worked for me, I hated cooking.

I had taken my experience working for the high school last year and managed to get a part time job a couple nights a week working as a handyman for an on call maintenance service. This gave me just enough spending money to go out on the weekends and still get all my school work and studying handled.

I made a friend not long after the beginning of the school year. I met him because he had been hitting on Katie. She had turned him down repetitively and asked me to talk to him because he wasn't getting the point. His name was Jeff and I went to talk to him to get him to leave her alone. I found someone not to unlike myself. We got to talking and I found out he lived at the frat house, but didn't quite fit in there. He said he was sorry and didn't mean any harm, he just thought Katie was cool and he had never had a real girlfriend. He said he would leave her alone.

After that he decided we could be friends. I wasn't that excited by that at first, but I soon realized he was cool to hang around with. When I had free time I would hang out with him in the frat house playing video games, and talking about girls with the frat brothers.

Jeff kept inviting me to parties but I told him I spent my weekends hanging around my weekends hanging around my sister and my girlfriend. The first time he met Abby I thought his eyes were going melt, he stared so hard. At that moment I got a kick out of calling her my girlfriend again, even if it was just a cover story.

I settled into a routine pretty early. I spent my days in classes, my evenings at work or in the school library studying and writing stories. I found myself escaping into my stories, I wrote primarily in the love and mystery genres. My writing teacher was often excited when I told him I had another chapter ready for him to review, he said he always couldn't wait to see how I would mix things up. College was shaping up to be pretty cool this year.

I spent my nights with my girls; they jokingly referred to themselves as my two girlfriends. Most nights I would be with one or the other at a time. It was only on rare occasions all three of us would get together.

I said earlier that both girls had very different needs. When Abby wanted it, she wanted it now. She didn't care what I was doing she wouldn't take no or later for an answer. She would grab my pants and the next thing I knew she would be riding me like she had a gun to her head. She was wild and tight and I could never last long with her.

Katie on the other hand, would ask me what I was doing or if I was busy. If I said I had time or wasn't doing anything she would lead me by the hand to the bedroom and we'd have sex slow and passionately. She was so warm and tight with her our love making would last for hours sometimes.

Even with all the sex I was having, I was lonely. The girls had each other. The rule was that having sex with one another was great and they both loved me, but night was their time together. They made a rule that no matter what was going on inside or outside the apartment they would always meet each other in bed at night.

I thought it was sweet. I could hear them in their room some nights making love to each other. It made me wonder how Abby was with Katie. Was she wild like with me or soft and slow like Katie? I tried not to think about it. They slept together every night, and in this case I'm meaning sleep, which I thought was sweet on a romantic level.

The fact of the matter was that I was jealous actually. They had each other and I spent every night alone. I'm sure they would have let me sleep in there with them but I didn't feel right about interfering with their alone time. So it was I spent all my nights in my twin size bed masturbating and passing out alone.

It was Christmas break in no time. I was alone at the apartment for once. Abby and Katie had flown home to Abby's house to come out of the closet to her parents. I opted to stay home for some peace and quiet. Truth be told as much as I loved having sex with them I was worn out and needed a couple days off.

I called home on Christmas and talked to dad for a while. He said he really missed having me around the house. He told me Linda had come up for a few days and they were all having a great time.

I talked to Lilly for a few minutes then I asked if Ash was around, not really knowing what I would say to her anyway. Lilly said that she and Linda had gone out for some last minute supplies for dinner. Then Lilly said that she really wanted to talk to me about something, but she would call me back later in the week. I wasn't sure if I should be worried about it or not. I wandered if Ash had said anything to her.

I was about to have lunch a couple days after Christmas when Lilly called me like she had promised. She explained that she had wanted to talk to me when my dad wasn't home to hear her.

"What's up Lilly?"

"I just wanted to ask if you had something you wanted to tell me." I wondered which one of the things she was curious about. The fact I was regularly having sex with her daughter or that I'd had sex with her sister.

"I don't know is there something I should tell you?"

"Did you lie to me when I asked you if you were having sex with Ash?" I thought back to that conversation two years ago.

"No. I didn't lie to you then. We weren't having sex. What brought this on, Lilly?"

"She hasn't been the same since you left. I recognize the signs Joey, I'm just looking for the truth."

"How has she not been the same?" I asked trying to keep my voice from cracking, "What signs?"

Lilly told me that since the day I had left for college Ash had done nothing but sit in her room crying. She goes to school. Her grades are only slightly just above passing. She comes out of her room to eat dinner and goes right back. Every time Lilly sees her she she's clutching a necklace I gave her.

Lilly said it was pretty obvious at first that she was sad to see her best friend go. But as time went by she wasn't getting any better. Lilly realized after time she was acting completely heartbroken, and she wondered what was going on. Lilly asked Ash about it and she wouldn't talk. All Ash would say to her was that after everything he didn't even say goodbye. This led Lilly to wonder what Ash was hiding from her. So she was flat out asking me.

"I truly don't know what to say here Lil," I didn't know what to say. I couldn't tell her the truth, "I knew were close but I didn't expect her to take my leaving so hard."

"Joey, I love you, but stop lying to me," She was stern and I could hear the anger in her voice, "I know this goes beyond just being friends, do you think I've been stupid all this time?"

"No I don't think your stupid," I was shaking, I really didn't know what to do here. I didn't want to betray Ash with our secret but I was lying to the woman who had been the greatest mom to me ever.

"It's ok Joey," Lilly said soothingly, "Just talk to me. I can't help her through whatever she's going through if I don't know exactly what happened."

"I loved her Lil," I broke. Months of holding back my hurt, burst from me in an instant, "I loved her so much I didn't think I could breathe without her next to me." I said angrily. I hadn't cried about Ash since that first morning I had spent in bed with Katie after I got here. Now it was coming out as anger.

"It's ok Joey," Lilly said softly, "I always knew that no matter what was going on in the house you truly cared for her. That's why I never really pried into what was going on between you two. I saw a lot more then you realize."

"Something that happened this summer, but I don't want to talk about it."

"It's ok Joey, I still love you, I'm not mad. I can tell you have real feelings for each other. I can hear two broken hearts in you guys."

"Thank you for understanding, Lil."

"Actually I'm not surprised I've been expecting this for a long time."

"I'm sorry I never wanted lie to you," I admitted.

"It's ok. I was only 16 when your dad and I got together the first time. I've been there. I know why you hid this from us."

"I love you so much Lilly. I wish you were really my mom too."

"Me too sweetie, but with all the tears I've seen from her and all the love I hear in your voice what happened?"

"I can't tell you that. I'm sorry." I wasn't about to tell Lilly about Ash's scheming and the fact that it had resulted in me banging Katie.

"It's ok, I think I get it. I can help her if she talks to me now."

"Lil, can you tell her something?"

"Sure sweetheart, what?"

"Tell her, I love her, and I was wrong."

The rest of Christmas break played out without incidents. By the time the girls were back I was so lonely I grabbed Abby at the door as she had done to me a few months earlier. I through her on the couch and I fucked her harder, more aggressively then I had ever had sex with anyone. When we were done she lay on the couch, giant smile on her face, thanking me but wondering what had brought that on. I shrugged and went into my room.

It was about a half an hour later that Katie knocked on my door. I told her to come in. It was rare for her to come to my room. She said Abby had gone to bed, complaining that she could barely walk after what I had done to her.

Katie had a sad look in her eye and asked me what had upset me so much. I shrugged and she told me that she could tell by the way I banged Abby I wasn't just upset I was mad. I told her the truth that I was upset by Lilly's phone call about Ash, I was lonely and I had missed my two girlfriends.

Katie crawled into bed with me. We never did anything in my bed. While Abby and I had done it everywhere in the house, Katie and I had only had sex in her bed. She started kissing my neck, and reached into my pants, lightly stroking me. She told me to keep talking about my feelings that it was about time I got them all out. She said if I didn't I might end up killing her girlfriend next time I banged her.

We both laughed at this. She always knew how to calm me down when I was angry. I talked to her for an hour or more. I talked about how much I needed love not sex. She continued to hold me and kiss my neck the whole time I talked. I told her I cherished these moments with her but she was Abby's girlfriend and I needed one of my own.

I loved being with her so much but I realized that night I needed to finally give her up too. I needed to move on, I needed real love and I needed a real girlfriend. I told her this. She kissed me on my forehead and said she understood.

We both knew this would be the end of our relationship with each other as anything other than siblings. I made love to her after that in my room. It was slow and had more love behind it then any time we'd had sex. It was the most passionate and delicate we had ever been with each other. We truly made love that night; maybe because we thought this would be the last time.

Katie kissed me deeply as she climbed off the bed. I knew I would miss her and what we had together. But I would never move on if I was dwelling on Ash and having sex with Katie all the time. I needed to break it all off and start over.

Since I decided that if I was going to stop having sex with Katie then maybe I should stop with Abby too. Abby didn't take things as well as Katie. She still had strong feelings for me and didn't want to give me up. We came to an agreement. As long as I wasn't dating anyone Abby and I could still have sex from time to time. She really didn't have to twist my arm that hard to get me to agree to that condition.

I told Abby I was serious though and I really thought it was time I enjoyed college and tried to find a girlfriend of my own. I told her it would definitely have to stop if I was seeing someone because I didn't cheat. She relented and said that's why she loved me, because I tried so hard to be an honest man. I again really wished in that moment that I could have loved her that way I wanted to. She deserved it from me after all this time.

The school year moved on and I still was no closer to finding a girlfriend. I found that most of the girls at school either already had boyfriends or were drunken partiers who slept with anyone. Jeff finally talked me into coming to his frat parties and I began to spend my fair share of my Friday nights going to those parties, after work, trying to meet a girl.

I actually lost track of the number of drunken, easy and moronic girls I hooked up with around that time. I was banging anyone who would have me anywhere we could get it on. No place was off limits to me during this time period. My old exhibitionism kicked into high gear I would get it on with girls in the frat bathroom, the pool, the girls dorm, the hood of a nearby car, once the front porch of a girl's parents house, I even had sex with one girl in the movie common room at the college with people in the room, generally anywhere a girl was willing to fuck me, we fucked. I'd have sex with these girls but it wasn't more than that. They weren't looking for a relationship after we'd fuck they would move on, I'd see them at the next party looking for the next drunken hook up.

I didn't blame them; it wasn't like I expected any of these hook ups to lead to the love of my life. The sex was really a way of getting through the week while pretending it was about looking for a girlfriend.

Abby and Katie had been dating now for a full year, I had stopped having sex with Katie after Christmas and I stopped having sex with Abby by spring break. It was about this time Jeff told me he had started dating his high school best friend. Her name was Jenny and she had moved nearby to take a job as a pharmacy technician. I guess they had gone out to lunch to catch up on old times and they ended up dating. I was happy for him but I was a little jealous that he had found a girlfriend and I still hadn't.

I gave up looking for a girlfriend after that. I wasn't much of a partier at heart and I quit going to the frat parties by spring break. Don't get me wrong it wasn't that I didn't like getting laid by random girls but it wasn't what I was looking for. If anything I was finding myself more lonely coming home smelling of sex, just to go to bed alone.

Just after spring break my writing teacher had given one of my short stories to the drama professor. The professor approached me about turning it into this season's college production. It was a murder mystery I had wrote that she felt would very easily turn into a stage play. It wasn't much more than an essay but it was a murder mystery with a twist ending.

I was so excited about the idea that one of my stories could be made into something real, that I said yes without thinking.

I agreed but only if I could write the play and help pick the actors. I had an idea in my head of how these characters were and I wanted to find actors I felt would embody the parts.

I found putting on a play was harder than I had ever imagined. Our college had an entire theater building with a large stage, and office and a number of dressing rooms down stairs. I spent the every night in the office trying to rewrite my story into a play; this isn't as easy as it sounds. The professor would lock me in every night so she could go home and I could do what I needed to. This worked out well enough I just had to remember not to forget my car keys because I couldn't get back in. I almost screwed that up on the first night. I had pushed open the door only to realize my keys were still on the desk.

We held auditions two weeks later; I had barely had time to finish the script by then. As the writer and script supervisor I was one of a small group in charge of the production, which included, the drama professor, a student director, a set designer, lighting and sound guy, and I talked Jeff into working with us as producer.

The six of us got together on a Saturday morning to hold auditions. It was, in my opinion, grueling. Time and again, line after line people would come on stage and just belt out the worst audition material possible. I had no idea how we were going to find all the people we needed from what came in the door. I was really glad it wasn't only my decision at that point.

It was Saturday evening and I was so ready to go home, I was beginning to rethink this whole idea, when she walked in. She didn't audition on the stage she walked up next to me and started talking.

I didn't hear a word she said, but she had her hand out to shake mine. I shook her hand while looking into her eyes; I had found what I had been looking for all year. She was an average looking girl, somewhat too skinny for me, plain face and what looked to be smaller breasts. What had me were her eyes, it's all I saw when she had walked up to me. As anyone knows by now I have a thing for captivating eyes. She said something else; I still didn't hear her, because I was in another world.

Jeff walked past me and put his arm around her and kissed her cheek. I was frozen on the spot. Jeff looked at me funny and walked away with his arm still around the girl. I wanted her. I wanted her not just for myself but for the play. But if she was who I thought she was I knew she couldn't audition. I had been so captivated by her I hadn't heard a word she said, but I knew she had to be Jeff's girlfriend Jenny.

I asked Jeff all about Jenny the next day. He didn't seem overly excited while talking about her. He explained that they had grown up together as kids and grew apart by junior high. He said in high school they had re-met in their sophomore year and became friends again. He said at the time neither one had any real feelings for each other they just remained close friends. Because they didn't have dates he took her to the prom senior year and they took each other's virginity after the dance. After that she went to trade school and he had gone off to college. It was just coincidence that she got a job in the same town now. When they had re-met again here they thought they should give the whole dating thing a try.

I was a little put off by how uninspired he was by her. In one second I had been completely lost in her aura. I didn't think he deserved her but I wasn't the kind of guy to steel a girlfriend was I?

Production continued and we eventually got this thing cast. I found a ruling about brining actors in from outside the college and I talked Jenny into playing the lead role. She didn't know if she would have time in her busy life, I told her I wouldn't do the production if she wouldn't agree to play the lead. Amazingly she found the time for me, I was more than grateful.

Once I was able to talk to her I found her even more interesting than at our first meeting. She was into books, which if you're this far into the story you'll know I like that in girls, and we spent our time discussing story plots, when we weren't going over lines.

As time wore on I found out she worked in a Pharmacy, did charity work, and had taken in her 8 year old cousin, Anne, because Anne's parents were drug addicted alcoholics and couldn't take care of her. She treated Anne as both cousin and parent. Anne still couldn't read yet and having had druggy parents she had a number of behavior problems. Jenny was taking her to therapy and trying to teach her how to read. I thought it was amazing that a girl not much older than me was doing so much and already being a parent. When rehearsing Jenny had to leave Anne with a friend until she could pick her up again she just found a way to make everything work.

I was so inspired by Jenny I went with her a couple times to the charity things she did. Jenny thought this was unbelievable, she had tried to get Jeff to go but he preferred to stay at home with his frat brothers and play video games.

I spent time with Jenny and Anne going to the park on a number of weekends. I used the excuse that we could hang out and run lines while Anne played with Jenny's dog. Jenny had a little mixed terrier ironically named Barky but the dog rarely made a sound. Jenny told me that it was nice to have the company, Jeff rarely liked going out if it meant taking Anne with them. He didn't know how to deal with her behavior and wasn't ready for with kids. Anne and I seemed to get along right away, we joked and I played with her and the dog for a while. Jenny said she thought it was adorable.

With only a few weeks to go in the school year we were getting close to having to perform this production. One week until we opened our lead guy got arrested on a 3rd DUI and was thrown in jail for 90 days. This left us without a main character actor. As the writer of the production I knew the lines better than anyone and they talked me into playing the lead.

I was petrified. I never wanted to be an actor. I was just fine behind the curtain but now I had no choice but to get out there and act with Jenny. The same reason I decided to play the role was the same thing that scared me about it. There was a love scene in this play. Nothing big, no full nudity or anything, that wasn't allowed, just lying in bed with her in a bra and me shirtless. All we did was mostly talk in this scene then a few minutes of kissing before going to bed. This took place just before the killer comes into

the house and I have a fight scene with him. Easy enough, but I was so enamored with her that I didn't know if I could stop once I started kissing her. Jeff joked that this better be the only time he caught me kissing his girlfriend. I just gave a quick laugh at that. When rehearsing we did this part with our clothes on and didn't actually kiss. We were holding out on doing it for real until opening night.

The night of the play changed everything for me. I liked Jenny but I wouldn't say I was in love with her. As far as I felt on that, I didn't love at all anymore. Don't get me wrong, I loved my sister and I loved Abby like a sister now, but that was different. I felt no more pain from my life last year and I wasn't ready to jump into the emotional pool anytime soon again.

But I liked Jenny a lot and I wanted to date her to get to know her. I felt like I had found a real person, not just another college slut. I wanted to date a real person. I thought back to Brooke. I really wish she was here or nearby enough to give that another try. But in the here and now was Jenny. It just would've been great if she wasn't dating Jeff.

It was opening night and I was jittery as hell. I knew my material and I knew my blocking, but I couldn't sit still. Jeff as producer had decided to hang out by the doors and great and talk to people as they came in. The cast had made their way upstairs hanging out back stage. I was upstairs and pacing around, sweating through my shirt.

I could see the auditorium filling up with people. I looked at my watch; we had only an hour before curtain. I looked around and I couldn't find Jenny. I decided to go look for her.

I found her in one of the dressing rooms she was standing still and breathing while moving her arms slowly. I asked her what she was doing and she explained about how she had learned breathing exercises when she was younger. She turned to look at me and saw how bad I was sweating.

"We need to get you another shirt," she exclaimed looking at me.

"Yeah, I guess this one's about ruined." With that she walked to me and pulled my shirt off. I felt guilty as she removed my shirt and I stood there half naked with her for the first time.

"I never liked that shirt as a costume choice anyway," she said shyly looking at me, "Let's find you something to make you look a little hotter."

"Well the shirt was picked for Ted when he had the role. I didn't bother with adjusting the costuming to me when he went to jail."

She smiled at me while looking through the extra clothing in the dressing room. She pulled a black long sleeve shirt off the rack.

"This one should fit," she said actually running her hand across my chest, she pulled away really quick when she had realized what she had done.

"Looks good," I said nervously, "Good choice."

I pulled the shirt over my arms quickly feeling awkward for some reason. Jenny stood in front of me buttoning my shirt for me. Suddenly we were kissing, I couldn't tell you who leaned in first or how long we had been kissing before I realized we were.

It was like I blanked out and when I woke up our arms were around each other and my tongue was flying over hers. I stood there kissing her, my shirt still half open, I grabbed her neck and held her to our kiss. She grabbed at the waistband of my pants, pulling me closer to her and unbuttoning them. I reached into her shirt and began to feel her breasts. My pants were open and she had her hand in my boxers stroking me, I unbuttoned her shirt and started kissing her neck while fighting with her bra hooks. Her bra fell forward reveling her small b-cup breasts, I reached for her pants. She pulled away from me and dropped to her knees.

I felt myself enter her warm and eager mouth and I was in heaven. She hadn't done this a lot, I could tell, but it was Jenny doing this for me now. That amazing Jenny whom I wanted so much, Jenny who was Jeff's girlfriend.

"Wait, stop, we can't do this."

"What............?" she questioned as I pulled her off of me.

"Not here, not now, not like this," I told her panting. My heart was racing so hard.

"I thought you............ liked me?" she asked turning her face away.

"I do, you're so amazing, but you're still dating Jeff," I told her pulling my cloths back together. I didn't know where this dose of morality came from. But I felt at that moment I couldn't betray Jeff.

"I'm sorry your right, Jeff's a good guy. It's just............" she bit her lip.

"What?" I asked tenderly caressing her cheek with the back of my hand.

"I've only ever been with him," she whispered as if she thought it was some terrible thing to have only been with one man, "I've never once felt passion like I felt just now in that moment."

"I felt it too."

"Then what do we do now? Do you want me to break up with him, I will, for you, your, such a sweet nice guy. I would break up with him for you."

"I want that so much. I really do. But I can't ask you to do that. What kind of friend would I be if I asked you to do that?"

"See even now you put your friends first."

"I won't ask you to do what I want. If you guys break up, I'll be right here waiting. If you choose not to then I understand, sort your feelings and do what makes you happiest." She kissed me again and re-hooked her bra. I left her there and went back upstairs until the play started.

We made it through opening night and the next two shows. Everyone told us the love scene looked hot, like we were really lovers. I smiled inwardly at that. I avoided being alone with her from opening night to closing night. I hadn't heard any bad news from Jeff so I assumed that they were still dating.

Closing night almost everyone had left the theater building and only the director, our drama professor and I were left. Jeff had gone ahead with Jenny to the cast and crew after party we were having at a local all-night restaurant.

I had made the comment that it had been cool to see my writing come to life and I wanted to hang out on the set and unwind before coming to the party. We had left the sets up as we were all planning to come back the next day and strike the set.

Our drama professor locked all the doors and said before I left that I should make one quick round to check and make sure no one else had stayed behind. I told her that was fine; I would only be a little while before I left. I walked around looking at the world that had sprung from my head. Everyone had really liked the story. I had something awaken in me that night; I knew what I wanted to do the rest of my life. I just didn't know how to get there.

I was sitting on the bed on set thinking about Jenny. She was awesome and I had enjoyed kissing her. I had really gotten into it tonight. I didn't know if I would ever have another chance so I made the most of our scene. I was thinking about her when the curtain fell on the stage closing it off from the auditorium. I turned to see Jenny standing at the curtain rope. I had no idea how she had gotten in but I was happy to see her. Jenny walked to me and sat down next to me on the bed.

"I did what you said," she said quietly looking down at her feet, "I thought about what I felt and I made a decision."

"What did you.............?" I started and she cut me off with a kiss.

"Does that mean what I think it does?"

"Yes, I choose you," she said taking my hand in hers, "But I haven't told him yet."

"Then maybe we should wait?" I questioned. She kissed me again softer, and longer.

"I would've broken up with him that night but he was so happy about how successful the play had turned out I didn't want to ruin his night. I want him to feel happy that the production went well, I'll give him tonight to party and then I will break up with him."

"I guess I can understand that. I still don't like going behind his back."

"I know............but I can't wait anymore," she said quietly pulling me to her. I couldn't hold back. I liked her too much to wait. We were kissing again and I realized I was a really bad friend to Jeff and I didn't deserve a girl like Jenny. But I was here in her arms and I couldn't turn away from that. I just rationalized that he had never understood her and had missed out on all the great things about her that had made me fall for her.

We were now acting out for real the love scene we'd been play acting the last three days. I pulled her shirt off of her as she unbuttoned mine. I kissed her more passionately as I removed her bra. We lay down together and began removing our jeans. We never stopped kissing as we wiggled out of our clothes. We had our eyes open as we kissed; I never broke eye contact with her as I rolled over on top of her. Without breaking our kiss I found her sweet love spot. I slowly entered her warm tight body.

She felt like no girl I had felt before. She was warm and tight without being crushing and burning. It was a perfect fit as I slid back and trust within her again and again. We lay there making love slowly, rhythmically, in sync with each other. I had never had someone raise her hips and meet me so perfectly with every thrust. It was like we were reading each other's movements and anticipating the next.

We moved together for hours, days, weeks, it could have been years, as I thrust between her soft loving thighs. I knew in that moment I would never give her up. She wasn't the girl of my childhood fantasies or my first love; I had grown up from those things. Jenny was the girl of my grown up hopes and dreams of a future and family.

I wasn't in love with her yet, I had learned now that jumping without looking only caused you to land on your face. I wasn't in love with her yet but as we made love the first time I had a vision of us in the future. I saw a real life with her, a real life with kids and a house and everything I could ever hope for.

All these thoughts swam in my head as we made love. I pushed away the emotional and began to focus on the physical, she felt so good under me. I thrust deeper and deeper, she moaned in my mouth as we kissed and it made me harder every time she did. I found her getting tighter and tighter with every moan I returned to her.

I, not surprisingly, finally came first. It wasn't more than seconds later that she finally came too. I lay down on top of her and we rolled over. Still not breaking eye contact or our kiss, we rolled over so she was on top of me. I was still hard inside her, when she finally pulled away from my lips and leaned back thrusting her hips forward on me. Her body tightened up on me in that moment squeezing me hard as she slowly moved up and down.

I'd had lots of sex this year, nothing compared to what I was doing now. There wasn't a word for what I was doing now. This was more intense then I could ever remember, more passionate then I had felt all year. I came in her again, exhausted. I was too tired to keep going but my body didn't slow down. My cock continued to respond to her riding me as the rest of me lay limp. She came again and fell on to me. This girl was amazing in life and in bed.

I looked at my watch, realizing why I was so tired; we had been here making love for almost 2 hours. I had lasted with her longer then I had ever lasted with anyone. I started kissing her again; our body's both to limp and exhausted to do anything else. I liked having her weight on me; it was comforting to feel her there.

We eventually had to get up and move. We, with much regret, got off the bed and gathered up our clothes. After we had dressed I sat down again and pulled her to my lap. We kissed and she told me she needed me to take her home. She had rode in with Jeff and didn't have her car. I asked her how she had ended up getting away from the party and back into the building. She explained that she had told Jeff she would get a ride out with one of the girls to the party. She said she had done it hoping to ride with me to the party so we could talk, but after she realized we were the only ones left in the building she thought this was better.

I told her that I really did feel bad about what we did to Jeff. She said she felt that way too, but she would take care of that tomorrow. We slipped out from the stage though the curtain and left the theater building. As we drove home I told her that my year was almost out and I would be going back home soon for the summer.

"But I'm going to come back in a month. I won't stay the whole summer."

"You're willing to give up the little time you have with your parents to come back to me?" she asked quietly but smiling.

"Yes. They will understand, besides I think the focus this summer will be on my sister and her girlfriend. Katie is going to tell the family when we go home this time."

"I hope it goes ok for them. Your sister and her girlfriend both sound pretty cool from the way you're always talking about them."

"Yeah, their cool," I laughed internally. I of course never told Jenny about my true relationship with the girls. Jenny did know however that Abby had been my high school girlfriend before getting together with Katie.

"But I'm not just coming back to spend time with you, I'm coming back to spend time with you and Anne," I told her and she smiled happily, "And little Barky of course." She laughed at me for a second.

I told her that since there was only a few weeks left of school; out of respect for Jeff we should keep things quiet for now. I told her when I came back this summer that would've been enough time for them to have broken up and for us start seeing each other. She thought it was sweet that I was trying to something to spare his hurt a little. I didn't know if I agreed with that but I didn't argue. I dropped her off at her house giving her a long kiss as she left the car.

When I got home that night Katie was at the door waiting and freaking out on me.

"Where the hell have you been?"

"What, Mom did I pass my curfew?"

"Ha ha, Jeff's been calling looking for you."

"I went out. I didn't want to go to the after party," I told her.

"Yeah, I know that look and you smell like you've been having sex."

"Does it matter? Why did he care so much where I went?"

"He didn't, he said Jenny never showed up at the party, he's been worried and trying to find her. Please tell me you weren't........" Katie frowned at me.

"I plead the fifth," I couldn't stop smiling.

"How could you do that to your friend?" she asked angrily, "I know you really like her, but I thought you were better than that."

"I do really like her, she's perfect," I started.

"Hey," Abby yelled, "What does that make us?" She was joking. I ignored her and continued.

"I didn't mean to come between them. She just started to like me too. I told her to make a decision; she's breaking up with him tomorrow."

"That's not the point; it's not tomorrow yet is it? You should've waited, Joey," she scolded me, "Just go to bed." I didn't argue with her I just went to my room and went to sleep.

I didn't see Jeff for a number of days. He finally turned up about a week and a half later telling me that Jenny had broken up with him the day after the play that's why she had disappeared and hadn't gone to the party. All she told him was that she needed a man who would step up to be with her and Anne, not bail on her when the kid came along. Not a boy who put video games before helping with charity. He was pissed and suspected she had someone else but didn't know who. I just said I was sorry for him and left it at that.

I waited until after I heard from Jeff to go see Jenny again. When I did see Jenny she sat me down saying we needed to talk. I was a little worried. Jenny sent Anne outside to play with Barky. She told Anne to stay right out front of the apartment.

As soon as Anne had closed the door Jenny told me that closing night of the play had been the most passionate night of her life. She told me that she was falling in love with me. She told me she had been falling for me from the beginning that's why she had performed the play for me.

"I felt the same passion for you that night too," I told her, "But I don't know how I feel yet."

"Oh," she said getting up and walking into the kitchen. I waited a moment then followed her into the kitchen. I put my arms around her from behind and kissed her cheek.

"I thought you were into me," she started quietly; "I thought that night meant something to you."

"Don't get me wrong, that night was one of the most wildly passionate things I've ever felt. I am into you, it did mean something to me, but I'm not where you are with this yet." I had hurt her. I could see it on her face.

I knew that the only guy she had ever been with had been Jeff. I knew they had lost their virginities to each other as an act of friendship not love. I knew the couple months they had been dating had been more out of long term friendship, not love.

I was very aware this was the first time she had told anyone she was in love. I just wanted to be honest with her, and not lie about how far along I was. I was too guarded to fall in love again so easily. But she had professed love and I had let her down. She wasn't crying and she wasn't pulling away from my embrace.

"I wish things were different right now," she said and I wasn't sure how she meant it.

"I want very much to fall for you," I told her, "I can see it happening, I'm scared of what that all means." I was honest and she turned around looking at me, my arms still holding her to me now around her back.

"Ssssh," she whispered, "You don't have to be scared." she ran her hand over my cheek.

"It's just I've been here before quite honestly, I'm just not ready yet, I'm sorry Jenny, I've been hurt." She kissed me passionately.

"I won't hurt you," she said softly. We kissed deeply until we heard the front door open. Jenny pulled away saying quietly she didn't want to do anything in front of Anne.

Anne came into the kitchen and smiled at both of us. She took a juice packet out of the fridge and skipped back outside to play again.

"I think what we need is time," Jenny finally told me softly; "You're going home soon maybe you need to take your own advice." she was smiling softly.

"What advice?" I questioned.

"You told me to take a couple days and think about what I really wanted before I broke up with Jeff. I did that for you now you need to do that for me. Go home and see your family, think about how you truly feel. Then come back and we can end this whole thing before we go any further or come back and ask me properly to be your girlfriend."

"Your right," I told her, "I'm sorry I can't sort this out and give you an answer right now. You deserve better than this." She kissed me again and told me that she knew the answer I just had to catch up.

I left a little while after that. I had fully gone to Jenny's apartment intending to leave having a new girlfriend, yet somehow that didn't happen. What was holding me back? Why couldn't I fall for her like I so much wanted too? She was practically the most perfect for me girl I had ever met and I still couldn't commit to that feeling yet.

I went home that night feeling like dirt. What was wrong with me? I talked to Abby and Katie about the whole situation, looking for some kind of advice. Katie told me that despite how I had gotten together with her the first time she sounded wonderful and I would be a fool not to date her. Abby smiled and said that I just had to get over myself, calm down and ask her to be my girlfriend now before she had time to think about it and run screaming the other way. We all laughed at that.

I turned twenty a couple days later. I awoke to find Abby lying in bed with me. She was snuggling her head against my chest at the shoulder and had her hand in my boxers rubbing my balls. I turned my head and kissed her forehead.

"About time you woke up. I've been here forever," she joked. I was surprised to find her here with me; we hadn't fooled around at all for a couple months. As I said before I had stopped having sex with her by spring break and Katie and Abby had decided to commit to each other. I thought that meant my time with them was over.

"I thought you and Katie had decided.........." I started not really knowing how to put it.

"I was really horny for dick and she said I could give you a special birthday present this one time."

"I don't know..........." I didn't really want her to stop but I was feeling guilty, like I was cheating on someone. But I technically didn't have a girlfriend, so I wasn't cheating technically but I still felt like I was betraying Jenny's trust. Those thoughts slowly crept out of my head as Abby began to stroke my cock.

"OOOh god I've missed you Abby," I moaned. Abby did have a unique touch about how she did things. I had missed our bond together this past couple months.

"I missed you holding me, while we play," she smiled back at me.

Abby stroked me slowly until I came in her hand. She pulled her hand out of my shorts and licked her hand grinning. She knew it turned me on harder when girls swallowed, and it makes me like steel when they licked cum off themselves.

"Happy birthday, "Abby whispered sliding down the bed and pulling my boxers down. I had a flashback to just three years earlier. Miles away, much younger and still both virgins, and not carrying the hurt we both had been though we had been doing this exact same thing on the morning of my 17th birthday. So much had happened and changed since then.

Abby took me into her mouth and my mind shut off the flashbacks and went blank. All there was for a few moments was the pleasure she was shooting thought my body, she really had learned how to use her tongue now, I guess dating a girl had helped that along some.

Abby sucked down hard and up again tickling me with the tip of her tongue on every stroke. I was shuddering when she pulled back, I could feel myself building again. Just before I was going to tell her I was about to cum she stopped and removed her mouth from me. I started to subside slightly as she took the tip of her tongue and lightly ran it along my length.

This was still shooting chills down my body but without her mouth directly sucking me my orgasm subsided completely. Abby went lower and took my balls into her mouth and began sucking them, using her tongue as she had on my cock.

Abby had never done this for me before. As I said before her style of love making was wild, quick and passionate. I had never experienced the slow intense side of herself she was giving me today. I was having shooting almost pains running up my spine, very few times had I ever had my ball sucked and never like what I was experiencing today. I was bucking with every pain up my spine. It hurt and felt awesome at the same time, I needed her to stop before I hurt worse but I didn't want her to stop.

At long last Abby took my ball sack from her mouth and began to suck my cock again. I only lasted about ten seconds before I grabbed the back of her head, sat up on the bed and came with real force in her mouth. She lifted her eyes to my gaze and looked me in the eye as she swallowed every bit of cum I shot into her mouth.

"Wow," was all I managed as I let go of her and fell back to the bed. Abby crawled up and put her head on my shoulder again. I liked her head on my shoulder. I knew I would miss this bonding with her someday when we had all moved on with the next phase of our lives. I really did love Abby, but I looked at her as a sister now.

"I think you were trying to kill me with that last one," Abby whispered joking with me, "Let me know when you're ready, I need more."

I smiled and slid down the bed. I knew she had been talking about sex but I thought I would return the favor while recharging again. Abby didn't complain as I opened her legs and moved in, flicking her clit with my tongue. She moaned loud begging me for more. I didn't give it to her; I flicked and teased her with only using the tip of my fingers and tongue for well over a half an hour, giving her multiple orgasms. Finally I gave in to her moaning and begging.

I thrust my lips forward licking into her hard, she gasped loud at the suddenness that I had gone from teasing to licking. I was ready to go again, only licking her for a couple minutes before pulling myself up onto her and sliding my aching cock into her soft pussy.

"OOOOOOOOOOHHHHH MY GOD," she cried out as I entered her, "I've missed getting a real dick so much." she whispered the last part to me.

I thrust deep into I had missed being with her a lot. I had banged so many girls this year and the only one that came near what I was feeling now was Jenny. But Jenny was on the opposite side of that scale. While none of the party girls could hold a candle to how good Abby felt right now, there was definitely something missing that had been there when I had sex with Jenny.

I was thinking of Jenny and I got harder inside Abby, this caused a response in her as she tightened down on me, contracting for her biggest orgasm of the morning. It caused me too finally cum one last time, this one inside her. I fell on the bed next to her; she snuggled up to me again resting her head on my chest.

We stayed like that until lunch time. Katie hadn't seen us come out yet she didn't want to interrupt us. She finally knocked on the door with a lunch tray of sandwiches, thinking we may be hungry. This reminded me of my first day here with them. Katie sat down on the bed with us and we ate lunch.

Classes were over and the school year complete, I hoped I had done well. I had a plan to change my major next year and a new career path I wanted to follow. I made a decision about Jenny but I didn't call her. I decided to stick to the plan and go home before talking to her about it again. I felt if I really liked her or more than those feelings would still be there in a month when I returned and if they weren't then I really had been fooling myself.

The girls and I had decided to fly home for the summer. None of us wanted to make the drive. The three of us got our plane tickets together and were flying home the same day. Abby was coming with us because the girls felt it was time to be open about their relationship to our parents and the world.

I couldn't wait to spend some time at home, but I mostly wanted to get the visit done so I could return and talk with Jenny. I just had no idea as we caught our flights that day at the end of June; our family life at home would soon be over.

Chapter Eleven:
Ashley's Diary Part 1: The Slumber Party

This is the story of Ashley's misadventures after I left for college. When I said I was going to write my whole story Ash brought me the diary she had kept in high school. She had started writing down her feelings and the events of her life as a way to cope with not having me around to talk to anymore.

I wanted to include them into the story but I wasn't there at the time and didn't live it. Here now with her permission are her diary entries, rewritten by me taken from her own words:

Ash awoke in her own bed; she hadn't remembered moving from the hallway. She shook herself awake looking around for a second trying to get her bearings. She had let go of the necklace sometime in the night and it was sitting on the bed next to her. By her other hand she found a piece of paper, it was folded and had her name on it.

"NO!" she cried out running from her room and across the hall. Joey's door was open and he wasn't there. Ash turned on the spot running at full speed down the stairs, past the empty kitchen and out the front door. Joey's car was gone she looked up in time to see him turn the corner at the end of the block. She dropped to her knees in the driveway, tears running down her face.

Ash realized it must have been the sound of the front door closing that had woke her this morning. Maybe it was Joe who had put her back into her bed. She was furious that he didn't wake her to say goodbye. She loved him, gave her virginity to him, had she meant so little to him that he couldn't even say goodbye?

Ash sat in the driveway until the early light had gotten bright as morning turned to day. Then she remembered the note next to her as she woke. She hadn't looked at it in her hurry not to miss Joe's departure. She ran back into the house past Lilly who was making breakfast.

Taking the stairs two at a time she flung herself on the bed. It was in the note, it would say that everything was fine and he loved her, everything was fine and things would be as they were when he came home at Christmas. She knew he loved her and the anger from yesterday would've subsided by now. It was all in that note, it had to be. She slowly, nervously unfolded the note:

> Ash,
>
> Nothing will ever change the fact that I love you. It's just right now I don't know how to feel about what we talked about. This is why I had said we should have waited for a few years to see how we really felt. Last week I would've died for you. Today I don't know if we were in love or if it was nothing more than a kid's game.
>
> I'm sorry if this hurts you. I'm just being honest with my feelings. That's one thing I will never do, I will never lie to you about how I feel. I never wanted to hurt you. I can't stand the thought of more tears running down your beautiful face.
>
> With me going to college today what we need is time. Time to sort out who we are and what were really feeling. What I'm saying, what I'm feeling, what I want to be

clear about, we need to break up. When I come back next summer we'll talk. We can see what we feel after spending a year apart.

I'm so sorry, angel, but I think this is all for the best. Don't think this means I don't love you. I love you more than life, you were my first real love and I will never forget that, ever.

Love you, Baby Girl,

Joe.

Ashley red the note three times before she tore up the letter and slamming the pieces down on her desk. How could he have broken up with her so easily and with a note? He just walked away from everything they had together, not even saying the words 'goodbye' in the note either.

Ash was more than furious now. She pushed her face into a pillow and screamed loudly. The pillow did the job to muffle the sound to the rest of the house but didn't stop her anger. Just yesterday she thought she might be carrying his child and today they were broken up. That bastard had left her behind like an old shirt he didn't wear anymore.

Lilly called her for breakfast a few minutes later. She didn't come down. She wasn't done screaming into her pillow, and couldn't face them right now. How could she face the world again knowing she had been used?

He had said in the note that he didn't know what was real anymore; right now she wondered the same thing from him. Did he ever really love her? Or had he played her making her think she was manipulating him? All she knew right now was that she was an angry, alone and confused 15 year old girl.

Ash stopped screaming and rolled over lying back on her bed. She felt more alone now then she had when she lost her parents. She had put her faith in a man who claimed to love her but still had slept with his sister when given the opportunity. Of course that was her own fault for her part in that. But if he really loved her would he have slept with another girl?

Ash lay on her bed confused and deep in thought when she heard a knock on the door. She didn't answer she rolled over and stared at the wall. She looked at the edge of the bed seeing the necklace. She didn't know why but looking at the necklace everything became clear to her. Her thoughts were interrupted as the door opened. Curse Lilly and her damn no locks on the doors rule.

"Hey sweetie," Lilly said soothingly, "I brought you a tray of food." Ash said nothing; she lay on her bed holding the necklace staring at the wall. Lilly set the tray down on the desk next to the bed and sat down behind Ash.

"It's going to be ok," Lilly told her rubbing her back, "He's only going to be gone for a while. Do you want to talk?"

"No."

"It's ok to miss people when their gone, I know you guys were best friends."

"No," Ash started though tears, "Best friends say goodbye. They give you a hug as their going away. After everything he couldn't even say goodbye."

Lilly didn't push her further that day. She sat and rubbed her back for a while

"Don't sit up here all day," Lilly told her as she left, "Eat something you'll feel better." With that said she left the room.

It was just after lunch when Ashley wondered down stairs she looked around realizing that everyone else was in the rec-room so she snuck into the study. The study had its own phone line and she needed to talk to someone who would understand. Unfortunately she only had one person who knew what was going on with them, she just didn't know if she really wanted to call Katie, on some level she was mad at her too.

In the end Ash gave up sulking on that point and called her niece. She called and told Katie that she and Joe had gotten in a fight and he had broken up with her in a note just before leaving for college. Katie laughed.

"Sorry I don't mean to laugh," Katie told her, "It's just I've been where he is before. When I left for college I left him a goodbye note as well" Ash saw the irony but didn't find it funny. Ash told Katie what the note had said and they talk about what it.

Katie told her that as much as it hurt maybe it was for the best at the moment. They were now in completely different places in life and in the country. Maybe space would help them figure out what they really wanted. In the meantime Katie said that she would find a way to make sure he was ok when he got to her.

Ash really didn't like Katie's advice but she couldn't deny that it would be next to impossible to work on their relationship when they wouldn't be able to spend any time together for a year. Even at that she was supposed to go to Linda's for the summer. If she did that she wouldn't really see Joey for over a year and a half. She had just turned 15 and it looked like she would be almost 17 before they had any real time with each other.

Ashley was a very smart girl she realized it was pointless to push for something that wasn't there now and wouldn't be. In the end she agreed with Katie that it was time she they needed. She told her niece that she would always love him but for her, for now it was really over. The girls talked for another half hour when Katie said she had to go.

Ash went back to her room and stayed there until school started the next week. Lilly had finally gotten after her and made her get up and get ready to go. She did as she was told and started her sophomore year of high school.

She found as the school year began she had no interest in classes, school activities, or her friends. Her friends all talked about their summer, crushes they had, and their first kisses. Ash found all this talk pointless. She had gone farther than the innocent kissing her girlfriends were doing at this age and she felt she had no one she could relate too. She found herself wishing Sara was still alive and she could call her to talk about the whole thing, but her old best friend was gone too.

The school year was passing agonizingly slow, yet miraculously it became Christmas break. Ash was still spending all her time in her room. She had agreed right away that the break up kind of made sense but it didn't stop the hurt or the void in the house his being gone created.

She came home every day and went to her room and continued staring at the wall. In the first few weeks she had tried reading and playing music. Nothing worked and in the end she had resorted to staring at the wall. Sometimes when she couldn't take it anymore and her feelings welled up so bad she couldn't stand it, she wrote pages and pages in her diary.

Lilly tried about once a week to come in and rub her back and talk to her about what was going on. Ashley wouldn't talk to her; she didn't want to betray Joey or herself. She felt saddened that she had to hide her feelings from her sister but Ash didn't want to take a chance Lilly would do something to Joe for having had sex with her so young.

Every week, sometimes a few days in a row, Lilly would come in with soothing words and a loving rub on her back as she lay down on her bed not looking away from the wall. Ash found it was getting harder and harder to not talk about it but she held tight.

Then Christmas break came and she didn't even get up or leave her room, except when Linda had come and almost forced her out of the house to run errands with her. Linda's visit had been the turning point of her isolationism and depression.

It was a few days after Christmas and Linda was going home the next day. Linda went to Ash to see if she would still come this next summer. Linda said she was sad that Ash was sad but really looked forward to spending the summer together. Ash said she would come. Lilly came in not long after and they three sisters talked.

Lilly told Ash that she had had a talk with Joe and that while he hadn't said what happened between them he had admitted that they had, had some kind of relationship. Lilly gave Ash Joe's message and she told Ash she didn't want the details that those should stay between her and Joe. After that the girls had a real talk about life and love and how to move on.

Ash was grateful to her sisters she had finally found someone who could relate to her problems on a scale her friends weren't able to yet. She really wished she had come to her sister long before. To Ash's surprise Lilly wasn't mad at Joey for being with her, in fact Lilly said she was ok with it because she could tell they really loved each other. Linda said some people take whole lifetimes or never experience love on that level, she was still waiting herself.

That talk made all the difference in the world for Ash. She started slowly to come out of her room more often. Then her grades started to come back up. Next she was taking Jessy to the park for walks alone but at least out of the house. Before long she was going out with friends after school to the library or coffee shop. She would take Jessy to the dog park for the whole day and sit under a tree and read, with one or two friends hanging out with her. Lilly said to her one afternoon that she was so happy to see her spending time with people again.

On weekends she started to stay at her friend Libby's house overnight. Before long Libby and Ashley were inseparable. Ash really liked hanging around Libby who was 15 like her, but more so she had developed a small crush on Libby's 14 year old little brother Jace. Ash wasn't in love with him by any means, she just thought he was cute in an innocent way because he was still a virgin and would blush

whenever Ash talked to him. She had stayed overnight wearing a tight shirt and a pair of shorts and had accidentally brushed up against him a couple times in passing. She began to notice each of these events had resulted in Jace running to his room and closing the door for a half an hour or more. She knew what he was doing, Joey had talked frank with her enough times she had no doubt he was stroking himself to the thought of having sex with her. Ash found that she was actually flattered and slightly turned on by it.

Ash thought it was so cute that he was so shy and nervous around her. She made up her mind that she wanted to take his virginity for him. She had been really horny for months now, and needed to do something about it. She didn't know if Libby would get mad at her for sleeping with her brother. She didn't want to lose Libby as her friend. So she decided she needed to come up with a plan. She knew Jace wouldn't mind, he was a boy after all, and what boy would argue about sleeping with the girl he's been fantasizing about? It took weeks before she had a plan in place that she though would work. It was completely juvenile but she thought it still might work. It started, as most of these things do, with a party.

Libby's parent's anniversary was coming up and they were going out for the whole night. They were trusting Libby and Jace alone in the house all night for the first time. Libby had invited Ash to stay the night and when Ash asked if Libby's parents would be ok with her staying over, Libby explained that she was told that they could each have one friend over.

Jace really didn't have many close friends, so by the time of Libby's parents anniversary Ash had convinced Jace to let Libby have his friend pick so two of her friends could come over, Ash told him that if he was nice to his sister that way Ash would be good to him in return. She had said it so sexy rubbing his arm at the time; he agreed and ran off to his room.

Libby's parents said it was fine for her to have two friends as long as they were both girls and that was it. Libby was excited and invited their friend Melanie, or Laney for short, to come to the slumber party.

Ash was excited now she had the place and time set up. She was going to seduce Jace in a way that Libby couldn't hold it against her. If she did this right Libby would be right there when it happened.

The big night finally arrived, it was a cold and rainy April evening when Lilly dropped Ash and Laney off at Libby's house. Ash had suggested to the girls that they wear only a shirt and panties to drive Jace crazy. The other girls giggled and thought it would be funny to see him all worked up nervous. So as soon as Libby's parents left, off came the clothes.

Jace had just come out of the bathroom when he saw the three girls running around; his eyes shifted obviously looking at each one while his mouth hung open. Ash noticed that his eyes stayed longest on Libby. Ash recognized that look on his face; she had seen it many times before on Joey. Ash thought this night was going to be more interesting then she realized. He might just get to live out a couple fantasies tonight.

As soon as he stopped looking at Libby, Jace spun on the spot running to his room and closing the door loudly. The girls all giggled knowing what he had left the room to do. Ash walked down the hall and stood by his door.

"Jace," She called sweetly, "Why did you run away, I wanted to play with you." She knew exactly what effect it would have on him. She heard a loud grunt from the other side of the door, the girls laughed from the living room. Ash didn't laugh she just continued, "Don't you want to come out and play with

me?" Another loud grunt and she knew he was hers tonight, there was no way he was saying no to her by the way he was grunting over her words.

Jace stayed in his room until Libby called him for dinner. They had ordered a pizza and gave the delivery boy something to look at when he came to the door. Ash actually kissed Laney as Libby paid for the pizza. The deliveryman had actually got a hard on as he took the money and left again. The girls all laughed at that, Ash was surprised not only at her own inhibitions but that when she kissed Laney she hadn't had a problem with it. Tonight might get really good.

Jace came out of his room wearing shorts and sat down at the table to eat, sitting next to Ash across from Laney and Libby. You could see the nervousness on his face as he walked into the room with them he had an obvious erection again sitting down.

He was eating a piece of pizza when Ash put her hand on his knee. Jace looked over at her and she shook her head slightly. He slowly faced forward again as Ash slid her hand back to the leg of his shorts. She could see sweat forming on his face as she slid her hand inside his shorts grasping his erection. If he hadn't have been chewing at the time he would've gasped. She stroked him slowly, not wanting the girls to see what she was doing. As she stroked him his body began to shake from nervous fear.

It took all his effort not to make a sound as Ash continued playing him. Within moments Ash felt warm sticky fluid covering her hand. She pulled her hand out of his shorts and using her other hand brought a napkin under the table to wipe her hand off. At the same moment she had removed her hand Jace shot up from the table and ran down the hall. The girls could hear him vomiting in the bathroom moments later, and then the shower came on.

When he came out of his shower Libby and Laney made fun of him for being so nervous around girls in their panties that he had to throw up. He didn't get upset by her joking instead he grinned and sat down on the couch.

It was time for Ash to start her real game. She told the girls they should play truth or dare. Yet again she thought it was a juvenile idea but sometimes the classic ideas still worked. The girls thought it would be fun and asked Jace if he wanted to play. He looked extremely nervous and said no he was going to play some video games. The girls decided to play right there in the living room with him there. Jace put in some kind of driving game and began to play.

"Ash, truth or dare?" Asked Libby.

"Hey, how do you get to go first?" Asked Laney.

"My house, my party, now how about it Ash?"

"Truth."

"I know you've had a boyfriend before, so have you ever given a blowjob?"

"OOOOH good starter question," said Laney.

"Yes," Ash said simply. She looked up and saw Jace looking over at her while she answered. She noticed the car in his video game was swerving all over.

"Now, Laney truth or dare?"

"Truth."

"Since you liked that question so much I will ask you, have you ever given a blowjob?" Laney turned red and said no, the most she had ever done was a hand job. The girls got excited and asked her who. She admitted that she had given one to a boy after a school dance last year. They had made out and she let him touch her boobs and she jerked him off.

"I could tell that wasn't your first kiss when we teased the pizza guy," Ash told Laney. Jace was completely staring at the girls now his car had crashed and he apparently wasn't even aware of the game anymore.

Ash smiled as she realized this was working, the tent in Jace's shorts said he was about ready for her game to take the next step; she only had to get the girls on the same page.

"So Libby truth or dare?" Laney asked her getting back to the game.

"I'll go truth this time."

"Ok back to the same question. Have you or not given a blowjob?"

"I............. I've never even kissed anyone," Libby admitted.

"Oh we need to fix that," Ash said leaning in and giving Libby a long kiss. They didn't use tongues but it was a real kiss. Ash looked up at Jace when she was done and he was crossing his legs trying to hide himself as he stared at them.

"Wow," Libby breathed out, "That was so cool."

"When did you get into girls?" Laney asked, "You've kissed us both tonight."

"I'm not into girls. I'm just not shy anymore and we're just having fun, right?"

The girls agreed that it didn't mean anything and it was all good if it was just for fun. The next few rounds had the girls responding to all kinds of truths and braver dares. Before long they were all laughing about what they had learned about each other and all three were out of their shirts and bra's only wearing their panties.

Jace had pulled the blanket off the back of the couch and covered himself. Ash could tell there was some slight movement under the blanket. It was turning her on bad that he was stroking himself in front of her behind the backs of Libby and Laney who couldn't see him.

"So Laney truth or dare?" Ash asked, she had, had enough and needed to fuck already. She had been so horny since Joey left and she felt safe with Jace.

"Dare."

"I dare you to kiss Jace for 2 minutes."

"Hey I'm not playing!" Cried Jace from behind Laney and Libby.

"No, I want to see that! He's been drooling over the show long enough," said Libby, "If you want to say out here and watch us anymore you have to play along, little brother." Libby's voice was stern, and had a slight longing in it. Ash was surprised; she thought she would have to coax Libby into this. It almost looked now as if she had been looking for an excuse to get here.

Laney in the meantime scooted over to the couch and standing on her knees pulled Jace into her. They kissed the whole two minutes, the whole time Ash and Libby could see his arm moving under the blanket. Ash and Libby looked at the movement and looked at each other as if a plan had been hatched right then. Libby also had a look on her face as if she was asking Ash for something she couldn't say out loud. After two minutes was up Laney came back and sat down again.

"So Libby truth or dare?" Laney asked keeping the circle going.

"Dare."

"OOOOh good I'm going to give you one further. Since you've never done it before you have to give him a hand job until he cums," Laney said with an evil grin.

"But she's my sister!" Jace unconvincingly exclaimed from the couch. All the girls could tell he had only raised the objection because it was the right thing to say, not because he didn't want it to happen.

"I'm ok with it," Libby said blushing, "It's all in fun, were just playing a game." She crawled on her knees to the couch and removed the blanket. The front of Jace's shots had a visible wet spot on them. He blushed but didn't fight it as Libby pulled down his shorts and his cock sprang free. It was bigger and harder than Ash had realized even from stroking it. Or he was more turned on by the three girls and the situation than he had been with her alone.

Libby tentatively reached out her hand and grasped her brother's cock. She stroked him up and down softly and he moaned.

"Grip him harder they like that," Called Laney trying to coach her a little. Ash thought she had to have given more than just one hand job before but didn't question her.

It only took a few hard strokes for Jace to cum on his sister. He moaned out a half warning as he shot cum onto his sisters tits. Libby squealed and backed off as it hit her. Ash went into the kitchen and brought back a roll of paper towels. She handed Libby a couple and she cleaned herself off.

Ash looked to Jace he was still hard and had a grin on his face which was completely red. He must be having the night of his life; Ash's moment was getting close.

"Ash, truth or dare."

"Dare," she said with a giggle.

"Then since you've done it before and I really want to see what it looks like, I dare you to give my brother a blowjob." Ash didn't even hesitate. She crawled on her knees over to the couch, taking Jace into her mouth sucking him hard.

"OOOOH GOD OOOOH GOOOD!" he cried out as he received his first blowjob.

"That's so hot!" Laney said as Ash sped up her sucking. Ash shifted her eyes to the side for a moment; she could see both girls had their hands in their panties, rubbing themselves. He plan had worked but Ash felt weird. This was the first time she had ever been with any boy other than Joey. Jace's cock wasn't as big and it felt really different, but she had made the decision to move on and that started now. She put all her effort into pleasuring this nice shy boy; she had enough experience to make his first blowjob one he wouldn't ever forget. After having just cum for his sister he managed to hold out for quite a while Ash thought. When he finally came in her mouth it tasted so different from what she had, had before. She took it all in as he went limp in her mouth, but she found she couldn't stand to swallow it so she turned quickly and grabbed the roll of paper towels, tarring off a piece and spitting into it.

"Oh MY God!" exclaimed Libby when it was over, "I'm so turned on right now!" She got up off the floor and pulled her panties down. She walked to Jace and pushed him down on his back laying him down. Libby sat down on her brother startling him. His eyes grew huge as he realized his sister was going to be the one who took his virginity. Instantly his cock came back to life, Libby felt it return and placed herself on him.

Ash was really happy with herself. She had wanted to have sex with Jace because he was really cute, sweet, and shy meaning he was safe and wouldn't hurt her. She had figured if she led a sexually charged truth or dare game then one of two things would happen. She could either get dared to have sex with Jace or she would dare Libby to. But Libby had fucked him without a dare. Now Ash could get with him without it ruining their friendship, Libby couldn't possibly hold it against her for having sex with him if she had herself.

It only took a few minutes of riding Jace for Libby to tense up and cry out in pleasure. She fell forward on her brother and rolled off of him. Jace was still hard, he hadn't cum with his sister, probably due to the fact he had been thoroughly drained already tonight, and the fact that being her first time she hadn't rode him that hard or for very long.

Before Laney could take her chance Ash crossed the room and sat down next on Jace's cock. Ash placed her palms flat on his chest as leverage and pushed down on him hard. He slid into her deep and it felt so good having him inside herself. She had needed to fuck for so long and now her need took over as she rode him for all she could put into it.

Ash grinded him harder then she could ever remember fucking before. She realized this was really the first time she had ever just straight fucked a guy, she finally understood the comment Joey had said the night they had finally made love about knowing the difference between having sex and making love. She had made love so many times yet never really fucked.

Ash fucked Jace hard for as long as she could hold on. He was moaning wildly, and crying out her name. He began to shudder almost violently driving Ash crazy; she drove deeper on his cock every time he did so.

It wasn't long before he found one more orgasm and shot a small amount of fluid into her. She didn't know where he had found more fluid at this point. Between masturbating, the hand jobs, blowjob, and the fucking he still gave her one last blast of cum. It was enough to cause her to clamp down on him and orgasm herself, her orgasm was powerful and washed over her whole body.

Ash collapsed on Jace she had only had one orgasm but after waiting for so long the need to cum with a man had caused one so intense her body couldn't take it and she fell to him exhausted. Ash opened her eyes and looked around the living room. Libby was rubbing her clit furiously and Laney had her had inside her panties still fingering herself.

Ash rolled off of Jace and noticed her had passed out from exhaustion. He had been awake just a moment ago. She watched as his cock went limp and his breathing came back down to normal. She loved him for what he had done for her. He was only the second boy she had been with and she would always have a special place saved for this sweet boy. She rolled onto the floor next to the couch trying to catch her breath. She was really content for the first time all year.

"That's......... so........ Not .... fair," Laney panted out in breathes as she continued to finger herself, "You............ Guys........ Got.......... Off............ and............ I didn't." Ash felt bad for her, she was right it wasn't fair. She considered for a moment going over to her and helping her out. While she didn't mind kissing a girl she really hadn't liked licking a girl when she had tried it before, but this was Ash's game and they had left out Laney. Her body was still exhausted as she leaned against the couch, but she tried to move to help her friend.

"OOOOH YES!" Libby cried out as she hit her orgasm. Ash looked over at her for a moment as Libby now done with herself started to crawl over to Laney. Ash relaxed again as she watched Libby reach out and pull Laney's panties down and position her head between Laney's legs. It was so hot to watch her best friends doing this. If her arm would've worked she would've had to finger herself too.

It didn't take long of Libby's tongue on Laney's clit before Laney was crying out from her orgasm. Libby rolled over on her back all three girls still panting hard. Jace was snoring softly behind her.

As everyone calmed down and the sexual tension in the room slipped away everyone started pulling their clothes back on.

"What the fuck did we all just do?" Libby asked when they had all their shirts and panties on again. She sounded excited and horrified at the same time. She had a good reason to be. She hadn't even kissed before and now she had kissed a girl, given a hand job, fucked her brother, and eaten out a girl.

"We played a game," Ash stated not knowing which direction Libby was going to take things.

"I want to play this game every week!" Laney said, "And next time I want to do more than just get kissed and eaten out."

"Hell yeah," said Libby and Ash calmed down. Her game had worked and it looked like Libby wouldn't hate her for playing this trick on her to get at her brother. It was only then that Ash realized that this whole thing seemed vaguely familiar, like she had played this game before. It was truly in this moment that she realized this was basically the same thing she had done to Joey and Katie. She had used the sister to get with the brother. It didn't matter it had worked and she had gotten laid and Libby couldn't break up their friendship over it.

The girls pulled the blanket back over Jace instead of dressing him, before going to bed. They all were so tired now, climbing into bed together hugging each other as they fell asleep.

Ash woke early the next morning and went to the living room, she found Jace still sleeping. He was hard again from morning wood. She looked down the hall and saw the girls were still in the room. Ash moved the blanket and climbed on top of Jace, moving her panties to the side. She slid up and down on his erection. Jace woke at the movement and she put her hand over his mouth.

It didn't last long this morning, but Ash had mainly just needed to feel him inside her again, it felt good to feel him inside her. He came what felt like gallons inside her and she slipped off of him. She told him he had better get into his room before his parents came home this morning and found him naked on the couch.

Jace didn't argue he picked up his shorts and ran down the hall to his room. Ash went to the bathroom and cleaned herself up then took a shower. She felt sweaty and sticky, but the water revitalized her making her feel soft and clean again.

Ash woke Libby long enough to let her know she was going home. She had accomplished her mission twice. She felt a burning in her cheeks blushing at her own actions. She slowly started walking home, it was still early hours and it was colder hen the jacket she had on, at least it wasn't raining.

She was swimming in her own thoughts, in the name of getting laid she had led her best friend to commit incest and become bisexual. The bisexual thing didn't bother her but the incest thing did a little. She didn't realize she would feel so guilty about it afterwards.

Then again she hadn't really done much to encourage them. Libby had jumped on her brother without a dare. He had been looking at her with both want and need. Jace had even gotten harder for Libby then for her, so maybe she shouldn't be so hard on herself for being the instigator.

As the school year was nearly at an end Ash really hoped for another sleep over soon. She had a physical need she had to fulfill and now that she and Jace had crossed that line she didn't see it as a big deal to do it again. As things turned out the whole plan backfired on Ash. They never got a night alone at Libby's with no parents to try playing the game again.

The way the game had backfired on her had been after playing that night; the line had been crossed with Libby and Jace as well. Libby confessed a short time later that she and her brother were having sex all the time now when the parents were out of the house. This was a familiar story to Ash. She remembered when she and Joey had been like that too. Libby said that she and Jace weren't in love or anything silly like that but they were having lots of fun.

The last week of school she found out how completely her plan had backfired. She found out that Jace had asked Laney to be his girlfriend because he really had liked her most of all Libby's friends. Ash was slightly disappointed when she heard that. She never told Libby or Laney that she had a small crush on him, but she was happy for Laney, Jace was a good boy who would treat her good and with Laney being in on their secret Ash guessed it all work out in the end. Ash was curious with Jace dating Laney and sleeping with his sister, were Libby and Laney still hooking up too? She wondered but didn't bother to ask.

It wasn't long before Ash had to fly out to go to her sister Linda's for the summer. She wasn't looking forward to going, she still had unresolved feelings she wanted to discuss with Joey and it wasn't going to happen if she was gone.

Two days after school was out for the year, Ash had all her bags packed and found herself in the car on the way to the airport. Lilly had taken her because Joey's dad had felt sick and too tired to go. The girls talked on the car ride, Ash really loved her sister who had become like her mother. Lilly meant the world to her and she would miss her while spending the summer with what she always called her fun sister Linda.

Lilly stayed with Ash all the way to the plane's boarding entrance. They hugged goodbye and both girls actually cried as Ash boarded the plane. Ash had no idea when the doors closed and the plane made its way down the runway she would never be coming back to this home again. Her life here with Lilly and her husband was over and Ash was now flying into her new life.

Chapter Twelve: Death In The Family

Lilly had come alone to pick us up at the airport. When the three of us arrived she ran to us hugging Katie first, then me and then Abby. She said she was so happy to have us kids home. Lilly explained that it had been extra quiet the last week with Ash gone as well.

Lilly said she was glad to see Abby too, she had been surprised when she got the letter saying Abby was coming with us, but she had really liked Abby when I was dating her and thought it was great we all reconnected. I thought to myself you have no idea.

Katie asked where dad was, and Lilly just looked down for a minute, she looked as if she didn't want to answer that question. When she looked up she said he was feeling a little sick and had stayed at home. I didn't like the look in her eyes but I didn't question it while standing in the airport.

It took another hour to get out of the airport and get on the road home. Baggage pick up was really slow and the traffic trying to get out of the parking garage was horrible. But we made it out finally and had an enjoyable ride home.

It was on the way home that Katie said that she had something she needed to talk to her mother about when she had a minute alone. I knew she wanted to tell Lilly about her and Abby first. Then they could tell my dad when Lilly had a chance to calm down.

Keep in mind that this was the mid-nineteen nineties, and people didn't have the social openness about being gay that people have now. It was still very much a hidden thing back then. Lilly was a great woman but he values and mindset was still from a different time, in that respect Lilly was much older than her actual age.

The girls and I had talked on the plane and I told them that Lilly had always been cool with me when it came to things she realistically should be mad at me for. I reminded Katie that she knew I had, had a relationship with Ash and it didn't piss her off. All Lilly had said was that if it was out of love then it was ok, I told Katie to trust her mother and if she explained she and Abby loved each other than her mother would probably approve.

Katie kissed my cheek and asked me when I had gotten so smart all of a sudden. It was me who had suggested that she go out to lunch with her mom by themselves and talk about it. I figured that dad would be the one who would be more open minded of the two and that if Lilly was already over the shock of it when they told dad then she wouldn't make a big deal out of it when he was told. If Lilly didn't make a big deal out of it then I was sure dad wouldn't make a big deal out of it.

Abby agreed that it was a good solid way to come out to them. When the girls had gone home at Christmas to come out to Abby's parents, her mother had broken into tear and her father the reverend had simply walked out of the room, got into the car and didn't come home for hours. It had been a hard vacation for them as Abby's parents didn't want to discuss it and repeatedly told them it was just a phase and the girls would grow out of it. Abby's mom told them that they were committing their souls to hell as they went through this phase. In the end Abby's parents told her she wasn't to return until she found a

nice boy to settle down with and start a family. They wanted to make sure this life style was behind her before she could come back home, as it was not the example they wanted for her younger sisters.

Both the girls had decided that it had actually gone better than they had expected Abby had figured they would ask them to leave right away. Even so the girls didn't want a repeat of last Christmas when they got home to our house this summer.

As soon as we got home I helped unload the bags, Lilly told Abby she could use Ash's room while until she returned home at the end of summer then we would figure something else out. I had to stop from giving a little laugh. I knew it would be worked out a lot sooner than that. I didn't even bother to put Abby's bags in Ash's room I left them in Katie's room with all of Katie's bags.

As soon as we got home I asked Lilly how Ash had been lately. She smiled and said that after our talk at Christmas Ash had finally opened up to her and come back out of her shell. She said that she had made new friends and had found a way to be happy again. I felt like a rock slid off my back, I had felt so bad for leaving her so upset. If Ash had bounced back and found a way to be happy I felt I could finally and truly move on now, I told Lilly I was glad Ash was happy now, she patted me on the shoulder and walked into the kitchen to start fixing dinner.

I walked into my room and it was just as I had left it one year ago. Old clothes on the floor and bed slightly out of place as I had moved it against the door the night before I left.

I left my room and walked into Ash's room, I don't know why I walked into the room, but I did, I sat down on her bed and thought about last summer. It was so long ago in my head, living in this house and being with Ash seemed like another life and many years ago.

I don't know why I laid down on her bed; it still smelled of her perfume I realized I only missed her by days. Memories were flooding back and I really didn't want them too. I had moved on from her and all of this. I was returning soon to be with Jenny, and start a real grown up relationship with her and Anne.

That felt weird knowing I was heading down the road to be in a relationship with a girl who basically was a single mom. I had never really thought much about having kids and now I was looking at a situation that meant instant family if things worked out the way I hoped they did for us.

Yet here I was lying in the bed of another girl, thinking of her. Was it even possible for me to have a real relationship? I'm was tired of having to choose between all these great girls. It was driving me crazy. As I lay on her bed Ash herself gave me an answer. I was laying there remembering, day dreaming and thinking of Jenny when I slid my hand under the pillow my hand hit something.

I sat up and lifted the pillow to find an envelope with my name on it. Good God this girl really knew me, I thought to myself as I picked up the envelope. It's like she knew I would lie on her bed and find this; I tore it open and began to read:

> Joe,
>
> I really hope it's you that found this, and that it's you who's reading it now. I wanted so much to be home and talk to you in person this summer, but I know I will be gone before you get here. I'm really sorry about what I did; please know it really was all out of love.

I was so mad when you left but I understand now you were right. It made more sense for us to move on if we couldn't see each other except a couple times a year. I just wanted you to know you were my first love too, and will ever be my one true love. But I did move on this year and I ask if you haven't moved on, that you find someone to love. You're an incredible lover and I mean that in the sense of loving someone with your heart and showing them with your actions, not just sex.

It would make me sad again to know you aren't sharing yourself with someone special, it would mean your true nature was going to waist. I miss you and I will see you at the end of summer when if you don't have a girlfriend you have a promise to fulfill that I'm going to hold you to.

Love you so damn much
Ashley

I read the letter and folded it back into the envelope. It was strange that I had found it just in the moment I was thinking of her and about the future. I wouldn't see her at the end of summer however I was leaving early to go home to Jenny.

I felt happy that I could see the girl who I had fell in love with in that letter, the girl who was always one step ahead of me. I was glad she had moved on and found a way to be herself again. I hadn't liked the sound of the girl I left behind whose light had burnt out and hid in her room all the time.

I got up from her bed and stuffed Ash's letter in my pocket. I had been home for about 20 minutes and I realized I still hadn't seen dad. I walked down stairs to say hi to dad thinking he was probably in the rec-room. As I came down the stairs I was passing the kitchen when Lilly flagged me down.

"Joey," she called as I passed.

"What's up?" I asked entering the kitchen.

"Katie and I are going out to dinner tonight by ourselves; do you think you can help Abby with your guys' dinner?"

"Yeah I can do that," I started to leave the kitchen.

"Make sure your dad eats something. Tonight," she said and her face turned worried, "Don't let him tell you he's not hungry."

"Ok Lilly what's going on with dad?" I asked kind of harsh.

"He's just been sick and cranky. He's been home in bed for a week and doesn't want to eat."

"Ok. I was going to see him I'll take him some toast or something and make sure he eats." I hung out in the kitchen and made some toast.

I walked up the stairs and knocked on the door. I waited for a minute and walked in. Dad was lying on his side sleeping.

"Dad," I called to him pushing his shoulder.

"Oh hey Joey," he said groggily sitting up, "When did you get home?"

"Not long ago, I brought you some toast," I set the plate down on the end table, "What's going on with you?"

"Nothing to worry, I've just been under the weather," he grinned slightly. I was less than convinced; I really wish someone would give me a straight answer.

"Dad, don't bullshit me," I said sternly. I never swore to my father, "If you've been in bed for a week or more, then something is wrong."

"Really, I went to the doctor with some chest pains and flu like sickness. The doctor ran some tests and we haven't heard anything, really don't worry I'll be fine."

I didn't push it farther but I stayed in the room talking with dad until he ate all his toast. I told him about my classes and about the play. I didn't tell him about the life decision I had made regarding my change in major next year. I didn't want to upset him while he was sick. So instead I told him about Jenny and how much I was starting to fall for her.

"That's funny," he said to me, "I was so sure you would end up falling for Ash." I was shocked I had no idea he even knew anything about all that.

"Why would you say that?" I asked a little unconvincingly.

"I don't know if you realized this, but I could tell she has quite the crush on you," he said smiling, "Don't think I haven't noticed that you've been a little sweet with her too."

"She's a great girl and all, but I've never been in to her that way," I lied.

"Too bad."

So my dad wasn't completely oblivious. He hadn't picked up the whole story but he noticed enough for me to laugh inwardly. I let it go there and started talking about Jenny again.

"I'm just glad to hear you found someone nice, as long as you're happy Joey." Dad lay down again on the bed.

"I'm going to let you sleep now," I told him. I picked up the plate and left the room. I got back to the kitchen as Abby was cooking us some dinner.

"Just in time," she told me as I set the plate down in the sink, "How's your dad?"

"He's not doing well. There's something wrong with him that he isn't telling me," I informed her.

"I hope it's not too bad," she kissed my cheek reassuringly, "Katie and Lilly just left, they decided to go to shopping before dinner."

"So what are we fixing?" Abby and I ended up making some chicken and pastrami wraps and eating in the rec-room. We put in a movie, a girly movie because I let Abby pick, and we snuggled together on the couch. She curled up with me leaning her head on my chest.

"I'm going to hate it when you pull your head out of your ass and actually ask Jenny to be your girlfriend," she said softly, "I'm sure she won't want you snuggling like this with your ex-girlfriend." I hated to admit that Abby was right. I would have to stop being so friendly with her, even in innocent ways like right now, if I had a full time girlfriend.

"Me too." I kissed the top of her head, "But we still have right now, sis." I had just recently started calling her sis from time to time as a way of acknowledging her relationship with Katie. I now completely felt as Abby was my sister too. I also felt bad she had given up her own family for Katie so the nickname was also a show of familial acceptance.

It wasn't long into the movie before Abby was asleep in my arms. I woke her and told her she should go to bed, she was groggy but she got up and went upstairs. I watched the end of the movie and went upstairs myself.

I was laying on the bed in my old room feeling like I was a couple years younger. I felt like I had come so far this year, I had met a real girl, I knew what I wanted to do for the rest of my life, and I had time to pursue it. I slipped out of my clothes and pulled the covers over myself drifting off into sleep.

It was late when my door opened I woke as someone slipped into my room. It was Katie. She was wearing only a shirt and panties. The sight of her like that still got my dick so hard, even after all these years and all the sex we'd had.

"What are you doing?" I questioned as she climbed into bed with me.

"I needed to talk and I didn't want to wake Abby," she nuzzled up to me feeling my excitement for her as she did so. She looked down at my tenting boxers, "I can see you really don't mind me being here." she joked but she had a sadness to her words.

"I can't help it if I love my sister," I said it to reassure her more then to be cute. I put my arms around her back hugging her tight, "Tell me what's wrong."

"I had the talk with mom at dinner, she hasn't really said much," Katie wasn't crying but you could hear the disappointment in her voice, "I feel like I let her down."

"Tell me what happened," I said calmly.

"I told her that the reason Abby was here with us was because her and I had started dating last year. Mom was visibly shocked but before she could say anything I told her that I really love Abby and she loves me."

"What did Lilly say?" I asked rubbing Katie's back now.

"She didn't say much she only really asked why I hadn't told her sooner. I told her I didn't know how she would take it. All she said was that we could talk more about it later."

"Lilly's cool, I love your mom, she will be fine, this was why you girls went out alone," I reminded her.

"Yeah, I just couldn't stand that she really didn't talk to me the whole ride home."

I didn't answer her I rubbed her back. I saw a single tear form in her eye and I wiped it away. We embraced for a while when she kissed me deeply, I was already so hard but I had to stop I felt like we were cheating on Abby.

"Abby.............?" I questioned pulling away from our kiss.
"Its fine, we talked, she said when I needed my brother to love me, she didn't mind. Just like I didn't mind when she gave you a special birthday gift a couple weeks ago. The three of us are so wrapped up with each other we don't consider being with you cheating."

It had been over six months since I had been with Katie, and I couldn't control myself with her tonight. I knew this all had to stop if I was to have a real relationship with Jenny, but like I had told Abby we had the summer. I just didn't know how I was going to live with them next year and control myself.

I pulled her shirt off and rubbed her breasts through her bra with one hand as the other reached up from where I had been rubbing her back and I unhooked her strap. She was just as amazingly beautiful as ever as her bra fell to the bed and she lay there mostly exposed. I thought it was ironic that we were here doing his in our parents' home now, after all the time I had spent jerking off in this very bed wanting to have Katie in it with me.

I had really thought the last time after Christmas break would be the last time we'd ever sleep together. But we had tonight, and I wasn't going to pass on the chance of another one last time with her.

I was kissing her neck and gently rubbed her nipples. I could still feel the tension in her body, her mom's reaction had really upset her and I decided it was my job to take all that hurt and make it go away, if only for a little while right now. I wanted to make her feel love and approved.

"I love you so much," I whispered in her ear. I could see tears in her eyes forming now. I slid my hand into her panties, "You're the greatest sister, I'm so proud of you, I love your spirit, your laugh and yes your body." I could see tears rolling down her cheeks now but she was smiling. I knew I was doing what I had set out to. Her body had started to ease down now. I was rubbing her clit while talking to her and her body was starting to respond.

"I love you so much, I'll always be here to show you how much I love my big sister, no matter what happens you'll always have me there, all you have to do is call me to your side," there were more tears as she pulled me into a very soft deep loving kiss.

"Thank you," she said quietly, "I can't imagine my life without my toy store boy, I love you too." She slid her hand into my boxers and began to stroke me slowly. I pulled her panties down and she removed my boxers. I continued to kiss her lips as I rolled on top of her. I wanted very much to lick her pussy again but with no locks on the door I had a real fear of someone walking in on us.

I pressed my forehead to hers and looked into her eyes as I glided my cock into her waiting pussy. She moaned out as my head passed her lips, she took in a sharp breath as I continued inside her. She was

so tight this time; I hadn't remembered her being so tight. I thrust deeper and deeper inside her until I was all the way in. I kissed her again as I pumped her body.

After a couple minutes Katie rolled us over and took charge. She pushed down hard and bit her bottom lip to not cry out as she pushed back against my thrusting up. It was only rare times we had ever done it this rough; Katie had always been the calm one when making love. But tonight we didn't make soft, slow and delicate love like we had before. She grabbed my shoulders and pushed hard on her down stroke. Tonight we were straight fucking. I thought she was going to break my cock the way she was thrusting herself on me.

She stopped suddenly her pussy tightening on me; she reached down behind my head grabbing a pillow pushing it over her face. A muffled scream could barely be heard as she finished her orgasm. I came hard and deep, releasing shot after shot of hot cum inside her as she dropped the pillow back to the bed. She lay down on my chest kissing my neck.

"Thank you, little brother," she said panting. I couldn't talk I was breathing so hard. This was the most wild we had ever had sex and I was awestruck I didn't know she had it in her. She lay there kissing my neck as I began to drift off to sleep again.

I woke to hear someone in the hall. Katie was still lying on top of me. I panicked a little I really didn't need Lilly to open the door and see us having fucked, especially on the same night Katie had come out to her. Lilly didn't have any reason to look in here but I was still panicked. I heard Ash's door open and close, then footsteps at my door. I yanked the blanket up over us as my door opened.

Abby stepped into my room and I sighed. She stepped over to the bed and sat down. She was smiling at me as she looked at the contentment on Katie's sleeping face.

"I was getting worried, I didn't hear her come home yet and it's late," she whispered to me.

"She had a bad night and didn't want to wake you," I explained feeling guilty. It was weird I hadn't felt bad sleeping with Abby a couple weeks ago but I felt like I had betrayed them by sleeping with Katie.

"It's ok Joey you don't need to defend her being with you. I actually understand, sometime you just really need to fuck and feel loved. You manage to do both when we need it." I nodded, not sure if that was a complement or not.

We gently nudged Katie, waking her. Abby picked up Katie's clothes and walked her half asleep girlfriend back to their room. I lay back down on the bed. Here I was again falling to sleep smelling like sex yet all alone. Now that the activities were done I fell asleep feeling lonely again.

It turned out that Katie's fears were unfounded. I got up the next morning and got to the kitchen while Lilly was making breakfast for everyone. Dad didn't come down Lilly said he was still acting out of sorts and she would take him a plate when we were done eating.

The day was already warm and Lilly was wearing a pair of shorts and a tank top that in the morning light coming through the windows I noticed just how much she looked like Katie, just a little older. She was after all only 18 years older than me. For some reason her legs looked really nice this morning. I pushed those thoughts out of my head as I felt my shorts getting tighter. I didn't know what

had come over me, I'd never really thought about her that way. She was like my mom not a real girl, it was bad enough I had slept with my sister; I didn't need to have thoughts of Lilly too.

Katie and Abby came down a few minutes later, both wearing shorts and tank tops as well. I thought it was a bad day to wear loose shorts as I looked at all of them. I managed to control myself this morning, I was happy I really didn't want to get too excited with Lilly in the room. Abby walked into the kitchen and looked to Lilly awkwardly. Lilly looked up from her eggs a little awkwardly too. It was like they both wanted to say something but neither knew how to start. Katie stepped into the kitchen just after Abby and saw her and Lilly gazing at each other. Katie looked to me as if to say, HELP ME! But I didn't know what to say any more than anyone else. It was Lilly who finally broke all the tension in the room. She broke the stare and walked to Abby and hugged her.

"Everything's ok then mom?" Katie asked tentatively.

"Everything's just fine," Lilly said reaching out and pulling Katie into the hug, "I love you so much, little girl, I'm just happy you found someone to love you as much as I do."

"But last night, you seemed so............."

"I was just surprised, that's all," Lilly told them letting them go from the hug and turning back to her eggs, "When you said we needed to talk and we had to go out to dinner for this talk I was expecting the, I'm pregnant, talk. I wasn't ready for the, I have an alternative lifestyle talk."

"You're not mad?"

"I'm mad that you hid it from me for so long," Lilly said to Katie then she turned to Abby, "I adored you when you were dating Joey, I couldn't be happier that Katie chose you for her girlfriend."

With all of that settled we decided to wait to tell dad until he was feeling a little better. We all agreed we still didn't know how he was going to take the idea of the girls dating and it wouldn't hurt to hold off a little while longer.

Before I knew it I had been home for three weeks. I was worried about my dad more than ever. He hadn't returned to work and had started working from home by phone and his computer; they had managed to hook his computer up to this thing called the internet. Keep in mind that the internet was still not a common thing in every house in the mid-nineties. I asked all kinds of questions about what was going on with his flu like illness and was told I had nothing to worry about.

I pulled Lilly aside and asked her about it. She said he had been talking to the doctor privately and that he told her the same thing he told me, that he was fine just under the weather. Lilly did tell me she was taking him to the doctor in a couple days and she was going to try to ask him personally what was going on with dad. I thought again about how much I loved her as a mom. I knew she wouldn't lie to me about it.

I still hadn't told Dad and Lilly that I was leaving early for school this summer; I kept feeling like there was never a good time to tell them. I was running out of time as I had already been there for 3 weeks. I finally sat down with Dad and told him that I was leaving in another week or so. I really hated to leave when he was so ill but I wanted to get back to the girl I had told him about. To my surprise dad was happy for me, saying that I should go and be with Jenny if I really loved her. I wondered for a minute

when he had gained a romantic side. But living with Lilly the last few years had probably changed him; she had that kind of vibe to her.

I got my ticket situated and a week or so later I got all my things packed as it was time to leave. It had just rolled over into August and it was a Wednesday morning and I went to my dad and wished him well and I gave Katie and Abby a hug goodbye. I told my sisters that I would see them in just a month and I loved them so much. Lilly drove me to the airport, we didn't say much about anything the whole ride. Lilly walked me all the way to the gate, giving me a big hug and telling me she loved me.

"I love you too, mom," it was the first time I had ever called her that. I could see her fighting back a tear as I said it. She smiled at me and hugged me again. I boarded the plane wishing I really didn't have to leave yet, but I had a promise to keep and I really missed Jenny.

The plane ride wasn't long and I was at home again. It was late in the day as I got home; I knew Jenny would be putting Anne down for bed soon. I decided that I would surprise them early in the morning tomorrow so we all could go do something. That meant I had a free night to myself at home. I reached the door and went inside. The apartment felt not just empty, but cold as I walked through it alone. It was now just August and the night was warm but I got really cold that night. It was about 80 degrees outside but I had to cover up with a blanket.

I woke on the couch, it was already over 70 degrees outside and I was freezing for some reason. I was beginning to wonder if I had come down with something, but I just got up and headed for the shower. I felt better as soon as the hot water hit my body. It must have been some kind of jet leg or something from the flight last night.

I partially unpacked my bag from the trip and thought to hell with it I will finish unpacking later. I got dressed in a pair of jeans and a light t-shirt, thinking the day was going to get hot from the look of things. I left the apartment and headed over to Jenny's place. The car ride seemed to take forever as I thought about what to say to her.

I had spent the last month thinking about her every day, thinking I couldn't wait until I could get back here and be with her. But as I drove the same weird feelings took me over that I'd had the last day we had spent together. I knew she would ask me how I felt about her and the closer I got to her apartment the more I was overwhelmed with fear. I was about to make a big leap of faith with her and I was scared. I didn't know where this fear was coming from. Jenny was really smart, she had a good job, she was kind, she had a big heart, and she was amazing in everything she did, from simply smiling, to charity work, to looking after Anne. I liked her so much I couldn't imagine a future without her, yet I still couldn't say I loved her, even in my own head.

I got to Jenny's apartment and sat in my car. What would I say to her when she asked me if I loved her back? I knew I was starting to but I wasn't ready, I was too scared to even think the words back to her. I finally left my car and walked to her door, I could hear Barky living up to his name as I knocked.

Jenny came to the door wearing a pair of shorts and a half t-shirt showing off her whole stomach, she looked hotter than I had ever seen her before.

"Your back!" Jenny cried and jumped on me, wrapping her arms and legs around me. She was hanging off my neck kissing me deeply, I could feel myself getting hard I already found myself willing

myself down, I didn't want to be hard in front of Anne if she came running to say hi, or be hard if Anne gave me a hug hello. I would've been horrified if that happened.

"Wait............" I pulled away from her, "We shouldn't do this now what if Anne........" She cut me off with a kiss. It was hopeless there was no stopping now. I slowly walked us inside and leaned over the couch; she dropped down and pulled me to her. I looked around the room scanning for signs that Anne might be there and see us.

"Don't worry," Jenny said caressing my cheek, "She's not here; my parents took her for a few weeks over the summer to give me a break."

I didn't need to hear another word, pulled her shirt off her and began kissing her again. I kissed her deep and aggressively our tongues dancing passionately as the need to be with each other was exploding within us. I had missed her so much more desperately then I had imagined.

I felt a sudden stab of guilt as I kissed her, I really did have such strong feelings for her, she was the most incredible person I had ever met yet I had slept with my sisters since the last time we had been together. I felt like some kind of a monster for caring so deeply for Jenny and still being able to love and have sex with Abby and Katie. I knew as much as I tried I would never be able to resist my sisters, I loved them too much. I made a decision as I kissed Jenny, I chose her, in that moment I completely chose Jenny meaning I would have to move out of my sisters apartment.

I started kissing her neck and she moaned in delight. She reached behind herself and unhooked her bra. I took the hint and began moving lower. I massaged one breast as I kissed her neck at the shoulder and moved lower. She pulled my shirt off and ran her hands over my chest. I ran my hand from her breast down to the crotch of her shorts. I began rubbing her through the fabric; she moaned louder and clamped her thighs against my hand grinding her hips.

I moved my kisses lower making it to the top of her breasts. Jenny and I had only ever made love the one night at the theater house and I hadn't had a chance to really go slow with her like I was doing now. I planned to take full advantage of our time now as I ran the tip of my tongue along her breast surrounding her nipple but not actually touching it, causing her to groan in anticipation and twitch slightly as I did so.

I really liked the response she was giving me, she was moaning insanely without asking for me to stop or move forward, she gave me complete control of her body. I finally lightly flicked her nipple and she shuddered with pleasure.

"Please don't make me wait anymore," she finally begged softly grinding her hips harder against my hand.

I sucked her nipple into my mouth and lightly bit down. Her whole body arched as I did so. I pulled my hand from her crotch and slid it up into the leg of her shorts over her panties. I could feel her soaking through the thin cotton barrier as I rubbed her slowly, teasing her body. She was moaning wildly back arching again.

"Your such an................" she didn't finish as she moaned loud and her body tensed up and her first orgasm hit her hard. I kissed her mouth again, "I didn't know I could get off that easily," she whispered.

165

"I know a trick or two," I said grinning.

"I think I'm ready for the next trick," she said grinning back,

I moved slowly back down her chest focusing my attention on her other nipple this time. She was moaning almost instantly as I sucked her nipple in, grinding her hips harder against my hand. She reached down and unbuttoned her shorts and pushed them off then did the same to her panties. I slid two fingers inside her and pushed her clit with my thumb. The reaction I got was a thrusting motion from her hips.

I decided I had played long enough I slid down the couch and began to lick her swollen nub slowly in a circular motion. She cried out almost instantly as I did that. It was like she was still a virgin the way she was reacting to me. I realized that she had only had one lover before me but how little attention had he paid her if she was still this sensitive to small teasing? I licked her clit hard twice and her pussy clenched up on my fingers as she had another orgasm.

"OH GOD OH GOD," she cried her back arching again then falling to the couch, "I need a minute," she panted and scooted away from me. She got up and wobbled her way to the kitchen as if she were dizzy; she opened the fridge and pulled out a gallon jug of orange juice, pouring herself a glass.

When she had finished her juice she walked more steady back into the living room and took my hand, leading me into the bedroom. We stood by the bed for a minute kissing as she undid my pants letting them fall to the floor.

"I've been waiting all summer for this," she whispered sexily in my ear. Pulling down my boxers and gripping me with her skinny delicate hand.

We lay down on the bed sideways facing each other and continue kissing, as she slowly and almost too gently stroked my cock. Lying in bed with her like this feels like heaven. I don't know what I ever did right that I deserve to be here now with her. My need for her now was burning but I let her take control with me now as she had let me control giving her pleasure a few minutes ago.

She was kissing my neck now, I massaged her breasts and she started humming softly. It was different; it was almost a purr as she continued down my body. She rolled me over on my back and kissed her way lower.

When she reached my cock she kissed the head gently, then the shaft working her way to my balls. It seemed like she was trying to do the same type of teasing I had done to her, but she hadn't much practice at it yet. It was still driving me crazy.

She sucked in one of my balls as she continued stroking me a little firmer now. I was willing myself to hold it in but I lost the fight and I came, one, two, three shots of cum shooting out of me running down her forehead covering her face.

"Wow," she said wiping cum off her face and licking it off her hand. I almost came again watching her do that. As I've said before, watching girls eat or swallow my cum is a MAJOR turn on for me. I stayed hard as she enveloped my cock in her mouth cleaning me and sucking me hard.

166

I lifted her head off of me and pulled her into a hard kiss. I rolled her onto her back, I couldn't wait anymore. I moved onto her body and opened her legs enough to slip myself inside her. It was as perfect of a fit as it had been the first time. She was so right for me in so many ways, but in bed she was perfect. I had said last time it was as if she was made for me, I felt so this time too. She was tight without being feeling like a vise and worm without feeling like she was on fire. I was back in heaven again, I was moving within her on a physical level but my mind was swimming in another world.

It was Jenny who came first this time, her body seized up on me squeezing my cock; I kept going through her orgasm, pushing her harder and deeper. Her back arched and she thrust back against me with more power then she had before. It was minutes later I came inside her. I didn't have as much as my first orgasm but I had given her enough it was leaking out as I continued pumping inside her. Only minutes later I felt her body tensing up again I knew she was close, I thrust as fast as I could trying to meet her and come together. It happened seconds later I felt her clamping down on me and I let loose my third orgasm. I came hard and fell over on the bed.

I looked at my watch as Jenny lay trying to catch her breath. We had been in the bedroom since morning and it was the afternoon already. I was shocked. It had felt like we made love for a long time but I wouldn't have guessed hours. Jenny was the only girl who I could last this long with. I literally had no idea how I had managed to keep it up this long.

Once Jenny had her breath back she snuggled into me, her back against my chest. I put my arms around her stomach and pulled her to me as tight as I could.

"I missed you so much," she said to me quietly, "I didn't know it could be like that, so intense, so loving and so long."

"I'm only like that with you," I told her honestly, "You bring it out of me." I began kissing her shoulder to her neck and back to her shoulder, just slow light kisses.

"I take it this means you want to ask me something………. Officially?" she asks both quietly and hopefully. I continued kissing her now on the back of her neck.

"I'm falling for you," I told her still feeling I was holding back slightly, "So much so in fact I'm starting to feel like I……" before I could say the last words she turned and kissed me to stop me.

"I love you, Joey; you're the sweetest guy I've ever met. You have and incredible heart, and you show love though your words and your loving, but don't say it if you're not ready," her words were soft but stern. Her face was worried, beyond tense.

"I love you Jenny, I fell for your heart when I was coming with you to your charity, I fell for your mind as we talked books and rehearsed the play, and I fell for your compassion for life somewhere long before that night in the dressing room," I paused to breath, I had said it, she was crying and now was the moment to be most honest with her.

"I was just scared to admit it before now because everything happened so fast. I've been deeply in love before and she……………" I didn't know how to put it exactly, at first I thought Ash had just played me, then I thought maybe she might have really loved me, but what I had come to realize is that no matter if the love we felt was real, our relationship hadn't been real. Even if the intentions behind it were meant

for good and there was real love there it had been a con game and I didn't know the real Ash. I couldn't explain this to Jenny, "............... It ended with both of us never speaking again."

"I'm sorry," she said sweetly and rubbed my cheek, "I can see you still love her."

"On some level I always will," I told her.

"I will never hurt you," she whispered in my ear, "I'm going to keep you forever." We began kissing again, our passion taking over, leading into our next love making.

Jenny and I stayed in bed for the rest of the day and the next. We only got up to get food and come back to bed. She called in sick to work on Friday so we could stay together the whole day. She said there was enough coverage on the weekdays they should be ok without her; she had missed me too much to leave me yet.

We talked and made love, ate junk food, made love again. It was nice to be in love, have a girlfriend and make love without having to be somewhere or worry about someone catching us. It was nice to finally go to sleep with someone in my arms, my girlfriend in my arms.

It was Saturday morning and Jenny had a weekend shift at work she had to get off to. We took a shower together that morning, I loved being able to wash her up and down, and I loved the feelings of her hands running across my whole body. We had to stop because I was getting too worked up and she had to get to work. After we got out of the shower and dried off I decided I would go home and get a change of clothes and hang out until Jenny was off work again and I would come back. We kissed at her door headed for our separate cars.

I thought I should actually spend the day looking for a job; I had quit mine at the end of June. Both Abby and I really wanted to go back to my parent's house this summer and our jobs had said that if we left for the summer they would have to replace us. Katie had been lucky, he firm she filed for liked her so much they were willing to let her go with the promise to find her something when she came back. So the three of us had talked and Abby and I quit our jobs. This left me needing work now that I was back. I decided to stick with my original plan and stay home and relax today.

I was actually content on the drive home that morning. I had, had a great couple of days. I thought I really was in love with Jenny. She was so amazing in all these ways who wouldn't be in love with her. It wasn't the crazy burning love like I'd had with Ash a year ago, but I was older and had gone through more life lessons. I felt like the love I had for Jenny was just as strong just in a more mature fashion.

I walked into the apartment and I found my answering machine light was blinking. Now for you young people out there we didn't have cell phones attached to our arm back then, so we often didn't know what was going on until we came home and checked messages. Now I had been gone for two days and there were a lot of messages on my machine.

I hit the button for the messages to play back and the tape started to rewind. I walked into the bathroom to take a leak as the first message started to play.

"Joey, its Katie are you home?................. Something's happened, come on pick up............... ok call the house as soon as you get this."

The next three messages were the same. I wondered what the big deal could be that she was calling me so much. I walked back into the kitchen and was looking for a can of something I could eat. I hadn't gone grocery shopping and the apartment had been empty for a month. The messages played on.

"Joey, pick up, did you make it home?" It was Abby this time, "Your starting to worry us, Katie has been trying to get a hold of you since yesterday. Come on Joey, please be home and pick up." Abby was crying and I knew something was really wrong. Abby wouldn't just be crying because I wasn't home. Katie had said something happened and it must be big. The messages played on.

"Joey it's Abby, I don't know what's going on with you right now but it's Friday night, we need you to call home, I didn't want to tell you over a message but something happened here, we need you back here. It's your dad and Lilly, call me!"

I didn't wait to hear the next message I turned off the machine and called my parents' house.

"Hello," Came Abby's voice, she sounded tired and like the life had gone from her.

"It's Joey, what's going on?"

"Oh thank god you're ok!" She exclaimed, "I was getting really worried, where you have been?"

"Let's just say Jenny and I had a long talk about our new relationship. So what's going on there?"

"Uh Huh, I know what that means, so can she still walk?" Abby asked, it seemed like she was stalling for time.

"So what's going on there?" I asked again.

"So did you tell her you love her?"

"Abby, quit circling around the question, what's going on?"

"I really didn't want to be the one to tell you," her voice dropped as she finished the sentence.

"Just tell me, for crying out loud!" I practically shouted.

"Your dad and Lilly are .... are in the .... Hospital."

"What happened," I fell down on the couch as I asked.

"They were on the way home from the doctor........................ when a bus ran a red light........... They got hit, your dad .... Your dad................... He won't make it much longer."

"What???" I was in disbelief, this couldn't be happening, "What about Lilly," I asked hoarsely.

"She's hurt, but they think she'll be ok."

"I'm on my way home. I need to talk to Jenny and I'm leaving now, I'm driving so I'll be a couple days."

"Are you sure you're ok to drive?" Abby asked.

"I don't care I'm not leaving you guys alone to go through all of this." I was already heading to my room to repack the bag I had brought home the other night, "Tell Katie I'll be as fast as I can." I hung up and finished repacking my bag.

I ran out the door going full speed to the car. I started the car and pulled it into gear and headed down the road before even putting my seat belt on. I was driving way over the speed limit and wasn't slowing down.

Chapter Thirteen:
Ashley's Diary Part 2: Summer Fling

It was a really hot afternoon when Ash got off the plane. Linda was there waiting as she came through the gate. Ash was happy to see her sister. Despite everything else going on in her life she did really like finally being able to spend some real time with her sister.

"I missed you so much!" Linda said to Ash as she pulled her into a hug.

"Me too," she responded, "So what's the plan sis?"

"I thought you would like to go out for dinner someplace nice tonight and this weekend I have some friends I want you to meet."

The girls went over to the coffee stand and bought lattés before they shuffled down to baggage claim and waited. It took only about a half an hour before they were on their way home.

Ash found it kind of exciting to be in a new place. She hadn't ever done any traveling except for having to move since her parents had died. She thought about all the changes in her life since then.

Ash was looking forward to spending time with her sister but she only wished she could have brought Libby or Laney with her too. She didn't know anyone here and it would be nice to have someone her own age to hang out with when her sister was at work. The first night with Linda was really fun they went to the movies and out to Mexican food dinner. Ash went to sleep feeling truly happier then she had in so many nights.

The next morning Linda told Ash she was taking her to meet her new boyfriend and his son. Linda told her that she had just started seeing a man named James, he was a couple years older than Linda and had a son who was 13 named James Travis who they all called Jt. Ash wasn't that excited about meeting new people but she didn't let it show, she acted exited for her sister.

Ash wanted to make a good impression so she decided to wear something nice, but it was looking to be a hot day already so she compromised. She chose a nice black short sleeve button up shirt and a black skirt. She looked pretty and the skirt would help her keep a little cooler today then jeans.

It was Saturday mid-morning when Linda led her across the apartment complex to James' door. Ash thought it must be nice for Linda to have a boyfriend so close to home. James answered wearing black Khaki shorts and a black t-shirt, Ash was immediately taken with his looks. She understood what her sister saw in him as she had to stop herself from staring.

"Ash this is James," Linda explained and Ash shook his hand, "And James this is Ash."

"Hi," she squeaked out weakly, he was hansom and had a really nice build, she could feel the dampness starting under her skirt. She pushed that thought out of her head, she was 15 and he was 20 years older than her.

They walked into the living room and sat down. James said that his son was in his room if Ash wanted to go introduce herself. Ash hung out in the living room for a few minutes as her sister and James talked, finding herself increasingly board with the conversation.

She found herself looking at James and her eyes slowly sank down to his shorts. She started wondering how big he was, if a grown man would feel better inside her. Ash snapped her head back up and looked at the wall past James. She couldn't figure out what was wrong with her, she had never been interested in older guys before, why would this man affect her now?

"I think I will go down and see what your boy is up too," Ash told them after a short while. She just wanted to walk away from James for a minute and this was the best excuse she could think of.

"Ok, tell him not to spend the whole day in his room," James said pleasantly, "It's nice out, maybe you can get him to take you to the park, and show you around the neighborhood since your new here." Ash knew James meant well but she really had no intention of wondering around the neighborhood with some teenage boy who, if he looked like his dad, would probably be all over her.

Ash knocked on Jt's door and waited. When no one answered she knocked again and went in. Sitting on the bed reading a book was a skinny freckled boy wearing pajama bottoms and a t-shirt, he looked like he was about 11 years old, but Linda had said he was 13. She instantly realized he wasn't what she had expected as James' son. She knew that even if this kid could work up the nerve to ask her out she could cut him off with a glance.

"Hi, I'm Ash," she said extending her hand. He nervously shook it for a second and pulled away as if he would be slapped.

"Jt," he muttered as he pulled away.

"Your dad said I was supposed to tell you to walk me to the park. So let's go to the park," she said. He smiled weakly at her and she liked him instantly, Ash smiled back and he looked like he would faint.

Ash's brain was moving quickly, she thought it was cute that he was so shy at 13. She knew right there her goal for the summer was to help break this shy boy out of his shell. She had done it before with Jace and she liked the challenge, besides this kid needed a back bone.

"Come on let's go," Ash said reaching out and taking his hand. Ash could actually see his pants tenting up as she took his hand.

"Ok," he replied quietly pulling his hand back as he stood up, "I need to get dressed first."

"Ok, but don't keep me waiting," she told him leaving the room and giving him a wink.

"So what did you think of Jt?" Asked Linda when Ash had returned to the living room.

"I don't know, I'll make up my mind if he decides I'm not so scary to talk to," she said and gave a small giggle.

"Yeah, I was scared of girls at his age too," James said smiling. Ash's body tingled again when he smiled at her.

"Just be nice to him, don't torture him too much," Linda said jokingly. She had no idea that Ash's plan was to torture him just not in the way Linda thought.

The idea of having a virgin to play with appealed to her, she figured if she was going home after the summer and she might as well have a fun game of him now. It was evil and she knew it but she liked the idea of being evil.

Jt came out of his room about 15 minutes later wearing jeans and the same t-shirt, his face was flushed and Ash knew exactly what he had been doing. She ran over and took his hand and led him to the door.

"Be back in a couple hours," Linda called to her. Ash nodded.

"We won't be back before two hours either," Ash told her nodding to James. She thought she would give her sister a couple hours alone with James. Ash pulled Jt out the door.

"Where to?" she asked and Jt pointed in a direction off to the left of them, "Its ok you can talk to me, I'm just a girl." She giggled and bumped her hip sideways into his as an acknowledgement.

"Ok," was all he managed.

The two kids walked without a word for about ten minutes when Ash realized she was going to have to put in real work to break this kid. She was still holding his hand and she couldn't tell with his jeans on if he was hard but she figured it was a good chance. She understood that it was embarrassing him and that's why he wasn't talking to her.

"So tell me about yourself," Ash said as an ice breaker.

"I'm Jt," he said and looked away from her.

"I think we accomplished that already," she giggled intentionally, "Tell me something other than your name, what do you like? What do you do for fun? Do you have a girlfriend?" Ash knew the answer to that but she was starting her game with him.

"Umm, I like to read," He was quiet but at least he was speaking, "I go to the movies for fun, and I haven't ever............ I don't have a girlfriend." He was blushing brighter than the sun.

"It's ok, I like books and I'm glad you don't have a girlfriend," she told him and winked at him. His face actually went redder then it already was. She really liked him, his shy nature was a real change from most boys at school who were always hitting on her or making inappropriate comments to her. That had been why she liked Jace so much as well, the shy thing really got her.

What she liked about the shy thing was that it gave her control to speed up or slow down things at her pace. She didn't ever want to be one of those girls who were pushed into things she didn't want to do, they usually ended up pregnant, raped or beat up. Shy nice boys like Jace and Jt wouldn't do that to her.

They reached the park and Ash led Jt to the swings and they both sat down on one and began to swing themselves. Ash noticed Jt looking at her legs as her skirt shifted in the breeze.

Slowly she got Jt to talk to her, and found that he had a lot of similar interests when it came to books and movies. Joey had gotten herself and Sara into reading when she was 13 and she was glad he had, she loved to read now. It seemed Jt had the same interests in reading and Ash felt it was nice to finally have a new friend that she could talk books with.

As they talked his innocence was intoxicating to her. She decided that she liked him, and wanted him as her pal for the summer. Since Libby and Laney couldn't be here she decided right there sitting on the swing the very first day of her summer at Linda's she was going to adopt this kid as he summer pal and if possible, fuck buddy. It would be the perfect summer fling she could tell the girls about when she got home.

After swinging for a while Ash took his hand again and led him to the park's party pavilion where they could sit down and talk all alone. They sat on the table top putting their feet on the bench seat. Ash almost wished Jessy was here to walk; it was a nice day and a great park for dogs.

As they were talking a gust of wind blew through the pavilion and blew her skirt up her legs revealing her blue panties to Jt. She pushed her skirt back down her legs and looked at him, as he turned red as a stop light. She giggled and took his hand holding it as they talked. She could now definitely make out the outline of his erection pushing against his jeans. She didn't know why that turned her on so much but it did.

Ash looked at her watch and realized they had been talking for a long time as their two hours were almost up. They would have to get going back to the apartment soon. With only a month and a half until she returned home Ash realized she was going to have to move fast with Jt. She didn't have a year and a half like she had taken with Joey or even the couple of months she had waited for Jace. If she wanted to play with him all summer, she would have to start now.

"We should be heading back soon," Jt said as he saw her look at her watch.

"We can't leave yet."

"Why not?" he asked.

"Because I've been waiting for the last hour for you to kiss me already, I'm not going back until you do." The look of shock on his face was unbelievable, it almost made her laugh, but she didn't want to upset him by laughing.

"But.............. I'm 13 and .... your 15!" he stammered.

"So what, you like me right?" She asked suddenly wondering why she was worried about the answer; this was just a game, a summer fling.

"I……… do." he said as he was nervously shaking, "I've never….."

Ash took control and leaned in and kissed him. He really had never kissed anyone before. She had to show him what to do as she gently used her tongue to open his mouth. It wasn't the best kiss she had ever had, but it was his first kiss and she was patient about his lack of experience. They kissed for about ten minutes as Jt really started to get the hang of it. When he started to finally get into it he was beginning to really turn her on.

Ash pulled away and looked around at the deserted park. They had a little bit of privacy where they were but that could change at any time. She was trying to decide what to do with him and how soon. She looked down to see a round stain on the front of his jeans. It looked like he had cum for her from just kissing. This made her a little wet, so looking around for people she pulled him back into another kiss.

Jt was really getting into this now, using his tongue, trying to taste every inch of her mouth. She unbuttoned her shirt halfway and reached for his hand, placing it inside her shirt. His body tensed up as they were kissing and she realized he came again touching her breast. The kissing heated up, god he's getting good quick, she thought to herself.

With his right hand caressing her breast though her bra, she took his other hand and pulled it up into her skirt against her panties. His whole body shuddered as he felt her wetness, and began to awkwardly rub the outside of her panties. He moaned as he first made contact and she thought he might have cum again. This was a big day for him; she actually found it cute he was so turned on by her and was couldn't control how often he had cum for her.

Ash was pushing herself trying to orgasm, but he wasn't experienced enough to get her there by himself. She would have to teach him where to touch when they had more time and privacy. For now she wasn't going to take any clothes off and show him the spots while people could walk by. She wasn't the exhibitionist Joey and Abby had been at her age from all the stories Joey had told her.

After about a half an hour of his rubbing she grabbed his hand and held it to her soaked panties and grinded her hips against it. It only took a couple minutes for her to cum that way; she squirted in her panties drenching them. She broke their kiss and looked around, seeing no one she pulled her skirt up and pulled her panties off using the dry area at the top to wipe herself off. She didn't want her juices getting though her skirt and making a wet stain on the front.

She through her panties in a nearby trash can and sat back down on the table top with Jt. He had stared at her wide eyed the whole time she had pulled up her skirt. She could tell despite spraying his underwear a number of times he was still straining the fabric of his jeans.

"Warn me when you're about to cum," she said unzipping his pants. Jt leaned back resting his palms on the table top, his eye staring so hard at what she was doing she thought his eyes would explode. Ash reached into his sticky wet pants and looking around again pulled out his hard cock. She began stroking it fast as his breathing was so erratic she thought he was about to have a heart attack.

"I um…………" he sputtered and she got out of the way quickly as he shot a huge blast of cum past her, then another and a third. It all hit the bench seat near his feet, some hitting his shoe. When he was done he quickly stuffed himself back into his jeans and stepped down off the table. He stepped into her and kissed her again. It was a really good kiss, she had set something off in this boy and he was not only learning fast, but getting over his fears fast.

"Um.............. Thank you," he said politely as he broke their kiss, "We need to get home." He was right they had now spent way past the time they were supposed to be out. They started the walk back home and as it turned out it was good timing as they reached the edge of the park a family with kids and a dog drove up and got out of the car. They might have been caught had the family been a few minutes sooner.

Ash felt really exposed as she walked home with no panties under her skirt. She felt like everyone who looked at her could tell and it made her very self-conscious. Jt now reverted back somewhat too. On the walk home he talked to her but his former shyness took front stage as their moment was over and he became actually more nervous around her after the fooling around.

Ash looked at his pants as they neared the apartment; he still had a large stain on the front. She had hoped the heat of the day would dry it out before they got home but it didn't. She looked down at herself checking for stains and realized her shirt was still half open. She fixed her shirt happy she had no wet spots she could see. It would be bad enough if Linda and James saw Jt, but she could pass it off like he was a shy horny boy and they leaked around girls some times. She wouldn't be able to bluff if she came home all wet too.

As soon as they walked through the door Jt walked quickly to his room and closed the door.

"You're an hour late," Linda said to Ash.

"Don't look at me I was lost," Ash told her, "I just followed him around town and didn't know my way back."

"Did you guys at least have fun?" James asked.

"Did you get him to actually talk to you?" Linda asked.

"Yes and after a time yes to both questions." She couldn't help smile.

"Wow what's your secret? I can never get him to talk to girls," James joked.

"I don't know I stopped talking to him and told him to tell me about himself, once he got going he started to feel ok talking to me, he stopped shaking and everything."

It was at that point Jt came back out of his room, Ash noticed he was wearing fresh jeans. She smiled inwardly at that.

"So did you have fun with Ash, Jt?" James asked, "You kept her out for a long time, anything I should know about?" James was joking but Jt looked at me and ran back to his room.

"Isn't that cute," Linda said, "I think he has a crush on you."

"I think your right," James said they both laughed.

Linda and Ash stayed until after dinner that night. The four of them sat around the living room watching a movie and talking while eating hamburgers James grilled up on the back deck. Jt hardly said a

176

word all night, he would only look over at Ash awkwardly and blush. Ash liked having a secret with him, her game had started well and she planned on playing it all the way through.

After dinner Linda and Ash returned to Linda's apartment and Ash went to bed right away, saying she was tired. She changed into a night shirt and put on panties. Once in bed her hand found her sweet spot and began rubbing. She had liked the feeling of his inexperienced hand against her. Joey had known too much when they had begun to play with each other and Jace and Ash had never had a chance to play as they had only had sex that one weekend. This would be a whole new game and some new experiences with him. Her body tensed up and she squirted some on her hand, she pulled her hand out of her panties and wiped it on her sheets. She was content as she fell to sleep.

The next day Linda and Ash spent with James and Jt, arriving not long after breakfast. Ash was wearing a denim skirt and a t-shirt, while Linda had on a tank top and shorts. When they got to James' apartment both the boys were wearing black Khaki shorts and t-shirts.

The four of them got in the car and drove to the mall were they went shopping. After looking around in some music and book stores, Linda told James that her and Ash were going to do a little more personal shopping and they would catch up with him and Jt in about an hour, James kissed Linda and took Jt to the movie shop for a while.

Ash had complained to Linda that morning she might not have packed enough of the right clothes for such a hot state. Linda was excited to take her out and buy her some cute clothes. Ash told her she had also forgotten to pack enough panties and wanted to shop for some of those too. Ash wanted to mainly replace the ones she had thrown in the trash and maybe find some sexy little panties that she could let Jt see soon.

The girls had fun trying on outfits for the next hour before they had to meet back up with the boys. Ash had gotten some very cute tops and a couple more skirts and six pair of sexy panties.

Once everyone was together again they had lunch at the mall food court. Jt was still turning red every time Ash spoke to him, which James kept jokingly picking on him about. After lunch they decided to make a whole day of being at the mall and headed over to the movie theater. They picked a family comedy, Ash and Jt went in to find seats while Linda and James went to get popcorn and drinks.

Jt sat in the middle of the theater next to the wall, Ash was next to him, with Linda on her other side, James on the end. The movie had barley started and James put his arm around Linda and she leaned into him. With Linda pulled away from Ash and looking up at the screen Ash decided to take another step at getting Jt over his shyness.

Ash reached over and held his hand, noticing his shorts lifting when she did so. He was so cute, so easily excited and so irresistibly nervous. She could feel him shaking as she set the back of her hand down on his thigh as he held her hand.

As the movie played Ash glanced over at Linda making sure she wasn't looking at her or Jt. Ash broke the contact from his hand and slid her hand up the leg of his shorts. He looked over at her panicking and she lightly shook her head then nodded at the screen. Jt got the point and turned his face back to the screen, his mouth was pressed shut and he felt to her as he might shake himself to death. She slid her hand under the leg band of his underwear and gripped his dick.

She moaned and reached behind herself unhooking her bra. He was still kissing her with his eyes closed as she fumbled with the hooks, finally getting them undone, she could feel his surprise as her bra fell and his hand ran across her bare breasts.

He broke their kiss and dropped his hand as he stared at her breasts, Ash knew this was the first time he had ever seen a real girl's breasts. She smiled as he gazed at her chest, his other hand still on the outside of her panties but had stopped moving.

"Happy birthday," Ash giggled as he snapped out of his stare.

"Um............ Thank you," he managed. Ash thought it was so cute, he had his hand on her panties, she was half naked with him and he had attacked her with a raw passion, yet when he talked he still had all the nervousness she had liked in him to begin with.

Ash leaned in and kissed him again. His whole body sized up when her lips made contact, as he had what had to be the biggest orgasm she had seen him shudder through. When he began kissing her again she felt his hand fumbling around her panties again.

She got up off the couch and took off her skirt and panties, her torn shirt still sitting on her shoulders. She sat back down on the couch again and guided his hand to her wet pussy. She showed him where and how to touch her. As with the first kiss he was a fast learner, and she could feel her orgasm building right away.

Ash was about to cum when Jt suddenly stopped, she looked up to see him sizing up again, he had cum again and she could see a large stain on his shorts. She grinded against his fingers as he sized up and her orgasm hit her. She shuddered slightly and her back arched for a moment before she fell to the couch.

They went back to kissing and Ash leaned him back on his side of the couch, slowly she slid her hand up the leg of his shorts feeling his hardness. She was going to take her game up one more level today and give him a birthday present to remember. She stroked his cock slowly and firmly and as before it only took a minute or two for him to cum again.

She pulled away from his lips and removed her hand, his breathing was heavy and she could almost hear his heart beating, punching the inside of his chest as she unbuttoned and unzipped his shorts.

Ash pulled his shorts and briefs down quickly reveling his still hard cock. She knew what kind of hair trigger he had so she didn't waist anytime teasing as she took his cock in her mouth. He cried out as her lips swallowed him down almost to the base, her tongue teasing as she sucked in hard.

Jt moaned wildly as he received his first blowjob, involuntarily thrusting up into her mouth as she came down on him. Jt only being now 14 wasn't really big yet and after a couple try's Ash found she could take his whole length into her. Even after having cum multiple times already it didn't take more than a few minutes before he shot rope after rope of cum in her mouth.

Ash waited until his thrusting stopped before letting him fall out of her mouth. He had finally gone soft, and was lying down on the couch exhausted, covered in sweat. She swallowed his cum down without meaning to, his cock just having slipped out of her mouth she sat up and swallowed. It wasn't too bad, Joeys cum she would never describe as good tasting but she didn't mind swallowing him because she

loved him so much, Jace on the other hand had tasted really salty and grimy and she had to spit it out. Now here with James, she wouldn't say she liked it but she found it wasn't disgusting either.

Ash laid down on Jt and took a short nap, waking in the late afternoon. She looked at her watch and found that they had almost over slept. James worked earlier in the morning and was always the first to arrive home; they had about a half hour until he should be home. While that was technically plenty of time to get cleaned up and dressed Ash still didn't like cutting it that close.

Ash woke Jt and told him to go put on clean shorts, while she got dressed in her skirt and re-hooked her bra. Ash was still wearing what remained of her torn shirt as she picked the buttons off the floor.

"Go get me a t-shirt I can wear home so I'm not flashing my bra at the neighborhood," she told him and he ran down the hall to his room, returning a minute later with the same shirt he had been wearing the day they had met. She put it on noticing it smelled like him, she started opening all the windows for some air flow.

"You can keep that shirt," he said quietly as his shy nervousness came back, "Maybe when you wear it........... you can think about me......... I will think about you," he said the last part picked up her broken shirt.

"You can have that, it has my perfume on it," she told him, "But go now and hide it in your room so it isn't seen." He did as he was told and went back to his room again; Ash thought it was adorable the way he wanted to trade shirts for each other's sent. She wondered how long he had been thinking about that.

He returned from his room looking like he wanted to say something to her but he would look at her open his mouth and look away again. She went to him and put her hand on his cheek.

"What Jt?" she asked softly, "Why can't you talk to me, after everything we've done your still so shy, tell me." Jt walked over and sat down on the couch and pulled himself into a ball, trying to speak but no words came out.

Ash didn't know what was on his mind, was he worried about what they had been doing? Was he afraid of them getting caught? She was a little afraid of that having come this close today; she would have to slip out in a couple minutes and go home and change her shirt before Linda came home.

"I just wanted to say................ To tell you.............. I mean I think................" he seemed more out of breath now than when they had been going at it.

"I love you!" He blurted out a minute later. He turned his face from her and pushed it into the back of the couch. Ash was taken back somewhat, she should have guessed this was what he was going to say, but it hadn't occurred to her because she wasn't in love with him.

Ash thought about her next words carefully before saying anything. She liked Jt a lot, she would even go so far as to say she had, had a crush on him since the first time they met, but she didn't love him, she admired him, she was passionate for him, but she had only ever loved one boy, and because of that she knew the difference in a way that poor Jt hadn't learned yet.

She realized her games had brought on more hurt again, as she had thought breaking him out of his shyness would be fun for her and she figured he would be grateful for all the sex, yet she never considered the emotional state of a fourteen year old boy.

"Jt, I............. I'm sorry," she said sitting down next to him and putting her arms around him. She kissed his cheek and he turned to her.

"When I was 13 I fell in love with a boy, and I told him. He told me the same thing I'm about to tell you," she paused and kissed him again, it felt weird to be on this end of this situation, "I love you very much, but I'm in love with someone else."

"You're not.....................?" He asked somehow more quietly.

"No. I want to be honest with you, I will never lie to you," she said feeling déjà vu.

"Now you hate me for telling you, you don't want to be with me anymore huh," he said and turned away from her again. Ash thought to herself, and they call girls emotional.

"I'm only here for this summer, I don't hate you, I care for you so much, and I do want to be with you all the time while I'm still here."

"Really?" He turned to look at her again.

"Yes really," she agreed and kissed him deeply again, "But right now pull yourself together your dad will be home soon and I have to go"

"Ok. I'll be fine if I know you still like me." Ash got off the couch and headed to the door.

"I'll be holding your shirt as I think about you tonight when I go to bed," she told him and gave him a wink as she left for home. Ash walked in the door and took off his shirt, stuffing it inside a pillow case on her bed. She knew Linda wouldn't find it because Ash did her own laundry.

The rest of July continued the same with only a small change, the routine now as on weekday Ash went over to Jt's house and they talked movies, books and music, but now they also played around with each other every day. They never went as far as having sex but she continued to blow him teaching him about stamina and he learned the finer points of eating out a girl.

The rest of the usual weekday and weekend routine stayed the same, she spent her nights with Linda usually at the apartment, and they spent weekends with James and Jt. Through all of this Jt still maintained a level of nervousness around Ash when his dad and Linda were around, it had lighted almost completely when they were alone but around his dad her still couldn't say hardly anything to her. She finally realized that it was because he was scared his dad would figure out what was really going on, and not let him see her anymore.

At the end of July Ash had some spending money she wanted to burn and she asked him to take her to the mall one morning. They rode the bus to the mall and she surprised him by saying the real reason they were there is that she wanted to take him to a movie he had been dying to see. They went to an early showing of the movie and then had lunch at the mall, before returning home on the bus.

When they got back to their apartment complex Ash asked him to come back with her to her apartment. Once inside Ash pulled him into her bedroom, and pushed him onto the bed. Jt had been so great to her in the last month she wanted to give him something more today. That had been why she had taken him to the movies and why she pulled him into her bedroom now.

They began kissing as she undressed him between kisses. She sat on top of his hips, her skirt covering then at the waist. She could feel his erection through his shorts pressing against her panties making her wet. She was sure the stain on his shorts today was going to be from both of them.

Jt's shirt was off and she unbuttoned hers as she kissed him, next unhooking her bra. His hands flew to her breasts as her bra hit the floor. He was caressing her nipples, and making her wetter, he had gotten really good at pleasing her in the last couple weeks under her training.

His hips began to grind up on her the fabric of his shorts scratching against her panties. They had played long enough, they had waited long enough, she had needed him since the first day they had met, she had needed him inside her, and she was so horny. Today was the day, today was the day she could no longer wait anymore. She was going to do what she had set out to do on her first day here at Linda's.

She rolled off of him, only long enough to remove his shorts and briefs, and then remove her skirt and panties. She rolled back on to him and their sexes touched together bare skinned for the first time. Jt was so scared now, she could feel it in his body, she could hear it in his breathing, and she could see it in his eyes. He boy was shivering from both anticipation and fear, so much so that he came only moments after she had rolled onto him. He cried out as it shot up thick hitting her stomach and dripping back down on him. Ash reached over and grabbed her shirt she had just been wearing and cleaned them off.

"I'm sorry, I ruined the moment," he apologized.

"Sssssshhh," was all she said as she moved up slightly and she placed him at herself sliding down onto his cock. Jt cried out again as her tight lips surrounded his virgin manhood. Ash took her movements very slow as she continued up and down on him. Jt seemed to have drifted off somewhere else as she continued to fuck him. She whispered his name but he was gone.

It was only minutes later his body convulsed and she felt his warm fluid inside her. It was enough for her to grind down hard on him as he came and hit her own orgasm. She squirted a lot of cum on his cock as she clamped down on it, he almost screamed out with pleasure, then his body fell limp and he began to shrink inside her. She rolled over and pulled the blanket over them.

Ash had fulfilled her game; she had succeeded in getting this shy introverted boy out of his shell and confident enough to not just touch a girl but to have sex for the first time. Now that they had finally had sex, they could do it every day until she went back home.

Ash leaned over and started kissing Jt with all the passion she had at that moment, she hadn't lied to him, she did love him on some level, even if she wasn't in love with him. She kissed him deep and genital. She was so into him she didn't hear movement in the house until her bedroom door opened.

"What the hell is this?" Linda was standing in the doorway looking at them, her face furious, "How could you be doing this behind our backs?"

Jt sat mortified unable to talk, he looked to Ash then to Linda and back to Ash. Ash looked at Jt, the wall, and Linda her mind was working as fast as ever, but she realized she was busted, there was no bluffing, excuses or talking her way out of this.

"I'm sorry Linda," she said simply, "I'm so sorry."

Chapter Fourteen: Commitments

I skid my car to a hard stop in front of the drug store Jenny worked at. I was distraught over my dad and I needed to get on the road home but I wasn't going to leave without telling Jenny what was going on. I practically ran through the building as I made my way back to the pharmacy.

Jenny was just finishing up with a customer as I ran up to the counter. Before I made it all the way to the counter Jenny looked up at me and I heard her tell her co-worker she would be right back. Jenny grabbed my arm and pulled me into the hallway by the restrooms, asking what was wrong.

I explained what was going on and told her why I had to leave again. She kissed me and said go, she would still be here when I got back. I kissed her back and told her I loved her so much and I was sorry I had just come back to her. She hugged me and said she understood.

I ran back to my car and smoked the tires on my way out of the parking lot. I ran through town at double speed, heading to the freeway. I felt guilty, I had a two day drive home and I didn't know if my dad or Lilly would still be there when I returned.

I felt guilty because if I had come home on Thursday I would be at dad's house about now. I didn't regret my time with Jenny the last couple days but I was mad that I had spent so much of the little time dad had left not knowing what was going on.

I made it to the interstate and pushed my car until it was shaking from speed. I finally calmed down a bit and slowed my speed down. I wasn't going to do anyone any good if I crashed or got busted for excessive speeding. I put a tape in the stereo and tried to calm down further as I drove.

I didn't stop all day as it turned dark I drove until I found myself falling asleep at the wheel. I pulled off the freeway at a nearby rest stop. I reclined my seat back and instantly passed out. I woke to the sun burning my face the next day, it was later in the morning then I had wanted to get going.

I got out of the car and walked to the restrooms, I was glad I had stopped here. I walked back out of the restroom and got a cup of coffee from the complimentary coffee and cookies they had for passing through motorists.   I drank my coffee and got back into the car, heading out as fast as I could push it. I wanted to make up as much time as possible. I did stop again at the next off ramp and buy a hamburger and fries. The food hit the spot and I felt like my energy had returned.

I drove over the speed limit all the way back home, it was amazing I didn't get pulled over. I felt relief wash over me as I arrived in town; I realized I hadn't asked which hospital dad was at. It was growing dark as I had no choice but to drive to my parents' home, to find out what was going on, I really hoped someone was home.

I walked into the house and dropped my bag at the door.

"Anyone home?" I called out. Katie came running down the stairs and hugged me, her face was red from crying. She didn't have to tell me, I knew I was too late.

"Joey, dad he.............." she burst out in more tears.

"It's ok, you don't have to say the words," I told her softly. I had accepted on the drive I would be too late, "How's Lilly?

"She's out of surgery, I left when the doctor said she would pull though. I just had to get out for a minute, I came home and took a shower and I was just about to leave." Katie through her arms around me and held tight.

I was sad about my dad but it really hadn't hit me yet that he was gone, at that moment I was relieved that at least Lilly had made it through. I loved Lilly as much as my dad and couldn't take losing them both; I had already lost my real mom.

I left with Katie for the hospital along the way she told me more about what had happened. Lilly and Dad had been coming back from the doctor when a little child ran across the road causing the bus to swerve into other traffic and running out though a red light, slamming into the side of Lilly's car. The bus hit on dad's side pushing them into another car.

It was a disaster, people on the bus were hurt, and so were people from other cars from small collisions from avoiding the accident. Then there were my dad and Lilly they ended up being the worst of all the accident victims. The little girl the bus swerved to avoid somehow made it across the street unscathed. By the time Katie had told me the whole story we were pulling up to the hospital.

"Did anyone call Linda and Ash?" I asked as we walked into the hospital.

"I called at the same time I was trying to get a hold of you," Katie told me with a hint of hurt in her voice. I knew she was mad at me about disappearing on them, "Linda got here last night she's with Abby upstairs now. I guess Ash is off at summer camp or something and couldn't come. Linda said she will tell her what what's going on after she returns home."

"That might be better, after what happened to her parents she doesn't need to be here to go through this right now too."

We made our way upstairs to Lilly's room. I rushed to hug both Linda and Abby. Lilly was asleep bandaged almost from head to foot. I could see bruising around her eyes and they had cut her hair. I was heartbroken to see her like this I loved my step mom so much.

The nurses had tried to cut down on the visitors but we had told them Linda was her sister and Katie was her daughter, we lied and told the nurse I was her son and Abby was her other daughter. They let us stay day and night after that.

Linda had to go home after a few days but we made sure that one of us, Katie, Abby and I stayed with Lilly all the time. Linda had to leave, saying that she couldn't be away from work anymore and Ash would be home again soon, she wanted to be home when Ash returned. I asked her how Ash was doing and I never got a real answer. It seemed to me like Linda was avoiding any questions about her, I thought maybe Ash had found a new boyfriend and Linda didn't know how to tell me.

As Lilly was recovering in the hospital Katie and I would only leave to handle all the death arrangements for our dad. We had him cremated then we took him home. Katie and I had known what our father's wishes were for his ashes but it would have to wait until Lilly was better.

Katie having gone to school for the last three years learning business and law so it made sense that she took charge of handling the financial aspects of what we had to deal with. We discovered that between the mortgage on the house, the wedding last year, the trip to Disney land, paying for Katie's and my apartment, my college, and his recent doctor bills there was almost no money left. This meant that all of our lives as we knew them were over.

I called Jenny that night; I was upset because the realization that I couldn't afford to stay in college had hit me. I didn't know when I could come back to her, as we had to give up the apartment as well. We talked and I told her I missed her and really needed her here now. She said that we would figure out our relationship later, that I should do what I could to help my family through this crisis. I thanked her and told her I would be home as soon as we had everything figured out.

Katie and I arranged a meeting with the bank and explained that our father had passed away and we wouldn't be able to make the mortgage any more. We made arrangements to move out and return the property to the bank. They felt for our loss and were willing to give us a little time to handle everything.

Katie and I had gone back to the hospital after our bank meeting and talked to Lilly, she was shaken by the financial situation but she said that we would all get through it somehow. Katie called Linda and talked to her for over an hour, when they were done it was decided that Linda would keep Ash at the end of summer and enroll her in school there.

There were insurance people from the city talking to Lilly since it had been a city bus responsible for the accident. They told her they would cover her medical bills and the cost of the death arrangements for dad. They also told her she was looking at a major settlement for both her pain and suffering and for dad's death.

Lilly decided to stay in town she said she would find an apartment for herself. Katie and I tried to talk her out of staying she should move near her sisters we knew Ash and Linda would love to have her around all the time. Lilly said she needed to stay at least as long as it took to clear up the entire medical bills, settlements and physical therapy.

Katie and I began to disassemble dad's office trying to go through everything deciding on what needed to be saved. Most of it was trash, but it was Katie who found some things that changed my life, I just didn't know the significance of all of it at the time. What Katie had found was a scrapbook of clippings and pictures from the time I was very young, it had my birth certificate and the paperwork from when my mom had died and dad received custody of me.

Most of what we found was standard paperwork that I was happy we had found because I might need my birth records someday. What struck me as most curious was that my birth certificate listed my first and middle names as David Joseph but my name was Joseph David. I made a note to myself to ask Lilly later if she knew why it was reversed. I realized by what was in the scrapbook it had been made by mom and been passed on to dad. It only covered the first four years of my life. The custody paper work from when mom died was the newest thing in the book.

Katie walked out of the room for a few minutes as I flipped through the book looking both whatever paperwork was there but also looking closely at the pictures. There were a lot of shots with me and a little girl, she looked like she was about a year or so older than me and she had the most beautiful yet familiar eyes.

As I flipped through the pictures I became more and more curious about whom the girl was as she was in half the pictures with me. Some of the pictures were labeled but some of the writing had faded away. The readable writing had claimed that some were taken at "the house on Hayford Ave "I could almost remember the house. Another picture showed a house by itself, it was small but looked very nice. The label was barley readable on this picture it read "Our house on Hayford Ave, HolBrooke island" I knew HolBrooke to be a small island town in the on the west coast, but I hadn't known I was ever there. Dad had once said that he had grown up there and left when he went off to college. The bridge that connected HolBrooke Island to the main land was only a couple towns over from where I had grown up with my dad and first step mom.

I was about two thirds the way through the pictures when I found one labeled "Joey and Jessica" I was shocked as I had young memories come flooding back to me. In my mind I saw the little girl about five or six years old grasping my hands and crying as we were pulled away from each other. I remembered that was the moment I was taken away to foster care while they found my dad. I was so little then only four years old. I never saw her again and I had forgotten her completely.

I had tears in my eyes as I still couldn't remember who she was or how I knew her. Katie walked back into the room and I told her what was going on. Katie said that HolBrooke Island had been where she had lived as a young girl.

Katie patted my shoulder as we looked through the rest of the scrap book together. Next were a few more pictures of the house and kids playing in the neighborhood, my first birthday, and me sitting on Santa's lap. Then another couple pictures with Jessica, it was on the sixth picture of about ten I found it labeled " Joey and his big sister at grandma's house " Katie and looked at each other, the girl in the photo wasn't Katie but I had never been told I had another sister.

I looked through the rest of the book without more insight. It looked like I had another sister in the world somewhere. I couldn't figure out why my sister hadn't come to dad to when mom died, why had they separated us and where was she? I wanted to find out everything I could about this girl, but we had more important issues at hand right now. I wrapped the scrap book up tightly and put it away in my duffle bag.

It was near the end of August when Lilly was well enough to return home. She had to use a cane to walk and would have to go through months of physical therapy but she was out of the hospital. Abby was an amazing help to us all during this time. While Katie and I were busy trying to handle the move and deal with family, it was Abby who took care of Lilly making sure she had everything she needed. Abby began cooking for us every day, which was both a blessing and a curse, It was great to have someone take care of the cooking but Abby's cooking was limited which meant we had some creative mystery meals for a while.

We still hadn't figured out what we were going to do about our apartment back at college yet. The rent had been paid through the end of September but as August was coming to a close we didn't have a lot of time to figure it out. Things at home weren't looking like we would be able to make it back to deal with the apartment anytime soon.

Near the end of August we had a garage sale, Katie and I boxed up all the personal effects from our rooms that we wanted to keep. Katie spent two hours on the phone with Ash one night discussing the personal things she wanted from her room and those were boxed up too. We put our boxes with the personal effects of Lilly in the garage. Knowing she was going to move into an apartment Lilly kept her whole bedroom set and the couch from the rec-room as it was her favorite. She also kept all the kitchen cookware and appliances. Almost all of my remaining things, along with Katie's and Ash's were put in the sale.

It was sad to see our furniture and things we had owned my whole life being carted out by strangers. As hard as that was we did manage to sell off most of our stuff and we gave the rest to charity leaving the house so empty we didn't have a place to sit or sleep anymore. Lilly's things were put into storage along with our boxes of personal effects. We cleaned up the house and called the bank telling them we were out at the beginning of September.

The four of us moved into a hotel for a place to sleep now that we were homeless. Katie went back to our apartment at college the first of September. She still had her scholarships to fall back on and she had a job waiting for her at the law firm she had been filing at for the last year. I drove Katie to the airport two days before her classes started, we decided that she would put all our stuff from the apartment in storage before our rent ran out, and she would move back to the dorm.

Abby had decided to stay to take care of Lilly, which was the best option as Lilly was long from being well again and Abby couldn't move in with Katie at the dorm. I felt bad for my sisters as it was hard to maintain a long distance relationship as I was now forced to do with Jenny. I hugged my sister goodbye and kissed her cheek, I was really upset to see her leave this time. I kept having a bad feeling as I stood in the window and watched her plane take off, I felt cold really cold.

It was on the way home from the airport I realized that Ash's 16th birthday had passed a couple days ago. I had forgotten with everything going on. I hadn't talked to her for a year and now she wouldn't be coming home, Lilly was in no shape to take care of her anymore. I told myself to remember to call her and at least tell her happy birthday.

We were at the hotel for three weeks, Lilly had started her physical therapy 4 days a week, and Abby would take her while I was spending all my time looking for a job. The insurance company was dragging their feet about the settlements and we were dangerously close to running out of money, then we wouldn't be able to stay in the hotel anymore. When Abby wasn't helping Lilly she was spending her time looking for a job too. Things were looking as bad as they could get and by the end of September it looked like we were going to be completely homeless before we could find jobs.

It was late September when I was going through the want ads I found an opening for an apartment manager. I had been a part time handyman and I had taken a couple management classed in my year at community college so I thought I would give it a shot. The job was for a manager/maintenance man for a 100 unit complex. The job came with a free small one bedroom apartment and a really good salary.

I took the job and the one bedroom apartment, then I rented out another two bedroom apartment to Lilly and I told them I would pay the rent on that apartment out of my paycheck. It was going to be tight on money for groceries but at least the girls and I had a place to live.

Lilly pulled her things out of storage giving the girls everything they needed for the kitchen, bathroom and Lilly's room. Abby had to sleep on the couch that we had saved before the garage sale but she said at least she didn't have to sleep on the floor like I did.

At the end of my first week of working my new job Abby drove me to the airport, and I used her unused return ticket to fly back to college and bring back our things from our old apartment.

I had called Jenny to let her know I was coming back. I left on Friday night and I only had two days to load a rental truck and get back home. I had to be back at work on Monday morning or I would risk losing my job already. I was so tired as my plane landed I just wanted to sleep.

I saw Jenny as I walked out of the gate. It had only been a couple of months but everything had changed. We ran to each other and hugged, I started kissing her as we embraced. I didn't care about the people around us as I passionately kissed my girlfriend. I was holding her to me tight kissing her, aching for her touch, as I felt myself growing hard, I didn't care if someone noticed, hell I would've fucked her right then and there had she not stopped me.

"Slow down baby," she panted as she broke apart, "I can feel how much you really want this," she said looking down, "But now's not the time."

"Yeah," I agreed begrudgingly.

We left the airport right away as I hadn't bothered to bring a bag with me. I was taking home all my personal belongings so it didn't seem necessary, right now I was so happy I didn't have to wait for baggage claim. As we walked I couldn't let go of her hand.

"So where is Anne?" I asked as we walked to the car, "I thought for sure you both would be here tonight."

"My mom drove up and got her a couple hours ago. I had talked to her about you coming home for just one night and mom thought it would be nice if we could have this one night to ourselves."

"I like that too," I told her squeezing her hand.

We made it to the parking garage and walked to the far end corner where her car was almost hiding between two big SUV's. We got into her car and I couldn't wait anymore, I leaned over and kissed her. Her hands instantly went behind my head pulling me closer to her; I could feel the need behind her kissing this time. It was more forceful then it had been at the gate more passionate.

I broke from her and climbed into the back seat pulling her hand to follow me. She hesitated looking around the car before deciding we were secluded enough in our spot she climbed in the back seat and laid on top of me. I was thanking god that she had tinted windows as we began kissing again. We kissed like two starving animals.

I was so hard as she ground her hips against me through our clothes. It had been so long since I had been with anyone; I had so much built up need I was running the risk of shooting my spunk in my boxers like a virgin boy. I didn't care, I was with Jenny now and that's all that mattered.

I slid both my hands up her t-shirt and massaged both her breasts through her bra. She responded by grinding her hips against my jeans harder. I knew she could feel my cock pressing against her because she knew just where to grind, it was driving me wild.

I couldn't hold back anymore and I froze up for a moment as I had the biggest orgasm I had, had in months shot after shots soaking my boxers. She pulled her mouth away from mine as I came and she giggled as she tensed up herself, I looked down to see the crotch of her jeans soaked through from her own orgasm.

Jenny reached into her shirt around my hands and unhooked her bra, as this one was a front hook type. Her bra opened and I resumed massaging her breasts focusing on her nipples with my thumbs. She resumed grinding on my crotch as I was still more than hard for her. My need for her was so great right now I doubted I could ever go soft again.

I leaned up to kiss her lips and she sat up away from me looking out the windows again. I didn't know if she heard something but moments later deciding no one was around she began unbuttoning my jeans, then she leaned in and kissed me again. I felt the zipper sliding down loosening my pants for my erection. We continued kissing as I felt her hand slide inside my sticky boxers.

"Wow!" she exclaimed as she felt my juices, "You must have really missed me." I didn't answer I just kissed her again as her hand began to stroke me. I unbuttoned her jeans and slid my hands inside her soaked panties.

"Your one to talk," I joked back at her. She actually turned red and simply nodded with a pouty, innocent look on her face. She pulled her hand out of my jeans and I groaned at her. She smiled big and stuck her thumbs in her waist band pulling her jeans down her legs around her ankles. She then did the same to me, both of us jeans down only wearing our shirts and underwear.

Jenny leaned over and kissed me again grinding her hips against mine again. I could feel her dampness against mine, it was warm and the car was beginning to smell musty, I was intoxicated with the feelings and the smell of our need for each other.

I closed my eyes and focused on the feeling of her on top of me, I was so exhausted from work and the flight that day but I somehow found the energy to grind myself against her too.

"Oh GOD, I love you so much!" she cried out as she had another orgasm. She tensed up on me for only a moment then reached down pulling my boxers down just enough to free my cock sitting her panty clad crotch on top of me. I moaned out and she didn't make me wait long as she slid her panties over and slid down on my cock.

My need was burning in me as I felt the soft folds of her inner walls envelope my hardness. She moved in slow rhythmic motions still kissing me while we made love. It wasn't the most romantic of settings but we didn't care. There was her and there was me and we were together here and now. I trust back within her and I again was struck by the thought of how perfect we fit each other.

I've said before that Jenny fit me as if she were tailor made for me and this time was no different, we made love so perfectly in unison it was as if we were trained to do each movement as if to the beat of a song. We knew without thinking about it what the other wanted and needed as we flowed together in the back seat of her car.

When her third orgasm hit her I was so ready for my second, she pulled away from our kissing and sat up. She put her palms flat against the roof of the car and pushed down against me as she sped up her thrusting, her pussy squeezed my cock so hard I thought it was milking me for the orgasm I had a moment later. My cum exploded out of me and wouldn't stop, I felt like I would fill her body before I stopped but I eventually felt myself softening as I gave her the last rope of cum.

She collapsed on me our breathing slowing down. She started to make a slight humming sound as if purring as her body came down from her orgasmic bliss. It felt good to have her on me I loved the feel of her weight lying there holding each other. Soon the sound of her purring turned into the sound of her sleeping.

I awoke and looked at my watch; it was after six in the morning. We had drifted off to sleep still in the back seat of the car. I didn't want to but I nudged Jenny awake.

"What time is it?" she yawned sitting up and realizing where we were, "OH MY GOD, did we really sleep here all night." It wasn't really a question just an acknowledgement, "We already spent all the time we had together didn't we?" she asked with a disappointed tone.

"Almost, I don't have to meet Katie until eight." I pulled her down and kissed her. I had woken up with my dick hard and pressing up against her leg. We were still mostly naked from the night before.

"I can't stand you to leave me again," she told me pulling away from my kiss and pulling her panties to the side again, "It seems like you only manage to be around long enough to make love and leave." She kissed me again as her outer lips began to envelope my cock, "I love you so much, I need you to tell me I'm not making a mistake." She was slowly riding me now; there was a different need in the way she made love to me this morning.

It took me a minute with her making love to me for my mind to click into place but I finally understood what she was getting at. The way we had gotten together had been hot and heavy, then I had made her wait to talk about my feelings, when I finally did I made love to her for two days strait and left her again. Now I was back only for one night. I realized from her point of view it could look like I only came back for sex and maybe I had told her of my feelings only as a scam to get back into her pants.

I gently kissed her neck and I rolled her over so I was on top of her. I pulled her shoes off and removed her jeans and panties completely. This would make things worse if we were caught but I wanted to make real love to her properly. I kicked off my shoes and pants as well and brought myself back to her.

"I'm not using you," I whispered in her ear, "I'm sorry for not being here for you right now. I need to take care of my family for a little while longer then I can come back. I promise you I love you." I kissed her neck gently leaving my hard self-outside her opening, I wanted to make love to her more but I was holding back I wanted her to hear my words and know I meant them before we made love again.

"I know," she said turning her head away, "I just really miss you, and I just need to hear it sometimes."

"I love you so much," I said again to her, as she slid her hand down and pointed me to herself again. I slowly pushed forward slow and deep inside her. I continued slow and deep I could feel my orgasm building but I maintained the slowness of this session. I wanted it to be as loving as I could. We

191

made love that morning for what seemed like years, after our burning need last night had been quenched this morning we returned to our normal selves. I could go for hours with Jenny when we were calm like we were this morning. I felt her orgasm building and I let mine loose I shot load after load inside her as she arched her back and cried out.

I collapsed on her this time breathing hard. She rolled out from under me and picked her clothing off the floor.

"I think we should get going," she said sweetly looking at her watch and rubbing the back of her neck, "I was supposed to be at work at nine." I looked at my watch shocked to find it was already nine. We had been making love for almost 3 hours.

"Yeah, we should go, I was supposed to meet Katie at the storage place an hour ago." We pulled our clothes back on and crawled back up the front seats. We held hands as she drove us out of the parking garage. We drove to the nearest pay phone were Jenny called her work and said that she had, had a personal emergency and wouldn't make it in that day.

"Now I can stay with you today until you have to leave," she said and kissed my cheek, "And I can meet this infamous sister of yours." For some reason I panicked a little inside when she said something about meeting Katie. I worried for a minute that she would see my feelings for my sister and she would wonder what that was all about. If Jenny figured out what was up with me and Katie, would she be ok with it or would it creep her out and make her not want to see me.

I rented a moving truck and we dropped off Jenny's car at her apartment so she could ride with me. We arrived at the storage place to find my sister there angry.

"Where the hell have you been?" She yelled at me as I was getting out of the truck.

"I'm sorry Katie......." I started but Jenny cut in.

"It was my fault," Jenny said extending her hand out for Katie, "I couldn't let him go this morning. You must be his sister he's always talking about. I'm Jenny."

"I'm the sister," Katie laughed, "And I'm not mad, I get it. It's just in light of what's been going on he should know better than to just disappear on me."

"Sorry," I said again.

"It's so good to finally meet you," Jenny said to her, "He told me so much about you and Abby."

"I certainly hope not," Katie responded giving me a questionable look. I shook my head slightly indicating I hadn't mentioned the relationship I had with my sisters. Jenny laughed at Katie's comment thinking it was a joke.

The girls both helped load the truck; they got along really well with each other. I was happy about that as I hoped to be with Jenny for a long time. Katie had already gone through everything and had taken from the apartment what she needed to stay at the dorm. I was bringing back our beds, couch, personal belongings and kitchen stuff. All of this was going to help out at the new apartments, as I had spent all week sleeping on the floor of my new place.

Once we had everything loaded I helped Jenny back up into the truck and I gave Katie a hug goodbye. I told her I loved her and kissed her cheek she said she would be home at the Thanksgiving holiday so we could go ahead and complete our father's wishes for his ashes. With that said she got into her car and drove away. I climbed back up into the truck and drove Jenny home.

It was about twelve already and I had two long days of driving to get back home again. I drove Jenny home and walked her to her door.

"I'd move to you if I didn't have Anne," she said fighting back her tears, "The main reason I moved here was so she could get the specialized classes her school has to offer."

"It's ok, I understand," I said wiping her eyes, "I would move in with you guys here if it wasn't for my job keeping our family alive right now."

"It's ok, I get that too." She held me tight, and I could feel myself getting hard again.

"I love you," I said breaking our embrace and pulling her into her apartment. I was finding it very hard to leave her too. I needed her again, badly, I knew I would kick myself later for leaving so late but I pulled her into the apartment and we made love again.

"You know this isn't forever, right?" I said to her as we lay together in bed, "As soon as Lilly can take care of herself again I will come back forever."

"I hope so." she said quietly.

"What's wrong?" I asked seeing a whole change in her demeanor.

"It's just that I............ Let's just not make any promises. I love you and our time together, but let's not go any deeper into this until you can be here with me.............. All the time."

"What are you saying?" I asked confused.

"What I was trying to say in the car this morning," she bit her lip and had more tears, "You seem sincere and I believe you mean what you're saying but................"

"You think I'm playing you?" I asked a little angry.

"No, well not exactly. I think you do care about me, and I think you mean well but I really get the feeling you're never coming back and I'm ...." she started sobbing now. I understood what she was saying. With everything going on I couldn't guarantee that I would be back or when I would even see her again. I had been in this situation before and it wasn't turning out any different.

"Are you saying we should break up until I can come back?"

"I NEVER said break up, you just did," she cried out, "Why would you say those words unless that's what's in your heart." She turned and buried her face in a pillow. This was her first real relationship and it wasn't going at all like she had thought it would. It was far from one of those fairy tale romances the girls watch all the time. She wanted me to choose her, right here and now, show her I loved

her by staying here and not leaving with all of my things. I got it but choosing her meant leaving my family without a means of support right now. I loved her but I couldn't hang them out to dry.

"Jenny................" I started rubbing her back, "I don't want to break up, I just thought that's what you were getting at."

"Just go home," she sobbed from under the pillow, "Go take care of your family, I won't ask you to stay when they are counting on you."

"But what about us?" I asked fighting my own tears now. She sat up her face all red and puffy she cleared her throat.

"There is no us, there never was, you've never been around long enough for us to have a real relationship. I can't just be your occasional whore."

"OH MY GOD!" I exclaimed in both shock and anger, "I've never thought of you that way! From the moment I met you all I've ever wanted was to be around you, to hold you, to tell you I was in love with you."

"That's why you couldn't figure out if you liked me or not before going home the first time this summer?" She was furious; I had made mistakes by not telling her in the first place. She had been holding this in since June, it was now coming out and she was shaking with anger.

"I knew then I was in love with you I was just too scared to tell you," I admitted. Despite how much I liked her I had been so scared to admit it even to myself, I should have told her in June.

"How do I know that's true?" She asked, "I broke up with my best friend for you, I had the best night of my life with you and I thought you did too. But you were just too scared?" I tried to hold her and she pushed me away, "Then you show up long enough to make me fall for you to my core, making love to me and telling me things I wanted to hear before you deserted me again for twice as long this time. Now you come back and do it again................" she stopped, breathing deep more tears falling. I said nothing; I really didn't know how to tell her I really did love her.

"Then you come back this weekend, I fall in love with you all over again, no one can make love like we do and not BE in love, my heart is breaking hard and you use the words BREAK UP when I try to be honest with you." I realized how bad I had just fucked up.

"Jenny ...." I was at a loss; she was completely right about everything. I had used her but I hadn't meant to. I loved her but I was walking away from her. I got off the bed and pulled my clothes on, once dressed I walked back to the bed and sat down.

"I never meant to hurt you," I told her and took her hand.

"I know, I don't know why I said all that," she said softly.

"You said what you feel; I can't get mad at that. I really don't know when I will be able to make it back," I told her and she looked down, "I promise I will return someday and we can have a real relationship but............" I stammered on the next part, "If you find someone and feel like you can't

wait.............I'll.......... Understand." I almost couldn't get the last part out, "I'll call you all the time, just tell me if you.............. Find someone else."

"I do love you so much," Jenny said looking down and away from me, "We'll see how we feel when the time comes. But you do the same as your telling me, if you meet a girl............. Just tell me."

"I won't, there will be no one who will catch my eye after you," I said lifting her hand and kissing it.

"Just leave," she told me pulling her hand away, "Just get going before you break my heart worse." I slowly walked to the door looking back at her again with my own heartbreak.

The drive home was long and quiet. The truck had no radio and I was stuck with two days of my own thoughts to keep me going. It was late when I found the rest stop I had stayed in on the drive home before. I stopped and took a few hour nap, When I woke it was still early morning. I went to the restroom and got a cup of coffee before returning to my drive.

It was after midnight when I returned to the apartment. I went next door to check on Lilly and Abby. Both girls were doing ok; they had been asleep waiting for me to return safely. I kissed Lilly and told her to go back to sleep. I went back out to the truck and dragged the couch off the back, pulling it into the apartment. I was sure as hell not sleeping on the floor any more. Abby appeared as I was struggling to get it in the door. She helped me get it in the apartment and we sat down.

"So what's wrong?" she asked me.

"It's nothing," I lied. She cut me down with only one look. I broke and told her everything that had happened while I was gone. It was usually Katie I went to in these times but that night Abby held me close I put my head on her chest this time as she had always done to me, as I actually started to cry.

I didn't just cry for Jenny, but for my dad and Lilly and the whole situation. I had held it together the last couple months I'd had some tears but I hadn't really cried since dad died. Abby was my hero that night as she held me close to her. I loved my new sister so much as we talked and I finally let it all go.

I woke just in time to take a quick shower before work. I had to wait until after work to unload the truck, but Abby came to me at lunch time and asked me for the keys so she could pull her belongings out while I was at work. When I got off that night I found she had unloaded everything except the furniture and had begun putting things away in my apartment for me. She really was great and I found myself wishing again I could have loved her in the way she had deserved from me all along. She really would make a great wife, but I still had in my heart that I would make it back to Jenny someday.

Abby helped me unload hers and Katie's bed into Lilly's apartment so she would have a bed of her own now. Abby had also taken all of hers and Katie's personal belongings from the apartment and moved them into the room at Lilly's. Other than what belonged to the girls directly everything from our old apartment came to my new one.

Abby helped out Lilly during the day while I was at work and I would go to their apartment after work for dinner. After dinner to give Lilly some peace and quiet and personal space Abby and I would go back to my place and hang out watching movies. Abby started spending the nights with me almost right away. She had asked me if she could spend the night with me, telling me she was lonely at night since

Katie had left. I said ok and we curled up in my little bed together. It wasn't long before she was staying in my house every night; we started out just sleeping and nothing more. I was still in love with Jenny and Abby had Katie.

I called Jenny a couple weeks after I came back, she was really happy to hear from me. She said she was sorry she had gone off on me and she had thought about our relationship. We talked for a few hours well into the middle of the night. What we came up with was that she had trust issues to begin with and she thought the reason she was having such a problem with me was because we had jumped into the relationship. We couldn't deny there was passion there but we really didn't know each other well. It was her solution that we spend the time away from each other talking on the phone and becoming friends first before more again.

I thought she had a good idea, she told me she had talked to Jeff again and was trying to repair their relationship so they could be friends again. I was indifferent towards that. I told her I would call her once a week no matter how busy things got, I would call her more but it was a once a week minimum. She liked that idea and told me that if I wanted to go out with girls I should, because were strictly friends now, she said she would not entertain the idea of the long distance relationship she believed those only promoted cheating and lying. I thought to myself I couldn't disagree with that.

The sad thing was as much as I truly loved Jenny I breathed a sigh of relief. I was free to do what I needed to for the time being. I vowed to myself I would return to her when I could and I would repair the relationship. I truly couldn't imagine being in a full blown real relationship with anyone else.

By Thanksgiving things had changed, Katie couldn't afford to come home like she had planned so it had just been Lilly, Abby and I having a nice Thanksgiving dinner at Lilly's apartment. By that time Abby's and I sleeping together was no longer innocent. Lilly asked us about the fact that she never slept at home and Abby said she just liked sleeping at my place. I don't know if she believed nothing was going on but we told her that Abby would never cheat on her relationship with Katie. Lilly believed that, what she didn't know is that the girls didn't consider being with me cheating.

So here I was a year later right back into the same relationship with my sisters as I was last year. Only this time I went to sleep every night holding Abby. I was so happy to finally be at a point in my life were I could hold someone all night as I slept. I was going to have a hard time giving this up when Katie came back.

I did feel a little guilty at the first time I had sex with Abby again. I felt like I was cheating on Jenny, but I wasn't actually dating her and I hadn't lied to Jenny when I said there would never be anyone new, Abby wasn't someone new Abby was someone I had known for years and cared for very much. So I felt there was no need to tell Jenny the next time I talked to her about what was going on. Besides Abby and I weren't dating we were just helping each other get over missing our true loves.

In late December we got the call that Katie was coming home at Christmas time. She had two weeks off and we would be so happy to see her. Abby and I had talked already to Katie and told her how things had been with us since she had been gone. She said that she was jealous of both of us but she wasn't mad.

Lilly was doing a lot better by then the therapy had done wonders for her getting around on her own. The insurance company finally contacted Lilly about ten days before Christmas saying they had come to a resolution they thought was fair. Lilly went down and had a meeting with the insurance people,

I was at work and Abby waited in the lobby but that night at dinner when I asked about it Lilly said she was going to wait until Katie came home to discuss it.

We all drove to the bus station to pick up Katie 3 days before Christmas. Abby ran to her grabbing her tight and kissing her deeply. I looked around seeing everyone looked in shock as the girls kissed at the station. Lilly wasn't shocked but her face turn red for a few moments. The girls broke apart and Katie hugged Lilly and I before we made our way to the car. On the way home I told Katie that Abby had been staying at my apartment every night and Katie said that it was no big deal she trusted us. Of course Katie already knew that but we had staged that conversation in front of Lilly so that she wouldn't think we were hiding anything from Katie or that anything was going on.

We sat down to dinner that night and Lilly came out with the news she had been holding off. The insurance company had paid out a lot of money. They had given her a huge sum of money for her personal pain and suffering as it looked like with her injuries she would never work again. They had also paid out a separate claim for the death of my father. She told us that she was keeping the money from her payout but she asked us what we thought we should do with the money from dad's payout. Katie and I looked at each other and neither quite knowing what to say. Lilly said that she had an idea and wanted to know what we thought.

"Go ahead," I told her, "What's your plan?"

"What I want to do is take part of the money and take a trip to finally fulfill your fathers final wishes, then I'm going to break the money up and both you and your sister will get half each." I was in shock; Katie had a similar look on her face. We were talking about a large sum of money, it wasn't like we were set for life but this was a game changer.

"Are you sure mom?" Katie asked finally, "You won't need the money at all?"

"No sweetie," she said softly, "He was your father; you kids should have the money, besides I won't need money with my end of things."

"Then I say ok," I stated, "But mom if you ever need anything you tell me and I will be here for you."

"Well said, and me too," Katie said.

"Me too," Abby agreed. Lilly smiled at all of us.

"I love my kids so much," she said looking at Abby, "All of my kids." The girls started hugging and crying then. I walked back to my apartment, this could change everything. I knew exactly what I was going to do with the money I had a plan.

It was a couple hours later when Katie and Abby came over to my apartment, they walked in locked the door and sat down on the couch on either side of me. Both girls placed a hand on either thigh and began to rub my legs simultaneously. I went from limp to rock hard instantly, only on rare times had I been with them both at once.

"I really missed my little brother," Katie said with a pouty look on her face, "I'm so jealous you got to play with my girlfriend so much lately and I didn't get to play at all." Abby giggled and Katie leaned in

and kissed me. It had been almost six months again since I had been with Katie, I loved our times together, and it made me feel special to be the only man she ever had sex with anymore.

As Katie was kissing me her hand went up the leg of Abby's skirt rubbing against Abby's pussy, which sounded wet already. All of this was making me harder. As Katie fingered Abby, Abby slid her hand up my leg rubbing my crotch through my pants. My right hand went up Abby's shirt to her braless breasts. My other hand went up Katie's skirt to her wet pussy.

Between what I was doing to them and what they were doing to each other I was severally over stimulated. Minutes later Abby had me unzipped and was reaching in my jeans to pull out my cock. As I was released and the air hit my swollen manhood I lost control and shot cum in the air, it came down on my jeans, my shirt, and Abby's leg. I was embarrassed but Abby simply wiped it off her leg with her finger licking it clean.

"My Toy Store Boy never fails," Katie said giggling.

"Toy Store Boy?" Abby said inquisitively as she began to stroke my still hard member. Katie and I both laughed.

"You never told her?" I asked.

"No, I'm surprised you never did," she answered. Abby stopped stroking me and looked at both of us.

"I'm lost what's the joke?"

"It's a long story it's how we met." Answered Katie, "I'll tell you tonight when we go to bed."

Abby grinned devilishly then leaned over licking the bits of cum off of my cock. I pulled Katie's shirt off then her bra, rhythmically rubbing her breasts. Katie scooted around and sat on the couch on her knees shifting up so I could suck her nipples. I gently twisted her left nipple while softly biting her right one. She moaned as I slid my hand back into her panties. Abby had moved from licking and teasing me to sucking now on the head of my cock.

I was lost with the feelings of both girls. I wished we could do this every day, I loved the physical sensations of it but I also loved the emotional bond I had with them. I was closer to my sisters than anyone else in the world. I loved being to express how much I cared about them this way. Whenever we had sex it was as much about strengthening that bond as physical pleasure.

Katie's legs clenched on my hand as she orgasmed causing me to explode into Abby's mouth, she gagged slightly from surprise and swallowed down the next couple shots. Watching Katie and I orgasm tipped Abby over the edge and she had her first orgasm grinding against Katie's fingers. It was intense as all three of us came at the same time fueling the others to cum harder. We all fell back on the couch when done. Abby curled up on me with her head by my heart on my chest like she so loved to do. I had cum so hard both times I was starting to shrink back down.

"Were not done yet," Katie whispered in my ear very sexily. She reached over and finished opening my jeans so I wasn't just hanging out of my zipper hole, she pulled hard removing my jeans then

did the same to my boxers, "I'm not going to sleep until I get fucked hard," she whispered in my other ear, "I so needed you to love me when dad died but........... You were involved, I didn't want to interfere."

I was really glad that Katie hadn't put me in that position then. It would have been really hard for me to say no to her. I loved my sister so much I would do anything for her whenever she needed but I don't cheat on girls, so it would have been a hard decision.

Katie rose from the couch sliding her panties down from under her skirt and sat down on my lap, her legs on either side of mine. Abby was still sitting close with her head on my chest as Katie climbed on top of me Katie's right leg squeezed between my left thigh and Abby's right thigh. This was so hot I had come back to life with a vengeance.

Abby moved sideways hugging tightly to my left arm as Katie sat up and slid back down on my throbbing dick. Katie wrapped her arms around my neck pulling our bodies together as she rode me slowly. She was so tight and warm I softly kissed her neck as her body moved with mine. I loved my bond with my sister, we had a special relationship, as much as I loved Jenny she would never understand how I felt about my sisters, I never wanted to break this bond.

"I love you so much little brother," she whispered in my ear clenching down on me slightly.

"I love you too, so much, I've always loved you sis," I whispered back.

"I love you both so much," Abby's voice sounded from my arm. Katie leaned over slightly and kissed Abby in response. As their kissing got heavier Katie sped up her rhythm on my cock. Watching them kiss right on my shoulder was so hot I couldn't take it anymore.

"Katie...............OH GOD!" I cried out as I had the most powerful orgasm yet today. I filled my sister with my cum as she clenched again clamping me to her so hard I couldn't slide out, she cried out and collapsed on Abby.

"I'm sorry Abby I don't have enough left tonight for your turn," I told her.

"It's ok I don't need you tonight, I want my girlfriend to take me when she's recovered enough," she responded smiling. We all lay on the couch for a while before Abby got up, taking Katie by the hand and walked her to my bedroom. I thought for a minute that they should have gone back to Lilly's apartment, as Abby had a larger bed there that she never used. But as the girls hadn't been together for months I didn't argue I let them have my room and I slept on the couch.

It was Christmas day when we made the trip to HolBrooke Island. As I said before my dad had grown up there, and his wishes had been for his ashes to be released from the bridge connecting the mainland to the island. I drove with Lilly riding shotgun, and Katie in the back seat. Abby had decided to stay home, saying that I should be the three of us. We told her she was as much family now but she insisted we all go alone.

The bridge was huge when standing on the walk path looking over the railing my fear of heights kicked in hard, as the water below looked like it was a mile down. You could feel the cold December wind blowing against you as you walked. It was cold and the day was grey as we spoke of our favorite memories of dad. We made our last goodbyes and I opened the urn and poured it over the edge watching dad's

ashes disperse in the wind. When the urn was empty I threw the urn off the bridge and watched it fall forever to the water. We walked back to the car without a word between us.

We stayed overnight on the island in a motel. It was then I thought about my sister, I hadn't even thought about her since the day I had found the scrap book. Being here on the island I wanted to learn more, but I didn't even know where to start looking. We sat around the motel that night talking about of dad.

I sat there listening to the girls talk and cry and my mind was going wouldn't stop thinking about finding Jessica. I really needed to learn what had happened to her. I finally decided to take a chance.

"Lilly what do you know about my sister?" I asked stopping their conversation short.

"She's right here if you have questions for her," Lilly said smiling.

"No, my other sister, Jessica, what do you know about HER," I asked again and I could see a change in Lilly's face.

"How did you learn about her?" Lilly asked. Katie got up and walked to the bathroom.

"It doesn't matter," I told her.

"Let me explain," Lilly started.

□

Chapter Fifteen:
Ashley's Diary Part 3: Punishment

Linda was furious Ash had been caught in bed with Jt and the room smelled of the sex they had just had. Linda and Ash locked eyes in a staring match; no one had said a word since Ash had apologized.

"Is there any way you'd believed this isn't what I looks like," Ash asked half joking half scared, she hoped to break the tension.

"You're not joking your way out of this," Linda said coldly, "Both of you get dressed and come to the living room." Linda turned and walked out of the room.

Jt turned and looked at Ash, he was crying now and she remembered just how young he was emotionally. She didn't regret her time with Jt, but she was upset about getting caught. Looking at her watch she realized Linda had come home a couple hours early today.

"I'm sorry," Ash whispered to him as she hugged him, "Its ok, we'll get through this."

"I love you," he said wiping the tears away, "My dad will never let me see you again."

"Its ok sweetie, we'll figure it all out," she was stroking his back gently.

"I love you so much.............." he said again and she realized he was trying to get her to say it back. But she wasn't in love with him; she didn't want to tell him she loved him and not mean it.

"I know sweetie. I care about you so much too." She knew it wasn't what he had hoped to hear. Jt got off the bed and pulled his clothes on, then walked out of the room.

Ash sat on the bed for another few minutes rocking back and forth, what now? Ash laid down covering her face with a pillow and screamed three or four times, she didn't know how to spin this situation. She had been completely caught with her hand in the cookie jar as it were. She sat up on the bed again trying to think, almost too scared to leave the room and face her sister.

She finally rolled off the bed and picked up her discarded clothes pulling them on slowly. She snuck her way out the door and up the hallway. She could hear Linda and Jt talking, he was crying and Linda was trying to calm him down.

"I understand sweetheart," Ash could hear Linda say to Jt as she reached the living room, her voice was calm and reassuring, "Just run home I won't tell your dad. I just need to talk to Ash right now."

"Um........ Thank you Linda," he said calming down. Jt got up to leave looking over at Ash for a moment before disappearing out the door.

"You sit down," Linda said sternly, her whole demeanor changing from the soft reassuring she had been with Jt to more cold and bitter.

"Um Linda..............," Ash started but she was cut off.

"Are you in love with him," she asked staring Ash down as sat on the couch.

"I really adore him."

"Don't word play me, are you in love with Jt," Linda's anger was building in her face as she asked.

"No, I'm not," she answered looking down on the floor. She was fighting back tears herself now then she added, "I wish I was he's a great boy, but I'm not."

"How could you then Ashley?" Linda asked, she had gotten up from the couch and was pacing back and forth around the room, "You realize Jt is completely in love with you?"

"Yes."

"Then how could you use him like that?" Linda was having a hard time controlling her tone now.

"I didn't use him!" Ash replied.

"The hell you didn't, Jt is such an emotional boy, how could you take his virginity for fun? How could you do that to him knowing he was in love with you?"

"I don't know!" Ash cried back at her, "I liked him so much; I wanted to be with him."

"You liked him but you're not in love with him. I could have let go what I saw today if you kids really believed you were in love, but this isn't right Ashley."

"I know I just really wanted to be with him. I thought I could help him."

"Help him how?" Linda asked her voice changed from mad to confused.

"I thought if I was really nice to him he might get over his fear of girls, I just wanted to help." Ash's brain had now found her angle to spin this situation; if she worked this avenue she might find a way to get herself out of trouble.

"Yeah being nice is one thing, but you ended up having sex with him to help him. How do you get to that point and rationalize it was just to help with his fear of girls?" Linda asked more confused and irritated.

"I don't know, it started out as just little things like hand holding and being sweet, then somehow we ended up here today.............. I really didn't mean for it to happen, I made a mistake."

"Yeah, you made a mistake, he's a confused 14 year old boy and you've really messed with his head. You've taken away from him something that should have been so very special."

Linda was mad but she had visibly calmed down. Ash thought her spin was working as her sister sat down quietly.

"I'm sorry Linda," Ash said still crying and looking at the floor.

"I know I was a teenager once too. Lilly got pregnant not much older then you are now. We weren't perfect either," Linda had completely calmed down now, "I would be such a hypocrite to tell you, you shouldn't be having sex at your age, but it shouldn't have been Jt."

Ash couldn't say anything to that as Linda was right; he wasn't emotionally ready for all of this yet, even if his body had been physically ready.

"I'm sorry," was all Ash could manage to say again.

"This could change everything," Linda began to explain, "Did you ever consider what he was going to go through when you went home in a few weeks?"

"No."

"Did you ever stop to think about when Jt fell apart heartbroken, how I would explain that to James?"

"No."

"Did you ever think about how that would impact my relationship to James if I have to tell him what you did with his son, he might not want to see me anymore. Is that fair to Jt, James or me?"

"No. Look I'm really so sorry."

"Not to mention if I ever got married to James, do you know how weird it's going to be to know my sister slept with my step son?" Linda finished.

Ash told Linda that she would break things off with him right away. Linda said just because she had calmed down didn't mean she wasn't still angry. Linda told her that it was going to break his heart when Ash broke things off but it was going to have to have happened when she went home anyway. Ash felt like she had dodged the bullet until Linda told her for the remainder of her visit she was grounded to the apartment.

James called later that night, he said Jt was even more quiet then usual and wouldn't come out of his room. He asked Linda if she knew what was going on. Linda told him that the kids had gotten into a disagreement over something Ash wouldn't talk about either. James accepted this answer and didn't investigate further.

As their weekend routine was the girls spent the weekend hanging out with James and Jt. It was awkward for everyone except James who was completely in the dark about what had happened. Ash and Jt hadn't seen each other since he had left her apartment the day they had slept together.

Ash pulled the boy into his room and they talked about what had happened and how she wasn't allowed to go outside unsupervised anymore. He told her how much he really loved her and she told him that they had to break up; she told him she really liked him but for the sake of her sister and his dad they needed to be just friends. Jt buried his face in his pillow and cried. Ash rubbed his back until he calmed down. When he had calmed down she hugged him.

"One last time," she whispered into his ear, and kissed him. They sat kissing for about five minutes when Ash pulled away from him and said she was sorry she had hurt him. He nodded and lay back down on his bed she could see the erection in his shorts and for an instant she considered giving him one last hand job but she decided it would only make things worse. He closed his eyes then told her to just go.

Ash walked out of his room closing the door. She walked out into the living room and sat with her sister and James the rest of the night. She sat in silence thinking to herself, she felt horrible, what she had done to him was what so many men do to girls. She had known he was in love with her and she still let things go too far, he was going to hurt so much for that. She didn't want that sweet, caring and emotional boy to go through any pain, yet she didn't know what she could do now. Linda was right; she was leaving in a couple weeks and might not ever see him again.

It was a few days later when Linda came home and said she had found an alternate punishment then having Ash locked up inside the apartment all the time. She told Ash she had signed her up for two weeks of bible camp starting the first of August.

This only left a couple days to get ready, Ash tried to think of a plan that could get her out of having to go, but she couldn't come up with a convincing argument. Eventually she stopped trying to get out of it; she had done something really hurtful to a nice boy as a game. Maybe this was karma catching up with her; maybe she needed a dose of morals to reboot her thinking. In the end she accepted her fate and got ready to go.

Linda had dropped Ash off at the church so she could take the bus with the other teens to camp. Ash had decided to dress somewhat conservatively, she wore her black skirt and her short sleeve black button up shirt, it was the same outfit she had worn the day she met Jt.

"I'm not doing this out of anger," Linda explained as they arrived at the church, "I just think it never hurts to slow down a little. You're almost too grown up for your age."

"I don't know," Ash said but inwardly though Linda was right. She was still only 15 and had been through a love affair and a pregnancy scare. Maybe a dose of wholesome teen activities would be good for her.

The girls got out of the car and Ash picked up her back pack and pulled it up on her shoulder. The sisters hugged each other, "I love you Ashley, and be good."

"I will."

Ash walked to the line of waiting kids and set her bag down on the curb. She was now getting nervous standing around looking at all these kids, not knowing a single one. She looked over to see three girls standing in a huddle they were wearing uniform looking pleated skirts and button up shirts and each holding their bibles.

Ash looked over at these girls with a contempted look as she felt a hand on her shoulder.

"Just hope you don't end up with them as you roommates," she the girl who had just touched her shoulder, "I had to share a room with them last summer, I about took my own life."

"It couldn't have been that bad really, could it?" Ash asked the girl turning to look at her. The girl was wearing an oversized t-shirt and ripped jeans with high top tennis shoes. Ash liked her already.

"You have no idea, they sit up all night and sing hymns and chant prayers. Or they sit all night and play the truth game, it's so fucking annoying you just want to kill them or yourself."

"I'm Ash by the way," she said sticking out her hand, "What's the truth game?"

"Terra," she responded and shook Ash's hand and cleared her throat as if to say something in an official manor, "The truth game is an important part of your spiritual bond, where you sit in a group of your most trusted companions and reveal when and how Jesus first touched your life." Terra broke down laughing by the end of the statement making Ash giggle as well.

"Don't make fun of the truth game!" Called one other three girls walking over to them, "Don't listen to her, she's a pagan anyway, I'm Brandy, and this is Mandy and Sandy." Brandy moved her finger to indicate which girl was which.

"Yeah," said Mandy, "All Terra did last year was tell us we were pathetic and make fun of us." Terra just smirked at them.

"Then I caught her sneaking around the boys dorm at night," said Sandy in a tone that indicated she thought that was scandaless.

"Well I was horny and you bitches were annoying," Terra laughed as all three girls gasped.

"God will forgive you if you ask him," Mandy said quietly. Ash realized in that moment, by the way she had said it, Mandy was hiding a secret.

"Why should I ask God for forgiveness, I was calling out to him the whole time I was fucking," Terra said as a joke but all three girls gasped again and Ash giggled.

"We do not need to hear about this," said Brandy in a snotty tone and walked away with the other two girls following.

"Ok I see your point," Ash said kind of amused.

"Yeah I learned almost too late that the only way to get them to go away is to talk about sex, I only said it to piss them off."

"It's ok you don't have to defend yourself to me," Ash told her. Terra pulled out a pack of cigarettes and lit one up; she offered one to Ash who simply shook her head no.

The girls became friends before the bus had even arrived. They sat together on the bus talking the whole trip. Ash found out the reason Terra was here was because her parents were ultra-Christian and sent her every summer since she was a little girl. Terra however had taken a different road and was actually agnostic but she continued to go to bible camp to appease her parents.

As the girls talked they shared different stories about themselves, they talked about boys, and they talked about sex. Repetitively they were shot sideways glances and glares about their topics of conversation, the bulk of the looks came from Brandy, Mandy and Sandy who Ash and Terra had now dubbed the Circle of Andy.

The Bible camp had once been a World War 2 army base that about 20 years ago had been converted into a camp, now it was owned by the church and had been renovated into a giant auditorium, dining hall, a boy's dorm and a girl's dorm. It had old bunkers that had been sealed off, there were 3 look out towers you could climb up to and look out at the ocean. The whole place was surrounded by trees and had a trail that led down to the swimming area at the ocean.

When they got there everyone was ushered into the auditorium and told to sit down with boys on one side and girls on the other. This was to set up for dorm room assignments. A pretty girl about 18 to 20 years old walked by with a shirt that said counselor, she was giving out name tags and was assigning rooms by rows, her name tag said Mary Beth. Each room had six beds and the room assignment was done simply by giving the first six girls in the row the first room then the next six the next room.

Terra was sitting next to Ash and she hoped that her six wouldn't cut off between them getting to room together. Ash looked to her other side, next to her was a girl she didn't recognize and next to her were all three of the Circle of Andy.

When it was their turn Ash and Terra did get the same room but so did the girl next to her, named Susan, and the Andy's.

"God damn it I knew this would happen," Terra said and the counselor stopped and glared at her.

"Don't use our lords name that way," said Brandi. Ash was never going to forgive Linda for sending her here.

Once rooms and name tags had been given out to the whole crowd was called to attention two people stood on stage, they introduced themselves as Pastor Randy and his wife Cindy. They were the camp organizers and spiritual leaders, Ash thought they were way too perky to be real.

Randy asked everyone to bow their heads and they started the started things off with the Lord's Prayer. After an hour of preying they were ushered off to their rooms and told to put their things away and head to the dining hall to sign up for activities.

Ash and the other girls found their room and picked their bunks. Each room was set up with three sets of bunk beds and six small dressers. Ash threw her back pack on her bed as did Terra and the two girls left the room right away.

When they got to the dining hall everyone was gathering around trying to decide on what activities they would like to do for the afternoons the next two weeks. Terra and Ash decided on

wilderness walks and archery. They thought those would be fun and as non-religion based as they could get.

After activities were picked the campers were given until dinner to run all over the camp and do whatever they liked. Terra wanted to go swimming and Ash thought that was all right. They went back to the room and got changed into their swimsuits and shorts; they grabbed some towels from the room and headed to the ocean.

Terra was worse than Ash when it came to guys; she was checking out all of them and pointing them out to Ash as they walked to the lake. They set the towels down and took off their shorts reveling themselves in their bikini's. The water felt really cold but good on this hot day.

It wasn't long before the water was full of scantily clad boys and girls. Ash was floating her eyes closed the sun on her skin from above and the cold water on her back, she was thinking maybe there would be something worth wile about these next two weeks. She was floating peacefully when one of the boys splashed her. She rolled over and stood up looking to see who had splashed her and found herself staring into the brown eyes of a very handsome boy with dark hair. He smiled at her and swam away; Ash looked around for Terra and didn't see her anywhere.

Ash followed the boy as he swam out of the designated swimming area, until they found a vegetative pocket along the edge. They swam into the pocket and sat on the edge of the water with their feet in. The sun was warm on their shoulders as they looked at each other for a long time without words. It looked like he was trying to say something but couldn't get the words out. She decided to let him speak first.

"So um...... I wanted to talk to you, I'm Derik," he sputtered finally. Ash thought this boy is too cute to be this nervous around girls, but this was bible camp. They started talking about nothing in particular, after a time she found that he was cute but she really wasn't that interested in him.

By the time they had been talking an hour she could see the bulge in his shorts and she was ready to head back to the camp, she actually preferred camp to talking to him anymore. She was polite and listened to him until he leaned over and tried to kiss her. She moved out of the way, stood up and walked back into the water. She swam out into the water heading back and leaving him there alone.

She had swum part way back when she saw movement under the old boat dock near the camp. She slowed down and floated slowly and quietly with only her head out of water. As she approached the dock she could see two people making out hard core. She found that she was close enough to shore she could walk on the ground now, she crept up further, she wanted to see who it was going at it so hard.

By the time Ash could see who it was she was swimming with her knees touching ground. She lay as flat as she could her head only above water so she could breathe. They were at an angle to her girl had her back mostly turned to Ash and she could see the girls top was off, she could see the guy fairly well, she thought she had seen the name Sean on his tag earlier in the day. He was standing near the middle of the dock the water at knee level, his shorts were pointing out at the girl.

In the time it had taken Ash to move in well enough to see them well the girl had moved down and was kissing his chest. The girl dropped to her knees the water level now just below her breasts. She began kissing his stomach running her hand up the leg of his shorts and he groaned loud.

Ash thought it was so hot watching someone like this, she knew she should've gone but her eyes were glued to the sight in front of her. Ash pushed back with her arms moving backwards in the water away from the couple so she could come around and get a better look at what was going on without being seen.

By the time Ash had made a long circle around and come back in near another dock post she could see everything and she knew she would be barely visible. The other girl was working his cock with her hand under his swim shorts and kissing the waistband, teasing him.

"Maybe we should................ OH GOD................. should stop?" he panted to the girl, "I've............ We could get caught."

Ash recognized the nervousness in his voice, this was probably the first time Sean had done anything with a girl, and he was scared out of his mind.

"Just calm down," the other girl told him, "I know what I'm doing, just relax, baby." The girl slid his shorts down do reveal what Ash thought was a very nice cock, and then the girl began to suck the head. Ash watched as the girl gave what looked by his reaction to be a very good blowjob. The girl played with and sucked the head without ever going lower. After about two minutes he cried out and she sucked him deeper into her mouth as his orgasm hit.

Ash slowly started swimming out away from them again as they finished and the girl pulled up Sean's pants. She had been lucky enough to come along when she did, she had dirt on the girl and her mind was turning as to how to use it.

After the couple had left Ash finished swimming back to the camp, as it was really close to dinner most the campers had already gotten out of the water.

"Where did you go?" Terra asked as soon as Ash returned to the room.

"I went for a swim further up the lake with Derik, where did you go?"

"I was board so I went to lay on the grass, when I looked up you were gone. Soooooo what happened with Derik?" she asked grinning.

"Nothing, he's cute but boring. He tried to kiss me and I left. But you'll never believe what I saw Mandy doing by the boat dock." Ash told her the whole story and Terra was shocked, she refused to believe that one of the bible thumping, virgins for Jesus, Circle of Andy's would be sucking cock.

"You sure you saw it right?" Terra Asked.

"Yeah, I could tell it was her voice too when she spoke."

"Oh my god, this is too good. Maybe there's hope for her yet." Both girls laughed at that as they walked to the dining hall for dinner.

The first week was truly uneventful as the daily routine was set from the first day on. Every morning Mary Beth woke the girls and Robby T. woke the boys and all campers were required to meet in the auditorium for morning prayers. Then it was off to breakfast. After breakfast they went to first

activity, which for Ash and Terra was archery. After first activity was Lunch then off to afternoon prayer. Next was second activity which for them was the nature hikes they had signed up for. After that they had a couple hours of free time to swim or chat and just relax or run around until dinner. After dinner was night prayer time, which lasted until the nightly hymns then it was bed time.

Ash discovered the first night what Terra had said about the Andy's as they sat on the floor in a huddle and read scripture to each other than they would sing. The girls would be up half the night doing this.

"SHUT THE HELL UP," Susan had finally yelled at them after midnight the first night.

"Profanity isn't appropriate," answered Brandy, "We'll pray for you."

"Jesus oh lord, please save me, please oh lord I repent, I repent save ME!" Cried Terra all of a sudden, "Save me from these fucking bitches and show me the way!" Susan laughed so hard she fell off her bunk, while Ash uncontrollably giggled.

During the day Ash and Terra sat in the back of the auditorium and talked quietly during most of the prayer time, Mary Beth would sometimes come through and tell them to be respectful and they would stop for a few minutes. The Andy's were just as annoying as ever, they constantly told Ash and Terra they needed to listen so that they wouldn't burn for their sinful ways. Ash caught Mandy's eye with a knowing look on one of these occasions, Mandy looked away like she had been caught yet Ash hadn't told her yet she had seen her and Sean.

At night the prayer sessions went on almost all night and so did the non-stop comments from both Susan and Terra. Ash never said a word at night during all of this for two reasons. First she couldn't get in a word between the Andy's praying and the girls jokes, second Ash was laughing so hard she almost peed herself more than once.

It was Friday night and Pastor Randy had said they had the whole day off on Saturday as was the weekly routine. On Saturdays they still did all of the prayer sessions but the campers were allowed to not attend because on Sunday they spent the day in prayer and that was mandatory.

Friday night the Andy's decided to play the truth game. Ash rolled her eyes and Terra though a shoe at them as they gathered on the floor. Ash had heard about this game but hadn't seen it. Ash would've rather played another type of truth game one with dares in it; she really wondered what kind of trouble she could lead these prissy bible thumping prudes into. But then again she suspected they had a hidden side to them. She knew Mandy did she had seen it.

It was after ten already and Ash was already annoyed listening to the girls play this game.

"I'm out of here," announced Susan looking to Terra, "Are you're ready?"

"Fuck yeah," she replied hopping off her bunk, "I wouldn't miss this, I lost my virginity there two years ago."

"Terra! You're not supposed to tell," Susan said sharply.

"You are heathens!" announced Brandy, "You guys will all burn for your sinning. You should stay here and recommit yourselves."

"I'm lost what's happening?" asked Ash.

"It's a camp tradition just put you shoes on and come along," Terra told her. Ash was all of a sudden so nervous she could hardly think.

"I don't know you guys, what's going on?"

"It's a satanic abomination that only whores participate in." Brandy spat as visible anger flashed across her face.

"Oh you're just mad because nobody would choose you. Come on Ash let's go," Susan said taking her hand.

"Fine I'll go, if it pisses off Brandy so much it has to be cool." The three girls walked out the door.

Terra stopped outside the door to light up a cigarette and she offered one to Ash and Susan. Susan took one and lit up too. They could hear the Andy's talking as they stood outside the door.

"One of us should bring them back." One of the girls said.

"I'm not going to THAT," another said in a snotty tone and Ash knew it was Brandy who had said it.

"I'll go," said a meek sounding voice, "I'll bring them back." Ash realized it was Mandy's voice this time.

"Are you sure?" Brandy asked, "You tried to bring Terra back last year and you got lost in the woods."

"I'm not scared, I'll go if it means saving them."

Terra, Ash and Susan walked away then, heading out towards the woods. After a few minutes Ash looked back to see Mandy was tailing them a few yards back. Mandy had a smile on her face and didn't seem to be trying to catch up with them at all.

They walked through the woods for about a half an hour before coming to a large clearing. There was a bon fire going near a large bunker that at one time had been the army barracks. Near the fire was a man and a woman dressed in dark robes wearing masks. All around the fire and going in and out of the barracks were a number of kids from the camp; everyone there was wearing a mask.

"What the fuck is this?" Ash asked somewhat panicked as they arrived at the clearing, "Did I just step into some kind of horror movie?" Both Susan and Terra laughed.

"No silly this is more like a masquerade party," Terra giggled. The girls reached the barracks and found a stack of matching masks. Each of the girls took one and put it on. Ash felt silly as they turned and walked to the bon fire.

"Attention," called the man in the black robe, "All virgins who wish to be chosen please step forward now."

Ash was really puzzled and scared now, what kind of cult bible camp had Linda sent her too? Susan pushed on Ash's arm as the man called for Virgins, and Terra laughed.

"Oh no, girl, she's no virgin," Terra told her.

"Oh, I didn't mean any disrespect."

"None taken, I'm glad I still come off that way," Ash told her, "But I'm still confused as to what's going on."

"It started from what we understand about 20 some odd years ago, at another camp," Terra started, "Basically this is for those of us who are stuck here and hate bible camp, on the first Friday night they hold what's called the deflowering ceremony."

"Yeah, some of the counselors that year realized that we are all teens with urges and the church teaches too much abstinence," Susan cut in, "So they started the Friday night thing as a way for those who want to lose their virginity can do so anonymously."

"You wear you mask and if you're ready you volunteer and go to the front, where a non-virgin can pick you," said Terra jumping back in, "Then when all the virgins have been accepted, all of us non-virgins can pick partners if we choose."

"It's basically an excuse to blow off some steam, get away from all that praying and have a major orgy," Susan said as the girls all walked to where they were handing out drinks, "Then as far as anyone here is concerned tomorrow, tonight never happened and were never to talk about it."

"I don't know…………." Ash started as she was handed a drink. She drank down a little of what the girls had given her and it burned a little. She coughed slightly at the taste.

The ceremony didn't last long as only a few virgins volunteered; there were about ten virgin boys and seven virgin girls. All the virgins were stripped down to only bra's, underwear and masks. Ash noticed one of her virgin girls was wearing a pair of panties with Brian the Bear on them. Ash thought that was an odd choice in panties for a night like this, Brian the bear was a beloved children's show puppet. Her thoughts changed back to the ceremony as one by one someone from the crowd would come up and take one of them by the hand and walk them into the old barracks building.

Ash thought this was a horrible way for anyone to lose their virginity. She was really happy she had lost hers out of love. She felt that even what she had done with Jt was more decent than this.

After the virgin choosing had completed everyone began to start choosing partners and losing their clothes. By the time Ash went back for another drink she already had to step around people committing sex acts in plain sight.

Ash suddenly realized that with all of the masks looking alike she had lost track of Susan and Terra when she had been watching the ceremony. Now she couldn't tell who was who just by naked flesh.

Ash was still dressed, for as much as she had liked sex, and liked her games she had played with Jace and Jt, this was almost too much. Susan hadn't been kidding when she said it was an orgy. Other than the people in the dark robes she had to be the last one dressed.

It was then that Ash remembered Mandy had followed them; she looked around but couldn't find any sign of the girl, would she have got scared and ran back? Ash remembered what she had seen at the dock on her first day, and Brandy had made the comment that Mandy should bring back her roommates like last year. Ash realized that innocent little Mandy had arranged this so she could sneak away from the Andy's, she was here somewhere. This made Ash grin, this whole orgy was proof of what she believed. The more you preached the worst you probably were when no one is looking.

Ash didn't know who was who or what to do, it seemed like everyone had hooked up, and she didn't think she could have sex with some random guy anyway. She had generally liked the boys she had slept with in the past, she may have played them and even used them, but she had liked them. She never had sex with a masked stranger before.

Suddenly two naked girls ran up to her and took her hands, she assumed it was Susan and Terra but they didn't say anything. They led her up the stairs to one of the barracks rooms. There were blankets on the floor of the room where a couple was having sex on the floor. She looked over to see a dark robe in the corner and she realized that the man who had held the ceremony was the guy here now.

Ash sat on the floor and watched as the man pumped hard into the girl, she was crying out wildly and Ash thought that she must be one of the virgins. Again she thought what a horrible way to lose your virginity, on a blanket on the floor of a dirty relic.

As Ash watched she felt herself getting turned on by the sight of the man's cock sliding in and out of the girl, she was focused on the point where they connected. She looked over at the naked girls who had brought her to the room; each had fingers in their pussy's grinding on themselves as they watched.

Ash not feeling self-conscious because of her mask slid her hand into her panties as well, finding herself more wet then she had realized. She began to furiously slide her fingers up and down inside her slit, taking in the sight in front of her.

Finally the girl screamed in orgasm, and fell limp on the floor trying to catch her breath as the man continued to pump her hole for another minute. He pulled out of the girl and burst, cum flying across her body. She scooted away and one of the other naked girls lay down in front of the man and began to lick the cum off his cock.

At the same time the other naked girl moved to the girl who had just finished fucking, adjusted her mask and began licking the cum off her body slowly. Ash found that she was just as turned on by the girl liking the other as she was by the guy getting his cock licked.

After a good licking the man was ready again, the girl with him lay down in front of him and he pushed himself into her. She groaned in pain when he slid inside. It wasn't a cherry pop kind of pain sound; more of a he had made a hard first thrust in her before she was ready.

On the other side of the room, the girl having now licked all the cum off the other had positioned herself on top of the other and they were now licking each other's pussy's deep. They had taken off their masks but with their faces buried in each other it was hard to see who was who.

Ash came hard soaking her panties, she hadn't remembered ever flooding herself this much before, but she had never seen sex like this in front of her before either. She had seen people having sex back at the slumber party, but that felt nothing like this did now. That had been some goofing around, virginal, inexperienced sex. This was something more but she couldn't put it into words, this was intense, and this man definitely wasn't innocent and knew how to fuck.

Ash removed her soaked panties and tossed them aside as she continued her self-exploration, she couldn't stop rubbing her clit as she felt another orgasm coming. The two girls in the corner both cried out in pleasure and the girl on top rolled off laying on the floor as Ash's fingers slid back inside her pussy, she was on fire in a way she had only ever been when she had actual sex. She had never been this aroused while simply masturbating before. Her second orgasm hit her hard juices flowing around her fingers.

Ash looked up to see the man looking at her now, he was still fucking the girl but his eye line was looking only at her, she burned deeper and wetter at this. She needed to fuck him now, stranger or not, she was going to have him. She had turned herself on to hard not to do it now.

The man pulled out of the second girl and sprayed her stomach with cum sticking his fingers inside her to grind against until she finally had her own orgasm. The man had now gone limp from his orgasms but Ash was burning to be with him, a man who knew what he was doing for a change. Virgins were fun but this was something different.

Before she could move the third girl moved in for her turn. The girl went to work sucking his cock deep and hard trying to return him to life for her turn. He continued to stare at Ash eyes burning into her, as the originally cum covered girl made her way over. Ash's gaze was locked into the man's so hard that she didn't notice the girl moving to her until she had slid her head in between Ash's thighs.

Ash's head snapped back as she looked down. Before she could say anything the girl had her tongue in Ash's wet pussy. It felt so good and she was so turned on she didn't care, she let it happen. Ash noticed the girls mask lying next to her leg but all she could see was the top of the girls head. It didn't matter who she was, she was good at what she was doing. She lay down on her back closing her eyes and letting the sensations fill her body.

The girl used both her fingers and tongue opening her and licking as deep as she could, it was incredible. She had been with Sara before and didn't like it; she realized now Sara hadn't known how to pleasure a girl like this person did. The girl using her fingers deep in her pussy moved up and began to suck on Ash's clit so hard it felt like it was growing.

Ash was so turned on that her pussy flooded the girls face, she looked down as she climaxed and saw the girl look up, it was Many who was licking her pussy, it was actually one of the greatest lickings she had ever had. As soon as Mandy pulled away she pulled her mask back on, but it had been long enough to see it was her.

Mandy went to the one girl she hadn't played with yet and began to lick her pussy now. Ash lay back down on the floor, panting and still so horny. She closed her eyes thinking of the man just a few feet

from her banging a random girl. She listened to the moaning in the room as her breathing returned to normal.

She started to drift into her own thoughts as she all of a sudden felt a cock rub up against her wet aching lower lips. She didn't opened her eyes as it must be her turn now with the dark robed man, she simply wrapped her legs around his back and pulled him down on her. He penetrated her deep, burying himself with the first thrust. His hips rocked back and forth thrusting hard, she felt so filled in a way she hadn't in so long. She hadn't been with anyone so big since Joey.

His thrusting was hard and all this activity was making her sore already, she would feel all of this tomorrow it had been too much for one night. Across the room she heard a man grown as if he was beginning to cum, but her man was still pounding away inside her. Her eyes flew open and she realized the boy fucking her wasn't her dark robed man, as he had just now finished with the third girl.

She began to panic; this was some other random stranger who had come into the room. Her legs dropped away from around his back. It was bad enough she was going to fuck one stranger but she thought she knew who dark robe really was, but this was a different stranger. Ash started hyperventilating and was about to push this boy off her when he pulled out of her and came on her upper thigh.

"Thank you," he said sweetly getting up and moving to one of the other girls.

Ash felt dirty, more so than ever before in her life. She reached over and picked up her soaked panties and used them to wipe off the boys cum. She threw the panties in the corner and got up. Her body was tired as she slowly walked from the room. She was disgusted with herself for having sex with someone she didn't know, but she couldn't blame the guy, that was after all the point of a masked orgy.

She pulled off her mask and through it on the ground as she walked out of the barracks. She slowly made her way back to the trail that led back to camp, stepping over and around people who were in the middle of all kinds of exhibitionism. She couldn't believe these were the same bible thumping kids she'd seen praying and singing hymens all week, this was the dark side of pretending to be good.

As she walked she couldn't help but wonder what was happening to her. Over the last couple years all she had done was manipulate people into loving or having sex with her. She liked Terra but she didn't want to become like her. Terra and Susan and even apparently Mandy, thought nights like this were acceptable. Ash didn't, she had done things tonight she already regretted.

Linda had sent her here to reflect on her behavior and think about the decisions she had made. It had backfired as now she had gone further over the edge that Linda had been worried about. What would her sister say if she could see her now, walking back to camp, no panties, cum stain on her skirt, and having enjoyed a bi-sexual experience.

Ash made her way back into her room sometime after 1 a.m. The room was empty, except for Sandy who was snoring quietly on her bunk; all the other girls had gone. This was strange as she figured at least Brandy should be here too. She wondered where she could have gone; it was improbable to her that Brandy went to the party.

It wasn't long after that Brandy slipped into the room her hair out of her usual pony tail all messed up. Ash peeked through mostly closed eyes pretending to be asleep as Brandy pulled her clothes

off to prepare for bed. Ash noticed Brian the bear on her panties and instantly knew where Brandi had been. She had been one of the virgins. This was just too good to be true, the queen of virtue had offered herself up tonight and lost her virginity. Ash rolled over and went to sleep.

The next morning was surreal, as Ash walked into the dining hall. It was clear why everyone wore the masks as she sat down at the table and tried to imagine witch of these proper innocent looking teens had been at the festivities the night before. She looked at the boys and tried to decide who had been inside her last night, it could have been any of them, it was pointless to try to figure it out as the boy wouldn't have known her either.

Terra and Susan came into the dining hall both looking disheveled and tired. Ash had worried when she had gotten up and not seen them in the room but was relived they were here now. The girls talked all through breakfast, but not a word was said about the night before, as Ash listened to the chatter in the room she couldn't hear one word of conversation from any table about what had happened. It was like the girls had told her, the next day it was as if it never happened. She wished she could forget it too.

As the day wore on the girls went swimming and spent the bulk of the day lying in the grass tanning in the sun. Ash liked being able to just relax all day without having to go to prayers today. After lunch she returned to the room and took a nap. She awoke again in time for dinner and left the room again to eat. After dinner she and Terra went sat in the grass and relaxed until bedtime.

Saturday night the Andy's again sat on the floor ready to play the truth game, as they didn't get to play then night before. Ash was astonished by the nerve of both Brandy and Mandy to sit there and play innocent for the whole room as they played the game. Terra was screaming at them to shut up as she needed sleep. The girls continued playing talking of their commitment to Jesus. Ash laughed and rolled over and went to sleep.

Sunday started with breakfast, which was a full feast, every type of breakfast food you could imagine was served. Once everyone was properly stuffed Morning Prayer began and lasted until Lunch. After lunch it was time for afternoon prayer which lasted until dinner. After dinner was evening prayer which lasted until bed. Ash went to bed thinking if she never prayed again it would be ok because she was stocked up now.

Monday started the exact same routine that the campers had, had last week. As they had last week, the Andy's sat every night praying and singing hymns, by the second week of this Ash found it incredibly annoying. She now understood Terra's comment about wanting to kill them or herself.

Before long it was Friday night again and the Andy's were parked on the floor in the room ready for another round of the truth game and committing themselves to Jesus. On the other side of the room Terra and Susan were getting dressed up in sexy clothes getting ready for a party.

It was already after eleven and Ash was torn, she couldn't stand the thought of staying in the room all night with the girls praying and singing, yet she had gone way to far the last time she went with Terra and Susan.

"Ash put on something sexy and move your little ass," Terra joked at her. Ash was wearing a black skirt and a t-shirt and felt she looked cute enough. She relented to her second option and put her shoes on to go with the girls.

The second Friday night tradition was called the light house dance. A mile or so outside the camp was an area owned by the city that had been turned into a state park, on the top of a large hill was an old lighthouse. It had been the look out during the war around the time they had built the military base that was now the camp.

After the long walk to the light house Ash was glad she had put on her running shoes instead of her flats that night. They arrived to a full out party. This was nothing like the deflowering party last week, tonight was more of what she had expected to go to the last time. There were lots of teens running around, drinking and dancing. Not all the teens were from the camp, some were local teens who liked to show the bible kids how to party.

"This is what's called the second week dance," Said Susan, "It's the camp version of prom."

"With lots of alcohol," Terra stated handing Ash a drink.

Ash wasn't really a drinker, but she decided to cut loose tonight, before she knew it she had, had four drinks already. There was music playing and kids dancing all around her. Ash was happy as this was much more what she needed.

Ash's legs were wobbly as she passed Terra; she was sitting on the stairs of the light house kissing a boy. Ash giggled as she passed them looking for a place to sit down herself. She finally sat down in the cold grass near the tower. She could see Susan dancing with a boy not far away holding a drink in one hand.

After a time Ash got up and walked to get another drink, a really cute boy handed her one and she walked away sipping her cup. This one tasted funny to her, but she hadn't ever had much experience drinking before and she thought it must just be the liquor.

Ash was about halfway through this drink when her world started spinning around her, all her senses fell apart at once, as she spun and fell on the ground. Moments later she felt someone pulling her arms, dragging her away. She looked to either side of her to see two boys pulling her to the light house tower.

These two boys were in their late teens and Ash hadn't seen them around the camp, they had to be local boys. The first boy moved the boards blocking the door to the light house tower stairwell the other dragged Ash in. They had drugged her drink with something. She could see and hear the world around her but she couldn't seem to move or speak. Her mind was so groggy she couldn't have made a coherent statement anyway.

They carried her all the way up the top of the stairs to the dome and dropped her down on the floor by what was one time the light lenses. Ash was helpless as she felt a hand run up her leg inside her skirt, touching her pussy through her panties. A set of lips began to kiss her gently. She wanted to cry out NO but between the drugs, and alcohol his touch was somehow making her wet.

It was a mixture of emotions as she was both scared and horny by this experience. Both boys were being gentle with her as they touched, kissed and teased her body. Her shirt was lifted over her head as one of the boys lightly caressed her body.

It was insane, she had been drugged and they were taking advantage of her but they weren't at all rough with her, she was angry but giving in to their touch. She had never been with two men before; it was horrifying and different at the same time. She felt her nipples being sucked in by the boys; this was incredible having both nipples sucked at once.

As her nipples received their attention she felt her panties being slowly pulled down her legs, one of the boys moved from her breast kissing his way down to the edge of her skirt, then slipping his head under it between her legs. She was confused, she had never heard of a case where a girl had been drugged so that the men could pleasure her.

When she realized she had been drugged she had expected to be mercilessly raped but this was nothing like that. This was exquisite almost loving in the way they were touching her, she was really afraid any minute her fears would become reality and they would hit her and be brutal.

The boy between her legs was licking into her slit as far as his tongue could reach; his thumb was caressing her clit. The two sensations together were amazing; she realized that the boy wasn't so much good at what he was doing as it was the drugs affecting her system heightening her sense of pleasure now.

The boy at her breasts removed his lips and sat up on his knees. He unzipped his shorts and pulled himself out of his zipper opening. Ash cringed as he moved his cock closer to her face, this was the moment she had feared, and this is when pleasure would move to brutality. The boy surprised her again, as he didn't shove his cock down her throat; he softly began to rub his penis head around her lips. With the boy still licking deep within her she was tingling all over. She managed to open her mouth, as if someone else was moving her tongue it snaked out of her mouth and liked the head of the boy's dick.

He moaned after a moment and leaned in letting the head of his swollen member slip into her mouth. She almost involuntarily started to suck. She tried but couldn't stop herself, the pleasure she was getting from the other boy was too much. Then it stopped.

She continued to suck the one boy's cock as the other left her dripping pussy and pulled back away from her. She could hear the zipper of the other boy's jeans as he pulled his own cock out rubbing it gently against her lower lips. The teasing was driving her crazy; she was dripping so hard she had a small puddle soaking her skirt under her ass now. She sucked harder; she could move her tongue but not her head, as he pushed more of himself in her mouth she was tickling him with her tongue.

The other boy was caressing her wet pussy lips with his cock but not entering her, the teasing finally became too much and she tried to move her body, she tried to thrust down but she couldn't move. The boy she was licking groaned loud, he exploded filling her mouth; she slightly gagged as she swallowed it down. It tasted salty and bitter to her but she had no choice but to swallow, as she couldn't turn her head.

The boy pulled back his dick softening; he was looking around as if only now becoming aware of where they were. He began to stroke himself watching her and the other boy, he seemed almost angry his cock had fell limp as he worked himself over trying to get hard again.

The teasing continued and despite the anger she had for them it felt physically good, as upset as Ash was she was that she was in this situation she just wished he would enter her already so it all could be over.

She moaned out loudly and the boy finally entered her. He wasn't as big as the boy last Friday or Joey, but he was still big. He slowly almost lovingly slid into her and pulled back. Softly yet deeply her pushed in and pulled back. She didn't know how long he had sex with her, but it was a long time. She hated herself for enjoying the feeling of him inside her. He was technically raping her but he did it with such gentle care it felt like they were lovers.

She moved her right arm to her breast rubbing her nipple, before she realized she could now move her right arm. This meant she must be coming out of her drug induced state; she wasn't the only one who noticed. The boy jerking himself called out to his friend telling him she had moved her arm and they should go.

The boy inside her pulled out a couple minutes later spraying the top of her skirt and her stomach with cum. A moment later the boy jerking himself moved in and sprayed her breasts and neck with his second load.

Both boys stuffed themselves back into their pants and ran hurriedly down the tower stairs. Ash lay there mostly naked covered in cum unable to move. She was upset for being here and letting this happen to her, she was angry with the boys for taking advantage of her, but it was her own fault for taking random drinks from strangers. She felt like a slut for liking the physical sensations as they took advantage of her, but she thought that had been the drug making things feel more pleasurable.

Ash could feel the tears running down her face as she struggled to regain control of her body. She had been completely used like a whore then abandoned. She felt empty inside, she felt cheap, and she felt dirty. She cried until she fell asleep.

Ash awoke lying on the floor of light house dome; the morning sun light was shining down on her now. She found she could turn her head but other than that she only had use of her one arm.

The sun was warm on her mostly naked body she looked down at herself as much as she could. She hurt emotionally as she looked at the dried seamen on herself, she had meant so little to them, she had been used as a cum receptacle, no more than that. She began to cry again.

She had no idea how long she lay on the floor, the shadows next to her had moved up slightly. She began crying again, but this time not for herself. She had come to a vast realization as she lay there. She cried now for Joey, Jace and Jt.

This feeling of having been used had made her realize what she had done to the boys she had been with before camp. She had genuinely loved Joey, but finding out she had tricked him, this is what he must have felt. This hole she felt right now as nothing to what she had probably made him feel. No wonder he hadn't talked to her all year. He hadn't even talked to her at Christmas.

Then she thought of Jace and the game she had played on him, but she tuned out those thoughts. Jace had, had one hell of a night with her and his sister then he had ended up getting a girlfriend out of the whole thing so he never went through the feelings of being used because of her game.

Then there was Jt, he was such a sweet and shy boy, and she understood only now what he must be feeling. He had to be sitting at home, crying, having a bigger emotional hole in his soul and it was her fault. But what was she to do about Jt? She was going home again soon, and she couldn't change the past. She would have to come up with something really nice to do for him before she returned to Lilly's.

It had to be mid-day and Ash was hungry. Since it was Saturday everyone had a free day she wouldn't be missed at prayers, they might figure she was out running around. She really hoped that Terra would realize she never made it back last night and when she couldn't find her today she would come looking for her.

Ash found her left leg could move now it wasn't enough for her to be able to get herself up but at least it could move again. She had begun to panic, thinking she would be permanently immobile, now she had an arm and a leg back. She pushed as hard as she could with the one leg and managed to slide herself to the glass wall. She used her good arm to push herself into a sitting position. This was so much better she could feel tingles throughout her body but couldn't stand up.

Ash managed to reach over by the wall and retrieve her shirt and one handedly pull it over her head one arm slipping into the sleeve easy and she picked up her other arm pushing the limp appendage into her other sleeve. At least now she wasn't naked, if someone found her. She looked over and could see her panties lying on the floor near where she had been laying but she wasn't going to get them.

Using her good leg and arm she scooted to the stairwell. She got to the first stair used her arm to balance and dropped into a sitting position onto the first stair. Ash spent the next hour slowly dropping one step at a time. When she reached the bottom her ass hurt from dropping onto the metal waffling of each stair.

Ash's whole body was prickling now; it hurt like a thousand needles were stabbing her skin. She used all her strength and pulled on the railing until she was standing. She hopped on her one good foot the ten feet to the door, pushing the boards aside and hopping through the opening. She lost her balance on the way out and fell. She lay on the ground deciding to not move again.

She had no idea how long she was on the ground when she heard someone walking around near her. She tried to call out to them but her throat was sore and she couldn't speak.

"OH MY GOD!" Terra screamed as she spotted Ash lying almost face down on the ground.

"What? Did you find her?" called someone else running up, "OH GOD! Is she dead?" Ash felt a hand on her arm shaking her. Between the climb down the stairs and the fall she had now energy left.

"I don't know she's not moving," Terra explained rolling Ash over. Both girls gasped.

"Oh my god, oh my god, oh my god," the other girl said over and over, Ash could see her now and was surprised to see the other girl was Mandy.

"What's .... Oh GOD NO!" Susan screamed catching up with the other two girls, "She'd dead?"

"No, look she's breathing," Terra pointed out breathing a sigh as she said so.

"Oh thank god," from Susan, "But what happened, she's bloody and she isn't moving."

"I don't know," Terra answered.

The girls picked Ash up and moved her to the stairs. Ash tried to talk but only accomplished clearing her throat. The girls looked her over and wiped the blood off her face.

"I......ok," Ash finally managed to croak out. Mandy was looking at her crying.

"We need to get her back to camp, but we can't get caught here," Terra said, "I'm going to run back to camp to find a couple guys who were here last night. They should help us without ratting us out."

"Good idea," Susan told her, "I'm going to get some water and something we can clean her up with. Mandy do NOT leave her side."

"I won't," Mandy responded meekly. The girls ran off in separated directions leaving Mandy and Ash alone.

"Thank........ You," Ash managed fighting for her voice to come back.

"I was worried. I..........," she said shyly, "I think you're nicer than those two." Mandy indicated Terra and Susan, "When they said they couldn't find you I overheard and wanted to help"

"Why..... You......... Pretend.....to be what..........you're not," Ash pushed her voice out.

"What are you talking about?" Mandy asked.

"I saw...... You and Sean......... At the dock. You...... And last Friday....... You licked my............."

"OH MY GOD! That WAS you!" she cried out her face now pail and she started shaking, "I thought I recognized your outfit. Please don't hate me." Mandy had tears in her eye.

"No, I don't hate you........... It was special," Ash said her voice coming back. Ash never in her life thought she would have to find the right words to reassure a girl about her sexual technique towards herself, "I just don't know why you play like your one of them when you're really one of us?"

"Brandy is my cousin, and she wouldn't understand. I have to act like her or she would tell my mom about anything I do. My mom is a crazy bible thumper like her too."

Ash told her she understood but to not let Brandy control her life. She told Mandy about seeing Brandy at the Deflowering Ceremony. Mandy was pissed, she stood up and walked around ranting about having to put up with all this Jesus bonding bullshit so that Brandy would approve of her, she had spent so much time covering her tracks just to have a little fun so Brandy wouldn't know and the whole time here was miss perfect running around fucking behind their backs.

Ash watched as a physical change took place in Mandy, she was visibly livid with her cousin. Ash wasn't sure if she had just opened the lid to something good or bad. She finally came back and sat down next to Ash.

"You saw me and Sean, and you knew it was me and you didn't use that against me?"

"No," Ash hadn't known why before that she hadn't used it against her but she did now, she liked the real Mandy under the fake Circle of Andy thing she did.

"You're not grossed out about me............ Doing that to you?"

"No," Ash said softly placing her one good hand on her shoulder, "I once had a special bond with another friend like we have now."

"I like that, I knew you were cool." Mandy smiled.

It wasn't long before Susan returned with some water; she tore a patch off the bottom of her own shirt and washed Ash's face down. Once the blood and dirt were gone she only had a small cut above her eye from where she had fell.

It was an hour before Terra returned with a couple boys. It was well past lunch time Ash was hungry and she still couldn't move her body completely. She had regained enough mobility in her other arm that she could now hold onto the two boys as they walked her back to camp. They supported her with their shoulders so she wouldn't have to hop so much.

It took a long time to walk the mile or so back to camp. By the time they reached camp the movement had circulated Ash's system around enough that she had the feeling back in her other leg again. She was still wobbly trying to walk but she could do so slowly. It was dinner time now and they headed to the dining hall.

Mandy sat with the three girls only to receive glares from the other two Andy's. Brandy was visibly pissed that Mandy was with them, she finally walked over to them.

"Mandy, where have you been all day? You missed the prayers today," Brandy said snotty.

"Go fuck yourself, you two faced bitch," Mandy shot back at her shocking all the girls around them.

"What....." Brandy said taken aback.

"Next time you want to lie to everyone's face, be more discrete, Brian the Bear," Many told her. Brandy had no response, she turned red having been caught and ran away out of the dining hall.

"About fucking time," Terra said patting Mandy on the shoulder, "So if you can talk good enough, what happened, Ash?"

Ash frowned and began to tell her tail. The girls were shocked and cried about what had happened to her. They talked about what she had been given. They all agreed that they had never heard of a drug that could make you paralyzed like what had happened to her. In the end they decided that it must have been a bad side effect due to the combination of the alcohol and the drug.

After dinner all four went and sat down outside in the grass until bed. This was their last night at camp and the girls didn't want to say goodbye they had bonded now, including Mandy. Brandy came back to the room talking only to Sandy who was very confused as to what was going on.

The circle of girls talking on the floor tonight was Ash, Susan, Terra and Mandy. After searching for her all day and thinking that she was dead when they found her, the girls had now formed a strong

bond of friendship. They sat up almost all night talking, they knew Ash was leaving town in a few days but all had agreed to keep in touch with her. About two a.m. Brandy threw a shoe at them and screamed for them to shut up and go to bed. All four girls laughed.

The next morning was another feast of a Sunday breakfast then off to morning prayers. This lasted until lunch time when they were sent to their rooms to collect their things before being able to get lunch. They were all handed a bag lunch they could eat on the trip home then they all boarded the bus.

The girls were quiet on the ride home giving Ash time to think. Linda had sent her to camp to think about her life and her decisions. She had done just that, after what she had gone through this last two weeks she had woke up to the harder side of life and re-thought her own actions.

Linda's idea to send her away had worked, just not in the way and by the methods she had envisioned when she sent Ash there. Ash felt she was lucky to be alive now. She wasn't going to take herself or others for granted anymore. She had, had sex long before now but she felt that she had lost her innocence over this last two weeks.

When the bus pulled up to the church Linda was waiting for her there. The four girls exited the bus and hugged each other crying. There was a bond between them she hated to have to break. Ash noticed Linda staying back and giving her both time and space to say goodbye

As Ash walked to great Linda she was excited to go home. It was only about another week and some that she was going to still be here, she would be turning 16 soon and be home with Joey, she loved him so much, she missed him so much, and she understood finally what she had done to him. She would just have to talk to him and resolve things. That time was so close now, after a whole year of waiting their time was coming.

Linda hugged Ash tightly, tears in her eyes. Ash was surprised to see her sister crying at her return. Maybe this meant that she had forgiven her. Linda opened her trunk and Ash dropped her bag in before getting into the passenger seat.

"We need to talk," Linda said in a tone Ash realized was quite serious, "Something's happened while you were gone." Ash's stomach sank as Linda began speaking; she knew this would be bad.
☐

Chapter Sixteen:

Ashley's Diary Part 4: Party at Christmas Break

Ash walked into her room and threw her back pack on her bed and jumped down next to it. She stuck her face into her pillow and sobbed; she had started crying in the car and now she let it all come out. Ash hadn't said a word as Linda told her of the events of the last couple weeks, Joey's dad was dead, her sister was in the hospital and she was now going to be living with Linda.

Ash cried for Joey's dad, she cried for her sister, she cried for Joey. She cried because she wouldn't be going home again, she wouldn't be going back to settle things with Joey, and she cried because of what had happened to her on Friday night. Now that she was home it all came crashing down on her. Her friends had helped her hold it together after they had found her but now she let out all the anger she had felt as the boys had raped her. She pushed her face into her pillow and screamed as loud as she could but it wasn't enough.

Part of Ash had died in that lighthouse, they had taken from her something she couldn't explain but it was lost. She sat up and started punching her pillows as her rage exploded out of her. She took her clothes out of the dresser and started throwing them against the wall with fury. She picked up her books now and started hurling them at the walls.

"What are you doing?" Linda exclaimed entering the room quickly having heard the noise, "Oh sweetie what's wrong?" Linda asked worried seeing Ash's face. Linda rushed to her sister and held her, "It will work out, and I know you're sad about Lilly and the family but it's going to be ok."

"It's...... it's......... it's not................." Ash stuttered through tears. She couldn't tell her sister what had happened. She would be in just as much trouble for leaving camp and going to a party where she had been drinking.

"Its ok sweetheart, did something happen at camp?" Linda asked softly in understanding, still holding her sister. Ash nodded against her shoulder, "Do you want to talk about it?" Ash shook her head as she began to sob against Linda's shoulder, "Its ok, you don't have to tell me, just know you can if you need to."

"Th...th...thank you," Ash replied softly. The girls held each other for a while until Ash pulled away and sat on the bed. Linda told her she was going to make dinner and she stepped out. Ash pulled the blanket over her head and curled up into a ball. Laying there in bed she felt the loss of everything she had. She felt like she had been dumped here unwanted and in the way as she was now going to be living with the sister she let down, and near the boy she had betrayed. She hated herself now; she hated what she had done to the boys in her life and she was furious at what she had let happen to herself.

She got off the bed after some time, she was hungry and needed something sweet to eat, and maybe that would help her feel better. It was then she felt a sudden surge of panic and ran to the dresser,

pulling the bottom drawer all the way out. Both items she had hid there were still where she had left them.

These two items were her most treasured possessions; she had only left them behind because she was afraid of losing them at camp. The first was a thin little box she picked it up looking inside before putting it in her pocket, and then she picked up the tattered slip of folded paper, putting it in her other pocket. With that done she walked out of the room to find something to eat.

After returning from camp Linda decided in light of everything that had happened Ash was allowed out of the house again during the day. She thought Ash had learned her lesson, saying the girl who returned home didn't seem at all like the one she sent away. Ash didn't have the heart or nerve frankly to tell her sister what had happened to her, after she had cried on Linda's shoulder they never brought it up again.

The Monday after she returned Ash ran across the complex and knocked on Jt's door.

"Come to say goodbye?" he asked bitterly.

"No I came to say I'm sorry and that I'm going to live with Linda full time now."

"I don't understand." He stated and looked like his face had softened slightly.

Ash told him what had happened at Lilly's home while she had been gone at camp. Jt looked sad and told her he was sorry. She hugged him when she was done talking he resisted at first then held her tight for a matter of minutes.

Ash told him that she was so sorry for leading him on and she felt bad about everything she then for some reason told him about what had happened at camp, she left most of it out but told him about the whole lighthouse incident. She didn't know why she told him but she did, and then asked him to not tell anyone.

Jt was such a sensitive kid that he was horrified by the whole thing, he said he was sad she had almost died and he hugged her again. Ash told him that she really did like him a lot but she didn't have the same feelings for him. She said that she would like it if they were best friends now that she was staying.

Jt sat quietly for a few minutes in thought then decided that he liked the idea of being friends with her. He said he felt special that she had talked to him about what happened to her, and that they could be just friends that had shared a secret special day. Ash liked that too and told him she would do her best to be a good friend this time and make it up to him.

It wasn't long before Ash turned 16, her day had finally come. She waited by the phone all day long hoping Joey would call, if only to say happy birthday, but the call never came. That night Linda, James, and Jt took Ash out to a fancy Italian restaurant for dinner. She tried not to be depressed as she sat there with all these well-meaning people but she couldn't focus on dinner, she thought only of Joey. It had been a whole year and not one word from him.

Her ordeal at camp had made her snap out of the mood she had been in. She had been so upset and heartbroken she had gone into a denial and had used both Jace and Jt without realizing her behavior

had been out of anger. She really didn't know much about what was going on in Joey's life right now. Did he have a girlfriend? How bad had he taken his father's death? Did he even still think about her? He had spent the last year with Katie; maybe they finally broke down and were dating each other? All these thoughts were driving her wild as she tried to eat her dinner.

Ash checked the answering machine first thing when she got back home from dinner; her sister had called to wish her happy birthday but no word from Joey. Ash went to bed early that night. She didn't even change into her pajamas that night as she lay on her bed crying. She reached into her pocket and pulled out the tattered slip of paper and read it. She hoped the words written on it would cheer her up, but instead it made her cry worse.

School started day's later still without a phone call from Joey. She realized that he had forgotten her completely. She deserved it and worse for all the trouble she had caused. As the school year began she sat in classes heartbroken all over again, this time she could only blame herself. She made up her mind right then that she loved Joey and always would, but if she mattered so little to him that he couldn't even call her, she was done. She was going to try to find someone she could love as much as him. She didn't know if that was possible but it was time to try. No more head games with boys, no more random fucking, just a real relationship with someone who loved her. She thought about Jt for a minute but realized that his love for her wasn't real. He had fallen in love with her because, like most young boys, he fell for the first girl to give him any real attention. It would have to be someone else, someone new but she didn't know if she could trust any guy again after the lighthouse party.

The one high point to the new life here was that Terra and Mandy both went to her new school, unfortunately so did Brandy. Ash had made as strong enemy in Brandy who took every opportunity to cut her down. It didn't matter because whenever she was down she had her two new best friends there for her.

Mandy turned 15 right after the start of the school year and Ash and Terra had taken her out for her birthday. They went to the movies and hung around the mall looking at guys and joking about what they would do with them. It was a really fun night and Ash was really glad she had met them. From that day on the three girls ran everywhere together, from the mall after school, football games, and just hanging out in the park.

Just for the hell of it all three tried out for the cheer squad. Brandy tried out for cheer too just to despite the girls. Brandy thought that being on cheer squad would be a great place to get back at the girls if they all made the squad. This backfired on Brandy however when Mandy and Ash were accepted and Terra wasn't. Ash and Mandy quickly quit because they didn't want to cheer without Terra, Brandy tried to quit but her parents told her she had made a commitment and she had to go through with it. So like it or not Brandy was stuck cheering for the whole year.

Life took a turn for the interesting when Linda came to talk to Ash in late October; she sat Ash down on her bed and told her that James had asked them to move in with him and Jt. James still had no idea what had really happened between Ash and Jt, but he and Linda had been dating for six months now and the girls spent so much time at his apartment now that he thought it was a good idea.

Linda had told James she needed to talk to Ash about it before she could give him an answer; she told James it affected her too. What Linda was really worried about was what might still be going on with the kids, she hadn't seen anything suspicious since Ash had come back from bible camp, but she still had a concern. Linda went home that night and asked Ash point blank if she was still fooling around with Jt.

Ash was shocked Linda had just come right out with it. Ash looked at her in surprise, she didn't have anything to hide but for some reason she didn't want to talk about her relationship to Jt.

"Look," Linda started, "I get that you've been really good since you came back from camp, but I can't move in with James if you kids are still having sex. This is just what I was talking about when I said that your affair could cause conflict with James and me." Ash understood but she didn't want the lecture right then.

"No," Ash answered looking at her feet, "I haven't wanted to be with anyone after............." She broke off her sentence and her face tensed up. Linda's face changed and she realized she had just picked at a nerve within Ash.

"I'm so sorry sweetie, I just had to ask," Linda told her pulling her into a hug, "I didn't mean to bring up something bad. You still don't want to talk about it?"

"No."

"Ok, sorry," Linda pulled away from the hug and sat next to her for a minute without saying anything, "So what do you think?"

"I think James is a great guy and we should do it. Jt and I are really just friends now. It will be ok."

It was the beginning of November and with the double income of James and Linda they found that they could afford to rent a house. They found a nice place with 2 bedrooms and two baths and a full basement. Ash liked the house it felt more like a real home to her then the apartment had. They had talked about the room arrangements when they had come to look at this house, James and Lilly got the master bedroom upstairs, Ash got the other room upstairs and Jt moved into the basement. He seemed really happy to have what he called his own apartment down stairs.

Ash figured she knew why he liked being all the way down there, as she had talked to Joey a number of times about what boys were doing at Jt's age. The basement was set up so that it was split into two parts, Jt had a living room type area just off the stairs where he could bring his friends and play video games and watch movies. They put a desk down in the front space so that he could study down stairs on his own as well. On the other half of the divider wall they had built was set up as a bedroom with his bed, dressers and end table. This arrangement gave him a lot of privacy to do whatever he wanted whenever he needed to.

Ash liked the house but she was tired of moving, it seemed to her ever since her parents had died all she did was move. This had been the fourth time in just over three years and she still didn't know if she would return to Lilly's once her injuries had healed. She loved Linda but she really wanted to go back home to her other sister and the life she had, had there.

It didn't take long to settle into things at the new house, Ash had stayed true to her word and not crossed the line again with Jt. Their relationship toward each other wasn't what you would call brother and sister but it wasn't sexual either. They had truly bonded and become like best friends. Ash usually hung out after school with Terra and Mandy at the mall but as soon as she got home she would run down stairs to tell Jt anything new that had happened that day. They would sit and do their homework and play

video games. In the first few weeks Linda would show up unexpectedly all the time to check on them, but by Christmas break she had begun to really trust them and leave them alone together a little more.

Everything was going great until a couple days before Christmas break. At dinner that night James told the kids that he and Linda were going out for a whole weekend that weekend and the kids would have to be on their own. Ash said that was no problem she had been on her own for weekends like that lots of times living with Lilly. Linda gave her a knowing look but she didn't say anything. Linda knew that she and Joey had made use of those weekends but Ash didn't plan on doing anything wrong this time.

Ash went to school the next day and talked to Terra about them being alone in the house this weekend, the first thing Terra said was PARTY. Ash told her no it was out of the question. As the day ended the ball had been set rolling and Ash had at least 25 to 30 kids coming over on Saturday night. Ash talked to Jt about it and he liked the idea of a party with girls, so he was in. Ash was all but shaking with fear at the idea of a party in her house; she still hadn't gotten over her last party. But this time Terra and Jt would be close by and not let anything happen to her.

Linda and James left Friday night; Linda talked to Ash privately and told her that she trusted her alone with Jt, and not to let her down again. Ash hugged her sister and said she wouldn't. That night was fun for the kids they ordered a pizza and sat down in the basement playing games and eating. They stayed up very late that night just enjoying being teenagers and having fun.

Ash awoke to Jt kissing her the next morning; she had passed out on his couch sometime during the late night. She was lying in the bend in the couch at an angle, not quite on her back but not on her side. Jt was lying partly on his side and partly on her and he was kissing her desperately as his cock was hard poking her bare leg as it had come out the leg of his shorts.

"Stop JT!" Ash said pushing him away, "We can't do this, and I promised Linda I wouldn't."

"But..... It's been so long," he whined looking her right in the eyes, "I've tried to be good too, but............ since we moved in here......"

"I know but I told you what happened the last time I........... I......... you know," she said shaking a little.

"I know," he said in a truly sorrowful tone, "But I need to so bad, PLLLLEEESSSEE." He was begging now and Ash felt bad. She had started this with him and taken it away, she could feel his need seeping against her leg. She sat in silence holding him back having a moral debate inside her head. She felt like if she didn't do this for him he would hate her, but she felt like if she did she would feel dirty and be betraying her promise.

"I like you Jt, you know that but I don't know.........." She trailed off in her sentence as he began to kiss her neck. It felt really good she had trained him well over the summer on how to hit her buttons. She started breathing hard as he gently bit the back of her neck. That was her melting point, she regretted teaching him that trick now, "Wait, WAIT!" she cried pushing him back again.

"I......... need you.......... So much.........you're so hot.........." He said between kisses attacking her neck again. She knew she was lost now. She had tried twice to stop this, but it was Jt and she liked him despite trying so hard not to. She pulled his shirt off and began kissing his shoulder, and then their

mouths met again kissing deeply. She reached down to his shorts and began to stroke his half exposed member.

Jt was still young and it had been almost six months, Ash expected him to go off on her right away then she might be able to end this but apparently his time in the basement alone had been working on lasting longer. Ash stroked as hard as she could with him sticking out of his shorts leg but he didn't pop.

Jt slid her shirt up her body reviling her bare chest as she hadn't been wearing a bra last night. His lips found her breasts and he began to suck hard on her nipple. His need for her was deep as he sucked her, he was both soft and aggressive in his approach to her now, and it was driving her crazy.

Ash pushed his shorts off his ass down to his knees, he wasn't wearing underwear and she wondered if he had planned this last night. She gripped him better with his shorts down and stroked him unrestrained, he was moaning deeply as he sucked her other nipple. It was only minutes later his whole body shook and gobs of cum shot out of him covering her legs, her shorts and the couch. He wouldn't stop Cuming, it was like he had saved it all since they had last had sex as he coated her shorts.

He finally relaxed kissing her mouth again when he had regained control. Ash felt sticky, dirty and wet as he kissed her, she wanted to stop now her mind flashed back to lying helpless at the light tower with cum coating her body, and she began to have a slight panic attack. She gently pushed him away from her and scooted herself into a sitting position pulling her sticky legs up to her chest.

"Ok, I think that's more than enough," Ash told him shaky, "I did promise Linda."

"But you didn't.............You know...........Did you?" he asked the shyness coming back again.

"No I didn't cum, it's ok, do YOU feel better now?" She asked trying to smile.

"Ummm...........yeah, uh.......... I'm sorry I couldn't stop............I woke up with........and you were there in those shorts........... I couldn't stop." Ash almost giggled at his stuttering apology.

"It's ok, we just shouldn't have, we just need to be more careful in the future," she told him quietly. She was as nice about the whole thing as she could be; he didn't know that she had such a hang up about sex now. She got up and left the basement room to go take a shower and put her clothes in the washer, the last thing she would need is for Linda to come home and find her cum stained shorts in the laundry.

Ash's fears started building that morning and didn't get any better by the time Terra had shown up, she was really worried about having a party at the house not just because of her own hang ups but because she thought it was betraying Linda's trust again. Jt seemed excited all day and when Terra had shown up and he met her for the first time he seemed to be unable to not look at her.

Ash actually felt a small twinge of jealousy at the way he looked at Terra but she put it away. If he liked her it would be fine, and it would clear up things like this morning if he fixated on someone else. They escaped from him long enough for Ash to change, she decided on her favorite black skirt and a really pretty hot pink button up long sleeve shirt. Terra was there for about an hour with Jt following them around before anyone else showed up. When people started coming they didn't stop, before Ash could think there were a houseful of kids filling every room.

Mandy had to sneak out of her house to come, so she was late. Ash thought it was funny when Mandy had made it because she was dressed just like Ash and Terra. It was almost like the three of them had planned it. All three looked hot in their skirts and Jt was still following Terra around when Mandy arrived and the girls joked about how cute it was. Terra told Ash if she didn't hook up at the party she might make Jt's dream come true and fuck him by the end of the night. Mandy and Ash laughed because they knew Terra wasn't actually joking.

The party was in full gear and Ash had begun to worry about cops being called and having the whole thing broken up, sadly she half wished that would happen. She had lost track of both Terra and Many as she had been trying to figure out who had brought all the alcohol, she didn't want the drinking in the house. This set off a chain of events where she began dumping out any alcohol she could and a number of people had gotten really mad and everyone finally left.

Someone had suggested that they move the party to some other place and the kids took the remaining alcohol and they all left. Ash was standing in the kitchen by herself looking at the mess in the house. She was a little pissed of that her friends had left her to deal with it on her own. She figured to hell with that she would go down and get Jt and make him help her clean up. He had been so keen on the idea of the party least he could do was help her now.

She walked down the stairs to the basement room and paused as she could hear moaning from behind the divider wall, she turned to leave thinking he was taking care of himself, when she heard a distinct girl moan. Ash was irritated had Terra really gone to him, she didn't like the idea of Jt getting with Terra; she was a little too wild for a boy like him. She wasn't jealous but she thought she should put a stop to it before Terra accidently broke his heart worse than she had last summer.

Ash walked to the divider and looked in, Jt had the lamp on next to his bed but a red shirt had been thrown over it giving off a low red glow to his room. Ash almost gasped as she looked up to see who was with him. Mandy was naked between his legs her head down sucking his cock deep. Ash's brain clicked into a memory of Mandy's tongue on her pussy and how good she had licked her out last summer. She knew that Mandy could use her mouth and by the look on Jt's face he was finding that out too. Ash could feel herself getting wet watching them, having been with both of them. She slowly moved backwards and left the basement, her hand in her panties rubbing herself as she climbed the stairs.

She ran up the second set of stairs to her room, she needed to take care of her dripping pussy. Jt had worked her up so much that morning she had never completely came back down, and now seeing them together she was halfway there already. She burst through her door hand still rubbing her clit to find someone in her bed. She pulled her hand back reluctantly and sat down next to Terra who was lying in the middle of her bed.

Terra sat up when Ash sat down, she could smell the sex radiating from Ash right then. Terra was drunk and as she sat up her and Ash locked eyes, neither said a word to each other they just sat staring into one another. Then they were kissing, both girls' tongues exploring each other's mouth, Ash didn't know what had come over her but she couldn't stop kissing Terra. Ash was confused as they kissed because she knew that Mandy was bi-sexual and she herself had played around a couple times but she had never heard Terra mention that she was into that at all. But for someone who never mentioned she was into girls Terra really knew how to touch her just right, her hands were in just the right places and Terra's mouth was now on her neck.

Ash had been half way there when she walked into the room and this was getting close to pushing her over the edge. She had never once thought of having sex with her best friend but here and now it seemed so right for them to be like this. Ash's need was flowing between her legs as they leaned back on the bed; Terra was now unbuttoning her shirt and ripping it as she did so. As soon as her shirt was open Terra's lips were on her chest, Ash thought she should put a stop to this in case Terra was too drunk, she didn't want to lose her best friend because of a drunken mistake.

"Terra, are you sure?" Ash moaned out as Terra reached behind her and unhooked her bra, "You've been drinking..............OH GOD DON'T STOP." Terra in one motion had sucked Ash's nipple in her mouth and found her clit with her hand.

"I'm not .... As drunk as......... I'm OOOOH GOD," Terra started as Ash's hand found Terra's pussy. Their hands slid into each other's panties and began to rub fast, kissing each other on the mouth again.

After several minutes the girls broke apart, Ash had been very close to her orgasm and moaned as Terra broke away. Terra pulled off her shirt quickly and threw it on the floor then she scooted up to pull off her skirt, panties and bra. Ash followed her lead removing her skirt and panties. It had been years since Ash had sat completely naked with a girl breathing hard ready to experiment. Not a word was spoken as they sat naked; they looked at each other again for a long moment before grabbing one another and falling into more kissing.

Ash hadn't wanted to be with a guy since her ordeal at the lighthouse but she hadn't ever considered that being with a girl would be the answer to her sexual hesitance. Their fingers found their way back to each other's pussies again and both girls moaned into each other as they began to clit play. Terra rolled Ash onto her back and started giving her slow supple kisses down her body.

Ash could feel her orgasm building again as Terra moved down to her stomach then on to her clit. Terra really knew what she was doing as she took Ash's clit into her mouth and sucked it in a way she had never felt before. Terra treated her clit almost as if she were trying to suck a cock, then her tongue snaked its way into her pussy, lapping deep and quickly. That finally pushed Ash over the edge, she sprayed Terra's face as she came harder then she had in over a year.

Terra didn't stop, she licked within her harder before Ash had a chance to come down from her orgasm, and within moments she was leaking more juices on the her best friends face. This only caused Terra to push harder again, Ash didn't know where she was finding this energy Terra used to eat her so thoroughly but it was the most incredible licking she had ever had. She hated to admit it but Terra was so much better at eating her out then even Joey had been and he had been so good when he had done it for her. When Ash's second orgasm hit Terra reached around behind Ash's back grabbing her ass and lifting it off the bed, pulling her pussy deeper into her mouth.

Ash lost any control she had left at that moment, she was crying out now and shuddering, she hadn't cried out like that for so long but she had never been through this before. Terra pulled her tongue back and replaced it with her fingers as she began to attack her clit again, sucking hard. Ash hit her third orgasm as more cum shot from her then ever had before. Terra's face was drenched now and it was dripping off her.

Ash's breathing was heavy and she was going in and out of consciousness as Terra continued her assault on her aching pussy. It was too much, too intense to crazy that this was even happening, she

230

couldn't believe she was here in this moment, it was too good to be real as she felt orgasm number four hitting her hard her body fell back to the bed.

"Ash? Oh my God! Ash?" She cried out in a panicky voice, "Hey girl are you ok?" Ash woke up staring into the eyes of a scared looking Terra.

"What's wrong?" Ash asked her voice weak.

"I thought something happened to you," Terra started, "You went limp and didn't respond, I didn't know what happened." Ash giggled at her for a second.

"I passed out; it used to happen to me when I was younger. Only one other person ever ate me so good as to make me pass out," Ash explained to her.

"I've never heard of a girl that did that, I was so scared when you stopped moving," Terra said quietly and Ash kissed her feeling weak she wanted to continue, she wanted to give back to her friend what Terra had just done for her, but her body had taken all it could and she needed to calm down, rest and recharge.

Ash could feel Terra's heart beating really hard as she laid her body against her own. They kissed as they both calmed down and slowly drifted off to sleep. Ash woke about an hour later, she was still tired but she was really cold, she gently slipped out from under Terra and pulled a blanket out of the closet. They had fallen asleep on top of the bed and she didn't want to move Terra to pull back the blankets. She covered themselves under the blanket and fell back to sleep.

Ash woke for the second morning in a row to someone kissing her. It was still mostly dark outside leaving very low light in her room. It was Terra kissing her today, focusing on Ash's neck instead of her lips. Ash was tingling already as Terra continued her gentle almost loving touching movements of her hands and lips. Ash was truly surprised by this degree of affection, in the few months Ash had known Terra all she had seen was a girl who moved from one guy to another, never showing any hint she cared about any of them.

Terra had become her crazy, outrageous, crude and kind of wild friend. Ash really liked being here with her now, being on the other end of Terra's soft side. She felt special that her friend was like this with her. Joey had once said that she and Sara had shared a special bond, and she had said the same thing to Mandy last summer, but both hadn't felt like this. This was so much more than just a friendship bond. Ash realized she had real feelings for Terra, she wouldn't say she was in love with her but she understood in that moment she had actually feelings for her.

"I wish I could wake up that way every day," Ash said softly.

"How are you feeling this morning?" Terra asked kissing her shoulder lightly.

"Really good right now," she said and gave Terra a smile.

"You're not weirded out?" Terra asked hesitantly.

"I was surprised last night, but it didn't weird me out," Ash paused she had something else she wanted to say but was really nervous, "In fact............. It felt right, I mean....... I mean........... I like you......

231

a little........ That way." She bit her lip afraid of how Terra would react. Ash only now realized how much courage it had taken Jt to say this to her last summer.

Ash had never before considered having a girlfriend, yet right now, lying in bed naked with her best friend she was considering. She had a crush on Jace but that hadn't been more than a passing interest. She liked Jt a lot, but she had never been in love with him. Right now as Terra paused Ash's heart beat fast as she talked to the first person she had really fell for since Joey.

"Can I be honest with you?" Terra asked after a long time, "I...... don't want you to hate me." Ash's heart felt heavy as she nodded to her friend, "I like to fuck guys, you know that, but I've only ever had a couple short term boyfriends, and I've never dated a girl."

"Ok," Ash said not sure where this was going, "But that couldn't have been the first time you ever did that, you were incredible."

"Thank you," Terra said a little embarrassed, "I want to tell you everything but............ I'm scared............ I don't want you to never talk to me again."

"I wouldn't, I............ I've been through a lot too," Ash explained. Terra turned away from her. Ash leaned in and kissed her neck, putting her arms around her friend. Ash could tell what ever Terra was hiding had been building up in her for a long time, needing someone she could trust to get it out.

Terra finally started speaking after a few minutes of Ash holding her, as she spoke Ash was again surprised at the change in her demeanor. This morning she was so soft in touch and words, as she told Ash that her mom and dad had broken up when she was ten and she had stayed with her mom and 15 year old sister, Megan. Ash had known that already but she let Terra start at the beginning.

It all started about the time that Terra was 12, she had just come home from playing at the park and her mom was at work. She was heading to her room when she thought she would go talk with her sister. She ended up walking in on Megan and best friend, Cammy, in bed licking each other. The girls were laying on her sisters bed faces buried in each other, Terra had never considered that girls would get together like that before and she found herself horrified and turned on by watching. Megan saw her standing at the door and Cammy jumped off the bed and grabbed Terra by the wrists and pulled her into the room sitting her on the bed. Terra was scared but she asked the girls what they were doing and the girls explained that when girls didn't have a boyfriend they could do what they were doing to help each other out.

Terra told them she wasn't sure she understood and was shocked when Cammy asked her if she had ever touched herself down there. Terra told her that she had never touched herself because it was wrong. Megan and Cammy laughed at her and she ran from the room crying. Megan came to her room a little while later to talk to her.

Megan asked her to not say anything about what she had seen to their mom because she could get in trouble. Terra asked her if she wasn't doing anything wrong why she would be in trouble. Megan explained to her that Cammy really liked boys but she also liked to play around with her too but Megan just liked girls. Terra was confused again and asked how a girl could like another girl? Terra had seen pictures of boys naked and she was excited for the day she could feel a boy's thing touching inside her, she told this to Megan and asked how girls could have sex without a boy's thing.

Megan smiled sweetly at her and told her she didn't understand because she hadn't ever played with herself. She told Terra that once she had gotten herself off a few times she would understand how more than a cock could make a girl feel good. Terra was shocked by the words her sister was using but she had made her curious. Megan left after Terra agreed not to tell on her.

During the course of her next couple weeks Terra began trying to understand what her sister had been talking about. She discovered after the first time she rubbed the nub above her opening that it felt good and she began to see what Megan was talking about. She spent most of her spare time alone in her room over the next couple months. She couldn't stop touching herself after she had discovered it, she needed it all the time, and she wanted more.

She had just turned 13 when she decided she couldn't continue alone anymore. She was asked near the end of the school year to a school dance by a boy who was a couple years older. She was excited to go and she accepted right on the spot she thought if the night turned out right this would be just what she had been hoping for.

The night of the dance had been really fun and she had enjoyed getting dressed up in pretty clothes and having him hold her all night. As he walked her home they stopped at the park and sat down on a pick nick table. Almost instantly he kissed her, it was ruff and he thrust his tongue in her mouth right away.

They lost track of where they were and the time as they were kissing. The whole thing was a little weird and awkward but Terra was enjoying the closeness she was having with this boy. She put her hand on his leg trying to steady herself as he leaned her back slightly. She could feel him under his jeans, hard and pushing against her hand. It made her feel special to know that she had turned on this boy so much.

Only a few moments after she had placed her hand on his leg he began to push against it and she pushed back making him kiss her like crazy. It wasn't long after that he unzipped his pants and placed her hand back down on his now open jeans. Terra felt tingly between her legs as this was finally going to happen. She reached in and grabbed his hard tool not removing it from his pants but gripping it and moving her hand as much as she could inside his jeans.

They had only been doing this for a few minutes as his breathing was getting really labored, Terra knew he was probably going to orgasm soon. It was then someone grabbed her from the back and pulled her off the table. Terra spun around to see Megan standing there angry. Megan grabbed her by the shirt collar and started to drag her towards home, the boy never said a word to them, he just zipped up his pants with an embarrassed look on his face and ran the other way.

As it turned out something had come up and Terra's mom had left that night for a family issue and left Megan at home alone waiting for Terra to come home. Megan had begun to worry when Terra was more than a half an hour late and had gone out to walk the ten minute walk that it took to get to the school. She had been more than angry to find Terra sitting there giving a hand job. Terra cried and told her sister everything from touching herself to needing more.

When Terra had explained herself she was surprised to see that Megan wasn't mad anymore, she told her little sister that she understood and Terra felt better. Megan told her to go to bed and they could talk more if she needed to later. Terra went to her room stripped off her pants and her nice shirt and pulled on an old t-shirt of her dad's that she slept in. She was still so turned on from playing with the boy and her fingers found her soft lower lips and began to explore.

Terra was into herself rubbing furiously when her door opened her head shot sideways to see her sister walking to her bed. Terra pulled the blanket over herself as Megan sat on the bed next to her. Terra's breathing was ragged and her face red, there was no hiding what she had been doing. She lay there mind spinning fast trying to come up with something to say, the silence was killing Terra from embarrassment. It was Megan who broke the awkwardness by making this even weirder. Megan leaned in and kissed Terra running her hand up her thigh before Terra could stop her.

Terra moaned out loud as Megan's hand found her clit. Terra was horrified and by what was happing to her but it felt so good she couldn't tell her sister to stop it was too amazing having someone else rub her. Megan reached over and pulled Terra's panties off then slid down the bed. Terra cried out as her sister's tongue slid insider her, as Megan continued rubbing her clit.

Terra's body arched as waves of pleasure spiked through her, she was moaning non-stop calling out Megan's name. Her sister pushed in deep and Terra's whole body shuddered but her sister didn't stop. Minutes later her body thrashed in pleasure and Terra's heart was beating so fast she thought she would die. After her second release her sister shifted her fingers inside her and began to suck her clit, the third orgasm hit almost instantly as this was the most pleasure she had ever felt. Her body arched deep then she fell to the bed exhausted.

Megan moved back up and began to kiss Terra again, slowly and lovingly. Terra pulled away from Megan her mind was returning back to normal and she was becoming horrified again about what had just happened. It took Terra minutes to finally talk to her sister about what was bothering her.

The girls talked and Megan had said that she didn't want to see Terra give into her urges this young and get pregnant. Megan said that she had been upset seeing her sister giving the hand job to the boy she felt she was too young to be at that stage yet. Megan said she had gone through something similar at her age and had almost become pregnant before deciding she liked girls. She thought if she helped her out Terra might be able to wait for sex until she was older. Terra couldn't disagree that it had helped a lot but she felt weird about it. Megan said it was ok if she felt weird but if she changed her mind or needed her help again then just to ask.

It took about six weeks before Terra couldn't stand it anymore, she could make herself feel good on her own but she couldn't get herself off all the way, and nowhere near like what Megan had done for her. She timidly went into her sister's room the first night that their mom wasn't home and asked her for help again. Megan said she would be happy to help her.

Over the next year the girls would fool around when they got the chance and would often have all night when their mom was gone. Terra was trained by her sister and had become just as good at giving pleasure as her sister. She loved the bond with her sister they would give each other pleasure then lay together all night holding each other. It was so special to Terra and as much as she was frightened by the idea she was falling in love with Megan.

Not long after Terra turned 14 Megan moved out, leaving Terra home alone all the time with their mom as flakey as she was. Cammy was going away to college out of state and Megan told everyone she was going with her so they could roommate. Terra knew the real reason that they had moved in with each other, and it pissed her off. Megan had chosen Cammy over her, and it upset her that she could just walk away after what they had been through.

That had been the cause of Terra's wild phase; she began running around with boys all the time after her sister had moved out. She started smoking, drinking and having sex looking for some way to stop the pain of loss her sister caused her. From that point until now it had been one party after another and one hook up to the next. Her mother was so out of it anymore and so flaky that she never noticed if Terra was home or if she had boys with her in her room, giving her pretty much the freedom to do whatever she wanted. The catch to all of that was that her mom still made her go to camp every year, Terra told Ash she only went to camp to feed her secret desire to be with a girl sometimes. Terra would make sure to hook up with one at the deflowering ceremony.

When Terra had finally finished explaining light had begun to come through the window and day was starting. Ash held her friend but Terra still couldn't look at her, she kept her head turned away.

"I'll understand if you don't want to talk to me again. I mean what kind of person does THAT with her sister?" Ash tried to hold back the smile growing in her face, it was way more common than Terra realized.

"I don't think any less of you," she said sweetly. Terra turned to her and the girls kissed sweetly for a few moments.

"You still like me?" Terra asked her voice trembling, "I've been so scared to tell anyone for so long."

"I still like you," Ash told her, "I think I would be a hypocrite if I held it against you." Ash went on to tell her the story of what she had done to get Joey and Katie together so she could have him herself. Ash hoped that Terra wouldn't think her the bad person now.

When Ash was done telling her story Terra kissed her this time. It felt nice to both girls to have someone so accepting of each other. Now having been completely honest with each other they kissed again slow and caring. Their hands slowly finding the other's breasts they lay down on the bed and their kissing became more passionate. It wasn't long before Terra's hand was rubbing Ash's clit again, it felt really good but Ash suddenly tensed up.

"I want to do this with you, I REALY do, but I've only ever tried licking once a long time ago," Ash said embarrassed, "I'm nervous that I................"

"Don't worry," Terra stopped her, "I'll teach you."

An hour later the girls both lay on their backs, breathing returning to normal, hearts beating madly and holding hands.

"Wow," Terra breathed out, "You learn quickly."

"So what now?"

"You're ready for more," Terra asked astonished.

"No, not for a while after that," Ash giggled, "I meant for us, what now?"

"I don't know."

"Me either."

They lay in bed until about 9:00 when Ash said she had to pee and got up put on her panties and a t-shirt and left. She had a lot of conflicting emotions on her mind and needed a minute alone. After using the bathroom she went down stairs for a couple of sodas. The house was a mess from the party and she would have to do a lot of work before Linda and James came home tonight but she had a little time now. She walked up stairs with the cans of soda preparing herself for the conversation that needed to come now.

It wasn't that Ash was into girls in a lesbian or bi-sexual standpoint. When her and Sara had fooled around it had been out of curiosity on both their parts. They had touched and licked each other but not really been into it. Ash had known the first time she did something with Joey she loved boys and LOVED him specifically. Last summer at the orgy she had let a girl, who happened to turn out to be Mandy, lick her pussy but that had been in the moment at an orgy it had nothing to do with being into girls.

Last night she had been so horny before Terra kissed her and her will was down, it had felt good and she hadn't wanted to stop. But with Terra things were different, she really liked her best friend, she had real feelings for her, but she knew she wasn't in love. She hated herself because she was going to hurt someone else she cared for again.

Ash paused at the top of the stairs leaning her head against the door frame; she didn't want to hurt Terra, for the first time in her life Ash had made love to someone without games, or manipulation or for just the fun of it. This time had been for real and she still had to tell the person that she wasn't in love and would have to hurt her.

"We need to talk," Terra said to her as she entered the room. Ash handed her the soda and sat on the bed next to her.

"Yeah, I think we do," she said softly.

"Look, I don't want you to get the wrong idea but what happened last night.............. It meant a lot to me but............" Terra paused biting her lip.

"It doesn't mean were a couple," Ash finished for her.

"Yeah," Terra said breathing out a sigh, "I just...... I don't know, it's so different with girls."

"I would say so," Ash exclaimed, "But I....... kind of feel the same way."

They talked about what everything meant for the next hour. Terra said that as much as she liked Ash she wasn't looking for a girlfriend she liked boys way too much to switch sides permanently. Ash agreed that was what she had been thinking too, both girls feeling a lot better for being honest. They decided for now they would just be friends, friends that sometimes made love which both girls seemed happy with.

Ash was just happy that she hadn't hurt her friend. It felt really good to hold someone and be honest with them without one person being more in love with the other and no games. They held each

other and kissed until about lunch time when Ash said that she was hungry and had to get started on cleaning the house in case her sister and James came home early.

Ash pulled on a pair of jeans, Terra got dressed and they both walked downstairs. To Ash's surprise Jt and Mandy had cleaned up most of the house in the time since she had come down for soda.

"Your still here Mandy?" Ash asked thinking her parents would be going nuts if they knew she was missing this morning.

"No, I went home early this morning and I came back to help you guys clean about an hour and a half ago," she looked over at Jt and blushed, "Are you two just getting up?" Mandy gave them a puzzled look.

"Yeah," Terra said nonchalantly, "I had a late night and Ash let me crash in her room."

"Oh," Mandy responded with a sly smile but she didn't question anything.

The four of them finished cleaning the house and Terra and Ash drove all the trash bags down the street and threw them into a dumpster at an apartment building. They didn't want Linda to come home and find the party trash.

After the house was back in order Ash and Terra sat on the couch in the living room and put on a movie, while Mandy grabbed Jt's hand and they went down to his room all afternoon. Terra looked puzzled when they left and asked Ash what that was all about and Ash told her what she had walked in on last night. Both girls thought it was really cute and they liked the idea of them being together it was a good match.

It was late in the day when Ash heard James' car pull up out front, she stomped on the floor loudly to warn Jt, and moments later he and Mandy came running up the stairs all flushed and red still pulling on their shirts. It was good that James and Linda had taken a long time to get the bags out of the car or Jt and Mandy would've been caught.

Linda came in that night and all four were sitting on the couch trying not to look guilty as Linda checked the house over completely. The girls stayed for dinner as Ash cooked spaghetti for everyone, Linda had started to cook but Ash pushed her away and said that after she had a trip she shouldn't have to cook. Linda stayed in the kitchen and the girls talked as she cooked, Linda had a suspicious look on her face the whole time.

The girls went home after dinner and Jt went back to his room, James went to the living room and watched TV as Linda and Ash cleaned up the kitchen. Linda told Ash she could smell the cleaning products when she came in the door tonight but as the house was left standing and their didn't seem to be any trouble caused she was going to let Ash and Jt get away with whatever they had done. Ash tried not to smile and just simply told Linda she had no idea what Linda could possibly be talking about. The girls just smiled at each other.

The day after Christmas Ash and Jt were alone in the house and trying to get all their chores done before Mandy and Terra came over that day.

237

"Um...... Ash....." Jt said softy. Ash still thought it was so cute that he was nervous around her, even after having sex with her and her friend he still had a hard time talking to her.

"What sweetie?" Ash asked patting him on the shoulder.

"Um I just wanted........ To thank you for....... You know........ Helping me..... Talk to girls and stuff."

"You're welcome sweetheart," she said amused, "And pretty soon you'll master it," she joked.

"Ummm yeah," he said turning red but realizing she had just been joking, "I just......... you know I'll............ I still........"

"Don't worry I will always love you too. You know what I mean."

"Umm Yeah," he said then paused, "You're not mad that I............. Like Mandy now?"

"No sweetie, I'm really happy for you," Ash said honestly and kissed his cheek.

That was pretty much all that was ever said about him dating her friend as Ash was happy that he found someone who liked him as much as he liked her. The hurt she had felt for using him loosened up a little, yes she had done something to him but in the end it had helped him end some fears of women, and that led to him having his first real girlfriend. She could live with herself again concerning Jt.

Not long after their talk Mandy arrived and she and Jt went straight to his room. Terra arrived at lunch time and they hung out in the living room watching movies for a couple hours. They hadn't had another event like the night of the party, they had talked about it and as much as they had loved giving each other pleasure they were still on the lookout for boyfriends. They had made the decision that on occasion it would be ok to fool around if they wanted to but it seemed they were just as content to be around each other. The four of them spent the rest of the vacation that way, Jt and Mandy in his room every day and Terra and Ash would hang around the house watching movies or spend the day at the mall.

The school year picked up again and things fell back into their normal routine with only one change, Jt now went everywhere with the three girls. This gave him a huge reputation at school because he was hanging around with the cutest girls in school.

Chapter Seventeen: The Tree House

"Let me explain," Lilly started, "I always wanted to tell you the truth, but your father made me promise not to."

"But he's been gone for months Lilly," I barked at her.

She paused but I just looked at her stone faced, "You have to understand, we didn't hide the truth from YOU, we hid the truth from everyone." She actually had a real look of fear and sadness in her voice.

"What truth," I asked feeling cold.

"Why don't we take a ride?" Lilly asked.

"To where?"

"I know this will sound completely cliché but if I'm going to tell you what happened then I think we should go back to where this whole thing started."

"Ok," I said wondering when I had stepped into the plot of a bad made for after school special.

"Katie," Lilly called out to the bathroom, "Were going out for a minute. Are you ok here for a while?"

"I'm fine mom," she said returning to the room. I grabbed the car keys off the table by the door and Lilly followed me to the car. I helped her get in and she pointed out were we had to go.

Lilly began talking about her childhood and how her family had lived on this island for many years, I had no idea what this had to do with my sister but I let her talk. She sounded like a weight was lifting from her with every minute she told the story; it started when she was a very little girl.

Lilly had spent the better amount of her child hood as a loner. There were other kids in the neighborhood but she didn't get along with them. She preferred to spend her time nature walking, sitting and watching the ocean and reading as most the girls seemed to play with dolls and watch TV.

By the time Lilly was ten and her sister was four, she had decided she would never have a best friend, but she hoped Linda would grow up like her so maybe they would be friends. She loved the idea of sisters who were best friends.

By this time Lilly spent most of her time at the house next door sitting in the tree house in the back yard. No one had lived in the house for as long as she could remember and she had filled the tree house with books and blankets to lay on she even made pretty curtains for decoration.

Like a lot of run down abandoned houses in every town, everyone was scared of this house. No one called it haunted or cursed or anything ridiculous like that, but at the same time the kids were scared

of the house. Lilly was the only child brave enough to go there, and she herself never went near the house, just the tree house.

School had just let out for the year and Lilly was sitting in the tree house reading when she saw movement in the house. At first she thought she had imagined it, until she saw the back door open. Out walked this small, shy looking girl, she looked like she was Lilly's age. She was nervously looking around the yard, when she noticed Lilly in the tree house window the girl jumped back in fright.

Lilly quickly climbed down the latter and apologized for startling her. The little girl asked her why Lilly had been hiding in the tree house and she explained about it being her secret hiding place as it were. Then Lilly asked the little girl why she had been in the house. The Little girl said her name was Cassie and she and her dad were moving into the house.

I knew what this had to do with my sister now. Cassie was my mom, though I really didn't remember much about her, and my dad never told me much more than her name. Lilly had already begun to cry as she told me what turns to make through town. The island basically consisted of one big town and houses running from town to the edges or the island.

I took a few minutes to cross town finally getting to the houses on the outer edge of the island. It was another few minutes before we pulled onto Hayford Ave. We stopped in front of the house from the pictures in the scrapbook.

I felt conflicting emotions as we got out of the car. It was Christmas and the island was very cold I found myself wishing I would've brought a better jacket with me. We got out of the car and walked up to the house, the doors and windows were boarded closed as it was obvious that no one had lived in the house for a long time.

We stood in silence looking up at the house before Lilly took my hand and led me around to the back yard. The tree house from her story was still there; it looked old and was in great need of repair. She slowly began to climb up the latter and I thought this was a bad idea with her mobility since the accident.

"I don't know if you should be climbing Lil," I said and she shot me a look, I backed down. After she had made it into the tree house I followed behind her. It was bigger and somehow seemed more stable than it had looked on the outside. There were shelves of withered books along the back wall and old tattered blankets on the floor; I could easily envision young Lilly here.

We sat down facing each other, Lilly wincing slightly as she sat on the floor. It was then that Lilly began to continue her story from where she had left off in the car. Now from here on out the story I'm writing will go into more detail then Lilly talked about that night. The story to follow is comes from 3 sources, first the story Lilly told me that night based off her own memory. Second Lilly told me of the missing years in her story as told to her by my father after they had gotten together at Linda's wedding. Third I got a lot more of the story filled in for me after Lilly gave me her diaries of her childhood years.

Lilly and Cassie talked awkwardly in the back yard for a while when Cassie asked if she could see Lilly's fort. Lilly told her it was ok because it was Cassie's house after all. The girls went up to the tree house and Cassie was shocked at how nice Lilly had made it, saying she loved it and wanted to keep things just like they were if Lilly didn't mind leaving them at her house.

Lilly's response to Cassie moving into the house next door was like something out of one of her favorite stories. It seemed too good to be true over the next few weeks, as the girls found they were both 10 years old and had almost all the same interests. Lilly had finally found a best friend to share in her adventures, and it usually was Lilly who led the way as Cassie was often shy or scared to do new things. But before long Cassie trusted Lilly and they began to go everywhere together.

When the new school year arrived Cassie attended Lilly's school but they didn't end up with the same teacher so they only got to hang out at lunch. For some reason Cassie had a hard time making friends, more so than Lilly. To Lilly it seemed like Cassie never tried to make friends, she was happy just having Lilly and didn't ever really talk to the other kids much. Lilly thought it was weird but she was happy she had a best friend now too.

Over the next couple years Cassie seemed to grow more quiet and withdrawn from the world, there were whole weeks were it seemed like she was crying all the time, but when Lilly would ask what was wrong all she would talk about was whatever book she was reading. Lilly ultimately decided that when her friend was ready to talk she would, she didn't want to push Cassie away by bothering her too much.

It was summer before again before Cassie finally said something to Lilly about what was bothering her. Lilly had just turned 13 when she found Cassie up in the tree house crying one afternoon, Lilly asked her what was wrong. Cassie said that her daddy had always been a really great daddy until her mom had died. Then they moved and he started getting angry and mean to her, she hated living with him. Cassie said she wished she could move in with her grandma but her grandma was very sick.

Lilly really didn't know what to tell her, she told Cassie that she could always stay the night at her house if she needed to get away from her dad. From that day on it Cassie spent more nights at Lilly's house then her own. Lilly's dad didn't mind he really liked Cassie and was happy to see his daughter have a best friend. In fact this helped his situation with both girls around the house for the summer he was able to leave Linda home with them during the day and not have to pay a babysitter. He trusted them because both girls were mature for their age and Lilly was really good with her little sister.

Everything was perfect that summer for Lilly and Cassie even seemed to come back out of her sell slightly being away from her father. Things were great and summer was almost over again, the girls were excited to go back to school until one Saturday afternoon when Lilly went to the tree house to fine Cassie inside alone with a boy. It was Cassie's 13th birthday and her dad had let her have a party, Cassie didn't have any other friends but the word had gone around that there was cake and a number of neighborhood kids had shown up anyway.

The boy Cassie was with was a local boy Lilly knew by the name of Travis who Lilly thought was about 14 years old. They were kissing so hard that they didn't even notice Lilly was there, Lilly was a little jealous because she had never kissed a boy herself. Lilly climbed back down the latter and returned to the party sitting alone reading under a tree.

About a half an hour later she slowly climbed back up the stairs and peeked in on Cassie and Travis. Lilly gasped when she saw them as Travis was lying on top of Cassie, his pants around his ankles, Cassie's skirt pulled up. The boy was thrusting on her and Lilly couldn't believe what she was seeing. She climbed back down the latter quickly and ran home.

Lilly was both shocked and turned on by what she had seen; she didn't know how she could ever look at Cassie again. She had a tingling down under her skirt as she made it to her room; it had made her hot seeing them doing it. She sat on her bed and pulled her knees up to her chest, images swirling around in her head.

Without realizing what she was doing she had moved her hand to her panties and begun rubbing herself. This was making the tingling feeling grow, as she slowly became wetter. She didn't know what was happening to her, she had never touched herself like this before, but she couldn't stop. Her rubbing became faster along with her breathing; she tilted her head back as she slid her hand under the fabric of her panties and rubbed the hard nub at the top of her slit.

Her body began sending waves of pleasure though she and she moaned out loudly. She was glad her dad and sister were at the party where they couldn't hear her moaning. She rubbed harder and faster, it was the most intense feeling of her life, she knew she was going to do this every day from now on, why had she never tried before? All at once her body tensed up and her toes curled as she let out the loudest moan yet, her body falling down lying on her bed.

Lilly's breathing was returning to normal and her mind began to wonder, if her fingers felt this good what must it be like to be with a boy? She was jealous again of Cassie because she wanted to know what Cassie knew right now. She wished she had the nerve to approach a boy and try kissing at least.

Lilly confronted Cassie about it a few days later, asking her all kind of questions about what it was like and how she could have gone that far with a boy. Cassie said that she hadn't really liked Travis but she had needed to be with him. Lilly didn't understand but didn't question it until a few days later. Things returned to normal after that and Cassie really didn't like want to talk about it. Lilly just had a million questions but Cassie seemed angry to answer them so she stopped asking. They went back to school and it was like the whole thing had never happened.

It wasn't long after that Cassie got sick in class one day and had to be sent home. Her illness was so bad that her dad had to pull her out of school for the next couple weeks. Lilly went to check on her every day but Cassie didn't seem that sick. Lilly couldn't figure out why she couldn't come back to school, she really missed her one friend being around all the time.

It didn't take Lilly much longer to figure out what was going on with Cassie; it was only a couple of months later that her small body started to show signs of growth. It was soon obvious what illness Cassie had, and Lilly knew why she couldn't return to school. In those days they would take the pregnant girls out of school and home tutor them as to not set a bad example to the other children. This was a small town and a pregnant 13 year old was a huge scandal.

It didn't take long for the blame to fall on Travis, Lilly never told anyone what she had seen in the tree house but, Travis being a typical 14 year old boy had bragged to everyone he could that he had slept with Cassie before the news was discovered she was pregnant. After she began to show the whole town turned on the boy and the criticism became so harsh his family had to move away.

Cassie's dad seemed to be disappointed but not upset about her pregnancy saying all children are a blessing. What surprised Lilly the most with the whole situation was her own dad. Lilly had expected her dad to tell her she wasn't allowed to hang out with Cassie anymore, so when she told her dad what was happening she expected the worst. He surprised Lilly telling her that when things like this happened that

you need to be there for your friends not walk away from them, he also talked to her about being careful herself so she wouldn't follow her friend into having a baby too soon.

It was nine months in no time it seemed to Lilly, and she was standing in the hospital holding a new born baby girl. It was so sweet and weird to be standing there holding a baby in her arms that had been born to a girl her same age.

Cassie wanted to call her River but her dad talked her out of the name and she named her Jessica. Travis came to the hospital the day Jess was born with flowers for both mom and baby. Lilly had left the room so Travis could talk to Cassie and her dad alone but Cassie later told Lilly about what had taken place. Travis was now 15 and very scared, he didn't know what he was supposed to do. Cassie's dad had told the boy to go ahead and start over in the new town they had moved to. He told the boy that he knew it had been an accident and that they didn't need anything from him. Cassie's dad had told him not to worry the baby would be loved and taken care of. Travis was relived as he walked out the door that day thinking he had dodged a bullet.

The school year ended and Cassie never made it back after having the baby. Summer had started and Lilly and Linda now spent most of her time hanging around with Cassie and the baby. They would sit out in the back yard or take the trail at the tree line of Cassie's back yard and walk to the ocean and sit on the beach. It was a nice summer as Lilly turned 14 and had developed quite a bit in the last couple months. The boys had started noticing her now but she still hadn't kissed one yet. Having gone through the pregnancy with Cassie it had taught her to be careful and she was waiting until she fell in love.

The four girls were out on the beach one afternoon playing with Jessica in the sand when he showed up. He was about their age and cute, Lilly felt her heart beat heavy as he appeared. Now he wasn't one of those hunky guys with a washboard stomach or anything, but he had shyness to him that Lilly was receptive to right away. Lilly waved to him and he looked behind himself to see who was there, before realizing she was waiving to him. The boy slowly walked over and Lilly introduced herself, Linda, Cassie and the baby. He said his name was David and he shook her hand tentatively then turned to Cassie and shook her hand. Lilly liked this boy right away; he was sweet, polite and talked to them without being crude.

They found out that David was 15 and that he and his mom had just moved to town, his grandparents had passed away leaving his mom the house. Times being tough for them they didn't have a choice about moving into a free house even if it was in the middle of a small island in the middle of nowhere.

It wasn't long before David was hanging around with them all the time. Lilly had a strong crush on him and it seemed he had a strong crush on Cassie. It was like all three were in love with each other; really it just seemed to Lilly that David liked Cassie best. He didn't mind the baby going everywhere with them at all, he always just seemed happy to have friends and that they were such pretty girls.

Life calmed into a routine by Cassie's 14th birthday, and school was starting again soon. Cassie talked to the day time babysitter that had watched Linda before she had started going to school and the woman was more than happy to look after Jessica so Cassie could continue her education.

The next two years moved very fast for the three friends, before they knew it summer had come again and Jessica had just turned two but she was unusually small for her age and didn't talk at all yet.

Cassie had been a little worried as her daughter was so tiny but the doctor had said she was healthy and just fine that she should not to worry the baby would grow in time.

The three of them had grown very close, none having any other friends. As it was a small town there was a lot of talk about what was going on between the three teens. When asked or teased by the other kids David would just smile and say that both girls were his girlfriend. When either Cassie or Lilly were asked if they were his girlfriend both would just answer yes. There were a lot of comments, dirty and disapproving looks in town.

For all the looks and comments there wasn't anything dirty or wrong going on. Despite the fact that they called him their boyfriend neither girl had ever gone all the way with him. Both Lilly and Cassie had started slow with David; it had begun in the first year of their friendship with little hugs and kisses on the cheek. Then by the end of the second year of their time together innocent kissing had moved on to not so innocent kissing and touching. By the time David graduated he had made out a few times with both girls only ever going as far as taking Lilly's shirt off, and feeling up Cassie through her clothes.

David had now graduated from high school and was leaving for college in the fall semester. At the same time Lilly's dad had taken a job off the island and they were moving away before the next school year could start. All three kids were heartbroken as this meant the end of everything they had been through together. David promised to come back as often as he could and see Cass and Jess, saying just because he was off to college didn't mean he would forget them.

Lilly said that they were moving across the state and that her dad was keeping the house here, they didn't know if they would be back but her dad couldn't give up the house that had been in his family for so long. Lilly said that she would be getting her license soon and would be back as much as possible.

Three weeks later Lilly showed up on David's doorstep, she was crying as he opened his door.

"Lilly what's wrong?" David asked as she walked in. He took her into his arms and held her as she cried on his shoulder.

"You know I'm moving tomorrow, and you didn't come say goodbye. I wanted you to come see me tonight.......... Don't make me be alone on my last night here."

"I......... you can stay with me, if you want too," he said shyly. She could feel him tremble with nerves when he said it, "But we have to be quiet because my mom's asleep on the couch." He broke their embrace and led her up the stairs.

"Thank you," She said as they walked into his room locking the door behind them. Lilly didn't wait she leaned into him and kissed him moving him back slowly to the bed. They had kissed many times before, and made out really hard a couple times but kissing him then felt different, she was sure he felt it too.

They lay on the bed side by side their tongues now exploring each other's mouth with a new passion for each other. They both knew she was leaving and there was no guarantee they would see each other again. They had tonight Lilly had come here for this purpose because he was too polite to make the move on her so she had decided to do it herself.

"I love you David," Lilly said pulling away, "I'm going to miss you so much."

"I love you too, Lilly," David responded quietly, "You're my best friend. I don't know how I can live without you girls next year." The smiled sincerely and they began kissing again.

"No, I mean I really LOVE you," she said with her heart jumping in her chest, "I should have told you before...." David stopped her with a kiss.

"I should've said it first," David told her shyly, "Both you girls have always meant so much to me but it was always you, Lilly, that my heart belonged to. I was just too scared to say it."

"Really?" She responded a tear rolling down her cheek, "I thought Cassie..." David kissed her other cheek as he gently wiped the tear from her face.

"No, it was always you, but I didn't want to hurt Cassie by choosing between you girls. I know she loves me too."

"I understand," she told him moving away from his face and began to kiss his neck pulling his shirt off and pushing him on his back. Her kissing moved lower as she kissed his chest she began to rub his stomach just above the waistband of his jeans. She could tell he was excited as she could see the bulge getting bigger in his pants. She slowly slid her fingers under the waistband gently rubbing just above his shaft.

"OOOOH God Lilly," he moaned out, "Please don't stop." She kissed her way to his shoulder reaching inside his pants taking hold of him for the first time, "Yes, ooooh god yes," he moaned out again then looked down at her, "I've wanted this for so long." Lilly to moved up and kissed him passionately like never before as her hand stroked his cock as hard as she could with his jeans on.

"I've wanted you to be my first since the day we met," she whispered in his ear.
"OHHHHH GOD!" David cried out in her mouth as he let loose his orgasm. Lilly removed her sticky hand from his pants and David turned red and rolled over, "I'm sorry Lilly, I couldn't hold back, it felt so good."

"It's ok," she whispered in her ear, "We have all night, you didn't ruin it." She actually thought it was sweet that she had turned him no so much.

"I just imagined this moment for so long," he said still looking away from her, "It's not going like I saw in my head." Lilly was overcome with love for him; he was so sweet she couldn't stand it.

"It's going fine, it will be perfect because I love you," she explained and he turned back to her again. They both sat up and began kissing again as he began to unbutton her shirt kissing her neck. It was Lilly's turn to moan as his hands went to her breasts massaging them.

After a few minutes David reached behind Lilly and began trying to unclasp her bra, and failing. After a couple minutes of fumbling Lilly reached behind her back and undid it for him. David turned red again having to have help, but as her bra fell off her breasts his lips immediately went to her nipples and began to suck them in gently. Lilly bent her head to his shoulder and bit down on it slightly as not to cry out with pleasure.

After David had thoroughly sucked on both nipples Lilly pushed him back down on the bed again, she started kissing his chest again working her way to his jeans, unbuttoning them as she moved down his body. When her kissing reached the waistband of his boxers she pulled his zipper down and stretched his boxers down. David sprang up right in front of her and she was surprised by the way his cock looked. Lilly had seen pictures but never had seen one in real life it was so thick and hard with need for her. She slid down the bed and yanked his pants and boxers all the way off, kissing her way back up his leg and thigh.

"Oh god Lilly, you're going to make me cum again if you keep kissing me." Lilly smiled up at him and continued working up his thigh, until she reached his balls. She had never tried this before but she had read so many sex scenes in her books that had given her ideas of what she wanted to try now. She grasped his throbbing manhood in one hand and began to stroke as she sucked in one of his balls.

"OHHH GOD BABY!" he moaned out, "I'm so close.............."

"It's ok, I want you to," Lilly told him. Lilly quickly took the head of his cock into her mouth as he hit his second orgasm of the night. She almost gaged as he exploded in her mouth the shear amount was almost too much to take and the taste was unlike anything she had ever expected. Slowly she waited until he was done then she picked up his shirt and spit it all out into his shirt she couldn't swallow it. David didn't complain he just laid back on the bed breathing heavy his cock deflating back down.

He had an embarrassed look on his face as he began to go limp as if he had let her down. Lilly moved back up the bed and kissed him again as he rolled her onto her back. It was his turn to remove her jeans and panties and he slowly did so with a big grin on his face.

David had never seen a real girl's pussy despite the huge amount of pictures under his bed. The sight of her nakedness made his body burn in a way he had never felt, he was in awe of her as he took his turn kissing his way up her leg and thigh. When he reached the top of her thigh he dove right in, plunging his tongue insider her as deep as he could, she immediately started bucking her hips against his face, as the feeling of his tongue was incredible. She had spent the last couple years with her fingers buried inside herself dreaming of this moment and now the feeling was beyond compare. She cursed herself for not taking this step with him so long ago, but she had been afraid he would tell her he really loved Cassie more than her.

"OH YYYYES," Lilly moaned out as his tongue slid out of her slit and his lips found her clit. She came on his face, splashing so much juice that it ran down his face, her legs and into the crack of her ass. He moved up the bed and kissed her lips again and she could taste herself on him. It was another odd and indescribable flavor just like he had been but it didn't gross her out half as much as she thought it would, so she kissed him back without reservation.

They kissed for a long time before stopping, lying on their backs breathing hard and holding hands both couldn't stop smiling.

"This has been the most wonderful night of my life," David said softly, "I hate that you have to go, I'm so sorry I never told you before."

"I should've told you too," Lilly whispered in his ear, "Let's not make this harder than it has to be."

"But........ Now that we've said it out loud what do we do?" He asked sweetly.

"SSSshhhh," Lilly said to him. She didn't want to have this conversation. She knew they could make promises to each other but with him in school and her moving away there was no guarantee that they would ever happen. Lilly was thinking realistic about the whole situation. She had read dozens of star crossed lovers tales, and she knew a thousand things could happen to make they're plans fail. Tonight she just wanted to say goodbye and love him as much as possible.

After a few minutes of silence she explained this to David. They would see where the future took them without making any promises. They talked about the future then of other things well into the night, it was well after midnight now when Lilly moved down the bed and took hold of his still soft penis and began trying to wake it again. She wasn't done with her first time; she needed to take him all the way tonight.

After a few moments she took his hardening member into her mouth. She had never done this before tonight and she found she had a hard time taking much more than his head into her mouth without gaging. It wasn't long before he was ready again and harder than he had been before.

Lilly held him in her hand stroking him as she rolled on top of him, leaning down against his chest and kissing him. She positioned him against her lower burning lips, rubbing him against herself. David was breathing so hard now he sounded like he was having an asthma attack. She pushed herself back the head stopping just inside her outer lips and he shuddered hard moaning out. At first she thought he had another orgasm but she realized he was just so nervous his whole body was locking up from fear.

"It's ok baby, I want this, I want you," she said leaning down and kissing him gently again. She sat up letting go of his cock still pressing just inside her outer lips, and began rubbing his chest. Slowly David's body began to relax again as he gained control over his nerves. Lilly reached back guiding him with her hand again as she pushed back taking him deeper within her. She froze as he touched her maidenhead she paused adjusting to the feeling of him being that far, she readied herself for the pain to come. She knew if she cried out and he thought he hurt her it would devastated him so she waited until she felt ready to push through it.

"Lilly, we can stop if you need to.........." He said quietly thinking she had maybe changed her mind because she had paused for so long.

"No baby, I'm just going slowly," she said as sweetly as she could. She pushed back hard busting through her hymen and sinking all the way down on his hard dick. It hadn't hurt anywhere near as bad as she had psyched herself up to think. He was all the way inside her filling her as she began to grind against him without moving up again. They both moaned as she ground her hips against his taking in the new sensations.

After a few minutes David arched his hips up lifting her slightly as he arched back down pulling out of her slightly before thrusting back up. She sat up off him a little allowing him to thrust up into her. This felt incredible as thrust after thrust was sending waves of pleasure through her. It felt so good the pleasure was coming in waves that were almost painful shooting across her back causing her to arch backwards her hands flat on the bed as her orgasm hit.

She had to forcibly close her mouth tight to not scream out in pleasure as her pussy tightened so strongly she lost her balance and fell back on the bed, her own juices running down her legs as she slid off

him. As her back hit the bed she reached out and grabbed his hands pulling him on top of her, her orgasm was still spiking as he positioned himself between her legs and began pumping her hard.

She liked having his weight on top of her as his cock moved quickly inside her. It was only a couple more minutes when he tensed up inside her and she felt his cum flowing out of him, it was so warm as shot after shot filled her pussy. There seemed like so much was going inside her but it was somehow fulfilling to her emotionally to feel his seed within her, it felt so right somehow. Drained now both physically and emotionally, they lay on the bed together kissing lightly holding each other, Lilly had never remembered being as happy as they fell asleep together.

David woke her around 4:00 that morning, saying that she had to go before his mom got up in a couple hours. Lilly agreed that she couldn't get caught there; she would get in trouble with her dad as well. They lay there naked in each other's arms for a few minutes gently kissing. The gentle kissing grew deeper, and then they were making love again. It was only a short time but before they knew it, it was 6 am when they finally stopped making love for the second time that morning so Lilly could go. She slipped out only a couple minutes before David heard his mother get up and head to the shower.

The next day Lilly moved across the state with her dad and little sister. David went off to college and Cassie was left alone with no friends and a baby to take care of. Cassie dropped out of school her senior year and got a job at a day care so she could bring Jess with her and still work. Cassie's dad had started drinking heavier that year and things around the house got far worse as he would get angrier and mean to her when he was drunk, and now he was always drunk.

Lilly had moved away and gotten sick at the beginning of the school year. She had wanted to try out for the cheer or drill team at her new school hoping to make at least one friend but when she got sick she missed a bunch of days she wasn't able to try out. It didn't take long for Lilly to realize that her illness was the same one her best friend had, had a couple years ago.

Lilly went to her dad first, telling him she thought she was pregnant. He was so angry with her he walked out of the living room and walked into his bedroom closing the door. She didn't know who he called that night but she could hear him talking on the phone to someone. It upset her that she had upset him, her father had always been the nicest most understanding person she knew. Linda now 11 years old came to her and asked why daddy was so mad. Lilly did her best to explain to her that she was going to have a baby just like Cassie. Linda thought the idea of a baby was really neat.

When her dad returned from his room he and Lilly sat down and had a long talk. He said he wasn't happy about another child in the house but it was her baby and they would figure it out somehow and make room in their family. What surprised her most was that he never asked her who the father was. Lilly imagined he didn't need to; it probably wasn't too hard to guess as David had spent practically every spare minute with her and Cassie for the last couple years.

Lilly next went in and talked with the school counselor and found that her school didn't home school the pregnant girls like they did in HolBrooke, they sent them to the alternative high school instead. This was a bad thing as the alternative school there had a bad reputation. Also in those days if you were looking to go to a good college or find a good job and they saw alternative school on your record they assumed there was something wrong with you and it hurt your chances. Lilly didn't want to hurt her future but it looked too late. The school had said that she could stay as long as she wasn't showing yet so she had some time left. Lilly had talked to her dad and told him she would rather drop out then go to

alternative school. He told her not to over worry and to take care of herself and they would figure something out.

Lilly's dad was on the phone a couple weeks before she was to transfer to the alternative high school, talking to his cousin when he learned that in the city his cousin lived in New York they didn't hide the pregnant girls, they let them continue to go to main stream school. Lilly's dad made arrangements for her to live there and finish school mainstream. Lilly wasn't sure about living in the busiest city in the world after coming from such a small island. Two weeks later she said goodbye to her dad and sister and was on a train to New York.

A year later Lilly had her baby and had graduated. She had been offered a job answering phones at a real estate office for a good amount of money so she took the job meaning she would have to stay in New York for a while. Her dad's cousin had enjoyed having her there so much she was happy to let her stay, also her dad's cousin had fallen in love with baby Katie and enjoyed being able to babysit for Lilly all day when she was at work. It seemed like a really good arrangement for her to make some real money for a while. She decided to stay there for the time being. She wanted to move back with Katie to the house on HolBrooke Island so she could be with her friend again, but that could wait for just a little while.

It was in that time while Lilly had her first full time job that Cassie had gotten pregnant again. It was the talk of the whole town because no one had ever seen her with a guy since David had left for college. As it turned out the innocent, shy, and polite boy David had been, had went away and found himself in college. He had come out of his shell and made a whole bunch of new friends and going to parties all the time. He spent his weekend's usually drunk and banging random party girls. His days with his two best friends were fading from his mind, he had loved them but now he was here in this moment and he was having more fun than he had ever had before and fun was taking over his life.

David's mom sold the house on HolBrooke Island and moved to the state where he was attending college. By the time his first summer vacation hit his mom was living in town and he stayed with her there instead of going back to the island, he figured the girls were just fine without him. He spent his days with his first real official girlfriend who he thought he was really falling in love with. He had truly loved Lilly but he hadn't heard from her since her move and he couldn't seem to get ahold of Cassie for quite some time either. He figured they had moved on and he decided he would too.

David had no idea that Lilly had gotten pregnant or that Cassie was pregnant again too but it had gotten so bad for Cassie on the island that she almost couldn't go outside anymore. People all over town were calling her names behind her back or wildly speculating as to who the father was but Cassie wouldn't say anything to anyone. She quietly suffered the whole pregnancy by herself missing her two best friends, who had abandoned her.

Cassie gave birth to me only a couple months before her 18th birthday. She was able to keep her job at the day care and bring her kids to work with her. She was really happy for the job because her father's drinking had him spending most of the money he made on booze. She was happy for the work because she couldn't stand the idea of being in the house with him all the time.

Jessica was four years old when I was born and she had still barely grown up at all. She still was tiny and looked not much older than me. Cassie's only real joy in life came now from her children. Jess was small for her age but she was really smart. As soon as she started talking she began asking questions, and Cassie found Jess had a real desire to learn. By the time Jess was six she actually now looked like a 4 year old girl and not a baby anymore and Jess had decided it was her job to help her mom with me.

Lilly paused in her story telling here, she told me that this part of the story was vague to her because neither her or my father had been around at the time, but what she knew came from phone calls Lilly had made to her during those years when she could get my mother to talk and from Cassie's journal.

"My mom kept a journal?" I asked Lilly,

"Yes, she didn't write in it much but she did have a journal of thoughts and feelings she kept over quite a few years."

"Where is it now? I would........ It would help me connect with my mom if I could read it," I was excited for this one thing that could let me understand who my mom really had been.

"It........ Your father burned it."

"WHAT?" I was pissed. How could he have done that?

Lilly started back with her story telling me that I would understand when we got to that point in the story. I was more angry then ever over this whole thing and we had been sitting in the tree house for what felt like all night I was really starting to wish she would get the point all ready.

So as Lilly put it, time moved on as far as she knew uneventful until I was four. Lilly was still living in New York but she had talked to her father and he had agreed to let her move back into the old family home on HolBrooke Island. Lilly was happy because she was finally returning to her best friend.

It was then that tragedy struck, Lilly returned home to find Cassie's house surrounded by police tape from the looks of things it something had happened quite a while ago and nobody bothered to remove the tape. The house looked cold and empty as Lilly approached the door finding it unlocked she slipped inside.

"I'm scared Mommy," said five year old Katie. Lilly picked her up and continued to look around. The floors creaked under her feet and every step stirred up more dust, and in the dim light she saw the dried blood at the foot of the stairs. Lilly hurried out the door and ran back to her house as calmly as she could as to not scare Katie.

It was days later that Lilly found out what had happened. As it turned out woman who had watched Linda as a small girl still lived in town, she was now running a full time day care. Lilly talked to her about looking after Katie from time to time and she agreed. It was during this conversation Lilly found out what had happened to Cassie.

It had happened only a couple months earlier, there was some kind of argument at the house, Cassie and her dad had been heard yelling by the closest neighbor who called the cops. When the police arrived Cassie's father opened the door, Cassie was at the bottom of the stairs bleeding out from her skull, her father said she had fell and that he had been just about to call an ambulance. The police radioed for an aid car and began questioning him.

It was a mad circus routine of people coming and going for the next couple of weeks. Investigators and child services all asking questions and not happy with the answers that Cassie's father

was giving them. It was about a month after Cassie's death that her father was arrested for aggravated assault, manslaughter and interference in an investigation.

The police had determined that Cassie had recently become pregnant again and she and her father had gotten into an argument when she had told him. The fight escalated and he was drunk, screaming soon turned to blows as he punched her. Cassie lost her balance and she fell down the stairs smashing her head against the bottom stair. It was then determined that he had let her bleed out while panicking over what to do until the cops had arrived. Had he called for aid when it had happened she might have been saved.

Lilly was crying as she told this part of the story, it was obvious she still really loved and missed her old best friend. Lilly went on with the story saying that the pregnancy was lost as she had only been a couple months along. Child protective services took Jess and I away and put us in a foster care home.

Child protective services then began tracking down other family of Jess and I hoping that they would take us in. Due to one circumstance after another no one was able to take either Jess or myself. Jess's father Travis had died over seas in army due to some kind of training accident and his family didn't want Jess. In the end they had no choice but to track down my father hoping he would take me. Jess and I were split up and she was taken away to be put in foster care or adoption. Luckily for me they tracked down my father who was really surprised he had a child, but it was his name on my birth certificate, he took me no questions asked.

I stopped Lilly at this point in the story; I was confused as there was a big hole in this story that didn't make sense.

"I'm don't get it, you said that dad went to college and never came back. I was born a year after Katie," I paused and Lilly didn't say anything, "I've done the math in my head, he can't be my father."

"No," Lilly said softly, "David was Katie's father, not yours." My whole last couple year's just crash landed on my face. They had told us Katie was my sister, I had loved her so much as a kid and it had been ripped away from us for no reason. Now it was too late, Katie was in love with Abby and I really didn't know how I truly felt about anyone anymore.

"Why the lie? Why did he raise a child he knew wasn't his?" I was starting to get angry she had finally got to the point but she was still hesitant.

"There were reasons, for one he realized that no one else was willing to take you and he was listed on the birth certificate. You were part of Cassie and for as much as David and I loved each other; he still really loved your mother too."

"So if my dad wasn't my father then who was? Do you even know?" I got up and began to pace the tree house back and forth.

"This was the reason for the lie; keep in mind David loved you. You were his son, it didn't matter to him that you weren't his blood, you were his son."

"My father Lilly, get to it all ready, it's almost morning."

"I came home and found out what had happened to Cassie and you kids. I had only missed seeing David by a couple weeks."

Lilly said that they had lost touch with each other and she was upset she missed him coming back to town. She wanted to tell David in person about having Katie but she had missed her chance. Cassie's house was eventually boarded up as no buyers could be found for it. It sat still boarded up as we sat in the tree house that night, no one willing to move in to the house where that poor innocent girl had been killed.

From what Lilly could pick up from around town my dad had shown up long enough to claim me and leave again. According to Lilly Dad didn't know who my real father was but he made the snap decision to raise me for Cassie. Dad and I never came back here until tonight. It was his love for Lilly and Cassie and that time in his life that made him want his ashes released off the bridge when his time came. He just had probably never expected his time would have come so soon.

It took months of being home again before Lilly had the nerve to climb up the latter to the tree house. Katie was playing in the back yard and Lilly decided that it was time to go back to her childhood fort. It seemed so cold without Cassie there, so empty and without love. It looked like the cops had gone through the tree house as well looking for whatever they could for their investigation. Lilly began to clean up and put the books back on the shelf she stuck her head out the window and looked to make sure Katie was doing ok before finishing up.

As Lilly was leaving she remembered that Cassie had a hidden spot in the trunk of the tree in the middle of the house. She got down on her stomach and reached between the crack of the tree and the house boards. Lilly knew of this hidden spot but had always respected Cassie's privacy about what she kept there. What Lilly found today was a small leather bound book; it was a journal that she had seen Cassie use to write in all the time.

Lilly walked back to her yard book in hand to find Katie lying on the grass playing with the neighborhood stray cat. She smiled as she watched her daughter frolic about with the cat, Lilly sat down in a chair and began to read Cassie's journal. Within minutes Lilly was horrified by what was written in the book fighting back the tears she didn't want Katie to think something was wrong she put the book away until later.

It was late that night when Lilly sat down in bed with Cassie's journal. Cassie had started writing sometime after her mom died. The more Lilly read the more she cried, she had no idea of what all Cassie was going through next door. By the time she had read the whole book Lilly had knew the truth about Jessica and me, she knew things that no one should ever have to know. She knew who our real father was.

"OK LILLY SPIT IT OUT," I barked at her finally I had enough.

"Look it's just hard to say it, as smart as you are you haven't put it together yet?" She said looking away from me. It clicked, I knew what she was getting at, I understood in that moment.

"NO, he didn't?" I gasped.

"Yes," Lilly said simply, "That's why David burned her journal. I won't tell you the details, I read the book and I've never been so emotionally disturbed by anything like I was by her words." I just looked at her, I would've read it because it was my mothers, but maybe dad was right to not let anyone see what was written there. I felt bad enough realizing what had happened to my mother without reading it.

"After your grandmother died," Lilly continued, "Your grandfather began drinking from there he began to hit your mother and by the time she was 12 he was raping her on a regular basis." I looked out the window as the sun was rising. I could feel tears rolling down my face. I felt sympathy for my mom and I was hurt for what she had gone through. I was mad at my grandfather he had done things that were unforgiveable and someday I would get him back for that.

"Cassie was already pregnant when she had sex with Travis. That's the only reason she slept with him. They set him up as a fall guy to cover that your grandfather was Jess' real father. Four years later they just simply wrote down David's name. Cassie thought if something ever happened having his name on the birth certificate would mean you would be legally his."

"Well she was right about that, as far as I'm concerned he was my father, not my grandpa. I understand why you hid the truth." I wasn't mad anymore. Dad knew that if I knew the truth it would have changed things between us weather we meant to or not.

Lilly and I climbed back down the latter leaving the tree house now. With the light coming up Lilly walked over and looked at her Dad's old house next door. It looked like it was in better condition than our old house. Lilly said they still owned her old house but the bank now owned my mothers. She said she had loved the house but life in this small town was hard and she said that she and Katie had moved out when Katie was ten years old. Lilly had started a new career and she couldn't continue living on the island.

Lilly and Katie had moved that year to the same town as my dad and I were living in but she had no idea until the wedding. Not long later Linda had moved from their dad's house and came to stay with Lilly and Katie. They were still living there when Linda had met John and had moved out to marry him bringing us to the beginning of this story.

"Thank you for finally telling me the truth," I told her, "Now what happened to my sister?" After this whole story I still hadn't learned the answer to the question I had asked in the first place.

"From what I understand, they wouldn't give her to your father because she wasn't his child or a family member. From what your father knew she was placed in foster care, from there I have no idea. Your father thought it best if you didn't know she existed as you seemed to have forgotten her."

"I get it he made a judgment call, but I'm not leaving this island until I find out what happened to her," I told Lilly.

"How……. Where will you stay and what about a job?" She asked.

"I will stay here at your old house, and when you transfer my part of dad's payout to me I won't have to work forever if I use it wisely."

Lilly didn't like it but I had made up my mind. We went back to the motel and I went for a walk with Katie, I felt she should know what's going on too. Lilly having stayed up all night went to sleep and Katie and I walked down the street to the park where I explained the story to her. She was sad for my mother and for what had happened. We were both relieved and saddened to find out we weren't brother and sister. I told her that no matter what blood said dad was always going to be my dad and she was

always going to be my sister. We kissed that morning holding each other and talking about life and what it could have been if we would have known 3 years ago we weren't blood related.

When Lilly woke up they took the car and drove back on their own. I lie down on the bed and fell asleep. I stayed at the motel another few days until Lilly could send me the house keys and transfer the funds into my account so I could begin the job of finding my sister.

I called Jenny, as I had promised to keep her involved in my life. She was furious with me for some reason. She said that I now had something else that I felt was more important than her. I told her I loved her but this was something I had to do; I had to find my sister. I didn't know why it was so important to me but it was. She said that it didn't matter and I should just let it go. She told me that I that she obviously wasn't as important to me as I pretended and we should just call the relationship over with. I was so shocked that she had no sympathy for my situation, and I didn't understand the level of anger I was getting from her.

I didn't say anything for a number of minutes and when I again tried to explain things to her she again said it didn't matter and that she said she was disgusted with herself for sleeping with me. In the end she was right, it didn't matter because she told me never to come back she didn't want to see me again. I told her I was sorry and I said my goodbye to her.

Chapter Eighteen: Lovers and Sisters?

I really didn't know where to start, I was in an unknown place and I didn't know anyone. Lilly called me at the motel when she and Katie had gotten home. They had time to talk about things in the car and they had come to some decisions about what was next for them since we had the money now. Lilly and I had a real and open discussion of things that night; I began to form a real plan.

I told her I would call my Job and tell them a family emergency had come up and I wouldn't be able to come back. Abby had a key to my apartment and she and Katie were going to pull my things out for me and put them in storage before Katie went back to college. Lilly in the meantime still had a lease on their apartment and money to pay the rent as they decided what to do from there.

My car was back with Lilly and Abby and even on this island I couldn't walk everywhere. I told to Lilly to go ahead and sell my car back home and send me the title with the keys to her family home. I was going to send it back signed so it would be ready for sale. Once I had the money in my account I planned on buying a new car here, mine was getting old anyway.

It took about a week for some reason to transfer the money in my name and get everything I needed and had asked for mailed to me. I'd had a nice week as I bought myself some clothes including swim shorts so I could spend part of my days soaking in the motel hot tub. I spent every evening eating at the bar in the restaurant next door. I would go over at lunch and sometimes stay through dinner talking to Gia the day time girl who ran the bar. It was a small town and they didn't get many day time customers so Gia was happy to have the company.

Gia was a really sweet girl about my age, who had grown up on the island and had moved back in with her parents last year. She thought it was amazing that I would want to live on HolBrooke Island as she had hopes to someday get away. Gia was about five foot eight, amazing green eyes and a smile that could melt steel. I found her very interesting from the beginning, I wanted to ask her out on a date but I found I couldn't get up the courage which was weird, I hadn't had this much trouble asking out a girl in years. So instead I spent my days hanging around the bar talking with her and singing along with the jukebox.

Gia was just as curious about why I was in town as everyone else I had met, but in her case she simply asked me as everyone else passed by me with suspicious looks. I found I didn't really want to tell anyone what I was really doing there. I didn't know anyone yet and in small towns like this if I told one person everyone would know. I simply told her that my step-mother had asked me to come and remodel her family home. I figured it was close enough to the truth and enough for people to know right now.

I had barely processed the truth about my family and I didn't want to talk about it with anyone other than Abby, Katie, or Lilly. I wished Jenny hadn't blown up at me because I felt like I would've liked to have her to talk to as well. I had really loved Jenny in the small time I had known her but we had different goals and things in our lives we both felt we needed to do. Maybe in a couple years if she would talk to me again things might be different.

Gia asked me which old house belonged to the family because, she explained, that with the times there were a lot of old houses on the island empty now. I told her where it was on Hayford Ave and she

asked if it was the one with the tree house or the one next door. I told her the one next door and she sighed, saying that she had always heard that the one with the tree house had been cursed. She said that she had grown up afraid of that house because people had died there. I told her I had heard that but didn't add on to the statement.

The day I received the keys I went over to the bar for dinner and talked to Gia again, I told her I was leaving the motel the next morning and she said she was sad that I wasn't going to be coming in to keep her company anymore. I promised her that she had definitely not seen the last of me and I would be by as often as possible.

"You'd better," she said with a little laugh, grabbing my hand and writing a phone number on my palm, "I want to hang out with you." She was smiling so sweetly and it was an almost perfect moment, so I shouldn't have been surprised when at that moment while she still held my hand that dumb ass song started playing over the jukebox.

"I............," I started trying to contain my growing erection. I didn't want her to see it, I was pissed that I was still reacting to the song, it was just plain hard wired in my brain now, song equals erection.

"Hold that thought," she said before I could say anything else, she looked down at my jeans and I knew she saw my hard on. She gave me a bigger smile and a wink as she walked over to help the customers who had just walked in.

I sat down and tried to calm down as the song played on. I was trying to breath slow as I watched Gia walking around in her shorts, her gorgeous legs not helping my situation. I thought about the timing of that damn song and I realized that this time it wasn't just the song that had got me hard it had been that Gia had been hitting on me when it started playing. Either way I was really embarrassed as the song ended and I slipped out the back door when no one was looking.

I went back to the motel that night and grabbed my swim trunks I changed and my erection still wouldn't go down and I thought maybe in the hot tub I might calm down. I grabbed a towel holding it in front of myself and I snuck my way to the hot tub without being seen. It was freezing outside I was crazy to go out in just my trunks to the hot tub room.

I slipped into the hot tub room and closed the door, I was all alone and I almost jumped into the tub after being out in the cold. The water felt incredible as the jets kicked in. I sat there thinking of Gia and her hot legs, and I couldn't stop myself, I pulled the front of my trunks down and began to stroke myself. It was only then that I realized where Gia had put her number on my hand, right in the palm that I was using to stroke myself now. It was like I was using the number to jack off, I liked that, I tilted my head back and began to speed up. I was so into it I didn't hear the door open and someone come in.

"I'm really glad I used permanent ink or you would've rubbed that off," Gia's voice came in a giggle. I snapped out of my thoughts and freaked out. I was really happy then that at least the jets were hiding my erection.

"Oh my god Gia, this isn't..............." I couldn't say anything I knew I had been busted.

"It's ok, were you........... Thinking of me?" She asked shyly.

"I........... Uh .... well," I sputtered.

"It's ok; I saw you're……. Reaction when I wrote on your hand in the bar."

"Oh," I simply responded, I was so embarrassed right then I wanted to die. That dumb ass song had struck again and caught me in a situation where a girl had seen me get hard for her because of it, "I was thinking of you, but why are you here?"

"If you would've hung out a little longer I was going to tell you I was off work, I just had to wait on that last couple. I wanted to……………" She paused and it was her turn to blush.

"What?"

"Well I don't want you to think I'm a slut…………. But I wanted to come over and hang out with you tonight," she explained biting her lower lip.

"You mean…………… You wanted to…….. Come back to my room?" I asked shocked. I knew we got along and I knew she was interested when she gave me her number but I wouldn't have thought a girl like her would want to do more than just hang out.

"Well maybe not to go……… all the way, but yeah," she said bashfully, "I know we just met and stuff but your such a nice guy, and so different from the jerks who live in this town."

"Oh," I said as the jets suddenly stopped and I was exposed to her as I hadn't put myself back into my shorts. I wanted to have sex with her so bad but I didn't want to come off like a jerk too. I paused without saying anything for a minute, it was an awkward situation, I was in the tub hard as ever sticking out of my shorts with a hot girl willing to do something about it. I wanted to pull her into the water with me and fuck her hard.

"So……" she said after a minute of awkward silence where she kept her eyes glued on my dick.

"I like you," I blurted out, "I really want you but I just met you, we don't have to do anything you're not comfortable with yet."

"See you're so nice even when you obviously want this." She said smiling and tilting her head to indicate my erections, "You still are such a gentleman about it. Don't worry about me I'm a big girl, no strings babe."

"Ok," I said simply and Gia began to undress. I somehow got harder as her shirt and pants came off. Then I thought my dick would burst from blood flow as she took off her bra and panties. I sat there in awe as this goddess stood in front of me. As much as I hated to admit it she had to be the hottest girl I had ever seen naked aside from pictures. Don't get me wrong all the girls I had been with were pretty but Gia was just a knock out. I couldn't believe this was happening this was a scene like what you read in a porn magazine, this couldn't be real. But somehow it was really happening. Gia turned the jets back on as she climbed into the water.

"OOOOHHH," she exclaimed stepping into the water. I went ahead and slipped off my shorts the rest of the way as Gia sat down. I couldn't remember being this nervous about a hook up like this before. I was shuddering in anticipation as I leaned in to kiss her.

Morning came all too quickly, as the room filled with light from the cracks in curtains; I looked next to me and smiled seeing Gia lying there. I kissed her cheek and nudged her slightly, her eyes opened opening only a little and she turned her face to kissed me on the lips.

Her lips were slightly dry this morning but soft, I caressed her shoulder as her kissing became harder. Her lips moistened up quickly as we fell deeper into one another. I slid my hand down from her shoulder to her back and pulled her closer to me. I began to rub her back while moving my lips down her cheek to her ear I kissed her ear before sucking on her lobe. She moaned out and her hand went to the crotch of my boxers and began to rub, I was hard in a second responding her touch.

"This feels so much better this morning," she said softly in my ear.

"Feeling less nervous?" I asked, "I know I am."

"Yeah, but I have to go babe," she told me regrettably, "I really want to do this now, but I have to run home and get clean cloths and a shower before work. If we don't stop now, I'll never leave sweetie." She ran her free hand gently across my cheek.

I looked at my watch and it was later in the morning then I had realized. I kissed her lips again as she got up and stepped off the bed. She pulled on her shorts and picked up her shirt. I reached out and took her hand, pulling her to me, kissing her again. She pulled away and put on her shirt.

"Don't forget to call me, last night was special." She said pausing at the door giving me a half smile for a moment before leaving. I thought about last night and what had happened. She had looked so good and I was hard when she stepped into the hot tub.

I had been really nervous, my hands shaking when I slid across to her. Our first kiss was awkward and short. She had stripped down and stepped into the hot tub with so much confidence but now I could feel her trembling, as I pulled away from her.

"Are you ok?" I asked.

"Yeah," She whispered. She lifted her hand to the back of my neck and drew me into another kiss. Her lips were soft and tasted like cherry; I could feel her tension lessening as we began to kiss the second time.

Our kiss this time wasn't as awkward, as her lips parted and I tentatively began to slide my tongue in her mouth. Her tongue found mine just as nervously. Little by little we both began to explore each other's mouths deeper, and it wasn't long before our tongues were dancing.

Once she calmed down she was a great kisser, I wanted so much more from her but I also never wanted to stop kissing her. As if reading my mind I felt her hand sneak between my legs and grip my dick, her touch was firm and her movements were slow. Her hand felt so good under the water it was a sensation like I hadn't had before. My hands found her breasts moments after she began to stroke my cock, they were just at the water line, I moved in with both hands timidly touching her soft mounds they felt so soft as I caressed her hardening nipples.

When the jets stopped again and I broke our kiss and pulled back, I intended turn the jets on and move my way down her body and suck her nipples but the look on her face stopped me. Despite the passion she was kissing me with, I could see that she had tears in her eyes.

"Gia, what's wrong?" I asked softly in her ear, "We don't have to do this............... if you're not as in to me as you thought we can stop." I didn't want to stop, but I could tell there was something wrong and I couldn't keep going feeling like she wasn't in to it.

"It's not you," she said looking down, "I do really want this..... I...."

"It's ok you can tell me anything," I told her pulling her into a hug. She put her head on my shoulder and I began to rub her back.

"It's stupid, you'll laugh at me."

"No. I won't laugh at you," I reaffirmed her.

Gia didn't say anything for a long time we just sat and held each other. When she finally spoke she explained that she was so nervous and she was happy I stopped she thought if she would've stopped me then I would've got mad.

"Why would I get mad at you?" I asked.

"I had a friend who changed her mind while she was having sex and wanted to stop the boy got so mad he hit her."

"I wouldn't ever.........." I began and she cut me off.

"I think I knew that, but I was still scared."

"So if it's not me, what's wrong?" I asked her softly kissing her forehead.

Gia was quiet again for a few minutes she explained that she had liked me from the first day we spent talking in the bar and she did really want to be with me. Her fear came from the fact that she had only been with two guys.

Gia said she hadn't been with anyone since her boyfriend because she knew and didn't like most the guys on the island. Tonight she had been willing and ready but the newness of our friendship and the difference in my touch had made her a little apprehensive she wasn't as ready as she thought.

I kissed her forehead again and held her. I didn't say anything for a couple minutes, and then I told her that I was fine with starting slow and we didn't have to do anything she wasn't ready for.

She leaned in and we began to kiss softly again, and our hands stayed around each other's backs holding one another. We kissed lightly for a long while when she pulled away from me.

"I'm so horny, and I can see you're still really horny too," she said quietly looking away, "But I'm still not ready." She started getting fidgety and I could tell something was on her mind.

"What?" I asked trying to get her to just say what she was thinking.

"Maybe we could watch each other? It made me hot watching you before......... I would be ok with that if you were."

I couldn't believe she asked me that, I simply nodded at her and moved to the other side of the tub. With the jets off we could see each other rather clearly, I gripped myself and stroked hard for her, she watched for a minute before reaching down and rubbing her clit in slow circles. Watching her touch herself was too much I had to slow down my pace as not to go off to soon.

After a couple minutes of rubbing her clit Gia pushed up out of the water and sat on the edge of the tub. I could see her so much better this way as she opened herself up and slid two fingers inside her wet pussy.

"The...... water was..... Not letting me feel this........ As good," she moaned out her fingers slipping in and out faster. I pulled myself out of the water and sat next to her on the edge. Gia leaned over and kissed me quickly as we continued to stimulate ourselves.

"OOOOOHHH," Gia moaned in my mouth as her orgasm struck her body. She used her other hand to rub her clit as her fingers slowed down in her pussy, her back arched and her head fell back, "OOOOOOOOH BABE!" She cried out and hopped off the ledge and sat back down in the water.

Watching her cum had put me over the edge too, my head fell back as I shot cum into the hot tub, once, twice, three and four shots flew out and landed in the water. I sat on the edge and watched my spunk get sucked into the side filter before I got back in. I moved next to Gia and kissed her, we began to kiss deeply again and I could feel her apprehension coming back.

"Sorry, I'm still nervous to kiss this way right now," she said pulling away, "I don't expect you to understand, but kissing is really personal to me, I'm just not ready for it to mean so much yet." She had a look on her face that clearly said she was seeking approval. The look on her face told me a lot about her and her last relationship and I realized she had been hurt emotionally by her ex-boyfriend.

"I understand, its ok," I told her taking her hand and giving it a kiss. She giggled at me and got out of the tub. I followed and handed her the towel as I rung the water out of my swim trunks before putting them back on. Gia dried herself off and handed back the towel, I wished I had brought more than one. She pulled on her panties and re-hooked her bra over her perfectly beautiful breasts before picking up her other clothes. I dried off my body and shorts as much as possible and we ran back to my room trying to get out of the cold as fast as possible.

This was the second time tonight that I realized Gia wasn't as shy about her body as most the girls I knew, running back to the room in just her bra and panties. As soon as I got the door open she ran and jumped into the bed pulling the disheveled blankets up to her chin to warm up. I walked over to the chair next to the bed and grabbed a pair of boxers and walked into the bathroom to change. When I came back to the room I lay down in the bed next to Gia and pulled the blanket over myself as she reached over and wrapped her arms around me for both heat and so she could stroke my hair.

I wrapped my arms around her and we lay there on our sides looking into the others eyes holding each other until we both warmed up. I reached down and held her hand as we rolled onto our backs and

turned our heads to look at each other, and then we talked. We talked about our past, though I held back a lot, we talked about our goals in life; we talked about everything until sleep took us both.

It was mid-morning and I needed to get started on my plans for the island. I was really happy I had made a friend but I put my thoughts of last night away for a moment and I decided to get dressed and get on with step one, buy a car. This was the easiest of step of the plan as I was 20 years old and now financially independent. I left the motel and I walked into town straight to the first car dealership I could find.

I walked onto the lot of a car dealership with the intention to buy a brand new car, but instead something else caught my eye, and I bought a black Jeep pickup truck. I had always wanted a truck as I liked them more than cars. My dream vehicle had always been the lifted Toyota truck from that 1985 time travel movie where the kid almost screws up his parents getting together. I always loved the truck he has at the end of the film. The truck I bought that morning wasn't quite the Toyota from that movie but I it was a lifted black pick up and that was close enough for now.

I used the dealership phone and called the electric company while I was working the deal out for my truck. I talked to the electric company and explained that I was moving into the house that day and would appreciate it if they could come right away and turn on the power. They said it would cost an extra fee but I said do it anyway, I didn't mind paying more money to have power by the time I got there.

Next I called for a phone hookup which they said would take a couple days. I then called for a satellite hookup for TV. Even with having made friends with Gia it was going to be lonely here without something to do, and TV had always been my friend in the past when I needed it.

I drove first to the grocery store and bought a few days' worth of food that could be eaten without cooking; I had no idea what I was walking into so I didn't want to have to rely on cooking to find I had no working stove. Along with the food I bought a barbeque and a big cooler and a lot of ice. I was sure that if the refrigerator worked it would have to be cleaned before I would want to put food in it, they were horrible to clean when having no power for a long time.

I drove next to the island town mall; it was a small building consisting of only a few stores. For any real shopping I would have to go off island to the nearest town but the island mall was sufficient enough that I bought a large TV, VCR (Like I said it was the 90s), a reclining chair, an air mattress, a thick blanket, a stereo and bunch of movies. My truck was loaded as I drove away from the mall. I had what I needed to get by for a while so I decided to quit stalling and I drove to Lilly's old house.

It was late afternoon already when I got to the house; I pulled into the driveway along the far side and parked in front of the garage. I looked over at my mom's old house and shook my head, I didn't remember living there but I had a cold feeling while looking at it. I walked up to the back door and unlocked it, dust stirred up as I pushed the door open, I flipped the light switch by the door without thinking and was surprised to see that the power had been turned on already.

The house looked twice as big on the inside as it did from outside. The back door opened into the kitchen on the opposite wall there were two doorways. I walked through the doorway on right and it led into a hall way. On the right was a large family room, on the left a stairway that led to the basement, at the end of the hallway was a foyer by the front door. Turning left in the foyer had a staircase to the second floor that sat above the stairs leading to the basement, just past the stairs I walked into another doorway

that was a large formal dining room. I walked through the dining room through the doorway at the back to find myself standing in the kitchen again at the doorway on the left this time.

I walked back through the hall and climbed the stairs to the second floor. Upstairs was a master suite and two more bedrooms a bathroom and a door leading to the attic stairs. I walked up to the attic and looked around, it was spacious and what surprised me the most was that the roof was high enough I could stand up in the entire attic. I walked back down stairs and then down to the basement, it too was spacious, the walls lined with shelves for storage.

What really surprised me was that the house was completely empty. I had expected to see some old furniture or knick knacks left behind, but there was nothing. It was all well and good as I had plans for how I wanted to redo the house, but it made the house seem much larger and gloomier then it really was.

I tested the stove and checked the refrigerator finding that both worked fine. The fridge had been cleaned out so well that it hadn't molded without power. I was happy as now I wouldn't have to use the cooler for my food. I went back out to my truck and began unloading; I put everything except the food into the family room as I decided to live in there for the moment.

I spent the first night and the whole first day just sitting in my chair watching movies wrapped in a blanket. It January and the weather was still cold and the house was taking a long time to heat up, I had closed all the doors upstairs and to the basement but it was still freezing in the house.

I left the next day and drove into town; I didn't have any idea of how you go about finding lost relatives. Writing this now I have to point out again the differences in technology in the last 20 years. Now a days you just type a name into your smart phone and a global search group will do all the work. But this was still the mid-nineties and the only thing I could think of was to drive to the county court house and try to track down records.

I had to fill out a special request explaining what files I wanted to search through and why, if I wanted to be granted access. While I was talking with the clerk she suggested that I have a licensed and bonded private investigator take over for me. She explained that she knew a guy who had an office at Port Howard who often did such investigations and she gave me his number.

Port Howard was a sea port town on the larger island of San Valo about a 30 minute ferry ride from HolBrooke. I wasn't sure I really wanted to travel all the way over there but the clerk had a point, I really didn't know what I was doing and if someone else did then maybe I should consider that. I had the money for to pay a PI so what was I holding off for?

I drove home and fixed myself a sandwich and sat in my chair to watch a movie. After lunch I went outside and walked over to the tree house climbing up and sitting down. I sat there and tried to imagine what my childhood would have been like had I grown up here. I also realized it wouldn't have been all peaches and cream living with a drunk child rapist either.

I looked around the tree house and I finally had my starting point. That tree house had meant so much to my mom, Lilly, and dad. I didn't know if I would ever have kids myself but I felt I really wanted to make this tree house really special. The problem was I didn't own the property; it wouldn't be practical to rebuild it then have new owners come along and decided they didn't want it and take it all down.

I went back to Lilly's house and made a list of supplies that I would need and I began draw up a picture of how I wanted things to look when done. It would be that greatest tree house ever built when I was done. I fixed myself something to eat for dinner that night and fell asleep in my chair watching movies.

The next day I walked over to my mother's old house, it had an old half unreadable real estate sign in the front yard; I called the number and found that the company was based out of Port Howard. I made an appointment to meet with the realtor at their office later that day. I drove down to the ferry and took the next one out to Port Howard. It was a rather unexciting trip as there was no real scenery to see along the way.

I had time to kill arriving on the island earlier then I had expected so I drove around looking for the address the clerk had given me at the court house. I found the private investigator's office and decided to at least talk with him. Thinking from movies I expected his office to be really cool, but it felt more like I was sitting in an accounting office. I only had to wait about ten minutes before Glen, the investigator met with me. We talked and I explained about my mother's death and my grandfather's arrest, leaving out the incest, and how we were sent to other homes. I explained that I simply wanted to find my sister.

We talked and agreed on a price, he said he had a strong work load but would find a way to fit my issues in. I thanked him and headed out to the real estate office. It took me about twenty minutes of driving around the neighborhood to find the right office and I was almost late.

I walked up to the door to find it locked with a note: Be back in five. I stood outside the cold seeping into my clothes, I debated getting back into the truck to wait, but the note had said only five minutes.

"OH my god, Joey!" an excited voice called out behind me. I spun around to see Brooke standing there, "What are you doing here?" She asked rushing over to me and hugged me. I moved to pull away from her and she kissed me firmly on the lips.

"Wow, what was that for?" I asked when she pulled away, "Not that I'm complaining."

"I just thought I would never see you again."

"Yeah, me too."

"What are you in Port Howard of all places in the world," she asked.

"I've got an appointment with the real estate office here but no one's here and the note says five minutes but it's been twice that."

"I meant how did you end up here? The islands aren't exactly tourist attractions, how did you end up out here?" she asked, "And as far as the note....." she reached past me and unlocked the door, "....... Come in sit down."

"I came out here after my dad died to start over; we have a family home on HolBrooke." Brooke sat down at the reception desk and I sat in the chair in front of her.

"Oh sweetie I'm so sorry."

"It's ok, how did you end up all the way out here yourself."

"I grew up on HolBrooke and my family moved to Port Howard when I was 10. I moved away with my dad when I was 17 that's how I met you at college. I came back here after college so I could be near my mom."

"Wow, small world," I told her, "I grew up here too. I don't remember living here though."

"I don't really remember much of my childhood on the island either," She told me, "You would think because I was ten when we moved I would but it's all blurry in my head, too much drinking in college I guess." She laughed at her own comment.

I talked to Brooke for a while when the phone rang. After a short conversation she explained that something had come up and the realtor had been delayed and should be back as soon as possible. I was fine with that as I was enjoying talking with Brooke that afternoon. I had really liked her a couple years ago when we had almost hooked up and I was so happy to run into her again.

When the realtor came back I talked with him about purchasing my mother's old house. I explained who I was and he explained that he knew all about my family and what had happened in the house. He said that the house had been completely paid for when seized by the state after my grandfather had been arrested; all that was owed on the property now was back property taxes. The property, technically as next of kin, belonged to me, all I had to do was pay the taxes and it was mine. I didn't feel right about clamming it all for myself so I explained that I technically had a sister that could claim the house too.

"I hate to tell you this," The realtor told me, "But as the story go's your sister...," he paused a long time, "She died."

"What?" I asked shocked. Why hadn't Lilly told me that? Only one thing made sense, Lilly didn't know.

"To my understanding of what happened," he explained, "Your sister was taken to foster care and her foster father abused her. I read all about it in the paper, the case broke open when your sister ran away from home and was found in the ocean the next day. She had drowned, it was a major incident as nothing like this ever happens on the islands and we had two cases of inside your family."

"You're sure about that?" I asked the whole reason I was there had just been blown apart.

"I can only tell you what I read in the paper and what I know from dealing with your family home," He told me sympathetically.

"I understand, so what do we do now?" I asked trying to get back to business. I intended to have my investigator look into the whole situation. He told me that I needed to bring back some proof of my identity and he could go ahead and turn over the paper work and the house was mine.

I asked him next the question that was digging around in the back of my head, "What about my grandfather? Would he have claim to the house if he gets out of prison?" I didn't ever want to meet my

grandfather, I thought if he ever turned up trying to lay claim to the house I might kill him for what he did to his own daughter.

"As my understanding the house was never his."

"What?" I asked more confused than ever.

"The house was actually owned by your mother, that's what my paperwork says," he said and paused as if waiting for me to say something, I just looked at him, "Ok, so as it says in my paperwork the house had been in your grandmothers family for many generations but your family had moved away from the island years earlier. So when your grandmother died she willed the property to your mom not her husband."

"Why wouldn't she leave it to him if they were married?"

"That I can't tell you, I don't know. I just have a copy of the will where it states that Cassie received all her money and property. That's all I can tell you."

"Thanks, so let's go over again what I need for the house to be in my name." I wrote down all that I needed and I left his office.

"Hey sweetie, what do you have planned for the rest of your day?" Brooke asked as I passed her desk.

"I have to talk to talk with someone before I leave the island but that's it."

"Good I get off in a couple hours and you're having dinner with me tonight."

"I am, huh?" I asked trying to sound playful but I was more upset than ever. I couldn't believe that my search might end this way and so soon.

"Yes you are, be back at 5," she told me. I smiled and walked out the door. I really didn't mind having a date with Brooke, I had always liked spending time with her, she was fun and wild I could end up doing something fun tonight ranging from something crazy that might get me killed to just getting laid. I was up for anything right now.

I drove back to the PI's office and explained all the details I had learned from the realtor, and he said that he would still look into everything and try to confirm about Jessica's death, and look into the full history of the house. He also was going to look into the family money the realtor had mentioned was willed to my mother. I thanked him and he said he was so sorry about all the tragedy of my family. I left his office and drove to the mall to buy some nicer clothes for tonight's dinner with Brooke.

I picked Brooke up right at five and she had me drive into town, she said there was an Italian restaurant that she had really wanted to try. We had a really nice dinner together, I had ravioli and she had the Italian Wedding Soup. The dinner was great and I enjoyed talking with Brooke, she told me about the conversation with her mom that made her come back to the island. She said that she was working at the real estate office to gain some experience while studying to get her real estate license. She wasn't sure where she would go but she planned on moving on from the island after she had her license.

I talked to her some about my dad's death and wanting to fix up both family homes. I didn't say anything about finding my sister or what had happened to my mother. Brooke thought it was great that I was spending my payout money to fix up the houses. She called that an investment in my future, saying it would be great if and when I met someone and decided to start a family.

Brooke asked me if I had a girlfriend and I said no, I thought about Jenny and Gia and told Brooke I had just kind of lost the girl I was seeing and I was interested in a girl I just met but officially I wasn't with anyone. I asked her about her love life and she giggled saying that there were a few boys chasing her right now but no real boyfriends. She playing her usual game with the boys and making them earn their way into her bed. She said she didn't like to settle on one person because she wasn't ready to slow down and pick one guy; she was trying to have as much fun as she could while she was still young. I laughed and told her she really hadn't changed.

After dinner I drove us back to Brooke's place, she lived in a small one bedroom apartment above a fish and chips restaurant. As soon as we stepped inside the door she kissed me.

"I'm so happy to see you again," she told me pulling away from our kiss and taking off her coat, "You've always been the sweetest guy I've ever know."

"Thanks," I said not really knowing how to feel about her. I liked Brooke, she was a great girl, I really wanted to have sex with her, but I had never had real feelings for her.

"I mean it, if I ever decide to settle down and pick a boyfriend you better watch out," she said and gave me a wink, "I'll be right back." She walked into her bedroom and I sat down on the couch. When Brooke came back she was wearing a pair of really short shorts and a tank top she turned on the TV and sat down on my lap sideways putting her left arm around the back of my neck.

There wasn't one word spoken and I didn't have to worry about feelings as she leaned in and kissed me firmly. I leaned forward slightly as she parted her lips and I slid my tongue in her mouth. She tasted like the mint we had eaten after dinner; it was sweet as my tongue danced with hers furiously. Kissing her reminded me of Abby, the two girls were both wild and Brooke had the same kind of energy.

I put my hand on her thigh and began to lightly caress her leg from her knee to the edge of her shorts.

"MMMMM," she purred as I slipped my fingers just under the hem of her shorts she opened her legs slightly so I could continue up but I ran my hand back down her leg. She broke our kiss and moved her lips to my ear, "I've waited a long time for you," she whispered lightly biting my ear. It was making me go so hard, but that was how Brooke operated, she liked to tease you until you were about ready to cum before she would give you what you were dying for.

I decided to play in turn as I slid my hand back up her leg and under her shorts, I had planned on stopping just outside her panties and lightly rubbing through them, but as I got there I found she had no panties on. Brooke wasn't having any teasing as she grabbed my wrist and pulled my hand forward grinding her hips against it. I found her clit and with my index finger began to rub it slowly as her grinding pushed harder against my finger.

"MMMMMM more baby," she whispered to me. She was so wet, already soaking through the bottom of her shorts. It turned me on so much when Brooke would flood for me; I took two fingers and found her slit, sliding them inside her.

"YEAH, Oh just like that!" she moaned grinding furiously, "Keep that up and your so getting fucked!" I have to admit my heart jumped as she said it. I could actually have sex with Brooke tonight, after two and a half years it might finally happen. She pushed against my hand gyrating as her ass lifted up off my lap slightly, she was leaking juice so bad I now had a huge wet spot on my jeans were she was sitting.

Brooke brought her lips back to mine and wrapped her other arm around my neck as her pussy clamped down on my fingers, cum gushing out of her. It flowed through her shorts, my jeans and ran down my leg on the inside of my jeans soaking the couch underneath.

"Wow, I needed that all day," she said sweetly. I was again in awe of the sear amount of fluid she produced. The last time she had literally created a puddle this was shaping up to be the same way. Brooke slid off my lap and off the couch and onto her knees in front of me. My heart was racing as she reached for my belt buckle.

I leaned over and raised her chin kissing her as she unbuttoned my jeans and brought down the zipper. I lifted up so she could remove my jeans and boxers, revealing just how hard she had made me.

"It's so nice," she said looking me in the eyes and gripping me with her right hand. I could see the juices still running down her legs into the carpet as she began to stroke me never taking her eyes off mine. If felt so good as she began to lick my balls with just the tip of her tongue. I didn't know how I held out but I did, I actually wanted to cum so bad but somehow I maintained, she knew just how and when to touch me to keep me from actually popping off too soon.

I closed my eyes and leaned my head back moaning out, as she began to suck my balls. I felt a bolt of pleasure shoot up my back and I twitched hard, and had a feeling like I came but I looked down and I hadn't actually shot anything out. The feeling washed over me and I began to build again.

"Cum for me," she told me, "Cum in my mouth." She didn't need to ask me again as she finally sucked in the head of my cock in her incredibly skilled mouth. I shot my spunk across her tongue filling her mouth. It had been so intense that I lay back against the couch, my dick softening. She looked me in the eyes again and opened her mouth showing me my load then she swallowed. It was so hot when women did that.

"I really hope you're not done yet?" She asked me and I shook my head, "Good. Can I ask............?"

"Ask what?"

"You're not still a virgin are you, it would be so cool to be your first," she said in a really sexy little girl voice, taking my cock and stroking me back to life.

"No, I'm not anymore. You were almost my first that night in the library."

"Oh, I guess I should've just taken it from you that day you woke up in my bed," she giggled. She was doing a good job and I could feel myself getting worked up again, "Can I ask who it finally was?"

"It was a girl I love dearly, she's............ like a sister to me."

"That's sweet, were you guys in love," she asked still in the same sexy voice.

"I love her, but we weren't in love," I explained.

"But at least your first time meant something," she said quietly. I wasn't quite sure where she was going with this.

"Yeah, didn't your first time?"

"Yes and no. I really liked the guy but, I wasn't in love. I've only ever once been in love. It didn't work out for us," she said dropping the little girl voice and almost turning sad. I couldn't help but wonder if she was trying to tell me something.

"Um, Brooke, I........... Don't want to lie to you............"

"Oh sweetie it isn't you, I wasn't hinting," she said amused kissing me on the head of my cock, "It was a long time ago, I really like you but I'm not in love with you."

"Oh, ok," I said relived and saddened at the same time. Brooke stood up and took my hands pulling me up. I stepped out of my pants that had been around my ankles and followed her to the bedroom. She slipped off her soaked shorts and lay down on the bed and I took off my shirt before joining her.

"I've really wanted to do this for a long time. Your one of the nicest boys I've ever known. I would be honored to be in love with you but I'm not, sorry." She had a real look of regret on her face.

"It's ok, that's exactly how I feel about you," I replied.

"So if we go do this it won't be weird? You're not looking for a girlfriend out of me are you?" I could see the concern in her face. I wanted to have sex with her but not if it would cost us our friendship and I told her that.

She told me she thought that I was too sweet, that I would walk away with a hard on if it meant not hurting her feelings. She said that only made her respect and want me more. Brooke rolled over on top of me and we kissed. As our tongues met I felt her hand reach down and take my cock lining it up with her soaked hole.

Brooke pushed back and I was inside her, she was so wet her pussy juices running down from her into the crack of my ass onto the bed. Her pussy felt so warm I felt like it would've burnt me had it not been for the amount of fluid she was leaking. It felt like her pussy was on fire, it reminded me of the first time I had sex with Ash. She moved her hips up and down on my cock without breaking our kiss, it felt incredible and I wished we'd done this 2 years ago. Then I remembered what stopped me 2 years ago. My love for Ash had stopped me from spending more time with Brooke then. Having sex with her reminded

me so much of what I had with Ash I could stop thinking of her, here I was having sex with a gorgeous woman and I couldn't keep my mind on what I was doing. The past was breaking through as much as I tried to put those thoughts out of my head I couldn't stop them from intruding.

I don't know if it was because Brooke was from the same time period in my life as Ash, but as I was having what could only be described as mind blowing sex my heart was aching to feel love not sex tonight. It had been so long since I had let myself think of Ash and now my mind broke and I couldn't stop the memories. I missed her so much and I hadn't even talked to her for a year and a half. I hated myself for just walking away and never dealing with it, I had gone away and put her out of my mind instead of dealing with my feelings.

"What's wrong baby?" Brooke asked me quietly, only then did I realize we had stopped kissing. I was still inside her but she wasn't moving anymore.

"Nothing," I lied.

"Baby you're crying," she said in a low tone then looked away, "Did I do something?"

"No, honestly you feel sooooo good," I didn't want her to stop but I wasn't into it anymore. Brooke pulled herself off me and lay down next to me wrapping her arms around me, holding me as my mind came back to the here and now.

"Do you want to talk about it?" she whispered. I didn't even know how to talk to her about it. What do I start with? Should I tell her about me having sex with a girl I thought was my sister? Or should I just start with the underage girl who used me until she thought she was pregnant? Maybe I should start with the fact that I was the inbred child of my grandfather? Or that my grandfather killed my mother? It was all too much and being with her had broken the emotional damn holding it all back.

"I'll be ok," I said smiling weakly. We lay in bed her juices drying on my crotch and under me until I fell asleep.

It was Brooke who woke me up the next morning. She told me we had to get going soon because she would have to head out to work today. I pulled her into a kiss and told her I owned her for last night and it had been nice to fall asleep in someone's arms, I had really needed that. She told me she hadn't expected the night to go the way it did but she understood I had been going through a lot even if I didn't talk about it. She said she was happy to be there for me but I would definitely owe her one later.

I took the ferry back to HolBrooke and drove home. I got back to the house and found the phone company there, I was happy that I would be able to call Lilly now and talk with her. I wondered how much of all of this she knew about; I really hoped she could shed some light on yesterday's events.

As soon as my phone was hooked up I called Lilly and she said that she really didn't know anything about my sister's possible death or why Cassie was left the house. I asked her to try to find my birth certificate, as I had left it in my dad's old paperwork, and everything else needed to turn the house over to me. We talked about the work I wanted to do to her house and she loved my plans for it, I was really happy she wasn't upset by the modernization I wanted to do. I talked to Lilly for over an hour before fixing some lunch and watching a movie.

The next month was really busy as I began work on the tree house, to keep myself busy I worked from morning until dinner, only stopping for lunch. I called and had the city put a construction dumpster between the two houses and I started pulling everything out of the tree house and tarring the roof off. I then took down the walls leaving just the original flooring. I re-enforced the original floor and began building new walls.

While building the walls I put in shelving and built window boxes on three walls with built in benches big enough to lie down on for sleep overs or for sitting and reading. By the time I re-built the roof the tree house was more than that, it was a full outdoor bedroom with a tree running through the middle. Instead of an open whole cut into the floor I build a locking trap door with a key for security and privacy. Lastly I took out the latter and made a set of real stairs instead, this would make it easier and safer. It was the kind of outdoor room any child would die to have, it was a perfect tribute to my mom and Lilly.

After the tree house I took a couple days off I needed the break and I really wanted to see Gia. I drove over to the bar around lunch time on a Friday to surprise her, but she wasn't there, the girl working the bar said she hadn't been in for a couple days but didn't know why. I was a little disappointed but thought I would call her when I got home. Since Gia wasn't at work I decided to forget lunch at the bar and I drove over to a fast food restaurant.

When I got back to the house that day there was a big moving truck sitting in the driveway. I parked next door at my mom's house and walked over to see who was parked at Lilly's. I found Abby sitting at the back door; she looked cold even with her jeans and winter coat on.

"Hey sis," I said walking up to her. She jumped at the sound of my voice brining her out of whatever she had been thinking. She stood up and we hugged.

"About time you got here, if Lilly hadn't told me about the tree house in the yard next door I would've thought I was in the wrong place."

"No, you found me. What are you doing here?"

"I brought all our stuff silly," she told me.

"Our stuff?" I asked.

"Yeah our stuff," she laughed, "You have yourself a new roommate."

"What?" I asked, she couldn't really mean she was staying could she?

Abby claimed that she and Katie had talked and so had Katie and Lilly. Lilly decided that it was time to break the lease on the apartment and use her money to buy a house. Lilly decided to move to were her sisters were and Ash was going to move back in with her there so Linda, James, and JT could live as a family. I guess that they didn't mind having Ash but it would be easier if Ash returned to Lilly which I heard is what Ash wanted too.

Again I thought that I really needed to call and talk to Ash and try to figure out what she was still feeling if anything after all this time. Since my night with Brooke I couldn't get her out of my mind, but I still held off on talking to her. I just couldn't figure out the right words and it always seemed like the

wrong time to me, and I made the excuse that with the time difference I wasn't sure what time it was where she was and didn't want to wake her at night.

Abby told me that since her parents had told her not to come home she had been left with a choice. Lilly said she loved Abby dearly and could've come to live with her and Ash. Abby had begun to love Lilly like a mom but she wasn't sure about it so she called Katie and they came up with the solution that she went with. Lilly told Katie she could have the house on HolBrooke that I was staying in now, Lilly didn't ever plan to return and she thought it would be a great home for the girls. Katie and Abby really liked the idea and Abby brought all of our stuff now while Katie finished her last year of college. I was happy to have all my things, and even more happy that I would have Abby's company.

Abby and I unloaded the truck and spent the rest of the day unpacking and setting up her room. It was nice to have a full kitchen full of plates and silverware and drinking glasses. I unloaded all of my things into the family room; I didn't want to set up a bedroom as I intended to move next door as soon as all of the red tape was cut. I did help Abby set up the master suite, she really loved the house and she was so happy to have her first real home of her own.

I was happy to have my own bed back again even if I was sleeping in the family room. I was lying in bed that night watching TV when I heard Abby walk down the stairs. I pulled the blanket back as she walked into the room and she smiled as she climbed into bed with me. Truth be told I had been waiting for her to come to me. I knew she hated sleeping alone and I knew sooner or later she would come downstairs. We were both really tired and I wrapped my arms around her kissing her neck. She let out a slight purring noise as she drifted off to sleep.

Over the next week I began work on Katie and Abby's house. I called and talked to Katie, letting her know my plans for their house. She loved every idea I had; she remembered living there as a girl and she really wanted to come home again to the updated house I had designed. Katie told me she was going to send me a check to cover the cost of remodel, I tried to argue but she told me that if I was going to do the work then she could pay for the repairs. I eventually gave in as it was her house and when I finally got my mom's house I would probably have to do the same amount of work, it would be better to not have to foot the bill for two houses.

Abby was a great help to me during the day she would cook for me and help me out as much as possible. At night we would cook dinner together, watch TV and she would sleep in my bed at night, I really loved having her with me to hold. Some nights we had sex, but most the time we didn't, we had the kind of comfort ability that we just liked being around each other and when we needed to be with each other we were. Our relationship had turned into one of the best of my life; I really loved my sister and was grateful she was her with me now.

Abby had been there just over a week when I got the paperwork in the mail that would allow me to get my mom's house in order. With the paperwork was a copy of my birth certificate and I had forgotten until I got it in the mail that my name had been reversed. I kept looking through the paperwork and found a court approved name change paperwork form. Sometime after taking custody of me my father had changed my name, reversing my first and middle but I had no idea why. I would have to ask Lilly if she knew anything about that, I'm just glad she had sent the name change info too, I was sure that would help with the house stuff.

I told Abby I had to go to Port Howard and asked if she wanted to come along, she really liked the idea of getting away for a while and decided to come to go. We left the next morning and on the way I

talked with her about my friend Brooke and what had happened the last time I had seen her, I don't know why it all broke out during the drive but I opened my sole to her, asking for advice.

Abby listened as I explained that I really missed Ash and needed to talk to her, I wanted to fix what had been broken and find a way to make it work. Abby had a tear roll down her cheek as I spoke; I asked her why she was crying. She told me that what I had just said was the sweetest thing she had ever heard me say about someone I loved, and she was crying because she wished I could feel about her what I did for Ash. She wouldn't ever leave Katie but she still had that piece that loved me too and she was touched by it. She said she would do what she could to make it happen with me and Ash.

I was again grateful for Abby and her presence with me, I had hurt this girl at one time and she still loved me enough to be honest with me and help me find real love. I wished, not for the first time, that I could've loved her the way she deserved.

We didn't talk much more on the ferry ride to the island. I drove straight to the real estate office and walked in. Brooke was there and was so happy to see me she ran from her desk and hugged me, only then noticing Abby standing with me.

"Girlfriend?" Brooke asked tilting her head towards Abby and pulling away from our hug.

"No, this is my sister," I explained, "Abby this is Brooke."

"OH," Brooke exclaimed, "I've heard of you, Joey talks about you and his other sister all the time. By the way everyone is out of the office for a few minutes, but please wait here and let's chat."

"OK," Abby said and sat at Brooke's desk and the girls seemed to hit it off right away. I sat down in the waiting area kind of nervous waiting for the realtor to come back.

When the realtor came back we walked into his office and set down to business, we exchanged paperwork and signatures for what seemed like hours. When things were all said and done I now owned a house, I finally had a home of my own to build a life at. I just hoped that the curse of the house wouldn't follow me home. I wrote a huge check to cover back taxes and he handed me keys and a title. He shook my hand and wished me luck.

I walked out to find Brooke and Abby giggling about something and I immediately regretted introducing them. I told them that we were all done and Brooke got up and hugged me again. I gave her a quick but sweet kiss on the lips and we made plans for as all to get together some time soon, with everything said and done we all said our goodbyes.

I decided that since I was I was at Port Howard I would stop in at the PI's office and see if he had found anything yet. I took Abby to lunch first then we made our way to the PI. Glen wasn't in but his secretary said that she would have him call me as soon as possible; she didn't believe that he had turned up anything significant yet but she would tell him I stopped by.

The ride home was enjoyable, Abby talked to me about Brooke, she really had liked her. I told Abby that Brooke and her had a lot in common and we both were looking forward to seeing her again we thought we would invite her over for dinner once the house was finished.

When we got back home I walked over to mom's old house or my house as I needed to learn to call it. I grabbed my hammer out of my truck and I pulled the boards off the door and used the key I had been given to go inside. The layout was almost exactly the house next door but my house felt darker somehow. It was in less repair than I had hoped and I would have to spend much more time and money to bring this house up to date.

I walked around the house, even in the afternoon light the windows were boarded up so it was still dark inside. I could see the dark spot on the light hardwood flooring near the stairs where mom had died. I tried to think back and remember living here as a small child but my memories failed me. Maybe it was for the best that I didn't remember those early years, from the tales I'd hear none of it was worth remembering anyway.

I felt Abby's arms wrap around me brining me back from my thoughts.

"You ok?" she asked.

"I'm good, just old ghosts filling my brain."

"The PI called, he's waiting on the phone," she explained.

"OK," I replied and walked back over to Katie's house. I picked up the phone and the PI had put it on hold as I could hear the hold music. After about ten minutes he came back on the line.

"Joey?"

"Yeah."

"Oh, good I'm sorry I missed you at my office, I've been meaning to update you on what I've found out."

"OH," I exclaimed excited, "Did you find her?"

"No, I have traced her birth records, and yours," He started.

"OK, but you can't find her now?"

"No, I found you both but as I was able to track you after learning of your name change, she disappeared sometime around ten years old, I can't confirm she died as there isn't a death certificate, but I can't find any record of her from there." I didn't know what to think, I had to give him credit for discovering my name change but that just meant something else was going on if he still couldn't find Jessica.

"So she could still be alive?" I asked my heart racing, maybe this wasn't for nothing.

"I don't want to get your hopes up," He told me, "The only real question I can answer so far is why your house passed down to your mom and not your grandfather."

"Ok," I said nervously, I don't know why but I felt this was about to be something big.

"From marriage and birth records I found out that your grandfather was your mother's step-father. Apparently he was abusive to your grandmother and she was going to divorce him at the time of her death. When she died she left the house to your mother."

"OH THANK GOD!" I exclaimed at the realization that my real father wasn't my biological grandfather, my sister and I weren't inbred.

"Um ok," Glen said confused.

"No this is just good news," I told him, "Thank you so much, just let me know when you have something else."

"No problem, good day Joey."

"Good day to you too."

Chapter 19: Katie Comes Home

The week following the phone call from Glen, he was able to find out what had happened to my families money. At the time of her death my grandmother's family had been worth quite a bit of money. Fearing that my mother's step-father would try to pull some kind of scam to take the money and run my grandmother had willed the house to my mother and had arrangements at the bank to have all the money put into a trust to go to my mother at the age of 25.

With my mother not making it to 25 years old the money had been sitting in trust since the time of my grandmother's death just accumulating interest and waiting for next of kin to claim it. Glen helped me set up the necessary appointments needed to claim my families lost money. I couldn't believe my luck as it doubled the money I had gotten from my father's death settlement.

I felt bad claiming the whole sum myself so I rolled half the inheritance into a trust to be given to my sister if and when she was ever found. I felt like it was the right thing to do. I set up the trust in a way that only two people would have access to the money, me or my sister with proof of identity. I was grateful to Glen for all his help now only having my sister to find left on his list of things I asked him to do.

I on the other hand had way too much on my plate to deal with now. With two houses to work on, I had come up with a plan to get all the renovation done. I had stopped the repair work on Katie's house long enough to remodel the master suite and bathroom in my house. Katie was going to be done with school in just a couple months and I wanted to be able to live in my house by the time she came home, I felt it was important that Katie and Abby have their own space together.

I figured if I completed my bedroom and bathroom then I could live in my house while finishing the rest of the restorations. The kitchen appliances were in dire need of replacement but I figured they were useable enough that I could use them if I had to. I really wanted to surprise Katie by having her place done when she arrived on the island. No matter how I added all up it equaled a lot of work in a short amount of time.

It was an unusually warm lunch time on a Saturday in April and I was sitting on the front porch of Katie's house eating a sandwich and drinking ice tea. I had just that morning finished the final touches to my bedroom and I should've been moving my stuff over to my house, but I was unmotivated. I had a breeze coming across the porch and the sun on my feet and it was an almost perfect moment, so much so I didn't think anything could get me to move all day.

I was enjoying having the house to myself as Abby was out with Brooke. The two girls had become friends and were often out shopping or just hanging out together if Abby wasn't involved with Katie I would've thought they would be a cute couple themselves. In reality I was really happy that Abby had a girl-friend to run around with, as much as we loved each other it was good for her to hang with someone else sometimes. I had dropped Abby off at the ferry dock this morning just after breakfast, and would have the house to myself until later that night when I would have to pick her up again.

I was sitting in a lawn chair with my bare feet up on the porch rail when a car pulled up in front of the house. I didn't move until I saw who got out of the car. It was Gia; I hopped up and walked across the yard to say hi. The soft grass of the front yard felt really nice on my feet right then.

"Hey," I called to her, "What are you doing here?"

"Well someone didn't come see me like he promised," she scolded me.

"I did but you weren't at work when I stopped by," I told her.

"SUUUURRE you did," she giggled and I hugged her.

"I did miss you, "I told her, "You want some lunch?"

"Lunch would be great."

We walked inside and it wasn't much but I fixed some sandwiches and milk, we had a pleasant time talking together and laughing. Spending time with Gia was always easy for me; it was like we never ran out of things to talk about and were always laughing, she was by far one of the most easy going girls I had ever met. I was hoping to have another moment like our night in the hot tub, but I was also really beginning to fall for her on some level too.

After lunch I gave her a walking tour of both houses and the tree house, we started with Katie's house, as I took her floor by floor and explained what I had done and what I was still doing. I had taken a bunch of Polaroid pictures and was able to use them to show her what I was talking about. I had originally taken the pictures to show the family before and after shots but I was happy to have them right now to show my friend. Gia was amazed at the work I was doing, she asked where I had learned how to do all the construction and I just shrugged and said I just told her it came logically to me how to do things.

After Katie's house we then moved to the tree house, Gia was awestruck again by the work I had done on the tree house saying that it was the most beautiful room she had ever seen. I showed her the before and after photos and she joked asking if she could rent it as a room to live in as it was nicer than her whole apartment. I thought about letting her for a minute, it would be nice to have a girl living at the house with me when Katie came home and I didn't have Abby all to myself anymore, or was I fooling myself that was the reason I wanted her around? I pushed the thought away for the moment and just tried to enjoy my time with her right now.

From the tree house I walked her over to my house, I had told her at lunch how I had inherited and was now the owner of the house and my plans to rebuild it. Gia for some reason was apprehensive to go inside, I asked her what was wrong and she told me that she had been raised to believe this house was bad luck. She told me that all the islanders always said it had a curse with it. I told her that was ridiculous and that I had been raised here and I was fine. I left out the part where my biological father had raped and murdered my mother; the less Gia or anyone for that matter knew the better.

When I finally got her to follow me inside she calmed down as we walked the whole house and I explained in detail my plans for each room. She really liked the work I had done on my room and she absolutely loved the bathroom, after looking at the before pictures for the bath room she said I should start my own remodel and design company. She said that there were so many old houses on the island and they didn't have any one local to remodel you had to call the main land for something like that. I

actually liked the idea, I had a ton of money now but I was spending a lot too it wouldn't hurt to start my own business and add some cash back to help in my later years. I put that thought to the back of my mind as well for the moment.

It was early evening when we walked back next door to Katie's house. We had just sat down to watch a movie when I got a phone call. I ran to answer finding that it was Abby saying that she was crashing at Brooke's apartment and not to worry about her coming home. That meant I didn't have to pick her up from the ferry dock that night.

I figured without having to worry about Abby I had the whole night so I asked Gia if she wanted to go to the movies. The island didn't have a movie theater meaning that we would have to cross the bridge onto the main land and hit the nearest city. I wanted to get away and I really wanted to take Gia out for the night, she was really sweet and I wanted to thank her for being so cool to me. To be honest part of me really hoped that I would have the opportunity to make out with her again; I really wanted to sleep with her too but it would be great to at least kiss her again. I knew I wasn't in love with her and I didn't want to hurt her feelings as I had the impression her ex-boyfriend had done, but I really wanted to be with her.

Gia thought it would be great to go to the movies; she was excited as I was to get off the island for a while and just go do something. She said that she hadn't left the island in so long she needed a night away. I told her we could get dinner while we were out too, and she joked saying it would be just like a real date. She leaned over and kissed my cheek and said lets go.

We hopped in my truck and I headed across town, 20 minutes later we made it to the bridge. It was another half an hour drive to get to Kayak Falls the nearest city after the bridge. It was like traveling in time to the future as we made it to the city I liked the islands but after being on them for 4 months returning to a major city it was like the islands were the land time forgot. However I hadn't missed crowds and traffic I realized as we pulled into the theater parking lot, it was packed.

We found a movie that we both thought looked pretty good and I bought our tickets. As soon as we sat down I took her hand and held it. She smiled at me and leaned into my shoulder. The movie was a comedy about two blonds who go back to their home town for their high school reunion. It stared one of the girls from that hit show about six people who hang out at a coffee shop.

We only made it about halfway through the movie before we were kissing, she was leaning against me and I simply lifted her chin and began to kiss her. Her lips tasted so good and I really couldn't believe this gorgeous angel was letting me kiss them. Our tongues teased each other as the movie played on unnoticed, as we missed the ending, only coming back to reality when the house lights came back up.

It was late when we left the theater and I asked Gia if she wanted to get some dinner and maybe get a room somewhere so I didn't have to drive back that night. She didn't say anything for a moment or two then said that it sounded fun and she was in no hurry to get back to the island. I could tell she had something on her mind she wasn't saying but she obviously wasn't ready to talk about it. We got some Chinese take-out and rented a motel room, we rented a movie on the motel cable and ate the food which wasn't the best ever but I really enjoyed spending time with Gia.

When we had eaten we lay down on the bed and began kissing again. Her lips were so soft to the touch and it wasn't long before my tongue was between them. She was a great kisser thrusting her tongue all the way inside my mouth; I slipped mine into hers as far as I could and she closed her lips on it and

began to suck my tongue. It was so erotic as she sucked it hard moving her mouth back and forth across it.

I brought my hands up to her breasts rubbing them through her shirt. I wanted to move slow knowing the last time moving to quick had scared her off. This time however it seemed like she was more comfortable and the more I caressed her the more her kissing grew passionate.

Gia moved her hands to my chest and began to caress me up and down, after a few moments she pulled back and removed my shirt. She leaned over and began to kiss my chest slowly sucking in one of my nipples as she reached it. I had never really had a girl full on suck my nipple and I found it to be quite erotic.

I began unbuttoning her shirt and she pushed me onto my back, moving her kissing down my body. I was so hard as she reached the waistband of my jeans and kissed all around the lower part of my stomach. I was aching for her to suck my cock by the time she began to unbutton and unzip me; she reached inside my boxers and pulled me out the hole, licking the head of my dick heavily and wet.

"You taste so good," she purred licking the pre-cum off the tip, she gave my whole shaft a full licking before slowly enveloping me in her mouth. Gia definitely ranked up there as giving one of the best blowjobs I had ever had. She sucked slow and hard her tongue grinding against the soft point right under the head. My eyes literally rolled back inside my head as I had waves of pleasure striking in sharp sudden spikes.

"OH GOD!" I cried out, "Keep that up and I'm going to cum so soon." Gia looked up at me pausing long enough to smile then returned to pleasuring me. I used every delaying trick in the book but in the end it was no use. I came hard shooting my seed across her tongue, she didn't slow down as I came she continued to suck my dick until she was sure I was out of fluid.

"MMMMM, so good," she moaned letting my cock fall from her mouth and sliding up on the bed. I was about to thank her when she kissed me it was slow and passionate as we lay holding each other. I reached out to continue to unbutton her shirt and she stopped me again, "I'm still……. Not ready to go too far tonight, if that's ok?" She said timidly thinking I would be mad at her for stopping.

"It's ok," I said kissing the side of her head by her ear, "We'll only ever go as fast or slow as you want." I would've liked to fuck her, but this was the second time I was denied that privilege. I stuffed myself back into my pants and re-zipped myself, I felt like if I played it cool now she would get comfortable to have sex eventually, and she had blown me so good I couldn't be mad.

"Thank you," she said soft and sweet, "I know most boys would be upset but you're so sweet to wait." She said and hugged me tighter, "I just really need to be held tonight." She had a need in her voice that told me she was seeking an emotional bond. I held her without saying anything, I thought she was really cool and she was fun to be with but I was in another situation where I knew I wasn't in love with the girl. I knew then this was going to end badly for us one day, tonight I just held her in my arms until we both fell asleep.

I woke to sun shining through the windows; I looked at my watch to find it was about 6:30; I kissed Gia's cheek and shook her slightly.

"Is it morning already?" she asked waking up.

"Yeah sweetie," I whispered. She wrapped her arms around me, hugging me really tight, "I'm not ready for it to be morning. I want to stay here with you for a while longer." It was very sweet but again I was worried that she was falling in love with me. I needed to talk to her, and now, today because I couldn't let this happen again and lead her on.

"Look Gia," I started pulling away from her, "I like lying here holding you and I think you're really cool............" was as far as I got before she cut me off.

"Don't do this," she said sharply, "Don't ruin our time together now. We can talk on the ride home. Please just hold me now."

"OK," I replied softly and held her quietly for a while.

It was after seven before we finally left the motel, I told Gia I had to get home and wait for Abby to call so I could pick her up at the ferry dock. Gia reluctantly let me go so we could leave. The ride home was in silence until we reached the bridge when she decided it was finally time to talk to me about us.

"I may have given you the wrong impression," she began looking out the side window, "I like you a lot and you're a really great guy but............"

"You're not interested in a relationship?" I asked cutting in. She looked at me and bit her lip without saying anything and nodded her head, "And you don't want to hurt my feelings." I finished for her. She nodded again.

"Don't get me wrong, I really like our time together, but I............" she stopped and I didn't push her to say more.

"It's ok," I started taking her hand and kissing it gently, "I kind of............. I sort of feel the same way. I just ended a relationship when we met, I loved her a lot and I don't think I'm ready to fall in love again." I was being honest with her and I hoped she didn't take it to personal that I wasn't interested in a girlfriend right now.

"Oh, ok," she said breathing out, "I really do like spending time with you, and I was hoping not to give you the wrong idea, but sometimes I just really need to be held by a man." I could tell for her this was really hard to admit and talk about I was honored she had chosen me for her friend and trusted me to be there for her.

"I get it, I'll be honest too, I would really like to have sex with you some day but I'm happy spending any time with you," I admitted feeling like I just wanted to put all cards on the table.

"I know, that's why last night I....... well I wanted to at first last night but I got scared again. I'm sorry, I've been through a lot," she told me and I gave her hand a reassuring squeeze, "I want to keep seeing you when I need someone to hold me and treat me so sweet. We will............ have sex when I'm ready for it, is all that ok? Can you wait until I'm ready?" she asked. I realized only then that it wasn't the last boyfriend that caused her sexual issues, something really bad had happened to her at some point but I didn't want to ask if she didn't want to tell me. But I could be her emotional fill in from time to time; I didn't mind doing that for her.

"Yes, sweetie, whenever you need me just come to me and I'll hold you all night. And yes I can wait," I told her and she lifted my hand this time and kissed it. By the time we were done talking we had reached my street; I pulled into the driveway and walked her to her car. She said she wanted to head home and shower before having her afternoon shift at the bar; I kissed her softly just before she got into her car. I stood on Katie's front lawn as Gia drove away, there was a mystery to that girl and I decided to figure it out, if it meant helping her I wanted to do what I could to understand her.

I went to get Abby at about 9:00 that morning; she was excited to tell me all about her time hanging around with Brooke. The two girls had really had a fun time together and had stayed up most the night just talking. I wasn't really that interested in listening as I had my own things running around in my head that morning; I just half listened and nodded my head often.

After bringing Abby home I spent the rest of the morning moving my things over to my house into my new room. When living with the girls at college we had shared things like dishes and furniture, and when I had moved into my last apartment I had used all our stuff from college. But now we had two houses to fill, and I decided to leave all of our old stuff to the girls. This meant I would need to buy a lot of furniture and necessary things. I spent the rest of the day setting up my new room and trying to find places to put everything. I set up my TV and reclining chair in that room for now as well. The master suite was practically as big as my last apartment and I didn't want to set up anything else until repair work was done on the other rooms.

I was in bed that night when I heard the back door open and close downstairs. I had given Abby a key to the house in case of emergency's so I expected that it was her. A few moments later I heard footsteps on the stairs and then my door opened. I had been right in walked Abby in her bathrobe which she took off and stood in front of me wearing only a shirt and panties. I lifted my blanket and Abby climbed into bed with me. I had expected this when I gave her the key, Abby hated sleeping alone and I knew she wouldn't like being alone in Katie's house. I rolled over and kissed her as soon as she lay down. An hour later I rolled off of her onto my side after making love to her, she rolled onto her side too and snuggled her back up to me. We fell asleep holding each other, content in my new room.

I went out the next day and bought new dishes, silverware, and bath towels. I bought a new larger bed for my room and moved my old one into one of the spare bedrooms. I had used this bed since I moved to Katie's apartment and it had always been too small for sleeping two people all the time, I loved the closeness I had with Abby but it was time to upgrade my bed. I decided to not buy anymore furniture right now until the house was done, so I would have to make due with a reclining chair and a bed to sit on. I was glad I didn't have to many friends here I needed to entertain yet.

I talked to Gia on a pretty regular basis for the next couple months and we went out do lunch a few times but I didn't really have a good opportunity to take her out on another date. Part of the problem was I had Abby sleeping in my bed with me every night. I knew all I would have to do was tell her I had a date and she would stay at home but I loved Abby so much and I knew she had a phobia of sleeping alone I just couldn't make her leave my bed at night. I knew it would only be a short time before Katie would be home again and they would have each other and Abby wouldn't be sleeping with me anymore anyway. A selfish part of me wanted as many nights with her before her and Katie were together the rest of their lives, I had gotten used to Abby sleeping with me this year.

I put all the effort I could into getting Katie's house ready by mid-June, as that was when she planned to return. I no longer had Abby's help during the day as she had found a job on the island at a local day care. With the money Katie and I had we told her she didn't have to work and we would take

care of her but she insisted that her days were too long sitting in the house and she wanted her own money. She did however let Katie send her the money she needed to buy her own car, I had told her I didn't mind running her around but I couldn't disagree that having her own car was a lot more convenient for everyone.

As far as getting a job for myself, once word had gotten out around the island that I had been remodeling the houses, I was began to get people stopping by to ask questions and check out the houses almost on a daily basis. Luckily for me I had the pictures and had built up a scrapbook which was now becoming a portfolio.

I was asked by several people on the island if I would be interested in doing remodels on their homes, and I believed this was because the work I was doing wasn't just some fixit work it was full on reconstruction. The island basically being from another time had so much updating needing done and no one to do it I couldn't help but wonder after the comment Gia had made how much she was to blame for all the new interest in what I was doing. I took numbers and I told people I would get back to them after I was done with my sister's and my houses.

I managed to finish the entire major repair and remodel work on Katie's house by the beginning of June. I was exhausted and wanted to take a break on remodels for a couple weeks, but there were a number of little touch ups and finishing work that needed done and the house was so close to being completed.

Katie called one afternoon she was hoping Abby was home because they hadn't got to talk for a while, with Katie in school all day and working in the law office in the evenings. Now that Abby had the job it made it harder for the girls to talk, I was sad to tell her that Abby wasn't home.

"So how are things going with the house?" Katie asked me.

"Things are busy, with Abby working I lost my help so I don't know if I will be able to have the remodel done by the time you graduate and come home," I lied to her. I wanted her to be really surprised when she got here, it was an old trick and she probably saw through it but I went with it anyway.

"It's ok Joey, I really appreciate what you're doing for me and Abby," she said sweetly and I knew my ruse had worked. I thanked her and asked when she was going to make it home and she told me she was leaving really soon, she didn't care to go to her graduation ceremony and her diploma was being sent to her house anyway, so she would be home the beginning of July.

"Why so late I expected you home in the next couple weeks?" I asked her confused, if she was leaving right away why would it take her so long to get here?

"That was my plan, I miss Abby and you of course so much," She started and I laughed inside as she added me to that statement. Of course she missed her girlfriend and I didn't blame her, "But since I'm driving I talked to Mom and I'm going to stop and stay with her for a couple days."

"She will really like that," I told her thinking about Ash again. I really needed to call her but some part of me wasn't ready even after two years, "I've thought about going and seeing them too, but I've been really busy here." I didn't tell Katie the truth, it wasn't the work keeping me from making the trip out to visit the girls, and it wasn't just Ash.

Part of me felt like I was losing the connection I had with Lilly since my dad had died. With all the revelations I had learned in the last six months I was having a hard time with my whole sense of family. Even talking to Katie that day I was starting to see her as a girl again on some level and not my sister anymore.

Katie and I talked for a little while longer before she had to go back to class again. I was somewhat sad when I hung up the phone because I realized just how much I missed her, my emotions were all over the place lately. I still loved Ash so much but she had hurt me and I was sure I had ruined that now from not dealing with it and just leaving her. Ash had to have moved on from me by now, forgetting all about me and our time together.

Then there was Jenny, I really loved her too but it was different from how I had loved Ash. Both girls were really special to me but in different ways, I had loved Ash so much but I never thought about our relationship past what was going on with us at the moment. With Jenny I actually saw myself getting married and having a family of my own with her. It was really confusing to have one love that was in the moment and another all about the future. I decided it didn't matter anymore anyway because both girls were lost to me, Ash and I had fallen apart and Jenny had ended things.

But in my life now there was Brooke, Gia, Abby and Katie. I really liked Brooke and Gia but both had made it clear that as much as they liked playing around with me they weren't interested in me being their boyfriend. I was ok with that because I knew that I wasn't in love with them but it still made things complicated inside my head.

Then there were my sisters, who weren't my sisters. I loved them both very much but again I wasn't in love with them. I had begun to consider a relationship where the three of us were together, I thought they might go for something like that because we all still made love all the time, but on an island this small it wouldn't take long for everyone to be in our business and that would be bad for us trying to live here. But that wasn't the only reason I was hesitant to be in a three way relationship with them. I really wanted a love of my own, and a real family. Katie and Abby had a real love between them and I would always be the third party on the outside of that, I wanted what they had together.

Lastly there was my long lost real sister out there, and she was the whole reason I had come here in the first place. I hadn't heard any new news on her in months, and I was growing frustrated with that too as I was beginning to wonder what I was paying the PI for. I understood that things took time but I had a feeling like I really needed this case to be solved, as if my future would hinge on what he found.

With all that in my head I felt as strange pull in my mind decided to go have lunch with Gia. I hopped in the truck and drove across the island to see if she was at work and surprise her. I thought about it on the way over and Gia was a really great girl and I realized someone had done something really bad to her and she was scared to move on, but I made the decision then that I would try to make it work with her. I decided to actually ask her out, she had said she didn't want a relationship but I figured it never hurt to try. She was a wonderful person and I could see myself falling for her in time, maybe for once I should try dating someone without being so blind stupid in love first to affect my decisions.

It was a mid-afternoon when I arrived at the bar, as I walked in Gia saw me and ran right to me throwing her arms around me and kissed me. The bar was mostly empty so there weren't many people to wait on so Gia kissed me for a few minutes before we broke apart.

"Wow," I said catching my breath, "That was unexpected."

"I just missed you," she told me taking my hand, "Tom I'm taking my lunch now." She called to the cook as she pulled me out the back door. Gia led me to her car in the alley behind the bar, and opened her back door, "I really, really missed you," she repeated to me running her hand over my chest.

"Gia um I......." was as much as I managed as she pushed me down onto her back seat. I scooted up all the way in the car as she climbed in on top of me and closed the door. I was really happy for the tinted windows as she began kissing me and pulling at my belt, "Right....... Now.............. Here......." I asked between kisses as she unbuttoned my pant.

"I only have a half hour lunch and I'm so ready," she said unzipping my pants and pushing them off my hips, "I've wanted to for a long time but I was scared," she whispered in my ear, "When you walked in just now I realized just how much I really needed you." She had my hard cock in her hand and was stroking me even firmer.

We kissed again and she let go of me long enough to pull her panties off from under her work skirt. I pulled my boxers off my hips as she grabbed my cock pushing herself down on it. Gia was everything that I had imagined her to be as I slid inside her warm firm love muscle. She was already dripping juices down my cock as she slid past the head, I couldn't believe how wet and tight she was. Gia was almost as tight as Ash had been and Gia was ten years older now then Ash had been at the time we made love.

Gia placed her hands flat on my shoulders and began bucking her hips as she rode up and down on me, pushing forward as she slid down. My head was so close to her door that when she bucked down the movement would send me forward slightly and I would lightly bump my head on the door. I didn't care she felt so good she could fuck me into a head wound and I would still take every minute of it.

Gia's pussy felt so good I actually found myself getting bigger inside her, I felt like I was larger than I had ever been before. Despite how wet her pussy was my new found size was making her so tight on me that it was becoming harder to move within her.

"OHHHHH FUCKING GOD," Gia cried out, "You're so big, baby, and it feels so good."

I didn't respond I began trusting up to meet her down strokes and she began moaning loud incoherent words. Gia moved her hands and wrapped them around my neck as she stopped moving and I felt her pussy actually tighten up around me as she hit her orgasm. After a couple minutes I began to thrust up pumping insider her fast my own orgasm building.

"Yes," she whispered in my ear, "Cum in me I want to work the rest of my day feeling you inside me." That was all it took and I shot my seed up and inside her waiting hot pussy. I felt totally spent as she lay on top of me kissing my neck lovingly. The whole incident had taken about ten to fifteen minutes but it had been one of the most unexpected and incredible moments of my life. I lay there with Gia our hearts beating really fast, my thighs all wet from her juices, and I couldn't help but wonder what had finally made her want this so badly.

"Wow, sweetie," I said to her, "That was............. Just wow."

"Thank you," she said shyly still kissing my neck, "I didn't even realize how much I've started to care for you until you walked in that door today."

"I care a lot for you too," I told her, "That is one of the reasons I came here today. I know you said you didn't want a relationship......."

"I want you," she said softly cutting me off, "I want to be with you. I was wrong not to be honest with you before. When you tried to talk to me in the motel I saw were you were going with the talk. I lied in the truck when I told you I didn't want this. I'm sorry, but I was scared of my own feelings." She snuggled her head in my neck and kissed me again.

"Gia I want to be honest, I really like you and I want to ask you to be my girlfriend but I'm............ not in love yet."

"It's ok," Gia said moving her kissing to my lips, "I'm not ready to be in love, that's the truth, but I am ready to be your girlfriend."

"Ok," I said simply and began to kiss her again. She pulled away from me a few minutes later and looked at her watch.

"I have to go clean up a little before I go back to work," she said with one last kiss, pushing herself up and off me. She picked up a shirt off the front seat and wiped herself off and handed it to me, "I'm glad I always keep a spare shirt in my car," she told me and gave me a wink. I wiped my crotch and pulled up my pants as she opened the door. We walked back in the back door and I kissed her as she walked into the bathroom.

I hung out and talked with her the whole rest of the shift. We both couldn't keep the smiles off our faces and I couldn't believe we had waited six months to get together. We talked and she said she was going to go home and get some spare clothes and come out to my house that night, she wanted to spend the night in my arms on the first night we were a couple. I told her that was fine and I would meet her back at home in a couple hours. I kissed her goodbye at the bar as we parted ways and I drove home.

I got home and I walked over to Katie's house to find it empty as Abby hadn't gotten home from work yet. I waited by the back door until she got home, and when she arrived she had a strange look on her face, she knew if I was there something was up. I first told her of the call from Katie and about her staying for a few days at her mom's house and Abby said she understood but she was a little saddened that she would have to wait longer to see her girlfriend.

Next I told her that we had to stop sleeping together, I explained to her that I had a girlfriend now. The one thing we had agreed to from the beginning was that it was going to shock the island bad enough when people learned about Katie and Abby as the island was many years behind an already intolerant world. We had agreed to not let anyone find out that Abby and I were sleeping together too and start even more rumors about the three of us. So Abby understood immediately what me having a girlfriend meant, we would have to act like nothing had happened and sadly move on with our lives.

I knew Abby wasn't happy with the idea of having to sleep in that big dark house by herself so I told her that she could come over and sleep on my extra bed if she really needed to. She giggled and said she would rather not be in the house for my first night with my new girlfriend, she said she would "Man up" as the term goes and just start sleeping in her own bed. I was grateful and told her at least Katie would be home in a few weeks and if she could make it the first week alone she would be fine. Abby leaned in and kissed me on the cheek and I left Katie's house and got back in my truck.

I drove back into town and bought a kitchen table and a few chairs, and then I went out for some groceries so I could cook something for Gia when she got to my house. I really wanted to make this a special night for both of us. I really didn't know where this was going yet but I still wanted tonight to be as great as possible.

Gia was waiting on my doorstep when I got home; she smiled at me as I pulled up and got out of the truck with my bags of food.

"I'm sorry if I made you wait," I told her.

"I've only been here for about a minute waiting; I got here a while ago and ran into your sister next door. I just walked back over." I was grateful to Abby for keeping her company but at the same time that did really feel weird.

I unloaded the food and stocked up the refrigerator before I went back out and unloaded my new table. I went to work on unpacking it and putting it together while Gia went out and pulled the chairs out of the back of my truck. I protested and said she didn't have to but she said if I had been nice enough to buy all of this so we could have a nice dinner she could help a little. It was about another half an hour to get my new table assembled but it looked great. I then began to work on cooking something great for dinner.

We talked as I cooked, Gia kept trying to help me but I would just tell her to sit down and let me get everything. Our conversation continued as we ate dinner and I realized I was happy, really happy for the first time since I had come to the island. I had been good spirited with my time with here with Abby but I was feeling really happy. After diner it was getting late so we decided to go up to my room and watch TV.

I was actually nervous as we climbed the stairs, and I didn't know why, I mean we had spent the night together before and she had been in my room too. But as we climbed the stairs preparing to go to bed it was all becoming real to me, Gia was my girlfriend and we were going to bed as a real couple. I realized that made me more nervous than having sex with her had.

Gia pulled back the blanket on my bed as I loaded the VCR with a movie, I put in the one with the sports agent who gets fired and starts his own agency with one employee and one client, it was also a cute love story, and I thought that would be good for us tonight. I walked to the bed as Gia began stripping off all her clothes, I did the same as I got to the bed I was really turned on looking at her naked body lying there. I climbed into bed and began kissing her; she wrapped her arms around me and buried her head into my neck. I understood and kissed her forehead before climbing over her so I was between her and he wall, now being behind her I put my arms around her and she snuggled up against me.

As we lay there watching the movie she took both of my hands from around her waist and placed them on her breasts still holding her hands against mine. I was really hard pressed up against her ass and she wiggled against me until my dick was between her upper thighs. I wanted to make love to her so bad but I held back and just held her to me as we drifted off to sleep.

Now that I had a girlfriend I decided not to take such a long break on my remodel, I didn't want her to have to keep coming over just to hang out in my room. I don't know why but it just became more important to have my house all finished at that point. Gia and I fell into a rhythm of things almost right

away. We both had felt like we clicked the first day we met and the way we thought and went about things was very similar.

We learned right away it was best for Gia to spend her work nights at her apartment after our making love in the morning had caused her to be late three days in a row. She would come over almost every day but she didn't stay over unless she didn't have to work the next day. The first day off she had we spent the whole day in bed holing each other and making love.

I pushed myself to get as much work done on her work days so we could run around and just be together on her days off. One Friday night we went back to Kayak Falls and spent the night in the motel after going to a movie again. We had so much fun just being around each other and I felt I had made a great decision to finally ask her out.

The first project I started on after the bedroom and bathroom was my kitchen, I went out right away and bought a new refrigerator and stove. I bought a dishwasher and put it in the garage for the time being, I had to remodel the kitchen to be able to install it as the design of the house had been built without one. I would've waited to buy the appliances until after construction but with having a girl over all the time and actually cooking it became more practical to have better working appliances.

In the meantime Abby was doing very well at being by herself at the house. I was happy she had found a way to start getting over her fears. As I was spending so much time with Gia, Abby started spending more time with Brooke on her weekends. Brooke came out to Katie's for the whole weekend to celebrate my 21st birthday with us and we all four had a great time together played cards, ordering in pizza and drinking beer. I felt a little weird at first having two girls I had slept with in the past there with my new girlfriend, but they were great and didn't say anything to Gia about it. It was great having really good people in my life to spend my birthday with.

At long last July arrived and so did Katie, she had called when she left Lilly's house and we knew she was on her way but we didn't know for sure when she would make it to the island, she finally arrived on a Saturday morning. Gia was in the kitchen around 9:00 cooking me a special breakfast for me and I wasn't allowed to come in until it was ready, I was sitting on my front porch drinking orange juice when I saw Abby, she had parked out front the last few days knowing Katie was on her way home to leave the driveway clear. I waved to her and she said she was going to the store and would be back soon.

It was about a half an hour later and Abby hadn't returned yet when I saw Katie's car drive past and pull into the her driveway next door. I hopped off the porch and ran after her; I got to her car as she was stepping out of it. My heart jumped at the sight of her and I could remember why I had fallen in love with her all those years ago. We both ran to each other and hugged; I had missed her so much over the last seven months. I realized in that moment I loved her so much and I never wanted to be away from my sister that long again.

"I missed you Joey," she told me pulling out of our hug. I just nodded and wiped the tear from her eye, "Sorry," she said referring to the tears, "It just means so much to be returning home here and to you and Abby."

"I get it," I told her, "It was hard for me when I first walked into my mom's old house too." She smiled at me happy I understood, "How was your time with your mom?" I asked.

"It really good I had missed her so much too. I had a tough time leaving her," She said and gave me an inquisitive look, "But that isn't what you want to really know is it?" I didn't say anything I turned my head and looked off the other way, "She's good Joey, she misses you much more then she wants to admit but she's good," Katie told me and I didn't know if that actually made me happy or not, "I have to tell you she has a boyfriend now and I think they are pretty serious."

"Thanks," I told her trying to hide the slight bit of hurt I was feeling, "Its ok I have a girlfriend." I had figured Ash would've moved on by now and I had now my second girlfriend since we broke up so I couldn't really be angry but on some level I was a little hurt to hear it.

"OOOh a girlfriend huh," Katie joked taking me out of my thought, "I have to meet her," she winked at me as she said it.

"You will, and speaking of girlfriends, yours should be back anytime. How about I show you the house and we unpack your car?" I asked her.

"That sounds great." She said giving me another hug. We walked in the house and her jaw dropped right away looking around the kitchen, "This is wonderful! It's nothing like I remember." I was happy she liked it; I didn't realize until that moment how nervous I was about it.

We walked the whole house from basement to attic and Katie couldn't stop telling me how happy she was. I had built in all the small details that she had asked for and more, she couldn't believe that I had the whole house done already. We walked back outside and began to unpack her car Katie had me stack everything in the living room telling me she and Abby would go through it all and put it away later. We were on our third trip to the car when Abby and Gia walked up the driveway, Abby rushed to Katie and jumped into her arms.

I saw Gia actually blush when Katie and Abby began to kiss right there in the driveway.

"That doesn't bother you does it?" I asked whispering to her. I had explained the situation to her months ago so I didn't know why she was blushing.

"No," she whispered leaning into my ear, "It actually turns me on a little." Gia was smiling ear to ear with her cheeks red. I couldn't help but grin back at her.

The girls finally broke away and I introduced Gia to Katie, the girls shook hands and talked for a few moments before we all went back to unloading the last of Katie's things from her car. Gia invited the girls over for breakfast and Katie and Abby just looked at each other, I answered before they could and told them to come by for lunch in a couple hours instead. The girls smiled and Katie said that sounded really nice, so I took Gia by the hand and we walked back to my house.

Gia pinned me to the door kissing me as soon as we got back home, her hands running across my body.

"That made me so hot," she told me unzipping my pants, "Fuck me, right here!" She began to kiss me with a wild spark I hadn't felt from her before. She had my pants and boxers down and I pushed her over to the stairs and yanked her shorts and panties down.

Gia spun around placing her hands flat on the stairs as I moved in behind her; I slid my cock inside her dripping pussy and thrust in all the way in one stroke. We fucked on the stairs fast and wild, as she pushed back as hard as she could against my thrusts. I reached around and grabbed her waist and used her as leverage to pump into her hard, this was the most wild we had ever been with each other. Gia had always been loving even in the back seat of her car that first time had been as caring as it was quick and passionate. As I pushed hard inside her, this was the first time I would describe our sex as straight fucking, and it was one of the most memorable fucks of my whole life.

I was breathing hard and my heart was pounding so fast as I felt her orgasm hit her, she clamped around me hard when I was in my reverse stroke, this caused me to slid out of her and I was ready to cum, I shot my juices up and across her back. We both dropped down onto the stares sitting next to each other, I leaned over and kissed her passionately until our breathing came back down to normal.

After our bodies settled down again we walked into the bathroom and cleaned up before we pulled our clothes back into place and she led me into the kitchen to finally eat the breakfast she had cooked for me. I was feeling so good and the food made everything just perfect, I don't know why but I turned to Gia and asked her, "Would you like to move in with me?"

"Did you really just ask me that?" she said in a baffled tone. I paused thinking I really had, I had so much fun with Gia and I just wanted to be around her all the time. My feelings for her had grown on me so slowly that I didn't realize how strong they were until that moment, but my feelings for her were so completely different than anything I had felt before. Our relationship was just as playful and fun, as it was loving and supportive.

"Yeah I guess I did," I finally answered her.

"And your just proposing living together not……….." she began.

"Yeah just moving in," I said quickly cutting her off.

"Is it ok if I think about it for a while?" she asked.

"Yeah," I replied in an even tone. She walked over to me and sat down on my lap and placed her hand on the side of my face.

"It's ok that you asked, I just have to think," she said kissing softly thinking I was hurt by her not saying yes right away. In truth I was happy she was taking a moment to think about it before jumping in. I had meant it moments ago when I had asked but truth be told I was nervous about going through with it.

She moved back to her chair and continued to eat, we didn't say anything for a long time, and I finally broke the ice.

"This morning was great baby," I said smiling, "If you got that horny from watching them kiss, imagine if you could see what they're doing now."

"MMMMM," she exclaimed and did a little shutter, "You don't think I'm weird that it turned me on."

"No, I don't think it's weird," I reassured her, "I've spent so much time around my sisters I don't even think about it anymore."

"Would you think I was weird..............." she stopped mid-sentence.

"What? Tell me," I coxed her.

"Well seeing it got me so.............wet," she spoke the last word softly.

"I got that when we got home," I said smiling at her and she blushed really big again.

"I.............. would you be ok if I ever wanted to try................ I mean be with........" She stopped short and I knew where she was going.

"You want to hook up with my sisters?"

"NO!" she said jumping up a little, "No, I wouldn't do it with them, but maybe if we ever met a girl we both could be comfortable with................. We could try...... something?" She was so shy and nervous about it I almost had to laugh.

"We'll see sweetie, it's not weird and I've done that before it's not that big a thing." She looked at me astonished she was so very shy with sex and the look on her face was so cute.

"You've......... Done that? You've.............. two girls............ Really?" She was on the edge of her seat waiting for a response. We had never had the how many and who conversation so my past sex life was still mostly unknown to her.

"Yeah, when I was in college I had a lot of fun and used to go to parties." I thought about telling her the truth but I held back. Now one but the three of us ever needed to know about my relationship to my sisters, and college was the perfect lie. I didn't want to lie to Gia but I thought it would be better in the long run to not tell her.

"Wow, I would never think you would do that, it's so hot!" She said grinning, "Did you do that more than once?" She was excited and I decided to be honest about that part.

"Well yeah, I had a couple of girl-friends and we all would get together every so often and have fun," I told her.

"Wow you've really lived, have you been with a lot of girls?" She asked and I could tell she wasn't asking me out of jealousy but because she felt it made me worldlier somehow.

"I've been with a few over the years," I held back, I knew she had only been with a couple men and I didn't want her to freak out if I told her all about all the girls in college. She didn't say anything but nodded with an inquisitive look on her face, she turned back to her food and finished her breakfast. I knew this whole conversation wasn't over but I had no idea of where it was going to go when we picked it up again.

I finished my breakfast and helped Gia clean up. I went out front and sat on the porch just watching the time pass until lunch time. Katie and Abby walked over sometime after noon, they were

holding hands and both girls had very big smiles on their faces. I had seen Abby smile in the last six months but not like this, both girls were truly glowing.

We sat down in my kitchen and had a nice lunch together, I was really happy to find Gia got along well with my sisters. We all decided to go out for a night on the town, dinner and maybe dancing to celebrate Katie's home coming. Abby suggested that we call Brooke and invite her too, Gia loved the idea too as she had really liked her.

After lunch Abby called Brooke and she loved the idea of finally meeting my sister and hanging out with all of us. She asked if she could bring her cousin Tommy who was staying at her apartment right now, Abby asked me and I said I didn't mind if she brought a friend because it would be more fun with more people.

We all met up at Katie's house at 6:00 and somehow stuffed all six of us in Brooke's car. Brooke drove and Tommy rode shot gun as Gia sat on my lap and Abby sat on Katie's all in the back seat. Abby and Katie were making out minutes after we left, by the time we hit the bridge Gia was so aroused she was grinding against my lap making me hard so I began to kiss the back of her neck making her grind me harder.

I was so horny as we drove to Kayak falls, I wanted to reach into Gia's skirt and play with her pussy but I didn't want to freak her out as far as I knew she hadn't done that kind of thing in front of people before so I moved slowly. I slid the back of her skirt from the bottom of her lap until she was sitting on my lap with just my jeans and her panties separating us. I reached under her ass and unzipped my pants, she could tell what I was doing and she turned her head and began kissing me hard as I slipped through my zipper and my cock popped up against her thigh. I could feel how wet her panties were against my dick as she wiggled herself against me, she had her hands at her sides to not give away what we were doing but wiggled her ass so her pussy rubbed my cock under her skirt.

I reached under her skirt and pulled her panties sideways and her tongue went wild in my mouth, she loved doing this with everyone in the car. It was so naughty and it was making her soaking wet as I slipped myself inside her, had she not been dripping I wouldn't have been able to enter her like this but she was so horny and grinded herself against me. I felt her pussy constrict after only a couple minutes, the danger of getting caught was so strong she had orgasmed almost right away. It was only then her sense of reality came back and she broke our kiss, looking at me then the car and back at me, she wiggle until I slipped out of her. I fumbled underneath her to stuff my wet hard on back inside my jeans and I felt her body relax when I pulled my zipper back up.

"That was fucking incredible," she whispered barely audible in my ear then gave me a long deep kiss.

I looked over and saw Katie and Abby were making out really hard core now; both had their hands up their shirts. I was happy they were making up for lost time, as I was sure they had really missed each other over the last six months. I looked to the front seat and saw Tommy had the passenger side visor down, it had a mirror on it and he was watching the back seat in the mirror. Looking down I noticed he had his dick pulled out of his jeans and was jacking off to the sight in the mirror, I actually laughed and nudged Gia and moved my eyes to point at what he was doing, she giggled as she saw him jacking.

"Are you almost done?" Brooke asked looking over at her cousin, "Were getting close to the city." I looked out the window and she was right Kayak Falls was coming up very soon. Katie and Abby pulled

away from each other looking around and seeing what Tommy was doing, they giggled and readjusted their shirts back into place.

"Yeah, I'm almost there," Tommy said somewhat grunting, and then he opened the glove compartment and pulled out a napkin, he came into the napkin and balled it up before putting himself away, "Fuck that was hot," Tommy said.

"What the lesbians or the couple back there trying to hide the fact they were fucking in my back seat?" Asked Brooke and all four of us turned red. Tommy just laughed and said all of it, he said after noticing both couples going at it he couldn't hold back. I said I wasn't offended and the girls said they could understand, Book just sighed and said it wasn't the first time she had seen him do that.

After the car ride dinner was a little less exciting, as we sat we joked, talked and had a really fun time together without any further sexual adventures happening. After dinner we went out to a night club were we could both dance and drink, this was cool because before I hadn't been old enough to go to a club like this. Abby and Katie were so into each other they were dancing really close and kissing on the dance floor, I could tell that even in a city like Kayak Falls they still weren't used to seeing two girls kissing so intently.

I made the choice not to drink because someone needed to drive home, which meant everyone else was free to drink as much as they wanted. I kept a tab open for all six of us and the girls began doing shots, as Tommy was drinking beer. I had a good time watching everyone dance as Gia and Brooke after a number of drinks began to dance together grinding their hips together as they danced.

I had an evil thought as I watched Gia and Brooke dance, I thought about my conversation with Gia that morning over breakfast. I thought about it and if Gia really ever wanted to be in a three way where we included another woman I thought about seeing if Brooke would be interested in being that third person. I thought it would be hot if I could get both girls at the same time and I knew Brooke was up for most anything.

We left the club at closing time, all five had drunk way too much and Tommy was so drunk that we had to carry him to the car, to the dismay of all of us. We set him in the front seat and the girls climbed into the back, Katie sitting on Abby this time and Gia sitting on Brooke.

Abby and Katie were making out hard core in the back seat on the ride home, I looked in the rear view and could see that Katie's shirt was pulled up and Abby was sucking her breasts, I could tell her arm was moving but with them right behind me I couldn't tell what else they were doing.

I looked behind me to my right and could see Brooke had her hand up Gia's skirt and was obviously stroking her pussy. I didn't know how to feel about the girls playing without me. Gia had her head leaned back, her eyes were closed and she was moaning my name, as drunk as she was I don't doubt she didn't realize it wasn't me. I knew Brooke meant no harm as she was just a wild girl who liked to play but I was a little indifferent about her touching my girlfriend without the three of us having talked about it first. By the time we made it back to my house I decided that I didn't really consider it cheating because everyone was drunk and it had been a crazy night with us all fooling around anyway.

I pulled up in Katie's driveway and Gia had fallen asleep on Brookes lap so I picked her up and carried her home to my bed then headed back over to Katie's. Katie and Abby were stumbling around the back door and they told Brooke she could sleep on their couch and she accepted. Abby got some blankets

down from her room and set them on the floor next to the couch, and put a pillow down as well. Brooke helped me carry Tommy inside the house and we placed him down on the blankets and Brooke climbed up on the couch, I kissed her on the cheek and she told me she had fun and she really liked my girlfriend. I told her thank you and went home.

I woke to the phone ringing the next morning; Gia was passed out next me sleeping peacefully looking so cute. I rolled over on top of her and picked up the phone, thanking myself for being smart enough to have had a line put in by the bed so I wouldn't have to run down stairs every time it rang.

"Hello," I said my voice cracking.

"Hey sweetie," Abby started, "I wanted to ask you and Gia over for breakfast.

"I don't know," I said playing in a joking tone, "Depends on what you're fixing, maybe I wanted to have my girlfriend for breakfast today?"

"MMMM sounds good," Abby joked back then said, "But don't fill up on that and come over for some eggs and pancakes we have news."

"Ok, sis we will be over in just a little while." I hung up the phone and rolled back off Gia onto my side of the bed again.

"So were going over for breakfast?" Gia asked just waking up her eyes still closed.

"Yeah, Abby said she has some kind of news." I started to get out of bed and Gia grabbed my arm.

"I thought you told her something about having me for breakfast, where are you going?" She asked grinning. I pushed her down on her back and began kissing her deeply.

It was an hour later when we walked next door for breakfast, we had played around, taken a shower and were dressed now. I was happy to see Brooke's car still in the driveway meaning I would have a chance to visit with her too this morning.

We walked in and everyone was around the table already, Gia and I sat down and Abby and Katie stood up facing the table.

"Well since we're all here," Katie started, "We wanted to tell everyone that I asked Abby to marry me," Katie went on and couldn't keep the smile off her face, "As you all know we've been dating for over two years now and she is my whole world, I love her so much."

"I love Katie so much too and I said yes," Abby said excited and blushing as she lifted her hand and showed everyone her engagement ring.

"That's so pretty," Gia said looking the ring over carefully.

"It was mom's, she gave it to me for Abby. It was the one Dad gave her a couple years ago when they got married," Katie explained.

"I thought it was so sweet," Abby told everyone, "It makes me feel so much more part of the family that Lilly let Katie have her ring. It's much more special then something new."

Everyone talked and had a great morning as we ate pancakes, Abby and Katie were much happier then I think I've ever seen anyone. We talked of the wedding the whole morning and it was me who finally brought up the dark side of the whole situation.

"I love you guys and I'm so happy for you but you do realize that it's illegal here for you to be married right?" I said and I had four girls look at me as if I had killed the mood in the room, Tommy just shook his head.

"We know, we talked about it ourselves," Katie said softly, "We know some people won't accept us as married but were doing it for us not them. We love each other and were going to have the ceremony legal or not."

"Good, that's what I was hoping to hear," I told her, "I love you both but I was worried because I don't want to see people hurt my sisters."

"You're too sweet," Abby said kissing my cheek, "But were tough we can take it, screw the haters we will be fine."

It was decided that they would wait until next summer to have the wedding as they wanted a lot of time to plan. They were going to have the biggest, prettiest and romantic wedding they could imagine. Katie said she wanted to get everyone back together at the lodge and have it where her mom had gotten married. I thought that was a great idea and I made the decision if I ever got married I wanted the wedding to be there too.

Chapter 20: One Year Later

It was a hot Saturday afternoon in the beginning of August and I was sitting on my front porch thinking about the last year, Gia was out with my sister doing god only knows what girls do when planning a wedding. The girls had lots of fun doing wedding stuff all the time but the date of the wedding kept changing due to the disappearance of Ashley. She had been gone for over a year now and Katie was still hopeful that she would return to us again, I was less than hopeful now.

As far as Ash was concerned, I called Lilly's place on Ash's 17th birthday, I felt it was time to finally deal with all this and talk to her again. I mean when it came down to it we were family and with Katie's wedding coming I felt it was time to let it all go and get back to being friends. I called Lilly's house to wish Ash a happy birthday and she told me that Ash had run away from home.

"She ran away?" I asked shocked, "What had happened? I thought the girls were very happy living together." When Katie had come home she had explained that Lilly had bought a condominium near where Linda was living and Ash had been happy to move back in with her.

Lilly explained to me that Ash and her friend Terra had started seeing some local boys in town and Lilly didn't like the boy that Ash was dating but she didn't interfere. Then one day Lilly came home to a note from Ash, it said that she was sorry but she had to leave and she would call soon.

That had been two weeks ago and Lilly was still without a word yet. Lilly said she had tried everything she could think of to find her, but even Ash's boyfriend didn't know what happened to her. The poor boy had come to Lilly's house trying to find out why she hadn't been returning his calls only to find out himself she was gone.

"That doesn't sound like the Ashley I remember," I told her my heart sinking in my chest. I was worried for Ash and didn't know what to do.

"I know, this is why I tried not to interfere with her boyfriend, I thought if I didn't get in her face about him she wouldn't do something this stupid."

"I don't know what to tell you Lil, she usually isn't that impulsive, what can I do to help you find her?"

"Nothing, sweetie, I filed a missing persons report and since she is underage the police are doing what they can. If nothing turns up in another week I will have an investigator try to find her."

"Ok," I told her and gave her the phone number for Glen, my investigator, and told her that maybe he could recommend someone in her area to do a good job.
"Make sure you keep Katie and me up to date on any news. Let me know if you need anything."

"Your sweet Joey, but I'm ok for now, she will turn up and be grounded until she's 18," She told me somewhat joking but I could hear real concern in her voice when she said it. I was worried for Ash,

but I figured that Lilly was right and she would turn up in a couple weeks and it would all blow over by Christmas.

I sat on my porch thinking enjoying the sunshine happy that I took the day off trusting Abby to run the store by herself today. Abby had come home only a few minutes ago and I had waved as her car passed by and she smiled back. She looked tired as she walked to her door and I was happy to be sitting at home drinking iced tea on such a nice day.

I thought back to last year at this time, I had worked as hard as possible last summer to get my house done by fall but as August was coming to a close I realized I couldn't get the whole thing done myself by fall and at the rate I was running into complications I wouldn't be able to finish by winter.

I didn't want my house all torn up as when the snow hit as I had heard rumors that if the island snowed it was really heavy. I made the decision that I needed to hire an assistant but the problem was I didn't really trust anyone to come into my house. The solution presented itself about a week later, I was talking to Tommy and he mentioned that he had worked as a maintenance man back on the mainland a for a couple years.

Tommy had only come out to visit Brooke for a couple weeks and had stayed for a couple months as he had been having a really good time hanging out with all of us. I asked Tommy if he would be interested in staying and coming to work for me, I told him he could stay in the house with me here for the time being and I would pay him construction wages to help out. Tommy agreed right away and he came to stay with me for a while.

We worked on the house on all Gia's work days and I gave Tommy the same days off that I took to spend time with Gia. He was really happy with the money and had no problem with the work schedule. We found that we worked well together and Tommy soon started to become my first real guy best friend I'd had since Jeff back in college.

Katie had been home for almost two months before she had decided it was time to go out and get a job. Abby had quit her job when Katie came home and the girls were hardly seen for the first month she was home. I smiled inwardly as I thought about the love they had for each other and how much it had meant to them to be with each other again.

It was early September and Katie set about trying to find a job at a legal firm like the job she had done in college the last four years. The problem was that the island didn't have any real big firms here so she set her sights on looking in Kayak Falls as well. I told her at the rate she was going it would make more sense to just start her own law office, she laughed and said she didn't have all school she needed for that but she though it was a fun thought.

It was October when Katie found a job doing accounting in Kayak falls, it was one of her second majors in college and she was really good with numbers. As it turned out that was another thing the island didn't have was its own accounting firm for taxes, to get advice or taxes done you had to Kayak Falls to one of the tax places there.

Even in the 1990's the island still was lacking a lot of the common businesses that seemed to be everywhere on the main land. The problem was that the population had grown so much more than the commercial side of things here and it was just waiting for big business to step in and get local. I think back to those days on the island and I really wish I could go back in time to those days, I look at

HolBrooke Island now and it feels like someone stuffed it full to the corners. I guess that happens to everyone's home town.

I had asked Gia to move in with me back when Katie came home but she had decided to wait on that until we had dated a little longer and the house was closer to finished. It was December when she finally moved in with me, she had been renting the apartment over the garage at her parents place and she talked with them and she had decided to leave her furniture there and just bring her clothes and personal belongings to our house. Gia introduced her parents to Tommy and set it up so that he could rent the apartment from them and move out of my house now that it was almost done.

Tommy had decided to stay on the island and I told him for staying to help me out I would cover his rent until he could find a job once the house was all done. He told me I had paid him good and that rent wasn't much so he was fine. I was still trying to figure out what I was going to do next as I wanted to start a business but I didn't know yet what it would be, but I told him once I figured it all out he would have a job with me.

I still hadn't any word on my sister, as Glen hadn't discovered anything new in the last year, I talked to him often and he said that he tracked Jessica to the point where she had supposedly drowned. I still hadn't told Gia about my missing sister yet and I didn't know why, but I wanted to keep the details of that all to myself for now, or at least until I had a whole story to tell.

According to Glen the whole incident shocked the island because the foster parents had been thought of as ideal people. After Jessica's incident it was found that the foster parents were running some kind of kiddy porn thing and both went to prison. Glen said he would've stopped looking but he couldn't find a death certificate and all of the kids living there at the time had seemed to have disappeared meaning they all probably had their names changed, this lead him to suspect the drowning of my sister was fake and he would look further. I thanked him for his efforts so far and he told me he would be in touch with more when possible.

I thought about all the people I had met on the island in the year and a half I had lived here, could any one of the girls here be Jess? I tried to put it out of my mind but I started looking at any girl around 25 to see if she looked like me. I did a double take anytime I heard the name Jessica or Jess but I realized that we both had different names since our child hood and I finally gave up my people watching as she could've been anyone.

Christmas had come and I bought Gia a new car as hers was beginning to have issues, she cried and told me that was too much but she couldn't say no. Gia had gotten me a bomber jacket that I had really liked when we passed it on a shop window; she said she thought I looked cute in it. Gia and I ate breakfast that morning and made love before going next door to see my sisters. We had a fun day watching movies and eating snacks and treats.

Katie and I called Lilly on Christmas night and talked to her for a while; she was happy to hear from us and wished us much love. There was still no word from Ash yet and Lilly was more worried than ever. She told us that Ash's car had been found in a used car lot somewhere in the Midwest and according to the dealership a man tried to trade it in without the title. When the man was questioned he said he had bought it from two girls who had needed the cash.

I had a really bad feeling but I didn't say it out loud as we finished talking to Lilly, I was of two minds of the situation. On the first hand if her car had turned up traded for cash and no one had seen or

heard a word from her since before her 17th birthday my rational mind said she was dead. I mean why else wouldn't she have called home or sent a letter or something? But in my heart I knew she couldn't be gone, there was something else going on here and it would all be ok in the end. I chose to believe the second thought until I heard otherwise.

It was January when Katie quit her job and bought an office on island. Developers had come in and built a strip mall, and the islands first apartment complex on the outer edge of town as part of the island growth that was going on.

Katie was the first person to take advantage of the new offices and she decided to buy one office to start her own accounting and tax firm. Gia quit her job at the bar and went to work for her to answer phones and set appointments. Katie had originally thought about hiring Abby for this job but I had suggested that working and living together might be too much for them over time and the girls agreed. Gia was happy to have a day time only job and weekends off and the girls could car pool every day.

It turned into a great thing for them both like working with your best friend. As it turned out there were a lot of grateful people happy to have a tax place right in town and not have to cross the bridge anymore. Her business took off fast and suddenly became too much for her to handle alone, so she had to hire another tax accountant to work for her. She ended up hiring her old boss from her job in Kayak falls because her old boss actually lived on the island too. This turned out to be a win, win situation for them because her old boss was really good and knowledgeable and she was happy to not have the drive anymore.

The offices filled up fast with all kinds of shops and businesses and I decided to buy one of the offices before they were all taken. I had a couple ideas about businesses I wanted to start and I decided that when I was done with my house I wanted a job of my own but I didn't want to work for anyone again. I had enough money to get started doing anything I wanted to do but I would decide on what my future would hold only when the house was done.

It was January when we went back to work on the house, I had taken December off while Gia settled in and for the holidays. I had run in to one disaster after another and the house had taken so much longer to finish then I had ever anticipated, but when you're talking about a remodel of a four level house it sometimes runs longer then you expect. In the end with Tommy's help we had the house completed by mid-February.

Once done I let Gia decorate the house how she saw fit. I wanted her to feel not only comfortable but that it really was just as much her house as mine. Gia had a good eye for decoration and had taken Katie with her when shopping, the girls had really become best friends and I was happy for both of them. In the end the house was a little more girly then I would have done it but Gia seemed really happy so I didn't complain.

I made a snap decision about what direction to take myself at the end of February, as I decided to open up a used shop. I had gotten into comic books in the last year and I always had to stop in at the one shop in Kayak Falls when I was in town. I would spend so much time talking to the store owner that Gia would often have to pull me aside and remind me that we had other places to go. The problem is that I did the math on what comic shops made and there was no way to open one on the island and make money.

The solution to my problem came to me while I was sleeping one night; it was so simple I was surprised it took me so long to think of it. I decided to open a shop that carried new and used items so I could have my comic books but I would also carry used VHS movies (keep in mind this was late 90s just before DVD took over), video games and books. I could buy and trade with people and help people order in what new items they might be looking for. I was really happy I had bought one of the larger commercial spaces in the strip mall as I would need a lot of it for my store.

It was the beginning of March when I found out about a major book sale going on from a closed library about 50 miles mainland. I drove out and over stuffed my truck full of boxed of books and movies. I had fun checking out garage sales and thrift stores all through Kayak falls looking for anything used I could use to start up my shop it really was like treasure hunting.

My store was one large room with four connecting rooms, one at each corner making the main room an octagon. The other rooms were set up so that they could've been offices but I took the doors off of the rooms and opened it up so I could separate out my items by type. The main room was books, corner room one was to the left as you entered I used it for comic books. Corner room two was in the back corner on the left I used it for games anything from card to video. Corner room three was to the right as you entered I used it for movies and music. Corner room four was in the back corner on the right I set up for old toys. I had found a number of old robot toys from the 80s and I thought about collectors out there and decided if I was going to run a used shop I should include everything.

At the back of the main octagon room was a door that opened to a hallway back behind the shop, I loved the layout of the front so much when I had bought the place I hadn't really thought much about the fact that the back half of the space was almost as big as the shop part. The hall way had two large conference rooms and a large office in the back with three smaller offices and a back door opening into the rear parking. I had no idea what I would ever do with the conference rooms and all the offices as I only needed one but I still liked my set up out front.

My shop opened officially in April and to my great surprise opening day was big, as it seemed like the whole island showed up to at least look around. Within days I had people in the shop all the time wanting to trade in their old books which was great for my inventory. I was so busy from day one and I only worked for a week by myself before I hired both Tommy and Abby to help me around the store so we could be open on Saturdays too.

It was about late April or early May when I had one of the local residents come into the store and ask me if there was anything I could do to help him remodel his house. Word had spread as nothing around this island is a secret and I now had somehow gained a reputation as a remodel specialist. I told him that I wasn't anything close to a contractor, I had simply done my own houses but he convinced me to come by and look at his house and see what I thought.

This was the beginning of my second business, as I began drawing up plans for people on how to repair and modernize their homes. Tommy started working with me on the house projects and we actually took on doing a home remodel for one of the island residents. It wasn't a construction rebuilding we were doing more over just a full internal face lift, as we began to update the style of everything from carpet to light fixtures.

This first remodel led others coming to us and before we knew it we were set for a number of jobs after that one, and we were set to make a lot of money. I set Tommy up as a partner in this business with me, because I had money and I felt the least I could do for all his loyal help was set him up as an equal not

an employee. We used the conference rooms in the back of the book store to run this second business and I felt like it was meant to be, I had a use now for both sides of the office space I had bought.

The problem was with two of the three employee's now working on the remodel business it left me shorthanded in the store, I tried to fill in as much as I could to give Abby time off but in the end I convinced Brooke to come work for me at the book store. I paid for Brooke to move to the island and she moved in to the new apartment complex near the strip mall, she actually was only the third tenant to rent there since it opened. We all took the day off from our jobs and helped her move, I was so happy to have all my friends right there on the same island and it was so nice for Abby to be able to work with her best friend.

Depending on what I had going on I would sometimes do shifts at the store and I felt like those were my favorite days as I loved talking books and movies with people all day. With the second business really taking off I really couldn't afford to work the book store as much as I liked and I was at a point where I was going to have to hire a third full time person. I put a now hiring sign in the window and I made Abby officially the assistant manager and told her to let me know if she found someone.

As I said I was now sitting on my porch thinking about the last year and how much things had changed, just enjoying the stillness of the street and life around me, it was great to slow down for a whole day and do nothing for a change. I had drifted off in my memories so I didn't notice how late in the afternoon it had become when Gia came home. I smiled at her as she walked over from Katie's house and she looked away, I wondered what was wrong as Gia always smiled and kissed my cheek when returning home.

"Hey sweetie, did you girls have fun?" I asked standing up and walking to her.

"I guess," She replied quietly walking past me into the house.

"What's wrong?" I asked following her inside.

"Nothing."

"Really baby what's wrong?" I asked again softly putting my arms around her from behind and lightly kissing her neck.

"I don't know, I've just been feeling........... I don't know...... I feel..... Joey where we going?" She said quietly her eyes starting to well up.

"I don't know what you mean? Where do you think we should be going?" I asked her.

"We've been dating for a year and you still don't talk to me."

I was shocked and I didn't know where this was coming from, "I talk to you all the time."

"You tell me about the house or the business futures, you talk to me but we never TALK........... We never talk about our future and you never tell me about why you really came to the island in the first place............... I don't know if I can stay with someone who has secrets."

"Gia......" I started, I did have secrets from her and I didn't know why I held on to them so strongly, "I don't want to lie to you but.........." She broke free of my arms and walked down the hall to the kitchen. She sat down at the table and put her head in her hands covering her face.

I stood in the doorway not saying a word trying to think about how to tell her everything. I still had never told her about my family history, I could hardly get her inside the house the first time I showed it to her because of her superstitions, how could I tell her she was right?

"I'll be right back," I said to her walking out the back door. I walked over to Katie's house and knocked on her back door.

"Joey what's wrong?" Abby asked answering the door. I told her I needed to speak with them really quickly and explained what had happened. I sat down at their kitchen table and I explained that I was tired of hiding the truth from Gia, and I was going to tell her everything.

"When you say everything do you mean about us too?" Katie asked me calmly placing her hand on mine.

"I think I should, we've had so many comments spoken accidently in the last year that I think it's time to come right out and tell her." I was shaking as I didn't know how Gia would respond to the news I had had sex with both girls I considered sisters. I didn't want to lose Gia but the secret had been chewing at me for a while and now it was killing me, I had hurt her by not being honest and it was time.

"Your right honesty is usually best, but if it gets out that we've had .... A relationship......... this is a small island," Katie said delicately. Abby took my other hand and put it on her heart, "Joey you're the only boy I've ever loved and I know how bad it hurt me when I thought you had cheated on me. Don't let her think that you've done that to her, go talk to her." Abby was right and again I overcome with love for my sister.

"She's right, if Gia can't deal with all of us having been together then maybe it's what's meant to be. If she tells the whole island and we become all the subject of gossip then so be it," Katie told me kissing my hand.

"No, if it were just me I would tell her about you," I said turning to Katie, "But I don't want to see people turn against you and your business fail."

"Then just tell her the truth about you and me," Abby said softly, "That should be enough for her to understand why you hid things from her."

"Thank you Joey, do what you think is best, I'm not ashamed of what we all meant to each other. I don't like to advise someone to lie to the person there in a relationship with, but maybe it is best that this secret stays between us," Katie told me.

"Thank you I love you both so much," I told them and pulled them into a hug.

"Come back over for dinner tonight if things are worked out. We have something to talk to you about," Abby said with a crooked smile.

"What....." I started but Katie cut me off.

"Go home and talk to Gia and come back later," Katie said pushing me out the door. I walked back home and Gia wasn't in the kitchen anymore, I walked around the house to find her upstairs in bed. She was lying on her side facing the wall as I sat down on the bed she didn't look at me.

"Before you say anything who's Glen? He called for you last night when you were working late again," she stated, "Why did you hire a PI? He wouldn't tell me, he just said he had news for you and to call him back."

"He has news?" I asked excitedly, "He didn't say anything?"

"I pushed him and told him I was your girlfriend but all he said was he found her," she said flatly, "But when I asked him who he said he couldn't talk about it and to have you call him back." I jumped off the bed and began to pace around I couldn't sit still, had he really found my sister?

"Oh my god," I breathed out, "I can't believe he found her." I was so excited that it took me a couple moments to realize that Gia was softly sobbing.

"Baby what?" I asked laying back down in the bed behind her. I wrapped my arms around her and she pushed me off.

"Don't pretend you care, all this time I thought you loved me and you've been looking for HER behind my back."

"What are you talking about?" I asked confused. I really didn't know what had brought all this on today and who she thought I was looking for.

"I asked Katie today while we were out why you had hired a private investigator and she told me I needed to talk to you about it," she said covering her face with both hands, "I hear comments between you and your sisters all the time and hushed conversations as I walk into the room. I'm not stupid I know there's more going on then you tell me."

"There's nothing going on Gia," I told her then thought about it and decided to rethink how to put it, "Well theirs things going on but not what you think."

"Next you're going to tell me some lie were you have a good reason for looking for your ex-girlfriend, but of course it's not because your still in love with her," She was crying so hard by this point she started coughing, "Go on............ Try to............ convince me your............. looking for her for your step mom........... Not yourself, tell me I have nothing to worry about and you still love me," she finally managed to say as her coughing calmed down again.

"Where is all of this coming from?" I asked finally understanding what was going on. She thought I hired the PI to find Ash and bring her home. I realized as she lay there crying that this was completely my fault because I couldn't be honest with her from the start. I sat thinking for a moment it was time to make some hard decisions, tell her the truth about all my secrets or let her go, "Why would you think I didn't feel for you everything I've said I do?"

"Because I've been through it before, I gave everything to my ex-boyfriend and ...... he betrayed me......... I just thought you were different," She paused crying into her hands again. I remember

thinking when we first started fooling around something bad had happened to her but in the time we had dated she still hadn't told me about what had happened with her ex-boyfriend. I suspected it was really bad as it caused major trust issues in her like tonight.

I lay down on the bed behind her and put my arms around her she didn't throw me off this time. I began to tell her about my family, how my grandfather married my grandmother when my mom was young, how he was my real father and how my mom died. Gia's crying turned to cries of compassion for my mother as I told her the story.

I went on to tell her about how my dad had adopted me and I hadn't found out about any of my history until a year and a half ago. The only thing I lied about was how I met Katie; I told Gia I had met her at Linda's wedding to John. I told Gia all about Abby and Brooke and how I had, had relationships with both girls when I was younger.

"It………… Finally makes sense," Gia told me wiping the tears from her eyes, "I always thought something was going on there."

"Not for a very long time," I replied slightly exaggerating. It had only been since just before Gia and I had gotten together the last time I made love to Abby but I slightly exaggerated it to sound like it had been since we were kids in high school.

"I can totally understand hooking up with Brooke, she's beautiful and kind of crazy, I'm not surprised there at all," Gia said. I was happy she was ok with the fact I had been with Brooke because the girls had become real friends in the last year. In fact it wasn't uncommon to see Gia, Brooke, and Abby run off to do things on their days off.

"I'm only surprised you picked me over her," She said as she looked up at me with a bashful look in her eyes. I knew she was fishing for a complement and I didn't let her down.

"I would pick you ten times over her," I said kissing the side of her face.

"Only ten," She joked, "Thank you for being honest, I do really understand why you hid these things."

"I'm sorry I should have told you a long time ago."

"SSSSSHHHH," she said and rolled over facing me. We began kissing and I pulled her tight into me. We kissed and held each other for a long time before our kissing began to become more passionate. I'd been so busy with things in the last few weeks we really hadn't had a chance to make love and I wanted her so bad in that moment.

It felt really good to have her not only understand the things I had told her but that she still loved me just the same. She began to rub my back and I became very hard from her light touching, I needed to be with her NOW so I slipped my hand under the waistband of her shorts, sliding my fingers inside her wet pussy. Gia moaned as I rubbed her clit with my thumb as I fingered her. I reached over with my other hand and began to pull at her shorts and her hands shot out grabbing my wrists.

"No, Joey, not now, I have some things to tell you too." I don't know why my heart somehow started to beat faster when she spoke, I don't know what I expected to hear but I knew it was going to be bad. I pulled my hand back and we lay down on the bed on our sides facing each other holding hands.

For the next hour Gia told me about her life growing up on the island, and her family. Her parents both having grown up on the island they had known each other their whole life. Gia's grandfather had left his grandmother when her father was a young boy and Gia's mom had grown up next door to Gia's dad. They had married right after high school and had kids right away; Gia was the youngest child of four, all older brothers. Things in the house were good for Gia until she hit about 11 years old and she began to hit puberty.

Gia began to shudder and I pulled her in tight to me as new tears began to roll down her face.

"SSSSHHH," I breathed out to her, "You don't have to tell me anymore if you don't want to."

"No I need to tell you," she cried softly into my shoulder, "It's just that when I told my ex he .... He........... called me a whore and left me."

"You can tell me," I whispered. I had a feeling I knew where this story was going but I wasn't going to stop her, "It won't change how I feel about you."

Gia looked up at me and kissed my cheek before she started talking again. She explained that her parents worked off the island and would get home very late at night leaving her alone with her brothers after school. This hadn't been a big deal until she was 11 and had walked in on her brothers one afternoon while they were sitting in the rec room downstairs masturbating.

She found out sometime later that her brothers would come home and hang out in the rec room and jerk themselves off whenever they felt like and didn't care if the other ones were in the room or not, if they felt the urge they just went for it. Normally Gia never hung out in the rec room as it was the boys domain to hang out but on this day she had gone down to see if her oldest brother would drive her to the mall on the main land.

Apparently all three brothers had gotten the urge at the same time that day as Gia opened the door to find all three with their dicks in hand. She was shocked at the site and she froze, she had seen pictures of penises and she had started masturbating herself a year ago but she had never seen the real thing like this. She froze looking in at them the door half open and in a horny moment of need her middle brother Rick grabbed her arm and pulled her into the room.

Without a word her youngest brother James grabbed her hair and pushed her down forcing his cock into her mouth, Gia tried to fight it but she felt hands on her shoulders pushing her back down when she tried to get up. Rick was holding her in place while James thrust his cock down her throat. Gia was crying and trying to call out to her oldest brother Lewis to help, he was her favorite brother and she knew any second he would put a stop to this.

Gia felt her ass being lifted, her shoulders were still being held down by Rick and James was still thrusting her mouth so the person bending her body up into this hurting position had to be her Lewis. This made her cry more as she felt her pants slide down her ass to her knees, of all the people in the world how could Lewis do this to her? She felt his hard cock push against her virgin slit, and the tears were blinding in her eyes, not Lewis, she thought, not the one person I trusted most in this world.

After she stopped fighting James they fell into a daily routine. Gia would come home and meet him in the rec room, where she would simply just strip and lay there while James forced himself inside her and grunted until he came. She didn't move, moan or give him any sign of pleasure; she just simply laid there and let him do his thing. Sometimes it felt good and she hated herself for enjoying her daily abuse but as it was the act of sex she couldn't help it, but even on those days she gave him no sign of pleasure. She really hoped that after a time or receiving no response from her he would grow board and find another girl to have sex with but it never happened.

As bad as that two years were it wasn't nearly as bad after she broke and gave in. He never hit her again, and she found that by submitting for a few minutes a day and letting him get himself off things were usually over within a few minutes and he left her alone the rest of the day. She hated herself but it was better than beatings and bruises, and she didn't have her older brothers to protect her anymore.

The only break she had over those two years was in the summer in between, her brother Lewis didn't come home that year as he had a girlfriend in the state where he was going to college and stayed with her. But Rich had come home that summer and even though she couldn't tell him what was going on, for fear of a real beating, his presence caused James to back off until he left again.

As soon as Rick was gone it was back to the same after school routine and she was back to hating herself and men for what James was doing to her. She simply didn't understand how he could be doing this to someone he claimed to love so very much, if he really did love her and felt anything for her as a brother she wouldn't have to submit to him daily.

After high school James joined the Army and went away. He rarely came home again after that and Gia was finally free of him, she still dreamed of killing him some day but as time moved on and she became an adult she decided that she would just move away from the island and never look back, never talk to him again and never return for any reason.

Two years later Gia had put a lot of her abuse past her, she had grown into a very beautiful girl and had many high school boys interested in her, but due to the abuse suffered at the hands of her brother she had never had a boyfriend and what made things worse was that all the boys on the island reminded her too much of her brother and she couldn't feel safe with them.

Gia was really excited when it was her turn to graduate and go off to college. She chose an out of state college in a big city, which was a major change for her but she was happy to be off the island and maybe start a new life that guys and dating were so far out of her mind that when she met Ken she was actually surprised to find she liked him.

Ken was the nicest and sweetest guy she had ever met to that point in her life, he treated her really nice and she was both happy and leery around him, she was so afraid he was going to change on her. She liked him very much but she was scared and made him wait a full year before she accepted his invitation to be his girlfriend.

Gia had gone home for the summer and upon returning to college she told Ken if he was still interested she would be his girlfriend. Ken was patient with her and waited until she was ready to have sex with him, which took her another couple months of them dating but that's when things changed.

Gia would often begin fooling around with Ken then have a panic attack and want to stop. Ken would get angry with her and tell her she was being unreasonable then storm out of the room and go home. He would call her later in the night and say he was sorry, and it wouldn't happen again.

It did happen again, every time Gia would freeze up he would get more and more angry which only made her not want to do things with him more, over the next year they only had sex a couple of times and she was always apprehensive doing it. She liked him but his anger towards her freezing up made her more upset and in the end she couldn't be with him anymore.

They broke up and Gia was so upset over the breakup of the relationship she hardly left her dorm room anymore. It was around this time that her best friend a guy named Court expressed that he was in love with her, and Gia realized she had some feelings for him too but she wasn't ready to try again.

It was just before summer vacation at the end of her sophomore year of college and she got a letter that her brother had been killed in a training exercise in the army. Gia was conflicted, she had wanted James dead for so long but she found she was really upset about the death of her brother. She went to Court to talk to him about it and they ended up making love that night, it was the first time in her life she had been truly comfortable having sex and she realized what he really meant to her. She thought she had finally found herself a real boyfriend.

Gia went home for the summer that year and when she returned to school she told Court that she was ready to make a real commitment to him and be his girlfriend. For the most part she didn't have the same issues with Court that she had, had with Ken when it came to being frightened in bed. Every so often she would freak out and Court didn't get mad at her as much as he didn't understand where it came from.

It wasn't until the end of her junior year when she was to leave again for the summer that she finally sat down and they talked about why she panicked from time to time. It was the first time she had ever told anyone about what had happened to her all those years ago, the first time she had trusted someone enough to share all of it.

Court's reaction wasn't good; he freaked out and told her she was a whore for sleeping with her own brothers. Gia tried to explain the whole thing but he said he was disgusted by the whole thing and it made him sick that he had fallen in love with a total slut. Gia fell to her knees and cried on her floor as she tried desperately to get him to understand, but he said he could never be with a girl who had sex with all three of her brothers.

Court walked out the door and he never spoke to her again. Gia went home and moped around the house for half the summer. That year her parents decided that they couldn't live in the house anymore after losing James and they moved to the other side of the island to a house with an apartment over the garage which they thought they might rent out to a border.

When Gia came back to campus to start her senior year word spread around that she was easy and that she had fucked her brothers, it only took a month before Gia quit school and moved back to the island for good. It didn't take long for Gia to find the job at the bar and she moved into the apartment over the garage as her parents had never found anyone to rent the apartment.

I held her to me and didn't say a word; I didn't know what to say to her. I understood what had happened to her and I felt really bad that her ex had thrown it in her face. We lay in bed the whole rest of the day talking and kissing softly holding each other.

Gia was happy that I accepted her for who she was and it didn't change things with us. I couldn't hold it against her without being a hypocrite because I had, had sex so many times with a girl who I had thought was my sister, even though the situation was completely different. We talked all night about where our relationship was going and Gia finally explained to me what was at the core of her fears.

I did begin to get nervous as we discussed our future and where things were going with us, it was time to really sit down and decide what we wanted to do. I knew one thing that night and that was from here on out things were going to be different, but I loved her and I looked forward to our time to come.

Sunday morning I was really happy I had made the decision that the remodel business would close on the weekends and the book store would be closed on Sunday so we all could have a day off together every week to do something outside of work if we wanted. Katie had chosen to close on the weekends too until tax season started again, so we all were home today. I let Gia sleep as we had talked pretty late into the night after telling our stories and discussing our future.

I pulled on a shirt and a pair of shorts and walked down stairs and began fixing us something for breakfast and it was only then I remembered that Katie had invited me over for dinner last night. I walked over to Katie's house and the morning air felt really good. Abby answered the door I apologized for missing dinner and told her they should come over for breakfast.

"How did last night go?" She asked with a hopeful look on her face.

"Were ok."

"What all did you tell her?" she asked quickly looking around.

I explained to Abby that I had told Gia about us but I had only lied about Katie and I's previous relationship. I told Abby so she could relay to Katie what was said so that we all would be on the same page, the last thing I needed was to get caught in a lie.

Abby said they would be over in a little while and I walked home. I thought about all that was said last night and the one thing I was really happy about was the fact I hadn't told her about my sister. In so many words while we were talking Gia had basically told me that because what had happened to her she was repulsed by the thought of incest. Blood sister or not I think she would have real issues with me and my sister.

Gia woke as I was finishing cooking the pancakes and bacon; she walked into the kitchen and sat down at the table. She smiled at me and I told her that the girls were coming over because they wanted to talk to us. She came up behind me and hugged me kissing my cheek.

"Thank you," she whispered.

"It's just breakfast," I told her.

"No for last night, thank you for accepting me for me," she said softly.

"It's ok, I love you for you," I kissed her cheek.

Abby and Katie came over for breakfast and we had a nice morning making jokes and enjoying each other's company, but the girls made us wait until we were all done eating before they would tell us what was up.

I was cleaning plates and putting things away when Katie finally began to talk, "Ok here's the thing, we were able to book the lodge for the second week of September. So were going forward with our wedding no matter what else is going on now."

"Ok," I replied, I knew that they had wanted to get married in July this year but with Ashley still gone they had waited. Katie didn't want her aunt to miss her wedding but it was looking like she had decided to go ahead without her.

"So with that only a few weeks away I wanted to ask Gia to be my maid of honor," Katie said smiling.

"Oh my god really?" Gia asked excitedly.

"Yes."

"Yeah, ok, I would love it!" Gia ran to her and hugged her.

"Ok with that settled I have a favor to ask you," Abby said turning to me, "We decided that Katie would wear the dress and I would wear a tux............ so I was wondering if you would be the best man." I couldn't help but laugh as I smiled at her.

"I never thought in my life I would be the best man to my ex-girlfriend at my sister's wedding, but I would be honored," I told her and she ran to me and hugged me. We all stood around my kitchen hugging for a while that morning before he girls went back home.

The rest of the day went by and Gia and I seemed to be back on track just fine after our talks on Saturday night. Monday I took the morning off and took the ferry to Port Howard to see Glen in his office, I was so excited that he had found my sister that I wanted to see him in person.

Glen was surprised to see me when I walked into his office telling me that there was no reason I needed to come all the way out to the island.

"Well the message I got was that you found my sister, I couldn't help it," I told him.

"I'm so sorry I think the message got a little miscommunicated," he replied, "I wish you would have called, I have found out something but I still haven't found Jessica herself."

"Well I'm here so what's going on?" I asked puzzled.

"I have found proof that she wasn't killed in the drowning, and I found some paperwork showing foster care records when she was 11 years old."

"If you found all that what's the problem?" I asked trying to hide the excitement I was feeling.

"Well that's just it, I found her case numbers and her records but for some reason it's been sealed, I'm trying to petition the state to have it opened so I can look at the info."

"Why would they seal her records?"

"Well they faked her death due to the abuse she suffered at the hands of her foster parents, as far as I can tell all the children of that home were given new names and fresh starts."

"Is this common?" I asked confused.

"No this isn't, usually they just remove the children and move them to new homes but for some reason they were all made to disappear. I'm looking into the reasons why that happened; it's an extreme action, something only done in severe cases like for a child porn situation or something to that effect."

"How long will it take to get access to her records?" I asked

"That I don't know, it's a lot of paperwork and I have to prove were not looking for her for some kind of malicious reasons. Give me time and I will have this all worked out, I'm halfway there now," he told me and I could see in his face he really wanted to help me resolve this once and for all.

"Thank you Glen," I told him shaking his hand and turning to leave his office.

I went into work that day with a lot on my mind, I was so close to finding my sister but at the same time I was getting a strange feeling like somehow this would end bad for me. I didn't know how but I was starting to wonder if it had really been a good idea to have Glen looking into the past, into things that maybe should be left dead and buried.

I checked in on Tommy out at the remodel site and he told me things were going fine, I told him that I was going to go check into the book store and to page me if anything came up. I don't know why but I couldn't focus and I really didn't want to be anywhere that day. I made the decision that if everything was ok with Brooke at the store I would take the rest of the day off and go to the movies; I needed to just get away.

Brooke was doing fine when I got to the shop and things were kind of slow for even a Monday afternoon. We talked for a while and she asked me why I was in such a down mood, I told her I was just feeling a little sick but I would be ok. I don't know if she believed me but she let the subject drop anyway.

Brooke suggested that we all get together and throw a bachelorette party for the girls that coming Friday. I told her that I thought it would be really fun and Brooke said she would handle everything. I thought about it and I realized that the last time we all had gone out to party had been the night Katie had come home last year. I decided I would close the store this Saturday so we could all really go out and have fun and not have to work the next day, we all deserved a good night of fun for all the work we had done this last year.

Also in light of the fact that Ash was still missing my sisters had really pushed back the date of the wedding and I knew her disappearance weighed heavily on Katie and a great night out with her friends

could do her wonders. I was really happy right then to have Brooke in my life looking out for my family, it was nice to have such a good friend.

I left the island as I had planned to do and drove out to Kayak falls, my uneasiness was getting worse and I felt almost agitated. I arrived in Kayak falls and I bought lunch before going to the mall. I did some shopping before going to the theater where I saw a really bad movie about a giant Japanese lizard that destroys Manhattan. After that I decided to go see another movie, so I went to see the 4th movie in the cop buddy series where the older cop was always complaining he was too old for this.

I got home late that night and Gia had my dinner ready when I got home. She had been worried about me being out and I told her that what had happened with Glen and explained that with everything going on I had just needed time to get away and think. She hugged me and told me not to be scared that everything would work out, and we would be fine.

"I know," I told her reaching into my pocket, "I love you and I want to marry you." I handed her a small box I had picked up at the mall while I was out.

"No............" Gia trailed off as she hesitantly opened the box, "Joey, I.............." She started crying, "It's all too good to be true, this whole last year has been the best of my life," she said and I wiped the tears out of her eyes and kissed her cheek, "Yes I'll marry you."

Chapter Twenty One:
Ashley's Diary: Part 5: The Road Home?

Ashley woke up with a jolt feeling cold. She thought she heard an odd noise outside, laying still she listened closely for any sounds around her but she could only hear raindrops on softly thumping against the roof of the van. She held her breath for a few moments until she realized nothing was trying to get inside then she finally relaxed.

She lay there knowing it was going to be a long day's drive if it was raining but she had no choice but to keep going. She looked at her watch finding it was only 4 a.m. she pulled the blanket back over herself, she realized she must have kicked it off in her sleep, not that it was much comfort against the cold on this late August morning.

Terra was asleep next to her breathing slowly and deep. Ash was jealous of her friend for being able to sleep so soundly because she found it was hard to go back to sleep. Ash could feel the itch between her legs telling her she really wanted to be touched, it had been a long time since she had fooled around with a guy and this morning she desperately wanted laid. She thought about waking Terra and fooling around with her but the girls hadn't had a repeat of the night they had spent together at Christmas time almost two years ago. Despite the fact that they shared a bed every night the most they did was sometimes hold each other as they fell asleep.

The night they made love at the Christmas party had made them very close friends but Ash and Terra had begun to date local boys not long after Christmas break. Despite how good they had felt and how much the girls had bonded from the experience they decided not to continue with the physical side of things anymore, even now that they both were single they still hadn't gone down that road again.

The fact that Terra was always with her made finding time to masturbate almost impossible now a days but thinking back to when she had made love to Terra only made her need worse. She looked over at her sleeping friend thinking she might not get a better chance and slowly slid her hand down her body. She unbuttoned her jeans and quietly as she could unzipped them, her hand slipped in under her panties and she found her clit right away.

A soft moan escaped her lips as she began to gently rub her swollen nub, it had been so long since she had taken care of herself and so much longer since she had been with a guy in any way. It felt so good to finally give herself some relief but her mind couldn't completely focus as much as she tried to close her eyes and just feel the pleasure she was giving herself her mind drifted to how all this trouble had started in the first place. Ash sighed loudly out of frustration and pulled her hand back, this line of thought wasn't helping her get things done.

Ash's thoughts went back to last year when she had first met Terra's boyfriend, Jake, and how much she had made fun of her friend for dating a musician. Jake was a high school dropout that was part of a local band "Bloody Kitten" who played all over the state and was working on getting a full on record deal.

Ash had told her best friend that it was so cliché that a wild girl like Terra was running around with a guitar player. Terra just shrugged it off saying that sometimes you can't help who you fall in love with and she loved Jake very much.

At the time Ash had her own boyfriend, he was a local boy she had met at school named Justin, and he was a direct opposite of Jake. He was a football player, sweet but not that smart and Ash wished she could say she loved Justin like Terra loved Jake but she really didn't know why she was dating him. What made things worse with the two couples is that Justin and Jake didn't like each other so the girls couldn't double date.

The problem with the guys was mainly Justin, he really hated Jake and told Ash often that Jake was a bad guy and needed to get Terra away from him. Ash had told him that as much as she made fun of Terra for dating a guitar player Jake really didn't seem that bad. What it came down to is it wasn't worth fighting with her friend over what the guys thought.

Part of that was Ash liked Justin and all but he was just a boyfriend and Terra meant more to her and she wanted to stay out of Terra's love life. Ash knew that Terra thought Ash could do way better than Justin but she didn't stay much trying to respect Ash's choice so the least Ash could do was respect her decisions too.

As far as Justin was concerned Ash had been taking things really slow with him. At that time she still hadn't had sex with a guy since the lighthouse incident. Justin kissed her and tried to get her to do things with him all the time and it had seemed the more he pushed the less she wanted to be with him.

They kissed and he felt her up all the time and on a few occasions she had let him reach into her shirt and play with her nipples. That had been the only things she had allowed him to do until prom night. That night she went so far as to let him suck her breasts as she gave him a hand job in the front seat of his car after they left the dance. That had made things worse because he wanted more from her after that.

Ash thought she should just break up with him because she was getting sick of him pushing her but instead she just began to spend less and less time with him hoping he would just move on, but he would simply call every day and talk like nothing had changed. He was just one of those people you had to hit over the head for them to take a hint.

Sitting in the van listening to the rain drops hitting the roof Ash had wished she would have paid more attention to Justin she realized after the events of the last year that he really had been a good boy. Clueless and not that bright but sweet and nice, she wished she would have been better to him. She wished she would have been better to all the boys she had known but she had used so many nice boys and done so many bad things she didn't think a nice boy would ever have her again.

As annoyingly persistent as Justin had become afterwards, prom night had been really fun. It had been nice to dress up again in a really pretty dress and shoes and go out to a very nice expensive dinner. The prom had been held in a ball room of a very nice hotel and she had enjoyed dancing all night. The fun and extravagance of it all had been so overwhelming that she had let her guard down as Justin drove her home that night.

They had pulled up to outside Ash's house and he kissed her, it had been the most romantic kiss they had shared up until then. Maybe it was just the night all coming together more than him but it had been a great kiss. Ash had closed her eye and fallen into their romantic moment so deeply that she hadn't realized he had pulled down the front of her dress and was caressing her breasts.

Justin pulled back and she realized she had been partially disrobed but before she could say anything his lips found her nipple and gave it a slight nibble. The feeling was so incredible that she leaned her head back and moaned. It had been Christmas since someone had sucked her nipples and she could feel herself getting very wet.

Ash lay in the van remembering prom night and she looked over at Terra again to confirm she was still sleeping. Her hand moved back into her panties and she resumed her earlier attempt to make herself cum. Thinking of Justin's lips on her breasts last year was starting to work as she rubbed her clit hard.

Justin had her wet and moaning when he took her hand and moved it to his pants, he had already unzipped and his dick was pulled out for her. Ash had been so into his ministrations that she hadn't noticed until he placed her hand on his throbbing cock. She hadn't intended to go this far with him but it had been a great evening and her hand was already there.

Ash was laying in the van the memories of prom working but not as well as she needed. She remembered trying not to giggle as Justin had cum all over his rented tux in only a matter of minutes. Her thoughts shifted then going back further into her memory, she remembered the first time she had put on a pretty dress and gone out for one of the greatest nights of her life.

She slid two fingers inside her wet slit as she remembered the dance she had gone to with Joey when she was only 13 years old. She had loved Joey at first sight but he was so much older than her and she knew he would never fall for her. It had meant more to her then anything in her life before it when he asked her to go to the formal dance with him. That night was still one of the best of her whole life. They danced and she couldn't believe it when she felt him aroused by her, Joey her one true love had been hard for her.

When they began to kiss that night her whole life had felt like it had led to that moment. She knew that she was still really too young to feel what she did but she couldn't help but be in love with him and when he kissed her it was the most perfect moment of her life.

She felt special and beautiful since the death of her parents she knew she was very fragile emotionally but she knew that this was real love. She leaned into him again and the second kiss wasn't as innocent as the first it was met with real passion. She kissed him and opened her mouth and he thrust his tongue forward, she squealed in both surprise and delight before she thrust hers into his mouth. She wrapped her arms around his neck and pulled him into her hard.

She was fingering her pussy as deep and hard as she could remembering the night of the formal, she remembered being so horny and curious at the same time. Ash had never seen a boy naked before that night when she was 13 and the desire and curiosity had taken over, as her hand had found his zipper.

When they pulled away breaking her kiss she thought Joey was going to be really mad at her only then realizing she had pulled him out of his pants.

"What are you doing?" he had asked.

"I'm sorry. I've never seen one for real. I just wanted to........." she said tentatively but never let go of his cock. It felt both weird and exciting to be sitting there stroking his dick, she was both curious and embarrassed doing it for him but she wanted to give him pleasure. He had made her so happy that night; she was so in love with him and wanted him to feel as happy as he made her.

"I'm so........... So close........." He had told her and not knowing why because the thought grossed her out at the time, she leaned over and put her mouth over his cock. Her fingers were going wild as she remembered the first time Joey had cum inside her mouth, and her orgasm finally hit her that morning. Ash's release was so strong that morning she that she completely soaked her jeans and forming a wet spot on the blanket beneath her.

She let out a loud sigh and realized she had been moaning loudly as she finished herself. She looked over to see Terra hadn't moved at all. Her breathing was still slow and rhythmic not showing any sign that she had woken up during Ash's morning relief. She sat up and rummaged through her bag for a dry pair of panties and some clean jeans, she slipped off her wet clothes and used her pant leg to dry herself off.

After changing into her fresh clothes she folded her blanket in half, length wise and lay back down. She reached into her pocket of her soaked jeans and pulled out a tattered piece of paper, instead of putting it in her pocket she decided to read it again, it had been a long time since she had actually read it. A tear rolled down her face as she folded it back up again, she was both sad and happy she had taped this note back together that morning.

Love was a big complicated mess; she gripped the necklace around her neck and thought for a minute about Joey, she wondered what he was doing right now. She knew from Lilly and Katie that he had moved to the island where he was born and had been rebuilding Lilly's family home but she didn't have a lot of details on that. Ash had been too busy dealing with her own things that she hadn't really asked many questions about him before she and Terra had left.

She knew that when Katie left last summer that she was going to the island to join Joey and Abby. Katie had told them that she and Abby were going to get married and that they had wanted to do that a year later, if they got married when they planned then that would have been about two months ago now. Ash was upset that she missed Katie's wedding as she loved her niece so much, and wanted to be there for her.

She thought about Joey living on the island with Katie, happy doing his own thing and living out his life anyway he wanted now that he had enough money to do anything. Before Ash had left town to protect Terra it had been almost two years since he had talked to her and she was sure that despite how much she still loved him he had forgotten her.

Ash knew Joey had moved on with his life and had, had a college girlfriend and he probably had one on the island now, she couldn't conceive of some girl not falling for him, he was a great guy. Another tear rolled down her face thinking about what might have been, but that time in her life was over. She wondered if he had tried to call her for her 17th birthday. He had missed her 16th but his dad had just died and things were busy, but had he tried to call on her 17th? If so she was sure Lilly would've told him about what she had done. Ash knew leaving like she did looked as if she ran away from home but there was not time to tell Lilly what had been going on. She was sure Lilly would have just told her no anyway and then Terra would have been on her own, and Ash wasn't going to let her go alone.

Ash looked up at the roof for a couple minutes before her mind went back to where this had all started, she had moved again when Lilly came to town, because Linda thought it would be better if Ash didn't live under the same roof as Jt if they had other options. Linda knew Jt had a girlfriend but she still thought separating them was a really good idea. Ash didn't complain as she loved living with Lilly and kind of felt like a third wheel to Linda's new family.

Linda was good to her word not to tell anyone what she had walked in on that day with her and Jt and only told Lilly that she thought Ash and Jt were a little too close and maybe it would be better to separate them. Lilly giggled at the idea and said she had already been through that with Ash and Joey and she understood and she would like the company around her new home.

With Lilly still not 100% back the full health after her car accident she had made the decision to not buy a house after all, she felt it would be too much work to keep up a house and yard, so she picked a very nice condominium a few miles away from Linda and James. The place was really nice with three bedrooms and two baths, a spacious living room, kitchen and dining rooms. It also had a study with pocket doors that Lilly decided to turn into an arts and crafts room, as she decided to get into scrapbooking and painting to fill her time.

On the first weekend Lilly and Ash had their new home; they drove down to the car dealership so Lilly could buy a newer car. She ended up buying a Chevy Malibu and then she looked at Ash and asked her to pick out what she wanted. Ash was in shock and she asked her sister if she really meant it, Lilly said that Ash had been through a lot and had been moved around so much without complaint so she wanted to buy her a late 16th and early 17th birthday presents.

Ash was so happy; she had her permit and was almost done with Drivers ED so she was only a couple weeks away from getting her license and never though she would have her own car already. They looked around the lot and Ash really liked a used black 1990 Mustang. Lilly called Linda and asked if her and James could come down and help Ash bring her car home, Linda was so excited for Ash she said they would be right down.

Ash woke again not realizing she had fallen asleep while remembering the events of last year, she was still hearing the sounds of rain on the roof. After looking at her watch again she nudged Terra, who rolled over grumbling something intangible.

"Come on get up," Ash said nudging her again.

"What time is it?" Terra asked looking at Ash and rubbing her eyes.

"About seven," she told her. Terra sighed loud and picked her clothes up off the floor and began to get dressed. Unlike Ash who liked to stay dressed in case of emergency, Terra always slept in her bra and panties. Ash actually admired the fact that her friend was comfortable enough sleeping like that as they were on the road, as Ash was really paranoid that something could happen at any moment.

The girls opened the van's side door and looked around before getting out. The dew was heavy on the grass and the air outside was cold but it looked as if the rest stop was almost completely empty. Both girls got out and Ash locked the doors before they headed to the restrooms, the rain soaking though their shirts as they ran. They used the restroom, brushed their teeth and tried their best to fix their hair, exiting they stopped and grabbed a cup of the free coffee each before running back to the van again.

Ash was eyeing one of the other three cars sitting in the rest area, she was sure she had seen it before but she couldn't pin point in her mind where from. She was leery as she unlocked the van and hopped inside.

"What wrong?" Terra asked as soon as they got back into the van.

"Nothing," Ash replied.

"Don't lie to me Ashley," Terra said sharply.

"I'm just upset this morning over the whole situation and I just want to get there."

"Oh," Terra said quietly, "I wish I had family who actually loved me waiting for me too, but I'm sure my family never wants to see me again."

Ash didn't respond she had gotten away with her lie and she didn't want to talk about what was really bothering her. She didn't want to scare Terra as they had been through enough this year as it was. Ash thought her friend was wrong, her family was a little crazy but they loved her and would want to see her again.

Ash truly did want to make it back to her family as this whole thing had been a major mistake she just hoped that Lilly and Linda wouldn't hate her and let her come back home again. The girls climbed into the front seat and Ash started up the van driving it out of the rest stop.

Ash looked into her rear view mirror after they had been on the road for about 20 minutes; she saw the car she had been eyeing at the rest stop was behind them. It could have been coincidence that they left at the same time, but she didn't think so. Ash steadied both her face and the van as she drove, she didn't want to give anything away if she was just being paranoid.

With her eye on the rearview mirror Ash drove on, heading across the state as fast as she could go without being pulled over. Originally she had been heading home again to Lilly's, but she wasn't sure she could face Lilly after being away for so long. Instead she had talked to Terra and the decision was made that the girls would seek out Katie first; Ash knew her niece would be able to help her talk to her sister before returning home again.

Ash had tried many times to call home since she and Terra had returned to the United States but she hadn't been able to get a hold of Lilly or Linda when she called. She could have left a message but she felt as if she needed to talk to her sisters herself and not by machine. She was happy this all was coming to an end but she was scared to go home and face them as well.

"I'm hungry," Terra commented, "Do we have enough money to go get some egg muffins?"

"Yeah," Ash replied, she felt guilty about how they had gotten the money and she had been trying to make it last as long as possible. In the last couple months the girls had done things for money that Ash thought they would never do.

In the beginning if the girls were in a town they were just passing through they would run out on the bill at restaurants. They also had stolen food at convenient stores. Ash wasn't proud of any of their

early choices but they girls were so hungry and needed to save their money for gas so they felt like they had no choice.

Circumstances sometimes dictated that the girls sometimes had to stay in a town anywhere from a day to a couple weeks at a time. It was then they found ways other than steeling to get them along. A couple times they donated blood and plasma. Other times they worked jobs as day laborers, which was why they would have to stay in town for a while, some places paid at the end of the week instead of daily. They would work for a number of days then move on to until they ran out of money then stay in the next town until they could afford to move on again.

Ash just wished that dinner dashing was the worst thing they had done but it wasn't. On a few nights Terra had stood outside bars and offered sexual favors for cash, Ash told her that she didn't like it and wouldn't do it herself, but Terra said that Ash didn't have to. Terra felt guilty and told her she had gotten them into this mess and if she had to blow a few guys to get them home then so be it.

Ash was disgusted by the thought and they did everything else they could do for money but Terra would sometimes still preform for cash. Ash thought that at least they would be on the island in a few of days then she could find Katie and all this would finally be over.

Ash was happy she had a really good memory for directions. Before her parents had died they had taken vacation trips to the island. Her dad figured that why own a house near a beach if you never use it. It was like renting a cabin you didn't have to pay for, so every summer from the time Ash could remember until her parents died they had vacation there one week a year. At this moment she was so happy for that as it was the only reason she knew how to find Katie.

By the weekend they had almost completely ran out of money and they were near out of gas. Ash explained to Terra they were getting close to the island but they might run out of gas before then. It was mid-day when they parked at the mall in a town called Kayak falls, the girls got out of the van to stretch their legs for a few minutes.

As they walked around the parking lot they talked about the money situation they were in, Terra said she would just wait outside a bar and do her thing one more time.

"No," Ash said firmly, "Were not that far away and we've gotten lucky so far, don't you remember what happened in Storms Rock?" Ash was referring to the last guy that Terra had sucked off.

Terra had been hanging outside a college bar one night and met a boy named Alex and after he agreed to pay her $25 to blow him she followed him to his car. Alex had just cum and Terra had grabbed the door handle to leave when he grabbed her hair and tried to push her down on the seat. Terra struggled and he slapped her, Alex still had his pants off and in a moment of self-defense Terra had grabbed his balls and twisted. Alex screamed in pain and Terra used the moment to get away.

"You would bring that up! I got away before he really hurt me, I can take care of myself!" Terra shouted back.

"This is a really bad idea and I hate it when you do this, we can come up with something else." Ash was pleading with her in word and tone. She was thinking about the car that had been following them days ago and for some reason she shuddered, "Please I have a bad feeling about it."

"How far away from your family are we?" Terra snapped.

"If I remember right, about an hour."

"Then that settles it, we need money now, not later," Terra growled, "It makes no sense to stay in town trying to come up with another way to make money when we can be there tonight."

"No," Ash repeated herself.

Terra stormed off heading the direction of some restaurants surrounding the mall in the distance. Ash climbed back into the van and lay down in the back, she had been driving almost non-stop for days now and she decided to lock the doors and sleep until Terra decided to come back.

It was dark when Ash woke up again; she looked at her watch to find it was after midnight. Ash climbed back up to the front seat of the van and looked around, the parking lot was lit up really well and all she could see was a car off in the distance. It was the car she had seen at the rest stop days ago, she knew it.

Ash clicked on the van lights and the car peeled out of the parking lot turned at the corner and disappeared in the night. It was then she noticed something lying on the ground. Ash started the van and drove over to where the car had been as she got closer she realized what the car had left behind and she began to scream.

Ash got out of the van and ran to her friend; Terra was on the ground covered in blood. Ash couldn't tell if she was still alive or not but she held onto her friends unconscious body.

"Terra wake up!" she cried, "Please wake up!" She clutched her friend to her chest crying, "Don't be dead, I'm sorry, please don't be dead."

Ash needed to get to a pay phone and call the police, but she couldn't let go of Terra, if she left her there she was sure Terra would be dead as long as she held her she could still be alive.

"I won't leave you," she sobbed into her neck, "I will never leave you." Terra didn't respond, she wasn't moving and Ash held her trying to find a pulse but couldn't find one.

Who was the person in the car and why had they done this? It was Ash's fault because she hadn't told Terra about the car, why hadn't she told her? Maybe she could've looked out for it. Ash thought she had just been paranoid at the rest stop, how could she have known.

Ash wasn't sure how long she sat in the parking lot with Terra before a mall security guard came by seeing her van parked with the door open and lights on. He came over to investigate the van and was almost right on them before he found the girls. Ash's face was swollen from crying as she still held Terra's limp body.

The security guard called the police and an ambulance right away. As they waited he began to ask her what happened, Ash wouldn't say a word. It wasn't that she didn't want to speak to the man who had come to their aid, but that she really didn't hear him. She wouldn't let go of her friend and just held her crying. It wasn't until the paramedics arrived that she finally, somewhat reluctantly, let go of Terra.

The paramedics began work on Terra right away checking her vitals and placing her on a gurney. Terra was still alive but her pulse was very weak, Ash fell to her knees as relief washed over her that her friend hadn't died. Ash wanted to go with her friend to the hospital but the cops told her that she needed to follow them back to the station for questioning.

The cops asked her all kinds of questions. They asked if she or Terra had been hooking and if that was how this all had happened but Ash played innocent while she lied and said they had never done anything like that. She was very convincing and had some pay stubs in the van from when they had worked day labor jobs.

Once convinced that the girls weren't hookers the cops seemed to be more willing to help her and treated her with more respect. She told the cops that she had taken a nap while Terra went to shop. She told them about the car from the rest stop that had been following them across the state and she gave them as much detail as she could remember.

Then next week was a blur of for Ash, she spent most of her time in the hospital at Terra's side. Her friend was alive but all the doctors knew was that she had been beaten with something heavy and stabbed in the side. Both Terra's legs, one of her arms and all of her fingers were broken. Her back and face were completely bruised and she hadn't woken up yet since she had been found.

Ash called Terra's mom as soon as the cops had let her go, as she suspected her mom was just happy to hear Terra was alive. Terra had said her mother would never forgive her for leaving but Terra's mom just wanted her to come home again. Ash detailed what condition Terra was in and her mom said she would fly out as soon as she could get money together and get a flight.

Ash tried a number of times to get ahold of Lilly and Linda but she couldn't seem to get ahold of either one of them. After watching Terra's mom forgive her daughter and really start talking for the first time in years, Ash felt even worse for what she had done to her sisters.

Ash only left Terra when the hospital staff made her leave the room. On those rare occasions she would go to the cafeteria and eat or she went a couple times to the blood and plasma banks to donate so she could have enough money to make it to the island. At night she slept in the van in the parking garage as they only allowed family to stay in the room all night.

It was mid-September when Terra's mom convinced the hospital to release her. Terra had finally woken up a week after she had been beaten; she was surprised and happy to find her mom standing there with her. Her legs, arm and fingers were all in casts and she had no memory of what had happened that night. Ash didn't say much about it until Terra's mom left the room, and then she explained everything that had transpired since that night.

Terra's mom made the case that she couldn't stay in town for long and as there wasn't much else the hospital could really do now that Terra was awake and mending anyway they needed to leave for home. Ash drove them to the airport and helped wheel Terra to the plane, where she parted ways with her friend. The girls cried and hugged as good as Terra could manage.

After leaving the airport Ash drove back through Kayak Falls finally on her way to see Katie. She hadn't been able to call Katie ahead of time because she still had been unable to get ahold of Lilly or Linda to get her phone number. She was sure her niece would be happy to see her and it would turn out ok.

Ash couldn't wait to congratulate Katie and Abby on the wedding she had missed this last summer, she thought it was weird the idea of two girls getting married but she found it great that the girls had found love in each other.

Ash was mentally exhausted as she reached the bridge leading onto the island. She was really happy she had a great memory for street names because the whole island had changed in the six years since she had been there. It was like things were newer and the island had grown, taller buildings and the trees were gone.

Ash followed her memory until she found Hayford Avenue. She drove the all the way down the road to the end and came back again. She was looking for her father's old house but for some reason she missed it on her first pass by. After she turned around and came back she saw it on the second pass, she realized that the reason she had missed it was because it was now a different color and had obviously been remodeled. She thought Joey must have been busy as she knew from Katie that he had been remodeling the house when she had come to visit them the summer before.

As she pulled into the driveway she spotted the tree house in the yard next door and she knew she was in the right place. The house and tree house next door had been beautifully redone as Katie's house. Ash remembered playing in that tree house as a small child as the house next door had always been abandoned. It didn't look that way anymore.

Ash excitedly jumped out of the van and ran to the door; she was finally back with her family. She ran up the porch and banged on the door then waited. No one answered, she banged again, and no one answered. An hour later she left the porch and drove into town, spending the last of her money on some food she could keep and eat in the van until Katie returned. Katie or Abby never came home that night.

Ash got up the next morning to find no cars had shown up and after knocking on the door there was still no answer. She walked around the house and looked to see if she saw anyone in the window of the house next door. After spotting no one she snuck her way over to the tree house. She found a beautifully made place to read and be at piece. She pulled a book off the shelf with the intention of returning it later, and then she snuck her way out of the tree house to her van and began to read.

It was late that night a cab pulled up to the house next door, a very pretty girl about 25 got out of the car and looked over at the van in Katie's driveway with a suspicious look on her face. Ash understood that a van at an empty house looked bad; she needed to find out where Katie and Abby were anyway so she decided to introduce herself to the girl.

"Um hi," Ash said running up to the girl, "Do you have a minute?"

"Maybe," the girl said cautiously looking at her very closely, "Have we met you look really familiar."

"No I just got here to the island yesterday, I'm looking for my niece, Katie, do you know her?" She asked and the girl's eyes got really big.

"Ashley?" The girl more exclaimed then asked and it was her turn to be surprised.

"Yes," she said slowly.

"OH MY GOD!" the girl cried out, "Do you know how worried your family's been about you!?" The girl cried out, "What are you doing here? And why right now? I'm Gia by the way."

"Nice to meet you," Ash said politely, "It's a long story but do you know where my niece is?"

"You don't know?" Gia asked, "She's at the lodge with the rest of your family, she's getting married tomorrow."

Chapter Twenty Two: It's Just A Jump To The Left

I awoke to the light coming through the curtains brightening up an already extremely white room. I was groggy from having too much to drink the night before and my head was pounding slightly. I rolled over to reaching out for Gia before I remembered she wasn't here with me yet. As my eyes adjusted to the light I began to regain my thoughts. I sat up and looked around the room thinking for a moment of the last time we had stayed here; it felt like so long ago.

I glanced over to the other bed to find it was empty. I wondered what time Brooke had made it back to the lodge last night and who she might have hooked up with. The club had been packed by the time we got there, it was a really fun idea Abby had for us all to go out and party the night before the wedding. I had left at midnight feeling tired and out of place being there without my girlfriend, so I made my way back to the lodge earlier than most of my family.

I smiled as I realized part of the reason Brooke hadn't come back last night was because Gia wasn't here yet and she didn't want any misconceptions. She was right though; I didn't want Gia thinking something had happened between Brooke and me without her here. I just wondered who she hooked up with to share a room last night. There were a number of single guys in the family and anyone of them would've jumped at the chance to hook up with a girl like her, I couldn't wait to find out who got lucky.

I pulled my duffle bag out from under the bed and pulled on a shirt then changed from my shorts I had worn to bed for a pair of jeans. I sat on the bed enjoying a moment to myself, as I looked around the room again I could hardly believe it was the same room I had lost my virginity in. The lodge owners had repainted the whole room and made it look much nicer then when we had been here just a few years earlier. But when the rooms were getting figured out for all the guests I had insisted on taking this room and with Brooke only staying two nights we offered to let her use the extra bed in our room so we didn't have to rearrange and get her a room of her own.

I walked barefoot downstairs enjoying the feel of the soft carpet under my feet; I headed off to the dining hall and sat down to order my breakfast. I was there for only a few minutes when Brooke came in looking disheveled in the clothes she had been wearing the night before, I covered my face to hide my smile. She sat down opposite to me grinning ear to ear, and I couldn't help but laugh softly.

"Long night," I asked.

"No, average night," she replied giggling.

"So which one of my relatives did you............. Talk to all night," I joked and she reached over and punched me in the shoulder.

"I met your cousin Chase," She said happily, "He's such a sweet boy. Reminds me of someone I met on his 18th birthday." She winked at me and giggled again.

"Really? You spent the night with Chase?" I asked somewhat in shock. He was only 19 and he was very shy, I was sure that Brooke made the first move on him. She did like to hook up with boys who weren't that experienced, she said they treated her better and were really grateful. She also got a thrill out

of being a guy's first time, she said that lasted forever. I thought she had really changed from the girl I met who used to make boys earn their way into her panties.

"So I guess the rumors about him aren't true?" I asked quietly.

"No," she said in a low tone herself, "He's very strait, just very shy."

"Well I'm glad you could help him........... CUM out of his shell," I joked slightly laughing.

"Oh shut up," she said trying not to laugh, "Let's just eat breakfast."

It was nice talking to Brooke outside of the book store were we didn't have to go over things or worry about the shop. It wasn't long before Chase came in, gave Brooke a quick kiss on the cheek and sat down next to her, she smiled at him and I thought I saw something there more than a sexual conquest. If I didn't know better I would have thought they really liked each other.

It was only moments after Chase arrived that Lilly came in to the dining hall, she still had a limp when she walked and I had noticed days ago that it was a little more noticeable in the mornings. I felt really bad for my step-mother knowing that she was going to have to live with her injures the rest of her life. I loved her very much and it felt bad seeing her still in this condition and I really wished there was something I could do to help her. I hadn't realized until she arrived here this week how much I had missed her too, I hadn't realized how much I missed my whole family.

Following her was Linda, James, Jt and Mandy. I had met Linda's new family when they had arrived a couple days ago and I thought they seemed to be really nice, Jt reminded me a lot of myself at his age. I liked James much more then I had ever liked Linda's husband John, James was really easy going and great to talk to. I hadn't really had much time as I wanted to talk to James's son Jt or his girlfriend Mandy, I knew that they had been friends with Ash but I tried not to bring up the subject, we still didn't know what had happened to her and I didn't want to upset them. I didn't know how they were taking her disappearance and I thought it best not to really say much.

We all chatted while we had our eggs, bacon, hash browns, toast and orange juice that morning, I couldn't remember a morning I had, had so much fun just hanging out with everyone. We were about halfway through breakfast when we were joined by Katie and Abby. Everyone got up and gave them hugs and told them how happy they were that the big day was finally here. I was happy for my sisters, they had waited for so long to get married and despite what the government said about same sex marriage nothing could stand in their way anymore. Tonight they would be officially married, even if it wasn't a legal marriage they didn't care it was real to them and I was proud to be here for them.

The only thing missing from breakfast that morning was Gia, I wished she could've been there but life had gotten in the way of her staying the whole time with us. Before we were supposed to leave her grandmother died and she wanted to be there for her funeral. Gia decided last minute not to come out to the lodge with me. Lilly told me she was a little disappointed that she hadn't come out with me because she wanted to get to know her future daughter-in-law; I thought it was cute that she had taken an interest in Gia.

The plan was that Gia had an open ticket for any time today so when she could get an available flight she would be back, since we didn't know when she would be back she had told me not to worry about picking her up, she would take a cab. Her big fear was that if she returned very late she didn't want

me to miss out on the wedding. It was then decided that if she hadn't returned on time Brooke would fill in as the maid of honor instead, Katie understood that Gia really wanted to stand there with her best friend but she understood what was going on.

After breakfast we all took a dip in the pool, it felt really good on this warm September morning. It was just like it had been the last time we were here, the music was playing and we all were having the best time. I swam around for about an hour before I decided it was time to get out. I was feeling a little too excited that morning looking at all the girls frolicking around the pool. There was Lilly and Linda still looking good for their age, Abby, Katie, and Brooke who I had made love too in the past, and Mandy who was young and looking very sexy in her tiny bikini not to mention all the other girls from Lilly's family. I was so enjoying the sight of all that flesh and I began to feel a stirring inside my swim shorts, all I needed was for that dumb ass song to start playing and it would be exactly like last time. I thought it would be safer if I just went ahead and got out now avoiding any future embarrassment this time.

I walked up the stairs heading back to my room; as soon as I entered I opened the window for some fresh air. I looked out the window for a moment before I began to strip off my wet swim shorts and dry off with a towel. I closed my eyes as I dried myself off thinking of the girls at the pool, how hot they had looked in those suits. I began to feel myself getting hard, it had been a couple days since I had taken care of myself and so much longer since Gia and I had made love. Even though I knew Brooke was at the pool I locked the door and sat on the edge of the bed.

I closed my eyes and thought, for some reason, about Mandy. Maybe it was because she was young, maybe it was because I hadn't made love to her, or maybe it was because she was Ash's friend but I began to think about what it would be like to make love to her. I thought about her walking in on me naked in my room and her getting embarrassed, I would tell her it was ok and to come in. I gripped myself and began to stroke my cock slowly as I thought about pulling Mandy to me and kissing her supple lips. I imagined running my hands down her back while we kissed and pulling the string to that very small bikini top.

I began to stroke myself faster as I saw her top fall way from her breasts in my mind's eye. I could see them being so young, firm and perfect as I would bring my hands up to touch them. I would spin her then onto the bed kissing my way down her body, kissing between her breasts before sucking on her tight and hard nipples. I would tease her body kissing her belly as I pulled her panties off, then moving slowly to her delicious slit. I would make her scream with pleasure before sliding my hard dick deep into her wet, tight and warm opening.

The thought of slipping into Mandy's pussy almost pushed me over the edge, I closed my eyes tighter as I stroked as hard as I could. I would pound her so hard that she would cry out with every stroke, like when Ash and I had made love here on this bed so long ago. That thought was all it took and I could feel my cum shooting through me, I thought about Mandy and Ash as I shot rope after rope of cum into the air hitting my leg, my foot and the floor between my feet.

I lay back on the bed opening my eyes, the visions fading away. I looked at the mess I created and laughed for a moment before wiping it up with the towel I had used to dry off with. I hoped the small wet spot on the floor would dry before Brooke came back to the room; I sat back down still naked trying to get my breathing back to normal and the heat from my cheeks to go away. I hadn't worked myself that hard in a very long time but I was really happy today and really horny. I was just very glad Brooke hadn't come back to the room and wanted in during that session. I unlocked the door for her for when she did return

then I reached over to the foot of the bed and began dressing in the clothes I had been wearing before we had gone to the pool that morning.

I decided to rest on the bed for a few minutes, so I turned on the TV for some entertainment. I soon found an old movie I hadn't seen for many years and just got comfortable. It was a movie about a boy from Kansas who goes to New York and ends up working in the mailroom in his uncles building then pretends to be an upper executive at the same time, it was one of my favorite movies with one of my favorite actors. I supposed I could have gone downstairs and tried to find some way to help out with the wedding but let's face it when it comes to planning and preparations it's usually best if the men just step back and stay out of the way. Thinking of planning and preparations I thought about my future and the next time I would be visiting the lodge, I had booked it already for the beginning of next summer for my own wedding. It was going to be a long year in the meantime but I really did look forward to coming back here again and taking that step with Gia.

As I relaxed I thought back on the last few weeks, we all had, had a lot of fun together and I had almost begun to let my guard down. It seemed to me that every time I felt things were doing well in my life fate would step in and make Katie my sister or something to that effect. So I was worried that fate was going to step in anytime now, with everything going on right now with Gia I was really scared. Things in my life had been as perfect as I could imagine up until a week ago, when Gia's grandmother had died, since then I'd had a looming feeling like my world was going to change again. With my luck what it was I would find out right after we got married that Gia was somehow the sister I was looking for. I knew of course she couldn't be as I had met both of her parents and she was their child but this was my life and it always hit a bump when I was happy.

We had, had our bags packed; loaded in the car ready to leave for the lodge the next morning and we were sitting in my kitchen eating dinner when the call came in. Gia got up to answer the phone and moments later she began crying, it was her mom on the phone telling her about her grandmother. Gia hung up with her mom and said she was going over to her parents' house for the evening. I told her I understood and asked if she wanted me to go with her, she said no and she would be back so we could leave in the morning.

Gia was late the next morning but I wasn't mad, we had a long drive to the lodge but I would have waited all day if we needed to for her to deal with her loss. We talked and she said she really needed to be home right now. I told her that I understood and since her parents were going to have the funeral the next Friday we decided that I would drive out to the lodge without her and try to enjoy the week with my family then she would fly out as soon as she could get an available flight on Saturday the day of the wedding.

The drive had taken a few days and seemed so much longer without a driving companion. To make the most out of my road trip and to have more fun I stopped at a couple tourist attractions along the way. We had planned a few stops for the ride there and a few for the way back, I didn't stop everywhere we had planned on the list but when I was near one of the locations and I needed a driving break I would stop and visit a place we had planned. I spent the first night at a really fancy hotel with a hot tub; I liked having the money to stay at a nice place where I could relax.

As far as my businesses were concerned I had originally made the decision to close the store for the few weeks we would be out of state, since all of my employees were my best friends and family it didn't seem fair for anyone to have to stay behind. The problem was in the end it didn't make sense for business to have the store closed for so long. After some conversations Brooke offered to stay behind to run the

store while we were gone. I changed the store hours for the time we were gone so she would only have to work eight hours a day and not the usual twelve the store was open. Then the arrangements were made and I bought her a plane ticket so she could fly out to join us on the Friday morning the day before the wedding and return Sunday after, that way I would only have to close the store for one extra day. I thanked her for looking out for the store and told her I would pay her double for her over time days.

As far as the re-model business was concerned Tommy really wanted to come to the wedding too, but he felt the timing was bad for both of us to leave for a few days. I had made him the same deal I gave Brooke to fly out for a couple days but he said that it was too much money for just one weekend. We had a number of things up in the air and he felt he should stay, he said his only real disappointment was he wouldn't be there to hit on the single ladies. I laughed and thanked him for taking care of things. I went Kayak falls ahead of time and talk with a temp agency to get Tommy some help during the time I was away. I felt things were going to be ok and Tommy would be able to handle things if there were an emergency.

I lay on the bed and the movie I was watching came to an end so I began to flip through the channels trying to find something on. I couldn't find anything good on so I decided to order a movie on the in room network, scanning through the list I came across "The Rocky Horror Show" and I couldn't resist ordering it. I had only recently become aware of the movie and I had become a fan after watching it the first time. It all led back to Brooke helping me break through my shell and do something I never expected.

I ordered the movie and sat back again thinking back to a couple weeks earlier to when we all had gone out for the bachelorette party. Brooke and I had originally talked about throwing a huge bash but as she began to plan what she called the party to end all parties she said something came to mind and we had to postpone things for a week. I was confused but she asked me to trust her and we would have more fun when she told us what her plans were. It was a week later when Brooke showed up at my house with a big duffle bag and a makeup case, she made sure she got Katie, Abby, Tommy, Gia and I together. Brooke opened up the duffle bag and began to pull out what looked like lingerie, I began to worry. She started with Tommy as she handed him a pair of golden shorts and gold boots, and I really got worried at that point.

"Cool I get to be Rocky!" Tommy said excitedly. I had no idea what was going on but Tommy seemed to understand. I looked at the girls and Katie and Gia looked as puzzled as I was, Abby had a grin on her face like she got the joke, I was wishing I did.

"So am I supposed to wear this?" Gia asked looking at the white bra, panties and slip Brooke had just handed her.

"I think it's sexy," I joked winking at her.

"Well if you like that then here's your outfit," Brooke said handing me a pair of new white briefs, a pair of white socks and a blue bath robe.

"You're kidding right?" I asked. She really didn't expect me to go out in public in that did she?

"I think it's sexy," Gia joked back at me grinning big.

"Yeah," Tommy joked winking at me and everyone laughed. I didn't say anything else as I still thought this was going to turn out to be a joke.

Next Brooke handed Katie a maids outfit, then handed Katie a pair of shiny shorts, a gold jacket and a top hat. I was more confused than ever as to what Brooke had in mind for the evening, I couldn't think of any reason for the costumes.

"How come she gets a maid's outfit and I get a bra and undergarments?" Gia asked eyeing Brooke suspiciously, "And what are you wearing?"

"Don't worry about it, you'll understand later tonight," Brooke replied, "And this is MY outfit." Brooke pulled one last costume out of the bag and I really wasn't surprised to see it looked like a teddy, a bad curly haired wig, black gloves, lacy stockings and high heels. Brooke told us all to go change; I shook my head but got up and put on my costume. Gia went with me to our bedroom and we both laughed as we looked at each other, I was feeling self-conscious standing there in my underwear. I didn't think I could go out in public that way, what made things worse was standing there in my briefs looking at Gia I began to get hard.

Gia was reaching for the knob when I wrapped my arms around her stomach and pulled her to me, kissing her neck from behind.

"Stop it we have company," she said quietly reaching behind her and running her hands through my hair. I slid my hands up her body and began to caress her breasts lightly and she let out a soft murmur, "We really shouldn't."

"But we haven't since the night that you said........." I started. Gia turned her head and kissed me gently on the lips.

"I know sweetie," she acknowledged, "And you know why, but I promise tonight when we get back, when were alone, I'll make it all better," She told me as she slid her hand inside my briefs giving my dick a hard squeeze then she opened the door to leave, "Come down when you've .... calmed down." She giggled at me before walking away. I sat down on the bed and pulled my cock out and began to stroke myself quickly. There was no way I was going to walk around in my briefs with a hard on all night, even if all the girls in our group had seen it before.

When I returned to the living room I couldn't stop laughing, everyone was wearing their costumes and we all looked like a bunch of people on the way to an orgy. Brooke took about an hour to do all the hair and make up for everyone, making us look even sillier. By the time we were all ready to go it was already after ten and I asked Brooke where we were going, she simply said to get into the car she was driving. We drove into Kayak Falls with Gia on my lap and Katie on Abby's lap like we had gone the night Katie came home, only this time I was so self-conscious there wasn't any sex in the back seat. The girls kissed but only a little because they didn't want to mess up their hair and makeup.

To my great relief when we arrived at the old vintage theater on the far side of Kayak Falls there were a whole bunch of people there dressed like we were. So many in fact that we would just blend into the crowd, at that point I began to think whatever this was might actually be fun. We got out of the car and began to mingle with everyone there, I could hear snippets of the conversations around me and people were pointing to others in the crowd talking about how close some of the costumes were to the movie.

A number of the people there didn't wear costumes and I kind of envied them a little, others that had shown up were in jeans and a leather jacket with a fake scar across their head. I thought to myself if that was a character in the movie, how come Brooke couldn't have set me up in that costume? There were a couple people there in wheelchairs dressed alike and I assumed they were in character also. It was all I could do to contain myself from getting excited looking at some of the girls in the crowd, there were some really hot women there dressed like Brooke, Katie and Abby. What I thought was really funny was there were a bunch of guys who showed up dressed like the girls too, wearing teddies and other lingerie.

We stood outside until almost mid-night when the doors opened and a very large man walked outside in a silky teddy and high heels, the man said that anyone who hadn't seen the movie in the theater needed to come to the front the line. Everyone in our group, except Brooke and Tommy, walked up front with a number of others from the crowd; one by one we all had a V pained on our foreheads with lip stick. Again I began to wonder what the hell was going on.

As it turned out, as some of you have figured out already, we were at the "Rocky Horror Show" and it was one of the oddest nights of my life to that point. It started with a host man dressed in an elegant evening gown, doing a pre-show where he embarrassed all the "Virgins" as those of us painted with a V were called. As it turns out anyone who has never seen the movie in the theater is a virgin by "Rocky" standards. The host started with making all the virgins dance, I could have killed Brooke for this. The dance we were taught was supposed to come up later in the film and he said anyone with a V was required to dance during the film or he would embarrass us worse after.

Next up was a costume contest, I wanted to sit down after being already red in the face embarrassed but they made all of us virgins go up and show off our costumes too. This contest took a long time and was done by audience response. I wasn't surprised that it was Brooke who got the most response from the crowd as she shook her ass and flashed her breasts to the audience. I was shocked to see her do that but I guess it was normal there as other girls after her showed their breasts too. After being more embarrassed then I had ever been in my life they contest ended and a man dressed in lingerie won, it was then we were sent back to our seats. The only thing I could think of was at least Brooke hadn't dressed me like some of the guys in the crowd dressed as women.

It was then the movie began, what I thought was really cool about this was that the theater group acted the movie out as it played on the screen. The other thing I thought was really different and cool was during the movie the audience calls out lines and comments led by the actors, I don't think I ever laughed so hard in years. The whole movie was really fun and I had one of the coolest fun nights ever. By the time we were half way into the movie I understood why Brooke had chosen which costumes went to each of us. Gia and I were given the costumes of the engaged couple from the film, while Abby and Katie's outfits had been chosen to imitate the two bi-sexual girls in the movie. I thought the choices were more than appropriate considering Brooke chose to dress as the craziest out of control sex crazed character in the film.

After the movie I was so excited, I had so much fun I just couldn't calm down. It didn't matter that it was almost three in the morning I just wanted to party or do something. Brooke wanted to go too but my sisters were ready to go home and Gia said that she was about out of energy. Brooke said she understood and we all piled back into the car, I had Gia on my lap again and as much as I wanted to play she was asleep within a mile of leaving. I looked over to see Katie and Abby making out really hot and heavy so much so I couldn't help myself as I began to get excited, Gia's head was nestled up against my shoulder and her ass was sitting right on my erection as I tried not to watch my sisters.

Tommy was in the front seat his head slumped against the window lightly sleeping too. I don't know why I was so pumped up but I really wasn't ready to go home yet but it didn't look like I had much of a choice tonight. It also didn't look like Gia was going to keep her promise to me that night about fooling around when we got home, I was disappointed but I understood. It was a long drive by the time we made it back to my house, Katie and Abby dashed from the car still holding hands and I knew their night wasn't over yet. I smiled about how much love there was between the two girls.

I tried to wake Gia up when we got home but she wouldn't budge so I picked her up gently and began to carry her inside. Brooke asked if her and Tommy could crash at my house and I said that seemed fine, so she woke Tommy long enough to get him to the couch. I told Brooke she could sleep in the guest room and I carried Gia to bed. I pulled off her bra and the slip from the costume and pulled the covers over her, she looked so peaceful as she lay there sleeping.

I woke to the door opening, I hadn't realized I had fallen asleep but when Brooke came back to the room I snapped awake. I looked up to find my movie was over, no wonder I had been dreaming back to the bachelorette party while sleeping through the movie.

"There you are," Brooke said, "We were wondering where you had disappeared to."

"Yeah I came up her to rest and I passed out," I told her while rubbing my eyes, "What time is it?"

"Time to get ready," she said, "I'm glad I left my clothes in here, if I hadn't come up to change you might have slept through the whole wedding."

"Yeah, and Abby would've killed me for that," I said and we both laughed, I groaned as I began getting up, "I'll let you get ready and I'll come back in a little while," I said stretching out my stiff back.

"What are you too shy to change in front of me?" She giggled, "You didn't used to be shy around me."

"More over you never used to be shy for the both of us," I joked, "But I'm more worried about Gia walking in here to find us both in our underwear," I told her. The truth was I would have loved to see Brookes naked body again as she changed but I didn't want any kind of comments going around that I might have cheated on Gia, "How come now one came to find me when she got here?"

"She still isn't here yet," Brooke informed me, "It looks like I get to be the maid of honor after all." She had a big smile on her face and I could tell it meant the world to her to be the bride's maid.

"She's not here yet?" I repeated wondering what had happened to keep her from arriving yet.

"No, so no worries you can help me get ready," Brooke said with a wink moving right up next to me.

"Brooke I……. I can't……" I began to stutter.

"Calm down killer," She laughed at me, "I was kidding, just give me a few minutes to change and then I can take my makeup case to the restroom down stairs. I breathed out loudly then nodded as I

walked out of the room. I wondered barefoot down the stairs not really heading anywhere in particular, before long I found myself walking into the lobby. I turned to find Abby sitting on the couch; I walked up behind her and put my arms around her neck from behind.

"What are you doing out here all by yourself?" I asked, "Shouldn't you be getting ready?"

"I just needed a few minutes alone but I'm really happy you came down."

"Are you nervous?" I asked her.

"Yes and no," she said simply and paused, "I just can't believe it's finally happening."

"Why did you think Katie would back out?"

"No, not really, it's just that we pushed the date back so much that I didn't know if it was me or just her aunt like she was claiming," she said quietly and she closed her eyes. I walked around the couch and took both of her hands pulling her to her feet and into a hug.

"She loves you so much," I whispered her in her ear, "And I love you both, don't ever doubt that the delays were because of Ash, my sister has no fears of marring you."

"It's not just that," she said with a tear forming in her eye, "I sent an invitation to my parents and it came back in the mail. They didn't even open it."

"I'm sorry," was all I could think of to say.

"I mean it's like I don't even exist to them anymore."

"That's rough," I acknowledged, "I lost both of my parents, but mine died, I kind of know what you're feeling but I guess not really. It would be harder to know they were out there alive, but lost to me."

"Yeah, I just thought............ I mean it's my wedding........." she began to cry and I held her tighter. It was unlike Abby to show this much emotion so I knew if she was this hurt on the outside then she was ten times worse on the inside.

"I'll tell you something that helps me when I think about how I lost both of my parents," I began and she lifted her head up and we pressed our foreheads together like we did many years ago when we were dating, "Lilly is the greatest mother I could ever have wanted, I lost my mom before I could remember, and my first step mom was an evil bitch who filled my head full of guilt. But Lilly made it all right in my life." I had never really put it into words how much I loved and respected my step mom before that moment but I meant what I was saying, "Lilly loves you like a daughter, if you let her she could help fill that space your real family broke in your heart. I know it's not quite the same but trust me it will help."

"Your right, this is all the family I will ever need, I love you all so much," she admitted, "I think you're the best brother anyone could ask for, you've always been the best guy I know," she said breaking the hug, "I sometimes wish we could've got married." Her face turned red after the comment and she looked away.

"It's not too late Abby we could go talk to Katie right now and we could get married tonight," I told her turning her face to look her in the eyes.

"Ok," she said in a very serious tone, "Let's do it, let's get married right now, tonight." We stared at each other not breaking our gaze for almost a minute before we broke out laughing.

"You almost had me," I joked.

"That's because I was almost serious, if I were ever to marry a man it would be you. You're the only boy I've ever loved," she told me with a real tone of truth then she kissed my cheek.

"In another time or place sweetie," I told her and kissed her cheek back, "So any word down here about Gia yet?" I asked changing the subject.

"Not that I heard, they are keeping me away from the brides side of the building so I don't see her in her dress," she said almost laughing.

"Well you are the groom," I reminded her, "its tradition."

"I know but the last I heard from them Gia still hadn't made it back and Brooke might have to fill in after all."

"Oh, I wonder what's held her up. I hope she made a flight out today," I was beginning to worry that she hadn't made it yet but we had planned for this. I had just expected her to be here by now and I really just missed my love and wanted her here with me tonight.

We talked for a couple more minutes until we were interrupted by Jt and Mandy walking into the lobby from outside. They were holding hands and looked like they had just gotten back from a hike, I wondered if they had found the spot Ash and I had made love at the last time we were here. I thought it was sweet that they seemed to be so in love with each other, I could remember being that age and in love, ironically the girl I loved at that age was getting married tonight to my ex-girlfriend. Life definitely took some strange bumps in the road as it went along.

"So I guess I should go and start getting ready now," Abby said, "And you too, best man."

"I guess so." I replied and turned to head back up the stairs.

I went back to the room and knocked on the door, Brooke answered wearing only a slip and her bra. I noticed her smooth tan stomach and I almost wished I was single for twenty minutes just so I could have her one more time.

"I can come back," I told her.

"No I was just going to put on the dress and I need someone to zip me up anyway."

I went in and closed the door, turning away from her I went to the closet and pulled out my tux. By the time I set it on the bed Brooke had put on her dress.

"I'm ready," she called and I walked up behind her and zipped it up for her. She smelled of lavender and her hair smelled like apples. It was an intoxicating mix of smells and I had to move away from her very quickly.

"I'll see you down there," she told me. She picked up her makeup case and left the room.

I pulled my duffle bag out from under the bed and pulled out a clean pair of boxers and an undershirt then walked down the hall to the upstairs bathroom. I took a quick shower and walked back to the room in just my boxers and t-shirt, I bumped into Mandy on the way back. We looked each other up and down and I could feel my dick hardening thinking back to this afternoon, she looked down and winked at me as a smile came across her face before we passed each other, I was actually flattered. I knew she was as much in love with Jt as I was with Gia but sometimes it was nice to know you got someone's attention.

I changed into my tux and I sat down on the bed for a minute after putting on my shoes, I loved my sisters but I had such a relationship with them over the years that it was somewhat sad to not be part of their lives in the way that we used to be. I don't know why it was getting to me in that moment as I had moved on with my own life, the next time I would sit in this room with a tux on it would be my wedding to Gia. So why then was I having a moment of reluctance to go down stairs?

Brooke came back up to the room to find me; I was still sitting on the bed. I had an overwhelming feeling all of a sudden that something big was about to happen, I didn't think it was just the wedding. I had a feeling like impending doom was on its way. I shook it off as nerves as Brooke opened the door.

"Are you ok," she asked looking at my face, "You look flushed."

"I'm ok, just thinking about the future."

"I don't doubt that, you have a lot going on right now, but don't worry she's ok, something must have just come up on her end," she told me thinking I was only concerned with Gia's non arrival. Was that the looming feeling I was getting? Was I just worried that because she hadn't made it out yet that it meant something bad?

"Yeah," I sighed, "Let's get this party going." Brooke just nodded at me and took my hand as I got off the bed.

We walked down stairs together then she turned to the bride's side of the lodge and I walked outside to the courtyard. It looked almost exactly like my dad and Lilly's wedding nestled in the trees. Abby was already at the altar looking very pretty dressed up in her tux; I walked up behind her and hugged her. She turned and smiled at me kissing my cheek.

"Thank you for always being the best man," she whispered to me.

Brooke walked up to the altar a couple minutes later and waved to the piano player to start, as wedding march began to play and Abby took my hand and held it tight. The moment was here and now the wedding was finally underway. All of a sudden back in the lodge someone yelled "OH MY GOD" really loud and there was a lot of noise and commotion coming from the building.

"What do you think that was all about?" Abby asked leaning over to me, "Do you think something happened?"

"I don't know, it could be the girls just having some fun while getting ready," I said trying to say calm myself. My natural curiosity was kicking in and I wanted to go look but I held steady. I looked over at Brooke and she shrugged back at me.

As we stood there waiting the wedding march played over and over again without Katie showing up, I was beginning to have a bad feeling about this. Abby squeezed my hand as the song began to play the seventh time with no sign of Katie. I didn't know what to do as I thought someone should go and see what was going on. I went to move at the same time as Brooke, she walked over to Abby and me when she saw me move.

"Stay here," she told us, "I'll go see what's going on."

"OK," I told her. I wanted to know what was up but she was the bride's maid so I left it to her to see what was going on. Brooke motioned for the piano player to cut the song and ran back up the rows into the lodge, and I heard more excited talking.

It was at least ten minutes later when and Abby was beginning to freak out, she was sure that Katie was backing out of the wedding. I was doing my best to calm her down and I told her we had waited long enough and I was going to find out what was going on. Just as I moved to leave again Lilly ran up with tears in her eyes and began talking quietly to the minister. Linda came out next and sat down in the front row, she was crying as she began talking to James, Jt and Mandy about something and I could see Mandy begin to cry too. Abby looked at Lilly then Linda and hugged me tight and began to cry with her forehead on my shoulder.

"It's over, she doesn't love me," she cried quietly into my ear.

"I'm sure that's not it," I whispered back, not sure myself.

Lilly finished her conversation with the minister and she turned and saw Abby, more tears filled Lilly's eyes as she leaned over to Abby's ear.

"Don't worry sweetheart," Lilly whispered softly, "Everything's fine." I was barely able to hear the words but Abby pulled away and looked at her soon to be mother-in-law, Lilly just nodded as she went and sat down next to Linda and James. Lilly pulled a tissue out of her purse and began to wipe her eyes. Brooke came back and sat down by Lilly, she had changed out of her bride's maid dress and had put on a very pretty sun dress, I was confused for a moment then I realized that Gia must have shown up at last meaning Brooke was relieved of bride's maid duties. Moments later a girl walked up to the altar, she was dressed in the bride's maid gown; it fit her just slightly loose.

I couldn't take my eyes off the new girl; she was the most beautiful woman I had ever seen in my life, that was no exaggeration. I realize I have said that about all of the girls in my life at some point throughout this story but this young lady was a true goddess of beauty. My mind was reeling I thought to myself that I should know the girl but I couldn't for the life of me remember where and when I had met such a beautiful creature. I couldn't believe this was happening again, I was engaged to Gia and here I was falling in love with another woman. It was more than just her looks, it was as if I was being drawn to her mentally and physically, I wanted her, needed her more than any woman I had ever been with. It was

wrong but I knew I had just met my future wife, but what do I do now? Gia was a great girl and I was already engaged to her.

I was still staring at her when the wedding march began again; Abby squeezed my hand really hard as we saw Katie appear. She was beautiful in her gown; she had chosen an off white dress instead of the traditional pure white. She began to walk slowly to us smiling bigger then I had ever seen her smile before, she was literally glowing with happiness as she reached us at the altar. Abby whispered a thank you in my ear as she let go of my hand and took Katie's so the ceremony could began.

The minister began talking about vows and I turned to look at the mystery girl again, she was looking back at me and if I didn't mistake my guess she wore the same look of longing on her face I probably had on mine. Then as I ran my eyes down her body again I saw it, I had over looked it until that moment, she was wearing the necklace that I had bought Ash for her 15th birthday. It hit me with a flash of recognition, I realized only then who she was but how did she get here? I hadn't seen her for three years and she had really grown and changed, she was taller and slimmer then she had once been, her breast had grown more and her face had changed a lot. I could see hardness in her face that told me she had gone through some rough times since we last saw one another. In that dress with her hair up she looked like a whole different person, all I knew for sure was she wasn't a little girl anymore.

Over the next twenty minutes the minister read the vows and one of Lilly's aunts sang songs, I really hated singers at wedding and made a mental note to not have that at my wedding. At long last the moment came for the rings, I gave Abby Katie's ring and she placed it on her hand and I have to admit a tear came to my eye. I had loved her so much in my youth and here I was watching her take vows and getting married, we had come so far together in the last nine years. Ash handed Katie Abby's ring and with the power invested in the minister the girls were married. I looked up at Ash and she looked at me, our eyes locked just as the minister pronounced them wife and wife.

The next hour was a mad house of hugs and congratulations to the happy couple. I really wanted to break away and talk to Ash but we both were stuck up at the altar talking with relatives. That was what happens when you're the best man and bride's maid I guess. So many people had arrived just for the reception that I didn't know or hadn't seen in so many years that I almost didn't remember them. I couldn't stop stealing looks at Ash every time I could get the opportunity to look in her direction, it was like a flood gate had opened in my heart and everything I had been repressing for the last three years came flowing back to me. I had the answer in that moment I had been searching for when I had left to college.

When I had left her I had wondered if I really loved her or had it all been the manipulation she had played on me, I knew with one look at her tonight it had been real love between us and I would never be away from her again. How I could have ever questioned my love for her? It was beyond me, but I had gone out and been with so many other girls in the last three years she wouldn't want me back now. I needed to talk to her; I needed to find out what if anything she felt for me.

The crowd at the altar finally broke and out came the champagne, we made our way back to the lodge so we could all toast the couple and they could cut the cake. Since I was the best man I was expected to give a speech as tradition dictated, I really didn't know what to say. I had tried for a couple days to think of what I would say but as everyone was looking to me to make the toast speech I just decided to wing it.

"On behalf of the happy couple I would like to thank everyone for being here tonight," I started, "I know it means the world to them," I paused for a few seconds, "Katie you were my first love and my sister and you will always have a special place in my heart," the crowd gave out an AAAAWWW at that not fully realizing in what way I meant the comment, "Abby I truly love you too and I'm so happy and proud to call you my sister, to you both I can't imagine being more proud of anyone in my life as I am for you on this day," I held up my champagne flute, "To the sweetest two girls I've ever known, may your love glow bright for the rest of your days."

I took a drink and everyone began to cheer, I thought I had bombed but everyone seemed to be happy and agree with what I had said as they began to drink. It was about a half an hour later they decided to cut the cake, the girls didn't smash it into each other's faces to the disappointment of many of the children, they simply took little bites from their pieces. Next came the tossing of the bouquet and the flinging of the guarder belt. I wasn't even trying to catch the guarder but somehow it landed on my head anyway, everyone laughed.

Next up was the dancing, the girls started it with the traditional first dance, it was so sweet watching them dance slowly with Katie's head pressed up against Abby's shoulder. I went to find Ash to dance with her and talk; I had so much I wanted to say to her now. As I approached her Lilly and Linda walked up to her, I could see the looks on their faces and they didn't seem happy.

"We want to talk to you," Lilly said to Ash.

"Right now?" She asked clearly trying to stall from the conversation they were about to have.

"Yes now," Linda said, "We didn't want to interrupt the wedding but now we need to talk."

I wanted in on that conversation, I was fairly certain that they wanted answers about where she had been for the last year. I wanted to know that too and how she had found out about the wedding and ended up getting here just in time. It was then Gia popped in my head again, she still hadn't made it yet, where was she? Did things not go well at her grandmothers' funeral? I hoped she was alright, but I thought it was well past time for me to find out what was going on with her.

I walked out of the banquet hall and down the corridor to the lobby and picked up the phone. I called my house hoping maybe to find her there but I didn't get an answer so I called the only other place I thought she might be, her mom's house.

"Hi," I said as her mom picked up, "It's Joey I'm trying to find Gia, did she make her flight?"

"No," her mom said kind of sharp, "She's still here on the island."

"Can I talk to her?"

"She's not here and she told me if you called to tell you she doesn't want to talk to you right now," she informed me.

"I don't understand..........." I began.

"Look Joey, she's been through enough," she said cutting me off, "After what happened with her brother............. She can't go through something like it again. Just leave her alone."

"I don't know what you're talking about," I told her confused, "What happened in the last couple days? Everything was fine when I talked to her last."

"I don't want to get in the middle of it," she said more gently, "I'll let you guys sort it out when you get home." With that she hung up on me. I sat in the lobby more confused than ever, what had happened this week? I couldn't think of anything I had done that might make her not want to come here or not want to talk to me.

I sat there for a few minutes when I heard the doors to the reception hall open up, I didn't want to talk to anyone right now except Ash so I walked out the front lobby doors and headed for the far end of the parking lot. I heard the doors open behind me but I didn't look to see who it was I just kept walking, I figured it was probably some relative just heading to their car. I got to my truck and I opened the tailgate and jumped up to sit on it, it was then that I saw Abby standing there to the left of me. She looked at me and smiled questionably.

"What's wrong sweetie," she asked, "I saw you leave and I could tell there was something bothering you." She climbed up on my tailgate with me, "You're not upset about the wedding are you?"

"No, it is a little weird to see the girl you lost your virginity to getting married," I admitted to her, "But that isn't the problem."

"Do you want to talk about it?"

"What I want is for you to get back in there for your reception," I told her.

"Joe," she said softly and I was caught a little off guard as that was the first time she had ever called me that, "You've always been there when I needed you, always letting me sleep in your bed or lean on your shoulder. I won't go back until you come with me."

"Thanks sweetie," I said and kissed her cheek, "But I just don't know how I can go back."

I told her all about my reaction to Ash and what had happened when I tried to call home to talk to Gia, I opened up to her in a way I had only ever done with Katie. Abby was the only person who knew my whole history with Katie and Ash and I needed real advice, I told her things some of which she knew but other things I had kept to myself. She took my head and placed it on her shoulder and began to run her fingers through my hair.

"You drive yourself crazy always trying to do the right thing," she told me, "It's clear that you want to be with Ash but you have feelings for Gia too, but are those feelings for her as strong as the feelings you have for Ash?"

"No," I answered without thinking it just came out.

"Then you just made your decision."

"But how can I just break up with a really great girl like her, she's been there for the last year and you know what's going on with us."

"I do know," she stated them paused, "Sometimes love isn't about what's right for everyone else it's about doing what's right for you."

"I know but......." I stopped trying to find the words.

"Look at Katie and I, the law says that we can't be married. Did we let the law stop us? Do you think that a lack of a legal document with our signatures on it means we aren't married as far as we're concerned?"

"No your marriage is as real as any I've ever seen."

"Thank you," she said kissing the top of my head, "So go to Ash and tell her how you feel. Maybe she will feel the same, maybe not. If she doesn't then you can go home and talk things out with Gia and nothing has changed since yesterday."

"But if Ash feels like I do.........."

"Then you go home and have different conversation with Gia." She kissed my head again, "You have to do what's right to be happy you dope or you will regret this moment for the rest of your life."

"Yeah," I sighed, "Your right it's just really hard to face it. What if Ash doesn't love me anymore, I would fall apart to hear it."

"But that's life mister, go face her and find out." She took my hand and pulled me off the tailgate and we walked back to the banquet hall. I somehow regained my composure and my smile by the time we walked back in the doors.

Everyone was still dancing and drinking when we returned, Abby quickly found Katie and they had a whispered conversation for a few minutes. As soon as the girls were done talking Katie came over to me and pulled me outside the doors again.

"Abby says you're having a bad night? Something about Gia bailing on the Wedding?" she asked me and I told her what had happened when I had called home.

"Did she say anything to you, ever, that might explain what's going on?" I asked once I had told all of what happened.

"I have no idea of what might have gone wrong; all she talks about is your wedding next year. But I would ask Ash because it was Gia who sent Ash to the wedding using her return ticket. That's probably why she didn't come. She might not have been able to get herself a ticket on such short notice," Katie explained. I had no idea how the hell that had happened, the girls had never met before and how had Gia found Ash at the last second? Now I really needed to talk to Ash.

"Wait, Gia gave away her ticket?" I asked Katie, "How did Gia find Ash?"

"I don't have the details, Mom just told me that's how she managed to make it here today," she said shrugging.

"Something just seems odd about that."

"I thought so too," Katie stated, "I wonder how they found each other but I'm sure we will hear the whole story soon enough that I'm not worrying about it tonight. I'm just so grateful to Gia that she got my aunt here to see me get married. Now are you going to tell me what's really bothering you? Abby wouldn't say anything but I see it in your face."

I talked to her about my feelings for Ash and she agreed with what Abby had told me, "I love Gia like a sister and would've loved to have her be part of our family, but you have to at least talk to Ash and see how she feels before you commit to Gia."

"I know, I know, I just don't want to hurt her."

"I love you Joey," she told me, "But how happy of a marriage are you going to have if you're truly in love with someone else?"

"I know I already realized that when Abby said it," I told her.

"Think about how guilty you felt when you were dating Abby and you were in love with me." That comment hit home hard, I thought I was so much more grown up since then but I was right back in the same situation as back then.

"Your right, thank you Katie," I said and I kissed her cheek. She smiled and patted me on the shoulder before going back into the reception. I followed her back inside and looked up to see Brooke talking to the DJ giggling about something. I had no idea what she was laughing about when she hopped down from his booth but she ran over to Abby and whispered something to her that made both girls smile.

I didn't have to wait long to get the joke as the song that was playing ended and "The Time Warp" from "Rocky Horror" began to play, despite my state of mind I actually smiled. Abby, Katie and Brooke went to the center of the room and began to do the dance, to my surprise so did a number of our relatives including Linda. For some reason I wasn't surprised to see Mandy jump into the group of people who were dancing, she seemed to be very familiar with the song.

I smiled as they all jumped to the left, under any other circumstances I would've jumped in with them but my heart wasn't into dancing right now. I broke myself away from the crowd and began looking for Ash, I figured now was as good of a time as any to find her and have the talk that was scaring the hell out of me. Never in my life, not even when I had found out Katie was my sister, had one conversation held the potential to impact my life as profoundly as what this one did tonight.

I spent the next hour wondering around the lodge looking for Ash to no avail, she had disappeared again. I hadn't seen Lilly in that time either, I had seen Linda come back to the reception but maybe Ash and Lilly were still somewhere talking. I knew Lilly well enough to know she would be both furious with her but also so happy she was home again. That talking to might go on for days.

I finally gave up and went back up to my room, it was early but I had enough merriment for today, I needed to sort my feelings alone. When I got back to the room I noticed that Brooke's clothes bag and makeup case were missing, I guessed she was now officially staying in Chase's room. I wondered when she had come back up to move her things out. I sat down on the bed and decided that I was going to leave for home tomorrow, I had intended to stay here for a few more days but I needed to get home as soon as possible to find out what had gone wrong on that end.

I got up to change out of my tux and I had just stripped down to my boxers when the door opened, I had forgotten to lock it. Ash walked in holding a shirt and a pair of jeans over her arm, she saw me and turned her head apologizing for not knocking.

"It's ok," I told her as I pulled on a pair of shorts and picked up my shirt, "What are you doing up here?" I asked.

"I needed a place to sleep and Brooke said I could sleep on her bed because she wouldn't be using her room she had made other arrangements." With that said she reached behind herself and un-modestly unzipped her dress and let it fall to the ground. I couldn't take my eyes off her body. She was wearing only a white bra and cotton panties, so I had a great view of her now grown up body. I felt myself getting hard so I sat on the bed and covered myself with a pillow. She always knew how to push my buttons and she was doing it now as I gazed upon her perfect body.

She pulled her shirt over her head and sat down on the other bed, her incredible legs hanging off the side, I had to stop myself from drooling as I was harder than I had been in a very long time.

"I..... I......" I started twice not being able to form a whole word, "I'm sorry," I finally blurted out, "I...... never should have left you the way I did." I hadn't meant to start by talking about us, I figured we would get around to it later but I couldn't stop myself.

"Joe, don't," she said tears already forming in her eyes, "I'm not ready to talk about......"

"I was just angry, I made the biggest mistake of my life," the words burst out of me before I could stop them, "I've been holding it in since I left, trying to find you again in other women, but they aren't you," I didn't realize what I had just said to be true until I had said it. I loved Jenny and Gia but they were patches over my broken heart, Ash was the one and only girl that had ever truly owned my heart.

"Stop it," she yelled at me, "You hurt me!" She was crying now, "I'm not the same little naïve girl you used and called it love!"

"I didn't use you," I said back quietly, "I really did love you."

"Then how could you not ever talk to me again? How could you move on and be engaged to another girl? How do you think I felt when I heard you had a college girlfriend? How do you think I felt when your fiancée told me about your engagement?" She was yelling at me and sobbing at the same time, "Don't talk to me of love when you didn't love me enough to ever call me again after you left, after what we had I didn't get one damn word!"

"I...... your right, what I did was wrong," I told her and I got up and sat down next to her. I tried to wrap my arm around her but she pushed me off, "I'm not proud of many of the things I've done in my life but hurting you is the one thing I wish I could do over. I still love you so damn much."

"How dare you tell me you love me," she said and she slapped me. I took the hit and didn't move, "You have no idea what I went through after you broke up with me, the hurt and the things I did trying to get over you. I became someone I didn't like. Where were you while I was going through all that? You were at college partying and FUCKING OTHER GIRLS!"

"Ash........"

"Don't even try to lie about it. I mean here you are tonight trying to use me again," she spat at me.

"What are you talking about?" I asked confused now.

"I saw you get hard when I was changing, you're here talking to me about love so you can get your dick wet before you return to your future wife. I'm not just some whore for you to bang on vacation. I won't be tricked so you can use me and return to your life." The rage on her face was intense as she yelled at me.

"I'm not saying anything but the truth, I still love you," It was my turn for tears; "I wouldn't ever use you. I thought I had lost you so long ago, I do have a fiancée but..........."

"But what?" she asked calming down, "Do you love HER?"

"Yes, but I've never loved anyone like you, that's the truth," I told her as tears rolled down my face.

"You're really telling the truth to me? You swear?" She asked her voice now becoming slightly calmer.

"Yes," I told her and walked over to the bed, I reached into the pocket of the jeans I had been wearing earlier that day and pulled out my wallet. Inside I removed a piece of paper, it was the note that she had left me under her pillow, the one I had found the day I had come home from college.

"I've carried this with me every day since I found it," I told her showing her the note. Her whole disposition changed at that moment, it was the piece of proof she needed to see to prove my feelings to her.

She picked up the jeans she had carried into the room earlier and reached into the pocket removing a taped up piece of folded paper. She smiled softly at me as she showed me the note I had left her on the day I went to college. I was stunned that she had kept the note for all this time too; I thought we really were so much alike at times. It was the one thing we both had held on to as a proof of our devotion to one another.

"I just don't know what to do Ash I really don't."

"Tell me what your heart says Joe," she said so tenderly I only began to cry again.

"I want you Ash, more than the world itself but I can't just walk away from Gia like she doesn't matter," I told her and she wrapped her arms around me and held me tight.

"I want you more than words can say," she admitted, "I've only ever loved you Joe."

I turned my head and we kissed, I was like electric fire shooting through my body and I couldn't believe this was real. I felt at piece kissing her lips, the world centered on us in this perfect union of passion and love. Ash was not just my love, she was a part of my soul I had been missing for the last few

years, and I needed her at my side for the world to be right. I don't know how long we kissed before we pulled back and put our foreheads together gazing into each other's eye.

"I've hoped for that for so long," she told me her arms still wrapped around my neck, "So what now?"

"I want this, so bad Ash but I need to talk to Gia and end things with her first. With what we have going on I can't just break up with her, but I can't be with her anymore," I replied.

"I don't get it," Ash said pulling away from me and letting her arms fall to her sides, "I don't want to play anymore games. I know she might hate you and it sucks to break up but how hard is it to just tell her you love me and break it off?"

"I don't want to play games or lie to anyone either but it's not as easy as it sounds," I wanted to explain it to her but I was having trouble getting the words out.

"How hard is it to tell her theirs someone else? You just say it, break the engagement and move on it's not like you have to hire a divorce attorney."

"No it's not that but......"

"Well what is it then Joe? I mean you're making it sound like it's more complicated than it is, it's not like you have kids together or anything."

I didn't answer her that time I just looked away with a guilty look on my face. We were getting to the heart of my real fears and I was afraid of Ash's reaction when she realized what was holding me to Gia.

"OH MY GOD!" Ash cried as the realization hit her, "SHE PREGNANT!"

"Yes."

"Oh god Joey I'm sorry for being so harsh with you," she said new tears forming, "I understand now, it would be hard for me to break up with someone if I was carrying his child."

"It certainly does complicate our situation," I joked trying to lighten the mood. She scooted back to me and began to kiss me again. I was hesitant because I felt like I needed to talk to Gia before giving into this. I wanted Ash so badly but I didn't want to cheat, even if I was going to go home and break up with my girlfriend cheating was cheating.

"Ash we need to stop," I said pulling back, "I need to talk to her first, I'm not that guy that cheats, and I can't do it to her not even for you."

"I know and your right but it's been so long since we've been here like this, I need you now and forever, "she said kissing my neck. I wanted to say stop but I couldn't, she felt so warm and so right kissing me. I wanted so badly to push her down and rip her panties off with my teeth before ravishing her beautiful young body but I managed to stop her.

"Ash I really can't, I'm not a cheater and would you really want me if I was?" I asked her, "Tell me the truth if I cheat with you now then somewhere in your mind you might think I would do it again someday."

"No your right," she said backing off; "If you can resist cheating with me then I know you're the right man, I love you for being that man, it just SUCKS right now."

"Yeah," I agreed and moved back to the other bed.

"But I know something else we can do."

"What," I asked.

"Well there's nothing that says we can't take care of our own needs while sitting on separate beds, as long as we don't touch each other it's not cheating."

"I can live with that," I told her. Somehow I didn't think Gia would agree that this wasn't some form of cheating but I had let it slide the night she let Brooke play with her pussy on the car ride home from Kayak Falls so it wasn't like she was a perfect angel either.

Ash didn't wait for me to say anything else; she lifted her shirt up exposing her panties and began to pull them down her wonderfully seductive legs. This was going to be a test of my resolve as I already wanted to break, run to her and make wild passionate love. It had been a few months now since I had gotten laid as Gia hadn't wanted to have sex since she had found out about the baby.

I slid my shorts down as I watched her take her finger and begin to rub her clit, I was so hard and leaking pre-cum down my shaft. She reached into her shirt and began to massage her breasts as two of her fingers found her wet opening and began to thrust in and out. I loved the sound of her sopping pussy as she grinded against her own hand.

I reached down and gripped my now well lubed pre-cum covered cock and began to stroke it in slow motions, I was already feeling like I might cum just from the sight of Ash's body so I tried to make this last as long as possible. Ash began to moan loud and I realized that she was getting close already herself. She turned her head and watched me for a moment as I sped up my hand speed.

"Cum for meeeeeee," she called out as she arched her back and her first orgasm took her over. Her hands began working faster and she ground her hips harder as her first orgasm began to subside, "Please baby cum for me," she begged, "I want to see you shoot big for me, show me how bad you want me," she said and licked her lips.

That was all I could take, I gripped myself as hard as I could and stroked as fast as my arm would go. Moments later I groaned loudly as my orgasm built up and released in an eruption of cum so big it seemed to go everywhere. It landed on my hand, thighs stomach and on the bed, shot after shot sprung into the air and back down on me.

"OH WOW!" Ash sighed as her hips bucked and she began to cum again, she screamed out loud as her body shuddered, "Oh god! I needed that, thank you Joe."

When I was finally done leaking cum I picked up the towel I had left on the floor from drying off and cleaning up earlier that day and began to wipe myself off. When I thought I had gotten it all I tossed the towel to Ash who wiped herself off with it and dropped it to the floor. She pulled her panties back up and I did the same with my boxers, I left my shorts off thinking it was no big deal after what we had just done.

"I have an idea of something else we can do tonight," I told her after a few minutes.

"Really what!" she asked excitedly.

"We can talk," I told her, "I would love to know all about you. What happened to you last year?"

Ash told me that the reason she had disappeared was because of her friend Terra's boyfriend, he was in a band and they got the chance to do an overseas tour. Terra's boyfriend had asked her to go with him but Ash had told her it was a bad idea to run off to another country with a bunch of boys all by herself. As hard as she tried Ash couldn't convince her friend not to go so she had made the last minute decision to go with them to make sure nothing happened to her friend.

Ash really didn't want to talk much about what happened when they were overseas but things had led to Terra breaking up with her boyfriend and the girls having to figure out how to make it back to the states. Then she told me the story of them traveling in a van across country to make it to the island and how she had met Gia while looking for Katie. Ash didn't know I was living in the house next door she had just been looking for someone when she happened across Gia late last night.

Ash said Gia had just been dropped off by her uncle Marty, who owned a cab company, and when Ash introduced herself she was surprise that the Gia knew who she was. She said it all made sense a few minutes later when Gia began to talk about who she was and that I lived in the house with her. Ash's voice waivered as she talked about how she had tried to keep from crying when she realized she was talking to my girlfriend.

Gia said that she was having some things going on with her family and that she felt like Ash should really be going to the wedding instead of her, Ash said that she didn't want to cause any trouble for anyone but Gia said that really she should stay and finish some things going on with her grandmothers death so it made more sense to give her the ticket. Ash was so happy to be going to the wedding that she actually hugged Gia for doing this for her.

I asked if Gia gave any indication of something she might have been mad at me about the night before, then I explained the phone call earlier tonight. Ash said that last night Gia fixed them dinner and they talked, Ash pointed out that the whole time they talked Gia seemed distracted as if something was bothering her, but she didn't ever say what it was.

Ash said that she had stayed in our guest room last night and Gia had gotten her up early and drove her to the airport so that Ash could try to get the earliest flight possible. Ash said that Gia's whole demeanor had changed that morning from the night before, she barely talked and her whole attitude was much colder. She dropped Ash off with only the clothes on her back and the plane ticket and drove away; Ash was both disappointed and relieved that she hadn't stayed with her all day. On the one hand it would have been nice to have company but on the other there was a tension between them and Ash would rather not have dealt with it.

I couldn't think of what might have been behind Gia's distraction other than the death in the family but that didn't explain why she hadn't wanted to talk to me when I called. Then it occurred to me that Gia had put Ash on the plane and sent her to us, why hadn't she called the lodge to tell us that Ash had been found? She hadn't given us any warning to look out for her or anything.

Ash slowly fell off to sleep telling me about her life the last few years and of the things that had happened to her. I was really tired by then but found I couldn't get enough of her talking to me. I was just so happy to have her in the room with me, and for the first time in our lives we were alone and didn't have to worry about a roommate or adult walking in on us. It was nice to be alone with her and not have to hide from anyone about it. I could tell when she was fighting to stay awake but I thought it was so cute the way her words just began to drift off as she fell asleep. I couldn't stop looking at her as I finally lost myself to sleep as well.

I woke only a short time later to feel a body against me, it was Ash. She had moved over to the big bed and lay down with me at some point, I wanted to wake her up and move her but I didn't. I put my arm around her and held her to me, kissing the back of her neck a couple times. She purred in her sleep nuzzling her butt up to me, I was glad I had put my boxers back on as I felt myself hardening between her panty covered ass cheeks. This was going to be a long couple days diving home trying to resist my little goddess.

Chapter Twenty Three: Beginning of the End

When I arrived home it was like returning to a dream, some unreal place that didn't seem like home anymore. I parked my car in front of my house and I ran to the door. The house was quiet, almost a dead quiet and I noticed right away that things were missing. I walked up the stairs to my bedroom and it was almost empty. I began to walk the rest of the house and I quickly realized that Gia had moved out, taking only things she had bought with her own money or special things I had gotten her.

I still didn't know what was going on; I had tried to call her on my three day journey home but hadn't been able to locate her at home or her parent's house. By the time I made my way to the kitchen I found the engagement ring I had given her on the table. I didn't need a note to tell me what that meant, things moved out and a ring on a table is a note enough.

I walked back upstairs and pulled the guest linen out of the closet and remade my bed. I wasn't mad about what Gia had taken with her; she could have everything in the house as far as I was concerned. I felt numb and I lay down on my bed and turned on my TV, I needed time to think and let this latest development set in. I only had a couple days left before Katie and Abby brought Ash back to the island. I had to find Gia and get this resolved before they got back.

I felt bad about how I had left Ash this time; I had snuck away in the morning while she slept again. I knew her well enough to know that she would be mad at me for that. I had woken up early the morning after the wedding, Ash was still lying in my arms, and I began to feel myself getting excited as I felt the warmth of her body pressed up against me. I didn't want to wake her but I had to move before I did something I would regret, I wanted her little body so bad but I couldn't give in to her. I leaned over and kissed her neck a couple times and she shifted in her sleep, rolling slightly onto her back. I used this opportunity to scoot back on the bed against the wall, moving carefully over her and off the bed.

I had made a decision as I lay there thinking that morning, I picked up my shorts from where I had left them last night and pulled them on before reaching under the bed and pulling out my duffle bag. I unzipped my bag and removed a clean shirt and put it on before I gathered up all my belongings in the room, just throwing them into the duffle. I quietly opened the door and slipped out, locking it behind me so that Ash would be ok alone in the room. Not that I didn't trust my family but I know I always feel safer with the door locked when I sleep alone.

I walked downstairs and headed off to the bridal suite, I needed to let Abby and Katie know why I was leaving. I wanted very much to spend the rest of the time we had planned out at the lodge but I needed to go and talk to my girlfriend. I knocked on the door loud enough to wake the girls, wishing I didn't have to but I wanted to leave before Ash awoke. I knew if I didn't Ash would break my resolve and I would take her into my arms and not let go.

Abby finally came to the door, she was wiping her eyes and she wore a look of concern on her face.

"Joey," she said somewhat surprised to see it was me, "Is something wrong?"

"No, not anything you need to worry about," I began, "But I need to leave. I have to figure out what's going on at home and ………. Well you know………. What we talked about last night."

"I get it, you go and get it sorted out," she told me as she patted my shoulder, "How did things go with her last night, I heard about the sleeping arrangements." She flashed me a guilty smile as she said the last part and I began to wonder how much of a hand she had in sending Ash to me.

"It went ok, we talked and I need to talk to Gia."

"WELL! Did you……. You know?" She asked excitedly with a slight giggle.

"No……."

"But it was Ashley, I thought for sure you guys would see each other and make mad passionate love, I kind of thought it would be incredibly romantic."

"Abby, I've got to go," I started changing the subject, "I just wanted to ask you…….. Well I just wanted to make sure that someone got Ash back to the island."

"Don't worry we'll bring her back with us. I promise," she told me and kissed my cheek, "Good luck with Gia and I'll see you in about a week."

"Thanks," I replied and kissed her cheek before I turned and walked towards my truck.

I stopped at the front desk and wrote a note for Ash, I asked the clerk to have it delivered to the room in about an hour. The note read:

> Ash,
>
> I wanted to tell you I'm sorry, I'm sorry for leaving you again while you slept without a word of goodbye. I love you so much that I couldn't leave while looking into those eyes but I have things I need to clear up at home and I can't stay.
>
> I made arrangements with Abby and she will bring you back to the island with her, if that's what you want. I would understand if you wanted to go back with Lilly and live with her. I hope you choose to come back to the island first. If you do, we can talk then I can send you to Lilly if you want to be there.
>
> I love you more than words can say; I just need to deal with my home life before I can talk anymore about OUR future together. I don't think it would be fair to you or my girlfriend if I didn't end one relationship before starting another.
>
> I'm sorry I didn't wake you to come with me, it's a two night car trip back home and I knew I wouldn't be able to control myself on the way home if I took you with me. I almost lost control this morning and made love to you in your sleep, there's no way I could resist two more nights. I hope you understand.

I love you so much and hope to see you soon.

Joey

I shook my thoughts out of my head as I lay on my bed, it had been a long drive home and I still hadn't had anything to eat that day. I walked back down stairs and began fixing myself a sandwich; I sat at the table and ate looking at the ring still sitting there. I couldn't get myself to move it yet.

Finishing my sandwich and placing the plate in the sink I felt it was time to try again to find Gia. I walked over to the phone and I saw a note written on the pad next to it. It had a shorthand note written on it simply giving the date and the name of Glen the P.I., I realized that the date listed was the day before the wedding. My other problems seemed to melt away for a moment as I let myself get my hopes up that Glen had found my sister.

I dialed the investigator right away; I needed a bit of good news in the middle everything going on. I closed my eyes and crossed my fingers as the phone began to ring; hoping today was the day I found her. His secretary answered telling me he was in a meeting and would call me back in about a half an hour. I opened my eyes disappointed about another delay but I said that would be ok.

While I was waiting I called Gia's parents house again, and was again told she wasn't there. I told her mom that I was home now and knew Gia had moved out, I asked her to let Gia know I needed to talk to her and find out what was going on.

I sat back down at the table and stared at the ring, Gia had made my decision really easy for me by moving out but I was still sad over the fact that our relationship was over. What were we going to do about the baby? If she wouldn't talk to me now how could we possibly raise a child together?

I was so lost in my thoughts I barely heard the phone begin to ring. I snapped out of my funk and jumped up to grab the phone.

"Hey," I said simply.

"Joey?" It was Glen's voice on the line.

"Yeah, I called because I found a note that you called a few days ago."

"I did call, but I gave all the info to your girlfriend."

"She didn't write it down and we........ She moved out."

"Oh, you're not upset I told her, I thought we had discussed sharing information with her was alright," he said nervously.

"No, it's fine I wasn't hiding anything from her. I just need to know what you told her."

Glen went on to tell me about how he had finally been granted access to the records and then he began to explain the process of tracking her down once he had her name. I really didn't care about the process and I tuned out most of what he said. I knew he was happy he had come through for me but all I cared about was the name and the address.

I let him go on as I didn't want to seem rude but I was getting really impatient by the time he finally gave me the name. At long last he finally told me who she was I didn't need the address; I knew where to find her. I was in shock, I knew my sister and I had known her for a long time.

"Thank you," I stuttered out.

"Are you ok?"

"Yes, I'm just happy to have found her, that's all."

"Ok, you sound a bit shaken."

"No, I'm fine," I told him. I couldn't tell him I was shaking because I had slept with my own sister, "Thank you Glen for all your help, you did a great job."

"No problem, so were done and I'm closing your case now."

"That's fine, thank you again," I replied and hung up the phone.

I had gone through so much emotional pain and trouble when I thought Katie was my real sister, dealing with the conflicting feelings of love and morality. Now in the end I found my real sister and I had slept with her, it was too much to handle with the break up I was going through. Was this the news that had made Gia leave? I knew this had to play a part in why she left but I was to numb at the moment to put it all together.

I thought about Jessica and I began to wonder why she hadn't told me herself? She had to know I was her brother, she had been old enough to remember her time on this island that there was no way she didn't know I was her brother. My thoughts were interrupted as there was a loud knock on the front door.

"Gia!" I exclaimed opening the door.

"Mom said you were back, we need to talk."

"I've been trying............"

"I didn't want to have this conversation over the phone," she told me cutting in and walking to the kitchen and sitting down at the table.

I closed the door and followed her into the kitchen, sitting down opposite her. Both of our eyes fell to the ring still sitting in the center of the table.

"Gia, what's going on?"

"I can't do this anymore. I told you before that I couldn't tolerate secrets and I know there is more you're still hiding from me."

"I told you everything that night......."

"Just stop now, if all you're going to do is continue to lie to me." Her face was red with anger and her tone was almost deadly, "I know you had a relationship with Katie."

"I don't know....." was all I managed to stutter.

"Don't deny it! I've seen you around her and I've heard enough comments."

"Gia, I don't know what to say about that. I........"

"I told you to stop! I understand why you would lie to the rest of the island as everyone thinks you're really brother and sister. But I know about your adoption and your real father! Why would you lie to me about it?"

"I did it for her," I explained, "I didn't want it to get out that we had a relationship."

"So you think I would've just blabbed to the whole island? Joey....... Justify it all you like but you couldn't be honest with me about her."

"Your right."

"Finally an honest answer."

"I'm sorry, Gia."

"I'm sorry too," she said with tears now forming in her eyes.

We sat at the table not saying anything for a long time, Gia laid her head on the table and sobbed into her arm. I couldn't believe that the reason she had left was simply my omission about Katie, there had to be more to it but I didn't know how to bring it up at that moment without upsetting her worse. After a half an hour of silence I finally said something, I had to tell her what was on my mind.

"Gia, about the baby, I'm not going to let you do it alone." This statement only made her sob worse.

"There's not going to be a baby anymore," she told me through her tears, "I had it aborted a couple days ago. I couldn't have it knowing what Glen found out."

"What?" I asked in shock. I was both relived and hurt in the same moment. I had come to terms with the idea she was pregnant when I asked her to marry me, I was excited to be a dad and now it was over. It probably was a good idea that I didn't have a child with her now as things were but my disappointment and hurt took hold over what was probably best.

"It all happened last Friday, I had come back home to get some things and I found your ex-girlfriend on Katie's door step," Gia began. She knew the family had been looking for Ash and was really happy she had turned up again.

Gia said that it was only a short time later that Glen had called and had told her the good news about finding my lost sister Jessica, he gave Gia her name and location and they chatted a little while longer. Gia hadn't thought much about it at the time and turned her attention to being a good hostess to

Ash. The girls had dinner and talked, sharing stories they both knew about me and just having a really good time.

She said that Ash seemed like a really sweet girl and they liked each other right away. She said that Ash hadn't told her any secrets but she had still managed to pick up some things from what Ash wasn't saying. She said anytime she asked Ash about Katie or our teen years Ash would almost side step the conversation or change the subject completely making Gia wonder what she was hiding.

The one thing that came through loud and clear that night to Gia was that Ash was still very much in love with me and knowing I was keeping secrets from her made things worse. It wasn't until the girls had gone to bed that night that Gia really thought about what Glen had told her and it clicked in her head were she had heard my sisters name before. Gia said she was so disgusted by the thought that I had fallen in love with and had sex with my own sister that she couldn't take it. After what happened with her brothers she couldn't stay here, with me anymore. She understood that when it happened we had no idea we were related but the thought that I might have slept with my adopted sister and that I had definitely slept with my real sister was just too appalling.

The next morning she had gotten up and took Ash to the airport, she was sure in her mind that once Ash returned to my life that our time was over. She could see the love in Ash's eyes and she knew from my stories of our past that the girl was a master manipulator. That fact coupled with what Gia had just learned mixed with the secrets I was keeping had pushed her over the edge and she came home and moved out the same morning.

Gia said that she was so emotionally upset that she just started loading her car without thinking. She moved back in with her parents who were a little surprised to see her come back home again. She said that she finally broke down and told her parents the truth about what had happened with James and she told them what was going on with me; her parents were sympathetic and took her back into their home with open arms. She said it was like a fire was burning in her as she moved her stuff out on Saturday and Sunday; she refused any help and wouldn't stop until it was done.

That same fire caused her to leave on Monday morning to a clinic in Kayak Falls and have an abortion. It was only after she had aborted the baby that the fire began to die down and she immediately regretted doing it. She had just acted on impulse moving out and trying to erase everything we had together but when it was done she had realized that it was all wrong but it was too late to undo what she had chosen to do. Gia stopped talking and began crying again, I didn't say anything to her.

"Gia, I wish you would've talked to me............" I started but she cut me off again.

"It dddosen't mmmatter now," she stuttered through her tears, "It's done and your with Ashley now."

"I....... I'm not with her."

"You're going to sit there and lie to me again and say nothing happened after she got to the wedding?"

"I didn't.......... we didn't........." I hadn't had sex with Ash but Gia still wouldn't be happy with what did happen. The fact that she slept in my bed would be enough.

"You're telling me NOTHING happened?" Gia asked her eyes narrowing.

"No, but I didn't have sex with her, I love you too much to ever cheat on you like that."

"I don't believe you."

"I didn't......."

"JUST STOP!" She screamed at me, "Just stop, I don't believe you and you can't change my mind. That's the problem here, TRUST; I don't have any for you anymore."

"I truly loved you Gia."

"I have no doubt about that," she said getting up, "But you never loved me as much as her. Don't even speak you know it's true." I just simply looked at her, she was right but I didn't want to say that to her. I didn't want to hurt her worse than I had already done.

"I think were done here Joey," she said walking towards the door, "I just need space right now so please don't call me." I sat there without another word as I heard the door open and close again. I had really love Gia and planned to marry her, on many levels I was hurt that the relationship was over.

I sat at the table deep in thought; it was amazing how your entire life could turn around in less than a week. One week ago I was engaged and about to be a father, now I was single and no kids in my future. At least in the end I had found my sister and Ash had come back to me, we could have a real relationship now. There would be no more hiding our love for each other; Ash and I were for the first time in our lives free to be ourselves.

Getting up I walked into the bedroom and laid down on my bed. I began to flip channels on my TV and accidently came upon the video to that dumb ass song. It had been years since I had seen the video, and my body reacted the same way as it always did. I lay there with my eyes glued to the TV as my cock began to grow, screaming for relief. I couldn't understand why I was still affected by this song so much after ten years but I reached down and slid my pants off.

After the day I'd I closed my eyes as my hand found my hard cock. I began to stroke myself slowly, savoring the feeling I was giving myself. I began to breath heavy as I sped up the speed of myself stimulation, I couldn't remember the last time jacking off had felt this good. It didn't take me long with that dumb ass song playing in the back ground, in only minutes I was firing off shots of cum landing on my stomach legs and hand.

I felt more relaxed then I had in days, I had needed this more than I had realized. I wondered to myself again if the song was a blessing or a curse on my life, as sometimes like right now it helped me out. I became so calm so quickly after masturbating that I fell asleep still lying there cum drying on my body.

I didn't wake up until early the next morning; I felt dirty and headed straight for the shower. I let the water wash over my body for until it ran cold, just trying to feel something but I was numb. I had come home with the intention of breaking up with Gia but I still felt heartbroken over it. For a brief moment I wondered if Ash had played me again, but I realized as the thought hit me that I really did love Ash above all others.

It was love that was my problem, I loved too much. I thought back to college and all the girls I'd had sex with during that time, and I thought about the girls I had loved throughout my life. I had loved Katie, Abby, Ash, Jenny and Gia. They were all great girls, the best and choosing between them had been so very hard over the years, but in the end at least they were all still in my life. Well maybe not Jenny or Gia anymore but I hoped to change that, I hoped that Gia would forgive me someday and we could be friends.

I knew Katie, Abby and Ash would be home sometime later in the day but I wasn't ready to see them yet. I wanted out of my house; maybe it was cursed, because all it did was remind me of what I had lost in the last week. I decided that I needed to see my real sister and talk to her; I needed to know why she lied to me and never told me who she really was.

I got out of the shower and got dressed, putting on my nicest jeans and sweater. I packed myself a small travel bag of clothes and I walked down stairs to write a note for Katie. I explained that something had come up and that I had to be out of town for a few days, I told her to apologize to Ash and I would explain everything when I got home again. I walked over to Katie's door and slipped the note under it before heading to my truck.

As I drove across the island I decided as I needed to stop in and check on my businesses. I stopped in on Tommy and talked to him for a couple minutes. He seemed almost nervous to talk to me, but said he could keep things under control until I returned home. Brooke had flown back home on the Sunday after the wedding as we planned and she was still running the store by herself, so she was happy to see me when I walked in. I explained to here that Abby would be back today and that I had to leave, I told her what had happened and why I was going and she cried for me giving me a big hug. She wished me luck as I walked out the door.

I drove to the airport and bought a ticket, leaving my truck in the long term parking. When my time came I boarded the plane, and I sat there as it took off. I was number than ever, I was nervous about how this would turn out. I didn't know what I was going to say to her and it felt so weird going to see her knowing she was my real sister. Unlike when I had thought Katie was my sister and we shared a common father, Jessica and I shared both parents. It was an awkward situation I was in because I had loved her so much.

It took me an hour after landing to rent a car and arrive at her doorstep; I stood for at least fifteen minutes before I could knock. In the end I decided it was pointless to make the journey to not knock on her door, so I did.

"Joey!" she exclaimed as the door opened, "What are you doing here? After all this time."

"I came to see my sister."

"Oh," she said crestfallen and turned away from me, "When did you know?"

"Only yesterday............ why didn't you tell me?"

"We should talk, come in, please."

She led me inside her apartment which hadn't changed much in the two years since I had been there before. Just as I was about to sit down on the couch I heard a little girl scream and I felt arms wrap around me.

"I missed you so much!" Cried the little girl.

"I missed you too, Anne," I told her.

"Did you come back to be with Jenny?" I had to admire how much Anne had grown in the last two years. She was a young lady now but she had the same little girl voice and innocence about her. I wished for a moment that I wasn't Jenny's brother and I could be with her, I would love very much to be this little girl's guardian parent. I would have to settle for uncle as it were.

"Anne, go play in your room or watch a movie, Joey and I need to talk."

"Awww alright," she replied pouting.

"Don't worry sweetie I won't leave without spending some time with you too."

"Really?" she asked perking up again.

"Yes, now run along."

Anne ran off to her room and Jenny and I sat down on the couch. There was an awkward silence between us for a long time, neither of us knowing where to start talking. I finally broke the ice and asked her why she didn't tell me, I told her I had spent a fortune trying to track down someone who knew all along what I was looking for.

Jenny said that she didn't know I was her brother in the beginning, because she had a brother David when she was little not a brother Joey. She told me about the years after our mother died and how she had been abused by her foster parents. She explained that she had grown up with Jeff there, which was how they had met as they were foster siblings. She paused a lot while talking about her foster years; stopping to cry as she remembered the abuse she and the others had suffered.

It all came to an end when she and Jeff had stood up to them leading to a very dark incident that ended with her almost drowning in the ocean. The truth came out about the foster family and all the kids were placed elsewhere and given new names. Jenny said that what followed was the first time in her life she had ever been happy, she was placed with a really great family who took her in and treated her like she was one of their own children.

She was happy when she found out that Jeff had been placed in a home not that far away from her and they were able to continue going to school together. She found it comforting to have a friend like him to count on, one who had lived through the nightmare with her and could understand things she couldn't talk to anyone else about. However despite the bond they shared after living through all this together she never could feel for Jeff what he felt for her.

It was living with that family that she was finally able to escape the island; they adopted her as soon as she turned 18. They had only waited until then because the foster care system could've interfered

until she was a legal adult. It was through her new family that Jenny became the person she was today, with the charity and kindness she bestowed on others.

She told me the truth about Anne as well, she had once said that Anne was her cousin's child and she had taken her in because Anne's parents were drug addicts. She told me the druggy parents were true but Anne wasn't her cousin's child. Anne had been a small child when Jenny found her in an apartment, both her parents had overdosed. They were her neighbors and the door to their apartment had been open for days and she could hear Anne crying, when she went in to look she found a half starved child and two dead parents.

Jenny took the child in until they could find her a real home but she fell in love with Anne, so her parents officially adopted Anne so Jenny could take care of her. Jenny said that she planned on adopting Anne herself when she turned 18 just like her parents had done with her. I could tell by the tones of her voice that she was relieved to be able to tell me the truth about her life.

I was more interested in why she hadn't told me who she was, but I let her tell me her story as it looked like she needed to get it out. Jenny told me she had been honest when she had stated that she moved to town because of the local schools being the best to help Anne and her learning problems, only then did she find out Jeff was going to college there too. They had lost touch after high school.

Jenny said that when she met me something had clicked inside her and she didn't know why but she knew she loved me. She could feel it the moment we saw each other. I told her I had felt it too. She thought it was weird as she never felt for someone like that before, again I told her it had been the same for me.

The whole time we had dated and made love she had no idea who I really was because, again, I went by the name Joey and I had been David when we were kids. I explained to her that my dad changed it when he took custody of me. I asked her how much she remembered of our childhood living at home, she said only bits and pieces. I asked her how much she wanted to know and she told me despite how awful it might be she wanted to know what I knew.

I told her about our mother and Lilly, how they grew up, all about my father, and how our step-grandfather was our real dad. Jenny cried and hugged me when I had told her the whole story. She had a vague memory of the beatings mom would get from our father, she also remembered our dad coming into her room at night telling her she was very beautiful. I realized that it was only a matter of time before our father would've turned his attention to my sister.

When she was done crying over our mother she explained to me that it wasn't until I told her about HolBrooke Island that she realized who I was. She told me that the night I had called her on the phone and explained about the house with the tree house in back and about a long lost sister she knew it was her. She told me that was the reason she had become so angry with me that night, she was disgusted with the fact that she had made love to her own brother. She apologized or not telling me but it had taken her a long time to get over the situation herself.

I told her I was sorry and she said it was fine she was over it now and actually didn't regret our time together. She said that after she had gotten over the shock of it she regretted not staying in contact with me and was happy I had come to her. It was a little weird maybe that we had slept together but she was more than happy to have me as her brother. I told her I was glad she wasn't upset about it anymore.

After a long discussion we decided that maybe the reason we had fallen in love so fast was because somewhere in our brains we recognized each other and our love as siblings was misconstrued into being lovers. I didn't know if that was it but I decided that was a good enough reason for what happened to us. After so many stories we needed a break so I told Jenny that I wanted to take her and Anne out to a fancy dinner. She liked that and called Anne back into the room. Anne walked in and saw the tears in Jenny's eyes and ran to her throwing her arms around her and asking what was wrong. Jenny was honest and told her we had just been talking about important stuff that had made her sad, but she was fine now.

I ended up staying with Jenny for a week as we talked more and I offered to build her a house on the island if she was interested in moving there to hang around me and Katie. I told her my sisters would love her to death. Jenny was happy that I cared so much but said that she would rather stay near her adopted parents who weren't that far away. She said that she would make it a point to come to visit whenever she could. I told her any time she wanted to come I would fly her and Anne out, she smiled and said that was sweet but she didn't want to spend my money.

It was then I remembered the trust I had set up for her from our family's inherence, I told her about the money and she tried to tell me she didn't need it. I insisted telling her I wasn't just giving her a hand out it really did belong to her. Once I convinced her that she really did deserve half of our family money she said that she knew some really good organizations she could help out with it. I told her it was hers to do with what she wanted.

I think the main reason I stayed for so long was I was nervous about going home again. It wasn't because Ash was there because I did really want to see her and be with her. It was more that I really didn't want to go back to my house. While I was staying at Jenny's place I drove out to the mall there and I bought a few things I would need once I got home again, I had started to form a plan in my head as far as what I wanted and how to make it happen.

When I had decided it was time to leave the girls drove me to the airport where Jenny and I said goodbye, I made sure to hug Anne really hard before I left. The plane ride seemed so short as it approached home, however it was long enough for me to finish thinking out my plan of action.

Soon as the plane touched down I ran for my truck forgetting my bag of clothes at the luggage pick up. The first part of my plan involved going to a real estate office, I stopped at the first pay phone I could find and looked up the nearest office and headed there. I sat down with the real estate agent; a nice older gentleman named Earl, and explained what I was looking for.

Earl and I spent the better part of the afternoon looking around town for offices that fit my needs, and looking at houses in town. By 10:00 p.m. Earl said that he needed to get going home for the evening, he apologized but explained that he made it a rule to cut the day off at ten. I told him I understood and I would be back in the morning. We shook hands and I drove off to a local motel for the night. I didn't feel like making the drive back home tonight, Kayak falls wasn't that far from home really but I didn't want to drive.

I thought about Ash that night, I had kind of bailed on her again, disappearing out of her life just as she had come back into mine. It was late but I couldn't wait anymore, I called Katie's house to let them know I was back from my trip.

"Hello," Abby answered kind of sleepy.

"Hey sis, it's me, can Ash come to the phone," I asked in my best childlike tone.

"Yeah, she's here," she stated and I could hear her call out to her, "So what's up? Where have you been?" I could hear the tone of concern in her voice.

"I will tell you both when I get home; tonight I need to talk to Ash."

"Ok, keep your secrets..... For now."

"Hello?" Ash said in a, who is this calling, kind of tone.

"Hey sweetheart it's me, you're not mad at me are you?"

"I wasn't until we got home and found another note, where are you?"

"That's why I called, I'm in Kayak Falls," I could hear her squeal on the other end; she knew just how close that was. I told her the name of the motel I was at and asked her to come out if she wanted to.

"I'm leaving now, I better not get there and find another note!" she joked and I heard the phone clank down hard in her excitement.

It took her almost an hour to get to the motel, I was pacing by the time I heard the knock on the door. I opened the door and grabbed her into my arms, kissing her with an animal passion I had never felt before. She responded with all the fury I was giving to her, she wrapped her arms around my neck and began run her hand through my hair.

My mind was swirling as we kissed I pushed her against the open doorframe, not caring if other motel guests saw us. I was kissing Ash again after so many years apart, here we were and this time we didn't need to hide from view. I ran my hands up her body massaging her erect nipple through her shirt; she moaned in my mouth and shifted her hips. I began to unbutton her shirt with one fumbling hand and the other hand slid under her skirt finding her bare skin underneath.

With her shirt now open I realized she had come without bra or panties. My dick throbbed in my pants as she began to grind her bare pussy against my probing hand. Her moaning grew louder as I began to kiss her neck, "I fucking missed this," she breathed out loudly.

"Me..... Too," I replied though kisses. She pulled away from me, pushing me against the other side of the doorframe and dropping to her knees. I made to move inside the motel room and she grabbed my side holding me in place as she unzipped my pants.

"Oh, god is this really happening," I moaned as she reached in and pulled my thick pulsating cock out and sucked it down all the way in one motion. I couldn't believe this was real, after all this time and out in the open where anyone could see us. I thought back to my younger years and this wouldn't have been uncommon when I was dating Abby. When had I gotten so old and conservative?

Ash had gotten so much better then I remembered her being with her tongue stroking my cock as she sucked. This was hands down the best blow job of my entire life. I realized that I had been with so many other women and she must have had relationships while we were apart too, right now I couldn't

complain about that. I was so overwhelmed with emotion and physical stimulation that I could feel myself tightening up; I was getting ready for one hell of an orgasm.

"Baby, you might want to stop," I started to warn her. She moved her head back long enough to say, "No." then proceeded to somehow suck me harder. I could feel myself touching the back of her throat as I began to release my seed, I came so much and so hard Ash began to cough and cum ran down her chin landing on her breasts. I was still shooting cum out in waves as she pulled back from me trying to swallow and the last couple shots hit her in the eye and hair.

I slid down the doorframe until I was sitting, totally exhausted. I looked over at Ash who sat down next to me, her breathing was calming down and she looked like such a mess with her open shirt and my cum drying on her face, chin, neck and breasts.

"I love you," I told her, "Thank you."

"I love you," she said taking my hand and licking her lips, "But I need a shower."

"Yeah," I joked, "You're so dirty."

"And that's my fault," she joked back. I lifted her hand to my lips and kissed it.

"Yes," I replied and she punched my shoulder. We both started laughing uncontrollably for no reason. It was a few minutes before we calmed down again and she got up heading for the shower.

I got up after I heard the water start running and closed the door to the room. I stripped off my clothes and walked into the bathroom. Ash squealed with delight when I pulled back the shower curtain and climbed into the tub with her.

We both held each other as we let the water run over our bodies. It felt so good in that moment, like the water was cleansing not just our bodies but our souls too. I couldn't remember the last time I had been this happy, the last time I had felt everything was so right. Ash began to wash my body and I began to feel myself getting hard again as she washed my cock. Ash slowly started to sink down to her knees again but I put my hands under her armpits and lifted her back up.

"Not yet sweetheart," I told her and took the wash cloth away from her. I began to clean and rub her body all over very slowly. I wanted to give her pleasure this time so I deliberately took my time with her. Ash was already shifting her thighs by the time I sank to my knees and began to wash her pussy. Making careful movements I could hear her moaning as I washed every inch of her legs working my way back up to her beautiful lower lips.

When I had made my way back up I leaned in and began to lick her slit gently at first until she opened her stance more allowing me to thrust my tongue deeper and more forcefully inside her. Ash grabbed onto the shower curtain rod and braced herself against the wall as she ground her hips into my face. She was moaning loudly and rocking herself into me.

"OOOOOOHHHHH GGGOOOOOOOOOOD!" she screamed as her thighs clamped down holding my head in place. I could taste her orgasm despite the little bit of shower water running down her body. She tasted better than I had remembered too, it was the most wonderful, intoxicating and addictive thing

I had ever tasted and I wanted more. I dove into her harder making her scream out again in pleasure; I couldn't get enough of this girl.

The water was beginning to grow cold when Ash gripped my head with the palms of both hands and pulled me back to my feet. She kissed me deeply and told me she needed a minute and it was time to get out. She turned the water off as I reached for a couple towels. We took turns drying each other off before we stepped out of the tub, not bothering to put on any clothes and climbed into bed.

"Thank you for calling me and asking me to come," She said really softly as soon as I had pulled the covers over us.

"I couldn't be away from you anymore," I said as I moved in towards her neck and began kissing her.

"I missed you so much," she said with a tone of sadness and kissed the top of my head.

"I'm sorry," I told her pulling away. I couldn't believe she wanted to talk about this now. I wanted to make love to her so bad at that moment I wasn't ready to talk about everything else, "I just had some things I had to deal with first."

"It's fine, I was just so upset when I woke up again and you were gone......" I could hear the hurt in her voice so I cut her off with a kiss. After a couple seconds I moved my hand lower and found her pussy, she was so wet and ready I slid my two middle fingers inside her and ran my thumb across her clit. We would talk about what happened but it would be later, now I needed to show her physically how much I really loved her.

Ash's moans were driving me wild; I was getting overly excited for her. I didn't know how long I could hold back but I wanted to really make her feel good before we actually made love. Ash didn't give me the chance as she pushed me off my side onto my back. She rolled up on top of me grabbing my throbbing love tool and pressing it against her waiting opening.

"Don't make me wait anymore," she whispered and I pushed forward. Somehow she felt tighter then I had remembered, it was an amazing feeling so tight and so hot inside. I remembered back to the first time we had made love and how she had been so hot that she had almost burned my cock. Ash placed her palms flat against my chest and began pushing back hard. Every stroke across my dick felt like a velvet gloved hand squeezing me, almost milking me for my impending orgasm.

It was Ash who had her orgasm first; she clenched my cock so hard it almost felt crushed. I could feel her fluid squirting out of her running down my balls and soaking the bed underneath. I reached up and pulled her body to mine, kissing her lips and rolling us over until I was on top of her.

I looked down into her amazing eyes as I began to thrust forward making her cry out with each stroke. I leaned down and nuzzled my lips into her neck and kissed her as I slid deeper and harder into her soaking wet love pedals. She was truly the most incredible girl I had ever made love to. So much had changed in our lives over the last three years and so had how we made love to each other. It was so much better now than when we were younger.

"FUUUUUUUCKING GOOOOOOOOD!" she screamed as her next orgasm took her over. I didn't slow down or stop as she tightened up again, I just kept thrusting as hard as I could. I was amazed at how

long I was holding out with her, maybe it had helped that she had given me such a massive orgasm at the door but I was lasting longer than I ever had with her. Ash hadn't come down from her last orgasm when another one rocked her body, her back arched and she shuddered all over as the next one took her over.

That was my breaking point, after feeling her grip my cock for the third time I burst. I flooded her body with my love, filling her until it leaked out around my dick. I didn't know I could cum so much in one night; I had never in my life from playing with myself or making love produced so much cum. I knew in my heart I had gotten her pregnant that night.

I rolled off of her exhausted; I pulled her into my arms and held her soft, warm and amazing body to mine. I was so happy to be there right then in that moment that I could've died a content man right then. The world was as it should be and nothing could ruin this moment for me, not even the thought of Ash being pregnant. In fact if she was that only made me happier, I hadn't known until Gia had the abortion how much I had wanted to be a father. Sleep took us both without words that night; it didn't matter as I still wasn't quite ready to talk to Ash about what had been going on.

The next morning was a whole different story, I took Ash out for a nice breakfast and I told her everything. I told her about my mom and Lilly, my real father, my real sister and about my life since we had last seen each other. I told her everything. I figured it was better to tell her all of it now then her finding out in bits and pieces later. Now Ash of course already new about Katie and I but she hadn't heard about what had gone on with Katie, Abby and myself in college.

She sat quietly when I had finished talking; contemplating to herself for a few minutes before saying to me that it didn't matter. She knew who I was, the real me, and her feelings for me hadn't changed one bit since she was 12 years old. She said it didn't matter who my real dad was, as far as she was concerned David had been my dad and Katie was my sister. She also said that if I wanted my real sister in my life she understood that too. She admitted she was more than a little upset that her real brother, Kevin, didn't acknowledge her as his sister. She said that she felt saddened by the fact she had no real relationship with her own brother and would never hold me back from seeing my sister.

Ash and I talked more as we ate and she told me some of what had happened to her over the last few years, she told me about the rape and the fact that she hadn't had sex with a man since then. I felt so bad for her I wanted to hunt down and kill the men responsible for doing that to her. She told me she was over it and that it had been a turning point in her self-destructive behavior.

I explained to her my most recent plan for things as we drove back to the motel, I asked her to stay with me here and help me with the next step in my life. When we got back to the motel I called Earl who agreed to meet me in an hour at another address to look at a house. Ash went with me to the house and we both fell in love with it right away. It would need some work but I was more than capable of doing what needed done myself. From there we met Earl at a strip mall where I found a place to open a new shop.

Once the places had been picked out I went back to the real estate office and bought the house and I leased the shop. I called Tommy and told him I was giving him the re-model business on the island and I wouldn't be returning to work. I told him I would have a lawyer draw up the paperwork and that it would be all his. He pointed out that without me he was just a construction worker and that it had always been my designs that brought in the customers. In the end I agreed to continue doing the house plans but left all physical re-modeling to him. We would still be partners but it left us both independent to get things done.

Katie had talked to Gia in the week I had been gone and Gia had still wanted to continue to work for her. It was a good job and she didn't want to give it up. I was happy that she didn't quit on Katie, as the girls were best friends too. I talked to Abby next and told her I was giving her the store to run full time. I didn't want to go back to the island and I was starting up a location here in Kayak Falls. Abby was more than happy to run the store and be the boss, I would still be owner but I left all decision to her on how to run the store.

After a late dinner we made our way back to the motel. I had spent the whole day between the real estate office and the new offices. I had also made plans with a moving company to move my things out of the house tomorrow and bring them to Ash's and my new home. Gia had been right when she called my mom's house cursed and I wasn't going to live there ever again.

As soon as we walked in the door I took Ash's hand and I dropped to one knee.

"OH MY GOD!" she exclaimed as I reached into my pocket. I pulled out a ring I had bought while I was at Jenny's house a few days ago.

"Ashley, will you marry.......?"

"YES, OH GOD YES," she cried out, dropping to her knees and kissing me deeply, "This is all I've ever wanted."

Standing up again Ash pulled me to my feet and to the bed. We stripped out of our clothes and made love. She was so beautiful and so wonderful that night. We didn't sleep at all only taking a break from our love making to get something to drink. It was the longest most emotional night of my life as we gave each other more orgasms then I could count. I could've lived my whole life in that motel room making love to her, my future wife.

Ash went to the new house the next morning and I went with the movers to help pack and get things ready. I had spent one night in that house in the last couple weeks and it felt like such a foreign place to me now, like someone else's home with my things in it. It was a shame to leave such a nice big home and I had put so much work into it but in the end I felt it was the right thing to do. It had been Gia's and my home and it didn't seem right to start a new live with Ash in that house.

I saw Katie and Abby before I left that day, I went over and told them what I had learned about my real sister and why I was moving. The girls were sad I wouldn't be next door anymore but said that they understood. At least I would only be as far away as Kayak Falls and they could visit anytime they wanted. I hugged them goodbye and got in my truck thinking I would never come back to the island again.

Epilogue: For The Love Of My Family

"Daddy, Daddy, Wake up!" spoke as soft yet excited voice from my side. I opened my eyes slowly looking out on the deck.

"What's wrong Cassie?"

"Sara fell and she's hurt," she said looking panicked.

"Calm down baby girl," I told her as she took my hand pulling me off the deck. We walked to the tree house where I found Sara laying on the ground by the stairs holding her bloody knee and crying.

"Sssssshhh," I whispered to Sara picking her up and carrying her back to the lodge, "You'll be ok sweetheart. Let's go find a band aid and get you cleaned up.

"Thank you uncle J," she said with her tears subsiding.

"There's my brave girl," I said walking in the side door and setting her on the downstairs restroom counter. I grabbed a paper towel and wetted it cleaning away the dirt from her scraped knee.

"Cassie sweetie can you open the first aid box there and hand me a band aid?"

"Ok daddy," she said and set about doing so.

"There we go little one," I said to Sara as I had cleaned up her wound. It wasn't that bad at all, a small scrape really, "You girls shouldn't be ruff housing so much on those old stairs."

"We weren't daddy," Replied Cassie handing me the bandage strip, "She just slipped on the third stair as she was coming down."

"Ok, well were all better now. So go back out and play for a while and I will call you back for dinner."

"OK," the girls said in unison. Sara jumped off the counter and they both ran outside. I followed after sitting back down on the deck chair again. I hadn't realized I had fallen asleep, that seemed to happen to me a lot lately. I reached over to the side table and took a long swig of my ice tea finishing it.

It was mid-August and the island was really warm today. Most everyone had gone down to the beach but the girls had wanted to stay at the lodge and play in the tree house so I volunteered to stay there with them. It made me happy to see how well Sara and Cassie got along with each other, I could see in them a young Lilly and Cassie playing in the tree house and it made me happy I had finally made good use of my families money and property.

I had never intended to come back to the island when I asked Ash to marry me but as life has its own agenda at times it was a fools notion that I wouldn't ever come back here. As I watched the girls play

in the tree house I was really happy I had changed my mind about staying away. I was happy they got along so well despite the fact that they really didn't see each other that often. Our schedules didn't link up enough now a days to allow the girls to see one another much.

I was just setting my empty drink bottle back down when I felt a hand on my shoulder. I actually jumped at the light touch as I had been so in thought I hadn't heard anyone walking up. I turned my head and smiled up at the new arrival to the lodge.

"Hi Anne," I said standing up and pulling her into a hug, "I'm so glad you guys finally made it out."

"Me too, I was so sad we couldn't come last year," she said giving me a fake pout and we both laughed, "Mom's up in the room and she will be down really soon. Where is everyone?"

"Down on the beach, your welcome to join them."

"I think I will, I'll come catch up with you in a little while," she said walking towards the trail to the ocean.

It had taken a couple years of asking to finally get Jenny to come out here and I was really happy she had finally chosen to come. She had already met Katie after my dad died but she was a little leery of meeting the rest of the family. Lilly was overjoyed to see her the first year she had come to the island, she actually cried to see Jenny/Jessica all grown up now. Jenny had only vague memories of Lilly but was happy to see her again as well. Jenny had come every year ever since only missing last year.

"Hi Joe," Jenny said walking up behind me as I was about to sit down again. I turned and hugged my sister.

"Hi sis," I said smiling, "Anne just walked down to the beach, the whole family is down there. Except the girls of course," I explained leaning my head to indicate Cassie and Sara.

"That's ok," she said walking over to the outdoor cool and pulling out a beer, "I think I'm fine right here," she told me sitting down on the deck chair next to mine.

"So I got your letter, I think it's great that your adoption finally went through," I told her.

"Yeah, it took a while but Anne is legally my daughter now," She said smiling, "As far as that go's it's great to see the girls getting along so well." I looked over towards them again to see them playing with their dolls at the bottom of the tree house stairs, "Do the girls know?"

"No, they're too young to really explain it all to them yet, but we will tell them when the time is right and they are old enough to understand."

"I guess you're right, how old are they now?"

"Cassie is 9 now, she had her birthday a few weeks ago," I began, "And Sara just turned 7."

Jenny and I talked for about an hour before she began to doze off in the chair, she decided after such a long trip she wanted to go back to her room and take a nap. I got up and walked to the cooler pulling out another ice tea and sitting back down.

It wouldn't be long before the family came back the lodge and began to shuffle around before dinner. I closed my eyes enjoying the last few minutes of relative quiet I had for the moment. I was always happiest when I was here with my family every year.

I thought back to how this phase of my life began. It started when Ash came back to my life. I had just asked her to marry me and we had moved off the island into our new house. The first person we called about our engagement was Lilly

"I'm not really surprised at all," She admitted giggling slightly, "You guys didn't do as good of a job hiding things from me as you thought."

"I'm surprised you never tried to intervene then," I replied with a slight laugh.

"Intervene?" she stated with a puzzled tone, "I was the one who told you to accept her flirting and be nice to her, I knew she loved you then."

"You little sneak!" I exclaimed.

"My only concern was that she was just to young then, as much as I wasn't opposed to the idea of you two getting together someday I thought she wasn't ready before you went to college."

"Yeah, and it was all perfectly innocent back then," I told her sarcastically.

"I know better than that, but I didn't want to interfere too much because I loved you both so much."

"Thanks," I told her sincerely, "We went through a lot to get here today and your blessing means the world to me."

"Thank you Joey, I hoped years ago that if I stayed out of it you guys would work things out. I'm so happy you did."

After moving in to our new home I opened my second used store location off the island in Kayak Falls with Ash as my one employee at that location. I had told Ash I was going to run this location myself until I found an employee and asked if she could help me from time to time. I had told her she could stay home and take care of the house but she was excited to help when I needed her. Before long the second location proved to be way more profitable than the island shop and it was too much for just myself and I found that I needed her more than we had planned.

What made things worse was that with me spending so much time at the business I didn't have time to help out Tommy with the remodel designs anymore. His projects were coming to an end with no new clients lined up. After about six months Tommy had closed out all of our jobs and decided he'd had enough of the island, he said he had made enough money to have a good start anywhere; he wanted to go so he was leaving.

It was around this time we found out that he was dating Gia, and they felt awkward about it. Apparently they had begun dating just after she had moved home. Tommy had still been renting the Apartment above the garage and with them hanging around all the time they had begun a relationship. I was fine with everything as business is business and personal stuff shouldn't come into play but they decided to leave together. I was happy for Gia as I knew she really wanted to leave the island and never come back. She had said so when we first met.

It was around this time Brooke also decided that it was time to get back to school; she had at one time been studying to become a real estate agent putting that on hold to come work with her friends. Brooke had also done something I thought was imposable, she had fallen in love. After Katie's wedding she had continued to see my cousin Chase and she decided to go back to school near him so they wouldn't be so far apart. I thought it was cute that she was finally settling down and I had no ill thoughts about her moving on with her life other than I would miss my friend.

This left me shorthanded at both stores however. I talked to Abby and we made the decision to close down the island location and consolidate everything to Kayak Falls. Katie now having lost Gia as her employee and Abby not running my shop anymore the girls decided it was time to move on as well. So that April Katie went ahead and sold her accounting business to a local competitor who was just getting started on the island.

Katie said that she loved the island but the girls had been taking a lot of criticism from the locals about her marriage and with me not living next door anymore they'd had enough and had no reason to stay. They took what money they had left from dad's settlement and her business sale and moved two states away. Katie decided it was time to use her law degrees from college and she got an entry job at a law firm. I was sad to see my sisters move so far away but I understood that we all couldn't stay in the same place forever.

In May of that year Ash's friend Terra came up to visit. She had recovered from all of her injuries and missed Ash terribly so I flew her out. After hearing what had happened to her I was really surprised that she ever wanted to come back to Kayak Falls but she said it hadn't been the town that caused that situation. She stayed with us in our guest room for a while and she decided she wanted to stay. It turned out to be good timing as Ash was so tired by then she couldn't hardly work anymore. I hired Terra to fill in for Ash over the next few months as things were getting close to time. After a couple weeks I even helped Terra find an apartment in town, she was excited by that as she had never lived on her own.

That June Ash gave birth to our daughter, I was so over joyed I sat in the delivery room and cried. I was finally a dad; I was so very happy, proud, amazed and scared out of my mind all at once. The baby had come a few weeks early and delivery was very hard on Ash and her little body, she came very close to dying giving birth. I held her hand during the whole delivery willing any strength in my body to her. In the end she pulled through very weak and her color pale form loss of blood.

The baby however didn't fare as well as her mother. Due to the complications at birth our daughter didn't make it. Ash and I were devastated at the loss of our child, she became so inconsolable she wouldn't even talk to me and told me to leave the room when I would come in. To make matters worse the doctor told us it would be highly unlikely we would ever have another child.

I was lost as I felt like my life was crashing down around me. This was the second child I had lost one way or another. What was worse was with Ash's anger towards me and the situation I thought I had lost her too. I was crushed about the loss of my family. I closed the store for a week and Terra stayed by

Ash's side the whole time she recovered. It was Terra who helped me through the worst of things that week. She told me to be strong and Ash would pull through this depression and I shouldn't fear losing her.

When things were at their worst for us Lilly showed up with Katie and Abby. It was Lilly who helped pull Ash out of her depression as she held her and talked to her telling her things would be ok and that she just needed to get well again so we could try again. Ash and Lilly cried things out together and in the end Ash asked for me to come back to the room.

"I'm sorry I made you leave," she said pulling me to her and holding me tight. I climbed onto the bed with her and we held each other, "I love you so damn much." She told me as she began to cry on my shoulder. I wanted to say something to her but felt like my words would only fall short. I kissed the top of her head and just held her all night.

Before Katie and Abby left the hospital I talked to them about my next plan. We had two abandoned houses next door to each other just going to waist on the island and I wanted to change that. I convinced Katie to officially sell me her house because she loved my idea so much. Katie sold me the house and land for only 10 dollars so that I would officially own the land but she said she felt like she was donating it to a better cause.

When Ash had recovered and returned home we had a surprise visitor come to see us. Terra was helping me bring Ash into the house when we found Mandy sitting on our doorstep, she had heard about the baby from Linda and come to see us. She had more bad news and wanted us to hear it in person. She began to cry as before she could get the words out and Terra held her tight for ten minutes before she explained what was going on.

When she could talk again she said that Jt had drowned trying to save a baby that had fallen into a river. Ash fell to her knees and cried as her two best friends held her. Mandy said that he managed to save the baby but as he handed her off to the people on the shore the current carried him down stream and he had drowned. I asked why Linda hadn't called and Mandy said she hadn't been able to reach us in the hospital and that she had told Linda that she would come to us and deliver the news. Mandy had missed Ash and very much wanted to see her and had already had the bus ticket to come, so she told Linda it might be better not to hear this over the phone.

The girls stayed up all night talking about Jt and the old times they had spent together and by morning Terra had invited Mandy to stay with her at her apartment for a while. I told her if she chose to stay she could work with the girls at the store. Mandy accepted right away happy to be reunited with her best friends even if it was under bad circumstances.

It was another month before Ash decided she wanted to get back to work by then it was almost time for us to close the store for two weeks and drive to the lodge. I had intended to rent the lodge myself for our wedding but Lilly insisted on paying for half of it. I tried to argue but she wouldn't take no for an answer and in the end I gave in. Ash and I drove out together holding hands the whole way like we had done on our first trip there.

This was my third time at the lodge for a wedding and this time it was mine. I insisted that Ash and I take the same room we'd had the last two times. The master suite would have been more roomy and elegant but that corner room had much more meaning to us. I had an extreme case of déjà vu as we pulled into the parking lot but I was so happy just to be there again.

The first few days at the lodge were a whirl wind of family and wedding decisions. I really wanted to have every detail like it was in the past two weddings, but the lodge planner had tried to talk me into doing things different. In the end it was Ash who put her foot down with the woman and explained that family was very important and we wanted to honor my lost father. When she understood we were trying to honor someone who had passed away the planner backed down and everything looked just like dad's wedding to Lilly.

The first week was really great with family and friends, Brooke and Chase had come early to help then Lilly and my sisters made to out by mid-week. I loved my time with my family so much and I was sad to see how upset James and Linda were when they had arrived. They put on a happy face for everyone but you could see they were still in great pain from the loss of Jt. Mandy ran up to Linda as soon as she arrived and they hugged for a long time.

The night before the wedding Abby and Katie kidnapped Ash and told her she wasn't allowed to sleep in the same room as me. The girls went out to a club in town as a bachelorette party and I ended up just hanging out in the bar with James. We talked and he gave me some fatherly advice about life, women and love in the end I was really happy to sit and talk to him that night I was sad my dad couldn't be there and James helped fill that missing spot.

Jenny and Anne called me that morning to wish me good luck and tell me that they were unable to make the wedding. I was sad as I would've loved to have her there and to be reunited with Lilly after so many years but that would have to wait. After her call I went to the pool and swam with my family for a couple hours before returning to my room. I changed out of my wet clothes and lay down on the bed to take a nap for an hour before I had to get ready.

Abby woke me a few hours later, "WAKE UP," she yelled in my ear, "You're supposed to be ready by now." I snapped awake and looked at my watch. It was only a half hour before I was supposed to be standing at the altar.

"Sorry," I said jumping out of bed still naked from stepping out of my swim wear earlier. Abby gave me a smile and slapped me on the but as I ran down the hall to the shower holding my under clothes in front of myself. I returned ten minutes later in my boxers and undershirt my hair still wet and messy from the shower.

"You really are a sight," she said giggling.

"I know, I'm going to be late to my own funeral someday too," I said pulling my tux out of the closet.

"So are you ready for this?" She asked.

"I hope so," I replied sighing, "If not It's too late to run away."

"You know it's not too late for us to get married."

"Yeah right," I responded laughing, "How would that work? You're married to my sister."

"Not legally and we could run away together," she said so straight faced I thought she was serious.

"Abby..."

"Oh you are priceless," she said falling back on the bed laughing, "I just wanted to screw with you one last time before Ash becomes the luckiest girl in the world."

"I love you Abby," I told her pulling her into a hug, "I'm so glad you're standing there with me today."

"Me too."

I finished getting ready and Abby pinned a rose to my collar. We held hands as we walked down the stairs and out the doors leading to the altar. It was that moment I was stricken with a fear unlike I had ever felt before. I closed my eyes and began to breathe deep trying to remember the advice James had given me the night before about remaining calm.

I still had my eyes closed when I heard the wedding march begin to play. I was shaking by then and I could feel Abby's grip on my hand tighten.

"It's going to be ok," she whispered in my ear, "Just look up." I opened my eyes to see Katie standing opposite us smiling at me; I looked down the aisle to see my love walking to me.

My heart skipped about three beats seeing her in her wedding dress. Instantly I stopped shaking and stood up straight letting go of Abby's hand, Ash was the vision of an angel in white walking towards me with the light shining behind her. She glowed brighter than the sun as she arrived at the altar. Lilly who had walked with her giving her away left her to sit down as our hands touched.

It was finally here, and it was now, our wedding day, the day I told the world what my angel meant to me. Our hands came together and we held on tight as we looked deeply into each other's eyes. The minister began the service reading the words we had discussed beforehand but I didn't hear a word I just saw my Ashley. When it was time to recite the vows he actually had to clear his throat to get my attention away from her so we could continue.

With the words said and the vows made he pronounced us husband and wife, I kissed Ash with an intensity we had never felt before. She wasn't just my wife she was my balance, she was the missing part of my soul now joined as one. I could vaguely hear clapping and cheering as our kiss seemed to last days.

"Alright get a room you two," Called Terra in a laughing tone, "You're going to make us sick."

"Speak for yourself they're going to make me horny," Joked Brooke back at her. It was only then I pulled away from Ash to realize our hands had moved and we were rubbing each other's sides. Ash stepped back almost embarrassed.

The rest of the day was a blur of congratulations, handshakes and hugs. There was a bouquet toss and a garter belt to throw, cake to smash into faces and dancing but it all went by so fast. Before we knew it, it was after midnight and we both were exhausted. Ash and I walked hand and hand up to our room and stripped out of our clothes before climbing into bed.

"I'm so beat," she said softly rolling over onto me, "I love you so damn much."

"I love you too my sweet wife," I said.

"What's wrong...?" she asked as I rolled her back onto the bed.

"Nothing, but I can see how tired you are. We don't have to do this tonight."

"You don't want...?" she asked confused and hurt, "We haven't...... not since we lost the baby."

"I know my love but I'm really beat too, tonight I just want to be loved," I told her grinning using the words she had used on me in the past.

Ash snuggled up against me and I wrapped my arms around her holding her as close to me as I could.

"Your right," she informed me yawning, "This is nice, but you better make it up to me in the morning."

We spent the rest of the week mostly in our room. We would come out for meals with the family and to go swimming occasionally but our time was mostly spent alone in our corner room where we had fist made love.

I actually was ready to go by the time we left this time. It wasn't that I was happy to leave the few members of the family who left the same time we did but I was eager to return home with me new wife. It took us two whole days longer to drive home then it had when we had drove up, as we stopped about every few hundred miles to make love again.

After returning home I focused all my time in the store, but as life had settled down I found myself growing restless. With three full time employee's working now I set about getting on with my next project. I had my mother's old house demolished along with Katie's house. I thought about all the money and time I had put into those houses but in the end I wanted to erase the "cursed" house from existence. I went through and pulled out anything savable and put it into storage then had a bulldozer level both homes.

It took me two years and a lot of money, in both supplies and contractors, to build the new structure. I had originally wanted to do all the work myself but as good as I was with remodeling standing structures I realized right away I had no idea of how to start from the ground up and build a new building so I contracted out a lot of the work.

In my original concept I was going to demolish everything including the tree house but when the time came I couldn't get rid of that. It had meant so much to both Lilly and my mother and I just couldn't take it down, I had rebuilt it into a tribute to them and thought it would be a great asset to the next generation of children to come. When the lodge was up and built I was really happy to have it still standing.

The lodge I built closely resembled the one where we all had gotten married as that place had meant so much to all of us. The only changes to the design were done for comfort or to make better use of the space I had available. The lodge we had gone to for the weddings was more of a large square design

outside; because I had kept the tree house I changed my design to into more of an L shape and added the deck off the back in the L pocket area near the tree house.

The place was a large three story structure with more than enough rooms for the family to come visit, it had an upstairs and downstairs large bathrooms, a dining hall and a large common room lined with couches for visiting, an entertainment room with a big screen TV and movies a game room with a pool and air hockey tables and since I didn't have room for a pool outside I had a hot tub put in. The reason Katie had basically given me the land was because she liked the idea of building a vacation home for the whole family, which is what it was. Any of our family was welcome to use the lodge anytime they wanted, but I had started an annual family reunion the very first year it was built.

Ash and I had our own room that belonged just to us; I also gave Katie and Abby a permanent room along with Lilly and lastly one for Linda James. All the other rooms were open for anyone to use at any time. The first year we had the reunion in late May for Memorial Day as I was happy to be done with the project and couldn't wait to get everyone out to the island. Terra and Mandy joined us that year as they were like family to us. Brooke and Chase came out too. It took a few years to get some of the more remote family to start to join us but they finally began to come out too, that made me happy because that was the point after all, to get everyone together.

It wasn't long after the lodge was completed and the first family reunion came to an end that Ash gave birth to our daughter. Knowing that her birth was close Lilly had decided to stay a few extra weeks staying at the lodge and enjoying some quiet time alone there. I would go visit here a couple times a week and often found her up in the tree house reading. It was great to have to have Lilly around for so long, she really was the greatest mother to both Ash and myself. Lilly had another reason to stay, as she knew as was about to give birth again any day.

Ash went into labor and had another harsh delivery; she again fought to stay alive as she tried to bring our baby into the world. I for the second time held her hand tight kissing her forehead the whole time telling her how much I loved her. I couldn't breathe as she pushed the baby praying that both mother and child pulled through this time. Ash's body went limp moments after the birth and the doctors rushed her out of room and into surgery. She had lost more blood this time and she was so white I knew she was gone.

I didn't know what to do when they took both mother and baby out of the room and away from me. Lilly tried to get me to sit down but I couldn't and I began to pace the whole floor, the nurses and staff tried to calm me down but I couldn't be consoled. I had lost another child and the love of my life; nothing had meaning anymore without her. I finally walked back to the room and rested my head against the wall tears running down my face.

It was only a half hour after the baby was born that they brought her out to me, it felt like it had been so much longer but they brought me my baby girl to hold the very first time. I looked over to Lilly and she was crying. It was holding my daughter looking at my step mother that I finally began to calm. Looking into the face of my baby girl my heart melted in a way I had never felt before, she was my baby, my little angel, and I would die for her. It was the happiest moment of my life tempered with what could be the saddest. I had lost family members before but this was my wife, my love and I was running through every emotion in the book at that moment.

Katie and Abby arrived by midafternoon and we still hadn't had any word about Ash. When they arrived they found me finally sitting down, my head against Lilly's shoulder crying. The staff had come

back and taken the baby to the nursery and given us as much information as they could. As soon as they took her I had broken out in tears again.

"Mom, what's going on?" Katie asked seeing us both crying, "Did something happen to the baby?" Lilly didn't say anything but looked at me. I sat up and Lilly stood up and hugged her daughter. Abby went straight to my side and hugged me.

"No, the baby is fine," I told them finally, "its Ash..." I stopped not able to say the words.

"She's in intensive care," Lilly finished, "She might not make it through the night."

That was the longest night of my whole life. I wouldn't sit down again until my sisters pulled me back down onto the couch and held me tight. Lilly finally went to sleep after midnight lying down on Ash's hospital bed, I was happy to see her get some rest. I refused to let myself calm down because I thought if I fell asleep I would wake to Ash being gone.

When morning came I went to the nursery and held my baby girl all morning just waiting for some new information on my wife. It was almost noon when we got word from the doctor that she had shown signs of making a recovery. They had given her blood overnight and her color had come back to her, the doctor said she still had a hard road to go but she had stabilized enough that he was sure she would pull through.

It was only then I was able to sleep, the nurses took my baby from me and helped me back to Ash's room. I passed out on the couch laying my head on Katie's lap and she stroked my hair until I had fully lost consciousness. I woke that evening to the doctors telling us we could go in and see Ash one at a time; I let Lilly go first knowing that when my turn came I wouldn't want to leave her side.

Lilly was only gone about ten minutes before she returned and Katie then Abby went to talk to her next. They all returned telling me that Ash was tired but seemed in good spirits, she was waiting for me next and I almost ran down the hall to see her.

"My angel," I said to her walking to her bed and stroking her hair, "I love you so much."

"I know," she told me smiling weakly and taking my hand into hers, "When I was in so much pain and I knew I was dying all I heard was your voice telling me how much you loved me." She paused and brought my hand up to her lips, "I focused on that through all the pain and it saved me from letting go." I began to cry as she spoke to me, I couldn't hold back as much as I wanted to be strong for her I could feel the tears rolling down my cheeks.

"I was so scared... I thought you had..." I tried to explain to her.

"It was you that made me fight; when I was sure I had no strength left it was you that brought me back." She gently kissed my hand again and I leaned down and kissed her cheek.

"I love you," I whispered to her again, "I love you so much there isn't a word for what I feel for you, because "Love" doesn't say it enough."

"I know," she said softly and I could tell some of her strength was starting to give way and she needed her sleep, "You're not just my heart, your my soul." We remained silent for a few minutes both of us crying.

"How is Cassie?" she asked when she had rested a couple minutes.

"Healthy and doing well," I told her unable to keep the smile from my face.

"Good, I can't wait to meet her." It was then the nurse came in and told me that Ash needed to rest and our visiting time was up for now. They told me I could come back in a few hours but I had to leave for now.

"Goodbye my dear wife," I whispered to her and she kissed my hand again.

Lilly took my sisters and I out for dinner that night, we went to a local Mexican restaurant near the hospital. I didn't want to leave my wife and child but Lilly convinced me that they were doing fine and getting out for a few minutes would be good for me. I don't know if it was the cooking or that I was relieved that things were looking up but the food tasted so good that night. I was grateful to have the three people I loved so much around me to help me feel better.

Ash was in the hospital for over a week as her little body recovered, she had remained in intensive care for another day before getting moved back to her room. Abby stayed the whole time but Katie had to return home to her job, she had just taken a week off for the family reunion not that long earlier and her job said they understood her relative had almost died but they needed her back. Abby's job had told her to return as well so she quit her job telling me family was more important.

I would only leave the hospital to go home to shower and change. On those occasions I would stop into the store and make sure Terra and Mandy were doing ok, they were handling things well and one or the other of them would come to the hospital when they weren't on shift. Linda and James flew out a couple days after Cassie was born both concerned with Ash and wanting to see the baby.

Once we returned home Abby stayed a couple extra weeks to help with the baby and make sure Ash was ok. This allowed me to take Ash's shifts in the store so the two girls didn't have to work all the time. It didn't take Ash long to get back on her feet after coming home which was great for her but I felt it was nice to have Abby in the house, despite her cooking, since the girls had moved off the island a couple years ago I didn't get to spend the time with them that I would've liked to.

Before I knew it Cassie was turning a year old and it was time for another family reunion again. I moved the date back from Memorial Day to August that year as to enjoy as much sunny weather as possible. Lilly, Linda and James were the first ones to arrive then Brook and Chase and finally Katie and Abby. Other family came and went as the week wore on and it was a great time as always with my family. Everyone was fawning over little Cassie as most of the extended family hadn't seen her yet, I don't think she was set down the whole week. Every time I turned around I saw my baby girl being carried around by a different relative, for her part she was a very happy baby and always had a smile on her face.

It was at the end of that week that Ash came to me with an unusual request.

"Joe, do you want more children?" she asked one night after we had made love.

"It doesn't matter," I said softly in her ear wrapping my arms around her.

"I'm serious, would you like more children?"

"Ash, don't do this. You know the doctor said you couldn't have another child," I told her not wanting to go down this road of discussion, "Even if you got could get pregnant again I wouldn't risk losing you again."

"That's not what I'm talking about," she said pulling away from me and turning body away from me looking at the wall.

"What are you thinking about a surrogate or adoption?"

"Not exactly..." she said biting her lip slightly.

"I'm lost then."

"Well... I was talking with Katie..."

"And...?" I asked wishing she would get to the point.

"Well she and Abby really want a baby."

"Where are you going with this?"

"Well... I guess they've really wanted a baby since Cassie was born but they, of course, can't do it themselves..."

"I get that," I replied sarcastically.

"So I might have suggested... that we could help."

"You're joking right?"

"No," she said sharply, "I love them so much and they love you so much."

"But Ash I can't father a child with my sister!"

"She's not your real sister," she pronounced sharply again, "Besides I know all about you guys in college so it's not like you haven't done it before."

"Yeah, but I wasn't married then," I said pulling her back to me again, "I would never cheat on you!"

"I wouldn't think of this as cheating," she informed me, "Not in this circumstance."

"How wouldn't it be cheating? I would be having sex with another woman."

"Katie always played a part in our relationship when we were young, and I would be giving you my permission this one time. I know you want more kids don't even say that isn't true. I can't give them to you and it would be so wonderful to give them that kind of blessing."

"But it really wouldn't be my kid if it was being raised to think of Katie and Abby as its parents."

"Joe, I know this is a hard decision," she said turning back to me and kissing my forehead, "Don't answer it tonight, just think about it. Look at how happy Cassie has made our lives. We have the opportunity to do that for them."

I told Ash I would think about it and that's exactly what I did. I thought about it all the time, the pros and the cons of what this would mean for my marriage and for my sisters. I can't lie and say the idea of making love to Katie again wasn't on my mind too. My first thought was if I did this for them I should get Abby pregnant not my sister but then I realized that wouldn't work, I remembered Abby saying that she couldn't have children.

Ash did good not to bring up the subject to me again until I went to her with my answer; it was about two weeks after the family reunion I told her that I would do it for my sisters. I called my sisters to tell them that I was agreeable to the idea and both were overjoyed that I would do this for them. The girls flew out to my house at Thanksgiving for the first attempt at getting my sister pregnant.

Despite having made love countless times in the past I felt really awkward as I led my sister by the hand into our guestroom. I had made the decision that if we were going to do this it wouldn't be in Ash's and my bed, I couldn't make love to another woman there.

"Thank you so much for this," Katie told me as we began to undress.

"Can I be honest with you?"

"Yes, please." Katie stood before me both of us fully reviled and I felt the old longing for her I hadn't felt since I was young.

"I'm scared."

"Joey..." she looked at me as I began to shake. She walked around the bed and held me tight, "We don't have to do this if you don't want to."

"I'm sorry Katie it's just that as much as I love you, my hearts not in this."

"SSSSSSShhh," she whispered in my ear, "Let's forget this, you don't have to do anything that hurts your heart."

"It's just that I love her so much and... I feel like I'm betraying her."

"I understand, it's ok, I know this is a lot to ask of someone who loves like you do."

"I want to do this for you... I really do... I just don't know what to do right now," I said resting my head on her shoulder. We talked without getting dressed for a long time; it was late when there was a light tapping on the door.

"Are you guys in the middle of anything," asked Ash in a low voice.

"No, you can come in Katie said pulling the blanket around us as she entered.

"What's wrong?" She asked taking one look at my face. Abby walked in the door behind her.

I told them I couldn't do it and I told them I was sorry as I got up and left the room. The girls talked for a while before Abby came into my room. She lay down on the bed next to me and took both of my hands in hers.

"It's ok Joey, we really love that you wanted to do this for us and I understand about feeling like your cheating. I felt that way so many times when we would make love when Katie was at college."

"Really? I thought you both were ok with our arrangement then."

"We were, but I loved her so much that some nights after we made love I actually cried when you had fallen asleep, I felt like I had totally cheated and I hated myself for it," she told me in a very soft tone. I could hear regret in her voice I had never heard there before.

"I never knew you felt that way or I wouldn't have..."

"I know, and that's why I never told you," she cut in, "You're always so noble and you try so hard to do the right thing. But on those nights I would wake up and call Katie the next day and talk to her about it. In the end she was ok with my being with you and I loved being held by you at night so much I never let on that sometimes it hurt."

"So what are you saying?" I asked confused.

"Just that sometimes I felt like you needed to hold me as much as sometimes I needed to hold you," she tried to explain but had a look on her face like she wasn't getting her point across like she was trying to, "I never told you that it hurt sometimes because I loved you too much to ever let you think you did something wrong. I never want you to feel like you did something wrong. If this all feels wrong to you then we understand."

I looked into her eyes and I rested my forehead against hers like we had done so many years ago in the library. My sisters had always been there for me when I needed them, always giving and loving without thought of reward, I made up my mind in that moment that I would give them their baby, I might feel like I cheated on Ash but I would carry that guilt if it made them happy.

I walked back into the room as Katie and Ash were still talking.

"I'm ready," I told Katie then turned to Ash, "Are you sure you're ok with going through with this?"

"I am," she said confidently, "I'll leave you two alone."

I went to my sister and kissed her gently on the lips. I held her as we kissed slowly laying her down on the bed. She moaned loudly as my hand made contact with her breasts, gently grazing her nipples. I slowly began to kiss her neck moving my way down her body. We had done this so many times before but that was years ago, and all my yearnings were coming back to me. We were here to make a baby but this was Katie and I couldn't just jump into having sex with her.

I kissed my way lower making my way to her breasts, I needed to taste them again but found myself teasing her instead, circling my tongue around her nipples teasing both of them before I finally took one into my mouth. Katie gasped loudly as I began to suck her nipple gently biting down on it as I did so.

"Oh MY GOD!" she blurted out, "I forgot how good you make me feel." I didn't respond with words I simply turned my attention to her other nipple and began work on that one.

I moved my kissing down her body, replacing my teeth and lips with my hands as I made my way down. Katie opened her legs wider as my lips made contact with her dripping wet slit. I slipped my tongue along her outer lips savoring her flavor. Her hips bucked as I began to turn my attention to teasing her throbbing clit.

"Please Joey I need you," she said pulling my head back up to hers kissing me with a fury, "I haven't been with a man in sooooo long, I need you now!"

I moved into position above her rubbing my cock on the outside of her pussy. I could feel how ready she was but I was feeling a little devious at that moment. I remembered those nights a decade ago when I was so horny for her and she would let me get so close to making love to her and then we wouldn't. I wanted to torcher her for a couple minutes before giving her what she wanted.

"Stop teasing me," she begged, "Please make love to me."

That was all the prompting I needed as I couldn't resist her any more. I pushed my way into her and began thrusting as hard as I could. She felt so good and yet so familiar; all the old feelings I'd had for her began to well inside me as I made love to my sister. I used those old feelings as a focus point as I tried to thrust deeper insider her with each stroke.

It didn't take long that first night for her to find her orgasm, her body bucked under me and she cried out in ecstasy as her orgasm hit her, feeling her body tense up caused me to explode into her. I shot load after load of seed into her womb until I collapsed on top of her.

"Thank you Joey," she whispered as I rolled off of her, "Thank you so much. I love you my toy store boy." I smiled at the nick name. It had been many years since she had called me that. We held each other and she stroked my hair. It was the middle of the night before I left her there dozing peacefully. I pulled on my boxer shorts and walked down stairs looking for something to drink.

I had just stepped into the living room when I found Abby laying on the couch crying to herself. She closed her eyes and acted like she was sleeping but I sat down on the edge of the couch next to her.

"What's wrong Abby?"

"No... nothing"

"Please tell me," I requested of her, "I can't stand to see you crying."

"It's nothing; I'm just having one of those nights we talked about."

"I thought... I thought you were ok with this?"

"I am, don't get the wrong idea. It's just been a while since we shared each other and I'm just having a hard time tonight."

"I'm so sorry."

"Don't be," she said harshly sitting up, "Don't be sorry, if this works out you will have given us a gift we can never repay."

I leaned over and held Abby until she fell asleep; she pressed her head into my shoulder as she dozed of whispering a very soft "Thank you" before she was taken by sleep.

I walked into the kitchen and drank half a carton of orange juice before returning upstairs to sleep at Ash's side. It was only when I climbed into bed next to my sleeping wife that the real guilt hit me. Looking at my sleeping angel I felt the first real stirrings of what I had done and I felt like a complete ass for going through with the plan. I just tried to focus my mind on what Abby had said, that it would be all worth it in the long run when I could be there to see the look on the girls faces once they had their baby.

By morning I was starting to feel a little bit better, I woke my wife and made love to her for over an hour before we got out of bed. I needed to be with her so much that morning. The next three nights were a repeat of my time with Katie making love again as to better her chance of becoming pregnant. The next mornings I always made sure to make love to Ash in intense sessions to reassure her who I loved best.

My sisters returned home after only a few days with us as Katie had to get back to work again. We called them every day for two weeks but to see if Katie had gotten pregnant only to hear that she hadn't. All four of us were disappointed as it seemed it wasn't meant to be. I felt really guilty now for having made love to another woman all for nothing. My mood took a turn for the worse as I felt like I had betrayed my marriage.

After days of sulking around the house Ash sat down with me one night and told me to stop worrying about it. She said that she wasn't upset with me and I hadn't done anything wrong as they had pushed me into this decision. She was very patient with me as I gradually pulled myself out of my depression. Part of what made me upset is that I had got myself excited to have another child and I had felt like I failed.

Katie and Abby came back for again at Christmas so that we could try again. I found myself less willing to try again. I still hadn't gotten completely over my guilt from the first attempt and I didn't think I could go through it all again. Ash again came to my sister's assistance; she suggested that if we were making a baby for my sisters then maybe both of them should be there for the conception of the baby. I pulled Ash aside to talk with her alone after this suggestion.

"Let me get this straight," I said confused, "You want me to have a threesome?"

"Well in so many words, yes," Ash stated, "You're doing something that affects both of them and last time I know your heart wasn't in it because of what you thought you were doing to both Abby and I. This time I think Abby should be involved and I'll be there with you to hold your hand and tell you how much I love you."

"I... I can't... make love to her with you there that's so... just wrong," I informed her, "Also I felt bad enough doing it with Katie, I can't cheat on you again with them both."

"I keep trying to tell you I don't see it as cheating!" She exclaimed, "Your sisters have always been wrapped up with our relationship in the past, I'm ok with doing this."

"But that was when we were kids; things were different when we got back together."

"Do you trust me Joe?"

"Of course my love," I said hugging her and kissing her cheek, "More than anyone else."

"Then trust that I have a plan and it will all be ok."

We all went out to dinner that night at a really great Italian restaurant. We had one of the greatest nights laughing and just enjoying each other's company. By the time we got back to my house we all were in a very comfortable mood with each other. My sisters went upstairs to the guest bedroom to get ready and I held Ash at the bottom of the stairs shaking. It wasn't the sex to come that scared me but what I had thought in my own mind it would mean.

"Come on Joe it's time," my wife whispered to me. She took my hand and led me upstairs. The girls were naked and laying on the bed when we walked into the room. Ash pulled up a chair next to the bed and sat down as I began to undress. I was so wound up at that moment that even with two gorgeous girls lying nude in front of me I couldn't rise to the occasion as it were.

"I thought this might happen," Ash giggled and she hit the play button on the tape deck next to the bed. I instantly began to laugh as that Dumb Ass Song began to play. The girls broke down laughing too and the mood in the room softened instantly. I began to have the usual reaction I had to the song as I climbed onto the bed.

"Now Abby you start kissing and touching Katie," Ash requested and Abby willingly complied. The girls began to kiss passionately and my reaction to the sight of them made me go harder, "Good, now Joey move in and... well you know what to do," Ash continued. I moved up Katie's body and slid into her warm and tight pussy.

"Now close your eyes Joe," Ash whispered in my ear. I did as I was told and Ash began to rub my back, "I love you so damn much." I made love slowly to my sister this time savoring every second. Ash continued to rub my back and tell me how much she loved me; with my eyes closed I envisioned I was really trying to conceive a baby with my loving wife. It was a total change from how we had tried to do this the last time.

It was one of those moments in time that can't be described or ever re-created. As much as I had felt guilty the last time we had tried this, it felt right this time. Here I was with the three girls who had ever meant more to me than anyone in the world. When I finally came I unloaded inside Katie, I released my seed into her with all the love I had ever felt in my life. It was an orgasm unlike any I had ever experienced before, when my body had let go every drop of my load I was so emotionally and physically drained I collapsed on the bed falling in-between Katie and Abby.

"I'll give you guys all a minute," Ash said getting up and walking out of the room. I woke sometime later to find Ash lying halfway on top of me. She was naked and had pulled a blanket up over us. I kissed her forehead and rolled her onto her side spooning with her and kissing her neck. She purred in her sleep a little and I stroked her hair until I fell asleep again.

My sisters left a day later we didn't attempt to conceive again on that visit. We talked about them coming back out in another month if there was no baby this time. We thought if it didn't work out in January then we would fly to them in February to try again then. I agreed at the time but thought to myself if it didn't work out on those four attempts then I wouldn't do it again as it would be obvious then it wasn't meant to be.

As it turned out my concerns were unnecessary as a week after Christmas Katie called us and explained that she had become pregnant. I talked to Abby too on that phone call and she was so grateful to Ash for suggesting she be there for the conception because she felt it was like they conceived their child themselves. In the end I had to admit Ash had been right, the happiness in my sister's voices made it all worth it.

The next family reunion was a big hit that year, Katie had just given birth to Sara and it was the first time Jenny and Anne came out to the island. It was also the year that Brooke and Chase announced that they were getting married. I was so happy for them and thought it would be really great to have Brooke as part of my family. Mandy and Terra joined us out on the island as well as their new boyfriends. I noticed a lot of our younger generation had grown up in the last couple years and many brought with them boyfriends or girlfriends. I was great to meet new people and see the start of so many relationships.

The lodge had its first marriage a year later at the next family reunion as Chase asked me to stand with him as his best man when he married Brooke. He asked me to be best man because he said if it hadn't been for my friendship with Brooke they would never have met. Brooke asked Abby to be her maid of honor because she said that the time she had spent with Abby at the store and on the island had been one of the greatest friendships she had ever had. The wedding was just as amazing as any we had done at the old lodge were I had gotten married.

By that time the store was doing very well, I had to change the hours to keep up with customer demands, meaning I had to work more hours myself. We had never believed in leaving our daughter with a day care service and when Ash and I both had to work we would bring her to the store with us. There were a few times when she was young that some costumers would be upset to wait if we needed to tend to Cassie but most felt it was really adorable that we had her in the store. By the time Cassie was three she spent most of her days in the store, she would sit behind the register and always thank the customers for coming in. It was the cutest thing ever.

It was only a couple months after the reunion that Mandy had become pregnant. She moved out of Terra's apartment at that point and moved in with her boyfriend. Mandy had saved her money well and had a great down payment for buying a house; I co-signed a home loan for her so she could raise her baby in a real house. Unfortunately Mandy and her boyfriend broke up not long after the baby was born and Mandy was left all alone, she almost lost the house but Terra came to her rescue. She had recently broke up with her boyfriend too so she gave up her apartment and moved into the house with Mandy to help with the baby and rent.

I shook off my memories when I heard the family returning from the beach, I looked up to see Sara and Cassie still playing with their dolls I reached over and drank down the rest of my ice tea before getting up to greet everyone. I walked over to the girls, admiring my children.

"Cassie, Sara come on girls it's time to go inside," I told them and reached down. Each took one of my hands as we began to walk inside. Ash ran up behind me and began to rub my shoulders as I walked the girls.

"I love you," she whispered to me.

"So damn much," I whispered back grinning.

Love, Lies, Sex And Secrets

Made in the USA
Middletown, DE
17 July 2022